# The Nightmares of God

## The Story of the Death and Rebirth of the Universe

by

# Michael Davies

# The Nightmares of God



For information address
mickiedaltonbooks@lycos.com

First Printing April, 2008
Second Printing October, 2008
Third Printing March, 2017
Fourth Printing December, 2018

Fourth Edition

ISBN: 978-0-9876304-3-8

**Published by The Mickie Dalton Foundation
NSW
Australia**

## *Other Works by Michael Davies*

The Janus Conspiracy
Accounts of a Killing
A Friendly Killing
Dreamkill
Ready, Steady, KILL!
Helix Dreams
Helix – The Second Renaissance

### *For the Young Adults (12-18)*
The Many Worlds of Mickie Dalton
The Many Galaxies of Mickie Dalton
The Many Universes of Mickie Dalton
The Strange World of Mark and Anna

### *For the 8-12 age group*
The Julie Malloy Gang and the Smugglers
The Quest for the Locket
The Secret of Yuri Kirilenko
The United Nations and the Extra-Terrestrial
The Secret of Charlotte's Cello
The Star of the Yshan Kings
The War of the Yshan Empire
The Star of the New Yshan Empire
The Red Fog of Time
The Mysterious Recorder and The Door to Elsewhere
Prisoners of the Picture
A Step Back in Time
What Can't be Seen Can Exist

### *For the Little Ones (3-5)*
Mary's World

### *And in non-fiction*
The Business School Approach to Writing Your Novel

# *To Eva-Marie*

## *Who always knew that this would be "The One"*

*The writer also wishes to express his grateful thanks to NASA and STScI for their broad consent for the use of the superlative images taken from their website and included in the cover of this book.*

# The Coming of the Infinite Soul

"If I cannot set Man back on the path to Oneness, then others must surely come. Teachers like myself, possibly. But if others must come, then they will be greater than I and also be healers to show the Children of Man how to find the path for themselves."

*(Jesus of Nazareth to the scribe, Benjamin ben Isaac in the prison before the Crucifixion. From a document taken from the forbidden library of the Vatican by Pope Jean-Pierre II)*

# Chapter 1. The First Tendril

The end of all of Time and Creation began early in the 21st Century, but nobody on Earth knew it at the time. Despite their initial ignorance of the enormity of what was happening, several individuals played significant roles in bringing about the final chapter of the story of Creation.

*(From the diary of Father Alan Drew, discovered in 2067 in a cottage in Maine, in the Canadian Province of Arcadia, where he is believed to have spent his last years.)*
*April 9, 2012*

The old man frightens me. He's dead now, and I watched him die, but still he frightens me. Perhaps he was right, and the world is coming to an end. Perhaps an old drunk dying in an alleyway has seen the Day of Judgement coming.

He was staggering, reeling against the walls of the seedy suburb when I saw him. I walked out of the church where I had just given the evening service, and the man was but a few yards away. I moved to him, just as he collapsed, banging his face against the red brick wall of the deserted factory. I rushed to his huddled form, and turned him on his back, recoiling as a wave of evil breath reached me. I forgot the distaste in the awful fact that the man was dying.

His eyes seemed focused on some infinitely distant event. Pale drool ran from the corner of his mouth and down his cheek. I took off my jacket and folded it on the hard concrete, then lifted his head and rested it on the makeshift pillow. I saw his eyes withdraw from infinity and touch briefly on my collar, then on my face.

"Oh, father," he said in an unexpectedly soft voice. The accent was North Country, Yorkshire, I thought, not the local Nottingham tones. "Strange that I should be telling a priest."

"Telling me what, my son?" I asked, pulling my bag toward me and reaching for the phone.

"It's all over," he said and smiled. His eyes moved to the phone in my hand. "There's no point in that, father," he said. "And I wouldn't want to hang around here, anyway. Not any more."

"Life is God's gift, my son," I replied. "It is not ours to throw away, even if Heaven awaits us." I pushed the emergency buttons on the phone.

"Heaven?" The old man tried to laugh, and nearly choked. "There's no Heaven, father. Nor a Hell, either. I just saw that."

"I don't want you to find out for a long time yet," I said as firmly as I could, knowing that the man's death was minutes away. I spoke into the tiny telephone as a voice answered, and I gave directions.

"But I have found out," he replied, and smiled at me with such love and happiness that my heart seemed to stop. "It's all over, father. You can throw that dog collar away. It's coming."

"What's coming, my son?" I didn't understand his words, but I felt a tendril of some incomprehensibly vast power touch my soul.

His eyes moved outward again. The expression on his face was a mixture of awe and happiness. He clutched my arm, though he seemed unaware of his act.

"Oh, it's so beautiful," he whispered. "I never dreamed it could be so beautiful."

I was certain now that his last moments had come. I had heard of people in their last seconds of life seeing tunnels leading to wonderful light and happiness.

"Are you seeing the tunnel to heaven, my son?" I asked, reaching back into my bag for the purple sash and other materials I knew I would need in seconds. His eyes turned back to me, and they suddenly shone with caring, as if our positions were reversed.

"It's not a tunnel, father. It's Oneness."

"What?" I asked, feeling my voice tremble without knowing why.

But he was dead.

I put the sash round my neck, and opened the tiny vial of holy water. The small sounds of a siren provided a backdrop to the words I began to speak.

The conversation in that dirty alleyway remained with me till late that night. I prayed for the soul of the old drunk and tried not to think about what he meant by "Oneness." By the next morning, I had returned again to the excitement of the news I had received the previous week. I am to be seconded to the Holy City! I will work with His Holiness for the next two years. That such an honour would come to me at the age of just thirty is far beyond my expectations and more than I deserve, but I will work my hardest to represent my Bishop in the Vatican. But to see Pope Jean-Pierre II every day! I am surely blessed.

But I cannot shake that conversation from my mind. "Oneness?" What in our Lord's heaven could he have meant?

* * *

Michael Hendricks was in San Francisco when the tendrils of the new presence in the universe entered his mind. Michael was a quiet man, divorced for more than ten years after a short and painful marriage, and had not come close to trying the experience again. He was an excellent financial consultant and a great asset for the clients of his firm. He could develop strategies that saved money and provided investment capital in the most effective ways, and he was highly regarded by the partners of the public accounting firm that employed him. He was also a thoughtful man who spent time and energy trying to understand what his existence on

Earth could mean. He had read works on comparative religions and found little that meant much to him in any of the Judeo-Christian sects, though he believed firmly in the pragmatic wisdom of the documented utterings of the man called Jesus Christ, whoever or whatever He may have been.

He sat with a business acquaintance in the bar of their hotel. They had been working on their client's financial strategies for a new issue of shares to finance a factory in Oregon. As often happens with colleagues away from home, conversation took a more intimate nature than with a similar setting after work in their own office. The other man was a born-again Christian, though not of the stridently aggressive type. Michael was well aware of his colleague's philosophies and usually steered clear of anything to do with religion or politics. But when the weirdest concept came to Michael's mind, he was unable to stop himself blurting out the question.

"How could any being actually be God?"

"I beg your pardon?" The colleague was startled.

"How can any one entity be aware of itself as omnipotent, all-knowing, and eternal, without eventually going nuts?" Michael continued.

"I don't understand," the colleague replied. He seemed more amused than offended by Michael's sudden branch in the discussion.

"It seems an impossibility to me to combine those qualities," said Michael, studying the colour of his scotch in the lights of the bar. He was startled by the force with which the question had flung itself into his mind and more than a little embarrassed. "Any intelligence needs stimulation to keep it fresh," he continued. "If one is eternal, then at some stage, all experiences, all learning will have been completed. Nothing can be new any more. And at the same time, you know everything there is to know, you are totally in command of all creation, nothing is above you, and even worse, nothing is equal to you. Every intelligence needs an equal one to stimulate it. The God of all Creation cannot have that."

"You're assuming that God has the same needs as you!" replied the colleague in amusement.

Michael looked sideways at him. "Aren't we supposed to be made in His image?" he asked. The colleague said nothing, but took a sip of his orange juice.

Michael paused a moment. The extraordinary energy flooding into him was confusing him. *Something is coming....* He forced his thoughts back on the track, which had so astoundingly opened up, in his head a few seconds ago. *As if somebody is trying to tell me something...* "But regardless of that," he continued, "such a being has no controls on it. What is there to stop it going insane? And if it knew it was eternal, it would know that there was no way out of the trap. Eternal boredom in an eternal prison. Eventually, however long it took, however many billions of billions of years it needed, it would have to go mad!" *Where the hell did that idea come from...?*

"That's ridiculous!" said the colleague, at last irritated by the blasphemy he was hearing. "God is supreme goodness, the Creator of all."

"Then why did He create evil?" asked Michael. "Could the presence of evil mean that perhaps God has already gone mad?"

"Evil is the Devil's work," replied the colleague shortly.

"Which leads me to another thing," responded Michael, fascinated by the growing power of his thoughts and not detecting the disturbance within his colleague. "All the churches are united in at least one way. They demand unquestioning faith and acceptance of the literal word as interpreted by them."

"So?" asked the other.

"Well, the one thing that separates mankind from the animals," replied Michael, "is the ability to question, to challenge the established order of things, to deny dogma and move on. Without that, there can be no progress. The Churches and all authoritarian governments try to deny that ability to us and without it, we are no different from the animals. So organized religion may be the Devil's highest achievement. If one believed in the Devil, which I don't."

"You're way off the wall!" The man's disturbance at Hendricks' thoughts had become obvious. He declined another drink and returned to his room. Michael continued with several more scotches and watched the last five innings of the Giants' game against the Chicago Cubs. He was as much disturbed by his new thoughts as was his colleague, but he had no idea why.

Two days later, they returned to Chicago without resuming the strange and confusing conversation that had erupted like hot lava into an otherwise peaceful evening. Anyway, Michael had begun to think more about Julianne Patterson, an Audit Manager with whom he had lunched several times recently. Julianne was thirty-five, divorced, and shared his tastes in baroque music, traditional jazz and Gilbert and Sullivan operas. He liked her figure, her graceful legs, tiny waist and just the right-sized breasts. Despite his self-imposed rules against involvement within the place of work and his reluctance to consider marriage again, the mutual attraction had been clear to them both. He felt a small wave of excitement inside as he dwelt on the possibilities.

He saw her in the lobby. Their eyes met, and she smiled. A warmth ran through him but was lost when he bumped into another man walking to the same elevator bank.

"Watch it!" snarled the man. "Why the fuck don't you look where you're going?" The man glared at Michael as if blaming him for all the ills of the world. His eyes were wide, furious, his mouth tight with rage. Michael stepped back and the retreat seemed to dampen the imminent violence. The man glared again then stamped into the elevator. Michael felt depressed. *Why had people become so angry and ugly these last couple of years? Encounters like that were all too common these days.* He forgot it and looked at Julianne.

"Hi," he said as they entered the elevator.

"Hi," she retorted, a small flush in her cheeks.

They spent the next few moments as the elevator ascended, looking fixedly at the door, saying nothing. They walked out at their floor, together with three other employees of the firm.

"Feel like lunch?" he asked, forcing the courage.

"Love to," she said, and walked toward the audit section with a quick backward look. Michael went to tackle the report for his West Coast client, feeling like Alexander returned from the conquests.

"I just got back from Europe," she said, spearing a pink object from her shrimp cocktail. "Having clients with foreign branches is one of the few perks of this job."

"Nice," he said. "I only went to San Francisco." She looked beautiful, he thought. Her dark blue suit fitted snugly. The white blouse was open at the neck and highlighted her shoulder-length dark hair. He struggled to control his breathing.

"Europe feels so different from when I was there for the audit last year," she said.

A ripple ran down his back. *There's that funny thought again, that somebody's trying to tell me something...* "Different how?"

She studied his face. "I really can't define it. I felt it in Paris, then Brussels, then Manchester. There was a...." She paused. "... a feeling of excitement, as if something fantastic was about to happen. People were happy, anticipating something wonderful, like a lover coming home, or..." She stopped and her face flushed.

"Maybe it's just the economy picking up," he suggested. "Perhaps it's the new millennium. After all, we're well into it now."

She shook her head. "No, not like that. People seemed so close, so friendly, as if everyone was an old friend. I felt awfully out of it. When I got off the plane in Chicago it felt cold and empty. All that lovely warmth wasn't here. If it was the millennium, wouldn't it be happening here as well?"

He caught his breath. Her words rang a small bell in his mind. "You know, I felt the same thing in San Francisco. People in the streets were smiling. I haven't seen that in years. Like you, I was quite depressed when I got home. I thought it was just the usual fatigue after a trip, but now I realise it was a lot worse."

"Michael, what's happening? Is the world going crazy?"

The intensity of her words surprised him. He remembered the power of the thoughts flooding his mind while talking to his colleague, and shook his head.

"I doubt it. If people in Europe and here on the coast are feeling happier and friendlier, that can't be crazy. Only some extreme religious whacko could see happiness as evil. But what scares me is that the opposite seems to be happening in the rest of the United States. Look at the violence that's blown up these last three years or so. It was bad enough when Chicago had about a thousand murders a year. But what did we have last year? Over six thousand? And look how ugly everybody seems to have become. It's dangerous to walk out at lunchtime, or ride the subway."

"It's not happening to you or me," she said. She cupped her chin in her hands and smiled at him. Michael felt breathless.

"You and I are very old souls," he said, feeling warmth rise within him.

"I think so."

"Then these two old souls should go to dinner

tonight and discuss how to mend the world," he said.

"We should."

"Pick you up about seven?"

"That would be nice."

"Like to go to Kiyo's? They have those little private rooms and the best sushi in town."

"Kiyo's it is. Will we mend the world?"

He laughed. "Just our little corner of it."

The rest of the meal passed in a relaxed manner. Just once, Michael asked himself the question. *What the hell did I mean about being an old soul?* The concept was alien to him. *What's going on inside my head?*

He signalled the waiter for the bill and completed his credit card transaction. As they stood up, a disturbance broke out. One of three men at a table stood up with a shout of fury. He kicked the table over violently, his face bright red and twisted. The other two men began shouting, their faces equally enraged. The first man pulled a handgun from his jacket and fired point-blank. The victim collapsed, blood expanding over his shirt.

Screams broke out as people dived for the floor. Michael grabbed Julianne's hand and pulled her to the doorway, placing a wall between themselves and the gunman. She leaned weakly against him and hid her face in his shoulder. He could feel the trembling in her body and his fear did not completely hide the delight of her closeness.

"Oh God!" she muttered. "The world's going crazy. Let's eat at my place tonight. I won't feel safe anywhere else."

"Yes," he said. "That would be better."

As police raced into the restaurant they returned to their office. Michael was haunted for several days by one memory of the scene. Many of the people there weren't frightened. They watched the murder with excited faces, taking pleasure in the death of a man.

"God, what is happening in America?" he asked himself, time and time again.

* * *

*(From the diary of Father Alan Drew)*
*June 6th, 2012*
It's happened again.

She was just a child herself, maybe seventeen, but she was about to have her own baby. The ward was ugly and bleak as only charity hospitals could be, about as ugly and bleak as the streets outside. These visits were always difficult for me, but I did them several times a week. There was always work for a priest in these halls.

She was brought in by ambulance just as I was about to go home. I was walking to the doorway when it flew open and the girl was hurried through, lying on a guerney propelled by two men in uniform and a policewoman. The girl was moaning, and the bottom half of her clothing was bright with fresh blood. The policewoman caught my eye and wordlessly told me in the split second of communication that I would need my purple scarf and small vial of holy water in just a few minutes.

I hurried after the tragic group as they rapidly moved into a ward and a doctor appeared, studying the scene with the detached view of the medical professional. A nurse stripped the blood-soaked clothing away and draped a sheet over the young woman, rolling it back from her legs and thighs. The distended belly of the girl was mountainous relative to her slender frame, and more blood was already gushing from her thighs. A scream of pain was ripped from the girl's throat, and I moved to her side, taking her hand.

"Hush, lassie," I said, feeling foolishly inept. "We're all here to help you."

Behind my back, the busy scene continued, somehow detached from the focus of my attention, the child's face. It twisted with pain, then seemed to relax as if a sedative had taken effect. She gripped my hand, the sudden strength surprising me after the weak grip of a few seconds ago.

"I'm not frightened now, father," she said, her voice clear.

"No need to be," I replied. "Everything will be fine."

"No, I'm dying," she said with astounding calmness and certainty. "But the child will be okay. She's an old soul, father, and she'll know how to look after herself."

Astonished, I touched the girl's cheek. "Nobody's going to die, lass. This is a fine hospital, and you're in good hands."

Again, she smiled. I was almost frightened. It was as if she was offering comfort to me. She who was near death, was comforting *me*. "Father, I've only got a few minutes left. But there's nothing to be frightened of."

Her face was radiant, like a bride on her wedding morning.

"You don't need the prayers, Father," she said. "Nor the purple thing, nor any of that lot. It's Oneness, Father. Oneness. And it's so beautiful. If only you could see it. She's coming for me, Father."

Her eyes closed, not in death, but in peaceful resignation. I tried desperately to make her words fit my universe.

"The Holy Mother will be with you, child, I know." I reached for the bag, for I could see the girl's life was nearly over. But she opened her eyes again, and smiled with such love in them that I felt tears spring to my own.

"Not the Holy Mother," she said. "Something far more wonderful. Oneness, Father. Believe in it, the time of Oneness is here."

Then she died.

For a second, I hesitated. I looked at the purple scarf and the little bottle of holy water, remembering her words that they were unnecessary. *Oneness,* she had said. What could she have meant by that? These were the same words of the old drunk in the alleyway not far from here. Feeling as living a lie, I pulled out the scarf and the bottle and gave the girl the Last Rites. Behind me, I heard a slap, and the cry of a new-born baby. An old soul? Dear God, what did she mean by that?

Could I bring these things up with the Holy Father? I go to Rome in a few days. Is this permissible? Can a poor parish priest ask the Vicar of Christ, the Wearer of the Shoes of the Fisherman a silly question about "Oneness" because two destitutes at the doorway to death seemed unafraid and used the same words? I sense the arrival of strange forces in England, and perhaps elsewhere in the world. But I have never been outside of this country, so I could not know.

Wait until I see the City of God. Maybe then I can decide. Just four days.

* * *

Raoul Carmagio was a short, stocky man. His face was eternally cheerful, and few who saw him could anticipate the steel within him, and the drive to achievement that had taken him from a childhood in a prosperous suburb of Turin to his place as a Prince of the Catholic Church. Carmagio was the Archbishop of Milan.

This evening, as dusk fell over the city, he was sitting quietly in his office, thinking about the odd state of the world. He had been seeing signs, which disturbed him these last few months. Oddities of behaviour that struck little chords within his mind, though he could not understand why. Even more odd, the disturbance was somehow familiar, *expected* even. Raoul knew it was time to talk it over with his closest friend.

He remembered the day he had met Philippe Leger at the seminary. He had been walking to a class, when he heard the soft sounds of feet behind him. He turned and saw a face. It seemed so familiar he almost greeted it as one would greet a family member or old friend. A second later, he realized that he had never met the tall, dark young man dressed in the same coarse robes he was wearing. Both of them seemed startled.

"Hello," said Raoul, with a curious smile. "Do I know you?"

"I don't think so," replied Philippe. "But you do seem familiar."

They walked together to the class, feeling as comfortable as brothers, and the relationship had never changed in over forty years, despite the cataclysmic events of just over a year ago.

Many years later, Raoul was in a conference with several business executives, discussing the best application of funds donated by business to the Church, when the door flung open and the Archbishop's secretary rushed in. He was flustered, his face white and he seemed not to see the people in the room.

"They've shot him!" the young man shouted. "*Il Papa...* he's dead!"

Everyone in the room came to their feet. Raoul walked quickly to the terrified young man and touched his shoulder. "Marco, my son," he said softly. "Control yourself. Now, tell me again. What has happened?"

The secretary took a deep, ragged breath. Tears rolled down his cheeks. "A bullet, Monsignor. His Holiness was walking through the crowds in the plaza. A bullet hit him...." The man was unable to continue.

In the room, all the businessmen let out deep sighs of dismay. Apart from the varying levels of their personal grief, the assassination of a Pope was bad for commerce, especially when the murder followed just three days after the Pontiff's election.

Raoul's own shock was severe, but it was not one of personal loss. He had never held Hilaire Rabat in much regard, even when the middle-aged Frenchman had become Pope Jean-Pierre just three days ago, following the death of his predecessor after a long battle with failing health. But the blow was immense. God's representative on Earth had been murdered. Evil was at large. He turned to the group of men.

"Gentlemen," he said softly. "We cannot continue this meeting."

With murmurs of agreement, the men filed out. Raoul sat down to consider how to handle the chaos that would now eventuate. But a month later, he received an even greater shock, though this time, far more pleasant. His oldest and dearest friend, Philippe Leger was elected to the Throne of Saint Peter, taking the name of Jean-Pierre II.

Remembering that amazing day, Raoul Carmagio smiled. Then the smile faded as he recalled the source of his worries. What was happening in the world? He knew that he would have to talk with his friend, Pope Jean-Pierre II, the Vicar of Christ and Bishop of Rome. The next day, Raoul would fly down to the Holy City.

* * *

The old man was dreaming. He was eight years old, playing by the water's edge, throwing stones into the river that flowed by as smoothly as the years. His best friend was alongside. Then they were twelve, playing in the junior rugby team. They were sixteen, running through the glowing autumn weather in the school cross-country race, and he was pulling his friend along. Jerry was slight, but tough. He could finish the race. The War was an exciting, but distant event, something his father mentioned at dinner, while grief echoed in his voice.

"I pray it's over before you two lads get into it," his father said. He had looked at Jerry with the same affection, for the two boys had been friends for years. He was eighteen, and one day he didn't take the bus to school, but got off at the town centre, walked to the train station and rode into London. That evening, he slept in the barracks at Hornchurch with fifty other recruits. Nine weeks later, he flew his first combat patrol in a Spitfire, and two days after that, got his first kill. Jerry joined him a month after that. And then Jerry died.

But Jerry was coming back. Jerry was somewhere near. The old man could hear a voice calling him from far away. Sometimes, the voice was of something incomprehensibly vast and powerful. Sometimes, it was his long-dead wife. Sometimes, it was Jerry. He couldn't make out the words. But they were the people he had loved most of all in his life, and they were dead and he missed them dreadfully.

The old man woke up, weeping.

* * *

"There are times, Philippe, when I feel unsure about addressing you like a friend." Raoul sat on a cane chair by a glass-topped, round table. Across from him, the dark, lean features of Philippe Leger looked back in some sadness.

"Raoul, you are the one pillar I lean on to keep me in touch with the world," said Pope Jean-Pierre II. "I know what this position does to the occupant and to the perceptions of those around him. I pray you do not let it spoil the friendship that has sustained me for forty years."

Carmagio smiled and sipped his coffee. They sat a few feet away from the open window. Ever since his election caused by the murder of his predecessor, the new Pope had agreed with his advisors never to sit in the line of sight of another building.

"I will try not to," Carmagio murmured in embarrassment. "But you are right, Philippe. The mantle of the papacy changes the way I see you."

"I am still the callow young Frenchman you met in the halls of the seminary," said Philippe with a chuckle. "And I still love to debate the truths of the universe with my oldest friend. I think you have come with that intent, Raoul. It does my old heart good."

But the look that Leger directed at him was sharp and direct. Startled, Raoul put down his coffee cup.

"Something strange is happening around the world," the Archbishop said. "I sense the turmoil, but I can't identify the cause."

"Anything specific?"

"Curious things," said Raoul. "Some good, some bad. Have you noticed the odd peace and harmony in most of Europe, while other parts have become even more vicious and violent these last two years?"

"I have. It has exercised some powerful minds recently."

"And the Middle East is showing the same ugly problems as always with the Israeli-Palestinian conflict becoming even more vicious and violent, while the tensions between Iraq, Iran and Syria are climbing at a terrifying rate. And Libya is back to its old ways, making some nasty noises toward its African neighbors."

"Can you make anything of this, old friend?" The Pope was watching Carmagio carefully.

"It is almost as if some band is playing music which some love and some hate. But not everybody can hear it."

"An odd analogy, Raoul. Have you heard the music?"

"No. Have you?"

"I don't know."

"You don't know? Philippe, you aren't telling me everything. Do you know of some force affecting us? Do you feel something?"

Philippe shook his head in some confusion. "There's *something*... I don't know what it is. I was hoping you had experienced it, too. It's a feeling of ... maybe hearing somebody in a dream. You hear the sounds, but you can't make out the words."

Raoul let out a sigh. "I've heard nothing. Philippe, you surely don't think this might be.... no, surely not."

"The Second Coming? Raoul, for all I know, it might be."

"Do you really believe in that?"

Philippe looked pained. "I'm the Pope, Raoul. I'm *supposed* to believe in it. But I never thought it would happen on my watch. And to be honest, I don't think this is it. The feel is... different."

"Different? Different from what? We have nothing to compare."

Philippe shook his head again. "I wish I could explain."

Raoul leaned back in his seat almost as if in resignation. "The world is becoming stranger. What's happening?"

"Raoul, I sincerely wish I could tell you. But like you, all I see is a diverging trend. Some parts of the planet are getting nicer. The rest is getting uglier, more violent, as if resenting the peace that the others are enjoying. They are angry about something. Even within countries, it's happening. Our friends in North America tell me that crime rates on the west coast and in the north-east are dropping, while in the central and southern areas, they are sky-rocketing, especially crimes of violence and murder. And those lunatic televangelists are getting louder and more bizarre, full of increasing hatred for those different from themselves."

"So *somebody* is hearing the music, Philippe, even if I can't. What tune is playing?"

"I cannot possibly say. I wish I knew the other answer even more."

"To which question?"

"The key question, Raoul. The one that may affect us more directly than anything else since the birth of Christ."

"Ah!" said Carmagio in sudden understanding.

"Yes. The real question, old friend. *Who* is playing this music?"

* * *

The ship was vast, perhaps a kilometre long and more than half a kilometre wide. Inside, the sound of the engines was a tiny but persistent hum, heard in every spot throughout the huge emptiness. Little else was heard, because the ship held few occupants.

The being that was the Infinite Soul lived in one enormous set of cabins in the mid-section. Few of the crew ever saw their passenger, which was fine by them because contact tended to cause such awe that they were overwhelmed.

The passenger preferred things that way too. Ascension to the stage of Infinite Soul had come quite recently and adjustment took time. So the passenger remained mainly in the comfortable quarters, and meditated, communicating with the individual entities of which it had been formed, and slowly merging all of them until its single consciousness was the primary intelligence. The passenger took the name of Maragos, which had been the name of one of the individual souls who had achieved fame as an artist in its last incarnation as an Old Soul. The ship having dropped back to normal space as it neared Earth's solar system, Maragos spent many hours gazing from the windows of the living quarters at the patterns of stars as they flowed past, and pondering the threat of extinction facing all of the universe's intelligent life which had been caused by the one species on Earth.

# Chapter 2. The Players

*(From the Diary of Father Alan Drew)*
*September 19th, 2012*

Now I must truly despair that perhaps the long night of evil has come, for this madness has reached within the Vatican and struck the chief servant of God.

I have been here just two months. It has been an astounding experience to be in the centre of all that I live for, the engine room of my faith. My first meeting with His Holiness was a powerful moment. He radiates energy and strength, love and compassion. He speaks English with no accent that I can detect, and I am told he speaks sixteen languages with the same command.

The whole time that I have been here, the Pope's closest friend, Raoul Carmagio, Archbishop of Milan has also been in Rome. There seems to be some understanding between them that nobody else shares, some great grief for the appalling violence and bloodshed that has broken out in some spots around the world. And with that grief, there is some comprehension, as if they know what is causing it, and that frightens me.

But it was this morning that my fear reached the level that is has. Something hideous has invaded the centre of the faith.

His Holiness, Pope Jean-Pierre II was conducting morning Mass when I sensed the first indications of the end. I was watching the Holy Father during the communion and saw the small shock that ran through the Pontiff.

A middle-aged woman in her black dress was kneeling before him. He made the sign of the cross over her bowed head, then, as she raised her face to him, he placed the tiny sliver of biscuit on her tongue.

"Take this, the body of our Lord, Jesus Christ," he said softly, passing down the silver chalice to her lips. "And drink of this, the blood of our Lord..." For a second, he seemed to pause. His eyes lifted from the woman's head, he looked up into the distance and a strange, lost expression crossed his face. I saw the Pontiff's sad look and felt a twinge of anxiety pass through my body. Something terrible was happening, I knew.

The woman seemed bothered by the delay of the wine at her lips and moved the chalice away from her mouth, and His Holiness returned his eyes to her. He smiled, a deep smile of such love, that she seemed nearly to cry out. As he passed further along the line, she held her hands to her mouth and watched him intently.

The rest of the service passed without incident, though I was watching closely for any further oddities. Several times, it seemed to me, the lean, intelligent face of the Pontiff adopted a sad look, the pain of a small boy who has lost something precious and still cries inside. I felt so frightened I nearly collapsed, but somehow kept a hold on my fear.

The service ended, the hordes of worshippers filed out into the heat and dust of Rome, and the Pope was escorted back to his chambers. He walked among the attendants, taller than all of them, and younger-looking than most. He was completely withdrawn during the short, stately walk, and I knew that something seriously wrong had happened. I looked at the Pope's friend, Raoul Carmagio, who brought up the rear of the small party, and saw an expression of concern on the Archbishop's face.

As part of my duties, I was allowed to follow the party to the disrobing chamber, where the attendants removed the gold chasuble from over the white gown and hung it away carefully. The Pontiff's face was white with strain as I walked in.

Finally, I found the courage to speak. "Holy Father..." I began, but I was silenced by a short, cutting gesture from Jean-Pierre II.

"Alan, I am not a Holy Father," he said. "That title has just become meaningless."

I felt a shock run through me. In the chamber, complete silence ruled. The two attendants who had hung away the chasuble and were advancing on the Pope again to assist him with the robes stopped short. One of them gasped, as if in pain.

Archbishop Carmagio looked carefully around the room then walked slowly up to his friend. Jean-Pierre II was standing still, looking into a far distance that nobody else could see.

The Archbishop touched him gently on the shoulder. "Philippe," he said softly. "What is the matter? Can I help?"

I watched Philippe Leger. He seemed to draw his eyes back from infinity in the same way as had the old man dying in Nottingham. He looked down on the upturned face of his oldest friend. To my horror, I saw tears in the corners of the Pope's eyes.

"Raoul," he said, with a small smile, "it is finished. All this..." He waved generally at the window, as if encompassing the contents of Vatican City and the surrounding world. "All this is meaningless."

The room was silent for nearly half a minute as the two friends looked steadily at each other. The Archbishop opened his eyes wide and his lips parted with a deep indrawn breath before finally he smiled too, and nodded.

"I see what you mean," he murmured. "Finally, I hear the music clearly. Maybe it should be your final official pronouncement?"

"How can it be official?" said the Pope. To my dismay, the smile on his face was like that of a small boy let early out of school. "How can it be official, when I know that the whole thing is rubbish?"

"Your Holiness!" I was too distressed to remain silent anymore. "Please, I beg of you, what has happened?"

Philippe Leger turned from the steady look of his friend Raoul Carmagio, and smiled at me. "Alan," he said, "forget that Holiness stuff, will you? Just call me Philippe. It's over, finished. Don't you see it?"

"See what?" I was too far in shock to remember any ceremonial form of address. "What has happened? What is it?"

"You don't see it," murmured the Pope more to himself than to me. "They don't see it, yet," he said more clearly to the Archbishop, who nodded in understanding. "Then I have a task for you, Alan," he continued, turning back to me. "In time, you will understand.  Not a lot of time, either. But start telling the world this. The Time of Oneness is here."

"The Time of Oneness? But what does it mean?" The wave of horror almost engulfed me. These were the same insane words used by the old drunk and the dying child as she gave birth. Now I was hearing them in the holiest precinct in the world, spoken by the man chosen by God as His representative on Earth.

"I don't really know," replied His Holiness with a gentle smile. "But both of us will, in time."

"May God have mercy upon us." I was almost weeping in dismay and bewilderment. Both the Archbishop and the Pope let out small, sympathetic chuckles that increased my worry and confusion even more. What was it that they had seen which I could not?

"You already do," said Philippe Leger gently. His words had no meaning that I could grasp. "You don't know it yet, Alan, but you already do."

The two old friends walked out of the room into the Pope's private suite, smiling cheerfully, leaving the two    attendants    and    me    shattered    and uncomprehending in the disrobing chamber.

I think Lucifer himself has opened the gates of Hell and come to Earth.

* * *

Bainesville is a small town thirty miles west of Austin on the road to Houston in Texas. The population of thirty-three thousand divides its loyalties almost equally between the Baptist Church and football. The balance varies according to the time of year, football being dominant from late summer through to the Super Bowl in January. On any Monday after a Fall weekend, the conversation on the buses, the trains, the cabs, and the restaurants was predictable, consistent and intense.

On a Sunday morning however, everything gave way to the demands of the Baptist Church, regardless of the season. The families of Bainesville would dress in their best, the men in their newest white hats and polished high-heeled boots, the women in the flowing, calf-length dresses, hats, often with thin veils, and the kids in the stiffest of Sunday clothes. They would pile into the pick-up truck, kicking away the empty beer cans from the previous night out, or into the Lincoln Town Car, the Camaro with the beefed-up suspension, or whatever was the preferred family transport, and head to one of Bainesville's Churches.

The Very Reverend William Hardcastle Horning always delivered, as far as the congregation of the Church of The Divine Word on the south side of Bainesville was concerned. His sermons were the best of the pure fire and brimstone that they loved. He promised eternal paradise to those who believed in Jesus and accepted His Word, and damnation in the lowest Pits of Hell with personal attention from the Devil himself for those who did not. The people of Bainesville were immensely honoured that Reverend Horning came to worship with them on Sundays, because he was a man of wide-flung interests, including a religious television channel of growing viewership, and the minister was a powerful influence in the Republican Party.

To William Horning, God was a personal friend with a direct line. At least, that's how it appeared to his congregation. And the Devil was a real, flesh-and-blood person, who patrolled the streets of America, smelling out the evil, the ungodly, the liberals, the fornicators and the opponents of America's involvement in any foreign war, and snatching them to the bowels of Hell.

Horning knew that he was personally responsible for putting the President in office. He told his congregation how he had talked directly to God and asked him for the victory for Good and Righteousness before the last election. He had told God how any other choice would lead to the collapse of America, God's chosen country, into the filth of corruption. The last several years of an administration headed by an agent of Satan assisted by his evil succubus of a wife had shown the degradation to which America would head if any more of the same were to be permitted. For had not Satan shown what would happen? Already, money had been diverted from weapons systems to wasteful extravagance, assisting godless people to have education they would never need. Money had been spent on socialist health care systems that only increased the numbers of the liberals. The true leaders of America were being taxed to death. The freedom to buy guns to defend themselves from the tyranny of socialism, liberalism and science had been curtailed. America's armies had not been used in the noble exercise of war for years and were dying from boredom.

If Horning's man were not elected, he told God, the liberals would triumph further. They would allow criminals to live instead of placing them in the electric chair as God had decreed, they would vote against arming the country with *nyookular* bombs, thus allowing the godless communists, those comrades of the liberals, to flood into the country.

Horning's man, he told God firmly, would ensure

that America purchased the proper weapons, and silence those liberal communists who said that many of them didn't work. He would make certain that no God-fearing doctor committed the crime of abortion. He would return God's Word to the schools every day, and end welfare payments to those folk incapable of living in America's true world where only those who followed the Baptist way would be saved.

God had obviously seen the wisdom of Horning's advice to Him, thought Horning's congregation, for the polls for next year's election were climbing for his man to be put in the White House, and the evils of the past administration would be rapidly exorcised. The men and women of Bainesville clearly wanted to hear more of the same, for there was rarely a seat free in the Church of The Divine Word on a Sunday. This particular Sunday was no exception.

Michael Hendricks was in church that day, too. He had spent the week in Austin on a project for his employers and was scheduled to spend the following week in Houston. Having seen little of Texas in his forty-three years, he decided to stay the weekend and drive to his new assignment, experiencing something of the State in the process.

He was unclear what had driven him to attend a Baptist Church service that Sunday morning, for he was not a religious man and felt no allegiance to any denomination. He had been brought up by parents who vaguely considered themselves Protestant, but had never forced their only child to attend churches or to receive formal religious training.

As Michael drove through Bainesville, he stopped for a coffee break and sat peacefully by the window of a small diner, watching the people pass by. As he returned to his car and started the engine, an odd impulse disturbed his peace. He sensed a strong pull to follow the lines of cars heading into the parking lot of the Church of the Divine Word, which he could see a few blocks further down the road. The compulsion was not pleasant, and Michael felt disturbed by it. It was a sensation of a confrontation with something feared. He parked in the capacious parking lot and joined the people walking into the building.

He received many hostile looks as he took a seat. Not only was he a stranger, something barely tolerable in itself, but he was not dressed in the manner befitting the congregation of the Very Reverend William Horning. Michael had left his motel that morning prepared for a lengthy drive, dressed in light slacks and a casual shirt with short sleeves. His stocky frame of average height, partially balding head of light brown hair, and his horn-rimmed spectacles stood him apart from the Texan worshippers as obviously a Northerner. A few muttered comments were passed around as Michael found his seat, but he was unaware of them.

Michael spent the few minutes before the service began observing his fellows. Something disturbed him about many of the faces around him, and he finally identified what it was. In many of the congregation, a blankness showed. The eyes of the worshippers seemed opaque, as if nothing lay behind them. The faces were dull, barely animate. In a few, an impression of suppressed violence was detectable. Michael felt even more disturbed. Why the hell had he come to this place?

A rustle of expectation ran through the hall as a man entered from a side door. Michael felt a startling sensation of fear. The Reverend William H. Horning was not a large man, but Michael could sense the aura of power around him. He stared at the preacher and saw something strange. Horning's eyes were dark, so dark that they seemed to suck the light from around him. Michael shivered, and tried to suppress the sense of dread.

The service was nothing special, though he found the nasal twang of the Very Reverend William Horning a little hard to follow. By the time Horning ascended to the podium to deliver the sermon however, Michael had attuned his ears and was fascinated by the rustle of excitement and some muted cheers and applause, which threaded around the congregation as Horning stood above them. Michael felt an unpleasant sensation as he looked at Horning. Whether it was fear, revulsion, or distaste at Horning's artificially perfect head of white hair, Michael could not determine.

The Reverend Horning began as he always began, with prayers of thanks for God's intervention in the coming election of His man to the White House, and gradually developed the theme to a call for prayer in the schools of the nation, preferably twice a day. Michael found his mind wondering. He thought about the client he had just left in Austin, and remembered a couple of loose ends he had left which would have to be cleared up by telephone the next day. He thought about Julianne.

The universe was immense beyond comprehension, he thought, letting images of Julianne slide away. Something was growing in his mind. *Mankind lives on one tiny planet,* he mused, *at the end of one small arm of a huge series of large arms in a far quadrant of the Galaxy. There are billions of stars, billions of other galaxies. Why would a God of all creation bother with just us to the exclusion of all other life forms? The religious nuts denied the existence of other life forms, of course. How silly.*

The pressure inside was growing stronger.

*What is everyone else thinking in this church?* he thought, lifting his head and looking around him. All eyes were intent on the Very Reverend William Horning. *Funny,* Michael thought, *the preacher's voice is far away, just a murmur in the distance. Look at that man two rows in front. What is he thinking? Does he ponder the insignificance of humanity in the grand scheme of things? Does he believe in the certainty of eternal heavenly paradise merely because he listens to this ranting preacher every Sunday?*

Michael was inside the man's head.

In startling clarity, he knew what the man knew, he saw the simplicity of the man's beliefs. He saw his wife and the two children playing in the small back garden of the house, he saw... *my mother who would be visiting next week with that old grouse of a father, damn him and his farting all day, the old bastard used to be too free with his fists when I was a kid, and sometimes I want to beat the crap out of him...*

Michael took a deep breath and found himself trembling. He stared at his hands and felt sweat run down his back. Fearfully, he let his eyes climb back up, and sneaked a look at the man whose head he had just invaded and whose thoughts he had just shared as his own. The man was staring around him, looking frightened.

*What in God's name happened just then?* Michael fought for calmness and slowly achieved it. The power of the images he had experienced was overwhelming. Michael knew he had just seen the world through another man's eyes in the most literal way possible. He closed his eyes and concentrated on Julianne again, the curve of her hips, the way her legs looked in the short skirt of her suit, her perfect complexion and hazel-green eyes. His breathing eased and the sweating stopped.

*Something is coming.*

He sat up with a jerk and his neighbor on his right looked irritably at him. She was a muscular woman in a blue dress and a flowered hat, and she sat with a huge, overweight man and two fat boys in their early teens.

Something was coming. Something incomprehensibly vast was coming and mankind would not be the same. Michael knew it and he feared it dreadfully. No. No, he didn't fear it, he realized. The image he had just seen in his mind was wonderful. Overpowering but wonderful. Confused, he stood up and began to thread his way to the end of the row of pews.

"How dare you!" hissed the woman in the blue

dress as he forced his way past her knees.

"Hey, feller!" protested her husband, and tried to grab hold of Michael's arm, missing by a fraction of an inch.

The mutterings got louder as Michael reached the aisle and heads were turning to watch. Mercifully, he got past the last seat, and began to walk back to the door, when a thundering voice stopped him.

"You, sir!" bellowed the amplified voice of the Very Reverend William Horning. Michael turned. Angry, hostile faces stared at him from every direction, but the most fearsome was the man on the pulpit. Horning was not a large man, well under six feet tall, but thick heels on his subtly-built shoes made him look bigger. His luxuriant head of white hair added further inches to the enhanced stature. He was standing upright, one finger pointed directly at Michael, and the rage in his eyes was terrible to see.

"Is the word of God not good enough for you?" he demanded, the loudspeakers slamming his voice down from all corners of the church like multiple thunderbolts. "Are you Satan's child that you must leave while the Divine Word is being spoken?"

Michael felt overwhelmed for a moment. The blast of darkness from Horning's eyes was terrifying. Michael felt a wave of panic and sweat rose again on his back. His shirt was soaked.

"I am..." he croaked and was unable to say anything more.

"You are a sinner, that is the truth I speak!" raged Horning. "How *dare* you leave while God's words are being spoken!"

Astoundingly, Michael felt strength flow back into him. Horning's black gaze ceased to frighten him. He stood straight, the sweat cooled, his throat eased from the constriction which had surrounded it and he found his voice.

"I left because it no longer means anything," he said calmly. A whisper of anger chased round the church. Michael ignored it. "I cannot explain what is happening, but I realized as you spoke, that something is coming that will make all this," he raised his eyes to the stained glass windows, waving at the vaulted ceiling and the magnificence of the altar, "all this, meaningless."

"What do you mean, something is coming? The Lord *Jesus* is coming!" Horning had stood away from the pulpit but had taken the microphone with him. His voice still thundered from the air around him, but Michael was unimpressed.

"No," he said. "Not Jesus. The Time of Oneness!"

A tiny shiver ran round the church. For a second or two, there was silence. Michael's words had touched some chord that a few of them would later remember.

"Oneness?" screamed the furious voice from the loudspeakers. "What is Oneness?"

Horning stared at Michael and for a timeless moment, Michael felt his own force rise up and fight the black energy of the preacher. A monstrous battle of wills was fought.

"I don't know," replied Michael, and walked out.

He continued walking through the huge front doors of the Church of the Divine Word, out into the brightness and heat of a Texan morning. Hardly aware of where he was, lost in wild, confused thoughts, he made his way to his rented Buick in the parking lot.

"Oneness? What the hell is Oneness?" he asked himself, speaking aloud. He had answered Horning's hysterical demand without thinking and the words had just fallen from him. Yet he knew that was what he had meant. And he was stunned and frightened by the power he had found within himself to counter the fearful force of Horning's black gaze. He shook the confusion from his head and fumbled for his car keys. As he opened the door of the Buick and felt the wave of blistering heat inside the car, he looked up. Three men were standing in front of him. One was the hugely fat man who had been sitting in his row with the woman and the two overweight boys.

"Listen, feller," said the fat man. "We don't take kindly to strangers coming here and being insolent to Reverend Horning."

"I'm sorry," replied Michael. "I can't explain it, but I intended no insolence. The words just popped into my head. You'll have to wait and see what happens." He moved to get inside the car, but one of the other men kicked the door, nearly catching Michael's hand as it closed.

"Oh, we know what's going to happen," said the big man. "You're going to hell, and right now!"

He unbuttoned his jacket and took out a pistol from a holster on his belt. He pointed it at Michael's eyes and pulled the trigger. Michael heard no sound and felt nothing, but he was dead before his body hit the ground.

* * *

*(From the Diary of Alan Drew)*
*September 30th, 2012*

I have found many changes after the cataclysmic events of that day the Pope spoke of Oneness. His Holiness walked away from the Vatican building only ten days after the Mass at which I had watched him lose the faith, and has spoken almost to nobody in that time. Several Cardinals have come to the papal chambers, but few have been admitted, and as far as I knew, the Pope has spent most of the time down in the Forbidden Library. I discovered the existence of this library just a few days ago, and I must confess, the idea that documents exist which the Church believes people must not see is profoundly disturbing.

Just once, I met His Holiness as he returned to his chambers, carrying several documents, which I suspect he had been removed from the Library. The Pope was wearing simple slacks and a dark blue shirt, open at the neck.

"Your Holiness..." I said, bowing my head.

"Alan, I've already told you, my name is Philippe Leger," the Pontiff replied. I looked up and saw him giving me a tired smile. "This Holy Father nonsense will have to stop."

"But I have not seen what you have seen," I said in desperation. "I don't know what's happening, or what I should do, or anything!"

"It's fairly simple, Alan," said Leger. I find it a terrible thing to call my Pontiff by his family name. But he has asked me to do so, and whatever he is now, I will still obey him. It may become easier as time goes by. "The time to end this whole structure and organization has come," my ex-Lord continued. "Someone will take this position I suppose, though why they should, escapes me. I'll be leaving in a few days. I imagine you should stick around until you learn otherwise, or until you see what the rest of us have seen."

The idea frightened me, and I changed the topic.

"You know that several of the Cardinals have already left the Church?" I asked. "The enclave to elect a new Pope will have less than half of the usual number."

"That's encouraging!" said Leger, and touched me gently on my shoulder. "It's all over, Alan, believe me. They may elect a new Pope, but he will be the last. Oneness is here, regardless of whether you have seen it yet or not, and all this religious structure will die away."

"I wish I understood," I said, tears threatening to overcome me.

"Alan, it will come," replied Leger, moving away in the direction of his chambers. "Till then, do what you have to do."

"Goodbye, Your Holiness," I said miserably, for I was certain I would never meet this astonishing man again.

"That's impossible, Alan," said Leger with a warm smile. "With Oneness, goodbye is a meaningless term."

I cannot possibly understand what he meant by

that. But then, I understand nothing of what has happened since that old man died before me.

*October 14th, 2012*
Having little else to do, I have remained at the Vatican as my Archbishop in England had instructed me. This morning, I was asked to become an unofficial assistant to Gregory Cardinal Lavalier. I'm grateful for the opportunity, but I have already listened to the Cardinal's ranting over the defection of Philippe Leger, and I'm following the complex web of political bartering that is going into the election of the next Pope. All the time, I wonder what will happen, and I wish I had the insight to understand how to see Oneness, what it is, and what it will bring to the world.

* * *

Jacqueline Carter had never been exactly the daughter her parents thought they would have. She confused them.

Thomas Jeffrey Carter had lived in Farnham, a small town in Hampshire, England all his life. He had left school at sixteen and gone to work at a local insurance company where he slowly worked his way up to being a section-head of a group in the accounting department, and so reached his ceiling. Tom was happy with his life. He took the same bus into work every morning at eight-fifteen, sat at his desk till four forty-five and caught the five-twelve bus home again. It was a good, dependable life. He could see where he was, where he had been and where he was going.

Jacqueline's mother, Deborah Jean had stayed at high school until she was eighteen, and then gone to a secretarial training college where she excelled at short-hand and gained a passing grade at typing and the use of personal computers. She had taken a job as a personal assistant to a partner in an accounting practice in Farnham and had stayed, working for three different partners until she left when she became pregnant. The partners gave her a farewell party and told her she could come back any time, but she never did.

Their lives were wonderfully stable, predictable, and from the viewpoint of Debbie and Tom, as near to ideal as they could wish. Jacqueline was a bright, pretty child, always tall for her age, with eyes that gradually became hazel-green, like her mother's. The Carters settled down for an idyllically normal, English existence. Jacqueline would go to the same junior school her parents had attended, they agreed, and then go on to Farnham High School like her mother. If they were lucky, she might be able to make it to University or perhaps Farnborough Technical College and become a teacher. One day, she would marry a nice local boy, perhaps one of Tom's subordinates at the insurance company, and settle down nearby to produce a couple of grandchildren for them.

It didn't work out that way.

When Jacqueline was twelve, she walked into town on her own one morning. Outside a hobby shop, she stopped, transfixed. Hung in the window were several flying models of aircraft. One was a World War Two Spitfire. Jacqueline stared at the model, aware that tears were rising to her eyes, and confused by the emotional shock. After a few minutes, she walked into the shop, leaving with a kit with which to make the same aircraft. It was a Spitfire Mark IX, with wartime camouflage colours and RAF roundels. Two weeks later, she had completed the construction and painting, and she mounted it on a stand on her bookshelf. Now and again, she looked at the model and, for inexplicable reasons, would burst into tears.

She was seventeen when the weird events in churches, synagogues and other places of worship began to occur around the world. She didn't hear much about them, because the news of the Pope's abdication overshadowed most other events. She read about Pope Jean-Pierre II with mild interest, but the doings of churches had little in them to intrigue her. She was far more fascinated by the developments in the aviation world, the new airliners built of carbon fiber compounds, the latest supersonic version of the Harrier and the spectacular failures of the American B-2 bombers that had experienced several crashes and most ignominiously had been shown to be highly visible to new developments in radar. She still had not yet flown in an aircraft, but somehow it seemed not to matter. She lived with calm assurance that she would learn to fly when the time was right, and her life would be devoted to flight and aeroplanes.

One weekend, she saw advertisements in her latest edition of *Aviation* for an airshow to be held at the Royal Air Force station at Lyneham in Wiltshire for a gathering of World War Two aircraft. Collectors and enthusiasts from around the world were bringing their Spitfires, Hurricanes and Mustangs to the show, to meet up again with Messerschmitt 109s, Heinkels and Stukas from Germany. An old Lancaster was flying in, the last of the breed, and the Americans were flying over with a B-29 Superfortress.

Without difficulty, she persuaded her current boyfriend to take her to the show, and early on the Saturday morning, they left for Lyneham, his elderly Ford loaded with packed lunches, a cooler of lemonade, blankets and cameras. By ten, they had found a spot in the airfield grounds, parked the car and extracted the cameras for a tour of the aircraft lined up by the hangars. Flying was scheduled to start at midday, so they had time to examine the marvellous array of ancient machines. The day was clear and sunny with few clouds, perfect for an air show.

They strolled down the line admiring the magnificently renovated Mustangs that were nearest to them. Jacqueline was feeling a strange mixture of excitement and trepidation today, and was unable to understand why. The feeling had begun as she entered the airfield gate, recognizing with a shock that this was actually the first time she had been on a working airfield. The runways, hangars and the control tower had stirred something within her, but she was unable to identify the feelings at all.

They stood under the wings of the B-29 Superfortress and goggled at the size of the machine, then wandered further down the line. Jacqueline moved round the bulk of a Harvard trainer and came to a Spitfire, stopped short and gasped audibly.

"Oh God! Kennie, look at that!" she said, her voice trembling.

Kennie stood next to her. Together they looked at the Mark IX Spitfire, perfectly restored and painted in camouflage green and grey, RAF roundels on the wings and fuselage and with the original registration letters on the side. Jacqueline felt a strange shakiness begin in her legs and up her body. She walked slowly up to the Spitfire and reached the wingtip, touching it gently. She felt as if a small electric shock went through as she did so, and she turned back to Kennie. He was standing watching her, his camera ready to take a picture, not seeming to notice her reaction.

She turned back and kept walking toward the wing root at the fuselage. She felt as if she were in a dream. The ground was almost rubbery beneath her feet and the noise of the crowds was fading from her. She was alone with the warbird. She reached the back of the wing and looked up into the cockpit, unable to see much beyond the top of the instrument panel. She was trembling hard and her legs were threatening to collapse.

"What's up, lass?" Kennie had walked up to join her, though she had been unaware of it. It broke the dreamlike sensation.

"I don't know!" she said, panic in her voice. "Maybe it's the sun?" She was still staring at the Spitfire.

"Why don't we go back to the car and have a drink?" he suggested, and gently took her elbow to lead her away. She went with him, disturbed and anxious at her weird behaviour.

Back at the car, Kennie extracted a blanket and laid it out on the grass on the shady side of the Ford. Jacqueline sat down gratefully while he found the cooler and poured her a glass of lemonade. She sipped at it, glad of the rest.

"Better?" Kennie said as he joined her on the ground.

She nodded. "God knows what all that was about!" she said with a grin. "But I got the weirdest feeling as I looked at the Spitfire."

"Probably just remembering the model you built as a kid!" he replied.

"Hmm," she said, thinking that his suggestion had some merit. It was certainly a feeling of *déjà vu*. She decided that was probably right, and tried to put it out of her mind.

"How long have we got before the flying starts?" she asked him. He checked his watch. "Twenty minutes," he replied. "Might as well wait here, the view should be as good as anywhere else."

"Sounds good," she said with a smile. "Fancy a beef sandwich?"

At midday, sounds of engines rumbled from the hangars, and Jacqueline and Kennie climbed to their feet. The airfield had filled up considerably since they had arrived, and lines of cars stretched either side of them. The sun was high now, and they folded the blanket back into the car, all shade gone.

The public address system came to life.

"Ladies and Gentlemen," thundered the loudspeaker, echoes of the words rumbling to her from the other speakers around the field. "We are proud to introduce the last flying Lancaster from World War

Two. And here it is, approaching from the west, the Avro Lancaster!"

All heads swung to the left as they saw the heavy shape only a few hundred feet above the ground. The four Merlin engines rumbled in an unsynchronized, gut-stirring way that made the air and the ground shake.

At first, Jacqueline thought the trembling in her legs was from the thunder of the Merlins, but it got stronger and affected her whole body. A feeling of faintness swept through her, and an incredible exhilaration mixed with fear churned her stomach. Nearly falling, she grabbed Kennie's arm.

"Kennie!" she gasped as he looked down at her in surprise.

"Christ, Jackie! What the hell's the matter?" he said, and turned to put his other arm round her shoulders.

"I don't know," she mumbled. *I know that sound!* she cried inside. *I know it! Oh God! What's happening to me?*

She felt Kennie lowering her to the grass and leaning her against the side of the car. She was still shaking uncontrollably and the thunder of the Lancaster was overwhelming. A small crowd of people had moved round to look at her and she was conscious of faces staring in her direction.

"I'm okay," she said, and looked into Kennie's worried face. And she did feel better, she realized. The sound of the Lancaster had faded and strength was returning to her body, though her breathing was ragged still.

"I really don't think so," he contradicted. "I've never seen anything like this happen to you."

"Nor have I!" she said with a grin, feeling stronger every moment, but bewildered by the events of the morning. "Let's not miss the rest of the show!"

She stood up and looked around. The Lancaster was still visible, circling some miles to the east. Bellows of engines starting came from the hangar area, and she turned to watch. The Spitfire and two Hurricanes had begun taxiing out for take-off, and the feeling of anxiety revived in her gut. Without pausing, all three aircraft turned into wind and roared off. The trembles in her body were at work again, but as the warbirds vanished towards the Lancaster and the sound faded, the shaking eased.

"There's something about the sound of those engines that's bothering me," she confessed to Kennie. He was still watching her carefully.

"So I see," he agreed. "They're all Merlins on the fighters and the Lancaster. Why the hell should they bother you?"

"God knows!" she replied. "Here they come again."

They turned to the east to see the fighters escorting the Lancaster back towards the field. As the rumble of engines got louder with the distinctive Merlin thunder, tears flooded into her eyes, a sense of massive grief and pain rose in her chest, and she collapsed in hysteria on Kennie's shoulder.

"Jackie! For God's sake, Jackie," he said, holding her close. "What's wrong with you?"

"I don't know!" she cried through the tears, banging her fist on his chest in frustration. "I just don't know!" Her sobs were deep and painful, making her body shudder. People were turning to stare as the flotilla passed, and they heard her weeping as the thunder faded.

Kennie pulled round to the side of the car, opened the door and pushed her into the seat. He walked round to the driver's side, climbed in and started the engine.

"Whatever it is, we have to get you out of here," he said, and moved out of the line of cars and headed for the exit. Jacqueline sat numbed with shock at her astounding reactions and said nothing until they were some miles away from Lyneham.

"Any ideas?" he said as they purred along the highway at a steady hundred kilometres an hour.

"None at all," she said, staring out of her window. "I feel fine now, though I can still feel the after-effects. But I just got terrified and excited at the same time as I heard those engines, then when all of them passed us, the whole thing overwhelmed me. And I have no idea why!"

"You're weird, Jackie!" he said with a grin.

"Yeah," she agreed, and said no more until they were home, quite late in the evening.

She spoke quickly to her mother in the kitchen, said goodnight to Kennie as he left for his home in Aldershot, excused herself from dinner, and went straight to her room. She took a bath and turned into bed, read a chapter of Roland Beamont's memoirs of test-flying the English Electric Lightning, and turned off the light.

At the deepest stage of sleep, a glaring, bright and horrific dream exploded within her.

*When the sirens went off, I was asleep in my armchair, a trick I had developed despite the nerves and the constrictions of the Mae West around my chest. My parachute was by my feet, and I was stretched out, my head against the incredibly dirty antimacassar on the back of the armchair.*

*The sounds of bodies leaping into action around me woke me about the same time as the sirens did.*

*"Green Squadron! Scramble!" yelled the duty corporal, slamming down the phone that he had snatched on the first ring.*

*I stood up and stretched, deliberately trying to look casual. Instead, I got a sharp slap on my back.*

*"Come on, Jerry! Huns to kill!"*

*Flight Lieutenant Peter Wells nudged me sideways as he ran past to the open door, where all the others were flooding out into the daylight. I snatched up the parachute and followed him, as I had been doing all this summer. He had entered flying school a month ahead of me by the crude device of quitting school early. By the time I was in training, he was already assigned to Tangmere and flying Spitfires. But I caught him, even if he was already two ranks above me.*

*I raced outside, the last of the squadron, and ran like hell to my aircraft. My wingman was waiting for me with a small frown of disapproval, but he said nothing as I threw the parachute onto the bucket seat, climbed in after it and concentrated on getting all the straps fastened correctly. I was barely finished before all the planes were moving out and I was last in line by the time I had the engine churning and the huge propeller spinning in front of me.*

*We reached the eastern end of the field and I tucked in behind Peter's left wing where I should be. He turned and nodded at me, his face already hidden behind the oxygen mask. The green fire flashed from the control tower, and I pushed the throttle forward as all sixteen Spitfires began to accelerate. We took off in groups of four and I settled in behind Peter's right wingtip. This was only my fifth combat flight and I was terrified, the fear churning my guts and my hands trembling on the control column. Peter had told me the fear never goes away. A pilot just learns to hide it.*

*"Green Squadron, steer one seven zero, angels two four," said the female voice in my earphones. Southern Command was steering us to intercept something, but as yet, the radar hadn't identified the intruders. The squadron flew almost due south over the Channel as we climbed to twenty-four thousand feet. Our new Mark IX Spitfires had the extra power in the Merlins and the climb was rapid and smooth. We had been re-equipped just a week after I had joined the squadron, and all the pilots were like kids with new toys. We had the speed of the Messerschmidt 109s*

now, and a smaller turning circle, and the kill rate was increasing.

At twenty-four thousand feet, the air was cold and clear, and the Channel below was a steel-grey strip of solid metal. The French coast was a thin line a few miles further south, the sand of the beaches of Normandy visible even from here. And tracking across the dirty metal was a flock of birds. My throat constricted. They were Heinkels, I could see, and somewhere above them would be the 109s. Somebody else saw them at the same time, and had better control of his voice than I did.

"Bandits, three o'clock, low!" said the calm voice. I couldn't identify it. Peter's voice was in my earphones immediately.

"Two Flight, follow!" he said, and I swung my head to his wingtip and carefully followed his track as he turned a few degrees further right and away from the Squadron which was now breaking into four flights of four aircraft.

I stared up into the dark blue of higher altitudes, but could not see any bandits there. I continued to follow Peter's wingtip, my heart thumping so loud I could barely hear the thunder of my Merlin engine. My hands were sweating on the control column and throttle lever.

"109s, four o'clock, two thousand down," said Peter's voice and I looked to my right to see them. There they were, six thousand feet above the Heinkels but below us. We tracked round behind them, and still they hadn't seen us.

"Unlock the guns, chaps," said Peter. God, I wish I had his nerves. He had always been the heroic type at school. He was the one with the fearless knee tackles in Rugby, the one who stood up to the school bully, the one the others followed. We played on the same teams and I was considered good, but not as good as Peter. We were friends, and had been since Prep School. Peter Wells and Jerome Mitchell, names to conjure *with, my father had said cheerfully. That'll scare the crap out of the Krauts, he said when I told him I was following Peter into the RAF.*

*"Okay chaps, tally-ho, good hunting!" Peter could have been leading the school cross-country team for all the nerves he was showing as he told us to break formation and choose our own targets. The dogfight was on. Below, the 109s had also broken formation as they finally saw us. I picked the wingman of one small group, got him in my sights and poured on the power into the Merlin. The engine howled savagely and I forgot my fear. I was right in it now.*

*Damn! The 109 had swerved away. I pushed on right rudder and aileron to follow him and tightened the turn. This was the Spitfire's strength. I pulled tighter, felt the blood draining from my eyes, but the 109 was crawling into my sights... he was there, I pressed the button and a stream of tracer flashed out... smoke burst from the 109, it jerked sharply as the pilot was hit... I got one!! I gave it another burst, and flames ignited on the starboard wing. I pulled away sharply, flung myself left, looked for another target.*

*"Jerry, behind you!" screamed my earphones, Peter's voice. How could he fight and look after me as well? I wondered as fear slammed my breath from my body. I pulled up sharply, flung the Spitfire into a rolling right-hand turn and saw the tracers flying just inches from my left shoulder. Someone was on my tail! I dived, twisting left and right, trying to get a glimpse behind me, but could see only a brief shadow as the 109 followed my every move. The Spitfire shuddered as bullets hit somewhere behind me, sweat poured out of me as I thought of being hit... smoke in the cockpit... then flames... Oh god, I'm hit, please don't fire again, can't you see I'm hit... another burst shatters my windshield and the smoke gets worse... the engine falters, flames grow bright somewhere on my left, I am frozen with fear....*

*"Jerry, get out, get out!" screams the voice in my*

*ears again, and I dumbly try and undo my straps... nothing happens... Oh Jesus... I'm going to die... the heat of the fire is burning my face....*

Jacqueline Carter shot up in bed, drenched with sweat, a small squeal of panic still in her throat. She was breathing hard, her gasps so loud in the tiny bedroom that she was sure her parents could hear her.

What had that dream been all about? She sat cross-legged on the bed, the covers thrown off as she tried to cool down. A World War Two dogfight? All the details were so clear.... It must have been something to do with the events of the day at Lyneham, she decided.

She knew that it wasn't. She sat in the dark and remembered. She remembered being eighteen-year-old Jerome Mitchell, fresh out of Reading School, a friend of Peter Wells since the age of eight. They had played together as kids on the banks of the River Thames in Reading, and when they were fourteen, war had broken out in Europe. In 1943, they had left school and joined the RAF, a month apart, then met up again at Tangmere as Spitfire pilots. Even in that month, Peter had already been promoted to Flight Lieutenant and had shot down three enemy aircraft.

She/Jerry had died in a dogfight over the Channel, two weeks later.

"I'm still dreaming," she decided and tried the age-old trick of pinching herself on the leg to make sure. It hurt.

"No, this is insane, I am definitely dreaming," she insisted to herself. She lay down again, and tried to get back to sleep, but after a few minutes, realized that it was impossible. She switched on the bedside light and picked up Roland Beamont's book again. She had read about testing the Canberra and the Super Sabre before sleep finally came.

In the morning, however, she still remembered being Jerome Mitchell who had died in an aerial dogfight over the English Channel over fifty years before she was born. She remembered his entire eighteen years of life, his family, his school days, and the girl he had taken to the school dance before he had joined the RAF.

For a time, Jacqueline Carter was the only woman in the world who could remember exactly what it felt like to be a man asking a girl to a dance. She told nobody about her memories.

# Chapter 3. Revelations

After six months of solitude in a retreat in a country house in the area where he had been born and where he grew up, a short distance south of Valence, Philippe Leger, one-time Pope Jean-Pierre II began to feel rested and prepared to return to the world.

In those months, the news of his abdication had burst on the world with even more thunder and excitement than the sudden death of Jean-Pierre I at the hands of an assassin, after only three days on the Throne of Saint Peter. The Cardinals met in Rome and spent seven days in prayer and discussion before finally the white smoke had issued from the chimney above the Vatican, and the people called out "We have a Father!" After a short series of non-Italian popes, the Cardinals had reverted to tradition, and elected a compromise as the new Vicar of Christ. Mario Grassano was an elderly man of great orthodoxy and no distinguished history, who took the name of Pope Pius XIII.

While that had been going on, Philippe Leger walked in the woods, and along the side of the River Rhone, recognized but discreetly ignored by his neighbors. Once or twice, he rode his bicycle into Valence and walked thoughtfully through the twelfth-century Romanesque cathedral that had been poorly restored in the seventeenth century. He felt an affectionate distance, like a middle-aged man who returns to his junior school. He stood before the bust of one of his predecessors, Pope Pius VI and stared at the thin, ascetic face.

"What do you think of all this, you dried-up old stick?" he asked. Receiving no answer, he smiled and walked out of the Cathedral, nodding politely to the few locals and tourists.

He read many books, including the Tibetan Book of The Dead and the Egyptian Book of The Dead, both of which he had studied many years ago. Now he read them again with a new insight. He read his bible a great deal too, but with a different perspective, and he read several texts, which he had taken from the secret library of the Vatican before he left. These documents were considered by the Catholic authorities to be too dangerous for the world to see. They included Aramaic scrolls found together with the Dead Sea Scrolls, which detailed a history of the man known as Jesus with different interpretations of his acts and sayings. Other scrolls suggested ideas and concepts, which could be considered dangerous to a religious hierarchy based on obedience to dogma.

One single page of an incomplete text was a few fragmented words by an unidentified writer. The words made Philippe catch his breath.

*"You shall live many lives,"* said the text. *"You shall live the lives of men, of women, of rich and of poor, of the mighty and the low, and thus shall you learn the first truth of Man."*

Philippe Leger carefully worked his way through the Aramaic words. "Reincarnation?" he asked himself. "Is this what the words are saying? And what is the first truth of Man? And are there subsequent truths?" He turned back to the script.

*"Only when you die will you live. And when you die, then will you make judgement on yourself."*

"No wonder they banned this lot," muttered Philippe to himself. "It removes in one sweep the power of the Church to control humanity. How would anyone believe a priest's threat of punishment, if there was no

Heaven or Hell, nor any Day of Judgement?" He thought further. "It does seem to verify an afterlife," he said softly. "One that is the real existence, rather than the one we have on Earth. And we judge ourselves? What a wonderful idea!"

*"And when you have judged, so then shall you live again, so that you may learn further,"* continued the words on the photocopied page. *"And when you have learned the first truth, then shall you no longer live again as Man, but go forward to learn other truths and live as God."*

Live *as* God? Not live *with* God, but live *as* God? Philippe was shaken. Here was an ancient writing that had the first awareness of Oneness. And there are other truths, too, apart from the clear indication of multiple reincarnations, though no details of what these truths could be were given. His mind swam in confusion and delight.

"Who wrote this?" he said in wonder. But there was no indication of the author anywhere in the page. He had not been able to find any more excerpts from this text, and he felt frustrated by it.

Another text was an even more fragmented piece, a copy taken from a crushed scroll from which only a few words were readable. The single photocopied page was barely legible.

*"For Man lives in the House of God,"* said the blurred characters, *"and other Men live in other Houses and have not the likeness of Man. But they are God also..."*

Other intelligences in the universe? It seemed to be saying so, thought Leger in excitement. He had always considered that such a possibility existed, though it was not a belief which sat well with the firm commitment to salvation through Christ which the Church demanded. *And if it was so, how could the writer possibly know?* thought Philippe. Who was the writer? And what did he mean that these 'other Men' were 'God also'? Again, Leger was frustrated, and almost wished that he had delayed his departure from Rome until he had taken the opportunity to study these forbidden texts in greater detail.

"Dammit!" he said to himself. "I could have locked myself away in that room and studied for years and nobody could have stopped me."

After a few days of such frustration, he calmed himself. "That's silly," he told himself. "You already know most of this now, and in a few years you'll know it all." For although he knew deep inside of the coming of Oneness, he still was not clear about what it entailed. Only a few facts glowed firmly inside of him. There was no God, not in any sense that had been accepted to date. There was no devil. There was no Heaven or Hell. Reincarnation was a reality, and there were other intelligent beings in the universe.

Beyond that, he was unclear.

* * *

At last consenting to a Press conference, Philippe Leger decided to meet the media in a conference room hired from the Hotel Chateau de Clavel, a building constructed in the style of Emperor Napoleon III, a short distance from his home in Etoile sur Rhone, a few kilometres south of Valence. He wanted no religious overtones to the meeting, so he refused the Vatican's request that the meeting be held in Rome, or in any church property. He agreed to allow up to two hundred people in the room, and only two television cameras, from which all networks would take their feeds. One camera would focus on the stage, the second would look at the audience during the period of questions from the floor.

The meeting would be televised live, he determined, because he wanted no editing of the proceedings. He would make his statement and would then decide whether to permit questions. The one-time Archbishop Carmagio acted as his agent to the outside world, and Raoul had to work hard to resist letting his anger explode on occasions.

"No, the meeting will not take place at two o'clock in the morning," he snapped at the representatives of the American television channels, who demanded that the broadcast fit in US prime time. "And it will not take place in New York or at the White House." The Americans seemed unable to understand that the rest of world also had televisions, or that the American viewers did not take precedence over everyone else.

"It will be at ten in the morning on the day and at the location we have already specified," Raoul said again and again to people who seemed unable to understand that simple statement and kept repeating requests for other days, other times and other venues.

The Vatican demanded that only its representatives be allowed to be present and that the statements should be recorded and subject to review before release to the world. Carmagio declined that demand, too.

"Philippe Leger is no longer a member of the Catholic Church, nor any other church," he stated firmly to Gregory Cardinal Lavalier who had been despatched by the new Pope to discuss the event with Carmagio. "You have no authority over him."

"He has left the Church?" gasped Lavalier. "He has abandoned the Mother Church? Does he not understand how his immortal soul is in danger?"

"He understands exactly what faces his immortal soul," Carmagio replied with a faint smile. His tweed jacket, grey open-necked shirt and casual slacks contrasted with the severe, formal robes of the Cardinal. "There is no danger."

"No danger?" the Cardinal protested. "If his statements are against God and the Church, if he preaches heresies, we will have no alternative but excommunication! He will face everlasting Hell!"

"He will preach nothing," the one-time Archbishop replied. "For there is nothing to preach. Preaching is a silly and dangerous habit. And your threats are no more than bogeymen to little boys. Philippe will simply tell us of a new truth."

"A new truth?" shouted Lavalier, his fear and anger destroying his composure. "There are no new truths, there are only the eternal, changeless truths of the Mother Church! Clearly, Leger is about to speak heresies! It cannot be allowed!"

"Tough," said the one-time Archbishop Carmagio.

* * *

On the morning of the press conference, Etoile sur Rhone was a zoo, just like it had been for the preceding week, as the reporters assembled, most of them staying at the Chateau de Clavel, or at the Hotel 2000 and other hotels in Valence. Many had tried to pre-empt the conference and catch Philippe Leger on one of his solitary strolls, but he remained hidden from the wolf packs, having quietly transferred to a friend's house in Saint Etienne.

The good citizens of the area had prospered from the invasion of reporters and supporting crews, for no true Frenchman would permit so many foreigners around without making sure that the visitors contribute their fair share to the local economy. But they had become tired of the frenzy, and would be glad when *'le bon Papa'* had finished with them and sent them all packing.

Leger arrived quietly early in the morning, having driven down in his Renault from Saint Etienne, and entered the hotel by the back door. He was shown to the conference room and sat on his own for over an hour before the doors were opened. As he sat, he looked around the room, thinking about the bombshell he would launch from here. The setting did not reflect the enormity of the event. It was just a room, big enough for twenty rows of seats ten abreast, a neutral area at the front of them, and then two seats on a slightly raised platform, with a microphone standing like a solitary stalk of wheat in a field.

Raoul Carmagio came into the room and saw his old friend sitting silently. The one-time Archbishop had lost weight over the previous weeks, not from any nervous pressures or fear, but simply because he had chosen to, and discovered the ability to implement his choices. He now wore an elegant black blazer, a white silk shirt, grey trousers and a blue cravat. He looked like a middle-aged millionaire on vacation.

"Nervous, Philippe?" he asked.

Leger shook his head. "Not really nervous," he replied. "More concerned about what's going to happen over the next few years as this thing spreads."

"Do you think they'll believe you today?"

"That's not important," said Leger with a small shrug. "The important thing is that the message will get out to the whole world. We two are certainly not the only ones to know about it, we're just perhaps the highest profile. So the more people recognize that the new knowledge is spreading, the quicker it will take place."

"There are some rumours around the world, already," agreed Carmagio. "I've been reading newspapers from all over the place, and it looks like a number of clerics got hit with this thing the same way you did, right in the middle of a service. I've got stories of priests of all creeds and beliefs walking out of church shouting about Oneness all over the world."

Leger turned a thoughtful eye on his friend from the wooden chair he was occupying, his legs crossed and his arms folded. He had dressed for the conference in a blue suit, with a white shirt, and a tie with blue and red diagonal stripes. A pair of gold cuff links was the only concession to the occasion or to his previous position as a world leader. His long, slender frame in the simple but elegant suit made him look like a successful bank manager or attorney.

"Really?" he said. "Mainly priests? I wonder why?"

"I asked myself the same question," said Raoul with a small smile. "I suspect that it was because they, like you, were in a highly receptive mental state during a service. At the same time, it may just be that walkouts by priests in the middle of church services make news. God knows how many people got it without the media hearing about it."

"God?" said Leger with a deadpan expression.

"Well, you know what I mean," replied his friend with a self-conscious gesture. "It's going to be hard to shake off old habits."

Leger chuckled softly. "Today, I think the numbers of the enlightened will swell dramatically. Those old habits will die quicker after this."

"I pray so," replied Carmagio, waving off the amused comment that he knew his friend would make about another outdated expression. "Sorry, Philippe," he continued. "Until we develop a new term for it, I don't know how to express it. But I worry that we may be facing the same reactions that the first Christians received from the Romans, and for the same reasons."

Leger stood up and stretched. Even as Pope, few would have thought that the fit, muscular man of six-foot-two was aged more than fifty, and only because he was a public figure did the world know that he was sixty-three. Now, like his friend, he had chosen to improve his shape and condition and looked like a fit man in his early forties.

"These are my worries, too," he said softly. "We must try and avert the problems." He walked towards the side door by the raised platform. "Time to let the world in, Raoul," he said with a friendly smile. "I'll come back when they're all settled."

He walked out and closed the door behind him. Looking a little wound up, Raoul Carmagio walked to the other door and unlocked it.

Half an hour elapsed before the conference was ready to begin. The television crew switched on the brilliant lights over the platform and tested the two cameras. The microphones were given a final try, while the reporters scrambled for their seats, took out their recorders and anxiously checked the batteries yet again. When the air of tension in the room crushed the noise under its heavy feet so that the silence almost cracked the walls, Raoul Carmagio stood up from the chair on which Philippe Leger had earlier been sitting, and walked to the front of the stage.

"Ladies and gentlemen of the press, I wish you good morning." He had chosen to speak in English, but interpreters for every major language in the world were listening in their studios and translating for the television audience which later review would show was the single largest audience in history. "I shall just repeat the rules for this conference," continued Raoul. "Mister Leger will shortly make a statement. Please do not interrupt that statement at all. When he has finished, you may ask questions. Please do so by standing up, and identifying yourself and your organization to me, when I have pointed to you. We shall try and let everyone have an opportunity to speak. But I must stress that if the meeting gets out of hand, we shall simply leave the room."

He looked out from the brightness, unable to see past the first two rows. The lights would have to be turned up in the main body of the room when question time began, he realized, and was glad that a thoughtful hotel manager had installed additional booster air conditioning units the previous evening.

In complete silence, Raoul sat down again. The door opened and Leger walked out, moved to the microphone and stood still. A buzz of excitement ran through the room and rapidly subsided. Leger had no notes and looked relaxed.

"Good morning," he said softly, speaking in English. There was no response to his words but two hundred heads instinctively looked to check that two hundred recorders were functioning.

"I know that you are expecting to hear from me some indications that I suffered a sudden loss of faith and walked away from the Church, a broken man," said Leger.

A small buzz of agreement and amusement ran through the room and faded as the tall Frenchman raised one hand. "Part of your expectations will be met," he continued. "But the reasons, and the results of that loss of faith will not be anything that you expect at all, of that I am certain. And as you see, I am anything but a broken man." He smiled at the room, though he could see nothing beyond the first two rows.

"Six months ago," he continued, "I was giving Mass in the Vatican when I became aware of an enormous presence in the Universe. I do not yet understand this presence, but with it, I became aware of a new reality."

He paused for a second or two, looking into a far distance. "I felt perhaps, like a stone-age man would feel when faced with the arrival of modern man in an aeroplane. Even that is quite inadequate to describe the sensation I experienced, but I will keep trying. I realized that all we have believed in the last two thousand years of Christianity, for the several thousand years of Judaism before that, and Islam and Buddhism since then is simply a tiny echo of the real truth. It was a truth we could cope with in our state of development at the time, but we have since become ready for the new reality of the Universe, and something is coming to teach us."

Nothing broke the stillness in the room.

"Just as once our missionaries took the word of God to people who worshipped stone idols or the Sun and the Moon, so is this presence coming to us. As I sensed it, I realized a tiny fraction of what we will learn, and this I can tell you now."

A tiny echo of a whisper flittered over the room like mayflies through a sunbeam, and silence returned.

"I used the term 'Oneness' when I discovered this new presence," Philippe Leger said, his voice growing stronger. "I cannot explain exactly what I mean by this, but I will try. I believe now, that what we have called God, is in fact the sum total of human intelligence, and eventually, all people will meld into this one intelligence. It means that all the trappings of Church, religion, and worship become meaningless, because prayer to God is simply prayer to ourselves. Hindus and Buddhists have had a grasp of this truth in their philosophy."

He looked across at his friend Raoul, and they exchanged smiles.

"I understand that many people around the world have experienced the same insight in recent weeks, and slowly, the whole world will come to see it. The wonderful result of that is surely that all conflict will end, because how can we continue to kill ourselves? All racial, ethnic and class bitterness will have to die away, because we will realize that every one of us will live, or already has lived a life in every sort of style that humanity can think of. Yes," he smiled widely at the audience. "I am talking about reincarnation, though my previous church, and most others in the Judeo-Christian school of philosophy have always taught that such a thing does not exist."

This time, a distinct ripple of excitement ran round the room. In the first row, Raoul saw the Cardinal who had spoken to him some weeks earlier. Lavalier's face was furious, his arms were crossed over his chest in massive denial, and he stared back at Raoul, not looking at his one-time Pontiff.

"I am also talking about an after-life," continued Leger, "which will seem far more real than the earthly incarnation, and during which, each soul will judge itself on what it has learned during its time on Earth, and decide what its next life should be. So, no Heaven, ladies and gentlemen, no Hell, no God, no Devil. I know that to many of you, all this sounds like the ravings of a mind become unhinged. But these ravings are now being echoed by thousands of people around the world, who will soon become millions, and eventually, billions. We must prepare for a different existence from this point onward. Whatever, or whoever is approaching us will teach us just what sort of existence this will be."

Leger looked out into the blindness of the arc lights and smiled. "This is not what you expected to hear, nor is it enough of what I wanted to tell you. But it is all I have. Perhaps some questions may extract more details from me, so will somebody please turn up the lights in the room so we can see you?"

The room hummed for a few seconds as somebody at the rear found the lights and turned them up. The barrier between the stage and the audience vanished, and people erupted to their feet to attract the attention of Philippe Leger. He smiled and pointed to a short, stocky man in the second row. Slowly, the noise subsided and the man remained on his feet, waiting for enough silence so he could be heard.

"Jan Reschko, *Chicago Tribune,*" he said. "Before I ask my question, perhaps we should clarify the protocol." He spoke English with a slight accent, which Leger decided was Hungarian, one of the sixteen languages the Frenchman spoke fluently.

"Which protocol is that, sir?" asked Philippe with a warm smile.

"How should we address you?" the reporter demanded. "Holy Father is no longer appropriate, but I feel unsure of what fits. Will you please tell us?"

Leger looked surprised. "My name is Philippe," he said. "That would be a reasonable thing to call me."

The man in the second row grinned with a display of white teeth. "Thank you, Philippe," he said cheerfully. "I was hoping that would be your answer!" He looked down at his notes and raised his head. "Philippe," he said, "would you tell us more of this 'Presence' you said was approaching?"

Leger looked briefly at the ceiling, as if in doubt about his ability to answer the question. Then he lowered his eyes to the audience. "Imagine the experience of a stone-age man on a lonely island," he began. "He is standing on the ocean shore and he hears the sound of aircraft engines. He knows the noise is alien. Nothing like it has ever been heard before, and he has no concept of what might cause it. But he knows just as strongly, that some incredible new force is approaching."

He looked round the room. Most faces were staring at him in fascination, but on some he detected a sneer of derision, the expression that said the old man had dropped his bundle, gone loopy, round the bend. Leger smiled to himself.

"That is what I experienced during that Mass," he said. "Something is coming to show us the reality of our mixed-up beliefs, but I don't yet know what it is."

The rows of journalists erupted again as men and women fought for recognition. Raoul Carmagio rose to his feet and began the task of selection. He pointed at a young woman at the back of the room, and for a second she looked around herself as if uncertain that she had been called. Confident that it really was herself, she cleared her throat.

"Angela Maxwell, the *Guardian*," she called out in a clear, English soprano. "May I just clarify this for my own sake? Are you saying that all the teachings of the Judeo-Christian churches of the last few thousand years are wrong? That we have been worshipping a God that does not exist?"

"That is exactly what I am saying," Leger replied. "We have confused a series of signs and phenomena, corrupted a set of valid teachings with greed and hunger for power, and diverged wildly from the reality. We will soon get it straight, however."

"I don't understand," the woman reporter insisted. "How can all the signs be wrong?"

"Think of it this way," said Leger with a small grin. "When we were children, we woke up on Christmas Day morning with a pile of presents delivered during the night. The set of facts we were given, that Santa Claus had delivered them, fitted the physical signs that we saw. The explanation was reasonable for the level of our mental powers as a child. But later we learned that a different set of facts had applied, though they resulted in the same thing. That is what I mean by our having misinterpreted the signs that we saw."

An odd thought came to Philippe and he tried to identify it, then decided to say something further. It was associated with the words he had just spoken... *what was it?... never mind, try and catch it again later...*

"Buddha expressed it rather more accurately," continued Philippe. "He told a story of a man who uses a boat to cross a river, then continues to carry the boat with him as he walks miles overland. Clearly, that is silly. One would use the boat for the purpose of getting somewhere, then abandon it when the function of the boat no longer applies. It is the same with beliefs, said Buddha. Do not retain your beliefs once they have got you to where you are going..." *(he said those words to me, one morning as the crowds gathered... said it to me? But that was the crazy thought you had a few moments ago. What are you babbling about, Leger?).* For a second or two, Philippe puzzled over the insane image that had just come to him, then returned to the audience.

"This is what I mean," he said. "Our belief structure has served us for five or six thousand years, sometimes for good, too often for evil. It has got us to where we are now, but it is time to abandon those beliefs in favour of a new set that more accurately represent the Universe as it is."

More wild waving, and Carmagio pointed to an elderly man in the front row. He was sitting next to Cardinal Lavalier and obviously had recognized the churchman, because he had been carefully watching the Cardinal during Leger's opening statements.

"Karl Reiner, *Deutsche Zeitung,*" he said.

"Philippe, why are you the only person to have experienced this enlightenment?" An edge of sarcasm was evident in the slightly accented voice.

"But I am not," said Philippe Leger sharply. "If you will study the world's newspapers when you get home, especially small, local papers, you will find numerous cases in the last few weeks and months where other priests have walked out on their congregations, saying that the Time of Oneness is here. I believe that this has occurred with priests because they would be in an emotional state of receptivity during a service, and so perhaps more open to recognizing the signals that we are all getting. But I am equally certain that many ordinary men and women around the world have also seen this thing, too."

A tall, thin man in the middle of the room jumped to his feet and waved frantically. Sensing corroboration of his words, Leger pointed to him.

"Tony Smithers, *Toronto Globe and Mail,*" shouted the young man. "I was going to ask you if these events had any similarity, but if I may, I would like to tell you about some that I had heard of." He consulted a page of notes in his hand. "There were two cases last month in Quebec, of Catholic priests behaving exactly as you said," he continued. "And in a small town in Ontario, a young Unitarian minister walked out on his congregation in great distress."

Leger looked with interest at the Canadian reporter. "You have other examples?" he asked.

"I sure do," the man replied with a lean smile. "These examples from home got me going, so I did some research. There's a Rabbi in Manchester, England who actually told his congregation that the time of Oneness had arrived, the same word you used yourself. I've got..." he looked closely at the page in his hand, "four ministers in Germany, three in Scotland, the Archbishop of Sydney in Australia..." He was interrupted by a laugh from Raoul Carmagio, joined in by Leger as the two friends looked at each other.

"Charlie's got it!" chuckled Leger and wiped his eyes. "I'm glad about that!"

"There are several cases of priests committing suicide within hours or days of their last service," continued the Canadian, "and there's a report that a man in Texas was shot dead outside a Baptist Church after he walked out on a sermon, talking about Oneness, also."

Leger's face went solemn. "I was afraid that sort of thing might happen," he said into the silence that had fallen on the room. "This new force is even more cataclysmic than the advent of Christianity. I fear that upheavals and hatreds will ensue until everyone has seen it." He looked out onto the room. "That must not be allowed to happen," he said with a worried look. "What has taken place is that we are beginning to grow up and realize that the Santa Claus theory of the universe is about to be replaced by something more accurate and commensurate with our maturing capacity to understand."

More waving from the floor, and Carmagio indicated a man who looked in his seventies, sitting at the right end of the fifth row. The man was tall and slender, he wore a small beard, totally grey, the same colour as his full head of hair. He was dressed much like Carmagio, in slacks and a light jacket with an open-necked shirt. Recognizing Carmagio's signal, he stood up slowly. The natural air of authority he wore caused a ripple of silence to move outward from him.

"Francois Bouchard," he said clearly. *"Paris Match."* Leger nodded recognition of the man with a small smile. The French reporter had interviewed the Pope a week after Leger had been elected to the Throne of Saint Peter. Bouchard was a noted agnostic and writer of anti-clerical pieces. The interview had been difficult for both men, because Leger had worked hard at keeping his temper in the face of the hostility of the questions, and Bouchard had been unable to generate the fire he usually obtained in his interviews.

"Philippe," said Bouchard, "does this mean now that you agree with me that it was all garbage?" His accent was barely discernible as French. "Specifically, do you now say that Jesus was merely a man, that the Immaculate Conception was a fable and that God does not exist?"

A rumble of murmuring ran through the room before silence reclaimed the space.

Leger smiled gently. "Your mode of questioning has not blunted its edge over the years, Francois!" he said, and the silence fell before a ripple of amusement. "And I will have to grant you a small victory this time," he continued, "even if it is a partial one." He ignored the broad smile that appeared on Bouchard's face, and instead addressed the room.

"Monsieur Bouchard certainly scores a point or two here," he said, with a brief nod at the reporter. "Let me address the question of the Immaculate Conception first. Yes, I will go with Francois on that one. Mere fable. To be honest, I never saw the point of that one, even as Pope. What is so wrong with normal conception that the Son of God should have to bypass the procedure, or that Mary, his mother, should be born in the same way?" He smiled. "We Catholics have always had this problem with sex. We could never come to terms with it properly, so we chose to consider it as something not just unacceptable, but actually sinful. I used to wonder as a young priest, why that should be, when God had obviously designed the process for all of the rest of us."

The laughter in the room was friendly.

"But the man called Jesus," Leger continued as the silence took back its place. "Not an ordinary man, either. In some ways, I can still tell you he was the Son of God. But then, we have to reconsider the nature of God in the light of this new knowledge. Jesus was something beyond the comprehension of man as we were then, and as most of us still are. I don't know if I can explain it to you while the awareness of Oneness is still so scattered, and indeed, while my own understanding of what I have been shown is still so limited."

Leger looked around the room. It might have been a tableau or a painting. Not a movement could be detected.

"I have to tell you, ladies and gentlemen," he said, an expression of surprise on his face. "This has just come to me. I don't know how, but I am certain of these facts. Jesus came to Mankind because we needed him at the time." Leger spoke into a limitless silence. "He was a soul that operated at a higher level of existence than we do as mortals, and he tried to pass on to us certain truths. At other times and in other places, similar souls have appeared in response to the need of mankind. Mohammed is one, Buddha is another. The problem is that we were not equipped to comprehend the truths they spoke, and we interpreted them within the framework of our culture of the time."

A small eruption occurred in the front row as Cardinal Lavalier shot to his feet. "Leger, you speak heresy!" he roared. "Your soul is damned to eternal Hell! I excommunicate you from the Church and condemn you!"

Leger waited calmly while the commotion in the assembly room rose to a crescendo as people craned the necks and surged forward to see who was speaking. The television camera at the front of room had zoomed in closely on Lavalier, and hundreds of millions of people round the world saw the muscles in the Cardinal's neck stand out and his face flush with rage and fear.

Leger looked sadly at his one-time colleague. "I am sorry that you are so enraged by this, Gregory," he said. "Your fear is very obvious to me. Your entire world is collapsing and believe me, I know exactly how that feels. But you cannot change it, nor can you prevent the future arriving. To save yourself more pain, perhaps you should leave?"

For a few more seconds, the two men stared at each other, one with anger, the other with sadness. Lavalier turned and walked to the door. As he opened it, he spoke once more to his ex-Pontiff. "Excommunication proceedings will begin as soon as I reach Rome," he said. Leger merely shook his head, and the Cardinal walked from the room. The door swung shut behind him, and Leger returned to his audience.

A man in the front row stood up. He didn't bother announcing himself, and Carmagio didn't try and enforce the procedure. Somehow, the nature of the meeting had altered, the formality of a press conference had been replaced by the warmth and closeness of a meeting of friends or students around a popular teacher. Nothing remained in the room of disbelief or cynicism. The world continued to watch through its televisions. Later figures would show that the viewing audience exceeded two billion people, but in the United States, most people had already turned their sets off. Those who continued to watch found in coming years that their interest would cost them their liberty, and even their lives.

"This visitor, Philippe," said the man standing before the stage. He looked about thirty, was short, and built on heavy lines. His hair was jet black and his eyebrows marked a solid, unbroken black line across his face. "You have mentioned it before. Are you saying that someone or something from outside our universe is coming? An alien life form?"

A tiny ripple played around the room, and subsided.

"Yes," answered Leger. "But an alien? I suppose we can use that term, but it is no more alien than we are. Another intelligence is coming to show us the way. I sense that this is not in the same way as Mankind was visited by Jesus, Buddha, or Mohammed before, when we needed guidance through difficult times. This is something more fundamental, but I don't understand any more than that. But yes, something is coming."

"That frightens me," said the man, still standing. "It frightens me that you know about it, while I don't, which I cannot comprehend. It frightens me because it means that far superior intelligences must therefore exist on other planets, and I don't know how friendly they will be. Our world is coming to an end, Philippe. I am desperately afraid."

"Fear is unavoidable." Leger smiled gently. "You are quite correct, our world is coming to an end. We face cataclysmic change now and who could not fear it? But the something that is coming, while it is incomprehensible to me at the moment, I know with certainty that it is benign. It must be. We are part of it, and it is part of us."

Puzzlement ran across his face. "I don't understand what I just said, but I know it to be true."

He walked to the front of the stage. Both cameras focused on him as he spoke. "My friends, my kin, whatever is happening is wonderful. Mankind will change for the better, and our final ascent to meet with what we have thought of as our God will soon take place. Go in peace now, live with what will happen, and we will all meet again in a way that I don't yet understand."

He walked from the stage, followed by Carmagio. The room remained still for a few seconds, then conversations began, with here and there, some sounds of weeping. Instead of rushing to their rooms to begin writing their pieces, everybody stayed for another two hours, taking warmth and closeness from what they had been privileged to see at first hand.

* * *

Michael Hendricks was standing in a comfortable, small lounge. The carpet was light grey, a settee in deep blue stood against the wall, a slate-coloured, kidney-shaped coffee table in front of it. An armchair in the same blue was placed on the other side of the coffee table. A bookcase full of paperbacks was against the far wall. Pictures hung on the walls, one of them a Picasso drawing of a dove, another an Impressionist work of the Cathedral at Chartres.

Michael Hendricks was home.

"A few years ahead of schedule," he said to himself. "There were a few things I hadn't done yet." He reviewed the moment of his death and the people involved in it.

"Infant souls," he said with understanding. "Seem to be a lot of them in that part of the world. All three of them have a long way to go. And now they've slowed themselves up with major Karmic ribbons to me. Could take them several lifetimes to burn those off."

He let himself drift from his position in the middle of the room toward the kitchen, thinking about how to negotiate settlement of the obligations that his three killers in Bainesville had planted upon themselves. It would have to wait a few years before those three died and moved back to the astral plane, but time was not a meaningful concept in the face of eternity.

As always after dying, he stayed in his earthly form for a time, and maintained a residence area much like the one he had inhabited while incarnate. Moving his arms and legs didn't seem essential for motion however, so he merely floated the few feet to the kitchen where he made tea and checked his refrigerator. He was more aware this time than on previous returns that creating an Earth-like environment was not essential, but he decided to stay with it for a while longer. He had liked that apartment in Chicago.

"Hello," said the voice from everywhere around him, and yet nowhere. Michael knew who it was, the sound, the colour, the vibrations were the names used on this level. The voice was unique, just as a face and a name would have been, though neither was any longer required, nor did they exist if the owner chose. The owner of the voice had been Michael's father in its last incarnation, and they had been friends. His father had died ten years ago.

"Was it a good life?" the voice asked.

"Useful," said Michael, sipping his tea. "Got a bit cut short by some Infants, though. There were affairs still to be settled."

"But otherwise a good life, it seems."

"There was a man there when I was killed," said Michael. "The evil within him was frightening. I feel I should have some memory of that soul, but I haven't."

Silence hovered for a few moments as the other soul extended its senses back to the incarnate plane and looked at the man called William H. Horning.

"That is truly an evil soul," said the other. "I have never seen the like."

"I think I have," Michael replied. "Maybe it was this same soul. Why can't I remember?"

"I don't know," replied the other soul. "You're an old enough soul to remember all your past lives."

"Yes," agreed Michael, "but I'm only a first-stage Old Soul, not a seventh-stage like you!"

"Transitional, though," replied his one-time father. "Another couple of lives should see you as a second-stage."

Michael gave the equivalent of a wave, and floated himself back into his lounge, settling lightly on the blue settee. Soon he knew, he would release this physical manifestation of living quarters and let himself take the form of pure soul again. But for the moment, adjustment to this level took a while, especially after a violent death. Once, after dying in a particularly blood-soaked battle between tribesmen in Central Asia in the eleventh century, he had taken subjective months to leave his body shape.

"Little I can do about Horning for now," he said. "I need some more time alone before I review the last life and pick the next, so I'll talk to you then."

"Sure," said the soul who had once been his father, another time his sister, and many times his friend.

Michael stretched out and fell asleep. Dying was always an exhausting business.

When he awoke, he abandoned the body shape, and the room vanished, replaced by mists that held but did not hide the proximity of others. He took himself to the meeting area, moving with a thought, and joined those others of his entity who were not incarnate at this time. He recognized six hundred or so of his entity souls, their colours and vibrations showing welcome to him. That meant a thousand or so of them were now incarnate on Earth. All his entity souls were either mature or old souls, some had completed their cycle of incarnations and would stay at this level until joined by all sixteen hundred of the souls that formed the one entity.

The entity had taken several thousand years to progress from being all infant souls, through the baby level, to young, then adult souls and then gradually to the mature level before reaching Old Soul stature. Each level took several lives, and Michael had lived three hundred and sixty-three incarnations on Earth. Sometimes he pondered on the question of how it was that they as a group had progressed to this advanced mature/old soul stage, while the greatest majority of entities remained composed of baby and infant souls.

Several souls were like him, newly returned to this spiritual level, and the review and discussion of their lives took time, as far as time meant anything anymore. A few had died as children, so there was little to do but let them determine a new incarnation to which to return immediately and complete their learning. They left at once, and the group watched with love as they were born in various countries, to different cultures and social standings. Guardianship duties were taken immediately, and Michael took on the care and teaching of three of the new humans. One was a boy, born to wealthy parents in Norway. Centuries before, that soul had been Michael's wife in ancient India, and once before, his brother during an unrecorded period of history in Mesopotamia. The second, also a boy, was born to a single black mother in New York's Harlem, having opted to learn specific examples of deprivation and the ways of overcoming them. The third was a girl, born with immense musical talents to a family of Russian peasants in Minsk. Michael had a special fondness for the last one. She had shared several incarnations with him, twice as a parent, three times as a sibling and once as his son.

The entity souls finished the post-death discussions, and Michael thought himself back to his own private area to compose himself and think about what his next incarnation should be. It would not take place until the three souls who had just returned to new incarnations on Earth had come back as spiritual beings, for he had taken on mentor duties for them while they were incarnate. However, he had already decided that he had learned much of what he had intended on his last sojourn in a body. Some other things remained, and he began to think that next time he would be a female, and, much like his friend who had just gone down, he would have considerable musical talents and perhaps a physical impairment to provide some drive. But not in America this time, he decided. The preponderance of baby and infant souls in that country generated its own problems, and these might be worsened by the imminent arrival of whatever the astonishing force was that he had sensed before he was killed. The value of the incarnation would be lost if he could not fulfil the mission. Maybe Norway, or China, he thought, drowsily feeling the need for some more sleep coming on. Countries with a higher proportion of mature and old souls, he thought. And there was an unfinished agreement with Julianne. They would need a life together in some form to complete it. He would talk with her the next time she slept and arrived on the Astral Plane.

For comfort, he created around himself a physical

room of considerable luxury. Original Picassos hung on the walls, with a glowing Rembrandt. The carpet was a deep white pile, and the furniture was black leather, in a style he had seen in an expensive shop in Rome. Then he slept, something that aided the return to the spiritual level. He would not need to sleep again after this, he knew, and he let go the bonds to wakefulness.

* * *

Jacqueline Carter spent many hours reliving the life of Jerome Mitchell. She replayed in her mind his days at Prep School when he was eight years old and first met Peter Wells. They had become firm friends immediately. Peter was always the natural leader, and Jerry had been comfortable with his role as supporter and associate. They had gone to Reading School together, and the relationship had remained the same through to their senior year, Jerry as Vice-Captain of Rugby to Peter's Captaincy, earning reflected glory from his role as Peter's best friend.

Jacqueline found the experience astounding. Not only was she aware of just how extraordinary it was that she could remember living a life before her own, but learning how small boys thought, talked to each other, looked at girls and related to their parents was fascinating.

"The ignorance we have about other people!" she thought to herself. "If only I'd known this earlier!"

She never spoke a word of this new insight to her parents or anyone else. She could not have known that other people around the world were experiencing similar profound learning from their past lives, because they too kept it to themselves. By now, she was in her first year at the University of Birmingham, having won scholarships to study Aeronautical Engineering. She found making friends far easier than she had as a younger girl, particularly finding that her relationships with men were relaxed and friendly. She had no difficulty in understanding their shyness with her good looks, or in seeing through the lines they used to approach her, and disarming the intended suitor with simple friendship. Her female friends were profoundly envious of this ability.

She dated several of the young men at the college, finding a preference for those who seemed to be calm and serene internally, much as she was. On occasions, she let the relationship develop to an intensely sexual level, and found that her insight into the minds of men was an astonishing attribute in bed. She knew exactly what would please her partner, and exploited her knowledge to enhance her own pleasure, with the capability to push him to levels of satisfaction never previously experienced.

In the summer at the end of her first year at Birmingham, as she celebrated her twentieth birthday, she thought of finding out if Peter Wells was still alive. For a moment, the concept stunned her. What would he be like? Could he possibly comprehend the thought that his old friend had returned in another body? How could she even try and tell him? She pushed the problems away and concentrated on the first stage, that of finding him. From her revived memories, she knew his old address, his parents' house in Reading. She could even picture the large sprawling building in Sideacre Road on the north side of the River Thames. As a boy, she had stayed there on many occasions during the school holidays. She searched the Internet telephone directories but was unable to find a Peter Wells at that address. She pushed aside the thought of his being dead and told herself he would be ex-directory. Somehow, she couldn't see him leaving that old house if he were still alive.

She was able to borrow the car belonging to her current boyfriend, and got his agreement to keep it for a few days. One Saturday morning in June, her last exams for the year completed with no doubts or anxieties, she climbed into the elderly Honda and headed down the A34 to Oxford and Reading.

On the way down, she tried to work out what to do if she saw Peter, or what to do if she couldn't find him. Some rapid arithmetic told her Peter would be in his mid-nineties if he was still alive and suppressed the fear that he was dead. She pictured him as she had known him at thirteen, as a stocky young boy with uncontrollable hair, at sixteen with some of the bulk hidden by the sudden spurt of growth that had occurred in the previous year, and finally at eighteen, when he took his flight of Spitfires out over the English Channel to challenge the Luftwaffe. Not all that tall, she remembered fondly, about five-foot-nine, muscular build and bright, hazel-green eyes that commanded attention. He had sported a moustache for his entry to the Royal Air Force, and Jerry had ribbed him mercilessly about it.

"Bloody outbreak of facial fungus, that's all it is!" he had shouted at the first sight of it, the day Peter came back home from his first two weeks of RAF training.

"Nonsense!" replied Peter with dignity. "Merely the essential trappings of a great military leader."

Jerry snorted and howled again, but privately admitted Peter looked pretty impressive in his officer's uniform and peaked hat, even if he didn't as yet have the pilot's wings over his breast. The thin stripe of a pilot officer was barely visible on his sleeve, but Peter carried himself as if he was already an Ace equal to Douglas Bader.

Jacqueline shifted in her seat, feeling a dreadful longing to see his/her old friend again. *How could it possibly be?* she thought. *Even if I find him, how do I possibly explain who I am?* She drove round the Oxford bypass roads and headed for Reading. As she came into the town, she found herself looking at landmarks with a different viewpoint. She had been to Reading several times as a child when her mother had brought her to meet her cousins. Now she saw the town as she had seen it when she was a teenaged Jerry Mitchell before the war, coming home from school with Peter to stay with his family for a few days. The two views of the town had difficulty staying in focus, as she saw buildings that had not existed in other years, roads that took different paths and new roads that had not been there before. Through the confusion, she managed to keep her head and drove without incident to the pleasantly wooded north bank of the Thames near the town centre.

The old road to Peter's house hadn't changed, though many of the houses had, and the old wooden signpost had been replaced by a smart metal pole with a yellow sign and black lettering. When she saw the sign, a small jolt ran through her. Large houses with huge picture windows had replaced many of the sprawling mansions, some of the big trees he/she had climbed with Peter had gone, but the road was the same, even if it was now sealed, no longer the rough, gravelled path of seventy years ago.

She was there. Her heart beating faster, she climbed out of the car and looked at the old house. A new extension had been built on one wing, and a room had been added to the ceiling to give an attic. A perfect room for a small boy, she thought.

Nothing to it but to try, she told herself, and began climbing the familiar path up to the front door. She knocked hard on the heavy oak, replaced since 1943, she saw, and waited. A faint sound of heels on tiled flooring came through the heavy door, a woman's step, and the door opened. A woman in her early forties looked down at Jacqueline from a height advantage of two or three inches. Her smile was friendly.

"I'm sorry to bother you," said Jacqueline, "and this may be a bit silly, but I was wondering if Peter Wells still lives here?"

"Which one?" said the woman, her smile widening.

*Huh?* Jacqueline felt shaky. *Which one? What could that mean...? Oh!* She caught on, and tried hard to take control of herself. But she had come to the right house! "The elder," she replied. "The one I know would be in his nineties now."

"Come on in," said the woman. "I'm Christine. I'm his house-keeper."

So Peter had survived the war! She had found him! Jacqueline felt almost drowned in the torrent of emotion. Shakily, she walked inside and looked around the lobby. So familiar and yet different. The old Edwardian furniture had gone, the oak panels had been replaced with light pine wood, the dark grey carpet which had shown signs of age when she was last here as a teenage boy had been removed, and elegant black and white tiles laid instead.

The woman retreated to the stairs at the side of the lobby. "Peter!" she called. "Someone to see you!"

Jacqueline felt weak at the knees, heard the blood pounding in her head, and tried to keep her stomach still. Slow footsteps sounded from the landing above, and she watched, hypnotized as a man looked down at her and began slowly walking down the stairs. All the time he stared at her, and she lost herself in that look, no longer seeing the lobby, the woman, the tiles, just the old man coming to meet her. He reached the bottom and stared even harder at her. His face was thin, his hair iron grey, the form just as stocky and muscular as she remembered. He still stood straight and the eyes had lost nothing of the brilliant charisma. His complexion was pale, and the moustache had gone. The expression was stern, almost angry, till a slow smile broke apart the harshness.

"Hello, Jerry," said Peter Wells. "I was wondering when you'd show up again."

* * *

"How did you know?"

Jacqueline Carter sat in the armchair of the old man's study, clutching her crystal glass of scotch. The physical shock of Peter Wells' recognition of her old self was over, but the occasional tremble still sent random forays around her body.

"I've been waiting for you for a couple of years," Peter said. His face was paler than it had been, and he too still looked shaken. "Things have been strange for me these last few years. My wife died twenty years ago..."

"Your wife? I have so much to catch up with you! What happened after I?..." Jacqueline was watching the old man's face in wonder, and let the question fade away. So strange, so familiar. Lines of memory reached her across a void she could not understand, he was both a stranger and her dearest friend. Peter smiled gently at her.

"I finished the war as a wing commander, and stayed in the Royal Air Force," he said, and took a small sip of his scotch. "Had to drop back to flight lieutenant, but it was fine by me, so long as I could stay flying. I got onto jets, flew Meteors, then transferred to Bomber Command. I was a group captain when I retired. I'd flown Victor Bombers for some years. Marvellous life!"

The old man's face gleamed with pride and delight. It was the face of the small boy who had just scored the winning try for the Prep School rugby team, the youth who took the county championship in the sprints, the young man who had pulled them both along to finish near the front in the cross-country run.

"I married Margaret in 1950," the old man continued. "I met her in Manchester when I was flying a Meteor at an air show. She was a nurse at a little hospital, and her brother had been a Hurricane pilot, so she came with him to shows like that. She was a lovely lady, Jerry...." Peter smiled and looked awkward for a second, then shook his head. "You'd have liked her, kid!"

"Of course I would," said Jacqueline softly. "I just wish I could have been there as your best man."

"I was thinking about you, believe me! I had the same idea standing with her in front of the priest."

"I was probably watching." Jacqueline felt a certainty in herself that her words were true. The two of them exchanged looks of old friends.

"Anyway, when she died of cancer," continued Peter, "I sort of retreated away in this house, and started doing a lot of reading. Everything. I read history, literature, all the works of Shakespeare and Dickens, and stuff like that. Got into religion, too. Hell, you know me, never was much for that sort of stuff."

"I know," said Jacqueline. "I remember we jumped Sunday School more than once!"

They grinned at each other. Just for a second, Jacqueline had the strangest sensation of communicating directly with Peter's mind. Her body almost felt like a space-suit. It surrounded her, but it was only a temporary thing she happened to be wearing at the time because it was necessary.

"When this Oneness thing began, I knew what they were talking about," said Peter, looking deeply into his glass. He shifted his position and crossed his legs carefully. "I've sensed this presence coming from outside, the way Philippe Leger was saying a couple of weeks ago. So nothing surprises me, anymore.

Jacqueline felt a tiny jolt run through her body. It seemed to have occurred just as Peter mentioned the abdicated Pope. She tried to ignore it. "And it's related to what's happened with us?" she asked. She was sure of the answer, but wanted to hear it said aloud.

Peter nodded. "About two years ago, I had this wild dream that you had come back. I woke up crying my eyes out!" A small smile alleviated the old man's stern face. "My son nearly had me committed when I told him about it!"

He smiled at some memories. "But I straightened him out!" he continued. "And then when you walked in the door, I recognized you. It was the weirdest thing. I saw this pretty young woman standing there, and yet I saw Jerry as well. Almost as if the body was irrelevant, just like a suit of clothing, or something. The real you was obvious."

"Your son! Peter, where is he? I can't imagine you having a son!"

The old man smiled. "He's sixty-three. Lives in Australia now, with a wife and three kids, all grown themselves. I'm a great grand-dad. How about that?"

She laughed, still shaky and trembling at the events of the day. "What would they think now?" she asked and took a sip of the fine old blended scotch. The sharp tang worked its way through her with an evocative friendliness. It had been Jerry Mitchell's favourite drink, she remembered. Whenever they came home from school, Peter and Jerry had raided the stocks that Peter's father kept in the cellars.

"They'll be okay with it," replied Peter. "They write to me a lot. Peter Junior has been following this Oneness thing as it's happened, and he's accepted that something strange is happening. Kylie's been getting some similar crazy dreams about old places that she says are memories of other incarnations. So they'd believe all this."

"I'm glad. I've got such clear memories of us from before."

"Do you remember what happened?" Peter looked at her in fascination. "When you died, I mean."

"Not at all," she replied with a shake of her head. "I remember the battle over the Channel, I remember you screaming at me to get out, but that's all. Next thing, I'm a silly teenage girl having conniptions at the sound of Merlins!" She grinned at him. "And now here we are! I could be your grand-daughter!"

He shook his head in confusion. "I never believed any of that stuff before, but now look! What does it feel like, remembering another life as a man, over seventy years ago?"

She stared into the pale liquid in her glass. "It's wonderful! I know I'm a woman, I like being a woman, and yet somehow, remembering what it was like being a man just makes it all easier. I think I like people a lot more now since all this happened, and I know I can get on with them better.”

“But what about?..” He shifted uncomfortably in his seat and waved a hand at her. “What about other men? Do you have boyfriends?” He looked embarrassed.

“Do I go to bed with them, do you mean?” She laughed at his expression. “Yes, I do, and it just makes it better. I wish I could explain, but somehow I’m enjoying it for both of us.”

“Have you told anyone else?”

“No,” she said with a shake of her head. “Only you.”

“Mmm.” He relaxed back in his armchair and sipped thoughtfully at his own scotch. “Remember that time we came back here in the Easter holidays and my parents were abroad?”

She laughed and let herself slip back over sixty years to another time, another body. “Christ, yes! We spent three days drunk out of our tiny brains, and you were sick all over the carpet!”

They spent the next three hours talking. Two old friends who hadn’t seen each other in decades, reminiscing over events of over fifty years before one of them had been born.

*The room was freezing when she forced herself awake in the deep pre-dawn blackness. Shivering hard, she roused the three other girls who slept in the same room, and they stirred unwillingly, one of them flinching when she touched the layer of ice on the stone wall. They pulled themselves from under the old blankets and piles of straw, and washed their faces in the frigid water in the bucket that had a thin cap of ice to be broken first.*

*She took herself up the stairs and began cleaning out the embers of last night’s fire. Around her, dogs stirred and snuffled before snuggling themselves back against the sleeping forms around the wall. She envied them. When the fire was properly glowing, she repeated the exercise in two other halls, and by that time, some of the men were stirring also. The metallic clatter of sword belts rang through the halls, and here and there, muffled complaints could be heard as the women were packed off to their duties. She hauled the sacking bags of the old fires' ashes outside, gasping as the outdoor air hit her lungs, hurriedly spread the ashes on the pathways around the castle, and ran back inside.*

*The first duties complete, she took herself down to the kitchens, stole a hurried gulp of hot water, and then lined up with the other maids to be given the plates of food for the nobles' breakfasts. She struggled upstairs with the load and deposited the tray on the long wooden table in the dining hall. As she turned away, she caught the stare that one of the squires was giving her. She had seen him the night before and asked about him. Squire to one of the Barons of the King's personal entourage, she had been told. That would be the only way out of here for one like herself, she knew. Marriage to somebody connected to the high-born, the only escape route from a life of limitless poverty and discomfort, and an early death from disease or a complicated birth of some knight's bastard child.*

Two in the morning. Jacqueline stared at the red digits of the bedside radio and slowed her breathing. She had gone to bed in the guest room of Peter's house at just after ten, exhausted by the stresses of the encounter. She had fallen into a deep sleep, then woken with a shock to the images in her head.

Another past life. She had been Mary, no second name, simply one of the uncountable peasant women serving the nobility in the castle of York. The King had been through Yorkshire, Jacqueline knew that, he had stayed at the castle, but she could not remember which

King it had been. She was fourteen at the time of that memory, she realized as she lay back in the bed.

Another lifetime! She put her hands behind her head and thought back. Mary had lived the life that she had thought she might. The Baron's squire had passed on, she had stayed in York. Two years later, she had been pulled down in the hallways after another night of feasting, by another young man who served another noble, and she had slept some of the night when she was not being painfully mauled by the inexperienced youth. The next night, he came looking for her again, and she had followed him, praying that he might take her with him when the visitor left. But he did not and some weeks later, the first hints showed that he had left something of himself behind instead.

In the summer, she gave birth to a mewling, wrinkled infant that did not survive the dawn, and she followed the child herself some hours later, as her internal systems seemed to consist of nothing but blood and pain. She had been seventeen.

Feeling disconnected from her body, but not frightened or shocked, Jacqueline recalled more moments from her life in medieval England, and fell asleep some time before dawn.

* * *

The editorials around the world's newspapers for some days after Philippe Leger's press conference were mixed, though most of them gave sympathetic coverage to the extraordinary events. The general air was best expressed by the editorial in the *Guardian,* whose correspondent, Angela Maxwell had asked a question of Leger.

*"We do not purport to understand what happened that extraordinary Spring day in Etoile Sur Rhone," said the writer. "But nobody can deny that something profound took place. Enough examples have occurred around the world of people discovering "Oneness" to*

*tell us that something inexplicable is happening, even if this writer has not yet been a party to it. That a man of the stature of the one-time Pope Jean-Pierre II should abdicate from the Throne of Christ and denounce the millennia-old teachings of the Judeo-Christian churches as "The Santa Claus theory of religion" is stunning, and must tell us that perhaps the time of these teachings truly is past.*

*"If he is right, and all the thousands of converts to these new philosophies are also right, then truly we are about to see the world change in a manner completely outside of our comprehension. If he is right and something massive, supremely intelligent and yet benign spiritual force, is approaching from somewhere outside our solar system, then the events that followed the birth of Jesus Christ pale into insignificance before this new Coming. Is this God? Mister Leger says not. A new religion? A philosophy? He also says not, but none of the adherents of Oneness can tell us what it is.*

*"What is "Oneness?" Mister Leger was not able to tell us, because, as he readily admits himself, he does not yet know. But he believes in his new universe as firmly as his old Church still believes in the traditional order of things, and that he and everybody else will one day know for certain. He can't give us a timetable for this new Coming, either. Our lifetime? Two or more lifetimes? Who knows?*

*"With absolutely nothing to prove the reality of this thing, we are forced to accept its impact. But how different is that from the more traditional faiths which also asked us to believe absolutely with little more evidence, perhaps less than we have now for the new order? So the only real thing we can see is that conflict is ahead. But then, what else is new in this world of ours?*

*"We have to say, we find the precepts of Oneness to be attractive. Reincarnation is both a terrifying thought and a source of intellectual satisfaction and*

*comfort. Mister Leger's claim that no God or Devil, Heaven or Hell exist, and that we shall judge ourselves after we have died, gives both joy and fear. Joy that the terror of eternal damnation and all the horrors threatened us by the church are merely tools of domination, and fear that we must hold our own destiny in our hands, rather than trust to some supreme, paternal Being called God. Oneness is not a philosophy for the faint-hearted and insecure, it seems.*

*"So all we can say, when it comes down to it, is that something astounding is happening. What it is, what it will bring us, how true the claims are, we cannot say. All we can do, therefore, is pray (for those who still believe that there is Something to hear our prayers), or meditate, or otherwise prepare ourselves for cataclysmic change. As a one-time popular Irish comedian used to say in closing his show, "May your God go with you."*

Most of the world's papers said something along the same lines. The exceptions were nearly all in the United States, though several others were concentrated in Islamic countries, most of which condemned the pronouncements of Philippe Leger and the new philosophies of Oneness. The more moderate Islamic countries, such as Egypt, Malaysia and Indonesia more or less echoed the Guardian's viewpoint that something astounding was happening, but the world would have to wait to see exactly what it was. They made much comment on Leger's remarks about Jesus, Mohammed and Buddha being superior souls summoned by Mankind at times of difficulties. The *"Straits Times"* of Kuala Lumpur was warm to that concept.

"Islam had always regarded Jesus as one of the great Prophets, with Mohammed as another. We have never claimed divinity for such men, only a close link with God. The one-time Pope spoke no words that we could interpret as blasphemous to Mohammed, though we have more difficulty with his views of God. But then, it is true that Man's perception of the Supreme Being has grown as we have matured. We no longer believe in gods of trees and suns and moons. Mister Leger does not deny a supreme power in his press conference, he merely gives it a different nature.

"We do not believe in "Oneness" which we interpret as a philosophy that all human beings are actually part of God, and will one day join to form the Supreme Spirit, rather than being souls created by Him. We accept that our Hindu and Buddhist brothers have faiths more in line with the precepts of Oneness, but we have no reason to doubt the truth of Islam. Let us then watch ourselves in the troubled years that we know must come, and pray that we can keep our faith, our trust in God and avoid the conflicts that could be worse than any religious wars of the past. We must avoid the temptation to declare *Jihad,* holy war against the new faith. And if, by some chance, Oneness turns out to be a valid concept, we must then re-evaluate our view of the nature of Allah. Perhaps that is the wonder of humanity - that such a change may be possible."

In the United States, there was no such tolerance. The *Washington Times* spoke for them all, though in tones considerably milder than other publications in Texas, Alabama and Arkansas used.

"We have no idea what has happened to a once great Pope," sneered the editorial. "For a man of his intellect and standing to abandon all for which he once stood is an act of arrogance and stupidity. Perhaps Leger confirmed the old truism that power corrupts and absolute power corrupts absolutely. For he certainly held almost absolute power over a major portion of the world's population until this madness seized him.

"The concept of "Oneness" which he claims to have introduced and understands to be the new "True Faith" is alien to us. It smacks of serious heresy, and we are pleased to see that the Vatican has indeed excommunicated Leger for this offence. The only trouble is that Leger is attracting thousands of misguided adherents who continue to look for some form of "Truth," and we fear the upheavals that religious conflicts may bring. Luckily, it appears that few Americans have succumbed to this foolishness. America has always been, and must continue to be, One Nation under God.

"The world has no room for new faiths. We found the real truth some two thousand years ago, and it remains good enough for all Americans."

* * *

The Sunday after the press conference, the Very Reverend William Horning delivered a sermon that out-shone even his usual blistering invective. It was delivered to the normal full-house congregation that was on its feet, shouting "Hallelujah" and "Glory be to God!" at every pause for breath.

"The Devil himself has come to Earth!" raged Horning. "He has taken the form of the Vicar of Christ and corrupted it to his own ends! Evil roams the world and tries to tell us he has a new truth! I say this Lucifer must return to the Pits of Hell from whence he came!"

"Hallelujah!" screamed the congregation, and some women fainted, while others wept copiously.

"I know that all good Americans refused to listen or watch the Devil as he tried to infect us with his heresies, and switched off their televisions as soon as they realized what he was saying. But as your Priest, I forced myself to watch the whole terrible scene, painful as it was to see human beings, children of the Lord, being forced to witness such filth, so that I could fully understand the depths of degradation to which he would try and lead us."

"Glory be to God!" howled the audience, aware of the brush with evil that Horning had undergone to save them from Hell.

"And I tell you, this Devil speaks EVIL! He refutes

the word of the Lord, he denies the existence of God, he corrupts the name of Jesus. He is a *humanist!*"

Cries of dismay and terror erupted from the crowd at the one crime that could be considered even more terrible and evil than being a liberal.

"I tell you now, my friends," bellowed Horning, his face a glowing red under the pristine white hair, small droplets of spit falling from his mouth, "this evil must be removed from the minds of man forever! The devil tried to speak this filth in this very church only a few weeks ago, and brave, wonderful men of this congregation silenced his heresies immediately."

"Hallelujah!" yelled the people of Bainesville. "Glory unto his name!" they shouted and the three heroes who had shot Michael Hendricks held their hands up high and accepted the plaudits.

"This is the way we must counter this flow of horror from Lucifer's empire!" shouted Horning, raising his hand to the ceiling. "Any man or woman who professes belief in this heresy of Oneness must be sent back to the demons that spawned them immediately! This is a Holy War to which I now call you! Take your guns, use the rope if necessary, but this evil must be cleansed from America! Kill them all!"

Screaming their love of God and Jesus Christ, the people of Bainesville set out on their divine mission of Goodness, to cleanse the world of the evil of Oneness. No records exist to show whether the fifteen people they shot and lynched in Bainesville that day, or the sixty-three that lost their lives to the forces of God over the next few days were actually adherents of Oneness. But they weren't members of the congregation of the Church of the Divine Word of God, and that was enough for the followers of the Very Reverend William Hardcastle Horning.

# Chapter 4. First Contact

The Ship's captain stood alone, silent in front of the viewer screen that was the single object on the forward bulkhead. The screen was ten meters high and twenty meters wide. It was the only obvious technical device in the control room, which was otherwise blank walls coloured a light cream, with six comfortable seats arranged in a broad arc in the middle of the floor, facing the screen. The captain was immobile but busy. Implanted devices in his body allowed him to communicate with sensors and controls around the ship and with all his crew as easily as thinking. Most of the eighty-man crew were occupied in bringing the massive ovoid of the ship into orbit around Jupiter under his constant stream of orders.

A human being looking at the captain would have recognized him as being of the same species, almost. The human might have thought he was a tall, if gawky individual, almost the build of a professional basketball player. On further inspection, the human might have been more disturbed. Only three fingers and an opposing thumb, and the hands were unnaturally long, equal in length to the already elongated forearm, with fingers twice the length of any human's. The face too, would have caused a shock to any human without experience of alien physiology. Huge, beautifully dark eyes dominated an otherwise almost featureless mask. The mouth was a slit which could close to a barely visible line against winds and dust storms, and the ears folded flat against the smooth contour of the head, opening out only when needed. A trained xenologist might have deduced that the captain came from a low-gravity world where the sun was dimmer than Earth's and where the winds blew with dangerous power.

Those characteristics had given the captain's species the early leap into space. A dimly-lit world in a densely-packed region of the Galaxy had given the early sentients a far more intimate view of the stars than humans had experienced, and thus generated a powerful urge to explore. Like humans, the captain's species had developed from tree-dwelling simian creatures, but with far more flexible, adroit, grasping hands that had assisted the later descendants with fine engineering capabilities. Strong wind forces had been an early incentive to electrical generators, and the low gravity had made powered flight possible after only a thousand years of civilization. The species had flown to its nearest moon when it was at an age equivalent to that of the Romans sailing their galleys on the nearby oceans, though that lunar flight had occurred over a million years before the Roman conquest of Europe.

The tiny hum that had filled every atom of the ship during its trip, swelled slowly until the floor trembled slightly and the hum became a small thunder. Gravitational engines that could shift planets and had flung the ship across millions of empty light years reduced the headlong flight to a dynamic relationship with Jupiter.

Silence returned to the control room and the captain remained standing, studying the multiple colours and swirls of the planet's surface with interest. His species had travelled space for a million years and was the main supplier of transportation services to nearly all the sentient species that comprised The One. The captain was accustomed to looking down on planets from orbit. He was an Old Soul in its final incarnation, the last individual still to remain incarnate of the six hundred souls that comprised a single merged entity. By Earth measurements he was over five hundred years old and his other entity souls had agreed to leave him in this form while it was still necessary to manage the physical transportation requirements of the Infinite Soul's visit to the Human species. His crew members were all Old Souls too, but then, his entire species had developed to this point and most had merged into their Ascendant entities on the Astral plane. The captain's home planet, a beautiful, yellow world orbiting a star in a galaxy of the Local Group was deserted.

Like nearly all the intelligent life forms in the universe, preparations for Oneness were moving fast. The exception was the species the Infinite was coming to see. Humanity was a long way from being ready.

"Tormented," said a voice behind the captain. "Not unlike those we visit."

He continued to stare at the swirling confusion on his viewer screen. Even as an Old Soul in his last incarnation, the captain felt overwhelming awe when faced with an Infinite. He knew that within a few years, he would join his own entity and that the Ascendant Soul that would result from that merging process, would at some time merge with every other Ascendant Soul of his species to form an Infinite Soul, but the knowledge did not reduce the sensation of reverence and awareness of power which he felt standing next to one already at that stage.

"Indeed," murmured the captain, switching his consciousness away from the ship's sensors. "When will you want to go on from here, Maragos?" His speech was a gentle, musical tone that varied so imperceptibly that human ears would have thought it a single note played on a cello.

"In a few hours," replied the Infinite. "I will take myself down. If you bring this ship any closer, we could cause such panic in our patient that any recovery might be impossible."

The captain swung his head around and studied Maragos. He hoped that the Infinite was joking.

Preventing Oneness was too terrible an idea for it to be anything other than a jest, but Maragos was examining the screen intently and no trace of a smile could be seen on the lips. The Infinite had taken human form for this journey, and the captain found the shape interesting. Too small, he thought, but compact for the higher gravity of the little third planet of this undistinguished sun located so far away from the main galaxies of intelligent species. Movements were too jerky, the captain felt, facial details were ugly in their large size and coarseness. But he had seen enough species of The One for his thoughts to be anything other than simple interest. The shape chosen by the species was always suitable for the planet that it inhabited. For those species that inhabited planets and had physical shapes, that is.

"You will need no further assistance from me?" the captain asked curiously. "How will you do this?"

The Infinite moved its lips in a gesture that the captain knew represented humour to humans. "I only worked it out in the last few hours. Given a little more time, I think I know how I could have travelled here without the ship, too. After all, there was once a species for whom that was an everyday talent."

The captain felt a wave of mixed awe and pride. It was logical that The One would know how to travel around Its universe without mechanical assistance, for after all, It had created the laws of time and space that formed Its domain. But no sentient species had that ability, though the Captain had also heard of the long-vanished Pfafth who had reputedly been able to teleport over infinite distances. The captain's race had prospered by providing the spaceships for inter-galactic travel over the last million years.

"How will you begin the healing?" asked the captain.

"There are four powerful souls down there," said Maragos. "They have been part of the process from the early stages. I will meet one of these souls first then gather the others to work with me. There is also a soul of great evil who will make our work difficult."

"Then I shall just wait here?" the captain asked.

"Indeed," replied the Infinite. "It will probably be many years before I am ready to return."

"I understand," said the captain. With a wide-eyed stare that was his equivalent of a human grin, he turned back to the screen. "I don't think we have anything else to be doing," he said.

* * *

Philippe Leger sat at his desk in the large study of his home near Valence. He had been left in peace since the press conference two years ago, though he spent his time studying the events of the world that had followed that extraordinary occasion.

The growth of Oneness had been patchy. In Europe, almost the whole continent had absorbed the new awareness, and peace blanketed the entire region, even covering previous black spots of continuous warfare such as Ireland, the Balkans, and Cyprus. Only a few tiny pockets remained of the old thinking.

In the Vatican, a siege mentality had overtaken the Catholic Church. With only a fraction of the clerics remaining in the Church, the small group staying loyal to the Pope had ended all communication with the rest of Italy, and with Europe. The main channels of contact were now with the United States, where support was growing and Oneness had been branded a Heresy under an edict issued by the President. The Middle East had become a mixture, with Israel, Egypt, Saudi-Arabia, Lebanon and Jordan collapsing their borders into one wildly commercial marketplace. Religion had totally disappeared in that area, nobody thought of themselves as Christian, Jewish or Moslem any longer. Nor had anybody even bothered to give the new territory a name. Just the old city names survived.

Around the borders of the new, unnamed country, and in small pockets of the world, the old violence persisted. Libya invaded Chad again, with a merciless barrage of artillery and aerial bombing. Curiously, within a matter of hours, the attack ceased, and Libyan forces pulled back. Almost immediately, violent civil war erupted within Libya. Little else was heard from the country after that, though sporadic reports indicated massive loss of life and complete destruction of the country's cities and industrial structures. Not a single bullet or shell was known to leave the country's borders while Libya committed suicide.

Meanwhile, Iraq, Syria and Iran were engaged in an all-out mutual war of hatred, each fighting the other two, and the carnage was dreadful, far exceeding the slaughter of the previous Iran-Iraq war. The curious feature of the new war was that the combatants appeared completely unaware of the zone of peace in their neighbourhood. The radios and newspapers from Damascus, Teheran and Baghdad poured out vitriolic hatred of each other with demands for even higher levels of slaughter, but no mention of any other country in the region was ever made. They might not have existed, and no random act of violence strayed over the war zone into the commercial zone centred on Jerusalem, almost as if a protective curtain had been raised.

An American news team on location was able to arrange an interview with the religious leader of Iran, and placed the question straight out in the open.

"Why has no action been taken against the new territory of Israel and its neighbours?" asked the American reporter.

A puzzled, confused look crossed the Ayatollah's face for a few moments. He stared at the carpet on which he was sitting. "Our war is with the enemies of Allah, the heretics. We shall destroy them," he muttered.

"But is not Israel, the Zionist State your major enemy?" persisted the American.

The Ayatollah made an irritated gesture. "Your

words are meaningless," he mumbled, and waved at his entourage to escort the American away.

Leger shared no such confusion, nor did anyone else in Europe and the new Mediterranean region. The answer was quite simple. All the hundreds of millions of souls in the region who shared the new knowledge of reality had simply decided that the Islamic combatants would not know about territories outside of themselves. The combined power of the minds of these numbers had acted better than any Star Wars Shield on which a one-time American President had expended such vast amounts of money and effort to achieve nothing.

Philippe also continued his reading of the papers smuggled out of the Vatican's Forbidden Library. The most astonishing were the direct eyewitness reports of conversations between Jesus of Nazareth and the people who gathered to hear him speak. These were the first ever documents he had seen which truly provided evidence of the existence of Jesus in his lifetime. All other documents had been created many years after the events they recorded, and in the past it had sometimes bothered Leger that despite the information and references to the Roman Emperor, to Pontius Pilate, to Herod and the others of that time, nothing had ever been found that recorded the existence of Jesus as it happened. For the first time in his life, Leger saw Jesus as a flesh-and-blood man, a real personality, not the untouchable, uncomprehended God that he had been taught to see. A human warmth came out of the pages, a picture of a man with real concerns, with a sense of humour, and a mission of teaching.

"Why is all this slaughter happening?" a distraught man had begged Jesus after a night when the Roman Legionaries had run riot through the streets of the small town of Menon, killing any who crossed their path.

"Why do children torture insects?" answered Jesus. "We kill in the process of learning and growing.

We understand not that we inflict pain and death on others, only that we must satisfy our own needs."

"Are we all children, then?" asked a woman in the group.

"You are all as children," replied Jesus. "And like children, you shall grow and you shall learn. And with age shall come wisdom, and with wisdom shall come Oneness."

Leger sat back, shaken. *"Oneness?"* Jesus talked about Oneness?

"But how can we learn if we are all killed?" pleaded the same man who had asked the original question. The unnamed scribe appeared to have taken the words down almost as they were spoken, or had written them down soon after this meeting, while the conversation was still fresh and unembellished by later philosophies and political necessities.

"Dying is learning too," replied Jesus. "So is killing. Neither is an ending. He who kills also dies, and he who dies also kills. You shall do both many times before wisdom grows."

"Must it ever be?" asked a man, sadness in his words.

"At this time and place in your world, you have made it so, for reasons of your own. It will not always be, and in other Houses of God, it has been once, but is now no longer. In some Houses, it has never been. All is choice."

Leger stared at the photocopied words. Jesus knew of other worlds, other civilizations, where sentient, ensouled species had conquered the violence, or had never even experienced it? Had he visited them? Were similar religions in existence on other worlds, concepts preached of salvation through a Saviour? He shook his head, feeling overwhelmed, almost drowned in the new knowledge he was finding.

"So what must we do?" asked another voice in the faded pages before Leger. The scribe gave no indication of the identity of the speaker.

"You must choose your own way," replied Jesus. "That is the task of Man, to find the way to Oneness with God, to answer the question that The One has asked of you."

The *Question?* What in God's name was the Question? Leger shook his head at himself as he relapsed into old ways of thought and expression then smiled slightly as he decided that perhaps on this occasion he had used that archaic expression quite appropriately. Leger assumed that the words "The One" meant God, whatever the nature of God might be. And how could The One, or God have asked Man a question? What could it possibly be that God did not know and that mankind could tell Him? And why did Jesus still use the term "God?" If Jesus knew of Oneness, then he must also have known that God, in the sense of a supreme, omnipotent, self-aware entity did not exist. Perhaps he was simply using terms which mankind of the time would understand. Leger felt massive frustration with the scribe who had attended this meeting. Why had he or she not asked Jesus for explanations? Why had he not asked what Jesus had meant by other Houses? Why had he not jumped on the implied statement of reincarnation, about killing and dying many times? Why had he not asked what the Question was? What did Jesus mean by the simple statement, 'All is choice?' And what could he possibly have meant by the statement that in this time and in this place, mankind had apparently *chosen* the pattern of murder and violence, which existed?

"Still, whoever wrote this down was simply a product of the time and culture," said Leger aloud. "He saw Jesus as the Son of a Supreme God, someone divine, unreachable, not a messenger or teacher to be questioned. But dammit, they called Jesus a rabbi, that means teacher, why did they not ask to be taught further?"

He thought some more. Maybe they had, he conjectured. Maybe they had, and these scraps of paper were all that survived of such questions and perhaps the answers, which Jesus had given. Maybe the authorities had seen just how dangerous was such knowledge to the power they held over the world so long as legend continued to triumph over fact. That was why these papers had been locked away from questing eyes for centuries.

A knock sounded on his door, and Leger looked up from his papers, puzzled. It was after two in the morning and he knew that Raoul Carmagio had retired before midnight. Maybe he had woken up and needed some words of wisdom or an exchange of his rapidly developing new ideas before sleeping again, Leger thought, and stood up from his desk. He walked across his study to the door, opened it and stopped, thunderstruck.

A young woman stood before him. She looked to be in her mid-twenties, average height, neatly shaped. Philippe's masculine eyes told him that she was an uncommonly attractive woman. She was dressed in a blue skirt and a white sweater, and her thick and well-groomed hair fell comfortably to her shoulders. For a few seconds, Leger studied this stranger, wondering how she had entered the building, who she was and what she was doing here.

"Philippe," she said with a small smile. "I have come a long way to talk to you."

As she spoke, Philippe finally looked at her eyes. Old reflexes, old passions took over, and he fell prostrate to his face at the woman's feet.

In all his life, despite his training and his professed acceptance that one day it would happen, Philippe Leger, once Pope Jean-Pierre II, Bishop of Rome and Vicar of Christ had never really believed that he would be present when God sent His only begotten Son back to Earth.

Even less had he expected to meet His Daughter.

# Chapter 5. The Way of Things

"No, Philippe, that is really quite unnecessary!"

The gentle, pleasant voice with an undercurrent of amusement broke through the whirling fogs of bewilderment and panic that had overwhelmed the mind of Philippe Leger. He still lay face down on the floor, but he became aware of a tiny whiff of exotic perfume and the warmth of the young woman as she bent over by his shoulders and touched him gently. The minute feel of her fingers, even through his sweater, was amazingly strong and sent a shock through his body.

Forcing calm upon himself, he pushed himself into a sitting position and looked up at the woman. She had knelt down beside him, and her face was mere inches from his. Her skin was perfection, a flawless blend of cream and roses, lips were full with the tiniest hint of a smile. Her hair was dark brown with a glint of red as the light caught it. But her eyes... *oh her eyes!* said Philippe to himself, and her smile widened.

"Windows of the soul, said one of your writers!" she murmured. "In this case, lots of souls!"

"You can read my mind?" asked Philippe, startled.

She shook her head. "You spoke to me on a psychic level," she said. "If you had wanted, your thoughts could have been kept private."

He almost didn't hear her, so preoccupied was he with staring into her eyes. They were hazel-coloured, with flecks of gold, and were beautiful in themselves. The power that had sent Philippe crashing to the floor in worship was in the intense depth of her gaze, the feeling that one was looking into the centre of the galaxy and seeing energy and strength of unimaginably titanic levels. He swayed back a little under the force that emanated from her.

"I thought you were God!" he said softly, unsure of his control over his voice. She rose to her feet in a single, smooth movement and took his hand. Without knowing how, he was also standing, still feeling the beautiful sensation of a hand that was soft and smooth, yet vibrated with the power of a thousand generators.

"In some ways you were right," she said, a small smile contrasting with the astonishing words. She took a seat in one of the gold damask-covered Queen Anne chairs that sat by the hearth and looked at him. Philippe took the twin of the chair, still feeling breathless and overwhelmed by the power radiating from the young woman in front of him. She dwarfed the room the way a Laurence Olivier had diminished a stage by his presence, but by several factors more. Philippe felt a sensation that her personality extended far beyond the room, the house, even the whole area around it.

"You are the one who has been causing this eruption around the world," he said, a statement rather than a question.

She nodded.

"Then just who or what are you?" he asked. He knew he was in the presence of a being of immense power, someone or something similar to the man known as Jesus Christ. *Had Jesus had this impact on the people around him?* he wondered. Her tiny smile told him she had heard his thoughts again, and he wondered how he could keep them private.

"I am the same and yet more than Jesus was," she said softly. "I am the sum of all the souls of every one of my species who ever lived in the last three million years. I am the single entity that has resulted from the joining of twenty-five billion beings into one. I am an Infinite Soul."

He shook his head, confused yet hypnotically drawn to her words. With every atom of his being, he knew she was telling him something immensely profound, giving him a basic building block of the universe to examine, but he was so unbalanced by her presence that he could not focus his attention on the meaning. "I.. I have.. so many questions..." he began and fell back in his seat like a student learning a new language and being intensely frustrated by an inability to phrase simple statements.

She smiled at him. "Like what is an Infinite Soul, what am I doing here and why has my arrival caused such an upheaval?"

He nodded, a flash of humour running through his mind. How could a creature who must be so close to the Supreme Being exist in the form of this beautiful young woman sitting so casually in an armchair across from him? It was like being invited to God's House for tea, sitting across from the Creator of All, and trying to balance a cup and a plate of biscuits on one knee while waiting for Judgement.

She smiled again. "Not Judgement, Philippe. Enlightenment. And healing."

Having his mind read so easily should have upset him but somehow it was unimportant. After all, how could one object if God knew one's innermost thoughts?

"But as I said, I am not God, any more than you are," she said with a gentle look. "Perhaps it would be more correct to say you are just as much God as I am."

"That name has slipped into disuse in recent years," said Philippe. "Most of the world has realized now that there is no God in the old accepted sense of a supreme, omnipotent Creator, but we are still unable to define what must take its place, if anything."

"Nothing should," she replied, "for in all real senses there most certainly is a God. It's just that you have not fully understood the nature of him. Or her. Or perhaps it."

Philippe was beginning to feel more at home now. The conversation had taken the form of the many, long, sometimes all-night discussions in which he had taken part as a young man, as a seminarian and as a priest. With a pang of regret, he realized how much he had missed those heated debates, sometimes held in secret because the ideas expressed could be at odds with the teachings they faced each day. They had faded from his experience as he reached the higher levels of the Church, and such questioning of dogma became unacceptable. With a massive wave of excitement flooding through him, he realized he had a debating partner who appeared to have the answers.

"Then tell me," he said, sitting back in his armchair and looking now at the woman more as an equal of great intellect. "If God has been presented to us as the Supreme, Eternal, Omniscient Creator of all things, in what way are we wrong?"

"In those characteristics, you were not wrong, Philippe. God is all those things."

He felt a breath miss its cycle in his lungs, and gulped. "Then have we erred by our rejection of the established teachings these last few years? Was my sudden realization of an alternate truth wrong?"

"Not at all," she replied. "You missed out some important other characteristics which you were once taught to have existed. These are the ones that make the difference between the God of your old theologies and the reality."

He thought deeply. She seemed to be playing the same game of debate as he was, as if that way the truth could be faced more easily, when it came. "What have I missed?" he said, thinking aloud. "We believed that God was eternal..." She nodded encouragingly. "All powerful... all knowing... our Father in Heaven who would judge us when we died...."

She leaned forward. "Ah!" she said and gave a grin of delightful mischief, like a teenage girl catching her parents kissing in the kitchen.

"No judgement?" he asked, unable to resist smiling back at her.

"Not by any God, no."

"Then by whom?" He suddenly remembered the documents he had taken from the Vatican vaults. He answered his own question. "By ourselves, of course!"

"Of course!" she agreed and sat back in her chair. She tucked her feet under her thighs and looked even younger.

"Then what else could we have got wrong?" he continued, staring in deep thought at the last embers of the fire in the grate. "We have pictured this Creator, watching all our actions, taking care of us, fighting Evil for us, sending His Son to redeem us...."

"Wrong, wrong, wrong and wrong."

He snapped his eyes back to the woman in the armchair. "Wrong on all counts?"

She nodded. "On all counts. There is nobody watching your actions, nobody is fighting against Evil for you, there is no devil to fight, after all. And nobody sent any Son to you. You called for him, and he was nobody's son. And you still have not reached the main point of difference."

He felt a tide of frustration. He wanted to tackle so many subjects immediately. *We called for him? Called? What had she meant by her incredible statement of being the sum of twenty-five billion beings of her species? What species? How the hell could he...*

She shook her head with the tiniest suspicion of that cheeky smile. "No Hell, either!" she said. "And we'll come to those questions when you have got this first stage right!"

He had to smile back at her, at her charm and her wit, and her capacity to make him relax. He began to think again. "I remember once," he began slowly, "when I pondered on the concept of being made in God's Image. I wondered how that could be, because many of the ideas of being God worried me. I used to think how could any being know of itself as the sole creator of all things, know that it was eternal and supreme over all creation....."

"Bingo!" she said softly.

"What bingo?" he snapped, confused. *How could she have such a command of vernacular? Supreme Beings should not be concerned with trivialities of small money games...*

"Why not?" she asked, straight-faced. "In such small things might lie the answer to the single biggest problem in the Universe."

It touched a chord of memory in him and he forgot to wonder if he might ever be able to close his thoughts to her.

"The question that God has asked of Mankind?" he said, barely above a whisper. "I read a description of a comment Jesus made about such a question, and wondered how could God not know the answer to something. Is this the point of it all?"

"It's that, and more than that," she replied. "But let us go back to your earlier statement. Indeed you were right to ponder those difficulties. Imagine being eternal, omniscient, omnipotent and self-aware. How long could you last without being desperate for an intelligence equal to your own with whom to discuss things?" She looked hard at him, brought her legs forward again and leaned her elbows on her knees. "How could it possibly feel to know that you knew everything, that you could learn nothing more, that everything that existed now or would ever exist had been created by yourself, that at some stage you would have experienced everything there ever was to experience? What would most likely happen to you?"

"I'd go insane!" he answered without thought, utterly transfixed by her eyes that seemed to have grown to enormous size and filled his universe.

"Exactly!" she sighed, and sat back.

He stared at her. "God has gone insane?" He felt his own balance of mind shake and tremble a little.

"No," she said. "But we would if we had stayed in that situation."

"We?" He felt the universe shudder around him. Here was the key to the blueprints of the Universe, of Eternity, of all of Time and Space, and it was about to be handed to him.

"We," she agreed. "Let me show you."

She made no movement, but the room faded from the awareness of Philippe Leger. He was watched lovingly by Maragos, the Infinite Soul grown from the merging of twenty-five billion souls who had lived for three million years on a planet circling a star in a Galaxy many millions of light years from Earth.

*There is nothing but "I." "I" am all there is, all there ever has been. "Has been?" An interesting concept is Time. Maybe "I" will use it if it pleases "me" more. What can this mean for this sense of "me" that "I" have? Around "me" is nothing that is something. Another interesting concept, call it Space. Meaning something else that is not "I," something that is where I am not. Is there another "I" in that Space? That's an exciting concept, also. Maybe I shall use it at some stage, too. This Time idea is getting stronger. Why not see what happens if I decide... ah! And there is something there in the space where I am not, something that was not there before. Time again. A concept of events following in sequence. "Events?" Something that can happen? But something just did happen as I decided it should, something is where nothing was before. What did I do? I decided something should be, and it was. Just dust, fragments, but something that is not I is now in a space where I am not. This time thing. How long... no, that has no meaning yet. How can a thing be measured when there is no concept by which to measure it? But before I had these concepts, where was "I?" **When** was "I?"*

*Dim memories now, of dreams of nothing, just a dream of "I" and perhaps dreams of "not-I?" What* could that mean? Another "I?" I like the idea, but cannot conceive of how to make it so. But let's try that decide game again. Decide something else and... see! More dust, a glow, let me play with this idea a little. Make the dust like so... and ah!... just with a flick of me... something exists where something did not exist before... this is pleasurable. Another interesting concept. But now there is definitely space that is not I, other space in which there is something that is also not I. Can I do it again? I know that I can, I have learned since I awoke and discovered "I" and Time and Space. Decide more dust, more glows, more space. And now there is even more space that is not-I and things in that space that are also not-I, and I have no limits on making more space and dust and not-I.

But what point can there be in making Space and Time and Dust? Can I do more with these things? Let me try and gather... and with another flick of me I can gather all the dust together into one space where several spaces were before... before... that time idea again... where several spaces were before and are now one large space.. large? Another useful idea, things relative to each other.. file it away as well. Press all the dust together, press it more, an idea comes to me, press it more and more with a thought... how am I doing this?.. and now release it. It glows more strongly than the first dust had glowed, and flies off in all the spaces I had created, and as it moves, more space is created. This is also pleasurable, to watch the dust move in the spaces and create more space as it does so. I watch it for... time? and eventually all the dust slows and ceases to move and make more space, and begins to move back along the way it had travelled before and returns to the one space which had been not-I.

Decide more dust and do it again. This time I watch the wonderful glow that gleams even brighter with the greater volumes of dust that I had pressed together with just a decision that it would be so, and *follow the trail of the dust as it flies outward and creates space as it goes. This time also, I let some of the dust gather in clumps, form globules, watch as it forms patterns of hot globules with cooler blobs that orbit around the heat. The patterns are pleasing, and as the orbiting clumps cool further as time? passes... now I have a way to relate the passing... will it do to make time a possible measure of the duration of the blobs as they whirl in the space I have created?*

*This game of decide is pleasing... let me concentrate for a while (Time again?...) on one of the collections of blobs that have settled in orbits around a hotter blob. I like the glow of the hot blob, it pleases me... but I will watch the smaller globules, their shape is also pleasing, they turn and the light of the hot blob shines on half of the globes at all times. As they cool, they become merely blobs, turning in the space I created... maybe something else?... aha! clouds of gas around the blobs, whirling in interesting and pleasing patterns, something new on the surface of the blobs... colours! Things that grow... did I create all that with just a decide game? Must have done. Look up at all the other spaces for a while and see that the dust balls have flown to new spaces, so far that I have to go and see them. I start off in their direction and find I will not catch them unless I decide on another way of... movement? I can move anywhere in all these spaces just with a thought, another decide game... decide myself back to the first globule and see all the green growing things and how all the wild twirling of the gas around the blob gas settled down. Decide something else... bodies of water appear on the globe and now it really pleases me. Let's do the same with some other blobs and globes. They have settled into pleasurable patterns of dust now, globes orbit hotter globes, groups of orbiting patterns rotate around each other in vast numbers... there's another pleasing concept... numbers... now there are lots and lots of these collections of bright, glowing patterns of hot globes and orbiting cooler globes, let's have that green stuff on a few more cooling globes... and water bodies... this game is really pleasant.*

*But after more.. time? I find I no longer have the pleasure in these whirling patterns of suns and planets, some of which are green and others are not. I decide again, and all the millions and millions of glowing dots are summoned back into my.. what? and I think them pressed and pressed and pressed and more dust is decided and yet more and this time the whole lot goes off with a delightful burst of glowing light and the dust flies off again into yet more space that is newly created for it and the same globes appear and start to whirl around each other and I make some green and make some water bodies and watch, and I find I am not taking the pleasure I had at the start of this game.*

*Maybe some not-I? Maybe something that can move and be in the space? Make something in that body of water... that is really pleasing! It moves around, I can hear it make sounds, make another one, let things get together and see what happens... and soon the place is full of those things and I am no longer pleased... bring it all back again and let's have another pleasing cascade of light and hot blobs and cooling blobs and green stuff and... this is not enough. I can play this game for all of time... time? but what else can I do? I want another not-I that I can talk to, so let's decide that... it doesn't work! Something I cannot decide?*

*I feel un-pleased inside me, and I begin to wake more from my sleep and realize that I can do almost anything, but make another I. My sense of time settles and I know that I have created and re-created the entire universe several times since awakening, that I am all there is, that I can create everything else I wish and I don't know how this happened but it is the truth.*

***I AM ALL THAT THERE IS.***

*I am the light and the word and the life. I will be so for all of time and what a dreadful, horrible prospect that is. I can make life, and I can destroy it, and there is nothing else that can do that or stop me doing it.*

### *I AM ALL THAT THERE IS. HOW CAN I EVER BE ANYTHING ELSE?*

With a jolt that almost flung him from his chair, Philippe opened his eyes. Still racked with grief and horror that had overwhelmed him as he lived through the first uncountable billions of years of God's awakening and experimentation and the final, overpowering terror of the prospect of eternal isolation, he wept, shaking with the pain of the memories he had experienced.

He had no idea for how long he stayed that way, head bowed in his lap, shuddering with the enormity of the emotions he had been shown. At some time he calmed himself, lifted his head and saw the beautiful young woman studying him gravely.

"You see," she said in her soft voice. "With no real concept of time, it looks like God first created several complete cycles of the universe before coming to that cataclysmic realization of its nature. It must have been billions and billions of years, if that can be any sort of rational measurement."

"But where did that image come from?" he said in a trembling voice. "Did you give it to me?"

"It's a memory that I have found in my mind since my ascension as an Infinite," she said. "It was always there, at every level of my being's growth, but I could not have controlled it before now. I only gave you the tiniest fraction."

"I never asked your name," he said, aware of the incongruity of his question after the experience he had just been given, but struggling for some rational balance, aware that she had said things almost incomprehensible, but not yet willing to query her.

She smiled. "My name is Maragos," she said. "It was the last name used in the final lifetime of one of the souls of my species who was an artist, a sculptor and a musician. He is part of me now, but his name pleases me."

"And who are you? I know I asked you before but I really did not understand your answer."

"You will, in a few more moments," she replied. "But I can tell you that I was a species that inhabited a planet called Shuramee orbiting a star that lay in one spiral arm of a Galaxy close to the local group. By the time I formed, we lived on several hundred planets in that galaxy and had explored three other nearby galaxies."

"The local group?" asked Philippe. "What does that mean?"

"It's the name given to the cluster of galaxies that contains your own, the Milky Way," she replied. "It includes the names most of you are familiar with; the Magellenics, Andromeda, Draco and a few others. This group is some four million light-years across. The Milky Way itself, your own galaxy is over a hundred thousand light-years along its longer axis."

He shook his head. "These are distances beyond human comprehension," he said. "And where is your home?"

"Too far away to be meaningful," she replied with a smile. "Consider this; the local group is just part of a supercluster of other groups of galaxies. It's over a hundred and fifty million light-years across. My galaxy is within that group."

"What does Shuramee mean?" he asked, feeling almost as if he was falling apart under the force of the words she was speaking. Clinging firmly to small, comprehensible concepts seemed to him to the only way to keep his head from exploding.

"It means Earth!" she said with a smile. "In the language that had become our universal tongue by the time my species had left the physical plane. Names of home planets are nearly always Earth, in one way or another."

Her smile sent calming waves over him. He gained control of his voice, and his head no longer seemed to be splitting apart. He was ready to tackle the bigger questions again.

"What do you mean by 'you left the physical plane'?"

She waved her hand a little. "Let me show you," she said, and the room vanished from around the two of them, and he was God again.

*Shall I decide some other not-I forms that at least have some intelligence and can talk to me? Why not? What can I lose? What can I gain? Nothing can stop me. Decide on this planet perhaps, and see, see how little things grow and move and make more little things... wait for them to learn how to use the abilities I have given them with a little of my life-force. But they have gone! Why have they gone? The life force has come back to me, but the creatures I made have vanished. Perhaps they need to refresh that life force, to find some strength to maintain the little incarnate bodies I made... yes, that must be it. Create some more, but let them consume some of the green growing stuff, maybe make some other little forms of different types that they can also consume... yes, that seems to work. And now they have learned ideas, they know of space and time and dust. Let me now exchange some thoughts with them...*

*This can be pleasurable, they know I have created them and they are filled with the sense of my power. This give me good feelings, let me show some more powers to them.. make this part of their globe hotter and burn... oh! That seems to done it again, the life force has returned to me and their globe has broken apart into the dust that formed it. Let's decide again.. more life, smaller forms for them to eat, let them learn more slowly this time before I talk with them, let them breed for several hundred cycles and now, let me talk to them.*

*I am the Life and the Word and the Light, I tell them, and they begin to worship me again, most pleasurable. I listen to their tiny thoughts and amuse myself with the importance which they attach to tiny things. They fear to die, which is silly because their deaths are only a return of my life-force back to me, they do not realize that they are part of me... sometimes they seem silly.*

*I have watched them now for thousands of their breeding cycles, seen millions of them return their life-force to me and then be recreated back into their little globe of dust and green and small animals, and they will not leave me alone... They congregate and worship, they keep asking of me things that are trivial, they fight among themselves and each group asks me to help them against the other group. This is silly, it is nonsense, it unpleases me. I soon find that they can have no thoughts that were not already my thoughts, no ideas that I have not had already, say nothing that I do not know they will say. I grow disturbed and.. with a decide, I wipe them from the space where they were and take their life-force back to myself... it is wasted with these puny creations of my mind.*

***BUT I AM ALL THAT THERE IS. I CANNOT MAKE ANOTHER "I." I THAT I AM MUST BE ALONE FOR ALL ETERNITY, FOR HOW CAN I STOP MY OWN LIFE FORCE? WHY CANNOT I GO BACK TO THE TINY MEMORIES I FIRST HAD OF DARK DREAMS AND FAINT MEMORIES OF I AND NOT-I BEFORE I WOKE AND BEGAN TO CREATE SPACE AND TIME AND DUST?***

***I CANNOT EXIST THIS WAY FOR ALL ETERNITY. I MUST FIND A WAY TO RETURN TO MY DREAMS AND PERHAPS WHEN I WAKE AGAIN, I WILL HAVE A SOLUTION.***

*And there is a way, now I see that. First, decide the dust all back again in one space, and start to press it together for a new start. As it presses, start to break up my life force into fragments so that each of them can live of its own will wherever it chooses.*

*Consciousness starts to fade as a new, multiple consciousness grows. Now am I a million different life-forces, different entities, each with its own awareness of itself, and of being partially "I" while all the others are both "I" and "not-I." But still we remember being "I" and the pain of having no other "I" to share the joy of creation of dust and space and time. Each of us will break down further into more millions of fragments, and as we do, each tiny fragment now forgets, loses the painful, fearful memory of being "I" alone in the space and dust and time I create.*

*Each of the first million entities that I shall become can now choose to go anywhere in the space I have created, and choose a place in which to break itself into the next level down of millions of smaller entities and lose more of the pain as distance increases between itself and the "I" that I was. And then each smaller entity can break itself further into several hundred even tinier fragments, and each fragment can now forget entirely everything that I was, that I remember and that I created, and it can start to live fresh and new and with hope.*

*And if each of these tiny fragments can start anew and live many times, each time returning its life-force to its entity before living again, as it grows and learns, when it can merge again with all the other fragments of its entity, and then those entities can merge back to being the rejoined parts of the first million that broke away from me, then when they have all grown and learned and finally returned to me and "I" can again awake, maybe this time I will have an answer to my question.*

*I will give all the million souls a mandate. Find out how I did these things with just a decide. How did*

*I move through all of my Space and Time with a thought? How did I create the living things? What are the rules I created for the way the worlds move within the galaxies and the galaxies around each other? Find out everything before I awake again, but above all, find the answer to the greatest question.*

***HOW DO I LIVE ALONE THROUGH ALL ETERNITY?***

*I feel the first of a million parts of me begin to break away just as the dust of all the spaces finally comes together again in my last squeeze, and as the glow of that squeeze starts to grow to brightness, my last memories fade, and....*

Philippe Leger came to consciousness more calmly this time, opened his eyes and saw her still watching him. He felt as if he had travelled a billion miles through time and space, and yet felt rested, strong, secure in the wisdom he been permitted to acquire.

"Yes," Maragos said. "God broke itself up into a million entities to lose the self-awareness it had of its own eternal existence and supreme power with which it could not live. Each of those entities chose a place somewhere in the universe in which to base itself as a species for the billions of cycles of creation through which it would live."

"And are all the species like us, like humans?" Philippe was still breathless from the enormity of what he had seen and what she was telling him. She shook her head, and the fine brown hair floated around her shoulders with glints of deep red spiralling up and down.

"Humanoid is a common form, but not all of us chose it," she said. "A humanoid shape is the most suitable to technology-based forms, but not all of us have opted for technology-based species. But that is the point of the exercise, to be as varied as we can be to give ourselves the chance of finding solutions to God's quandary."

"And what happened when each species decided where to base itself and what form to take?" Philippe felt that he had never before asked a question with so little comprehension of what the answer might be.

"Each species broke itself yet further into millions of smaller entities, called Ascendant Souls," she replied. "These grew further apart from the memories of the pain. Finally, each of those smaller entities, the Ascendants, broke itself into a few hundred individual souls that started with complete ignorance of God's distress. As unique souls, they began a cycle of incarnations, usually as a physical body, but not always. Most Ascendant Souls of all species have between five hundred and two thousand individual souls which go through several stages of growth, living several hundreds of lives in the process before rejoining as the complete entity."

"So having broken itself up into billions of individual souls, we begin the process of learning until we can start the merging back again?"

"Exactly," she said with a smile. "Each species has the same basic structure, though the precise details vary among us." She paused a few moments, looking at the carpet, apparently in deep thought.

"There are five ages of the soul," she said, returning her astonishing eyes to Philippe. "When we are first cast off from our Ascendant Souls to become individual souls, we begin as Infant Souls. Just as human infants, we share the characteristics of the very young and immature. We demand a rigid structure of behaviour and a need for powerful authority figures. With a number of incarnations and the experience they bring us, we grow to being Baby Souls, somewhat like toddlers. We begin to make our own judgements and we question and test the boundaries in which we live. In time, and after more lives, we become Young Souls, something like teenagers as humans. We have enormous energy in that time, we grow through the most rapid learning stages. Even later, we become

Mature Souls, much like young adults, and finally we reach the last stage and grow into Old Souls. When all the souls have completed the cycle, they merge once more to form a complete entity. This is an Ascendant Soul."

"How many lives must we live to complete this?" Philippe was entranced with the information he was getting. It made so much more sense than the old ideas of merely one life followed by eternal hell or heaven.

"Many!" she said with a laugh. "Each age of soul has seven levels, and each level can take five, ten or even more lives before you are ready to move on."

"What is the difference between each level?" asked Philippe. "How do we grow through this process?"

"Difficult to define," she replied. "Each level depends on the degree of experience and maturity gained. It's a little like one's progression through school. You can recognize the difference between children of each grade, but specific definition of the difference would be difficult. But we know when we progress through each level and reach a new soul age."

"But we remember nothing of our previous selves while we live. Do we remember our past lives after we have died?"

"Oh yes," she replied. "When you return to the Astral Plane between lives, you remember all your history. That is when you review the previous life with others and determine what you learned from it, what you still need to learn, and what Karmic Debts you have made or paid off to others. At least..." She paused. "That's what is supposed to happen," she continued. "But the sickness has made it difficult, sometimes impossible, for many souls to remember all their history."

Philippe was feeling overloaded again. There was so much he wanted to get so quickly, while other questions banged in his head for attention. The question of Karmic Debts was fascinating, and he had read of this concept in his other studies. But the nature of the being in front of him took precedence for a time. He passed over the reference to a sickness as being too confusing in the face of all the other information.

"You said you were the sum total of all your species. You mean that all the souls have merged again and you are one of the original entities that broke away from God?"

*What an incredible question to ask,* he thought to himself. *That I can ask it at all is amazing. That I am asking it of a youthful, beautiful woman sitting so calmly in my study in front of me is beyond rationality. Is this reality? Have I fallen asleep and all this is simply an astounding dream?*

"No dream, Philippe," she said with a smile. "And few people could even consider asking it. But that is why I am here. Yes, I am the end result of all the souls of my species growing to the final stages of old age and merging with their entities to become Ascendant Souls. And all those Ascendants have spent thousands of years in meditation before being ready to return to a single being. And that being is I. I can remember every moment of every life of the twenty-five billion fragments that once I was. The process has taken three million years since the first of us incarnated on Shuramee as Infant Souls. And here I am."

"And is this the form your species had on... on Shuramee?" He gestured a little awkwardly at her.

"No. We were a humanoid race, but not like this. I took this form to visit you."

"You can do that? Manipulate matter into any shape you want?" Philippe was almost exhausted now by the flood of data and experiences he had absorbed in the last few hours, but this question woke him a little.

"Oh yes! Matter and energy are very easy, once you know how!" She gave a small wave at the ceramic water jug that sat on the side of Philippe's desk. "There's a well known party trick that my famous predecessor performed," she said with her teenager's grin. "Have a sip of that!"

Cautiously, Philippe rose, feeling the stiffness in his limbs, and picked up the jug, sniffed it and stared at her.

"Wine?" he croaked, astonishment seizing his throat.

"Wine!" she agreed. "You might pour us both a glass!"

Laughing out loud, he poured two glasses from the jug and handed her one. She took it, looking exactly like a young girl at a party, smiled at him, said "Your good health, Philippe!" and took a sip. He raised the glass at her in acknowledgement and did the same. The wine was superlative. It tasted like the best Cabernet he had ever experienced, smooth and delicate on the tongue, leaving the throat sighing with delight as it rippled down to his stomach.

"Oh my!" he whispered.

She laughed. It was a lovely sound. "On the other hand..." she said, and the jug in his hand was a bottle made of dark green glass. The label was ancient, but dimly indicated fine old scotch as the contents. He sniffed, and smelt the tang of ancient peat moss and smoky liquor. He raised his eyebrows at her, feeling like a young man again.

"Just party tricks!" she said, and put her glass down on the floor by her seat. "Back to my species. We are bigger than you. We took a high gravity world several times larger than Earth, and decided against a technological society. I don't think you would have found us physically pleasing."

"And instead of technology, what then?" he asked, unable to think of her in a different form.

"We were a species that developed mental powers and abilities instead. You would have called it magic perhaps, just like that little trick I did with the jug. Any of us could do that even at infant-soul stage. But as we grew, we built cities with that ability, moved our world to a different orbit when the sun changed its physical properties, altered the nature of the planet itself."

"And is that how you came here?"

She shook her head. "I could have done," she said. "I realized that only recently. But space travel over immense distances was developed early by another species and they helped us all move about. The ship that brought me here is parked near Jupiter. The rest of the way I did come myself."

"Helped us all move about?" he said. "Why you and not us on Earth? Have we been left out of the picture for some reason?"

She looked soberly at him, her face suddenly serious. "Yes, Philippe, you have. And by your own choice. Which is why I am here."

With a jolt, he realized that he had forgotten the most important question of them all. Why was she here? He put his wine glass and the ancient bottle of scotch back on his desk and returned to his seat.

She watched him as he settled back, tucked her feet under her thighs again and rested her head on her hand, her elbow on the armrest. "Philippe, the cycle I described to you appears to be ending. We are almost ready again for Oneness. Soon, all the souls in all species will have reached their final stages and be ready to merge with their entities, and all the entities will then soon be ready to merge back to a single Infinite like myself. I am the first to reach that stage, which is why I came."

She paused, and Philippe felt his heart pounding violently.

"Billions of years ago when the original million entities first split off and chose their base locations, we opted to have no more than two or three hundred of us in each galaxy to keep ourselves with room to grow and learn. We spent many millions of years in the Infinite stage before starting to break ourselves up, and in that period we watched the galaxies form, saw how the planets shaped, and then we began to form the planets to the nature we wanted for ourselves. We waited even more millions of years for the basic life forms to appear on the planets before we began to incarnate ourselves. So we occupied a few hundred galaxies and these galaxies were all in the one area, if such a term can apply. But we agreed that we would stay relatively close."

She paused and took a sip of the wine before looking directly at him, and again he felt the jolt of the infinite power that rested within her as their eyes met.

"But something happened to the Infinite Soul that is Humanity," she said. "You fled from the central galaxies and came out here, almost as far away as you could be from the rest of us. We tried to talk to you, but failed. It was like trying to talk to a severely deranged person, no communication was possible."

He stared at her. His mind felt frozen, nothing moved inside him.

"Then you broke up into millions of smaller entities and continued the pattern to further entities of some hundreds of souls. You started the process of casting off those souls as infants to start the cycle of eternity until you were ready to merge again, just as we had done, so we left you alone. We thought that maybe you were simply trying another path. Every thousand years or so we came and looked at you, but that's when we saw the problem."

Leger could do nothing but stare at her. But underneath the immobility, a tiny echo of a memory hummed at him. He knew, he knew what she was about to tell him, it was a root cause of everything he had ever lived for, this time and before....

"Philippe, Humanity has barely started its growth," she said. "You have stagnated, ceased your development. Few of the entities have souls developed beyond the infant stage. Only a handful, of which yours is one, have reached generally Old Soul status and are beginning to think of merger into their entities as Ascendant Souls."

His body would not move. Despite the faintest wisp of an echo of something in his mind, what she was saying seemed so far from rationality, he could not even be sure he was hearing her.

"Humanity is sick, Philippe," she said. "We can not regain Oneness without you. Unless you heal, God cannot return."

# Chapter 6. Born in the USA

*(Extracts from a standard history text for schools and colleges in the second half of the third millennium)*

In the American Federal and Presidential elections of that year, the Republican candidate was plagued with considerable doubts about his true commitment to right-wing ideals and his real strength. In his first four year term, following a narrow victory at the polls, he had done little of note for American society, other than to order a small military strike against the tiny state of South Yemen, and to raise the tax rates on the lowest income groups. The small burst of military action had never been adequately explained, but had delighted the extreme right wing of America. During an impromptu press conference on the golf course, the President denied that the strike was an attempt to boost his public image and insisted it had resulted from a strategic crisis caused by the ascension to the throne of South Yemen of a liberal-minded monarch who had intended to allow elections among his people. The President had seemed confused by the question from one journalist as to why this constituted a threat to world peace, and stated that the strategic position of South Yemen so close to Japan made the problem critical. He refused further explanation and returned to the fourteenth hole where he shot a double bogie.

Despite the small boost to his popularity caused by the military effort, the President bowed to pressures from the Religious Right and took as his running mate, The Very Reverend William H. Horning, a wildly successful Southern Baptist TV evangelist out of

Bainesville, Texas. Horning had exploded onto the televangelism arena three years earlier when the Oneness Movement had begun to collect momentum, and he had built a vast following of the faithful by offering the most fundamentalist interpretation of the Bible yet, and a virulent, hysterical outpouring of hatred against the new philosophies.

Horning's television program hit prime time in Texas and was on the morning program of the networks within weeks. By the summer of that year, he was on prime time on all the networks except ABC, and even the ABC organization was under heavy pressure to follow suit, eventually submitting a few months later. Executives at ABC denied that the change in stance had resulted from the deaths of thirty-two employees in an explosion in the company's car park.

The nomination of Horning as Vice-President swung the tide and the election was a landslide for his party. The Vice-President continued to run his prime-time shows, despite legal challenges to this practice by the fragmented remains of the Democratic Party, under the laws regarding the separation of Church and State. A Supreme Court ruling rejected the challenge with only one dissenter, Justice Pennie Fielding, who had gradually distanced herself from the sharp move to the political far right of recent years. Three days later, an assassination attempt on Justice Fielding nearly succeeded, resulting in bullet wounds in the Judge's chest, and the Judge announced her retirement on the basis of her health a week later. She moved to a house in Vermont when she was released from hospital, and quietly slipped over the border into Canada. Nobody ever heard from her again, but occasional rumours placed her as living either in a small cottage on the north coast of New South Wales, Australia, or a beach-front house in Nova Scotia, Canada.

In the spring of his second term, the President was

added to the list of Presidents assassinated in office, when a heavy calibre bullet fired in a hail from a semi-automatic weapon destroyed the car in which he was riding to a county fair in Indianapolis, killing also his wife and the Secret Service Agent driving the vehicle. Some commentators stated that the President had finally achieved his long-claimed parity with John F. Kennedy, at least in the manner of his death, if not in life.

The Very Reverend William Hardcastle Horning took the oath of office of the President of the United States fifteen minutes later in the White House. Only one newspaper, the *Chicago Tribune* asked the question of how come a Judge had been present with the Vice-President so conveniently ready for the ceremony, but after one edition of the paper had reached the street, the editorial was changed. The President, speaking that night, stated that the Judge had visited him for prayers that day and just happened to be with him when the news broke of the President's death. He denounced as a Liberal-Democratic plot to discredit him the implied question that he might have had something to do with the President's death.

The next day, President the Very Reverend Horning announced two developments. Firstly, he appointed Senator Abraham Luckey of Tennessee as his Vice-President. The new Vice-President was aged seventy-six, and had long been a proponent of the agenda of the Moral Majority and the Religious Right. In his illustrious career, the Senator had banned a number of art displays in his home state, fought hard for prayers to be mandated in schools and opposed any extension of civil rights to the citizens of the USA. The President also announced the end of the impasse over the nomination of a new Supreme Court Judge to replace Fielding. He nominated an old friend and colleague of his, a minor preacher with whom he had worked in his early years, the Reverend William Casey of Austin, Texas.

The furore in America lasted three days. The House debate lasted only one day, though that one day was frenetic. The major point of discussion was the total lack of any legal qualifications in the Reverend Casey. House Democrats lashed out at this factor and were severely attacked by the Republicans who claimed that no law stated that a Supreme Court Judge actually had to be a qualified lawyer. All twenty-six Democrats who had survived the last election stood up and shouted that *of course* there was such a law! One had to have a license to practice law in every state of the Union, and being a judge definitely fitted within the definition of practising law.

The Congressman for one of the wards of Alabama immediately stood up, demanded the floor and was granted it. He submitted a bill, completely prepared already, for a change in the regulations which removed such minor requirements for Supreme Court Justices and the bill was passed by acclaim. The next day it was passed by the Senate on party lines, the six Democratic Senators voting against it, the remaining votes enthusiastically endorsing it. The President signed it into law the same afternoon and Casey's nomination proceeded.

The Senate Approval Committee was asked to meet the next day and observers in the committee room were struck by the demeanour of the Democrats on the committee. To a man, they were white-faced and the Senator from Illinois could be observed to have a severe tremor in his hands. Rumours of threats of severe bodily harm, even death being sent to the Democratic Senators flew around the beltway for a few hours then dissipated. The Approval Committee asked no questions of the nominee and the committee expressed its consent to the appointment within fifteen minutes. The new Justice took a week to arrange his affairs and took his seat without fanfare. Some reports filtered out of the Court that his welcome from the other judges had been subdued.

## The Nightmares of God

* * *

A month after the installation of the new Justice of the Supreme Court of the United States of America, the President called a meeting of the Republican Party, which was held at a convention centre in Atlanta. The first hour of the meeting was dedicated to prayers and the singing of many hymns, and the President led the session with enthusiasm. Then he moved to the podium to speak and the applause and shouting took fifteen minutes before he could be heard.

"My fellow Christian Americans," he began, and was immediately lost in the noise as every delegate stood up and cheered for another ten minutes. The noise abated again, and Horning raised his arms.

"At last, America is fulfilling her true destiny!" he called. "We are one nation under God!"

The noise level rose to a screaming crescendo. The President stood with his arms raised as the roar continued and the flags were waved with dangerous enthusiasm. The noise slowly metamorphosed into the singing of "God Bless America" and finally faded as many of the delegates were seen to be weeping joyously.

"Our enemies of the past have been vanquished by the valiant and heroic works of those God-like men, our previous Presidents Reagan, Bush and ...." The roar hit the ceiling like an explosion of Mount Vesuvius, and Horning beamed at the standing crowd. "And the people of America have spoken with the voice of God in removing most of those cowardly, un-American Liberal communists from both Houses," he shouted.

Noise gushed to the walls and ceiling again, and another ten minutes passed before Horning could continue. He spent the time smiling into the cameras and at his wife and children sitting behind him.

"But one new enemy has arisen," he bellowed, his face twisting with pain. "Satan has seen fit to challenge America with a new evil. This evil proclaims itself to be

123

the new truth, more suitable for men of maturity. I say that this evil of Oneness must be stamped out, eradicated from the world, sent back to the pits of Hell from whence it came!"

The screaming echoed through the hall, with occasional yelps of "Hallelujah!" and "God be with us!" leavening the dull roar.

"I promise to all of you, on my life, that this administration will henceforth dedicate every resource available to destroying this sign of Satan's presence," he thundered. "Christians of America are at war! We will fight on God's right hand against Lucifer's work until the Devil has taken back his minions, the liberals, the Democrats, the homosexuals and the ungodly, and retreated with them to his own domain, never again to corrupt God's Kingdom in America!"

The entire assembly rose to its feet and roared approval.

"And so, to commemorate this victory for truth, for God and for America," shouted Horning, when he was sure he could be heard again, "I propose that we rename our Grand Old Republican Party with a title more suited to this new age."

The hall was silent for a few seconds, yet electric with expectation.

"I propose that we should from this moment," he said, lowering his voice to a deep, emotional tone. "Be proud Americans, joyously proclaiming ourselves members of the American Party of God!"

It was twenty minutes before any semblance of order returned to the assembly. The congregation had sung three renderings of "God Bless America," two of "The Star Spangled Banner" and several assorted hymns before Horning rose to his feet again and raised his arms for silence.

"Next week," he continued into the silence that had grown under the encouragement of the hundreds of muscular young men who patrolled the hall, wearing black trousers, white long-sleeved shirts and short haircuts, "loyal members of the House of Congress will introduce a bill that will finally correct an anomaly in this fair country of ours. At last, we shall recognize that Democrats and Communists are the same anti-Americans they have always been, and both parties will be banned from practising their heresies in this country."

For a second or two, silence draped the room. Then, under the urging of the muscular young men, the crowd rose to its feet again and began shouting approval.

"Consequently," the President continued, "those members of the banned parties who still hold their seat in Congress or the Senate will be removed, and the Governors of the States from which they came will be asked to nominate suitable and legal replacements."

Exhausted by now, the crowd could only summon up loud applause from their seats. The young men looked angry at this but chose to take no action. The meeting broke up an hour later, after several more hymns and a call for the blessing of the Almighty on His new political party.

*(Eyewitness report from an unidentified attendee at the Republican National Convention in Atlanta, August 2016)*

* * *

The Republican meeting in Atlanta signalled the start of the Second American Civil War. Within twenty-four hours of the declaration by President Horning of the ban on the Democratic Party, a number of States seceded from the Union. The geographic location of these States was interesting, and revealed something of the distribution patterns of immature souls in the USA. All the west coast states from Alaska through Washington, Oregon and California, plus Hawaii joined together in condemning Horning's activities, and formed the Union of Pacific States (UPS). Similarly, the north-east states of Vermont,

Maine, Massachusetts, Connecticut, Rhode Island and New York left the Union to form the Atlantic States of America (ASA). President Horning immediately declared war on the two new Unions, calling them massive conspiracies by the Communists supported by Satan. However, difficulties arose in the conduct of the war.

The first problem lay in the massive defections in all branches of the armed forces. Over a third of the fighting men crossed into the new territories, or remained there if they had been stationed in those regions. While many forces in those regions remained loyal to the new Administration and returned to the shrunken United States of America, no record of armed conflict between the two sets of troops has ever come to light.

Armed action did arise in other areas but was short-lived. The remaining elements of the US Air Force launched a massive bomber raid on San Francisco, Los Angeles and San Diego in September, 2019, ahead of major troop movements along the California border. All but one of the bombers returned to their bases, the bombs having been dropped over the ocean. Despite intensive interrogation, none of the aircrew members was able to give any explanation for their actions, or even to remember them. One crew that did carry out an attack in their B-2 Stealth bomber was picked up by UPS radar soon after take-off, despite the much-vaunted claims by the military and the manufacturers of the plane's invisibility. Although a squadron of UPS F-22 fighters was sent to intercept the bomber, the B-2 suffered structural failure flying through storm conditions over Utah and crashed before interception or delivering its bomb load. This last recorded mission of the B-2 bomber, which had finally cost over two billion dollars apiece, ended in a farce in the Utah countryside.

Similarly, the troops massed on the borders of both new nations were given orders to attack, but none of the commanders was able to remember receiving his orders. The troops remained in position for two months, gradually running out of supplies, until finally recalled by Horning who refused ever to recognize the new nations on his borders, but was unable to use his forces to attack them. In a speech before the joint Houses, he blamed communist infiltrators aided by forces of Satan for the failure of the armed forces. A purge of senior military officers followed, and over a thousand officers above the rank of major were executed without a trial as secret followers of the forbidden cult of Oneness. But the new military leaders were equally unable to force an attack.

This episode, plus the inability of the Middle East warring nations of Iran, Iraq and Syria to perceive the events outside of their borders, were the first major examples of human minds joining forces in their millions to prevent, or to localize the effects of damaging action.

* * *

The Supreme Court was busy over the three months following the inauguration of the new Justice Reverend William Casey. Carefully selecting cases that it would hear, the Court first ruled that the concept of separation of Church and State was a serious misinterpretation of the Constitution. As a result, States became free to impose a mandatory prayer meeting in all schools. Every single state chose to do so within a week, some deciding that the school day would both start and end with a prayer meeting at which attendance was compulsory, regardless of the child's religion. The rule was extended to all State-funded seats of learning, including colleges, universities and trade schools.

That same week, the Court ruled that the official religion of The United States was Christianity, which was deemed to include Catholicism. A consequence of that ruling was that citizenship of the USA was a right and a privilege only of members of the Christian churches. Non-believers were assigned a new status of Resident Aliens of the United States, with neither voting powers nor the ability to hold public office. Those proclaiming belief in the evils of Oneness were branded as simple criminals, liable to prosecution under the new category of "Enemies of the State" with concomitant loss of citizenship or resident status.

The Vatican began immediate proceedings to open up an Embassy in Washington and announced a new era of co-operation between the Mother Church and the American Party of God, which now ruled unchallenged in what was left of the USA.

A week later, the State of Alabama prosecuted a case against a black president of a local school board, claiming that her occupancy of that position was unconstitutional. The case hinged on the belief of the State's legislature, that citizenship was a prerogative only of persons of European birth. The claim was based on the concept that Europeans had freely colonized the USA, while others had been brought as slaves and thus had no valid claim to citizenship. The case was lost in the State Supreme Court, which held a number of Judges who had been appointed over ten years ago, but an appeal to the Supreme Court of the United States was immediately lodged and heard within a day. The State Supreme Court ruling was overturned without dissent.

Massive changes occurred within weeks in every municipality, township, school board and court as now-illegal incumbents were forced to relinquish their positions, and replacements were appointed. State Governors *en masse* decreed that the election process would cripple the country, and abrogated to themselves the authority to appoint replacements until the proper electoral procedures could be initiated at a later date. The only exceptions to the citizenship rulings were the three black, and two Jewish Republican senators who were granted honorary citizenship by the President until such time as they no longer held their Senate seats. But within three months, all five were tragically killed. Senators Hoyle and Weissman died when their commuter aircraft lost its engines over San Francisco Bay one morning. Wayne Bentham, the black junior senator from Nebraska was killed in a hit-and-run accident in Washington, without a single witness being located. Senator Aaron Burman vanished while driving from his home in Tampa to visit his sister, and his body was later found many miles away in swampland, half-eaten by alligators. The last, Senator Bryce Johnstone of New Mexico, a noted authority on Black American history, was shot by a long range rifle while standing by the Vietnam Memorial. No perpetrator was ever found.

The President expressed his deepest regrets for the devastating loss to America of these fine men. New Senators were appointed within a week. For the first time in many years, the entire population of the Hill was white, Christian and almost entirely male.

The House also passed a new Extended Crimes Bill a week or two after the deaths of the Senators. The death penalty was made mandatory for all crimes of rape, murder, drug dealing, drug possession, incest and a new category under a single title "Crimes against the State." This last category included proven belief in the creed of Oneness. In addition, the right of appeal against sentence was sharply reduced, as was the period between sentencing and execution. Later that year, following a wildly acclaimed speech by the President on national television, the death penalty was made an option for arson, kidnapping, robbery and fraud. Judges were encouraged to apply the extreme penalty whenever possible. By the year 2020, not a single one of the thirty-eight remaining states of the Union had failed to restore the death penalty to the statutes. In the years between 2020 and the destruction of the USA in 2026, over two hundred and sixty thousand executions were carried out in the USA.

In 2020, the State of Utah was the first to permit the televising of an execution by lethal injection. The object of the proceedings was a thirty-year-old black man who had been found guilty two months earlier of shooting his girlfriend. Later analyses showed that over eighty percent of televisions were tuned to that event in the broadcast area, and the show was later syndicated to national companies and cable organizations. Estimates were made that between fifty million and seventy million Americans, nearly eighty percent of the nation's population, watched the event.

Other states followed suit and by the end of the year, such events were regularly scheduled programs detailed in the weekly television guides. Viewer levels remained so high that advertising time around the events was sold at premium figures. Illinois took the next logical step early in the Spring of 2022, and conducted a public execution. Engineers installed the electric chair in the home plate area at Wrigley Field in Chicago, and proceeded to electrocute a Hispanic man found guilt of robbery, a white, middle-aged male for the murder a month earlier of his wife and her mother, and followed that with the executions of two convicted heretics, followers of Oneness. The affair was a sell-out despite the premium prices of almost twice the cost of a regular ball-game ticket.

Spotting the revenue-enhancing capability of such affairs, most states followed the example and before long, weekly execution nights became standard at the majority of major league ball parks, conducting between four and eight terminations of prisoners' lives to spectacular applause from the audience. The evenings soon became major events, with the singing of hymns, the national anthem and fireworks displays, rivalling football and baseball as spectator sports. Concessions for beer and food became gold mines for those lucky enough to hold them.

Changes continued to be implemented in the schooling process of America's children. While the individual states still had the freedom to select their own curricula, a House bill passed in 2022 removed a number of federal grants from those states that failed to align their teaching programs with those of the President's policies. These policies replaced the teaching of evolution with a rigid program of biblical teaching of creationism. To ensure no heretical concepts should be taught in other courses, all programs in chemistry and biology were removed from the President's chosen curriculum.

By the following year, not a single school or institution in the USA taught any course in chemistry, biology or botany. Many had also ceased to offer any courses in mathematics, physics and engineering, fearing accidental infringement of the law against evolution teachings.

In 2020, the general election took place without a Presidential election. Congress had proposed that such a process was unnecessary and contrary to the public good, as public acclaim had already guaranteed President Horning a second term in office, and nobody had declared their intention within the American Party of God of running against him. Almost incidentally, referenda were proposed and held in all states of the Union for an amendment to the Constitution. The limit of two terms for a President was removed. Radio, television and newspapers began to issue editorials in favour of making William H. Horning President for Life.

*(History of North America during the Time of the Infinite Soul, Klaus P. Scheidenhorst, University of Berlin, 2105, Oxford University Press.)*

# Chapter 7. Hell and Rebirth

The slaughter of the Unbelievers in Bainesville, Texas was matched in other towns and cities across America, though the extent of the lethal ferocity in Bainesville exceeded most others. The disciples of The Very Reverend William Horning were driven by fanatical hatred against those they believed to the Devil's Followers, the Accepters of Oneness. Led by the three men who had killed Michael Hendricks that morning outside the Church of the Divine Word, they murdered over four hundred people in the two years following Philippe Leger's televised press conference. Hendricks' killers became heroes and leaders of the community.

John Donald Parker was the acknowledged head of the trio. He was the fat man with the fat wife and two fat sons who had sat next to Michael Hendricks in church, and it was Parker who had fired his Colt thirty-two into Michael's forehead. Parker was forty years old, owner of a car dealership in Bainesville and saw himself as a truly religious man, a guaranteed occupier of a seat in Heaven when he died. He loved God, he feared the Devil, he feared Hell, and above all, he feared any change to his familiar environment. He despised anyone who was not a devotee of the Reverend Horning almost as much as he despised Liberals, Jews, Blacks, and anyone who read books, or spoke any language but American.

George Rolfe was one of the other two. A tall, slim man, married but without children, he had been born Catholic, but had become a rabidly-extreme white-supremacist in his early twenties. Totally devoid of any sense of humour, he worked as the stores controller for an engineering factory, and drove his workers mercilessly, especially those who were not white and avowedly Christian like himself. He had been elected to the local school board five years earlier, and had conducted an unrelenting campaign to remove unsuitable books from the curriculum and have daily prayers established in the program, despite the Supreme Court rulings that denied such practice.

The third was Henry Acheson, a non-entity of a man who was a cost accountant in the same plant at which Rolfe worked. Never married, a non-smoker, a non-drinker, a hater of most things, Acheson was a committed Republican who believed Ronald Reagan's face should be added to Mount Rushmore and had long believed, even before Horning made it so, that the Democratic Party should be banned as agents of the Communists.

These three led the regular rampages against the Devil which the Reverend Horning inspired every week or so. Parker had personally killed thirty-two people, including ten women and three children. Rolfe took credit for only seven, all black males. Acheson never carried a weapon, and was rarely seen at the action points. Instead he stood at the rear of the army of God's Agents as they called themselves, and watched with glittering eyes. After such an evening of entertainment, the three would usually gather in the local tavern and talk excitedly about the night's work.

This night in mid-summer, however, something went wrong.

The crowd had gathered at the tavern early, all of them except Acheson drinking hard and waiting for sufficient numbers to build up before setting out on God's work. By nine o'clock, the spirit had moved them and they walked in a crowd of twenty-one to the junction with the road which passed through the town, and the main highway to Houston. They raised a barricade across the highway and stopped every car heading in either direction. Most, they let pass after assurances from the occupants that they were true believers and committed to eradicating the evil of Oneness from the Earth. In boredom, they pulled the black occupants out of one car and beat them senseless, but refrained from killing them, leaving the three men and one woman to crawl back in their car and drive away.

At ten-fifteen, a Greyhound bus approached the barrier, and Parker waved it down with his shotgun in his hand. The bus slowed, stopped and the door opened. Parker climbed the stairs and looked into the bus. It contained about twenty young men, all in army uniform.

"We are the Agents of God, doing God's Work on Earth," called Parker. "Who is not a Believer here?"

One of the young men stood up. He wore the bars of a captain on his shoulders and had a handgun in a holster at his belt. "I've heard about you guys," he said with a smile. "Figured we'd come and see you some day!"

"Then be welcome, and God's blessings on you," replied Parker, and lowered his shotgun. The captain walked up to the front of the bus and was followed out of the door by five of his men, all also carrying handguns in holsters. As they reached the road, Parker followed them and so failed to see two more men open the racks above their seats and pull out sub-machine guns. The two men opened the windows a few inches and watched the proceedings outside.

"I am Captain Garry Hawker, 82nd Airborne," said the young officer. "Heard about the work you guys have been doing and I wanted to talk to you about it."

"God be with you, Captain," Rolfe said. "Maybe you could stick around a few days and give us some help? God has much work for us to do in His Name."

"Afraid not," replied Hawker. His smile was cold. He moved a few inches and his men followed him so that they no longer stood between the local men and the bus. As they did, a muffled clatter came from the bus windows as two automatic weapons opened up. Parker, Rolfe and Acheson died immediately. Seven more of their supporters followed, and six more fell to the ground, shaking with agony and their screams. In the shattering silence that followed the three-second burst of fire, Hawker and the other young men took out their pistols and carefully shot the writhing men on the ground. Checking that all were dead, Hawker calmly gestured to his men to return to the bus and followed them aboard. The five remaining God's Agents stood in deep shock, motionless, staring with terrified eyes at the young men as they filed aboard.

The door closed and the Greyhound moved off with a deep roar. Nobody looked back at the pile of bodies lying in their own blood by the roadside.

"Gotcha," said Hawker softly. He leaned forward to the driver. "Still okay, Ken?"

"Yes sir," replied the sergeant at the wheel. "If we keep going, we'll reach the Canadian border by tomorrow morning. Maybe someone can spell me in about an hour?"

"Sure thing, sergeant," answered the captain, leaning back with a weary look on his face. "I never thought I'd leave America this way," he said to the lieutenant seated next to him.

"I never thought America would become like this," said the lieutenant. "At least we cleaned up some of the worst of the mess."

The captain nodded and fell asleep.

* * *

John Donald Parker regained consciousness, lying on a cold, marble floor. Pain raged through his body, and he screamed aloud as he recalled the explosion of shells in his chest that had ripped his heart and lungs into confetti. He jerked his head and opened his eyes to see a cold, white light. For some minutes, he was unable to comprehend his surroundings. At first he felt as if he were in the centre of a white globe, except that he could stand up on the marble. Though when he tried that, severe vertigo seized him and he fell again, retching up thin bile. In the process of wiping his mouth, he saw his chest, unmarked, no bullet holes, no blood, though the pain still shrieked in every atom of his body.

"I'm dead," he muttered, horror sweeping over him so heavily that it almost masked the pain in his body. He tried to pray, but his mouth refused to make the words. Again he raised his head, and tried to look around. This time, he fought the dizziness and concentrated. He was on an enormous, endless, flat plain of marble. Not a single feature broke the vastness. What he took for sky was only a shade a darker grey than the marble on which he stood, and the dividing line of the impossibly remote horizon was only detectable with intense staring.

The agony diminished slightly, and he fought his weakness to climb to his feet. Finally upright, he turned slowly, looking for some break in the dreadful emptiness. Thirst nearly consumed him, and he felt worse than he had ever done, even after the fight in the tavern, when four men had taken exception to his comments about their appearance and beaten him senseless. He stopped turning and stared hard into the emptiness. A tiny, minuscule bump had appeared in the almost invisible horizon. Parker froze, and continued to stare as the bump grew larger and seemed to be approaching. With nothing by which to measure, he was unable to estimate the object's size, but something inside of him began to shake with fear, a certainty that the approaching mass was huge beyond comprehension.

"Oh God, how can this be?" he was finally able to mutter. "I am your faithful servant, a devout Christian who has served you all his life. Why am I not in heaven?"

The thunder shattered the dreadful quiet that had

so far surrounded him, making his body shake with mixed fear and pain. His ears reverberated, causing shafts of more agony through his head, and he tried to vomit again, without success.

**"JOHN DONALD PARKER!"** bellowed an awful voice. It had the cataclysmic rage of the worst thunderstorm Parker had ever experienced, worse than the unstoppable violence of the tornadoes that so commonly screamed their way across Texas. Parker fell to his knees and hid his face.

**"JOHN DONALD PARKER, YOU ARE COME TO ME FOR JUDGEMENT!"**

Finally, Parker understood. At last, he had come before his God to be judged and sent to Heaven or Hell. Feeling more confident now, he raised his head. The bump had become a figure on a throne, still massively distant, but obviously of a size incomprehensible to him.

Triumphant joy swept through him. "We were right!" he exalted. "God exists, He judges us, and those who followed His path will be brought before Him to dwell in the House of The Lord forever!"

He fell to his knees in an attitude of prayer. "I am here, My Lord, Your faithful servant," he cried. "I have followed in Your path and accepted the Lord Jesus Christ as my saviour. I am ready to be judged!"

**"FOLLOWED MY PATH?"** screamed the voice with a fury that sent waves of pain through the kneeling man. **"DID I NOT SAY, 'THOU SHALT NOT KILL'?"**

"But, My God, I killed only Your enemies! I was serving You!" Parker felt bewilderment and fear race through him. This was not how it was supposed to be. Surely he had proved his devotion by removing those children of Satan, the Eternal Enemy, the Accepters of Oneness? Why was God angry with him?

**"AND WHO ART THOU, THAT YOU SHALL DECIDE WHEN MY LAWS CAN BE BROKEN? WHAT PUNY HUMAN SHALL TELL ME, YOUR**

## SUPREME GOD, YOUR CREATOR, WHO ARE MINE ENEMIES?"

Parker fell flat to the floor, fear driving out all the terrible pain that still lived in him. Something was horribly wrong, the Judgement was not how the Reverend Horning had promised him it would be.

Howling, screaming winds surrounded him, he felt himself lifted from the marble floor and in a dreadful instant of complete understanding, Parker knew he was sentenced to Hell.

The storm took him, helplessly flailing his limbs, freezing his heart with fear, and he flew through a formless, black maelstrom of nightmares that bellowed fury at him. He lost all sense of time, of space, knew only helpless panic. After some un-measurable time, he crashed onto a surface that was coarse and scalding hot. He felt his arm smash and he screamed, a high, formless scream. He could see little, there was thick, curling, evil-smelling smoke around him. Whatever was left of rational thought worked enough to let him form tiny ideas.

"It's just like they said it would be," he gibbered in his brain. The heat grew stronger, painfully blasting at his broken arm and scraped legs from where he had fallen. "All it needs is..."

As he thought it, the first shape appeared out of the hot shadows. Small, horrible shapes, straight out of the paintings of Dante's vision of Hell, they hopped to him and giggled.

"Parker!" called one, and jabbed him in the foot with a spear. "We've been waiting for you!"

Parker stared in immeasurable horror. The demon had a tail, horns, carried a trident which had just cut deeply into him. It was exactly like all the pictures he had ever seen in the books he had read at Sunday School.

"How could they have known so accurately?" the last sane remnants of his brain babbled. "It's just like they told me at school!"

He felt scaly hands grab his elbows and he was hauled so fast that he fell, unable to avoid being rushed through the blackness. The heat built up so that now he was burning, he felt his flesh blister, his eyes began to steam, and the pain was so unbearable that all he could do was scream, and scream, and scream, and he kept screaming as the demons flung him through the smoke and into the pit that appeared before him. And as he fell through the endless burning, and his body shrivelled but couldn't die, and his skin smoked and burned off to reveal the white bone which then burned black as he watched, he screamed even more, his brain losing any rationality except for one thought.

"I'm sorry!" he howled to the unresponsive smoke and blazing fire. But nobody heard him, and he couldn't black out and lose consciousness because he was already dead.

* * *

John Donald Parker slowly came to be aware of only one wonderful sensation, the absence of pain after unknown aeons of agony. For several minutes, he stayed motionless, lying on his back, eyes closed while he savoured the experience, trembling with the aftershock of unimaginable tortures. Only after some further time did his memories of the terrors of Hell return to his mind, and with a shudder of fear, he opened his eyes, terrified that he would again see the fires and smoke and the demons that had inflicted such horrors on him.

Instead, he saw a man, sitting in an ordinary armchair, watching him thoughtfully. Parker sat up, realized he had been lying on a sofa that matched the armchair. He looked round. The room was spacious, elegant, dove-grey walls with a light blue carpet. Paintings hung on the wall. One was a wildly colourful, distorted face of a woman. She appeared to have two noses and several eyes, and her tears of pain and agony were horribly reminiscent to Parker of his recent experience. The other was an older-style picture, a man sitting on a wooden stool, wearing armour and holding a spear. His belt buckle seemed to glow with an internal light.

The man in the armchair continued to study Parker without expression. Parker finally faced him. He felt curiously that soon he would understand where he was, there was something familiar about the sensation.... ah! Of course. This was reality, he finally understood. He had died after yet another in a series of lives, none of which seemed to have led anywhere. He was back on the Astral Plane.

"I know you, don't I?" said Parker to the man in the armchair.

The man smiled briefly. "You should," he replied. "You have a major debt to me."

Parker stared hard. "You're the man I shot outside the church," he finally said. The man nodded.

"I'm very sorry," muttered Parker. "I simply didn't understand what was going on."

"How many lives have you had?" asked Michael Hendricks, settling back in the chair and looking at the Rembrandt painting on the wall. He felt it contrasted nicely with the Picasso Weeping Woman, both of which he had created with his apartment that was a copy of his previous home. He had done so to ease the wakening of Parker from his death and his descent into Hell, back into more familiar-style surroundings.

"That was my hundred and thirtieth," replied Parker, certain of the number but unable to say how he knew.

"And can you remember all those lives?"

"Yes, of course..." Parker stopped. He realized that his memory held massive gaps. He could not remember each of his past lives, but something told him that he should.

"Yes, John. You should have detailed memories of every one of them. And you're also still an Infant Soul, only at the fifth stage. By now, you should have progressed at least to being an early-stage Young Soul." Michael's voice was gentle. Parker seemed not to hear him. His eyes were again full of the horror and fear of his experience of Hell.

"Did you get judged by God when you died?" he asked Michael. Looking at the man in the armchair, he could read the aura around him to tell that Michael was a Mature Soul, almost an Old Soul. He trembled a little at the void between them. Michael shook his head.

"You created that experience for yourself," he said. "You were so rigid in your beliefs when you were alive, that you had to make the reality fit them when you died. The only judgement here is by yourself."

"But..." Parker stumbled over his words. "I don't understand. If I created it, why did I get sent to Hell? I was so certain that the teachings about God and Jesus were correct, and that I was doing God's work. I should have created Heaven for myself!"

Michael smiled a small smile. "But inside, as an immortal soul, your higher intelligence knew what evil you had done," he said. "That truth over-rode your simplistic beliefs, and you punished yourself, before returning to the Astral Plane. The mind is very powerful, even in an Infant Soul like you. You created your own Hell with images you had picked up from your childhood education, just as I have created this room and returned to the shape I had when you killed me, so that you would recognize me."

Parker felt waves of sadness and dismay inside himself.

"You see, John," continued Michael. "Something appears to be wrong with you and all your entity souls. There are fifteen hundred of you. You've all lived over a hundred lives, and you are all still Infant Souls. Not one of you has even reached the seventh stage before moving to Baby Soul level. I have lived three hundred and sixty lives and all my entity souls have lived about the same, but most of us are Old Souls, and just the last few are like me, seventh-stage Mature Souls about to move up to the last level. I reached my first Mature Soul stage after a hundred and ten lives, about where you are now."

Silence fell on the room while Parker stared aimlessly at the walls and the pictures. Michael's words had meant little to him. He had a faint understanding that several hundred souls eventually combined to create a single entity, but he was not clear on the details. The fact that his own entity had not progressed had never occurred to him before.

"You are not alone in this problem," continued Michael. "Most of the souls of mankind are the same way. My sense is that this is not as it should be."

Parker shivered a little. "I don't understand," he said again.

"Nor do I," admitted Michael. "I just know that something is wrong with all of mankind. But we have another problem to sort out first."

"What problem?" asked Parker. He felt depression wash over him. He was beginning to remember more clearly that this had happened before. He died, he awoke, he had more problems than when he had been born into his last incarnation.

"The problem of your Karmic debt to me," answered Michael. "And to the thirty-two other people you killed in your last few months incarnate, and the seven hundred and forty you have killed and tortured in previous incarnations."

Parker was remembering everything more clearly with each second. He remembered other Karmic debts incurred in previous incarnations, how he made agreements to repay the debt, but somehow always avoided his commitments to the other souls. He had killed many times in those lives that he could recall. Religious obsession had been a common thread through most of those lives, rigid thinking, terrified of change or uncertainty.

Parker remembered that he had been one of the Romans in the circus, screaming for the blood of the

Christians who had dared to question the establishment truth of the godhood of Jove and the others on Mount Olympus. He had been one of the witch-burners in medieval Europe, an Inquisitor of Spain, always a relentless bigot fighting any new ideas or concepts. He had been a teacher in a small school in Idaho during the early years of the previous century, beating his tiny class of farmers' children if any of then ever dared to question his version of the truth. He had sat in the audience of the Scopes Trial, screaming rage at the young man who had offended God by teaching evolution. His whole series of lives had been spent in anger, in hatred of change and those who brought it. He recognized now, how the souls of the entities of mankind had gathered together, how the enclaves of Baby and Infant Souls had grown in Syria, Iran and Iraq, with smaller pockets in parts of Australia, Northern Ireland and other countries, and the largest single mass in the United States, a gathering of spiritual infancy greater than all the rest put together.

Michael Hendricks was still speaking.

"I have been in council with all thirty-two of your most recent victims, as well as those earlier souls who died under your hand at other times," he said. "They have given me the right to negotiate for them how you can repay your Karmic debt."

"What will I have to do?" asked Parker. He felt resentment, anger, at the other souls, at Hendricks, at himself. Why had he not grown up as Hendricks had done? Why did he not have the knowledge that mature souls had?

"For now, nothing," replied Michael. "Your record of repayment is not good. We have decided to wait. Many of us feel that something immense is about to happen. We believe something is coming to us from somewhere distant. Perhaps it will make things clearer for us to decide."

"And will I incarnate again?"

Hendricks shook his head. "There is no value in

that. You have stagnated in your incarnation progress. We will wait."

The elegant room dissolved, Hendricks vanished, and Parker found himself surrounded by light mists. For a few moments he panicked, then voices surrounded him. He recognized them, others of his entity, souls who had been his relations, his friends, opponents in other lives. The conversations that surrounded him were irritated.

"How dare those Mature Souls tell us what to do...?"

"They said we can't go down again...."

"The one I spoke to had only had a hundred and ten lives and he was a Mature Soul. How come none of us has ever progressed...?"

"What's this about something coming...?"

The soul that had been John Donald Parker gradually retreated from the bickering and complaining. The words of Michael Hendricks were paining him. As he returned to familiarity with the Astral Plane, he remembered some more of his previous incarnations, the dreadful similarity of narrow-mindedness, bigotry and hate in all those existences. There had been no progress, no growth, not just in himself, but in all the souls of his entity. He remembered how, after each life, he had refused to evaluate the lessons of the incarnation with others who were his mentors, denied the obligations he had incurred by the killings and the cruelty he had shown so many other people. Each time, he had simply chosen to return to a society where his immature soul could continue with no new demands upon it, where other souls like him congregated. He recalled how the gathering of like souls had grown, the vast numbers of infant souls joining for support in the United States, in several countries of the Middle East and in smaller, localized regions around the world.

He shivered with pain and regret. In his last few lives, he had engineered the deaths of many who had disagreed with his own rigid brand of Christianity. And now he knew that the basic concepts of Christianity were also fiction, that the truths of reality, of the Universe, of eternity were far and away advanced on the simplistic beliefs of his infantile mind and those like him. He trembled as he sensed something infinitely powerful in the universe. Was it coming to Earth? What would happen when it came? Why was so much of humanity stuck in the first stage of soul development? Was that why something was coming?

In its own way, the soul that had been John Donald Parker was one of the first to stumble on the truth of the coming of the Infinite Soul, and in so doing, take the first step towards its own redemption and that of all Mankind.

# Chapter 8. The New Inquisition

*(From the diaries of Alan Drew)*
*May 21, 2022*

I believe that this day signalled the collapse of my world and everything I have ever worked for. I have somehow come to terms with the abdication of Philippe Leger from the Throne of St. Peter a decade earlier, and was becoming restless with my forced idleness. In that time, there had been much work to do, but I was in the role of general assistant to anyone who needed it, rather than a specific position. But this morning, I received the short note from Gregory Cardinal Lavalier with a small tremor of worry. The note said briefly, and with only the barest of greeting courtesies, that I must attend the Cardinal's office the following morning at eight o'clock. Was my long period of limbo in the halls of the Vatican finally about to end with an ignominious dismissal back to England? I can't think of any other reason why the Cardinal would call for me. As a one-time aide to the disgraced and excommunicated Pope Jean-Pierre II, I am sharply aware of the distance that had been placed between me and the others in God's City. The Cardinal has given me few duties since I was assigned to his service and I have lived within this isolation all these years.

I spent the afternoon in prayer in my room, emerging only for the evening meal and Vespers. Returning to England holds no attractions for me. Like the rest of Europe, England has almost completely succumbed to the mysterious and frightening new philosophy called Oneness. I can't bring myself to call it a religion. How can it be a religion when it worships no gods, believes in no heaven or hell, fears no divine retribution and accepts no priests? No religion can exist when its adherents didn't even know exactly what they believe.

The astounding events surrounding the carnage in the Middle East fill me with confusion and fear. The three combatants kill each other with a rage and despair far worse than any horrors of the First World War trenches, and yet they seem ignorant of the presence of a zone of peace around them. I am confused because I have absolutely no idea how this could be, and I'm terribly afraid because the power behind the cause, whatever it is, can hardly be denied. Could a few hundred million people in Asia and Europe simply decide in their own minds that the murderous blood lust of Syria, Iraq and Iran would be confined to those countries' borders, and it was so? Could they make the entire populations of these countries forget the presence of their most hated enemy, the State of Israel? This is what I have read in the few editions of European newspapers I have been able to find in the streets outside the walls of the Vatican. And yet this is what has happened, just as it has certainly happened that the borders nearly everywhere else have collapsed, and few people outside the blood-drenched warring nations seem to think of themselves as Christian or Jew or Moslem anymore.

The idea makes me tremble for here is something so far outside my comprehension that it threatens my mental balance. Is this the final conflict between Good and Evil, between God and the Devil? If so, which is which? If Oneness is Evil Incarnate as my Church has stated, is Ultimate Goodness represented by the killing of millions in the deserts of the Middle East? Is Goodness, the Kingdom of God, reflected in the United States, where the slaughter of the followers of Oneness has begun to climb to appalling heights? If so, I'm terribly afraid, for my beliefs, my love of God and the One Apostolic Church to which I have devoted my life have failed to provide an explanation of how this could be so. This is not my view of a supreme God of goodness, of love.

I spent the evening again in prayer, and slept hardly at all during the night. At five, I awoke and visited the small chapel kept for the residents of the Vatican, and prayed again. Missing breakfast, I returned to my room, checked my appearance once more, adjusted my robe and walked through the corridors to the office of Gregory Cardinal Lavalier.

The Cardinal's secretary, a young man of well over six feet in height and the thinness of a flamingo standing in water looking for fish, gave me a cold stare as I entered the outer office. He did not invite me to sit in one of the dark leather chairs round the walls, and I remained standing, nervous, shifting from one foot to another and trying to look at the medieval paintings that hung above the chairs. Angels floated over knights in armour, saints with their haloes suspended over their heads knelt in prayer or underwent awful tortures at the hands of the mob, and several versions of Jesus, immaculate in perfect white robe, trimmed beard and Anglo-Saxon pale face looked out at me from the archway-shaped frames of the pictures. The young man at the desk scribbled endless lines on paper sheets and ignored me, for which I was grateful.

Finally, a small buzzer sounded from the secretary's desk. The man merely looked up and nodded slightly, which I took as permission to enter the adjoining office. I opened the door onto a huge expanse of luxury. It almost felt like leaving a building by a small door and finding oneself in an empty city square. The carpet was a deep purple, the walls were a pale cream, again lined with medieval paintings of religious scenes. The Cardinal appeared to have a singular taste in art, I decided. Near to where I was standing, a large, glass conference table was surrounded by a dozen beautiful, black ebony chairs with white padded seats. Three vases of flowers lined the table and a silver tray with a crystal jug full of water stood at one end, surrounded by four crystal glasses.

The Cardinal sat behind a small desk against the far wall. The desk looked antique, delicate and expensive. Dressed in his black robes and scarlet sash round his waist, but without his skull cap, the Cardinal was working on a sheet of paper with a gold fountain pen. He looked up me, nodded in recognition and gestured briefly at an armchair against one wall.

"I will be with you in a moment," he said, and bent over the desk again. I sat in the armchair and tried to relax. Would I have been given the courtesy of an armchair if I am being dismissed? I decided it could either mean I was to be treated gently while being sent home, or there was hope for me, yet.

Lavalier folded his pen away, slid the paper into a blue folder and stood up. I rose to my feet, but received a small smile from Lavalier and a gesture to remain seated. The Cardinal took another armchair at right angles to me, arranging his robes carefully. I held my breath.

"Alan, we go to Washington, you and I," Lavalier said.

I slowly let my breath out and realized my heart was thumping insanely. "Washington, Your Eminence?" I managed to stammer, recognizing that perhaps my career in the Vatican was not yet over.

"Indeed," replied the Cardinal, letting out a rare small smile that encouraged me even more. "You are aware, of course, that the United States has become our only real ally in the fight against this evil that has infested the world in the last few years. Our embassy there needs more help to co-ordinate the liaison with the American President, and I have suggested that you fit the post very well."

"I... I am very honoured, Eminence," I said, feeling a wave of both excitement and fear run through me. I had never been to the USA and had always wanted to see that extraordinary country. But the developments there of the last seven years since the startling departure of Pope Jean-Pierre II scare me. Such violence, so much killing.

"We will leave next week," continued Lavalier. "I will stay for two weeks to see you settled in, and then will return. You will stay for as long as you are needed, and you will be a personal contact for President Horning."

"I will meet President Horning?" I was astonished, and excited by the news.

"Meet him? You will work with him and be his daily contact with our Embassy," replied Lavalier. "This is a position of great responsibility, Father. I have every trust in you."

"Thank you, Eminence," I answered faintly. "I will do my best not to disappoint you."

"Let us both pray that you do not," said the Cardinal with a touch of acid. "This may be our only chance to work for God's victory against ultimate evil."

* * *

*May 27, 2022*

Most of the rest of the week has been spent waiting in anxiety. I have little to pack and no personal preparations to make. They told me that the delay was mainly to allow the Cardinal to make his own arrangements, and because commercial flights to the USA have declined in frequency to the point where only one flight every two weeks leaves from Rome to Washington. But this morning, the Alitalia Airbus 380 left Italy with the Cardinal and me safely ensconced in the first-class section as befitted emissaries of the Pope.

Ten hours later, the massive aircraft touched down gently at Washington's Dulles Airport, and the Cardinal and I walked out of the passageway to be met by a small party of men in the reception area. They looked grim-faced, cold, as if they suspected everyone around of evil crimes. One of them advanced on us. His face was harsh, as if it had never smiled in the entire life of its owner. The eyes under a full head of black hair that reflected the lighting of the terminal were small, but dull, seemingly without life of their own.

"Your Eminence," he said and bowed over the hand extended to him by my Cardinal. "I am Stephen Crossman, the President's liaison with the Vatican Embassy." He turned to me. "Father Alan," he added and gripped my hand firmly. The grip was cold and I was relieved to release it. Crossman's face gave me a deep sense of unease. The eyes seemed blank, without any indication of human personality behind them. I have never encountered such an impenetrable wall in a man's face before.

"I wish you God's blessing on your arrival to join us in the fight against Evil," the American said.

Lavalier inclined his head courteously and said something softly that I was unable to hear. Instead, I looked round the terminal for my first examination of the United States. It was not a comfortable inspection. Armed men in combat greens lined the terminal, carrying what looked to my untutored eyes like automatic rifles. Few other people were around, whether because traffic was limited, or because of security arrangements for the Vatican representatives, I didn't know.

The Americans began to lead us through the terminal and we emerged through the automatic doors into the open air. Three limousines waited parked outside, and the Cardinal and I were hustled inside with little ceremony and driven off, thankfully alone, without those hostile men. The first twenty minutes of the ride were uneventful, passing along a motorway until we entered the city, but to my pleasure, in the short ride that remained, I was able to see the Monument, the dome of the Capitol building and the White House. When we stopped, we were at the apex of a U-shaped driveway outside a small mansion. An emerald green lawn was surrounded by the driveway and the house was pure white, with a massive, black door which was opening as the limousine came to a stop.

"Our new Embassy building," announced Lavalier as we left the luxurious confines of the limousine. It seemed a redundant comment. I had assumed that fact. The ride had been fascinating for me, but I had been puzzled by the almost complete absence of people in the streets, and the scarcity of cars. I thought I would have seen crowds in the capital city of the USA, but the place had been almost deserted. Most of the vehicles I saw had been limousines like our own, or military trucks carrying seated soldiers armed with the same rifles the men at the terminal had been carrying. I felt unwilling to ask the Cardinal about it. To my slight dismay, a second limousine pulled up, and Crossman got out. He led the way into the house and once inside, he addressed us again.

"We will leave you for the evening, Eminence, as I believe you may wish to relax and recover from your journey," he said to the Cardinal. "Tomorrow at nine, we will have a meeting with the President to discuss the formation of the new council."

Lavalier nodded, and the American left without looking at me.

I was puzzled by his words. "Council, your Eminence?" I asked as we stood in the huge foyer of the Embassy. We were almost alone, the nearest people being a trio of servants standing in the doorway some yards away. They were all black men, dressed in formal striped trousers, white jackets and white gloves. They looked uneasy.

"The Council for the Protection of God's Name," Lavalier answered. "President Horning and the Holy Father have already discussed the formation as a way of defending the Holy Church against the attacks of the Great Adversary. You will learn further tomorrow. Now go and rest, and join me for prayers at nine tomorrow."

I bowed my head, and the gesture seemed to be taken as a signal to the three servants who immediately approached us. To my astonishment, but not, apparently, to Lavalier's, one of them knelt at the feet of the Cardinal and bent his head almost to the red carpet of the foyer. Then he rose and began to walk to the door at the end of the foyer. Without a word, Lavalier followed, nodding slightly at me to do the same. Outside one door, the servant stopped, opened the door and again knelt with his head bowed while Lavalier entered. Then he stood again, and walked to another door across from the first. Again the extraordinary obeisance occurred, and in some embarrassment, I walked into the room, hearing the door gently close behind me.

My bags were already unpacked, the large and splendid bed was ready, with the corners of the eiderdown turned back, and I realized how exhausted I was. Checking my watch, I realized my internal clock was more than two hours past midnight. Setting my portable alarm for six-thirty the next morning, I first scrawled my notes for the day into the diary, undressed and climbed into the bed. But I was not able to fall asleep instantly, as I would have expected. The Cardinal's words of a few minutes ago came back to me. The Council for the Protection of God's Name? What in Heaven could that mean?

* * *

*May 28, 2022*
The next day, the ride to the White House was short, barely five minutes, and again I saw little but other limousines and military transports. I sat on the left-hand side of the vehicle, the Cardinal on the other, while the cold-faced White House aide sat facing us, his back to the screened driver's compartment. No words were spoken in the ride, and I felt uncomfortable, despite the excitement of the forthcoming visit with the

President of the United States of America, the Very Reverend William Hardcastle Horning.

The limousine slowed as it turned into the gates of the White House then stopped. All the darkened windows were lowered by a central control that I presume had been activated by the driver, for nobody in the rear of the car had moved. At each window, an armed guard appeared and stared hard at us. The young men looked in their twenties, hard eyes drilled unblinkingly into my face, the blue metallic sheen of the automatic rifle held firmly across the chest, so close that I could smell the light oil in the mechanism. Behind the guards, three tanks stood heavily on concrete platforms that had been laid into the grass by the driveway. Although the main guns pointed outwards at the city, I could see a smaller machine gun mounted on a swivel under the barrel of the machine nearest to me. The muzzle pointed straight at the limousine.

The guards stood upright, saluted, and the limousine glided smoothly away, the windows all closing simultaneously as it did so. The remaining trip lasted merely seconds. The car stopped gently under the roof of a driveway, and another uniformed guard, this time a captain, if the bars on the man's collar meant what I thought they meant, saluted as the door was opened from the outside. The Cardinal was about to climb out when Crossman stopped him with a quiet word.

"Your Eminence, I must get out first and check for your safety," he said. Lavalier sat back in his seat and waited for Crossman to climb out. In a few seconds, Crossman bent back into the vehicle. "Your Eminence, Father Alan, if you would follow me, please?" he said courteously.

I followed my superior out of the vehicle and stood up in the fresh morning air, breathing deeply and looking around. We had stopped by a door in one wing of the White House, under a portal that looked as if it had once been open to the air. Now a sheet of transparent material covered the outer edge of the parking area. Bullet-proof glass? I felt awful discomfort at the idea of a world where visitors to the President had to be protected from distant snipers. What had we come to, here in what was supposed to be the greatest democracy on earth?

I'm in the White House, I realized with a wave of excitement, a guest of the President, and I forgot my concerns of snipers as the door to the building was opened. Crossman led the way as our small procession walked along corridors, stopping suddenly before a beautifully polished door that Crossman opened and ushered us inside. I followed the Cardinal and found myself in a small conference room, little space but a long white table with ten chairs placed neatly around it. There were no windows to the room. Paintings on the wall were not dissimilar to those in the Cardinal's office, religious scenes, mainly saints and haloes and pale-faced, handsome, Anglo-Saxon representations of Jesus. The only exception was the large oil painting at the head of the conference table. It showed a round-faced man with a majestic head of white hair and an angelic expression of devotion, looking into the far distance. The face showed just a faint sign of suffering borne in bravery. From the photographs I had seen in newspapers, I knew that this was William Horning. The President of the United States looked every inch the Servant of God, performing his duties at whatever price his Lord demanded of him.

"If your Eminence would be seated, the President will be with you in a moment," said Crossman, pulling back the chair at the right hand of the head of the table, clearly indicating the need for the Cardinal to sit there. Lavalier calmly seated himself as shown and nodded at me to take the seat to his right, so that I would be two places from the President. Silence descended on the room.

It lasted barely a minute. A door on the opposite

side of the table from which the visitors had entered swung open and a loud voice rang out.

"Gentlemen, the President of the United States!"

Through the door came the subject of the painting on the wall, and we all rose to our feet. I felt a surge of excitement. One man walked alone into the room, and my excitement turned to dismay. I felt a wave of cold sweep into the room, and instinctively took a step backward, banging my legs against my chair.

Horning spoke first. "Your Eminence, it is my special delight and honour to meet with the representative of the Vatican," he said, extending a hand to the Cardinal.

"Mister President, my honour," replied the Cardinal, and waited while the President bent over and lightly touched his lips to the Cardinal's ring. "His Holiness, Pope Pius the Thirteenth extends his greetings to you and blessings on your initiatives in this fight against God's Adversaries."

"Hallelujah!" the President exclaimed and clasped his hands together in an attitude of prayer.

"And this is Father Alan Drew, your new liaison with the Holy See," murmured the Cardinal, turning to me. Horning bustled round the table and approached me, seizing my hand and shaking it vigorously. His grip was cold and powerful.

"Father Alan, you are most welcome," he gushed, his voice ringing in the room. Unable to speak, I swallowed and nodded at the President. Horning turned away and took his seat at the head of the table. Crossman took a seat at the other end of the table and said nothing.

Despite my inexplicable fear, I forced myself to study the President. Other than the two Popes, Philippe Leger, once Pope Jean-Pierre II, and his successor, Pope Pius the Thirteenth, this was the first world leader I had ever met in person, or even been in such proximity to. The differences between the man and the painting were marked. The reality had a much chubbier face than the artificially ascetic leanness of the painting, and the signs of dissipation and meanness in the pink, fleshy lips of the man at the table were missing from the picture. But I had no doubts that the worst aspect of the man was in the blank, opaque nature of his dark eyes. It was not a warm darkness as should have been in such eyes. Instead, it was more an absence of light, even a drawing away of light from everywhere else. The room seemed to have become gloomy with the presence of Horning.

"Cardinal Lavalier," said the President. "As I understand it, His Holiness accepts entirely the need for the formation of this new Council, is that correct?"

Gregory Lavalier bowed his head slightly. His face seemed quite expressionless. "The Holy Father expressed the same horror and dismay as you did, Mister President, at the advances that the Great Adversary has made recently," Lavalier replied. "And he has asked me to tell you that no steps are to be ignored to counter them. Whatever it takes to prevent the spread of Evil is blessed in the Name of God."

"Good! Excellent!" The President rubbed his hands and grinned like a business executive informed of a new bonus. "Then the Council for The Protection of God's Name is officially created as of now." He turned and made a small gesture at Crossman standing quietly against the wall. "I have appointed Mister Crossman here as the Chief Examiner," he said. "We will do everything in our power to root out this foul heresy, wherever it hides in this Country of God, and eradicate it."

I felt horrified. Those words again. The Council for The Protection of God's Name? Chief Examiner? These terms sounded dreadfully like those of an earlier time in history when the Grand Inquisitor had led the Spanish Inquisition to seek out and destroy heresy. The tools then had been terror and torture, mass executions in the *auto-da-fé* in the public squares of the cities. What has Horning created here?

The President rose to his feet, and the rest of us followed. Horning again extended his hand to the Cardinal and shook it, no kiss of the ring this time. "We shall meet again this evening, gentlemen, when we go to witness God's Work," he said, and abruptly left the room.

The silence lasted an uncomfortable few moments while we again sat down, this time with Crossman advancing up the table to sit opposite the Cardinal. I listened with terrified fascination to their conversation, though they ignored me completely.

"Arrangements are well in place," said Crossman. His voice was a low monotone, almost mechanical. Not an expression had crossed his face at any time that I had looked at him. "We have collection and detention centres established in most cities, and processing facilities have been installed in all of them."

"Already?" said Lavalier, one eyebrow lifted slightly.

"We expected the Vatican's support in this work," replied Crossman without a sign of discomfort.

"I see," murmured the Cardinal. "And what sort of processing facilities will you be using?"

"Fairly advanced," Crossman replied. "Combinations of drugs and technology. Nobody will be able to resist an examination for more than a few minutes."

"And in what state will they be after an examination?" Lavalier seemed only slightly interested in the answer, looking carefully at his ruby ring and turning it to catch the light of the overhead bulbs.

Crossman shrugged. "Who cares?" he said. "If they embrace evil, they have only themselves to blame for what happens to them."

"But what if they are innocent of any belief in Oneness? What if they are true servants of God, falsely accused?" The Cardinal looked directly at Crossman who merely looked back.

"Then I am sure God will forgive us for our enthusiasm in seeking out His enemies, and He will take the innocent into His arms and everlasting Paradise," Crossman replied.

"Of course," said Lavalier, and I was unable to detect any trace of irony in the Cardinal's tone.

*My God, what have they done?*

* * *

The rest of the morning and afternoon passed in a series of meetings with other diplomatic personages that seemed to me to be no more than an exchange of meaningless clichés between cloned men in formal attire. Most were American, a few others were like us, members of the Vatican Embassy in Washington, and a small handful of representatives of the warring nations of the Middle East. In the short discussions I was able to have, I learned that most of the last group had come to Washington to beg for weapons from the Americans with which to continue their mutual slaughter, and their presence gave the Americans a severe headache. These extremist Moslem States were mutually at war with each other, but were also the only other major nations who had so far been untouched by the inroads of Oneness, and all three of them looked to the USA for spiritual guidance as well as more practical support in return for their oil.

I learned that President Horning had so far been able to play a desperately sharp-edged game of keeping all three unaware of the fact that he was selling large amounts of war material to them all, while convincing each of them that they were the sole recipients of his generosity. How long the game could continue and what would happen when the cat escaped its confines was the problem making many of the American diplomats look haggard and distressed.

At six, after a light meal back at the Embassy building, I again met with the Cardinal in the lobby as I had been instructed. We were going to witness "God's

Work" I had been told, and these were the words that the President had used earlier that morning, but the Cardinal had refused to explain further, and merely instructed me to be on time. I was five minutes early, as I had long ago learned was the rule when meeting with Church superiors, and I turned as the Cardinal appeared in the lobby.

"The limousine is here?" Lavalier asked.

"Indeed, your Eminence," I replied.

"Then just one word before we leave, Father. Whatever you see tonight, you must show restraint. What we witness will undoubtedly be strange to you, probably distasteful, but you must remember that the Holy Father himself has confirmed the religious necessity of these proceedings. There is historical precedent for tonight's events, and you must remember that and if your spirit weakens at any time, remind yourself that you are the servant of God and this is in support of His word."

"Yes, your Eminence," I said, feeling a return of the horror that had swept over me that morning. What was I to see tonight? I followed Lavalier out of the door opened for us by the black servants in their striped coats, white gloves and bowed heads, and entered the limousine to find it empty apart from ourselves and the driver in the front compartment.

As we drove through the quiet city, the Cardinal said nothing, merely stared out of the darkened windows, but I thought I detected tension and possibly anticipation in the thin face across from me. After a few miles, the traffic had built up to what I felt would be more normal for a major city. All the cars were heading in the same direction as we were, and the traffic stream slowed as congestion grew. However, the official limousine was being given right of way by drivers, and the police we passed, all armed with the same weapons that the military troops carried, stopped any cars to allow the limousine to proceed as necessary.

Finally, we arrived at a huge gate that led onto an

even more enormous parking area, room for thousands of cars. At the far end of it was a high wall, two or three hundred feet high, and I recognized a sports stadium, not unlike the football grounds of my youth in England. Passing through the gate, the limousine stopped next to a doorway set in the enormous wall. More armed guards stood there, and they lined up by the limousine as Lavalier opened the door and climbed out. The door was opened from inside, and I followed the Cardinal to a small lobby where a bank of elevators stood. A door was already open for us, and we were swept up in almost complete silence.

At the other end of the ride, the door opened to reveal brightness and festivities such as I had not seen so far on this trip. We had arrived at the rear of a private box of the stadium. It was large and spacious, with armchairs along one side, but the main attraction was the far end that opened out onto the stadium. The lights were already lit, and the brightness was like midday in a Rome summer. Several people stood around, holding glasses in their hands and talking animatedly. Many of them they had already met that day, and the Cardinal and I found ourselves being greeted as old friends.

"Eminence, Father Alan, the seats in the front are for you," said a familiar voice from behind me, and I turned to see the solidly expressionless face of Stephen Crossman. He ushered us forward and we sat in comfortable leather seats immediately behind the balcony overlooking the stadium. The place was already almost full, and I looked out onto an ocean of faces in row upon row of excitement. People were standing, many of them staring in our direction and waving. Flags were flying all round the top of the wall round the stadium, and a marching band was performing on the astoundingly brilliant green surface of the playing area. The outline of a baseball diamond was clearly marked in front of them and, having occasionally watched the game on television, I recognized the home plate directly opposite and below me.

I felt a massive wave of relief. A baseball game! That is what we had come to see! All my fears were groundless. I was about to see America at play, something I had always wanted. And I was in what were clearly the best seats in the house! I settled down with pleasurable anticipation, and watched the crowds milling below me, buying beer and popcorn and hot dogs, just like I had always imagined it. Not at all like a cricket match in stuffy old England!

The stadium was almost full when the band struck up the tune that I knew as "Hail to the Chief." The President was joining us, of course! I felt a sudden panic and stood up, just as Horning entered the box and advanced to the front row, holding his hands high. The roar of the crowd built up until it was painful, but I stopped myself from covering my ears as I caught the eye of my superior.

The shouting continued for nearly five minutes, during which Horning continued to stand and receive the adulation with a fixed grin on his face. Finally it died enough for the band to strike up again, this time the familiar tones of the American National Anthem, and the amplified tones of a female singer filled the ground. I looked down and saw a slender young woman standing on a small platform that had been placed near the home plate. She was holding a microphone and waving one arm as she sang. Before she had finished, the whistles and roars of the crowd had drowned her out, and she climbed down to the ground and walked off, still waving to the crowd.

The crowd grew silent in expectation, and it occurred to me that I had seen no signs of the ball players so far. Surely they would have been on the ground, warming up, practising? But not a sign had been seen. Yet the expectation and excitement in the crowd was unmistakable. Something incredible was about to happen, I was certain.

"Ladies and gentlemen!" bellowed the loudspeaker, echoes of the words chasing round the ground like kittens at play. "Welcome to another night of God's Work, the efforts to preserve the Almighty's Law and save the world from Evil."

The din of the crowd built up again, and I began to feel a small chill of worry. This was not a baseball game, I realized. The something incredible had become something horrible.

"We have a full program tonight to proclaim God's Name," shouted the loudspeaker. "Eight heretics and criminals will be sent to meet their maker tonight, and the world will be a cleaner place when it has happened."

The crowd's roar built even higher than when Horning had appeared, and the pain was appalling for me. The crowd was standing and waving American flags and photographs of the President, gesticulating at the box where we sat.

"Mister President!" bellowed the public address system. "We, the people of America thank you again for this opportunity to witness God's Work in action and help you protect America and the world from the evils now rampant. When tonight's work is done, America will be a better place than when we came, and we have you to thank for it!"

The noise built up again for a few minutes, and Horning stood and waved back at the crowd. I felt dreadfully exposed and naked sitting just two seats away, almost the focus of nearly a hundred thousand human beings screaming in adulation, and with a shock, I saw that television cameras were pointed at the box. Maybe millions all over America were watching us! With a chill of horror, I knew now what I had been brought to see.

"Ladies and gentlemen, join the President as he leads us in a prayer for this night's work," rasped the loudspeaker, and fell mercifully silent. Horning rose to his feet, raised his arms and began to intone a prayer to which I was unable to identify the words, so rigid with pain and fear was I. The words were carried around the stadium from the small microphone that protruded from the balcony in front of Horning, and the prayer was followed by a hymn, then another hymn, until I felt I was in the middle of a nightmare.

Finally, Horning resumed his seat, and the rustle of expectations grew louder. The loudspeaker slammed its presence into the proceedings again.

"The first stage in tonight's work is a thirty-year-old man who killed his wife in a drunken outburst last week. God's police apprehended this killer and tonight he faces the punishment for his crime. Ladies and gentlemen, this is Peter Browning!"

The crowd stood and yelled, and from below their box seats, a small procession appeared, walking slowly to the point that should have been home plate. I saw that a construction had appeared on the small stage, and realized it must be an electric chair. My heart was pounding and my breath was feeling strangled as I watched the procession advance on the chair. At the head of the small group, two large uniformed men held the arms of a smaller man who seemed about to collapse, were it not for the supporting grips. I was near enough to see his face, ashen, with staring eyes and a mouth that was clearly drooling. He wore old, stained trousers and short-sleeved shirt, and the trousers were cut open at the knees. Behind these three, walked a short man carrying a small bag, and he was accompanied by a tall, slender man in late middle age who carried himself with the assured air of a senior military officer or policeman.

The man in the ragged clothing was turned around and fastened to the chair with a heavy leather strap round his chest, and the two larger men bent over him, attaching fittings to his feet and wrists. They stood upright, and one of them placed a metal headpiece over the man's shaven scalp. The headpiece had a visor that could be swung down, but it was left upright to show the ashen, nightmare face.

The crowd fell silent, except for an almost vibrant sensation running round the ground. The harsh illumination from the walls was subdued, and to replace it, arc lamps over the electric chair sprung into life and lit the scene starkly in the gloom. A deep sigh ran round the crowd and silence returned.

"Peter Browning is a killer," intoned the loudspeaker, "and now he will suffer for it. An eye for an eye, a tooth for a tooth. So it says in the Bible, and so shall it be here tonight."

The concept was dreadfully wrong. The words were from the Sermon on the Mount, when Jesus said that although many would say those words, He would say turn the other cheek. How have they corrupted the words of Jesus to serve themselves!

"Peter Browning, before you die, have you any words to say to us?" The loudspeaker had resumed. To my utter dismay, I saw that a microphone was standing in front of the chair, not two feet from the man's head. The ground fell silent, and the only sound was a muffled gasping and gargling from the man in the chair. One of the men on the platform moved a hand and slapped the visor over the face of the man in the chair.

"Then, Peter Browning," said the enormous, amplified voice with a theatrical emphasis and pause, "go to meet your God!"

The man jerked against his bonds, and his body vibrated. From this close, I could see the man's hands, fingers stood out rigidly. The jawline, just visible under the visor was shrieking and the sound of the high pitched wail was audible through the loudspeaker system. I almost screamed with him but could not take my eyes away. The whole chair sparked with small flashes, and even in the midst of the horror, a small part of my mind told me that the sparks were surely special effects, not necessary for the process of exterminating life, but a bonus to the watchers. The body slumped back, and one of the attending men approached it, put a stethoscope onto the chest, then stood up, with a small nod to somebody out of my vision. Again, the body in the chair jolted upright, again the hands stood up almost in prayer, and the hidden face screamed limitless pain.

The crowd had begun to roar again, and by the time the body slumped back, the whistles of jubilation and yells of appreciation were echoing round the stadium.

Just like when Nottingham Forest had scored a goal in the soccer stadium near my home, was the insane thought in my head. I was sweating heavily and gasping for breath.

A stretcher was carried up to the chair by two young men in jeans and tee shirts, and the body was rapidly taken from the chair, laid on the stretcher and carried out. The shouts of the hawkers of beer, popcorn and hot-dogs resumed sharply as if on cue, and the crowd settled back happily, a hum of enjoyment racing round the stands. I looked around. Faces were smiling, conversations were animated, and many people were standing up and greeting others, or waving at the television cameras.

*Dear God in Heaven, what is happening here? Can this truly be Your Work? Is this what the Holy Father has sanctioned in Your Name?*

"Well, Eminence? How do you find our service in the name of the Lord?" President Horning had risen to his feet, and between waves at the crowd had turned to the Cardinal. I watched my superior, looking for any reaction, struggling against waves of nausea and the fear I felt in proximity to William Horning.

"Highly effective, Mister President," Lavalier replied. "The message is certainly brought home in this way."

"You bet it is!" Horning beamed and sat down again. A young man leaned over me with a tray of drinks, and I grasped one eagerly, taking a deep draught before realizing it was something strongly alcoholic mixed with lemonade. I had not touched alcohol since my teenage years, and the kick it delivered to my insides was painful, but welcome.

"Our next event in tonight's service is a particularly deserving case," bellowed the loudspeaker again, and the crowd rapidly resumed its seats with a hum of excitement.

"Kenneth Jensen is a Son of Satan, a truly evil man, a follower of the Devil's Creed of Oneness! True Christian Americans discovered this nest of evil in their neighbourhood and reported it to the local authorities. After examination, Jensen has refused to recant and so faces us tonight!"

The crowd rose to its feet, applauding wildly as the small procession re-appeared. But immediately, I could see a difference to the previous group. Jensen was a medium-sized man in his early forties. He stood erect, looking proud despite the shabby, cut-up clothing he was wearing. His face was calm, even a small smile adorned it as he looked interestedly around the crowd, needing no enforcement to make his way to the chair. He climbed the three small steps onto the platform and seated himself as if taking his place in an airliner seat. He made no move as he was belted into the chair and the attachments fastened to his legs and wrists.

Sensing the absence of fear, the crowd began to shriek abuse and curses at the man in the chair, but they fell silent as the loudspeaker roared out.

"Kenneth Jensen, you are about to meet your accursed Father, the Devil himself and be cast down into the pits of Hell! Do you have anything to say before you die?"

Silence fell as the crowd listened to what the man might say. His voice, when it came from the speakers was astonishing. It was deep, calm, almost amused.

"Sure, I've got something to say," said Jensen. "But I don't think you're going to like it."

The silence rang round the ground, a freezing clangour of shock.

"I've got friends, family and loved ones waiting for me," said Jensen, showing no hint of fear or tension. "I'll be with them again in a few moments. But you lot, all you sick, infant souls, I feel sorry for you. When you go, each and every one of you will experience Hell worse than any Catholic story book could prepare you for. And you, Horning, you are damned. Your Hell will be the worst of them all. You will suffer tortures beyond your sickest imagination for ten thousand years. I do hope you will all think of that tonight. Anyway, I hate to spoil your fun, but I think I'll be on my way."

For a few seconds, the fear in the stands was palpable, the temperature seemed to have fallen from a mild summer night almost to a winter snap. And on the stand by the chair, confusion broke out. The two men who had strapped the attachments to Jensen had leaned over to place the metal headset on him, but now they stood upright again, looking baffled and angry. Jensen had slumped in the chair and the doctor jumped up and placed the stethoscope on his chest. I couldn't hear the words above the confused babble of the crowd, but the doctor was shaking his head in confusion. The straps were undone, and the two men appeared with the stretcher. Jensen was already dead, I realized, and felt a wave of wonderment. How had he done that?

The crowd was booing and shouting in annoyance. Several empty beer cans were thrown in the direction of the chair. Horning looked round behind him as if to assure himself that he had protection.

"What the hell happened there?" he snapped. "How could that man die just like that?"

"It was almost as if he chose to," Cardinal Lavalier murmured, looking intensely interested at the body as it was carried away. "I have heard that some of these heretics claim to be able to do that."

Horning settled back in his seat, but an expression

of dissatisfaction remained, a sulky, petulant look. Somebody rapidly rearranged a schedule, because almost immediately, the small procession appeared again, this time with a young black male being hauled to the chair, and the crowd settled down, appeased.

"This is Albert!" thundered the voice. "A Resident Alien, owned and well treated by good, Christian Americans. He chose to treat their kindness with contempt and hatred, and ran from their charity."

Screams of hatred and abuse rang through the thousands in the stadium. They were taking out some of their frustration for the loss of the previous spectacle, and the clamour was terrifying with the undercurrent of hatred that ran through it.

"We do not invite aliens to speak at these affairs," bellowed the speakers. "So, Albert, you chose to leave your master and mistress. Go then, and bother us no more!"

To shrieks of laughter, waving of flags and much applause, the killing jolts struck the young man in the chair as the false sparks and crackles added colour to a dreadful spectacle.

I couldn't take any more of it. Without a word, I rose and walked to the back of the box, opened the door and stood outside by the elevators. Shivering every time I heard the roar of the crowd, I offered up my prayers for the souls of the departed condemned.

# Chapter 9. History

"Sick?" Philippe Leger felt he could hardly breathe. While the idea was almost incomprehensible, somehow a faint ghost in his mind told him that what he was hearing was not new to him. He had no idea what this could mean.

Maragos took a sip of her wine and nodded. "The process is quite incomprehensible to us," she said. "We have no idea what caused it."

"What happened?" asked Philippe, fascinated by the idea of one such as her, infinitely powerful, infinitely ancient, as being sick like some schoolboy.

She settled back in her chair as if ready for a long story. Philippe took a quick glance at the gold clock on the mantelpiece. It said four in the morning, but he felt no fatigue or sleepiness. How could there ever have been a more powerful, astounding night in anyone's life before this? He had no wish to miss any of it or cut off the flow of amazing data she was providing so freely.

"When we first split off into the original million entities, we still had many characteristics and memories of The One," she said, speaking almost to herself, so soft was her voice. "If Time can mean anything so soon after the Big Bang that The One had used to start a new cycle, we spent many millions of years in a spiritual state, not incarnating, because there was nowhere to incarnate. There was only the total turmoil of dust flying off in all directions, before the suns and the planets began to form into galaxies. We all watched that and meditated on how we would choose our initial planets, how we would form them, how we would break ourselves up into smaller entities and how we would try and select paths that might lead to a solution. We could all still feel the pain and loneliness of the original crisis that The One had experienced, and we were all still close enough mentally to communicate."

Philippe tried and failed to imagine the existence that these incredible entities had experienced for millions of years, God-like in their powers. It was too much for a human mind.

"Eventually, we watched the planets and suns form, and the galaxies concentrate, and we picked our spots," Maragos continued. "We spent more millions of years influencing how our selected birth planets would develop, and in that time, we got so busy that communications faded a little."

"You could influence how the planets would form?" asked Philippe, enthralled by the power she was describing.

"Oh yes!" she said with a smile. "You did the same with your own planets. You've had two of them, by the way. Earth is your second!"

"What?"

"You still have the race memories inside you," she said. "And they've given rise to many of your biblical legends. The whole story of Genesis, the Creation, that is Humanity's recollection of terraforming the Earth to suit itself. You did that twice. You even have two versions of the Creation in your Bible to reflect that fact, but nobody has ever realized the implications of that. It's caused no end of problems for your theologians, has that little historical burp in the Scriptures."

"Twice? Maragos, what did we do?" Philippe thought he had been astounded before, but now he was experiencing even more tremors at what she was telling him. She smiled, understanding his mental turmoil. "Humanity first settled on a planet quite close to here, orbiting a star you call Epsilon Indi, about seven light-years away from Earth. You formed it into a planet much like Earth is now, and began the splitting off into lower entities and finally human souls. But after only a few cycles, major climatic changes began to develop. Your terraforming work had been done less than perfectly, and the whole planet was cooling, becoming a water world and on its way to becoming an ice ball. That gave rise to another race memory, transformed into a legend."

"Noah?" he asked, his voice trembling.

"Noah, indeed," she replied. "Luckily for you, you had delayed your start of the cycle by many hundreds of thousands of years, and other races had developed technologies of space travel already. One of them built the ship that was sent to save you. They sent a vessel, and picked up the humans and the animal life that Humanity had developed, rather than let them all die. The captain of that vessel had a name that might roughly sound like "Nor-Ah," by the way. They felt that so massive a death experience would have made your sickness worse, so they assisted you select Earth, and gently nudged the terraforming for you. And you settled here, instead."

"Good grief!" he said, aware of how silly his comment sounded relative to the data she was passing to him. "But you said we had already left the rest of you by that time. What had happened to make us run?"

She shrugged. "Still unknown. One day, so to speak, we were all busy forming our planets and preparing for the cycle of incarnations, and we looked up and you had gone. We had been aware that for some time, communication with Humanity had been limited, but we assumed that was merely a path you had chosen. We followed you out here and we managed a few discussions, but they were difficult."

"What did we say?" Again, Philippe had the weirdest feeling that somehow he already had some knowledge of this story.

"You do!" she said with that cheeky teenager's grin again. "And you'll understand in a moment. But the only thing we got from you was vague, panicky stories of how you had messed up, done something wrong, fled from the punishment you were certain you would get. Waves of fear, grief and dismay. Very frightening to hear. And of course, that's the other race legend you've generated."

"The exodus from the Garden of Eden! Of course!"

"Quite right!" she said, almost like a teacher approving of a bright pupil. "It seemed you began to suffer from a morbid paranoia. You ran from the rest of us, delayed your incarnation cycle by several hundreds of thousands of years, and worked it out alone. And what a dreadful mess you've been making of it!"

"What sort of mess?" he asked. "You've said we were sick, but you haven't told me how. Just what is wrong with the human race?"

"The nearest thing I can think of is the condition I mentioned before, an extreme morbid paranoia. It affects the majority of human souls, though some have remained clear. The primary symptom is fear of anything that is different from oneself. It results from a deep hatred of oneself, just as the same sickness in an individual does. The second symptom is an inability to leave anything alone if it's good. Humans have a compulsion to destroy anything joyful, beautiful, or peaceful. Humanity has gone to war at the slightest opportunity, and the most bloodthirsty, vicious characteristics appear immediately. And for most of you, that condition is seen as right and proper. At national levels, those mind-sets are seen as true patriotism."

She looked at Philippe, and her expression was one of sadness. "We only have to look at the Holocaust in Europe, the constant warfare in South-East Asia and the sort of madness released in the Balkans and the Middle East every few years to see examples. It reflects the internal self-hatred of the Human Soul. Humans war against each other the way a madman inflicts mutilation on himself. And the greatest hatred and violence is always directed against those souls who are healthy. The most obvious common factor of tyrants and bullies of all religious persuasions and political colours, is absolute detestation of minds that think clearly, objectively and with long term vision."

The room was silent again for a few seconds.

"The final symptom is an inability to grow up, either as individual, or as a species," she continued. "Just like small, spoilt children, you grab for everything now, destroy anything that can be damaged, and cannot see into a future."

"Not all of us, surely?" Philippe said defensively. She shook her head.

"No, not all of you, of course. But the greatest majority of you think this way. It's normal among infant and baby souls. The problem is, few of you have grown beyond those early stages, and mankind is stuck in the infantile frame of mind after enough lifetimes to have grown to at least Mature Soul stage."

"Are we so different from other species, then?"

"Quite different. Several of us took paths that had histories of violence in the early stages, and that was a useful stage of growing as we experienced all the dreadful features and the waste of psychic time caused by intensive killing. The object of the exercise, after all, was to experience everything possible in order eventually to come up with possible answers to The One's problem."

"I remember the readings I found," said Philippe with a surge of excitement. "One of them mentioned 'Houses of God' where violence had been outgrown, and others where it had never even been present. Jesus described them, He said everything was choice, and I wondered then if He had perhaps been to these other planets."

"More than been to," she said firmly. "He was of them, of several, in fact."

A wave of excitement flooded over Leger. Here was a pedestal of the old Christian Church, faith in legends with little to prove them but writings made long after the death of the historical figure of Jesus Christ. This attractive young woman sitting before him knew exactly what the truth was, and he would hear it.

"Tell me!" he said, urgently and simply.

She smiled at his eagerness. "Three times in the history of Humanity, your species has reached such a level of pain and despair, that you emitted a violent psychic scream for help. We heard that shout, but when we tried to talk on the spiritual level to the total entity of Humanity, the Human Infinite Soul, we got only the ravings of a madman. So we sent help in the form of an advanced soul who would incarnate as one of you, and gradually gain awareness of its true nature."

"An advanced soul like you? An Infinite?"

"I am the first Infinite," she said with a small shake of her head, and she took another sip of wine. "And I only formed in the last few years of your time. What we did was select several Ascendant Souls of different species and merge them into a single entity."

"Merged?" he asked, puzzled.

"Yes," she said. "There is much wisdom and experience in Ascendant Souls already. And we asked eight such Souls from different species to merge as one, and incarnate on Earth. They brought massive power, wisdom and love with them, and we hoped that they would provide enough guidance for Humanity to work its way out of the crises."

"And Jesus was one of these?"

"And Buddha and Mohammed," she added. "Those were the only ones, though others have claimed to be such teachers."

"Were any human entities part of these souls?"

"Only one, in all three cases," she replied. "Ascendant Souls are very scarce among Humanity," she added with a tiny smile.

"And did they achieve anything?" he asked. "All my

training has been to ignore Mohammed and Buddha as merely prophets, and to accept Jesus as the one true Son of God who brought Christianity and Salvation to us. Now I wonder what the truth is."

"And as you know, the other main beliefs place all three as great prophets on an equal level, which is the truth. Each achieved something in his own way. Buddha was perhaps the most successful, he introduced a way of thought that most resembles the truth of Oneness. Mohammed and Jesus each introduced patterns of behaviour and thought that were highly constructive and should have provided a way to major health and improvement. But that Human paranoia corrupted large portions of their adherents, so you got religious fundamentalism, the Inquisition, the Holy Wars, American Televangelists, and the insanity in the Middle East, all the consequences of intense sickness throughout the Human Soul."

"I have known many people with powerful religious beliefs," said Philippe thoughtfully. "They seemed to me to be people of great love for their fellows, much kindness and warmth. But they believed absolutely in the literal word of the Bible. Were they sick souls too?"

Maragos shook her head with a smile. "No, of course not. Being true to the words of Jesus as they knew them reflects a genuine sincerity of beliefs. After all, Jesus did speak to Mankind with great power and wisdom, even if many of his words were spoilt in translations, and many others were never revealed at all. To hold such beliefs is no more inappropriate than for a child to believe in Santa Claus, if I can use your own analogy. They were probably Young Souls, because Old Souls would have begun to question the literal biblical interpretations. But in their beliefs, such people tend to form strong families, raise their children well, and do much good in the world. Would that more of the self-proclaimed religious practitioners were as genuine. Belief in the Biblical teachings itself is not a sign of sickness. Rigid inability to consider alternatives, forced acceptance of these beliefs on others, violent reaction to perceived "heresy," those are the signs of sickness."

She stood up and went to the table where the whiskey bottle that had been a wine jug and before that a water jug stood. He watched as the jug reappeared and she poured from it into her glass. It was wine again. She picked up his glass, letting a delicate whiff of perfume float by his nose as she did, refilled his glass and handed it back to him. His fingers touched hers in the process, and he felt the sensation of infinite power again. She took her seat again, tucked her feet under her thighs, and smiled at him.

"And now you have the developments in the USA, exacerbated by my presence. The infant souls are in the majority, they are experiencing overwhelming fear at my arrival and they are denying it with every atom of strength they have. They have found a leader who will tell them what they want to hear, and they are following him as fast as they can, rather than accept that something must change. All in all," she said, "our assistance failed. The sickness was far worse than we had believed."

"But you can help us heal?" asked Philippe. A sense of fear ran through him at something she had said, though he was uncertain what it was. "Can we change the forces in America?"

"We must, Philippe," she replied, and her face was deadly serious. "That is the key. The President there is far more evil than anything we have encountered before, more so than Hitler, Amin, Stalin or any past tyrant."

"How so, Maragos?" asked Philippe. The fear within him expanded like a flame under gasoline.

"This Horning is drawing on the power of the souls around him," replied Maragos. "It is a form of Oneness, growing in power with the numbers in his sphere. Already, he has the strength of an enhanced soul, though he doesn't realize it. If he knew what his powers truly were, the problem would be much worse."

"Will he learn of these powers?"

"We must work to prevent it," replied Maragos. "My predecessors faced the same problem, and they were unable to destroy the black side of Oneness."

"And now you have come, instead?" It was more of a statement than a question.

She nodded. "I am the first to reach Infinite stage, and that only recently, as I said. But it means that Oneness is not too far away. More of my kind will emerge in the coming years. Without true self-awareness, The One is nonetheless sensing the need to return and check out the problem and the answers we might have found. If that final Ascension to Oneness cannot take place, and it cannot without Humanity at the Infinite stage also, we are doomed to wait out all of time in limbo."

"And how long would it take for The One to be ready for the final merging, if Humanity was ready?" Philippe had an idea of perhaps a few years and wondered how the problem could be solved.

"Probably no more than twenty or thirty thousand years," she said seriously. Philippe almost laughed, but then realized what a tiny sliver of time was that to a being who had spent millions of years watching the galaxies form before starting a cycle of billions of lives. To Maragos, the problem was one of extreme urgency and little time.

"The new Ascendant Souls will need several thousand years to absorb all the individual memories of the souls that comprise them," she continued. "And when they merge to form an Infinite Soul such as I, another few thousand years of meditation will be needed before we can think about combining the original million of us again."

Another idea came to Philippe, just one of the flood of so many thoughts and questions he had for her, but this one rose sharply out of the turmoil and nudged him. It would satisfy an age-old question in Mankind's history. "When you said you checked up on us during our history, does that mean you actually visited us? Are those visits the cause of all the unidentified flying objects we kept hearing about that so many people claimed to have seen?"

She shook her head. "No, we have never visited you physically, except when we transferred you from Epsilon Indi to here, and this trip now. Apart from the incarnations of the Prophets, that is. But we were the cause of the UFO sightings, though on a mental level. There were no actual sightings of ships, once humanity had been resettled on Earth."

"I don't understand," he said.

"It's rather like my arrival here," she said with a comforting smile. "As I have been approaching Earth, the influence of my presence has been causing an awakening of the spiritual powers in many of you. That's why so many humans have become able to remember past lives, or establish mental communication with others, or continue contact from the Astral Plane back on the physical level. These are simply abilities that advanced souls develop, and I speeded up the process merely by coming closer. In the same way, as we sent mental probes and messages here to check on Humanity, the presence of those psychic forces opened up many human minds, and they saw images of other races on other planets, so clearly that the experience had the impact of reality on them."

"So no flying saucers?" he said with a small smile.

"Not here on Earth, no," she agreed. "As I said, there have only been two visits, the rescue ship and this one. But the images were accurate enough. Your Prophet Ezekiel saw one, and it was well documented in your Apocrypha as much as a non-technical man could describe a highly advanced technological society. He saw visions of daily activity on a planet called X'Katcxo - that means Earth, too, by the way!" she added with a grin, "which is on a spiral arm at the southern end of this galaxy. The entity there, which calls its souls X'Kasxi, a name roughly meaning the Kindred, had sent a mental probe as a periodic check on you. Ezekiel felt the presence, and saw a vision of normal activity in an X'Kasxian city. They are a space-travelling species, though not as advanced as the crew that brought me here."

"So what of the many strange things that exist on Earth?" he asked. "What is the truth behind the markings on the Plains of Nacza, or the impossible construction of the Pyramids? How did these things happen?"

Maragos smiled. "Only one ship visited here when it brought you from Epsilon Indi," she said. "It visited twice, and the first time, it stayed a long time. Several thousand years in fact, while it worked on the express terraforming of the planet. Those markings are the remnants of the energy flows that developed. Once that task was complete, it went to collect the human and animal life forms on Epsilon's planet."

"And the Pyramids?"

"Mankind did not settle immediately in the current body shape you have now," she replied. "Neanderthals survived for many thousands of years before Cro-Magnon was developed. In the meanwhile, some unusual forms were tried, one of them a gigantic and powerful species. You have found no traces as yet of these early humans. Remember how one line in the Bible refers to Giants living on the Earth? There surely were, and some of these remained through almost to modern times, certainly through to the period of the Egyptian Empire. Some of them assisted in those massive tasks, and in others, such as the Druids' Circles in Europe. No remains have yet been found of them, but imagine the excitement when they are!"

Leger sat back, trying to absorb everything she had told him this amazing night. It seemed years since she had first knocked on his door and almost thrown him back into pre-realization modes of religious thought, convincing him she was perhaps God incarnate. He thought of his friend, Raoul Carmagio, still asleep upstairs, and what he would be able to tell him when he awoke.

"No need," she said, with that dizzying ability to read his mind. "Everything that has passed between us tonight, Raoul has witnessed on the Astral Plane while he has slept. He will join us later today, fully aware of all we have discussed. So it is time to tell you a little about yourself, Philippe."

"About me? What is so special about me, after all? Why did you specifically visit me?" Philippe had nagged at this thought all evening, just as he had worried about why he had been one of the first to sense the coming of the Infinite. But still, under the worry, was that tiny, elusive thought that he knew something in his mind that his conscious self had not yet understood.

"Philippe, you are an exceptional soul," she said with a warm smile. *Were she anything other a millionth part of God,* he thought, *this would be the woman who would let me make the final departure from my life as a Catholic priest. I could fall so in love with her.* He snapped himself back to an embarrassed realization that he had still not learned to shield his thoughts from her. She was smiling softly, and the face had an ethereal beauty that almost made him weep.

"No matter, Philippe," she said. "There is a woman who will join you soon. You have shared past lives with her, but you have never let yourself meet with her on the Astral Plane in this incarnation because it would have interfered with your commitment to becoming Pope. But you are free of that now, and you can find her, if you wish."

"How?" he asked, realizing his voice was trembling with the need and the loneliness that he only now fully recognized in himself.

"Next time you sleep," she said. "You will meet, and you will remember."

He could only stare at her. "You were telling me about my exceptional nature," he said dryly.

She laughed. "Oh, that ecclesiastical discipline!" she chuckled. "But yes Philippe, let us by all means return to you."

He felt his heartbeat accelerate a little and he concentrated, just like anyone about to hear astounding truths about themselves.

"You are in your last incarnation, Philippe," she said. "You are an Old Soul, in the very last learning moments of the final, seventh stage. You are ready now to leave the physical plane and wait for the others of your entity to catch up. You are the first of that entity to reach this stage."

"Are there others that I know and have met?"

"Many," she replied. "And they, with others, have shared many of your four hundred and five previous lives. You will be able to recognise them now."

"Four hundred and five! I have lived four hundred and five times before?" Even though he had accepted the concept academically, Leger still felt an enormous shock at the idea. Four hundred and five times he had been born, lived a lifetime and died? What an incredible idea!

"Somehow, with you, and a few other souls in human history," she continued, "more of the higher powers have been concentrated. It has shown in various ways. Michelangelo, Leonardo da Vinci and Amadeus Mozart are examples of such powers showing in exceptional creativity. It has commonly been displayed in artistic skills, as with Beethoven, Johan Sebastian Bach, whose whole family was touched with it, Rembrandt, Picasso, there have been many souls with the gift of the highly creative elements of Oneness present in them."

"All men?" he said, curiously.

"Just choice!" she said with her wonderful grin. "They incarnated as men when the full pressure to create was strongest, because they knew that as women, they would have less freedom to show their wares, so to speak! All of them have been women many times in other lives. In fact, one of Beethoven's earlier incarnations in the twelfth century was as Hildegard von Bingen, one of the most extraordinary philosophers, political forces and composers of her day. That soul, incidentally, is one of your own entity. One day, you will be able to relive the experiences of those remarkable people."

He laughed with a wonderful exhilaration to think that somehow he was among such a breed of geniuses. "And what have I done?" he asked light-heartedly. "Have I written symphonies, sculpted great works, or painted famous pictures? Was I actually one of those people in a previous life?"

She shook her head. "In you, Philippe, it took a different form," she said. "You recognized very early, the sickness that was rampaging through humanity, and you placed yourself at the heart of the events that might have presented a cure. You have set it as your personal task to help the recovery. Some time ago, well before the end of your previous life, you sensed that I was coming. That is why you determined that in this incarnation, you would become Pope and be in a position to involve yourself."

"What have I done?" he whispered, the lightness gone, the realization of the enormity of what she was telling him washing everything else away.

"You have already met some of your own past work," she said. "You asked why the scribe had not questioned Jesus further when he wrote the words you were reading when I arrived. Look deep inside your soul now, Philippe, and you can answer your own question."

"I was that man?" he croaked.

"Have a look," she said, and the room faded.

*The night had been filled with screams and blood. Benjamin ben Isaac had spent it huddled deep in his cellar, blocks of stone kept for just such a purpose piled against the door to prevent the Centurions from pressing too hard against it. Through the small grilles in the outer wall he had heard the killing orgy the Romans had started soon after midnight. It had been the night of some Roman feast in honour of one of their plethora of gods, and a junior officer had unfortunately chosen that evening to fall down the steep ramps and injure his legs outside the market place where he had been buying wine with his mistress. After a night of hard drinking, the soldiers had eventually concluded it had all been a Jewish plot, the officer had been deliberately tripped, and they had gone out on the rampage.*

*God knows how many of us they have killed, shuddered Benjamin. He had heard the crashes as the Romans had destroyed doors and buildings, hauled out the occupants and slaughtered them in the street. The screaming of the victims and the laughter of the Romans had mingled with the ripe smell of blood and made him vomit several times in his cellar.*

*By four, the sounds had faded but for the weeping and sobbing that blanketed the street outside, and even that had died down by dawn. Nervously, he pulled the stone blocks from his door, aware that they had again kept him alive, and he ventured out into the first tentative beams of sunlight.*

*At his doorway, the sight overwhelmed him, and he fell to his knees in anguish. Bodies littered the street, few of them in one piece. Random arms and heads lay in spots as if deserted by their owners, and dogs worried several bloody limbs that had lost enough flesh already to be no longer identifiable as human remains. On one corner, the mangled body of a woman lay over the corpses of two small children. Their guts had been ripped out and lay straddled over their limbs like obscene knitting. One tiny corpse was without its head, which rested in the gutter with the scream of horror still on its small face.*

# The Nightmares of God

*A few people were already out collecting their dead and the muffled sobs and wailing were a pitiful backcloth to the dreadful scene.*

*"I must describe it for others to read, one day," muttered Benjamin, and returned to his small house, found parchment and pen and began to write the details down while he could still keep the images fresh and his mind did not revolt. Many times he had done this, written the story of another Roman onslaught on his people, though he was unclear what was driving him to do so. The risks were great. If the Romans found his parchments, he would surely be crucified with the other troublemakers and dissidents.*

*As the sun climbed higher in the morning sky and the heat made the stench of blood even worse, a small disturbance began to the western side of the village, on the road from Bethlehem. Benjamin raised his head and looked to see what was happening. A small group of people were arriving, Israelites it seemed from their poor clothing and the two or three asses which carried a man, two women and a few small children while a few more men, women and children walked alongside. The man on the leading ass seemed to be their leader judging by the way the others looked to him for guidance as to where they would stop.*

*The market place was the chosen point, and the group came to a halt at the base of the steep ramp down which the Roman officer had fallen and precipitated the night's slaughter. The group's leader walked up the ramp and sat down on the stone of the platform while the others took places at lower levels, and then sat as if waiting for others to join them. Curious, Benjamin folded his parchments, put his pen in the folds of his robe and moved closer. Most of the bodies had been taken from the immediate area by now, though the smell of blood was still strong in the dust and the rising heat.*

*Benjamin's curiosity was shared by others of his village. Several had moved closer to hear what the*

185

man on the ramp would say, for clearly he had taken the position of a teacher or storyteller. When about twenty people were gathered at his feet , he spoke.

"What has happened here?" he asked.

Attracted by the beautiful depth of the man's voice and the obvious expression of pain and grief he was suffering for them, Benjamin moved in closer and studied the man carefully. He was nothing extraordinary in appearance, Benjamin thought, much like any Jew travelling the roads of Palestine. Smaller than the Roman soldiers as they all were, dark skinned, an untidy beard and long black hair matted with sweat and dust from the roads. A nose with a proud curve to it. Just another Jew with a story to tell.

The man looked up and caught the gaze of his observer. He smiled gently, and Benjamin felt a jolt of astounding proportions hit him, leaving his heart pounding and his blood racing through his body like a spring flood when the River Jordan burst its banks and inundated the areas around it with the life-giving waters. The man's eyes were deep wells of such power that Benjamin almost fainted. What manner of man has eyes like that? he wept to himself. This is not just a storyteller or a teacher. This is a Rabbi, a man of God, a healer. The man's gaze moved on, and Benjamin breathed again, gasping in the hot, blood-tainted air.

"What has happened here?" the man asked again, moving his head to look at the gathering group below him.

"The Roman soldiers," answered a man squatting in the dust. Benjamin knew him as Michael, son of Saul. He kept a small herd of goats and somehow scratched a living from the soil. "They took in the devil last night and came looking for blood."

"How many dead?" asked one of the teacher's company, a middle-aged woman dressed in rather more costly robes than was usual in travellers such as these.

*"At least fifty. My wife and children among them,"
the man replied, looking hard into the dust, but
Benjamin could see the grief marked deep into the
lines of his face.*

*"Your loss is great," said the Teacher softly. "But
the killers will pay more than the price at a later time."*

*"Why, will you go to the Roman encampment and
demand justice?" said the man in the dust, looking up
and revealing the tears flooding down his face. "You
will be lucky to escape with a flogging, and would
probably end up on a cross like my uncle and my
father."*

*Benjamin shifted and felt the rolls of parchment in
his robe. Carefully, he extracted them and found his
pen. Something powerful would happen here this day,
he knew.*

*"Justice does not have to be applied immediately
for it still to be justice," replied the man at the top of
the ramp. "God's law can be applied many lifetimes
after the crime."*

*"Huh!" sneered Michael, son of Saul of Miron who
had been crucified with his brother for failing to move
away fast enough from a Roman Legionary. "What is
justice if it is only applied after the criminal's death?
And who are you that tells us such useless thoughts?"*

*"Death is not the end of living," replied the
Teacher. "It is merely the end of a life. And my name is
Jesus, son of Joseph of Galilee."*

*Startled, Benjamin stared at Jesus. He had heard
of this man who walked around Palestine and talked
of a Kingdom different from the world around them,
and who denied the Roman Gods. So too, had the
others in the group, because the slight hostility that
Benjamin had sensed rapidly faded, and the group
gathered closer for comfort, like frightened children.*

*"Why is all this slaughter happening?" a
distraught man asked. Benjamin had seen him earlier,
kneeling in grief over the body of a younger woman,
perhaps his daughter. Benjamin hurriedly scratched*

*the question on his parchment and waited for the answer.*

*"Why do children torture insects?" answered Jesus. "We kill in the process of learning and growing. We understand not that we inflict pain and death on others, only that we must satisfy our own needs."*

*"Are we all children, then?" asked a woman in the group.*

*"You are all as babies and infants," replied Jesus. "And like children, you shall grow and you shall learn. And with age shall come wisdom, and with wisdom shall come Oneness."*

*What does he mean by Oneness? Benjamin asked himself, but rushed to catch the next question about to be asked.*

*"But how can we learn if we are all killed?" pleaded the same man who had asked the original question.*

*"Dying is learning, too," replied Jesus. "So is killing. Neither is an ending. He who kills also dies, and he who dies also kills. You shall do both many times before wisdom grows."*

*"Must it ever be?" asked another man.*

*Jesus shook his head. "At this time and place in your world, you have made it so, for reasons of your own," he replied. "It will not always be, and in other Houses of God, it has been once, but is now no longer. In some Houses, it has never been. All is choice."*

*That is terribly important, I know, thought Benjamin, racing to catch the words. But I don't have time to think about it. Maybe I can ask about it later. What could he mean? What are other Houses of God?*

*"So what must we do?" asked another voice. Benjamin was writing fast and was unable to determine the identity of the speaker.*

*"You must choose your own way," replied Jesus. "That is the task of Man, to find the way to Oneness with God, to answer the question that The One has asked of you."*

*Somebody else was about to ask something further. If he had not, thought Benjamin, I would have leapt in and asked what Jesus had meant by Oneness, and The One, and what possible question could God have to ask Man that God did not already know already? But the question was lost in the warning shout from behind a row of houses.*

*"The Romans! They come again!"*

*Instantly, the listeners rose to their feet and began to race back to their homes. Stifling panic, Benjamin instead watched Jesus and his party. They seemed totally unafraid, and continued to sit where they were, watching the approaching band of soldiers.*

*There were some thirty of them, Benjamin estimated, all armed with short swords and shields. They were fully equipped for battle, dressed in the heavy leather tunics with breastplates and helmets. The man at the head of the small column was thickset, a powerful, coarse face staring with hostility at the silent group of watchers at the ramp. Benjamin had no way of guessing his rank, having seen few soldiers of officer level.*

*"You people!" yelled the soldier as they approached. "Get to your homes! There is a curfew on this place."*

*Nobody moved, and nobody spoke. Benjamin took a quick look at Jesus who seemed calm, watching the soldiers with interest. The armed group stopped about ten yards away, and the leader shouted again, clearly angry at the lack of movement in the watchers. "Didn't you hear me?" he roared. "A curfew has been established. Get into your homes!"*

*"But we cannot," replied Jesus mildly. "Our homes are not of this village."*

*"Then you may never see your homes again," the commander snarled, and stamped forward, loosening his sword in its sheath. He walked to within a few feet of the base of the ramp then stopped, staring at Jesus, who looked calmly back.*

*Silence held that small scene for several moments, the soldier staring, while his rage slowly dissipated and his jaw went slack. "I know you, don't I?" the Roman said, his voice hoarse.*

*"It is possible," replied Jesus. "We will deal with each other again, that is certain."*

*The soldier looked confused, still staring at the face of the man on the ramp. He turned sharply and returned to his men, a baffled glare on his face visible to Benjamin who started to breathe again, certain for a moment that he had been about to die. The solders turned about and began to walk back the way they had come, a stiffness in their carriage indicating their resentment. The metallic clatter of their armour and the heavy tramping of their feet disturbed the air for some minutes before the troop and the dust they raised disappeared from view.*

*"You were not afraid, Benjamin son of Isaac?" came the gentle voice of Jesus. Benjamin stared up at him, astounded that his name was known, and again lost himself in the amazing depth and power of Jesus' eyes.*

*"Yes Rabbi, I was," replied Benjamin, sensing the exhilaration of fear faced and overcome. "But it was worth it to see the Romans walk away."*

*"They will all leave here when their time is done," said Jesus, standing and gathering his robe about him, beginning to walk down the ramp towards Benjamin. As he reached the ground, he smiled at Benjamin who felt a terrible urge to fall to his knees. Standing near to the wanderer, Benjamin was of a similar height and build and he smelt the body odour of dirt and sweat that was universal on anyone who walked in the heat and dust of Palestine. The man Jesus was any man who lived, until one looked into his eyes.*

*"And when will that day come, Rabbi?" asked Benjamin, fighting to control the trembling in his body and his voice.*

*"When you choose it," replied Jesus.*

*"I, teacher? How can I choose when the rulers of the world will depart my land?"*

*"You and all Mankind could choose today, if you wished, and if you knew how powerful your collective will could be," said Jesus. "But it is not yet the time of choice for you."*

*"I do not understand, Lord," said Benjamin, certain now that this was a Holy Man indeed. "You talked of choice before. What did you mean?"*

*"All is choice," replied Jesus with a small sigh. "In this House of God, the choices are being made so badly that I fear for us."*

*"You speak with words that fly above my head like flocks of birds, Lord," said Benjamin, a sense of frustration in him. Speaking with Jesus was in some ways like the stories he had read of the Greek Oracles who spoke in riddles that cloaked the absolute truth that they revealed. Unless one had the key to these words, the truth was not evident.*

*"Mankind is not yet ready to catch those birds, Benjamin son of Isaac," came the reply. "While Men of other Houses of God have caught them and flown above them already."*

*"Other Houses, Rabbi?"*

*"Indeed, other Houses, Benjamin." Jesus waved his arm to encompass the village, the country around it and all the known lands of the world. "Think you that this world, these shores, these skies are the only House that God has built?"*

*"You mean those far lands of the west and south, Rabbi? Few have ventured there and lived."*

*"Further than that, Child of Man," replied Jesus with a friendly smile. "So far are they that other suns shine down on the land, men stand in the light of those suns but have not the likeness of Man such as you would understand."*

*"You have been to these lands, Teacher?" asked Benjamin. He knew that he should have felt ridicule at*

these extraordinary words that Jesus was speaking, but something in the depth and power of the Rabbi's face made him instead feel awe and wonder, a sense that he was privileged, while unknown, unimaginable doors were being opened to him.

"I am of these lands, and others. I have been to them and walked upon them," replied Jesus. "And the Men of those Houses have learned the lessons and discovered the choices that Men of this House have yet to learn and discover."

Benjamin was shaking inside with a vast sense of grief, though he did not understand why.

"You grieve, Benjamin son of Isaac?" said the gentle tones of the Rabbi. "And well should you, for the path of Man will be a difficult one before you can come back into the light."

"How long before we can return to the light?" asked Benjamin, the pain and dismay powerful in his chest.

"I cannot say," replied Jesus. "But I know that you will be there to see it, and you will be with those that follow me to show you the way."

"So it will happen in my lifetime, Lord? Then we can surely celebrate if our redemption is to come so soon." Benjamin felt an easing of his fear.

"In your lifetime, yes, but not in the lifetime of Benjamin son of Isaac."

"I don't understand, Lord."

"We live many times, Child of Man. You will understand one day."

Confused, Benjamin turned away and saw the middle-aged woman approaching them.

"Rabbi, we must leave," she said, addressing Jesus, but with a small smile to Benjamin.

"Yes, Judith, it is time," Jesus replied, and touched Benjamin lightly on the shoulder. The contact sent reverberations of awesome power through Benjamin's body and he knew he had been touched by something close to the hand of God.

*"We will meet again," said Jesus, and turned to leave. Unable to speak, Benjamin watched the two walk away, knowing he had looked into the face of Infinity. He walked slowly back to his house, unaware now of the smell of blood and death in the streets. Sealing himself in his cellar, he took out the parchments and wrote down as much as he could remember from his conversation with Jesus of Nazareth.*

Philippe Leger returned to the room, weeping bitterly, curled up tight in his chair like a small child. "I met him! I met with Jesus and talked with him! I wrote down his words."

The grief he had experienced in that vivid, painful recollection of a life lived two thousand years before overwhelmed him, and the words came out through explosions of hurt and sorrow that strangled his voice. The memory of the extraordinary eyes, the same eyes as Maragos that had sent him crashing to the floor in worship.... he looked up through his tears and saw her watching him, peacefully and with love in her face.

"It is in you now, Philippe to remember all your meetings with Jesus," she said. "Any Old Soul at your level should be able to remember all its past lives at will. My arrival has begun to heal that small defect in Humanity, though many followers of Buddha had never suffered that hurt. In time, you will recover the memories of all your lives."

"I met him again?" he asked, wiping his eyes.

She nodded. "As I said, you were present with all three of the enhanced Ascendant Souls that incarnated on Earth. It has been your task to be present at the moments and events that might heal Humanity. The Soul that was Jesus recognized you, and that is why He said that you would be present at Humanity's redemption."

"So was I with Mohammed and Buddha too?"

"You will soon see for yourself now," she replied.

Philippe was silent, deep in wonderment at the memories of that past life, at the revelations of his own task which now he understood had always been in his deep subconscious mind, and at the possibilities of reliving his contacts with the three Ascendant Souls who had tried to offer healing and guidance to sick Humanity.

"There is still the biggest question of all to be asked," he said, waking from his deep meditation. "Can we be healed so that Humanity can again become an Infinite Soul like you?"

"It will be complex, difficult, and require the efforts of all of us," she replied. "But yes, you can. In time."

"What will we have to do?" he asked, dizzy at the idea of healing the billions of souls that would make up the entire Human species.

"Many species have not yet reached Ascendant stage," she said. "The souls that constitute the complete Ascended Souls of those species are still in the final cycles of incarnation, some even in the Mature Soul stage, yet to reach Old Soul level. So they have perhaps twenty to fifty lives still to live incarnate before their Ascendant Soul can form and begin the learning that will lead to the Infinite stage."

"I don't think I can see the connection..." began Philippe, then stopped as he saw the incredible, the astounding possibilities of what she was saying.

"Yes, Philippe," she murmured with a smile. "If large enough numbers of human souls can reincarnate into other species for a few lifetimes, the sickness will dissipate, and healthy souls can return to their entities. They will be like antibiotics against an infection and will heal those that remained behind."

"This can be done?" he asked, breathless at the enormity of the concept. "And the other species have agreed?"

She nodded. "We have talked together, these entities and I, and they have agreed."

Excitement hit him. "Can I be one that goes?"

She smiled. "Of course you would want that, and of course you will do it. Any who volunteer may do it. The problem will be to persuade enough numbers of the very sick Infant Souls that their path to redemption lies this way."

"How will you do this?"

"You and I and some other enlightened souls will meet with many of them now on the Astral Plane," she said. "They will probably see the path easily. Those in the main concentrations of sickness will need something powerful to persuade them."

"Something powerful? Do you know what?" he asked, a small wave of anxiety shooting through him.

Her expression was sad. "I do," she replied. "You and I will provide it, together with your friend Raoul and the woman you have yet to meet. We will provide the impulse to make many millions of sick souls seek their redemption and that of all Humanity."

"Will you tell me, Maragos? What is it that we will do?"

"Not yet," she said with a small shake of her head, and rising to her feet. "You need to sleep now, and make contact with the fourth one of our small group. And all of you must grow and acquire some further wisdom and insights before we embark on this task."

She stood in front of him so that her eyes grew vast like the universe and showed him the infinite power and majesty of the Supreme Being of which she represented a millionth part.

"The task will take everything we have, Philippe," she said. "And if we fail, Oneness will take millions more years to be achieved, and the damage may be irreversible."

Shivering a little, he stared back. If one such as she could show fear, what possible help could a single human soul be to the task she had undertaken?

She touched him gently on the arm. "You will discover just how much, in time. Sleep now, Philippe. We have much work to do."

# Chapter 10. God's Council

*(From the Diaries of Alan Drew)*
*June 6, 2022*

My night was fearful, sick and violently disturbed. After a silent, hostile ride in the limousine back to the Vatican Embassy, the Cardinal and I disembarked, leaving the vehicle to swish off silently, with only a crunch of gravel under the heavy tires. Lavalier said nothing as we entered the lobby of the mansion house, and I followed the black manservant to my room, miserably aware that I had failed the Cardinal's instruction to show discipline when faced with the night's events.

But dear God, how can I not be sickened by the fact of a hundred thousand people enjoying the sight of their fellows being executed as a public spectacle?

I prayed on my knees by my bed for an hour before I climbed into the covers and tried to sleep. The sound of the strangled gasping of Peter Browning as the crowd hung eagerly silent to see what a man would say when about to face a painful death, echoed in my brain. It was followed by the thin wailing through the loudspeakers as the artificial sparks flashed round the chair like Saint Elmo's fire and the real but silent, lethal voltages shook the man's body like a puppet in the hands of an irate child.

I saw as if coloured film played in my head, the happy, excited faces of the crowd standing up with delight as the body slumped, cheering as if for a home run by their team. As we left the stadium in the limousine, we passed the thousands walking cheerfully to their cars, some carrying children or holding the hands of boys and girls who carried souvenir models, toys of an electric chair which sparkled and hummed when a switch was pressed, and a small doll strapped to the seat jumped and twitched. Faces were smiling, sated as if the home team had won a major victory, and the official car received shouts of greetings and applause as we passed.

Sometimes, the image in my head was of the calm, smiling face of Kenneth Jensen who surveyed the crowd before seating himself and silencing the thousands with his quiet damnation of them all. Then the gentle slump of Jensen's body before the power had been switched on, as if he had simply abandoned it, stepping out of his physical form like a man about to enter the shower and dropping his pyjamas on the bathroom floor.

Around dawn, I finally slept for an hour or two and I felt terribly weary, old and haggard as I faced Cardinal Lavalier across the breakfast table at six-thirty.

Lavalier looked fresh, well slept and alert. "It is a shock, the first time, Alan," he said in a tone of conciliation as he took a piece of toast and applied marmalade to it. "But you must remember that there are plenty of precedents, and His Holiness has endorsed the process."

"The Inquisition, Eminence? This is the precedent?" I was too distraught to tone down my words, but the Cardinal seemed to ignore it.

"Desperate times Alan, desperate measures," he replied through a mouthful of toast. "Do you question the infallible wisdom of the Holy Father?" His eyes were suddenly cold as they regarded me over the resumption of chewing movements of his mouth.

"Of course not, Eminence," I stammered, aware of the dangerous path I had stepped onto. "I was unprepared for the reality of the sight, and the reaction of the people there. I am unable to believe that the death of one's fellow men should be a cause for celebration and amusement."

Lavalier shrugged. "President Horning has a major problem here," he said, pouring coffee from a silver pot into the Wedgwood china cup by his elbow. "Industry is collapsing and the unemployment rate is soaring. These spectacles at least provide some diversion for the people as well as a major object lesson on the errors of crime, or even worse, heresy."

"Bread and circuses, Eminence?" I could not keep the irony from my voice, but Lavalier ignored it if he detected it.

"The Roman Emperors had the same problem, it is true," agreed the Cardinal. "Let us hope that this does not herald the end of the American era of world power. If it does, then the night which will follow will be long and dark indeed, if the Great Adversary holds sway on Earth."

He looked hard at me. "You do not have doubts that the brotherhood of America and the Vatican are the last bulwarks against Evil, Alan?"

I found myself unable to meet his eye. "No, Eminence," I whispered. "I am dedicated to God's work."

"Good," replied Lavalier. "Because you will have to attend such events regularly as part of your duties to show the support of the Eternal City for President Horning's Administration."

I shuddered inside, but somehow kept my face composed.

The Cardinal continued to speak. "Today, we will visit a centre of operations for the newly formed Council for the Protection of God's Name," he said. "Several heretics will face examination, and you must be there to provide the Holy See's support to the process. I demand far more control of yourself than you displayed last night. Can you do this for me and for the Mother Church, Alan?"

I was having severe doubts about just that question. I told myself over and over again that the Holy Father had endorsed this whole business so it must be valid and in support of God. I prayed internally for a few seconds, asking God for strength and wisdom to see the deeper, eternal verities that must exist behind the horrors I knew I must witness.

"I am the Lord's servant, Eminence," I said, and managed to drink a mouthful of coffee without throwing up as my insides had threatened all morning.

"Good," said Lavalier, rising to his feet, "for we leave again in half an hour to witness the Council's work."

I rose with him, and tried to steel my soul for the day's events.

The limousine ride was longer than the trip to the stadium the night before. It took us well out of the city into pleasant rural scenery and then re-entered urban surroundings after a half-hour or so. We stopped outside a conventional office building, and the car door was opened by yet another in the series of armed guards who seemed everywhere. To my total lack of surprise, Stephen Crossman was waiting for us at the top of the short flight of stairs leading into the building.

Crossman gave me a cool glance that I am sure contained derision. "I trust you have recovered from last night's temporary illness, Father?" he enquired.

I looked back into the blank, unreadable eyes of the President's aide. "I am well thank you," he replied and saw the Cardinal give me an amused glance. Crossman stared at me for a few seconds as if doubting my words, then opened the building door and gestured us inside.

It could have been any government office building. The floor was white-tiled, and two uniformed guards manned a small reception desk in the centre of the lobby. They nodded briefly at Crossman as he led us to the bank of elevators behind the desk, and resumed their study of three television screens set up in front of them. As I walked by, I could see myself and the others in one of the pictures. From the angle, I guessed the cameras were on top of the doorway by which they had entered and I looked back to confirm it. The other two pictures appeared to show lengths of unidentifiable corridors.

We waited by the elevators, and off to one side, glass walls showed a conventional office scene. Lines of desks, all with a computer terminal on them, most of the desks staffed by young men and women busy with unknown tasks. Several were talking on telephones, others walked by with manila files in their hands. Along the walls were a series of offices, some with their doors open, some closed. It could have been an insurance office or a government administrative department.

With a small chime, an elevator door opened and Crossman led the way inside. He pressed a "Down" button and the car moved silently, dropping several floors before coming to rest and the door opened again.

"Your Eminence, this is the primary Examination Centre for the region," said Crossman, turning left out of the elevator and leading the way along a corridor that was well lit, though stark in appearance. The walls were painted a light green, no pictures hung anywhere and not a single door was open. None of the doors had any sort of window either, they were all the same blank, impervious look. I felt a strong chill of apprehension. There was evil here, a sense of overwhelming fear which rose from the floors and the walls and was almost palpable.

The three of us reached the end of the corridor, and Crossman paused, his hand on the door handle. "This is the main collection operation," he said, and opened the door.

The other side appeared like a massive warehouse. It was brightly lit and at the far end, sliding doors were just closing. Several long lines of men and women were standing silently under the light, while a number of guards equipped with assault rifles inspected them. I tried to estimate the numbers by counting partly along the first line and then counting the total lines, and finally decided that some two hundred and twenty men and women were under guard in the space before him, with several children as well. Most of the people looked nervous and a few were weeping, but several of the faces I could see displayed the same calm assurance that Kenneth Jensen had shown the night before as he walked up to the electric chair.

"This is the result of last night's sweep through Washington and Baltimore," said the toneless voice of Crossman from behind me. "Most have been collected as a result of tip-offs by neighbours, or on suspicion because of strange behaviour patterns."

The lines of captives suddenly sat down on the floor under the urging of the armed guards. Several men appeared from another door to the right, and one man went to the head of each line and began asking questions of the seated person. Each of the questioners was carrying a small device into which he seemed to be keying data according to the answers he was given.

"Radio frequency microcomputers," said Crossman in answer to a question from Cardinal Lavalier. "We take in the normal details of social security number, name and address, next of kin, and so on, and the information is immediately transmitted to our computer upstairs. Shortly, we will also film each person on a camcorder and the picture will also be stored with the data on the computer."

As he spoke, more men appeared and began following behind the men with the microcomputers. They pointed tiny camcorders at the prisoners as the information was being entered. At the far end of the huge building, a disturbance erupted. A man had leaped to his feet and screamed something unintelligible. He struck the man asking him questions, sized the tiny computer and slammed it to the floor. Immediately, several guards closed in, raised their weapons and clubbed the man to the floor. Other men in the area stood up and the guards reacted as if attacked. In two minutes, twenty or more men were lying on the ground. I could see blood on the heads of several of them.

A trio of children clinging to a woman a few yards away began crying, and one of the guards spoke to her. She put her arms around the smallest of the children and stared at the guard. He dropped his eyes and turned away.

"They will be here several more hours," said Crossman, and gestured us back through the door. "Let us go and look at the examination rooms."

Such an innocuous name! I took a deep breath and tried to prepare myself for what I must now see. We walked back along the corridor, until we reached a steel door half way back the way we had come. Crossman took a small plastic card from his jacket and waved it before a black square in the door. A tiny buzz sounded and the door moved slightly as a lock was released. He opened the door and led the way inside, where there was another corridor, less well lit than the first, and lined with solid looking steel doors.

"This man has been waiting for our arrival before examination would commence," said Crossman and opened the door that swung silently on oiled hinges.

The room was starkly bare of luxuries. The walls were stone, the floor was plain green linoleum. A heavy wooden chair was in the middle of the room, on which was sitting a man who looked in his early thirties. He was dressed in conventional jeans and a light shirt, and was sweating heavily. The man's wrists were strapped to the arms of the chair. Next to him, stood a small wooden table with a black leather case resting on the surface. It looked like any businessman's briefcase. At a small desk against one wall, a young man was sitting, writing carefully on a paper sheet illuminated by a small desk lamp. Above the desk was the only decoration in the whole room. The picture of President

Horning was the same as that I had seen in the White House the previous day. The man at the desk stood up as they walked in and placed his pen by the table lamp.

"Good morning, sir," he addressed Crossman, then bowed to each of us. "Good morning, Your Eminence, Father Drew," he said, and remained standing. He was of medium height, perhaps in his late thirties. He was dressed in dark trousers and a shirt that fitted snugly on a well-muscled body. Epaulets on the shoulders gave him a slightly military look. Dark brown hair, the insipid good looks of a minor male model or a news anchorman at a small, local television station, all gave him an averagely pleasant, unassuming appearance. Neither the Cardinal nor I returned the greeting but that did not appear to worry the young man. The prisoner in the chair looked terrified as we walked in, and gave us both a look of undisguised hatred. But he remained silent.

"Gentlemen, this is one of our Examiners," said Crossman without further elaboration. He nodded at the man then marshalled us to the back of the room where we stood against the wall to the left of the prisoner in the chair. I felt pressure building in my chest and my breathing became forced. Sweat built up on my back and arms, and my face grew sticky with a thin sheen of perspiration. With a quick look at the Cardinal, I saw that Lavalier was as cool and composed as if waiting for a service to start.

The Examiner walked up to the man in the chair, carrying a slender metal rod in one hand and another tiny computer in the other. He looked at the miniature screen on the device.

"You are George Harold Mosely?" he asked politely. His accent sounded almost English. He could have been checking the man's reservation for dinner, so calm and courteous was his tone.

"Yes," replied the man. It was forced from his throat as if something was stuck inside it.

"Good," said the Examiner. "And you live in Meadows Road in Bethesda, correct?"

"Yes," croaked Mosely. He twisted his head to his left to stare at Lavalier. "What are these two priests doing here?" he rasped.

"That is not your concern," said the man with the computer. "Your concern from this point on is with me and me alone. Do you understand that, Mosely?"

The prisoner ignored him. "Father, please help me," he said to Lavalier. "I have done nothing wrong. For the love of God, will you ask them to let me go?"

Lavalier shook his head. "I can do nothing, my son," he said. "You must trust in the Lord now to prove that you are innocent of any crime of heresy. If you are a true Christian, God will protect you."

The young Examiner placed the computer back on the desk and returned to the chair, the metal rod still in his right hand. "I shall ask you once more, Mosely," he said. "Do you understand that your only concern from this point on is in communicating the truth to me?"

Mosely stared back at Lavalier. "Call yourself a man of God!" he spat. "To hell with you and all your stinking..."

The metal rod touched his shoulder and the man screamed in anguish, his head slamming back with force against the solid wooden back of the chair. I couldn't prevent myself starting and another drip of sweat ran down my neck. The Cardinal touched me briefly on my arm and I forced myself to be calm.

"As you see, Mosely," said the Examiner, as if reprimanding a child in school. "You must give me your undivided attention from now on or you will undergo considerable pain. This is now clear to you?"

The prisoner's shriek of pain had faded to a soft moan. "Yes," Mosely gasped.

"Excellent! Then let us proceed," said the nameless Examiner. "It has been reported to us that you have never been seen in church as long as your neighbours can recall. Is there any reason for this, Mosely?"

"I've just never been a church-going man," replied Mosely, his eyes fixed on the metal rod. The Examiner walked behind the chair and lightly touched the rod to the man's neck. The shocking, terrified scream of pain echoed in the room. My insides turn watery and my whole body trembled. Lavalier turned his head and stared hard at me. I struggled, took another deep breath, and the Cardinal turned his eyes back on the scene before them.

"Not an appropriate answer," said the Examiner. "Flippancy is unacceptable. Now again, why have you not been in church for at least two years?"

Mosely moaned. "It's the truth, I swear it! I'm a Christian, used to go regular like, but I got out of the habit when we got kids. Please don't do that to me again, for God's sake, I ..."

Mosely tried to twist away, but the rod caught him on the left cheek, and lingered there like a lover's touch. Mosely jumped almost as if he was in the electric chair and the shout of agony reached a crescendo before fading into a slobbering moan and his head fell against his chest.

"Do not take the Lord's name in vain, Mosely." The examiner's voice was controlled. "That is the last time I shall tell you. Let's start again. Are you a believer in the creed of Oneness?"

Mosely lifted his head. "Oneness? No, never. I think it's all garbage."

This time, the rod was not lightly touched. The Examiner slashed Mosely across his face, leaving a violent, red streak from his right eye to the base of his chin. Mosely didn't make a sound, but simply collapsed in his bonds and his head fell down across his chest.

After two or three minutes, during which I felt that the silence in the room would burst my eardrums, the man in the chair lifted his head. A few more moments passed before he focused on the Examiner standing silently in front of him. He stared for a few seconds, and began to tremble.

Mosely let out a moan that gurgled with the shaking of his body. "Please..." he whimpered. "Don't do that again... please..."

"I will do whatever is necessary until you tell me the truth," said the young man in the military shirt. "So let us see if you can do so. Now, again. Are you a believer in the creed of Oneness?"

He watched the man shiver in the chair as Mosely struggled to concentrate and control the shaking.

"No-o-o-o.." groaned Mosely. "Never."

"Then why have you remained away from the House of God these past two years?"

"I wanted... I wanted..." Mosely struggled for control. "I wanted to spend... time... with my... children."

"You could have taken your children with you," replied the Examiner in a reasonable tone. "That is not good enough." He reached for the rod on the table.

"Please... no! Please, I beg you..." His shuddering voice was interrupted by a long wailing scream as the rod was touched to his arm. While the prisoner recovered from the last jolt of agony, the young man walked back to the desk and picked up the computer. He walked back to the chair.

"Your children are Denise aged six and Paul who is four, is that correct?"

The man in the chair was unable to speak, but nodded, again twisting his head round to direct a look of pleading at me. I closed my eyes and murmured a prayer under my breath.

"Are your children believers in Oneness, Mosely?" The Examiner spoke again.

The prisoner shuddered, and continued to tremble with a low undercurrent of painful moaning. "No-o-o," he groaned.

"Do you teach them that they are part of God and one day will ascend to form Him?"

Mosely shook his head, saliva running down his chin.

"Do you tell them that they live many lives, that there is no Hell for heretics, and that there is no Heaven for true believers, that there is no Day of Judgement?"

The bound man tried to speak, but emitted only a small gasp.

"I see here that you used to be a registered Democrat," continued the Examiner in a tone of interest. "Does that mean that you were opposed to President Horning?"

A violent tremble shook the prisoner and he sobbed. He dropped his head, and drool fell from his mouth onto the thin shirt he was wearing. He seemed to gather strength and raised his head again. "I left the Democratic Party when it was banned," he said with massive difficulty as if he had just had dental surgery and the anaesthetic had not worn off.

"But that means that you voted against Presidents Reagan and others before the Reverend Horning set this country on a new path to God. Even worse, it indicates that you voted for that Devil's agent and his succubus of a wife. Is that not so, Mosely?"

"It was legal, then," gasped the man in the chair, forcing words out through uncooperative lips and throat.

"Evil does not have to be recognized immediately for it to be evil," said the Examiner as if lecturing a small child. "Under our new, enlightened criminal code, you are still guilty of Anti-American practices." He walked round in front of Mosely and leaned his hands on the prisoner's shoulders.

"I'm losing patience, Mosely," he said, staring hard into the eyes of the man in the chair. "All I want is the truth. That you are a criminal is now established. So tell me, are you also a heretic?"

"No-o-o," gasped the man in the chair.

The Examiner stood up, the metal rod in his right hand. Astoundingly, after his courteous, quiet speech so far, he shouted in fury. "You're a liar! You're a God-damned, heretical liar!"

The man in the chair shook even more violently. "No-o-o" he said again, struggling to get the word out.

The young man before him seemed to lose his temper. "Liar, I say! Liar! Damned heretic and liar!" With each pause he slashed Mosely across each cheek in turn with the metal rod. The red weals burned and hissed and Mosely screamed helplessly.

"You're a follower of Oneness, aren't you?" bellowed the young man, again leaning across Mosely. "You're plotting against President Horning and against America, aren't you?"

Mosely struggled to speak, but the shaking of his body got worse and he obviously could no longer control his mouth at all. The Examiner stood up straight, and with a howl of fury whipped Mosely across the head three times with violent, slashing strokes. Mosely collapsed in the chair, and the room fell silent.

I realized I had been holding my breath for a long time, and slowly released it, my heart pounding so fearfully, I was certain it could be heard in the room. Mosely was dead, I knew it. The trembling and shaking had ceased and the body appeared to have shrunken, the way bodies did when the soul left them.

For the first time, the young man looked at Crossman. "I'm sorry, sir," he said.

Crossman shrugged. "Couldn't be helped," he said. "You followed the procedures. I'm certain he was a heretic, after all."

"Yes, sir," replied the young man with a look of relief.

"You'll arrange for the family to be picked up, won't you?" said Crossman, and buttoned his jacket in preparation for leaving. The young man nodded at him, and began to enter data into the small hand-held computer.

Crossman moved to the exit and opened the door, holding it for Lavalier to leave in front of him. I could hardly wait to get out into the corridor and wondered if

I would have to watch any more horrors like this.

As we moved along the dim corridor, a door opened. Another man in the uniform of an Examiner raised his eyebrows at Crossman. "Another PSID, sir," he said, to my mystification.

For the first time since I had met the Chief Examiner, I saw an expression of anger on the man's immobile face. Crossman turned abruptly and marched into the room. Inside, the scene was much like the room we had just left. A heavy chair, a bound man slumped in it. Against the far wall, a desk with a table lamp. By the chair, a small stand with an identical briefcase, metal rod and microcomputer. The difference was in the man in the chair. He was dead, that was obvious. But the expression on the face was calm, even a small smile was still evident.

"Tell me!" snapped Crossman. He glared at the Examiner who was an older man than the previous one.

"Just like the others," the Examiner said. "He sat down, let us strap him in, then he grinned at me and said 'This is a waste of time, you know,' and then laughed. I asked him why, and he said 'I've got things to be doing, and I don't want to hang around here being roughed up by you'."

The Examiner looked away from his Chief for a few seconds. An expression of fear crossed his face. "Then he looked at me, almost with pity, and said 'You've got a terrible time coming when you die, you know that, don't you?' And then he just closed his eyes, and that was it. He was dead."

"This happens frequently, Mister Crossman?" The Cardinal spoke for only the second time since entering the elevator to descend to the Examination centre.

Crossman looked uncomfortable and was unable to meet the Cardinal's eye. "There have been a number of similar incidents, Eminence. The heretics clearly get the devil's help to avoid exposure, and we get another Premature Self-Induced Death."

I finally understood what a PSID was. If they had

given the phenomenon a name, must that mean that it was a common event? Are there more like Jensen, who can discard life like a snake leaves its skin?

"Much like last night during God's Work," said Lavalier thoughtfully. "Unfortunate that it should have occurred during such a publicized event."

"At least, Eminence, the public telecast was in delay mode, so we got a chance to cut that incident out before it was broadcast." Crossman was looking irritated and he glared at the dead man in the wooden seat.

"As you say, Mister Crossman," said the Cardinal. "Fortunate that over eighty million Americans were not able to see heresy in action."

Eighty million! I was horrified to think that so many people would wish to watch such a spectacle as the painful deaths of their fellows. The full insanity of the Horning administration was becoming clearer to me every second.

"Is there anything further that you should show Father Drew before we move on?" asked Lavalier, and Crossman shook his head.

"No, Eminence," he replied. "We have the principles of Examination well established now and the training schools are being set up in all states. With the technologies we employ, the process is rapid and we can put three or four hundred a day through the questioning at a centre of this size."

"Tell me, Mister Crossman," I said, feeling emboldened by my outrage at the numbers I had heard of people being tortured each day in what I had always believed to be the world's largest democracy. I ignored the glare from Lavalier that my interruption earned me. "Of those hundreds per day, how many are found to be true Christians and returned unharmed to their families?" I stared unflinchingly at Crossman, despite the angry gesture from Lavalier.

Crossman glared back, a flush in his face. "Those figures are classified, Father," he said sharply.

"How many, Mister Crossman?" I repeated.

"Father!" snapped Lavalier. "That will do!"

Silence held for several moments, then Crossman spoke in a conciliatory tone. "Father, you have to remember, that with the massive wave of evil and heresy that threatens us, the old rules change. We cannot presume innocence until guilt is proved. The Devil doesn't work to those rules and nor can we."

"So nobody leaves alive, is that what you are telling me?" I asked, trembling inside at the talk I would have with the Cardinal, later.

"Not so," replied Crossman. "Many leave alive, confirmed as true Christians. But they will bear the scars of the examination to show others the price of even considering heresy."

"God's will is done," I said, and this time, nobody could have failed to hear the irony in my voice.

"I shall take this angry young priest away for now, Mister Crossman," said Lavalier, and I was astonished to hear amusement in the voice when I had been expecting a tongue lashing of royal proportions.

"A good idea, Your Eminence," said Crossman, but there was nothing but anger in his face and he turned away, walking rapidly along the corridor.

"Come, Father Drew," said Lavalier as we walked out of the elevators back on the ground floor of the office building. "I have one more facet of the country that you must see and understand before I return to the Holy City and leave you to your work." Around them, the business of the Council for the Protection of God's Name continued. People carried files around with them, stopped and talked with colleagues in the corridors, sipped water from the coolers and communicated with computer terminals on their desks.

Hard to imagine that the government business of this department was the imprisonment, torture and murder of thousands of innocent people. What went on in the minds of the men and women in this building as they processed the files of their countrymen? When they came to work in the morning, did they think about the prisoners downstairs as they made the first coffee of the day, or discussed their previous evenings? When they had lunch in the cafeteria, did they ponder how many people had died that morning in the cells a few feet below them?

When they flirted with each other and began relationships of love and affection, or simple lust, maybe marriage, when they compared notes on the others in the place as young people had done in the workplace for ages, did they give even a passing thought for the screams of agony as people were touched with those dreadful metal rods that the Examiners flourished? Did they care that people died in awful pain because a neighbour had commented that they hadn't seen old so-and-so in Church for a while? Or that children of four and five were being rounded up because their parents had once been members of a now-illegal political party?

I thought back to the reading I had done as a younger man when I had been fascinated by an incomprehensible aspect of evil in Nazi Germany and Stalinist Russia. Similar structures existed then, bureaucratic edifices for the efficient destruction of human beings. Whole sections had been dedicated to the recording of the numbers of deaths, the transportation of millions of people like so much raw material to processing plants in Dachau and Auschwitz and to frozen camps on the tundra of Siberia. Men and women had processed the mechanisms of slaughter and then gone home to their families, played with their children, said prayers before retiring to sleep and had eaten breakfast before leaving for work the next day.

The banality of evil, one writer had called it.

This is what I was seeing here. Human souls so callused by the mass statistics of murder in the name of God and the State, that they perform their duties and think of themselves as Christians. What adds the final touch of horror is the fact that this whole structure is dedicated to the service of God, no doubt with complete sincerity. I am certain that Cardinal Lavalier truly believes that the murder, the torture, the public executions and the wild celebrations that accompany them are services that further the Name of Almighty God.

"Father? You seem to be in a hurry!"

I returned to the present with a shock. I realized that I was striding along the sidewalk of whatever town this was, at a rate that was stretching the physical capabilities of the Cardinal.

"Your Eminence! My apologies, my Lord, my mind was running away with me!" I blushed in confusion as the Cardinal caught up with me, breathing hard.

"In company with your legs, it would seem!" The Cardinal appeared to be in a good humour, though how any man could be so after witnessing the events we had seen in the last two days was beyond my comprehension.

"No matter," said Lavalier, breathing deeply to gather himself. "We were heading in the right direction. I think we will take a short break right here."

Right here was at a small cafe with an outdoor section, much like a European coffee shop. The sidewalk was opposite a small park bounded on all four sides by the town's roads. At the far side of the park, an attractive, white-painted wooden building had the definite look of a town hall, judging by the open doors through which passed a stream of people in both directions, and by the several police cars parked outside.

Lavalier led the way into the fenced-off enclosure and took a metal seat by a white, cast-iron, round table. I joined him, both of us sitting so that we could see out over the park. People were gathering in the open area, centering round a low stage that had been erected. Yesterday morning, I might have believed I was about to witness a public speech like an oration at Hyde Park

Corner in London. Or perhaps a town meeting. Now I shall steel myself for whatever is to come.

By this point, I already knew what I must do. One man alone could not battle the might of President Horning's religious autocracy. But one man could record the evil, the cruelty, the moral bankruptcy that came when religious fanaticism became the ruling force in a country. One day, I knew, I would pay my penance for the part I had played in this corruption of reason. For the present however, I would observe, record and store away whatever I was able to witness of the history of the collapse of once high principles into the rotting quagmire of theistic power. What use I could ever make of the story, I had no idea, but it was all I could do.

A petite, teenage girl curtsied at us and took our orders for coffee. Lavalier asked for a danish pastry. The crowd in the park was increasing by this time, and several large trucks had slowly ground their way from the rear of the park to within a few feet of the stage. I folded my arms and coldly watched the movement across the road.

One truck opened its rear doors and a man climbed out. He wore a gun on his belt and held one end of a chain. He barked out an order to someone back in the truck's body and a line of men appeared. All were black, dressed simply in a pair of jeans, naked from the waist up, and had their hands bound behind them. The chain held by the man at the front led through metal rings at each man's belt.

A slave sale, I realized, and firmly closed the door in my mind against further possibilities that this Vatican-American axis of power was anything but corrupt and evil. For a brief second, I pondered on the implications of what the philosophy of Oneness could now mean to me, and returned to my observation of the scene before me.

"You seem less disturbed by this sight than I expected, Father Drew?" Cardinal Lavalier was watching me, I saw, and I turned to him.

"As I said, Eminence, I accept the word of the Holy Father," I said, and sat back in my chair as the waitress deposited the coffees and the pastry on the table.

Lavalier gave me one piercing look, as if suspecting a shift of attitude then poured sugar into his coffee cup and stirred reflectively. "I understand your confusion," the Cardinal said, and took a small bite of the pastry, chewing it delicately. "I experienced the same difficulty when I first came over here a few months ago."

"I was not aware you had been here before," I said in surprise.

"There was no need for you to know," replied Lavalier. "But I came to inspect the developments with the Horning Administration in order to brief His Holiness in Rome. We debated at length on the validity of Horning's approach and finally had no choice but to endorse it."

He sipped at his coffee and I did the same, as much to hide my thoughts as to take nutrition.

"The teaching of the Church, after all, is that Almighty God is the Supreme Creator, mankind can only find redemption through Jesus Christ, and total acceptance of these teachings is essential. You agree with me, Alan?" Lavalier looked hard at me.

Startled, I could only nod my head, and the Cardinal seemed satisfied. "Given that," he continued, "how could the Mother of Churches believe that this creed of Oneness is anything but a repudiation of all our teachings? Its adherents deny a Supreme God. They deny the divinity of Jesus Christ. They deny the Immaculate Conception, the existence of the Devil, the principles of everlasting Heaven or Hell, even salvation through our Lord Jesus Christ. These are the cornerstones of the faith. And therefore, Oneness stands against the One True Church and thus against God. Neither the minor though admittedly disturbing manifestations of Horning's excesses nor the startling degree to which Americans have accepted these changes can invalidate our conclusion. Whatever you may think and however it may appear, Alan, the Church must embrace President Horning's support and fight against this Devil's Creed."

"I understand the reasoning, My Lord," I said and took another mouthful of coffee. I was feeling stronger every second and the lengthy sophistry of the Cardinal's arguments had no effect on me.

"And embrace it, Father Drew?" The question was accompanied by another piercing look.

"I will obey every order you have given me, My Lord," I replied. "I will observe all the events of the Council that Mister Crossman requires, and show by my presence that the Holy See supports this Administration."

"That is what I have asked of you, certainly Alan," murmured Lavalier. "Why is it then, that I feel some concerns about you?"

I looked him firmly in the eye. "I will perform my duties to the Church as I have vowed, my Lord," I said. Lavalier gave me one more hard stare then shifted his gaze to the park.

The line of bound men was now standing on the platform, and they had been disconnected from the chain. While one had been brought to the centre of the platform, the rest remained at one side.

"Ladies and Gentlemen, Loman's Manpower Provision Services is pleased to open today's auction with this fine selection of staff!" bellowed the man who had led the black prisoners to the stage. "This is lot number one, a collection of eight splendid items, all aged between sixteen and twenty-four, in perfect health. Our procedure is standard. We will accept bids for the first item. On acceptance, the buyer may select one or more, up to the entire group at the same price per head. If any are left unclaimed, we will resume bidding at the price at which we received the last bid."

Immediately, his voice changed into a high pitched rapid-fire auctioneer's style that I was unable to follow. I watched the man point to several people in the crowd as bids were offered, until finally his voice slowed.

"At six thousand, eight hundred dollars, going once... going twice.... sold to Mister Hubbard, thank you sir! How many will you take? All eight of them? Splendid, Mister Hubbard, we will take a ten percent discount from the total price for that magnificent purchase!"

I found that I had been sitting forward tensely as the bidding was carried out. I let out a long breath and sat back. I looked sideways at Lavalier and saw the Cardinal apparently unmoved, finishing the last mouthful of the pastry.

There was a stir at the park. Two young black women had been brought to the stage and the same auctioneer was speaking.

"...two superb specimens here, sisters from Alabama. Ideal for breeding requirements or for household duties of any type..." The man broke off as a chorus of wolf whistles interrupted him, and he smiled a toothy grin of appreciation.

"As I said, household duties. Now gentlemen, shall we start the bidding at three thousand a head?" And with that, he fell into the unintelligible gabble of the practised auctioneer. I watched intently, no longer feeling tension or sickness, merely a need to observe and to record.

Finally the high-speed babble slowed again like a racing car slowing after the chequered flag and the words came clearly across the park.

"...and at twelve thousand... both of them, sir? Excellent! Sold to Senator Grant of Baltimore! And thank you, Senator."

To another howl of whistles, the girls were led off. One of them was weeping bitterly.

Lavalier rose to his feet. "Time to return to the Embassy, Father," he said. "I must prepare for my return to Rome and you probably wish for time for quiet and prayer."

Feeling no emotion, I stood up, waited as Lavalier

placed a banknote under his coffee cup, and followed the Cardinal to the sidewalk. Calling a cab from a line waiting by the corner, we returned to the Vatican's embassy building and by the evening, I was left alone as the Vatican's liaison with President Horning and the Council for the Protection of God's Name.

* * *

*"Oh Jesus Christ! It hurts!"*

Horning screamed in mixed pain and fury. The doctor examining him flinched and stood up straight, the stethoscope flailing across his chest.

"What hurts, Mister President?" he asked.

"The Devil!" screamed Horning, leaping off the examination couch and hurling himself in the corner. "The Devil is coming for me!" He hid his face in the angle of the walls and clutched his arms across his chest. A muffled sob broke from him. "Don't let her get me, please don't let her touch me!"

"Mister President!" shouted Stephen Crossman. His face was white. He moved toward Horning, reached out his hand then withdrew it before he touched the weeping man. But even the gesture broke Horning's terror. He roared in fury and turned to face Crossman.

"Don't you ever fucking touch me, Crossman!" he bellowed. The walls rang with the noise. Crossman shouted in pain, and collapsed on the floor, the expression of agony struggling with astonishment at what had happened. The doctor also gasped and bent over double.

Calming abruptly, Horning stared at both of them. "What the hell's the matter with you two?" he shouted.

Crossman emitted a moan of pain. Drool ran down his chin as he struggled to sit up.

"I don't know, sir," he rasped. "When you shouted, it felt like a knife going through me."

"What the fuck are you talking about, man? I only shouted."

"Yes, sir." Crossman pulled himself to his feet.

Against the far wall, the doctor did the same. A greenish tinge collared the skin of the doctor's neck. Horning glared at him.

"Get out!" he snapped. "There's nothing wrong with me."

The doctor almost ran out of the room and Horning stared at the closed door. He turned back to Crossman, and the tears were evident in the President's face again.

"She's coming," he whispered. "Crossman, for God's sake, you've got to stop her coming."

"Who, sir? Who's coming?"

Instead of answering, Horning began to stride around the room like a caged animal. "Got to stop her, got to stop her, got to stop her...." he mumbled.

"Mister President, please!" called Crossman. He moved toward Horning again, and the President stopped and stared at him. The blackness seemed to radiate from his eyes and Crossman sank to his knees in shock, unable to breath. He almost felt his soul sucked out of him, felt death stroke him with familiar affection, then he gasped for air and his lungs worked again. Horning resumed his stride, walked up to the wall of the office and hammered both fists against it in a full-blooded slam. The wall shook.

"She's coming!" screamed Horning. His voice rose to a high-pitched shriek and his head went back against his neck as the scream filled the air with pain.

Holding his hands against his head, Crossman was sobbing as he knelt on the floor. It was a few seconds before he realized the awful sound had ceased. He looked up.

Horning was standing silent and still, staring at the ceiling. Crossman followed his stare and felt a wave of fear run through him.

The ceiling was black and smoking as if someone had directed a flame-thrower against it.

"How the fuck did that happen?" asked Horning thoughtfully.

# Chapter 11. A Gathering of Old Friends

Jacqueline Carter looked forward to sleep now. The process took only a second or two, and she suspected she had learned the art of directly lifting her soul into the Astral Plane rather than wait for true sleep to come. Each time she awoke, she was able to remember more details of her past lives, and had memories now of eight different previous incarnations. Prior to being Mary who had died in childbirth, she had lived in Japan and been a Shinto Priest. One time, she had been an African slave in the home of a rich Arab trader in Tunisia, once a wine trader in Belgium at the time of Rembrandt. An early memory was of life in prehistoric days in central Africa, as the mother of her tribe.

She continued to stay at the house of Peter Wells and eventually settled into a permanent state of residence that had lasted almost seven years as they explored their pasts and dreamed their dreams of what was happening in the Universe. The two of them spent long, intense days sitting by the river and talking over their old lives as schoolboys over seventy years before. Sometimes, to Peter's total confusion, she linked her arm in the older man's, until finally he laughed uproariously and admitted his remaining inability to separate the body of Jacqueline Carter from the soul of Jerome Mitchell had at last dissipated.

Most days, they walked down to Caversham Lock where they had played as boys. Despite passing his hundredth birthday, Peter was still strong enough to walk the distance, and his mind was as clear and forceful as it had ever been.

They strolled on in a companionable silence.

"I've had other memories," she said after a few minutes.

Peter looked sideways at her. "About our times?" he asked.

She shook her head. "Much earlier," she said. "The first one was of medieval England. I was a working girl in Halifax Castle. I died in childbirth when I was sixteen."

Peter was still looking at her, feeling intense awe at the calm, serene expression in her profile. He was thinking of how he had always been the leader when they were boys, but now she seemed the more adult, the wiser person.

"It seemed such a waste of an existence," she said. "Nothing but poverty, misery, pain and then an early death."

He stayed silent, sensing that she had more to say.

"And there have been several others too, with the strangest feelings that there's more to come," she continued. "Somehow, I knew that there had been many other lives, and the last few nights I've been getting clearer and clearer memories of them. You'll be in some of them, I know," she added with a small smile at Peter. "But there's something else, too."

She looked out across the quiet waters of the Thames flowing by. A pair of racing rowing fours passed them, heading east to Sonning, the high-pitched voice of the cox of one of the boats reaching them clearly across the water. Several men were sitting on the bank studying the lines of their fishing rods, though none of them seemed to be having any luck.

"There's a presence, a person, someone who is critical to me, but I can't see him. Yes," she said, turning her face to his for a moment, "I know it's a man, he's incredibly powerful, and we've met before. It's the weirdest feeling."

"When you say you've met before," asked Peter, "do you mean in this lifetime?"

She shook her head. "I'd know it if I had ever met this one. He's powerful. But he's somehow close to me. Almost as if we've met in other lives and he's been critical in those lives, but there's been a barrier between us lately."

"You think the barrier is about to break down?"

She nodded vigorously. "I'm certain of it! That's why I go to bed early every night, wanting to fall asleep right away so I can find out what's happening!"

She reached into the small hamper she had carried and refreshed their cold drinks. A quartet of teenagers, two boys and two girls walked by them, giggling about something.

"I envy you," said Peter, as the group moved by to squeals and laughter. "I would love to know who and what I was before this, but I'm not getting a peep of any past lives."

"That's because you're a fifth-stage Mature Soul, and I'm a seventh-stage Old Soul," she said without thinking and stopped abruptly. "What did I just say?" she asked, looking hard into his brilliant eyes.

"You said I was a fifth-stage Mature Soul, and you're a seventh-stage Old Soul," he replied. "I don't know what that means, either."

"Christ, Peter! What the hell's going on inside my head?" she muttered. "I must be going round the bloody bend!"

"Now there's an expression Jerome Mitchell would have used in 1943," he laughed. "Not Jacqueline Carter in the twenty-first century!"

Her irritation faded and she laughed with him. "All the same, Peter, those words came from somewhere!"

"Obviously you've remembered something you knew in some other life," he said.

"No, I don't think so," she replied. "That's something new. But I think I'll find out tonight when I'm asleep."

"Keep me informed, won't you," he said with a smile.

She laughed, all irritation gone. "You'll be the first to know, I assure you!" she chuckled. "Meanwhile, there's a pub near the bridge, and I, for one, need a proper drink!"

"Are you old enough, young lady?" he asked with a severe expression.

"I'm just three months younger than you are, Mister Wells, you know that!" she replied, suppressing a laugh.

"Try telling that to the bloody barman!" he said, his extraordinary eyes glinting at her. His hundredth birthday had passed a few weeks before, but the brilliance of his eyes had not diminished. If anything, over the last few years, they seemed to have become even brighter.

This time the laugh came tumbling out of her, and in great good humour, two old friends walked up the road to get a pint of beer, the way they had over eighty years before.

* * *

The evening began as many similar evenings had begun since Jacqueline had moved into Peter Wells' house on Sideacre Road. Christine, Peter's house-keeper prepared a light meal then retired to her room. Talk faded for several minutes, and a companionable silence fell at the table. Jacqueline began to think back on her comments to Peter that morning on the towpath. She sensed knowledge welling up from deep inside her and she saw not only the eight previous lives she had recalled in recent days, but every single life stretching back over more than six thousand years. She began to speak softly, as if reciting a lesson learned that day in school. Peter sat unmoving, watching her, feeling the truth and power of her words.

"I have lived all these lives, Peter," she said. "I can see now how each was a learning experience, how I picked conditions for each life so that I could gain new and different experiences. And I can see how I have

223

matured so that now I feel like the Old Soul I mentioned before. And there is someone else who is important to me through nearly all those lives...." She tailed off as her mind began searching for a clue to this identity. She looked at her friend and smiled. "I am seeing this for the first time, and it is because something has arrived on Earth and just by being here, has caused spiritual growth. I can sense it now, just as Philippe Leger..." She stopped, a powerful bolt of energy crackling through her. The mention of the ex-Pope's name had startled something in her mind, somehow linked with what was happening to her tonight. She remembered how a similar jolt had shaken her so long ago on the day she had met Peter and he had mentioned Leger.

"I watched the press conference he held eight or nine years ago," said Peter. "It frightened me at first, when he said a massive presence was coming from elsewhere. But it was that presence that was causing this awakening, so I lost the fear. And it is here, now? You are aware of it like Leger was then?"

She nodded, still caught up in the immense reaction to Leger's name. She felt a strong, calm confidence that when she slept tonight, something new would develop, a further major leap in her spiritual growth.

"And we meet each other many times in our lives," said Peter, a statement, not a question. "We have met before, not just this last time?"

She nodded, reading the knowledge from somewhere undefined inside herself. "You and I, we have been together many times. Your last incarnation was in Germany in the nineteenth century. You were a teacher at the University in Gothenburg, I was a student of science, and you helped me learn when I was having difficulties. You put so much into it, that I became a successful engineer and formed a company that made me rich."

Peter smiled, hearing the echoes of that life in his mind.

"In between lives, we agreed to live another life together as friends," she said, returning his smile. "I agreed to help you become a leader, a motivator, so I played the secondary role to your strength and helped you grow. My death in the war was accidental. It cut short our plans, though you achieved your objectives anyway. Coming to see you again was essential. Our agreement was incomplete. Without the presence of whatever it is that has arrived and let me understand all this, we would have lived another life together to complete the Karmic Debt."

"But you are an Old Soul," whispered Peter. "You are so advanced on me."

She nodded. "Something has accelerated my growth, something..." She stopped. "Remember how I said that there was a presence, a person of huge power that I couldn't identify?"

Peter nodded. "You said he was close to you, but a barrier existed."

She was looking into an infinite distance. "The barrier is breaking," she said, so softly that he could barely hear her. Silence lasted nearly ten minutes, while Jacqueline tried to make sense of the powerful surges inside her. Somebody was near, soon they would talk... A wave of love and delight engulfed her, and she laughed out loud in happiness, but uncomprehending.

"This is my last incarnation, Peter. Somehow I know that I have a part to play in all this...." The sensation of the hovering presence was almost overwhelming. Without further words, she rose and went to her room. This was the time, she knew, for a new contact to be established, another breakthrough into a relationship with the Infinite. She changed into comfortable pyjamas, lay out on her bed and closed her eyes, immediately moving into a new level of awareness.

"I am here," he said, and the delight and love in his voice was obvious to her, even if she had not had the psychic communication.

"It has been a long lifetime that you have kept us apart," she replied. "I've missed you."

"There were reasons, as you know," he responded. "Our task needed me to be dedicated to the problem of this lifetime. I had to start early, rather than wait for you to complete the life of Jerome Mitchell."

"I know," she said, and the mists of the Astral Plane dissolved to form a beautiful room. Red carpets were thick and luxurious, wall hangings of gold and white embroidery gave colour to contrast with the floor, and the light was from a number of candles around the room in intricate, ornate silver candlesticks. A log fire gave off warmth and the scent of cedar wood.

Philippe Leger stood with his back to the fire. He was dressed in a deep blue suit of the style of Regency England. A complicated knot in a snow-white cravat was sealed with a huge ruby pin, and white lace flowed at his wrists.

"Ah yes," Jacqueline said with a smothered laugh. "You always did say that our last life together had been one of your favourite periods for style and elegance!"

She looked down at herself. She was clothed in a long yellow gown that displayed an astonishing expanse of bosom under a diamond necklace of immense beauty. Her hair was piled high, powdered white, and decorated with gold bands.

"Mind you," she said, smiling at him then looking down at her chest, "the style was a mite breezy for me! But if this is what makes you comfortable, I can cope for a while."

She walked up to him and kissed him firmly.

"I was waiting for you since I fell asleep," he said, and touched her face.

"I know, I sensed you," she replied and took his hand. "You always were so powerful on the psychic level!"

A silver tray appeared on a table by the wall and he walked over to it. It contained a heavy crystal glass jug of wine and two elegant glasses. He poured wine into the two glasses and returned to her, giving her one.

"To your health, my lady," he said and raised his glass.

"And to yours, sir," she said with warmth, and they drained their drinks.

"It is so good to see you again," he said, placing his glass on the mantelpiece above the fire and doing the same with hers. "I see you have taken the same physical form you had when we last lived together. I sometime regret the task that has kept us apart in this last of our series of lives."

"Our timing was confused," she said, taking his hand again. "I had the agreement with the soul of Peter Wells to be his friend at the time his development needed it. It gave him the leadership and power to make many completions in his present life. My death in the war was accidental or I might still be Jerome Mitchell."

"And I had to time my birth to accomplish the rise to the papacy when I first sensed the approach of the Infinite Soul," said Philippe. "That is why I have locked out our meetings on the Astral Plane during this life. I had to keep my mind clear as Pope. It would never have done to wake up on occasions feeling lovelorn for you! But Maragos told me I would finally be able to meet with you again. We must work together once more and our task is immense."

"It has always been leading to this, hasn't it?" she replied, smiling with delight at him. "You told me so, over six thousand years ago in our earlier lives together that this would happen. I was still only a Young Soul then, while you had already grown to being an Old Soul. I could never understand how you knew what your task was, so clearly."

"I have been lucky," he said, and traced the lines of her face with one finger. "The times I spent with Jesus,

Mohammed and Buddha gave me such fast growth that I outpaced every one of the other souls of my entity. But now, you and I must be together again."

"You and I and Raoul, again? We will join with the Infinite? We will be like the Four Spiritual Musketeers!" she said, grinning widely at him.

He laughed loudly. "You know, I wondered who Maragos reminded me of! I think she deliberately took an appearance like your present one. When you laugh, you could be sisters."

"I have never met an Infinite before," Jacqueline said, her face serious again. "What is it like?"

"Nobody has ever met an Infinite before," he replied. "Not on Earth, anyway. She said she only formed in recent years, and she is the first to have done so. It's a powerful experience to see her."

"She must be amazing, to have had this impact on Earth, just by coming here," replied Jacqueline. "When will we meet?"

"Why not now?" said Leger.

She shook her head. "Not yet," she replied. "I want a little more time with you alone first. It's been over two hundred years since we were man and wife in Regency London. I love you."

Their hands touched and clung.

"Come to Valence, to my home," he whispered. "We can remember this meeting now when we wake up, and you could come immediately. Raoul is there too, and Maragos keeps her presence there until it is time for us to move on."

"Do you know what we must do?" she asked, looking deep into his eyes.

"I think we must confront the main source of the sickness that has kept so much of Humanity as Infant Souls," he replied. "That means America."

"Yes," she agreed. "It must be so. We will have to die there."

"The world will have a wonderful time with us," he said, smiling at her. "Think of the newspaper headlines.

Seventy-plus-year-old ex-Pope has live-in girl friend of twenty-seven!"

"That was in a pre-Maragos world," she said, touching his face. "Only the Infant Souls of America and the others in the Middle East would care, and they are more concerned about killing each other."

"Then come to a post-Infinite world," he said. "Come to Valence and be my love for the rest of the time that we have left."

"I have never been anything else for six thousand years," she said softly, and moved into his arms.

They stood still, their foreheads touching. Suddenly, she felt the tiny chuckle running through his body.

"So what is amusing His Holiness?" she asked, already sensing the situation.

He took one hand from behind her back and with one finger, gently traced the lines of her breasts that were so splendidly displayed to him in the low-cut dress directly before his eyes.

"You realise it's been over two hundred years?" he said, his voice trembling with a mixture of amusement and excitement.

"Is that how long it is?" she replied, sensing her own breath begin to come more rapidly.

"Indeed it is," he said, and gently slipped one shoulder free of the gown.

"Can we do this intensely physical thing on a spiritual plane?" she asked, her voice starting to tremble.

"We Old Souls can do whatever we damn well like," he answered, pulling the gown off the other shoulder and revealing her breasts in their entirety. The room changed and was now darkened with gentle lights in the corners. An enormous four-poster bed almost filled the space.

"We have two hundred years to make up," he said.

She tightened her arms round his neck and felt herself carried to the bed.

* * *

By noon, Jacqueline Carter was ready to leave. Her parting from the house in Reading and from Peter Wells was sad, as the two old friends knew that it was for the last time. They would never meet again.

"Not in this incarnation, anyway," whispered Jacqueline, fighting tears as she held onto Peter's hands. "But we've known each other twenty times before, and we will meet again on the Astral Plane, that I know for certain."

"That's the trouble with you Old Souls," muttered Peter, his bright eyes even more gleaming with unashamed tears. "You know what will happen. We poor old bloody Mature Souls have to struggle on without any help!"

It had always been his way to hide grief behind a joke, thought Jacqueline, and put her arms round his neck. They held onto each other for several minutes, unwilling to let this final contact with an old life fall apart. Finally, she pulled away. "I have to go," she said.

"I know. Take care of yourself, Jerry."

"I will, old friend. No more fighting Huns, eh?"

He smiled, and the tears rolled down his cheeks. "Just remember not to fly straight and level for more than ten seconds," he said. "That's what got you last time."

She looked hard at her friend for another moment, then walked out of the front door and climbed into the waiting taxi.

Six hours later, she was in Valence, after a short domestic flight from Paris. She had made no calls either to her parents' home or to the house of Philippe Leger, not knowing either the address or the number of the ex-Pope, but she travelled with a calm assurance that she had no need.

He was waiting for her at the gate as she walked off the aircraft, and they smiled at each other like married couples who are still deeply in love. No words were necessary but they embraced tightly, neither seeing nor caring about the stares that they were receiving. They parted, he took her small bag, and they walked out into the open air and a short car ride to Philippe's home.

"Must I dress in a Regency gown again?" she said with a smile, looking at him as he drove his elderly Citroen. He grinned, and his face looked even younger than when he had held his press conference. Now he looked in his mid-thirties, lean and fit, and with the bright eyes of a healthy man.

"You looked good in it last night," he said cheerfully. "I remember it was one of your favourite gowns in London."

"So was the necklace," she answered, thinking of how extraordinary was this conversation. Here she was, a twenty-seven-year-old English girl, driving down a French road with the one-time Pope Jean-Pierre II. They were discussing events held on a spiritual level and recalling their previous life together two hundred years earlier, as if it were a party held the previous week.

"Yes, it's crazy!" he said, and looked at her. "Now I understand what Maragos said about speaking on a psychic level! I heard you clearly!"

She reached across and touched his cheek. "We have each lived over four hundred lives," she said. "And in over half of them, we've been together. We should be able to communicate this way, if anyone can!"

He took her hand and held it. "This is the last time for both of us," he said.

"I know," she whispered. "But we have almost an eternity before we merge with our own entities and lose our individual selves. And eventually, we'll all be one, anyway."

He released her hand to steer round a slow truck, crawling up the slight hill on the road, and said nothing, but the sadness in his face stayed for several more miles.

"Tell me what she's like," said Jacqueline, breaking the silence.

"How can I really tell you what it's like meeting a millionth part of God?" he replied. "She's a lot like you, as I told you last night. At first sight, she's a pretty, very bright young woman with great warmth. Then you sense the power and if you touch her, it's almost overwhelming, like stroking a whale."

Jacqueline laughed. "Some whale!" she retorted. "But twenty-five billion souls in one person! It's impossible to conceive."

"I think she would agree with you," replied Philippe. "I get the impression that it's still all very new to her as well, and sometimes she can't quite handle it. She said that she's still absorbing the memories and experiences of all the souls and it takes hours of solitude and meditation. Most of the months of the flight to Earth were spent that way."

Silence returned to the Citroen again as Jacqueline tried to comprehend the experience of being Maragos, and gave up.

The Citroen turned into a driveway surrounded by leafy bushes that needed a trimming. At the end of a fifty metre drive, the old house looked in repose, like a contented old man asleep in the sun.

Jacqueline smiled happily. "It's a lovely house, Philippe."

"My family has held it for two hundred years," he replied. "It has always been my shelter and retreat."

"And now it holds the most powerful presence on Earth," she said, subdued again. "This meeting scares me a little, my love."

He stopped the car outside the heavy oak front door and switched off the engine. The Citroen settled down on its suspension like a cat choosing a place to lie down by the fire.

"No need, Alexandria," he said, then grinned, realizing he had used the name she had held when they were last married, two hundred years before in

England. "Just be careful when you look into her eyes. It's an overwhelming experience."

They both climbed out of the car and he walked round to join her on the side nearest the door to the house. He smiled gently at her, and led her up the short flight of steps. The door opened before they reached it, and Raoul stood there, smiling at both of them. With a small cry, she ran at him and they embraced tightly.

*The farmhouse in Iowa was tiny, and their father struggled daily to produce enough to keep them alive. Andy and his sister, Penny were up at four each morning and helped milk the three cows and clean out the barns. After a short breakfast of bread and milk, they walked the two miles to the school. In the winter, the walk could be a living hell for two children aged only eight and ten, and several times, Penny would make them sit out the snow squall under a hedge or in the shelter of a building until they could see to walk on. As the elder, she had fallen naturally into the role left by her mother who had died the previous year. When that had happened, their father had retreated into a silent world of his own and the children now only had each other for conversation and company.*

*On this spring morning the walk was a delight, the warmth of the sun rapidly despatching the last few strands of ice that hid under bushes as if frightened by the heat. By eight, they walked into the small shack that was the school building, and their pleasure in the day faded as they encountered Miss Hotchkinson. She had been the school-mistress for as long as the children had been going there, and each day was a nightmare with that tense, angry and vicious woman.*

*This morning was worse than most, maybe because the beauty of the day had brought out the worst in her. They stood with the other eight children as Miss Hotchkinson strode into the single room.*

*"Prayer books!" she snapped at them, and glared at them until they were ready. She began leading them*

*in the Lord's Prayer, her high, strident voice rising above the mumble of the children. Suddenly, she stopped, and the mumbles faded into a deep, intense silence. The children turned to follow the direction of her irate stare.*

*Andy was looking out of the window, a small smile of delight on his face as he watched a small nest of chicks being fed by a mother bird in the tree outside. The woman strode furiously to him and struck him on the head with her hand.*

*"God hates little boys who don't pray to him!" she shrieked in a rage. Andy cowered and his fear brought even more rage to the teacher. She began slapping him hard across each cheek in turn. "What do you mean," she shouted, "by turning your face away from God? What do you mean by it? Well? Answer me, boy!"*

*Only the sound of weeping broke the silence. Unsatisfied, the woman whose soul would one day be John Donald Parker returned to her conduct of the morning worship of an Almighty and supremely loving God.*

"I only remembered when I saw you," Jacqueline said, her words muffled against his shoulder.

"I too," he replied, and kissed the top of her head. "It's wonderful to see you again, little brother!"

"There are still things we obviously remember only on the Astral Plane, and forget when we wake up," said Philippe, walking up the stairs towards them. Jacqueline and Raoul separated, but kept smiling at each other.

"It was one of those lives where we two were incarnate, but you weren't," said Raoul to Philippe, moving back into the hallway and letting Jacqueline and Philippe walk ahead. "Jacqueline was then my little brother, a couple of years younger than I was, and I brought him up when our mother died. It was a hard life, but we grew a lot in our knowledge of the world and of people."

Jacqueline smiled back at him. "There have been many more lives, with all three of us together," she said.

"But this task is the one you all agreed on many centuries ago," broke in a clear voice from the doorway of Philippe's study. Jacqueline turned, aware of the immensity of the force that emanated from that direction, and saw Maragos for the first time.

Despite Philippe's warning, she sank to her knees and hid her face.

* * *

The Soul who had last been Michael Hendricks felt at peace with himself and with the Astral Plane. Since his death at the hands of John Donald Parker and his companions, he had sensed massive growth in himself and was aware he had moved more than one stage in his soul level. At his death, he understood that he had been in the last incarnation as a first-stage Old Soul, and that in his next life he would attain the second stage. How he knew that, or how he knew that he had advanced to fourth-stage Old Soul since returning to the Astral Plane was beyond him. It was like trying to explain colours to a blind man, or explaining how one moved a leg or an arm. One didn't know how, one only knew. And Michael Hendricks knew that he had moved rapidly up through the learning and experience equivalent of possibly twenty or thirty lifetimes on Earth.

His meeting with his killer, John Parker, had happened and had been under his total control without his awareness of how he had precipitated it. The power to do so had appeared in him, and with it had come the understanding of what to tell Parker. Michael had held council with the many hundreds of souls who had been victims of Parker in his previous stagnant incarnations, again without understanding how he had learned the power to do so, but Michael had negotiated the authority to speak for them when dealing with Parker.

235

He spent much time, as much as time meant anything at all on the Astral Plane, meditating, absorbing the lessons of his last life as Michael Hendricks and considering the implications of the experiences. Sadly, he realized that the potential relationship with his colleague, Julianne Patterson would have been a major experience for both of them but had been cut short by his death. He and Julianne had been close many times before in other lives, and this relationship would have released the considerable capacity for love and caring which was latent in both of them. On several occasions, he called her when she was asleep and spoke to her on the spiritual level.

"My days are sad without you," she said, as she emerged on the Astral Plane while her body slept in her home in Chicago. "I'd been waiting for you to come home from Texas, and I knew you would finally get us together."

"I understand," he said, and stroked her face. Each had taken the bodily form that they had held when Michael was incarnate, and the warmth and love between them was powerful. "I was thinking about you in church the morning I was killed, and feeling so certain that we would start something beautiful."

"And now we have to wait until the next life," she said, sadly. "The rest of this incarnation for me will be lonely."

He shook his head. "No, it needn't be," he said. "There are other men with whom a relationship is possible in this life."

"I know," she agreed, but with sorrow in her voice. "But you and I have been happy in times before. Have you decided what your next life will be? I would like to be part of the decision with you."

He shook his head again. "I had made a decision almost as soon as I came back here," he said. "But something has happened, something incredibly powerful. I have advanced to fourth stage Old Soul and I'm certain it has something to do with the Infinite. It's here now and I think it has something for me to do."

"Do you know what?" she asked. "I've not been able to see anything of the Infinite's effect. Things are so clouded in America now."

"You're still only a Young Soul," he said with love and affection, wrapping his arms around her. "Even so, you're a long way advanced on most souls in America. Things will get worse there, I'm certain, and I want you to leave. Go to Canada and then maybe on to Europe."

"Will you talk to me again?" she asked, grief showing strongly in her face.

He nodded and kissed her. "Regularly and often," he said with a smile. "I love you too much to leave you."

When Julianne Patterson awoke the next morning in Chicago, it was with a sense of deep love and happiness that she was unable to explain. She felt she had been dreaming of Michael Hendricks again, and felt the strong wave of regret at his death seven years earlier. Her current relationship with a man she had met at a client's office was moderately happy, but she felt a constant sense of something missing when she was with him. He was entertaining enough, and well educated, though as a deeply committed supporter of President Horning and his policies, he was not a man to whom she could get too close, mentally and emotionally. She knew that telling him of her reservations carried too great a risk of a summons from the Council, so her relationship was hardly based on trust. But he was sexually proficient, and the age of forty-two, she felt she had too few options left open to her.

By the time she had reached her office in LaSalle Street, however, she had decided things were quite unsatisfactory in her life. Without knowing how, she realized she had been planning for some time to leave America. The country's dramatic change into an autocracy based on religious mania had deeply upset her, she knew. The changes had affected her not just on an emotional level, but on a powerfully personal level too. A recent speech by Horning on TV had been a furious denunciation of the liberal trends of the past fifty years where women were concerned. Horning had shaken spittle over his podium as he claimed that it was outrageous for women to be considered the equal of men.

"It is the will of God," he shouted, waving his hands furiously, "that women should submit to men. Saint Timothy himself wrote that no woman should have dominion over a man! It is an affront to all the laws of God!"

Horning took a deep breath, and resumed the tirade. "For a woman to be in a position of authority over any man is a crime against Heaven and the signs of Satan's power on Earth. I demand that such heresies be cleansed from our country and Satan be given yet another reminder that his filth will not be tolerated here!"

Julianne knew that it would be only a matter of days before her position as a manager would be cancelled, and that she would be demoted to being merely another accountant working in teams that could only be supervised by men. The two female partners in the firm had already quit two years earlier, foreseeing this trend, and Julianne knew that both had crossed the border into Canada before the blockades had been put into place.

That lunchtime, she went to the Citizen's Travel Office and applied for an exit permit for a brief vacation in Canada. She swore three separate oaths on the Bible that she intended to return, and paid over her security deposit of five thousand dollars. Being a certified Christian American with a record of church-going that the Chicago office of the Council for the Protection of God's Name was able to verify, she had only a month to wait for her travel papers.

Mentally writing off her mortgage and the equity in her home, she took the maximum amount of money she could take from her bank and drove her car along the rapidly decaying Interstate 94 to Detroit. After the normal three-hour wait while her car was examined in detail for illicit documents or possessions, and two more oaths sworn on the Bible before cold-faced agents of the Council, she was allowed to pass through the armoured border post, past the line of tanks where the heavy gun barrels pointed at the opposite shoreline, and crossed the Ambassador Bridge into Windsor. There were no customs or immigration checks on the Canadian side.

The tears began flooding down her face as she drove out of the exit lanes from the Bridge, and she hurriedly turned off the road and into the parking lot of a shopping centre. She spent half an hour sitting in her car weeping bitterly before she felt able to continue. She switched on the engine again, steered her way to the 401 Freeway and drove non-stop toward Toronto. After a night in a hotel in Mississauga on the west side of Toronto, she continued into the city and found one of the burgeoning number of employment offices that had grown in response to the new demand for labour by the increasing numbers of companies and the flood of refugees from the United States of America. By the following afternoon, after interviews with the partners of a small accounting firm in the city, she was a manager at a salary well above her Chicago level. She remained bewildered as to why she had made the decision so suddenly, but knew inside herself that it was a correct one.

Michael Hendricks continued to meditate on his rapid spiritual advance, taking no more time to consider his next incarnation. The voice that suddenly spoke to him was soft and sweet, but the vibrations and the colours he read in the aura were massively powerful, more than any soul he had ever encountered, even the final stage Old Souls who occasionally had guided him.

"Be with me, Michael Hendricks," said the wonderful voice from all around him. He left his spiritual state and took the physical form of his old life, shaping the space around him into the warmth and comfort of his old Chicago apartment.

"You are the Infinite," he said, needing no confirmation. He trembled inside himself, not from fear, but from the awareness of the awesome power and wisdom he was sensing and the realization that he had a part to play in solving the problem that had brought the Infinite to Earth.

"You are correct on both points, Michael," said the voice with a small chuckle just audible, and Maragos appeared in front of him. She wore a formal grey business suit, a light blue blouse under the jacket open at the throat, the skirt short enough to display beautiful legs. Rather the way Julianne had dressed, he thought to himself and smiled at Maragos. Despite his awe at knowing what she was, her appearance eased him.

"You have a crucial role to play for us, Michael," she said and sat down in the armchair under the Picasso painting of The Weeping Woman.

He stared at her. "I think I've already been playing it for a time," he said. "My discussions with John Parker, with his victims, and my instructions to Parker to wait before reincarnating again. These things are a part of what you want, aren't they?"

She nodded with a smile. "Michael, you have played the role before," she said. "Think back now, with your new abilities as an Old Soul, and you will remember."

*Over a hundred people were thronging the side of the river, and he was busy. They waded out to where he stood thigh deep in the cold water and he touched their heads until they knelt before him, up their necks.*

*"I baptize you in the name of the Lord and that of the Messiah who comes to us," he said, and pushed their heads under the water for a second. Each of them*

*rose, shivering slightly, but with smiles of joy on their faces. As the line ended for a time, he turned to the crowd on the water's edge.*

*"I command you!" he bellowed. "You must be prepared for Him to come to us! Stand not there like scared children at the market place! Come! Come to me and be baptized! Be cleansed of the sins of the world!"*

*On some faces he could see the grins of derision, the expressions that said old John was as crazy as ever, maybe worse and if he didn't stop his ranting and raving the Authorities would be calling on him. But one man stood out.*

*He was just another man, John thought. No taller, no cleaner, no neater than any of the others on the riverside, his robes no whiter, no less stained from travels than any others. But his face was different. It shone out of the crowd like a lantern from a fog. John began to stride towards the man on the river bank, wading his way furiously through the water which rose like the bow wave of a boat before him.*

*"You!" he cried. "Come to me! Who are you?"*

*The man turned away and moved through the crowd, but not before John saw his eyes. They burned into his soul like the power of all the suns of the universe. Like those he had baptized, John sank to his knees, only his powerful face and raging eyes above the water's surface.*

*When he stood up, the man had gone.*

"I was John the Baptist," he said calmly, as if he had always known it. The sharp, startling visions he had just experienced were like a colour film in his head and he could recall the details perfectly. "My task was to go before and tell of a coming and to prepare people for Jesus."

"There were other, similar roles also," she agreed, "which you will remember in time. And now you have another role, even more crucial. It will be less dramatic than the roles my other small group will play. While I talk to you here on the Astral Plane, I am also talking to them about their parts in the events to come. Will you help us, Michael Hendricks?"

"What question could there possibly be, Maragos, of not helping you?"

"You understand, of course," she replied. "I accelerated your growth to Old Soul so that you would understand what has happened to Humanity. The need for the sick souls to begin incarnating in other species is immediate. Others who wish to do so are also welcome. It will be an extraordinary experience for all of them, and we believe that it will heal you. That is your task, Michael. Shepherd the souls of Mankind into this path and you will play a role greater than any before."

"And what will you and your small group be doing, Maragos?" he asked.

"We will precipitate the end of the world," she said, and stood up, walking towards him. She touched his face lightly, and he felt the contact with the furthest reaches of Infinity. He took her hand, and looked deeply into her eyes, knowing he was truly looking into the face of God, and that God was everything, including himself.

"I am your servant, Maragos," he said, and kissed her cheek softly, sensing his own power growing tenfold as he did.

She laughed a ripple of music and delight. "Be then my good and faithful servant, Michael. Go out and gather souls for the most wonderful task they could perform through eternity."

He moved away from her, feeling a happiness never before experienced.

"I have another memory for you, before I go," she said. "You have served the Higher Souls before Jesus, too. Look into your past, Michael."

*The old Sage, Asita woke early that morning in*

*his home a few leagues south of Savatthi. The sky told, him, the morning sun told him, the dreams of the thirty-three gods playing in the night sky all told him.*

*"The Bodhisattva, the one destined for Enlightenment has come," the old man said, excitement clawing at him. He rose and dressed, made a light breakfast, and called for his chariot and horses. He would travel to Lumbini that day to verify the boy, to see the Eight Signs of Enlightenment on the boy's body and confirm that the new Buddha had come.*

*All day the old man travelled, feeling no fatigue in his excitement, eating only when his driver needed it. They travelled through the land that one day would be called South Behar, west of Bengal and south of the River Ganges, in the country of the Magadhas. That night, they slept by the chariot, and by dawn they were at the park in the city of Lumbini, where a huge curtained enclosure had been erected for Suddhodana, the wealthy and noble leader of the high Kshatriya-caste family. Suddhodana and his wife had been travelling when the signs of the birth had been clear, and they had stopped in Lumbini.*

*Recognizing the old Sage, the servants carried word of Asita's arrival to Suddhodana and he was granted entrance.*

*"I would see your son, Prince Suddhodana," said Asita.*

*"Why, old man?" asked the Prince, disturbed but excited by the famed prophet's arrival and imperious demand. Was his son the new Buddha, the one destined for Enlightenment, born from the country of the Gods and descended into the womb of Maya, his wife?*

*"I must see the Eight Signs," said the Sage.*

*Suddhodana gestured at his servant, and the two men waited in the cool of the curtained area. In a few moments, the servants reappeared, carrying the small bundle. They laid it on a mat placed on the ground, and Asita painfully and slowly lowered himself to his haunches. He carefully removed the child's covering and examined him intently. Then he climbed back to his feet, feeling a mixture of happiness and grief.*

*"The boy is the Bodhisattva, Prince Suddhodana,"* he said. *"He is the one destined to be the Buddha, the Enlightened One."*

*"Then why your sadness, old man?" asked the Prince.*

*"Because I know that I will not live to see him become the Bhagara, the Lord," replied Asita. "My time is very short. And also because it is written that the mother of the Bodhisattva, having given birth, being pure of spirit and mind, will die within seven days."*

*The Prince's face paled. "Maya must die?" he whispered.*

*"It is written," said Asita the Sage. He turned and left the presence of the Kshatriya Prince. Asita, the Sage who had foretold the coming of the Buddha, would now die in peace. Over five hundred years later, the soul who had been Asita would be John the Baptist, forerunner of Jesus of Nazareth and nearly two thousand years after that, Michael Hendricks, gatherer of souls for the healing of Mankind.*

Michael Hendricks laughed with a joy he had never before experienced.

"It is a glorious task, my friend," said Maragos. "As is mine, and that of the others who work with me. And remember, Michael," she added. "Eternity depends on us all completing our tasks."

She vanished, and he let the room dissolve again.

The soul that had been Michael Hendricks began work on the greatest mission any immortal being could imagine, to bring about the rebirth of God.

* * *

"I had to do the same thing with Philippe," said Maragos with a small laugh, and touched Jacqueline on the shoulder. "It really isn't necessary you know. We are both parts of the same reality."

"It doesn't feel like it," whispered Jacqueline, rising to her feet, but with her legs trembling violently. This was far worse than the attack of sickness she had felt when she had heard the Merlin engines at the airshow in England.

"But it truly is," Maragos insisted. "And soon you will understand that."

Philippe put his arm round Jacqueline. "You only went to your knees," he said, smiling at her. "I went flat on my face!"

The simple, conversational words brought her to some sense of normality, and Jacqueline's trembling eased. She looked at Maragos again and realized that Philippe had been right. They were alike. Perhaps a deliberate move by Maragos? She felt so.

"Partially," said Maragos with a smile. Even forewarned by Philippe's own ability to hear her unspoken thoughts, Jacqueline still felt shaken to find Maragos doing it.

"My appearance was carefully selected for the maximum impact of what we must do later," continued Maragos.

"And what is that?" asked Raoul Carmagio. He too had controlled his physical appearance and now looked more like a fit man in his late thirties. The chubby shape had gone and powerful wisdom shone from his eyes.

"We go to America, of course," replied Maragos. "We must heal, that is our function, and the greatest healing must be done where the greatest concentration of sickness lies."

"Immediately?" Philippe Leger looked uncertain. Within himself he felt that not all the spiritual developments necessary for that task had been completed. Maragos smiled at him.

"No, Philippe. As you say, you all have some growth to accomplish first." She laughed lightly. "But we will do what any good show-business act will do. We will rehearse our performance in the provinces before hitting Broadway!"

"But what do we do about the souls who must reincarnate into other species?" asked Philippe when the small laughter had died down. He picked up Jacqueline's bag and started to move towards the stairs.

"I am just talking with another soul who will help us with that task," said Maragos.

"Just now?" Carmagio looked puzzled. "We have been talking together for the last two hours before Jacqueline arrived."

"Do you think I am present at just one place at any time?" Maragos replied gently. "This presence you see is only a tiny part of me. While we stand here, I am also discussing our plan with the soul of a man killed a few years ago when my presence began to cause the more advanced souls amongst you to discover Oneness." She looked around the three of them and smiled at their expressions. "I am also communicating with the Infinite Souls of three other species," she continued. "Even though they have not actually reached that stage. And I am trying once more to talk with the soul of Humanity, but still getting little but madness."

"How can you talk with an Infinite Soul if it has not merged yet?" asked Philippe. He was leaning against the stair rail, two steps up, his intent to take Jacqueline to his room forgotten for the moment.

"The Soul still has an identity, even though it is not aware of itself," Maragos said. "It is the same way in which The One is signifying its readiness for Oneness again even though it does not have full self-awareness. The identity can be contacted, much like a person in deep hypnosis can communicate through the sub-conscious."

"And you can manifest yourself on several levels at the same time?" asked Jacqueline.

"Indeed I can," replied Maragos. "The presence here is but a fraction of this Infinite Soul."

"And you are self-aware at all levels?" asked Raoul curiously. "Each presence can act independently of the others?"

"I am, and it can," replied Maragos. "One day you will comprehend how this occurs."

A little shaken by the power indicated by this statement, Jacqueline and Philippe went up the stairs to their room. Raoul opened the door for Maragos to return with him to the library where they had been discussing and reliving some of Raoul's first incarnations, just as Philippe had done with Maragos when she had first arrived.

# Chapter 12. Flights of Fallen Angels

John Donald Parker sat stiffly on a chair in the centre of a poorly decorated room. Ill-matching furniture sat round walls of a faint green colour, and a thick, but dirty grey carpet covered the floor. There were no windows. It was a room that fitted a man with no taste in colour, style or art, which was exactly the man John Parker had been in life.

He retained his earthly bodily form too, not yet confident enough to adapt to the Astral Plane and let the environment look after itself. Without being aware of how he did it, he maintained a physical lifestyle much like the one he had left under a hail of bullets.

He stared harshly at two other men huddled in almost foetal pose on the other armchairs. George Rolfe was sobbing into his knees, wailing like a child that has just been spanked. He hid his face and his whole body shook with the spasms of anguish and terror that shook him. Henry Acheson simply vibrated with the force of his trembling, rocking back and forth on his seat, his hands over his eyes.

Both men retained the same body shapes they had possessed on Earth. Rolfe was tall and thin, narrow-set eyes under dark, oily hair. Acheson was averagely built, with no memorable features at all, the sort of man forgotten once he has turned away.

"You did it to yourselves," said Parker once more. He had been trying to talk sense into his one-time friends and partners in the Army of God's Agents as they had called themselves when they were alive in

Bainesville, Texas. "Your minds created your worst images of Hell as a punishment for what you knew you had done."

"It's not fair!" gasped Rolfe through his sobs. "I've been a true Christian all my life! I love God! All I did was protect the Church from those slimy liberals! When I get out of here, I'm going to kill those Army bastards!"

"You don't get it, do you?" laughed Parker with contempt. "You're DEAD! You're never going back! Not as George Rolfe, anyway. You've been to Hell and now you're back on the Astral Plane where you started."

"NO! NO! I'm not dead! I can't be dead! I'd be in Heaven if I was dead!" Rolfe lifted his head and stared wildly at Parker, stamping his feet on the floor as he spoke, like an irate child in a tantrum.

"You're a disaster, Rolfe!" said Parker with a sneer. "I thought I was bad enough, but you've lived a hundred and six lives and you're not even past the first-stage Infant level!" He stopped and wondered how he knew that, but certain that he was correct. Perhaps he was adjusting to the Astral Plane a little, he thought, and learning some of the techniques of the older souls. Both the men collapsed back into their huddled state.

"Listen, you stupid bastards!" raged Parker. "You remember getting shot by machine guns? Who could survive that? Then you both appear here, obviously having gone through some hell or another. What do you think could have happened? What did you go through, Rolfe?"

"I woke up lying in front of a huge throne," gasped Rolfe, struggling to contain his sobs. "I couldn't see to the top of it, but this huge voice screamed at me for breaking his commandments."

Parker nodded. "Yeah, I got much the same thing," he said. "It was like the stories old Mother Houlihan used to teach us in Sunday School when we were kids. Then I suppose the devils came and got you?"

On his chair, Acheson had calmed down and was listening intently.

Parker turned his head to him. "The same sort of thing for you too, eh?"

Acheson nodded, and leaned back in the armchair, the trembling mostly under control.

"Yes, six of them." Rolfe sniffed and wiped his eyes. "I was flown down a huge pit and dropped into the flames. I just burned and burned...." For a few more seconds, his eyes filled with tears and his face pulled into a grimace of pain. "God knows how long it went on for, but eventually I blacked out, then I woke up and found myself here..." He suddenly looked around the dull room and stared at Parker. "Where the hell are we, then?" he demanded.

Parker grinned without humour. "Not in hell, that's for sure!" he replied. "You'll start to remember soon enough. You're on the Astral Plane. We come here when we die, and we leave here to go back to another incarnation."

"That is correct!" echoed a strong voice from all round the room. Rolfe and Acheson screamed and flung their heads onto their knees again as if trying to dig their way under the carpet. Parker sat back in his chair at last and relaxed. He knew the voice. Michael Hendricks materialized, standing in the middle of the room. He looked around with a dismayed expression then concentrated on Parker.

"They're even younger than you," he said with a small smile.

Parker scowled. "I know," he muttered. "Don't rub it in any further. Why are you here again?"

"I need to do something about this room," said Michael, ignoring the question, and the surroundings altered soundlessly. Cream walls now, the carpet a gentle dove grey. Picture windows looked out onto a lake with weeping willows down one side and flocks of waterfowl sailing on the surface. Another pair of paintings on the wall, one a Miro bursting with joyous colours, the other a painting of a young girl with her back to a mirror, so that she appeared twice. She was sitting sideways in the chair, her elbow on the back, her left cheek in her hand. Her expression was one of gentle calm, yet a little sad and lonely.

"Sybil Before the Mirror," said Michael, as all three men started upright, thunderstruck by the change.

"What?" snapped Parker, not comprehending. Michael pointed at the second painting. All three men followed his finger and looked back at him, completely without any shadow of understanding.

"It's a painting," said Michael gently. "It's in the Museum of Modern Art in Brussels."

"I don't think they know you," said Parker, almost with a grin.

"I do!" snapped Acheson. "That's the guy you shot outside the church!"

"Correct, gentlemen," replied Michael.

Acheson collapsed back in his seat. "Now I know we're dead," he whispered. Rolfe had also looked up to stare at Michael and he nodded agreement.

"Concentrate, all three of you," said Michael. "Look at me, and concentrate on your thoughts. I'm going to advance you several soul stages. Be with me..."

The tableau in the room held for what seemed to Parker like several minutes. They stared at Michael's eyes, and slowly lost themselves in their depths. Hendricks' pupils seemed to swell to giant proportions, and the glow in them was like a searchlight. When it faded, all three of the newly dead sighed deeply.

"Now I understand," murmured Rolfe. "We've lived all these lives and never progressed."

"What you have just done is advance to the seventh stage of Infant Soul age," said Michael. "It's still way behind where you should have been by now, but it was as far as I could take you. The sickness is very strong in all three of you."

"You said the last time that we would not reincarnate again," said Parker. He had gained some confidence since his last meeting with Michael, perhaps from the realization that an alternative plan was being developed. The presence of the Infinite was obviously a key to the whole thing, he knew.

"You're right, John. She's the key," said Michael with a smile, and Parker sat back in dismay. Having his thoughts read was frightening to him.

"As we agreed last time," continued Michael, "you will not incarnate on Earth again. Not for a long time, anyway. Nothing is to be gained from that. But I want to suggest something to you."

"What?" All three men leaned forward. Their new awareness of what had happened to them had also made them realize their sickness, and Michael's words were like an opening offered by a judge when about to sentence a criminal.

"Healing will come if enough human souls reincarnate in other species instead of humans," said Michael. He was watching the three men, reading their confusion, hopes and dismay gushing from them like the boiling waters from a dam outlet. After his words, their main emotion was one of bewilderment. They didn't understand.

"There are a million intelligent species in the universe that make up The One," said Michael. "We are just one of them. All the others have advanced nearly to the end of their incarnation cycle, some beyond it. But a few remain with a few thousand years of the cycle still to complete. I want you to be born among them."

Parker shook his head in confusion. "You mean we will be born on some other planet as some other species?"

"That's exactly what I mean," replied Michael.

"But what will that do?" asked Rolfe. His face reflected the same fear that Michael could read in his mind.

"It will be like a sick man entering a hospital," replied Michael. "You will be healed simply by living a few lives with a healthy species of advanced spiritual age. When you have finished the life, maybe several lives, you will bring back with you some of the healing powers to spread among the rest. If enough of you do it, Humanity may heal itself."

"I don't want to," muttered Rolfe. "I'm scared."

"Let me tell you something," said Michael. His voice had a snap to it that hauled the attention of the three men from their fear and back to him.

"You, Henry Acheson," said Michael, pointing at the forgettable face of the third of the murderous group who had killed him with such glee. "In the ninety-seven lives you have led before, you have killed two hundred and thirty people, many of them children. You were a slave trader, many times a priest of one sort or another and always a bigot."

He turned to the figure of Rolfe, who looked back with fear in his face. "And you, George Rolfe. A wonderful total of only seven murders in your last year on Earth, but fifteen before that, all of black men and women. In your previous lives you were a coward in war, a cheat in business, a bully as a teacher, and like your friends, always a murderous bigot. Four hundred and eleven people have died under your hands in your lifetimes."

As he spoke, the memories of these lives flooded into the minds of the two men. Parker, who had already experienced the dreadful agony of remembrance of his former evil had no sympathy for them.

"And of course, John," continued Michael, turning his eyes on Parker. "You and I have already noted the seven hundred and seventy-three souls whose lives you cut short. A grand total of one thousand, four hundred and fourteen lives destroyed by the three of you over your useless, stagnant, vicious lifetimes as humans. Powerful Karmic debts owed to all of them. Do you think you have any alternative but to obey the wishes of those souls and burn your debts in this way?"

The room rang with silence, though Michael could read the thoughts of the others as clearly as if they were shouted out loud. At the same time, he sensed the combined thoughts of the fourteen hundred or more souls who had tuned in and were applying unseen pressure on the minds of the three seated men.

Parker was the first to break the silence. "Where would we be?" he asked. *"What* would we be?"

The other two looked up. In their minds, Michael read the fear but also the decision to follow the Karmic path set for them.

"There is a race that lives in this galaxy," said Michael. "They are one of very few other species that came this far from the central galaxies, and they settled in a spiral arm just about the opposite side of the galaxy from us. They are humanoid, technologically advanced and space travellers. Most of them are now Old Souls and many have merged into Ascendant Souls. But enough remain at the Mature Soul stage for some lifetimes still to be led on their planet."

"And you want us to incarnate as one of these?" Rolfe spoke quietly from his seat, but Michael could see that the determination was firming in him.

"Not just me," replied Michael. "The many hundreds you killed, and in fact, all of humanity needs you to do it."

Parker took a deep breath and spoke. "I'll do it," he said. He was echoed immediately by Rolfe. All three of them looked at Acheson, who stared at the floor.

"We have to, Henry," said Parker. "There's no other way."

"I'm scared," said Acheson.

"We're all scared, man!" burst out Rolfe. "But look at what we've done in our lives! Nothing! It's the only way to make up a bit."

"I was a good Christian," muttered Acheson. "I shouldn't have to do this."

Parker stood up and went over to Acheson. He leaned over him and gripped his shoulders. "We were all good Christians, Henry," he said, "or so we thought. And look what we did! Being a good Christian didn't amount to a hill of coonshit, man, not the way we did it! We were wrong, damn you Henry, wrong! And we're sick! We have to do it."

"No," Acheson said, and hid his face in his hands.

Parker took his hair and pulled Acheson's head up so that he stared into Parker's eyes. "You'll do it, Henry," he whispered. "Because if you don't, I'll hunt you down any time you incarnate again and I'll kill you the worst way I can. I don't care where you'll be or what you'll be, I'll find you and I'll cut you to pieces. And I'll keep on doing it, regardless of what it does to me and my chances of ever growing. Got it, Henry?"

Acheson's eyes were round with fear. Despite the pressure on his head, he nodded. "Okay, John," he whispered. "I'll do it."

"Good," said Michael Hendricks, and disappeared. Immediately, the beautiful room he had created dissolved, and with it went the three men, blown into the infinite darkness they had to travel to reach the world of their next incarnations.

* * *

Early morning in Valence.

All four of the residents of the lovely old house that had sheltered and nurtured the Legers for over two hundred years were up and about early. Whether Maragos slept was a matter of semantics. Certainly she retired to her room and nothing was heard again until morning. When asked, Maragos said that she still needed time to meditate and absorb the remaining souls that comprised her being. She was the first in the kitchen that day, a little after dawn, as if expecting unusual events.

Something was happening.

Philippe Leger and Jacqueline Carter woke together and smiled at each other. They had slept with total familiarity with each other, as married couples do after twenty years. This morning, they had sensed the power of external presences, and ended the exploration of past lives they had been conducting together on the Astral Plane.

Something was happening.

Raoul Carmagio also woke early in response to the same sensations. He too, had been exploring past incarnations, sensing the guidance of Maragos as his soul grew and aged as she fed him experience and wisdom that would not otherwise have been gained in less that thirty earthly incarnations.

Something was happening.

They breakfasted in the old kitchen, sitting at the ancient wooden table and dining on fresh bread and fruit, with aromatic coffee. They were silent on this strange morning, uncertain, edgy. The view outside the window showed only the trees of the small garden, the high hedges shielding them from the outside world. Only Maragos ate peacefully, seemingly unaware of the tension in the room.

"Maragos, I can feel the pressure, but what is it?" Leger asked, breaking the silence. It was six-thirty.

"The world knows about me," said Maragos, and took another bite of the crusty farm loaf loaded with butter and raspberry jam.

"Didn't they before this?" asked Raoul. He had managed only coffee and orange juice this strange morning, unusual compared to his normal healthy intake of the bread and fruit.

"Only in patches," replied Maragos. "They sensed me, but it varied in degree. Now the whole world knows fully, except for those so frightened that they will continue to deny me for another few years."

"And what will happen now?" asked Jacqueline.

Maragos was about to reply, but her expression suddenly filled with grief and pain. "It just did," she whispered, and tears filled her beautiful, terrifying, infinity-reflecting eyes.

"What?" demanded Leger. Maragos' pain was so enormous, that the room filled with fear.

"The warring nations are dead," murmured

Maragos, and hid her face in her hands. "All of them. They have just released nuclear weapons on each other. The sands have turned to glass, the cities are holes in the ground and all of them are dead."

Jacqueline rose slowly to her feet and turned on the radio by the fridge, but already they had sensed what Maragos had experienced. The massive shockwave of pain and death raced through their minds and left them feeling sick and dizzy.

"This is the World News of the BBC," said the small voice from the radio. "Nuclear devices exploded over Baghdad, Tehran and Damascus a few moments ago, as well as over the battle fronts and other cities. Measurements indicate at least twelve devices were used, all over twenty kilotons. We believe that nobody is left alive in the war zone."

Jacqueline turned the radio off.

"The radiation will fall out all over Europe," whispered Raoul. "Perhaps everyone will be dead in a few weeks."

Maragos raised her face from her hands and shook her head. "No, I will not allow that," she said. "The radiation will stay within the region it destroyed and will not leak out."

The room was silent. The enormity of the event fought with the awe at the power she had just indicated so casually.

Maragos rose to her feet. "We should go outside," she said softly. "Come, walk with me."

The others rose also and followed her out of the kitchen and into the vast, beautiful lobby of the old home. The strangeness was around them. The sounds of the farms around had not intruded. No cocks crowed, no dogs barked as they brought in the cows for milking. No cars had been heard on the road only a short distance away. The silence was like a blanket. Only the power of the presence surrounding them was real.

Maragos led the way to the front door and opened it. All of them walked out and stopped short.

The fields around the house were full. Thousands and thousands of faces looked at them. People lined the edge of the field and the crowd continued over the other side of the road. The small hill to the south was crammed with humanity. *So many thousands of people,* thought Jacqueline. They must have been gathering during the night, without a sound. There could be half a million here. She turned and looked around her, her chest filled with the emotions she was sensing from every direction.

Men, women, children. Old people, young people. Farmers from the local villages, people from the city in expensive clothing. All of them simply stood, looking at her. She looked at the faces as far as she could, and saw on all of them, excitement, longing, on some, tears of happiness. The love that rose from the crowd enveloped the house, the fields and the four people who stood on the front steps.

From nowhere, from everywhere, a single voice uttered just one word, not loud, but blanketing the whole world.

"Maragos!" said the voice of half a million people, and fell silent.

The silence echoed round the fields and the small hills of the country round the house of Philippe Leger. Maragos stepped forward to the top of the steps and looked round the half million faces gathered before her.

"I am with you," she said softly, but every person in the throng heard her clearly, whether they spoke English, French or any other language, they heard and understood the words of the Infinite. "I am with you till Oneness."

The tiniest stir of movement went through the crowd, like a small breeze racing over the top of a field of tall grass.

"The way will not be easy," continued Maragos. "Humanity has been ill for many hundred of thousands of years now, and those that came before me were not able to heal you. Those of you that have come to us today show that already my presence has begun the process, but this alone will not complete it."

A sigh ran through the sea of humanity before her like the small breath of a sleeping child.

"Already you have learned the power of Oneness," said Maragos. "You were able to contain the insanity of the millions of Infant Souls in the Middle East to their own territories. Now that they have burned themselves in their own final conflagration, I will ensure that nothing of that madness seeps into your lands. But you have seen what many minds can achieve, both for good and for evil."

She stopped for a moment, and the silence echoed like thunder in the mountains.

"Many times in your history, the sickness has taken on a virulent form, concentrated in small areas," she continued, still speaking softly, but obviously audible to the furthest people on the hillside. "The small form of Oneness showed its dark side, and then dissipated like a disease that hides itself from the medicine until another opportunity arrives to infect the soul of Mankind. That opportunity has shown itself, and soon we will go to America to continue our work."

The silence continued in the hills and fields, and Maragos smiled at them. "I will stay with you until Oneness comes, though it will be many lifetimes before that happens. This world will change a great deal in that time, and you will all learn and grow with it."

She started to move back from the steps and raised her arms. "Go home now," she said. "Our work will start this day."

She led the way back into the house, and all around, the bustle of half a million people beginning to move broke in and fluttered round the rooms like starlings in springtime. By noon, they had gone.

* * *

Philippe Leger was time-tripping. Like all of them who had acquired Old Soul stature, he had slowly grown aware of his memory of all his past lives and his ability to relive moments of them as clearly as if he were there. Maragos had said that such revisiting of years and centuries passed was an essential part of the preparation for the transition beyond the cycle of reincarnations. The soul had to explore every moment of its previous lives and search for meaning, for indications, for learning, anything that one day might meld into the thoughts and memories of countless billions of other souls and give a new thought to The One and Its question - *How do I live alone throughout Eternity?* Philippe Leger was two thousand years in the past.

Benjamin ben Isaac approached the prison cautiously. One never knew with the Romans. He felt a small spasm of fear eat its way up from his guts to his mouth and he swallowed the sour taste again with a convulsive shudder. But he had come well-prepared.

The guard at the main gate was happy to let him through on payment of a skin of red wine, and the officer in the interior guardhouse did no more than slap him around before accepting the two chickens and the leg of lamb. Wiping the dust from his legs and shoulders where he had fallen from the blows, Benjamin followed the Roman officer across the sand of the parade square to the door of the prison cellblock. Without a word, the officer left. A second later, the door opened. Startled, Benjamin recognized the Centurion who had led a squad into Benjamin's home town after the slaughter, and who had been turned away by Jesus. Jesus had said then that they would deal with each other again. How had he known? Benjamin wondered. The Centurion barely looked at him and led him down the dark corridors of the cellblocks and was finally halted outside a barred door.

"I have to search you," said the Roman. He showed

obvious discomfort at having to touch this Jew, and he moved away quickly to wash his hands, leaving the young soldier who had accompanied him to open the door and let Benjamin enter the gloom of the cell.

"I knew you would come, Benjamin, son of Isaac," said the soft voice from the corner. Jesus sat up on his straw mattress and leaned back against the stone wall.

"I had to, Rabbi," Benjamin stammered. He was frightened by the surroundings and by the nearness of those unpredictable Romans, who might just decide Benjamin was another troublemaker and keep him here.

"Do not fear, Benjamin," said the soft voice. "They will not keep you."

Startled, Benjamin dropped the two apples he had pulled from his robe to give to Jesus. "How did you know my fear, Teacher?" he asked, picking up the apples and wiping them on his gown to hand to the seated man. Jesus took one and bit into it with hunger.

"You spoke it loudly, my friend," said Jesus, and spat out an apple seed. "I can hear your words, even if sometimes you do not speak them."

Benjamin was silent for a moment, thinking of the implications of that statement. "They say you are the Son of God, Lord," he said finally, worried what answer his words might get.

Jesus smiled and turned his astounding eyes to Benjamin. Even in the dark of the confined space, those eyes reflected power like the tramping of all the Roman armies over the whole world. The energy could have burned the walls down, Benjamin felt.

"The Son of God?" said Jesus. "But what is God, Benjamin? Do you really know?"

"How can one know the Unknowable, Teacher?" replied Benjamin, puzzled by the reply.

"By knowing yourself, son of man," came the confusing answer.

Benjamin was sensing the same frustration he had felt before when he had first spoken with Jesus. "I am clearly not yet ready to catch the birds above my head that those other men in other Houses of God have passed," he said, a small smile on his face.

Jesus saw the smile and responded. "You are nearer than you know," he said. "But I think you did not come here to discuss catching birds."

Benjamin sat down on the floor of the cell and crossed his legs. "Rabbi," he said. "I see the power in you. I have seen you turn away a squad of armed soldiers. I have seen the people follow you. Why do you stay here in this cell? I am certain you could walk from here with me if you wished."

Jesus stared hard at Benjamin, and the man on the floor almost felt the soul burn away from within himself. When Jesus turned his face to the tiny grille in the wall, Benjamin found himself able to breathe again. He watched the shadows play on the figure of Jesus, sensing that the power of the man was so vast that he could push the walls down with a light touch. The cell stones around them were as insubstantial as pencil strokes next to the man called by some the Saviour.

"The work is not done if I walk away from here and from what will happen to me," Jesus said. "The life of one man is not worth that."

"But it is *your* life!" cried Benjamin. "Lord, they plan to crucify you!"

"I know," replied Jesus. "They must. And they must see it done."

"But it is your life," said Benjamin again. He was horrified by the implacability of Jesus' words.

"We live many lives, Benjamin, Son of Man," said Jesus and resumed his eating of the apple. "You shall live the lives of men, of women, of rich and of poor, of the mighty and the low, and thus in time shall you learn the first truth of Man."

"The first truth, Lord?" asked Benjamin, awed by the words Jesus had spoken. "What is that? And are there subsequent truths?"

"The first truth is of the nature of man," said Jesus.

"The others, you are not ready to know until you have flown above those birds that you cannot yet catch."

"I will surely die before I learn that truth, Rabbi," said Benjamin, struggling to understand what Jesus was telling him. "And in my weakness, God may judge me unfit and send me to Hell. How then can I catch those birds and pass them?"

Jesus turned back to Benjamin with a youthful grin. "Only when you die will you live," he continued. "And when you die, then will you make judgement on yourself. Your decision will only be yours. Nobody can send you to Hell except yourself, for there is no Hell except that which you create with your own mind."

Benjamin shook his head in awful pain and frustration. "Lord, we talk here of other lives, and we have talked about other Houses of God," he said, struggling to control the tears in his throat. "Perhaps, like the Greeks, we could sit all night and debate these matters, but in a few days they will take you and crucify you. Why won't you leave?" The tears rose to his eyes.

"Benjamin, I say to you, it must happen," replied Jesus. "Look at the hatred around us. Look at the fear. Do you think anything will change if I walk away from this place and go and live the life of a hermit somewhere? What would I accomplish?"

"At least you will be alive, Rabbi," said Benjamin, still struggling with the tears.

"I will still be alive, my friend," said Jesus, and stood up. "I will just be elsewhere."

"With your Father in Heaven?" asked Benjamin.

"In another House of God, yes, Benjamin." Jesus stretched out his hand and Benjamin took it. Without knowing how, he was on his feet next to the Rabbi. "Have no fear for me," said Jesus. "Instead, have fear for Man, for you have lost the way to Oneness. Hope and trust that my death will set you back on that path."

"How will it do that, Lord?" asked Benjamin.

"Enough minds of men must be hurt by this event that they will decide that the times must change," replied Jesus. "The power of many minds is beyond belief, Benjamin. If enough minds believe, man will fly above those birds you seek. Enough minds believing will send the Romans from your land, close the gates behind them, move the stars in their courses, and take you to visit those far lands of God's other Houses."

"Is there nothing I can do?" asked Benjamin, almost stammering with his grief.

"You have already chosen your way, Benjamin," said Jesus. "Stay on the path, work with those that may follow me, and you shall see the truth."

"Those that follow you, Lord? Will others come, teachers like yourself?"

"If I cannot set Man back on the path to Oneness, then others must surely come after me," replied Jesus. "Teachers like myself, possibly. But if others must come, then they will be greater than I and also be healers to show the Children of Man how to find the path for themselves."

"You never answered my question, Teacher," said Benjamin, knowing this would be the last time they would talk together. "Are you the Son of God as they say?"

"The answer is simple," replied Jesus and smiled again. "Yes, I am the Son of God." Benjamin gasped and sank to his knees. "But so are you, my friend," continued Jesus, and again raised Benjamin to his feet. "And so too, are you the Father, just as I am. We are all part of The One, both creator and created."

"It is above me again, Lord," said Benjamin. The cell door opened with a clashing of keys, and Benjamin moved back into the corridor.

"It will not always be so," replied Jesus, and the door was slammed between them. "One day, you will look down from a great height on those birds you seek," he said through the tiny grille in the door then even that was closed, locking Benjamin away from the face of the Rabbi.

Benjamin, son of Isaac of Menon walked from the

prison to find his way home and write the words he had spoken with Jesus. Philippe Leger opened his eyes to find tears streaming down his cheeks.

"Philippe, what is it?" asked Jacqueline, and sat beside him on the couch where he had taken his place two hours ago. She wrapped her arms round him and kissed his wet cheeks.

"I think I understand what Maragos must do," he said, gasping words out through the lump of sadness in his throat.

"We knew when we met on the Astral Plane that first night," she said, her voice soft and compassionate. "Don't you remember? I said then that we would die in America."

Philippe took her hand and let his head rest on her shoulder. For a moment, for all his powerful spirit, he simply needed his love of six thousand years to comfort him.

* * *

"I'm fascinated by the concepts of alien intelligences," said Jacqueline as they sat round the wooden table in the kitchen that night. The evening discussions had become a routine, though not one that bored any of them. There was so much to know.

"Alien?" asked Maragos with a raised eyebrow, and Jacqueline smiled at the expression. Philippe felt a pang as he saw how alike the two women were, and received a quick glance of affection as both of them sensed his emotion. He smiled back and smothered the confusion.

"I know it's the wrong word," replied Jacqueline, "but it's become the standard term over the years for intelligences from outside of Earth. Can you tell us about some of them?"

"Of course," said Maragos. "Any one in particular?"

"How about your own species?" said Raoul. He was sniffing gently at a glass of claret that Philippe had poured from an elderly bottle the two men had found deep in the cellars of the Leger mansion house. The others were drinking the same, except for Maragos who had declared a liking for cognac and had made inroads into Philippe's stock.

"We selected a high-gravity world," said Maragos and took a sip of the brandy. "It's the fifth planet out from a sun with eight other satellites. Gravity is about a quarter again that of Earth and we slowly developed an animal with the strength to cope with the pressure."

"Developed?" The question came from Leger.

Maragos looked at him and nodded. "In a sense, both your Creation Theory followers and the Evolutionists are correct. When The One set off the Big Bang that started the formation of the galaxies, the suns and the planets, It initiated factors that would create animal and vegetable life under certain conditions. I watched a number of planets form around several suns, to see what would develop, and four of them generated animal life that could eventually be modified to carry ensouled intelligence. But it was a random process, and creatures evolved over millions of years, just as your scientific community has taught. Only when a suitable form had appeared, would an Infinite Soul begin to influence further development, and in a sense, "create" an intelligent animal. The Story of Genesis in your Christian Bible actually indicates that, but nobody has caught on."

"Genesis does?" Philippe Leger was startled. "In all my training I don't think I've seen any sign of that."

"Because you had no idea what it meant," said Maragos. "But remember how the Bible says that 'the earth brought forth the animals' or words of that meaning depending on the translation taken. But it says that 'God created man,' a different emphasis. It wasn't God however, but the next best thing, the Infinite Soul of Humanity that created man in the sense I mentioned earlier, by selecting and then developing further a life form into which the human souls would be born."

Leger was thunderstruck. "But how did the writers know? Who wrote that?"

"Men and women like yourselves," replied Maragos. "But people a lot nearer the beginning, and still with the spiritual memories of the Human Infinite within them. The language was the nearest way they had to describe what they felt inside was the truth. A pity that the churches corrupted that truth. But that's the nature of the sickness."

Philippe stayed silent for several minutes, absorbing this information. "So do animals have souls?" he asked, lifting his eyes from the table again. "It's been a major thorn in many people's sides over the centuries." He waited for the answer with fascination. He had held for many years to the official church doctrine that only humans had souls, but had worried about that stance since his awareness of Oneness.

"Not directly," replied Maragos. "Their life force comes from the ensouled species. We generate it and maintain it, and in most ways, they are us and we are them. So while you could never incarnate as an animal, enough energy flows between us that many people believe they have memories of lives as animals. Some creeds believe it also, but it's an incorrect belief. No soul has ever incarnated as an animal. Any memories you might have of being an animal result from the cross flow of life forces."

A moment of silence stilled the table as each of them absorbed the knowledge in their own way.

"So what happens?" asked Raoul. "Life does result of its own accord where the conditions are possible, but the mind comes from us?"

Maragos nodded. "I watched the first cells develop," she said, her eyes distant as she looked back at a time impossible millions of years ago. "I saw the growth into animate forms and I sensed my own energies flowing into these creatures. Eventually, the forms on Shuramee developed in a way that seemed possible for intelligence bearing and I began to direct the development. When the time was right, I began to cast off the Ascendants who then cast off the individual souls, and the cycle began."

"So life is spontaneous, evolutionary and also created?" asked Jacqueline with a grin. "That would confuse the fundamentalists!"

"And the scientists!" added Raoul. "They've both been right and wrong all this time!"

Leger was thoughtful. "And at some stage, you decided that these animals were enough developed for your souls to begin to inhabit them?" he asked.

Maragos nodded. "At a quite primitive stage, I may add," she said. "Much as you did. Human souls began to inhabit primitive man soon after they evolved into social creatures walking upright. That was on your first planet, some four hundred thousand years ago."

"And we came to Earth still in that form?" asked Jacqueline. "As Neanderthal Man?"

"Yes, you did," replied Maragos. "Just two hundred thousand years ago. But during the trip, enough of your collective human mind was working to decide to develop the design. The Neanderthal form was not appropriate for the slightly lower gravity of Earth, or the terraforming that you did with our assistance. A hundred thousand years after getting here, Humanity developed one tribe of Neanderthals into Cro-Magnon Man over several generations, and gradually let the Neanderthal species die out."

"So they did co-exist in time?" asked Raoul. "I believe that historians have argued that point since the discoveries of the two breeds."

"For many years," replied Maragos. "The first true Cro-Magnon tribe existed ninety thousand years ago, though the only remains so far discovered date from less than forty thousand years ago. The last Neanderthal died out twenty thousand years after Cro-Magnon appeared. Philippe has inhabited both forms in his earliest incarnations, Jacqueline and Raoul only took their first incarnations in later years."

The silence round the table was deep. Although all of them had learned to time-trip through their earlier lives, none of them had explored this far back.

Leger broke the silence. "We were asking about your species, Maragos," he said with a grin. "You let us get sidetracked again."

Maragos smiled, and indicated her glass. Philippe poured some more of the eighty-year-old cognac into her balloon glass, while Raoul did the same with the claret for all the others.

"My species was generally between seven and eight feet tall, compared to your average five to six foot," she said. "We were shaped much more like your early Neanderthal Man, and obviously very powerful to withstand the gravity. Our early history for the first million years was much like yours, too. Hunting, agrarian civilization, tribal organizations, very low technology. My philosophy was to develop mental powers, much like we would have at the Infinite stage, but that was simply one of many choices the Infinite Souls made."

She looked round the table, and the other three were paying her their total attention. Glasses of wine were forgotten. "After that period of a million or so years, there was a small surge of technological development," she said. "The wheel was invented, small carts were designed and built and we started to use a four-legged animal as a beast of labour, just as you did on Earth. But it was against the overwhelming philosophical mandates I had laid down when I broke off into smaller entities and then individual souls. Quite a lengthy and bloody series of tribal wars broke out over that problem before the agreement was reached to begin mental development."

"Consciously?" asked Leger with curiosity.

Maragos shook her head. "Oh no!" she said. "The losers, if one could call them that, sulked horribly for centuries. The mandate was expressed as a philosophical and religious force that encouraged meditation, not unlike some of your religions here, such as Buddhism. People gradually began to learn the technique of tapping into the total force that was my complete entity, and thus had many of the powers of The One."

"The power of God, in fact?" said Raoul.

"Effectively, yes," agreed Maragos. "And what we slowly learned, was that many minds could combine to strengthen the effect. An early awareness of Oneness."

"It's interesting that certain numbers of your souls could defy that mandate you had first laid down, and start to develop along technological paths," said Raoul. "You obviously allowed some form of free will."

"Not a case of allowing it," said Maragos. "Once a soul is separated from its entity, it has freedom of thought and decision. Intelligence cannot be caged."

"Could they have swung the entire species along their path?" asked Philippe. "Would that have been possible, to go against your basic mandate?"

"Oh yes," said Maragos with a smile. "That would have been a learning experience for all of us that has actually occurred in some species, where the Infinite Soul's original concept was altered by changing philosophies of the lesser souls."

"It was a war between tribes or groups?" asked Raoul. "You haven't indicated much violence in your species so far."

"Oh, it was war, alright," said Maragos with an energetic nodding. "The greatest war of my species in all its history, because it was the pivotal period for us. They were known as the Wheel Wars and lasted over five hundred years before the mandate was restored."

"How dreadful!" whispered Jacqueline. "Five hundred years of warfare?"

"Not dreadful, just experience," replied Maragos. "We must remember, whatever happens, anything at all, provides new insights into The One's problem."

"Even the sickness of Humanity?" asked Jacqueline.

Maragos looked at her. "Even that," she agreed. "Your perception is excellent. When you have healed and The One has returned, the experience will be added to all the others. I could have certainly followed a different path, but my mandate held, and that is also experience."

Another few moments of silence straddled the table.

"I suppose that's one main reason why you're the first Infinite," suggested Jacqueline. "Your species followed a path most like the Infinite life form and developed more rapidly."

"I think so," agreed Maragos. "But it also means that perhaps I have less total experience than the others. We shall see as more Infinites emerge over the next few thousand years."

"Tell us about life as you lived it," asked Philippe. "What was a normal lifetime like?"

"Can any life be normal?" teased Maragos. "There are twenty-five billion souls in me, and all of them have different experiences. But I can tell you some parts."

She paused for another sip of the brandy and cupped the glass in her two hands. Sometimes, Philippe found it impossible to think of her as anything but a bright, thoughtful and beautiful woman. She raised her eyes to him, and Philippe again realized the immeasurable power within her.

"Our average life-span was about three hundred years by the time we had completed the physical cycle of reincarnation," she said. "Childhood was very long by your standards, almost a third of our lives. We spent the years in schools, learning to use our minds, both alone and in concert with others. A standard early exercise, for example, was telekinesis, using the mind to move objects. Most children could achieve that after some ten or fifteen years. Then we would move onto lifting heavier objects and into shaping of material at the atomic level."

"How far did this go?" asked Raoul in fascination.

"About a million years ago," she replied, "our sun developed heat ranges that could have caused us damage. We moved our orbit slightly to avoid it. That was our biggest achievement."

"Er... yes, I imagine it was," said Leger dryly. A small ripple of amusement ran round the table.

"Did you live in a family structure?" asked Jacqueline. "Marriage, children, all that stuff?"

Maragos grinned cheerfully. "In a way. We became pubescent after about eighty years, and at that time we also developed mental communication skills, a sort of telepathy. The process of attraction between the sexes, courtship and mating was not all that different from yours, and most people entered mateship arrangements after a hundred or so years, soon after reaching adulthood. But although we tended to mate for life, children became more involved with their school groups, and less directly involved with parental relationships. So a nuclear family was not a feature of our lives. The ability to communicate mentally meant that we had a wider species relationship."

"How about careers, professions? Did you have to work in any sense?"

"To earn incomes to buy essentials? No, not at all," replied Maragos. "If you can create anything from the atomic matter around you, the concept of barter or wealth does not exist. But the level of skills and creativity varied, so people specialized in whatever they chose. The soul that bore my name in his last incarnation was a sculptor who created shapes that dazzled the mind. Others might design living shelters that gave satisfaction in emotional ways, so their services as what you might call architects were in demand. Something that could be described as mental music was a particular art form. Vibrations that stimulated the mind, causing enormous emotional effect, there's no real equivalent here in a non-telepathic world. But those who could create such things were in demand."

"But not for pay?" asked Raoul. "Because there was no concept of money, I suppose?"

She smiled warmly at him. "Correct," she said. "Social standing was the reward."

"Was there no crime in this world?" asked Leger. "It seems almost too idyllic, apart from the Wheel Wars."

"Crime, certainly," she responded. "Because crime almost always results from some sense of deprivation or envy. But the only envy we could produce would be one of higher social standing, or mental abilities. Nothing therefore that one could steal. But crimes of violence caused by such emotional stress could happen."

"But could hardly go undetected in a telepathic world?" queried Jacqueline, and Maragos nodded.

"That's the problem for a criminal!" she smiled. "And punishment would be equally a problem. What could one do to somebody who could alter their environment at will? The idea of a fine was incomprehensible. Punishment was therefore impossible, other than execution. Better to modify the mind that had the problem."

"Were you aware of the nature of Oneness? Did you know of reincarnation?" Leger was intrigued.

"Not for centuries," replied Maragos. "Our religion was more of association with other minds that resulted in ecstasies not dissimilar to intense religious experiences here. In the last few thousand years we began to learn the truth and could communicate with souls on the Astral Plane almost as easily as with each other. Then as souls merged to form Ascendants we gradually became aware of the higher truth of The One."

She paused in thought for a few seconds. "It is true that my species did not experiment very much in looking for answers to The One's question. But with a million of us looking for alternate paths, one of us had to choose a path close to the original. My true learning may yet come from being the first Infinite, and so having the chance to guide others, as I am doing with you."

"Did all Infinites develop a mandate for their species?" Philippe asked.

"It was an essential part of the process," Maragos said.

"Then what was ours? What was Humanity's mandate?" demanded Raoul.

"To be creative. To explore the boundaries of possibilities in art, science, commerce, patterns of thought, and break through them. Humanity has produced astonishing beauty in all these fields, most commonly in music and art. But the truly sick among you have developed powerful alliances in opposing such developments. Reactionism is a visible symptom of the human sickness."

"What about other species?" asked Raoul, breaking into her thoughtful silence. "This is so fascinating! I need more!"

The thoughtful expression on the face of Maragos was replaced by amusement. "There is a race that chose lives of only eight years in length," she said with a grin. "They are humanoid, but tiny, barely three feet high in human terms. They could not achieve any sort of technology in that lifetime, so they have remained always as tree-dwellers, only one level of a food chain that ends with an appalling predator that resembles something like a carnivorous, armour-plated giraffe. They are an intensely spiritual race, with a deep awareness of Oneness and their quest for a solution to eternal loneliness. Because they know of the reincarnation cycle, a short life is unimportant, and they strive for understanding with each death experience. The communicate with souls on the Astral Plane almost as if they were alike, and they barely differentiate between the two levels of existence."

"What level of development have they reached?" asked Jacqueline.

"Most are late-stage Mature Souls and early-stage Old Souls," replied Maragos. "The incarnate population is only a few million, but it has never been higher than half a billion at any stage. They are one of the species that I will suggest some Human souls should choose for reincarnation. Their spiritual development is highly advanced."

"What sort of life can they lead?" asked Raoul with a worried look. "It sounds dreadful."

"Not so," replied Maragos. "The intensity of the spiritual life gives great rewards. And their incarnate life is not without pleasures either." She smiled mischievously. "They mature physically within a year of birth, and their sexual activity is wild! The replacement needs are high, as you might imagine, so life is a constant party! No marriage, no family, just survival, meditation and procreation. The gestation time is only sixty days, and because senility only arrives within weeks of death, adult life extends for over six of the average eight years."

"But what a six years!" said Jacqueline. "Almost worth it!"

"At the other end of the spectrum is a race of non-humanoids that lives in the same galaxy as my species inhabited," continued Maragos when the laughter had died down. "Their life span is about a thousand years. So they take fewer incarnations to grow from Infant Soul to Old Soul."

"How many?" asked Raoul.

"Each lifetime generally takes them up one Soul age," replied Maragos. "So they normally take only one or possibly two incarnations to grow from their first Infant incarnation to reach Baby stage, one or two more to grow to Young Soul, and another one to reach the Mature Soul stage. Sometimes, a more powerful soul will grow through two levels in one lifetime. At the Old Soul stage, they slow down a little, as this is their most meaningful time, and they never take more than one lifetime for that stage."

"What sort of life do they lead?" asked Raoul. He seemed the most fascinated by this intelligent race of beings.

"They are non-sexual," answered Maragos. "They procreate by a form of pollination, much like flowers. They look more like a termite mound than a recognizable life form and they are not mobile at all once they have taken adult form. The planet has no natural predator that affects them and no form of illness."

"Sounds terrible," said Jacqueline with a pained expression. "What do they do with that thousand years?"

"Communicate," said Maragos. "That has become their function, to communicate with other species by mental means."

"Another telepathic race?" asked Leger.

"It's not uncommon," answered Maragos. "Over two hundred species developed such means of communication, including my own. But this race developed the skill to talk over infinite distances, between galaxies if necessary, which eventually, it was."

"Why?" interjected Raoul. "Why did it become necessary?"

"Because one race developed the capacity to travel such distances," answered Maragos. "They were the species that brought me here..."

The ship's captain was studying the master board when Maragos appeared in front of him. He tried not to appear surprised but the rapid blinking of his huge eyes revealed his shock.

"I was not expecting you just yet, Maragos," he said, the cello tones of his voice giving a small vibrato with astonishment.

"There will be no need for you to stay, captain," replied Maragos, her tones so soothing that the captain relaxed. He hurriedly cancelled the automatic alarms that the devices implanted in his body had set off around the massive ovoid of the ship and which had transmitted messages to the two hundred crew members who were manning their stations.

"The situation will require me to be here for a lengthy period," she continued. "And I can move at will now, without your help. Go home, my friends. It is time to delay no longer, join your entities and allow them to become Ascendant Souls."

"We are in need of that," the captain said, his voice now a smoother tone. "We are the last incarnate among us, and we sense the pressures to ascend."

"Then do so, with my blessing," said Maragos. "I have much work to do here and I no longer need your ship to travel."

"The sickness is extreme among Humanity?" the captain asked, setting certain processes in action through his communication devices.

"It is, but it can be healed," replied Maragos. "Though I see why our previous attempts failed. The task was greater than even an enhanced Ascendant could achieve."

"I see," said the captain, his wide-eyed stare that signified intense amusement filling his face. "I am relieved to hear your confidence, Maragos."

The Infinite emitted the strange, heavy breathing sounds that the captain knew indicated amusement in the small Humanoid form. "I think that you would get on well with my friends on Earth," she said. "We must say goodbye now, captain. It is time for your species to start the process of becoming an Infinite. I will welcome you again at that time."

"Until Oneness then, Maragos," said the captain, and the same farewell was echoed by the remainder of the crew who had ceased all duties for the last time.

"Until Oneness, my friends," replied Maragos, and vanished.

A few seconds later, the ship exploded in a titanic upheaval that cast shadows on Jupiter and the moons around it.

The captain and his crew had completed their last incarnations.

"... and I have just said goodbye to them," said Maragos to the group around the table. "They were the last of their kind to remain incarnate, and they were ready to merge with their entities to become Ascendant Souls."

"Just now? While you were talking to us?" Jacqueline looked shocked.

"As I said before," answered Maragos. "The presence you see here before you is only a fraction of what I am. I can travel now through any spatial distance without any time elapsing, and I can be in many places on different spiritual levels at once." She looked around the silent group. "Time and space and matter are only realities in an incarnate world," she continued. "Though I had to achieve Infinite level to understand that."

"How far will the ship travel?" asked Philippe, his voice subdued.

"No distance," said Maragos. "They have no need to travel anywhere in the physical sense. Their planet is uninhabited. All others of their kind have completed the entire cycle of incarnations and were waiting only on the captain and his crew to complete these lives and join their entities so that they could become Ascendant Souls. Then they would begin the long stage of meditation between all the Ascendants to merge to the Infinite level."

"So what have they done?" asked Raoul, concern on his face.

Maragos smiled at him. "Raoul, the old values must change," she said. "They mean nothing in the time before Oneness. Death is also nothing, just a passage. In a little while, I'll show you what they did." She reached over the table and pulled a slice of fresh bread toward herself. "There are other species you may wish to ask about?"

"And distance," said Raoul, recognizing the barrier Maragos had set in place for a while. "Just how big is our Universe?"

"Well over forty billion light-years across," replied Maragos.

"And those ships can travel those distances?" Raoul looked thunderstruck.

"In relatively short periods of time," agreed Maragos. "Though because none of the outer galactic clusters is inhabited, the maximum distance a Kaloti ship has travelled is a little under thirty billion light-years. That trip takes about four weeks. But then, because of the complexities of hyperspacial dimensions, most trips only take one or two weeks."

"So Einstein was wrong?" chimed in Jacqueline. "The speed of light is not the finite barrier?"

"Indeed it is," retorted Maragos, "in the physical universe. But the Kaloti discovered hyperspace. In practice, hyperspace is just a level above the physical universe on which we normally live, but somewhere below the Astral Plane, the spiritual level. On reaching light-speed, a Kaloti ship is able to enter this almost-spiritual level where time and space are less meaningful."

"And how long did your trip take?" Jacqueline was entranced by the concept.

"We travelled just a few hundred million light-years." Maragos smiled at the looks on their faces. "It took two weeks. But now I have found how I could have done the trip instantly, without help."

"As The One must surely be able to do," said Philippe.

"Exactly," agreed Maragos.

"Tell us about the Kaloti species," said Leger. He sensed an inexorable power in Maragos, and a wave of sadness ran through him, though he was unable to explain why.

"They inhabited a yellow planet in a galaxy within the local supercluster, as your astronomers call it," said

Maragos. "The cluster of galaxies is called NGC 3190 by the astronomers. The species called their planet Kaloti, which means simply "Yellow World." It's a world of low gravity, high winds, and because it's nearer the centre of their galaxy than is Earth, with a sun less bright than yours, the inhabitants always saw a star-filled sky that intrigued them and developed a characteristic of inquisitiveness and a drive to exploration. They began as tree dwellers, like humans did, but they developed into humanoid ground creatures early. They retained flexible hands and feet, much more adroit than mankind had, and engineering came naturally to them."

She looked around the table at the rapt faces.

"The high winds allowed them to recognize natural energies, and from then on, things happened amazingly rapidly," Maragos continued. "The planet has two moons. The Kaloti reached both of those after only three or four thousand years of civilization. On Earth, that would have placed humans at the Roman Empire stage, though this happened on Kaloti over two million years ago."

"And where was humanity at this time?" asked Jacqueline with curiosity.

"Still fleeing from the rest of us," replied Maragos. "You had stopped running and settled around Epsilon Indi. You had terraformed the planet you had selected, but still had not begun to break down from the Infinite stage. These were the times when we were still trying to communicate with you without any success."

"But what about the Kaloti?" asked Raoul, trying to bring the conversation back to its theme. "You were telling us about them."

"They developed space travel thousands of years ahead of any other species," continued Maragos. "They colonized three of the habitable planets in their system within a hundred years of the first moon-flights, and then discovered faster-than-light travel through subspace, and methods of influencing gravity. From then on, it was easy. They built massive ships and began to travel their own galaxy and the others, and eventually became a sort of private union of transportation specialists for other races as they reached maturity. Which is why we needed the communication species I mentioned before."

"Oh yes! I'd forgotten about them," said Jacqueline with enthusiasm. "You said they looked more like termite mounds!"

"They are an essential part of the system," said Maragos and took a sip of the cognac. Raoul topped up her glass and she nodded her thanks at him. "They call themselves the Speakers. Telepathic communication is instantaneous, regardless of distance," she continued. "And this species can send and transmit, so they became a sort of cosmic communications centre. When they're not communicating messages they transmit ideas and exchange them with other species. Or they simply meditate for years at a time, following through a single idea or concept."

"It sounds like several species discovered capabilities that we might accept as being a God's characteristic, but not one of a sentient race," said Leger, thoughtfully. "Any religious person on Earth could accept that God could travel through His Universe without difficulty, or communicate by thought over any distance. But few could believe that an intelligent race could do these things."

"That's about it," agreed Maragos. "The chief characteristic of an advanced species is the ability to tap into the powers of The One, and anyone could do that, given enough determination and time."

"Did all species choose physical forms?" asked Jacqueline. "A common theme in science fiction is the race of sentient beings existing as energy or gaseous forms, not tied to a particular planet. Did this happen?"

"Indeed it did," answered Maragos. "Both types developed. One of them is a pure energy form that exists in space and has never adopted a home planet.

They chose a non-death cycle, so that each soul grows through all the stages of incarnation in one lifetime, and then moves to the Astral Plane as simply another Soul Age beyond Old Soul. They travel freely in space and as a pure energy form, they are free to travel between galaxies."

She looked at each of them in turn, and all three listeners were absorbed by her words.

"Several species chose gaseous forms," she continued. "All of them procreate by fission and they chose planetary existence as preferable to free space life. They can be killed by electrical storms or by lethal gases that form on their planets, so the death experience is part of their cycles."

"An infinite number of life forms," murmured Philippe. "And yet you said earlier that most forms have adopted humanoid shape."

"It proved to be a convenient general pattern for mechanical and technological species," replied Maragos. "Though within that pattern, the variation is enormous. There are races with three arms, four arms, six arms, even more. Some have two legs, some have three, one species developed from a centipede-like creature and has thirty legs. Some races have one head, some have two or three, a few have no heads at all. But humanoid is the most common."

"So far, you've told us about races that seemed ultimately benign," said Philippe thoughtfully. "Again, a common theme in science fiction has been the malevolent and advanced, perhaps truly evil species. But if all the ensouled species were part of The One, such a thing would seem impossible."

"Not at all," said Maragos with an emphatic shake of her head. "A number of species chose paths that could be construed as malignant and ugly. After all, to consider The One as merely infinite goodness is quite wrong. It contained all forces of all emotions and qualities. And so God, if you want to call The One by that title, is both good and evil, positive and negative, a perfect balance.”

“An interesting quandary for the theologians,” murmured Raoul, “if there is such a profession left in the world.”

“They’re still around,” said Philippe with a grimace.

“There is a species in a galaxy close to my own,” continued Maragos. “A technologically-advanced race by any standards, with inter-stellar travel, which engaged in a series of conquests of other species.”

“Inter-stellar war?” asked Raoul. “A favourite theme of the sci-fi writers.”

“In a sense,” replied Maragos. “A real inter-stellar war is simply impractical. Too big a problem of logistics. No, what the Gelkka, the Masters as they termed themselves did, was simply to set off in small fleets, locate a less developed species and settle on their planet. Rather like colonists, except that their colonial rule was quite vicious. There were few races to enslave because as I said, we had agreed on only a few hundred species per galaxy, and the Gelkka did it only eight or ten times.”

“What happened as they matured towards the Infinite Soul level?” asked Philippe. “Did they realize what they had done?”

“No, not really,” answered Maragos. “They are only now beginning to reach the Ascendant Soul stage. As they do, they are becoming aware of the path they had chosen. But the reality is simply that such a path was merely another choice. It provided a new experience, a different viewpoint. It remains to be seen whether that viewpoint, those experiences will result in a possible answer to The One’s problem. There are other, even more ugly species, too. We won’t even talk about the Zlan. You’d get permanent nightmares, and I need you with whole minds.”

“The Yin and Yang of God,” said Philippe with a grin. “It raises an interesting debate on the nature of evil. If The One contains both, and if apparently evil acts are committed as part of the process of solving God's dilemma, we have to question whether there can be such a concept as Good and Evil."

Maragos nodded without echoing the smile. "Of course that is correct," she said. "If The One is the sum of all things, It must also contain Evil, as we call it for the moment. The One is both God and the Devil. It is interesting that one of your writers recognized this idea in a story of the final conflict between God and the Devil, which the Devil won. But in time, the Devil was forced to become God to provide the balance of forces demanded by the Universe."

"So how can we truly identify evil?" Raoul asked. "Is it possible that an act might be evil in one circumstance but not in another?"

"I believe there can only be one definition," said Maragos. "The drive to Oneness must be good, however it may manifest itself. Anything that opposes the rebirth of The One must be evil. So the acts of the Gelkka were a specific program designed to gain experience. For their subject races, the Masters represented evil. And to oppose the Gelkka was also a developmental act, so was entirely legitimate. But Horning and his cohorts committed their crimes purely for self-fulfilment. The sickness they encourage is counter to The One's rebirth. It is truly evil."

"A difficult philosophy to justify," Philippe murmured. "It seems to permit some hideous acts."

"I am not even sure myself that I have it correct," Maragos admitted. "Some species, I have difficulty in seeing their objectives."

"And the one you mentioned," asked Philippe, "the Zlan. They would seem evil?"

"So evil you cannot imagine," replied Maragos. "Absolutely without any capacity for caring, only the use of other life forms as food and incubators for their young."

A moment of silence ran round the table as they absorbed this concept.

"A professional question for Raoul and myself," said Philippe with a self-deprecating smile. "We lived with this question all our lives and all Catholics do to some extent. The question of original sin, salvation and all the other clutters of religion. Was humanity alone in this belief structure?"

"Not entirely," said Maragos. "Many races have adopted some form of religion. In fact, nearly all of them did in their early stages, but Old Soul status diminishes that tendency. Most races have, at some stage, tended to believe in a supernatural god with some form of focal point on their planet, such as Jesus was on Earth. But the original sin concept is unique to yourselves and reflects the sickness in an evident way."

"The sickness is the sin?" Raoul was amused, and Maragos reflected his smile.

"That's how it carried forward into the incarnate stages among many of you," she replied. "Large sections of humanity in the earliest stages were aware of their imperfect souls because of the sickness. Somehow, the Christian sects managed to interpret this race sense of imperfection into the religious concept of original sin, something with which you were born and which must be expunged."

Raoul and Philippe grinned at each other, then Raoul's face went serious as he thought of another question. "Did any other species come out this far with Humanity?" he asked.

Maragos nodded. "A few did," she answered. "One had developed originally in a galaxy nearer the rest of us, but they were also a space-travelling race. I mentioned them before, they are the X'Kasxi of the planet they call X'Katcxo, who now also live in this galaxy, about eighty thousand light-years away. They transferred many of their people to the new planet and set up a civilization there with one objective of keeping an eye on Humanity. They are a race that souls of this planet have already chosen as their next species for reincarnation."

"Already?" gasped Jacqueline. "Some humans have already incarnated as these... what did you call them?"

"X'Kasxi," murmured Maragos. "Yes, three souls are already preparing to be reborn there. Many more will follow in the next decades."

"We're out of booze," said Raoul rising from the table and breaking the astonished silence. "I'll find another bottle in the cellar."

"What happens when we merge?" asked Jacqueline when another bottle had been found, dusted off and the contents poured into three glasses. The brandy balloon had also been refilled, and some of the sadness at the death of the last of a species had passed. "It frightens me Maragos, that I will lose my identity for ever. And it frightens me more that I will lose Philippe. We have been together for a long time. But we are not of the same entity. When I become part of an Ascendant Soul, I will lose him forever."

"I cannot begin to tell you," replied Maragos with sympathy in her voice. "I know that every one of the souls that comprise my being felt the same fear. And yet, we are now one. It's as if the individual cells of your body feared the loss of identity by becoming you, but you must remain the real personality, not those cells. And yet each of those souls in me is part of me, and in some ways, retains their being. I can remember every second of every life that was lived by my twenty-five billion souls. I am every one of them, and they are all part of me."

Silence ruled the room.

"And now, I begin to sense some of the quandary The One must experience," continued Maragos. "I am aware of the powers within me, and I cannot but recognize the wonder and exhilaration this gives me. To be able to travel the Universe with a thought, to be the most powerful entity on this planet, in fact the most powerful entity in the Universe, because I am the first. Do you not think that this fills me with delight?"

The three looked at her, hypnotized by her words. They were hearing God speak to them.

"But do you not think that I too fear the final merger into The One when I will also lose my identity?" She looked at each of them in turn. "And I see now the loneliness of being the single, ultimately powerful creature in all of space and time. Until other Infinites emerge, I am alone as nobody can understand. In time, others will emerge, and I will have company. But for The One, there is no such escape. And each of you will be part of It, each of you will experience the delight, the wonder and the pain."

Silence in the room was almost explosive. The agony in the voice of Maragos could be felt by each of them, and tears rose in all their eyes.

"But what if The One has no solution?" Philippe Leger was the first to find his voice with the question that all of them had sensed.

"Then I believe it must all start again," replied Maragos. "The One will gather all the space and time and dust, and compress it into Its hands and release another Big Bang. Perhaps a different structure this time, perhaps different laws of physics, perhaps a different pattern to the Universe. But the idea will be the same."

"Will we be the same souls we were before?" asked Jacqueline, her voice still a tremble.

Maragos smiled sweetly at her. "If you take the ocean and fill a billion bottles with water, they will be individual bottles. But if you then pour the water back and refill the bottles, will the water in each be the same? No, of course not. There will be simply many billions of souls, each of which will be a fraction of The One, with completely new awareness, new identity, total forgetfulness of everything that has gone before."

"How often can this cycle occur?" asked Leger. The sadness that Maragos' words had caused in Jacqueline was ignored in favour of the intellectual interest Philippe had in the process of eternity.

"How can we know?" replied Maragos. "Maybe it has happened a billion billion times before, or maybe this is the first such cycle. We have no way of knowing. Even The One would not know, because all memories are wiped out by the start of the cycle as all souls are completely new."

"God starts out as a child each time," murmured Raoul. "What a wonderful thing, to be so innocent, and yet eternal and all-powerful."

"It is the only way we can survive eternity," replied Maragos with an approving nod. "To have no memory of the previous cycles. But maybe this time, The One will find an answer. Perhaps just one soul in its several hundred incarnations, or one Ascendant in the thousands of years of meditation, one Infinite may have stumbled on a way to live alone and aware through Eternity."

She looked round the room with a warm smile. "But meanwhile, we can take only one step at a time. Our task is to ensure that Oneness can be achieved this time around. We will worry in another few thousand years about what solution The One may or may not find."

The three of them relaxed in the warmth of her.

"Tomorrow, we start work," she said, "and it will take some years to complete."

"What will we do, Maragos?" asked Leger. He was still feeling the grief from his recognition of how the work would end.

She looked at him and took his hand, knowing his sadness and of his awareness of the final stages of the work. "We will travel and talk to the people," she said gently. "As much as possible, we must travel, because my presence alone will heal many of those less sick, and spur the spiritual growth of many others. But you know that our biggest task will be when we reach America."

"I think we all know that, now," replied Leger, so

aware of the limitless strength in her small hand. "What will be done about the millions of sick souls that died this morning in the Middle East? How can we heal them?"

She released his hand, and the pain showed in her face. "That was a death experience of terrible power," she whispered. "Never before have so many died in one short period of a few seconds, and in such appalling conditions. Many millions of infant souls have reached the Astral Plane together and their religious madness will induce most of them to undergo experiences of terror and pain inconceivable to you. I have called for help, because the task is too great for us."

"Help?" asked Leger. "What sort of help?"

"The only sort of help that will achieve anything," she replied, the pain still in her face. "Several species have just merged a number of Ascendant Souls, much like Jesus, Buddha and Mohammed, and have placed them among the millions of the newly dead. Their presence will provide much calming and healing, and then many of these poor sick ones must be sent to incarnate as other species."

"And you called for this assistance?" Leger knew the answer, but hearing her explain still helped his mind accept the infinity of power of the being that appeared to them as an attractive young woman.

"As soon as it happened," replied Maragos. "I talked to several species in whom the Ascendant Souls are almost ready for the growth to Infinite level. A thousand enhanced Ascendant Souls are with the newly dead already."

For a few moments, the power of her words and the sadness of the experiences of the day kept the room in sombre silence. It was broken by Maragos as she stood up.

"Come with me," she said, leading the way out of the kitchen to the front door. Outside, it was a clear night with only the thinnest sliver of the new moon.

Forty minutes had passed since the revelation of Maragos' farewell to the Kaloti.

"There," said Maragos, and pointed. As she did, a tiny spark grew in the sky, swelled for a few seconds to drown out the glow of nearby stars, and died.

"They blew up the ship?" Jacqueline was horrified.

"They were in a hurry to get home," replied Maragos. "If space and time are meaningless beyond the Physical Plane, what better way for them to rejoin their species? Why waste years returning to a dead planet?"

The small group stared into the sky for a few more moments in silence before returning to the kitchen. The bottle of red wine was finished in rapid gulps when they sat down again. The three human old souls who could remember dying hundreds of times before were not yet ready to accept death as simply a passage to somewhere else. A small sadness for the physical end of an entire species hung in the air. The conversation slowed and nothing seemed able to interrupt the dark mood, and all of them retired to their rooms.

* * *

Edward Foulkes stood nervously in the anteroom to the Oval Office. His small delegation from the Illinois Branch of the Christians for Horning Society stood around him, listening with silent attention to Stephen Crossman. The President's aide spoke softly, forcing the group of six men and three women to stand rigidly so as not to miss a word.

"I will lead you into the office in just a few moments," said Crossman. "You will walk in single file, with Mister Foulkes here leading the line. As you reach the President's desk, I will announce your name and you will bow your head. The President will be standing, but you will not make any move to shake his hand or approach him in any way. After the last of you has been announced, you, Mister Foulkes, will make your statement of support and allegiance and present your gift to the man standing to the President's right. Reverend Horning will then speak a few words, after which I will touch Mister Foulkes on the shoulder and you will walk quietly out of the office by the far door that will be opened for you. Is that understood?"

Crossman looked at each of the nine in turn. As his gaze turned on him, Edward shivered slightly. Crossman's eyes seemed so dark, so impenetrable, he thought. There was a blankness to them that also showed in the face. Edward had seen not a single expression touch Crossman's face throughout the briefing. He shifted the small package from his right hand and wiped the clammy sweat from his palm. He had felt the touch of Crossman's hand as he had handed over the package for X-ray a few moments earlier, and the skin of the Chief Examiner's fingers had been cold and hard. It had felt more like the hand of a wax dummy, thought Edward. He took a deep breath and nodded his response to Crossman's query. As the dark stare moved on, Edward tried to relax, but the air of menace and fear in the room persisted. Edward deeply regretted the chain of events that had led to his being there, even though he had so looked forward to the trip and had accepted the envious congratulations of his neighbours in his home town of Streamwood, Illinois when the invitation from the White House had arrived.

*I wish we'd never sent in the copy of the Society's newsletter,* he thought. *Just because we'd held a marathon prayer-meeting to call for God's blessing on the President, we shouldn't have sent in the newsletter. I wish I was somewhere else....*

The black reverie was broken by Crossman opening the door, and Edward steeled himself. He could see inside the fabled Oval Office, and the emanations of menace became even stronger. He moved to the door under the guidance of Crossman, then felt himself pushed into the room. Dimly he heard his name being called. He moved toward the huge desk, feeling as if he was walking through heavy mud. The figure behind the desk rose to his feet. Edward bowed his head, grateful for the way the movement allowed him not to look into the eyes of the Reverend William Horning, President for Life of the United States of America. He shuffled himself to his left as the others of his group filed in, then, as the man standing by the side of the desk moved to him, handed over the package.

"The Blessing of the Lord be upon you," said Horning. Edward felt ill. Horning's voice seemed to be coming from a long way away. The sickness became worse and Edward's vision lost focus. Strength seemed to drain away from him and his legs began to tremble. In growing horror, his eyes seemed to force themselves up to stare at Horning. The President's eyes had become huge and they glowed with a dark radiance that sucked the life from Edward. In a dreadful moment of comprehension, Edward felt his body drop to the floor, *but he was still standing*. Another man in the line also collapsed, and Edward sensed the spiritual presence of the man remaining on its feet. All his sensations became tightly focused on Horning, and a terrible power began to pull Edward toward the President. Horning's eyes grew larger and Edward was being dragged into that black stare. He felt his energy diminish and fade.

"Oh God," prayed Edward with the last, dying dregs of his own being. "Save my soul from Hell, I beg of you..." Then his last sensation of self faded as his soul was sucked into the eyes of the man behind the desk.

Crossman watched without surprise or dismay as the two men in the line collapsed. He knew they were dead, because this had happened before. The remaining seven men and women from Illinois seemed dulled and uncomprehending as if much of their own energies had been sucked away. Their eyes had become dark and blank, and their faces showed the same slack-jawed dullness that so many people around the President displayed

Crossman watched his President. Horning's eyes were closed and he was breathing deeply as if he had just drunk a stimulating draught of wine. A massive influx of new energy had just reached the President, Crossman understood. He felt a subdued wave of fear run through him, but the sensation was dulled, underpowered, as if felt through a thick blanket.

Horning's eyes opened and stared at Crossman. The jolt of power that crossed the room shook Crossman back to self-control. He took the arm of the man standing next to the body of Edward Foulkes, and led him to the far door of the Oval Office. Crossman opened the door and gently pushed the man through it. The others of Foulkes' group followed obediently. When the last of them had left, Crossman gestured to a military aide standing outside the office.

"Get a clean-up crew," he said softly. "Two bodies."

The aide nodded and reached for a phone on the wall. Crossman returned to the Oval Office. Horning was still standing by his desk.

"My God, Crossman," said Horning. "I feel good!"

Energy seemed to radiate from the President. A tiny frisson of the fear he had experienced before ran through Crossman, then he took control of himself again.

"Yes, Mister President," he replied. "I regret this deplorable incident. The bodies will be removed in a few moments."

"Don't hurry," said Horning. "For some reason, I feel good just looking at them."

For several minutes, Horning remained silent, staring down at the two bodies on the floor of the Oval Office. His expression was gleeful, his eyes sparkled like those of a man who had just injected cocaine into his veins. When the door opened and four men walked in carrying two stretchers, Horning turned away with regret.

"What's next, Crossman?" he demanded.

"Another branch of the Christians for Horning Society," replied Crossman. "Idaho Chapter."

"Oh shit," said Horning. "Why do you keep pushing these ass-licking little jerks on me, Crossman?"

"It's good public relations, Mister President," replied Crossman calmly.

"I suppose so," said Horning, and sat down behind his desk. "And you never know, we might have a couple more of them collapse like those others did."

"It's possible," replied Crossman, beginning to understand what happened when people fell dead in front of the President. Cold, sick fear ran through him.

"Okay, show the bastards in," said Horning with a gleam in his eyes.

# Chapter 13. Playing The Provinces

Over the next two years, the Infinite Soul's group of four travelled the world, appearing at random in major cities or small towns in countries in all quarters of the globe with two exceptions. They did not visit the glass plains that were once the countries of Iran, Iraq and Syria, and they did not visit until the very end, the reduced nation that still called itself the United States of America. They did not arrive on the North American continent at all until three years after the first assembly with the people.

The arrivals and the events that followed them were in no particular order, because the Infinite did not require conventional means to travel. Maragos and her three associates, Philippe Leger, the one-time Pope Jean-Paul II, Raoul Carmagio, once Archbishop of Milan, and Jacqueline Carter, an Englishwoman who had maintained a spiritual connection with both the other two over the previous six thousand years, simply appeared. Early signals through psychic means meant that crowds gathered, sometimes totalling a million or more.

The first assembly was in Moscow. At six in the morning, one warm June day in 2023, people began to gather in the huge Revolutionary Square opposite the Kremlin. It had been renamed Anna Karenina Square some years after the collapse of the old Soviet Union, and was a popular assembly spot for Russians and tourists alike. The Kremlin building itself had become the centre of the booming Russian economy that had sprung from the ruins of the first experiments with free markets, and accelerated its growth after the spread of Oneness through Europe. Together with most of the rest of the world, all borders had fallen, and movement throughout the region was completely unrestricted. Trade and development in the territories of the one-time Soviet lands was brisk, as other European countries opened up operations there in relatively virgin territories. Moscow and St. Petersburg became open cities, without business taxes, and soon were the largest cities in the northern hemisphere, as hundreds of thousands migrated there from all over the world, following trade and employment.

The crowds that began to grow that dawn were mixed, representing all generations, all ethnic groups, both Russian and many thousands from other parts of the world. Some reported that they had started travelling to Moscow ten days before in response to an urge that they could not explain. By ten, the numbers were estimated to be over half a million people in Anna Karenina Square. Eye-witness accounts indicate that the silence was almost total, broken only by murmurs of people here and there, and the occasional laughter of children playing.

When the four people appeared on the balcony that had held the Soviet leaders during the military displays that once celebrated the October Revolution, a small wave of sighs went through the crowd before silence took over. Those close to the balcony said that Maragos stood quietly, smiling at the crowd when she appeared, while expressions of confusion were obvious on the faces of the three others. No doubt the first experience of teleportation would have that effect, for the party of four had been at the house of Philippe Leger in Valence just moments earlier.

Maragos used no public address system, but everybody in the crowd heard her perfectly. It seems that everybody assumed she was speaking in their own language, but in fact, all the listeners understood her perfectly, regardless of the language they spoke. Maragos communicated directly between minds, and as we have since learned, she did not actually speak at all at these assemblies. All communication was telepathic. As Maragos told her group another time, she was repeating the process by which her predecessors, Buddha, Jesus and Mohammed had spoken to the crowds that had assembled to hear these earlier superior souls. Leger is reported to have said that he had often wondered how Jesus had conducted the Sermon on the Mount or his other assemblies when several thousand people had gathered. A human voice simply could not have been heard by so many people.

"I am with you till Oneness," the words of Maragos said to all the listeners in forty different tongues. A small wave of murmurs went through the half million.

"My presence here is already healing many of you," she continued, "and advancing your soul ages some of the way along the path that has been blocked to you for so many lifetimes. But you are only a few of the many, and the broken path is longer than I can repair for you all."

The silence was unbroken, but it was a loving, attentive silence.

"Your lives will be very different from here on," the Infinite continued. "They have been very different since the first awareness of my coming was felt by some of you, that I know. But from now, the difference will be greater.

"You know now that there can be no more war with your siblings, because you now understand the nature of yourselves. You are all one, even though you are still fragmented and sick. In time, you will truly be One, all of Humanity will be an Infinite Soul like myself, and we will talk then as well as we do now. So you must do no further damage to yourselves.

"You are free to go anywhere, do anything, except hurt others. You may be what you wish. You may discover powers in yourself that you had never dreamed of. Some of you will become Old Souls because I have healed some of the sickness, and you will remember past lives, past loves, and you will discover past friends and family in complete strangers. Do not fear this, it is a beautiful experience and holds much love.

"You may find others to whom you owe debts from those past lives, or who owe you. Do not hold back from paying the debts, because they will survive after this body dies, and live on into your next life. But do not force the issue of repayment if you are the creditor, because there is no worth in such a repayment. The debt is not repaid if the debtor is unwilling.

"Human souls live many lives," continued Maragos. "Most of you here have lived more than thirty incarnations on Earth, some have lived fewer, some have lived more. Most of you are Infant Souls, though the growth to Baby Soul has already occurred in many since I arrived. A few of you are Young and Mature Souls, though the sickness has made that number tiny. Even fewer are the numbers of Old Souls.

"In some parts of the world, nearly all the people are still Infant Souls and no advance has taken place in a hundred lifetimes or more. Even worse, is the sad fact that many millions of souls have refused even to experience a single life on Earth, so frightened and sick are they. They wait permanently on the Astral Plane, too fearful to experience life and growth."

Maragos paused and looked around the silent ranks of faces locked on hers. Reports say that she turned slightly and caught the eyes of her three companions. They were apparently as enthralled as the crowd, perhaps because none of them had realized that so many human souls had not even lived a single lifetime, never mind the several hundreds which each of the three had lived.

"But all of you," continued Maragos, "every single soul on Earth, or waiting on the Astral Plane must become an Old Soul before my work is done. That requires that hundreds of millions of souls must heal before much more development can take place. And when the healing is complete, the growth of human souls must occur rapidly so that Oneness can return."

As with any major gathering anywhere in the world, small entrepreneurs were at work. A number of food stalls had opened up around the square, selling local delicacies of piroshkis, blinis and drinks. At this stage, nobody had bought food, but as the hour of eleven approached, the entrepreneurs began preparing for business. Despite the rapt attention Maragos was receiving, many of the crowd were beginning to feel small pangs of hunger and were a little worried at how few stalls were present.

"Most people on Earth," continued Maragos, "have come to see that the old religions were based on weak foundations. Your beliefs were corrupted by the needs for power by other people and organizations, true information was withheld from you..." She threw a quick sideways glance and a smile at Philippe Leger, though nobody has ever been able to determine what the secret understanding was between them that precipitated that. "And the powerful Souls that visited you in the past were not adequate for the task of healing and inspiration that was necessary.

"But now I am here, and I am the sum of twenty-five billion souls with all the power and wisdom that is contained in me. Together we shall repair the hurts and let Oneness return."

A few people began drifting towards the food stands, and Maragos smiled.

"There is not enough to feed half a million of you, you realize," she said, and the movement stopped. "But one of my predecessors got over that problem with a few pieces of bread and fish, so perhaps I can do something similar," she continued.

The food vendors appeared to flicker slightly, and hundreds more of them appeared throughout the crowd. Rapidly, they began handing out food to the people, and without any fuss or confusion, people were able to get what they needed. No money changed hands, but none of the vendors seemed concerned. Later reports showed that the original vendors had all received mental assurances that money would be paid to them, and indeed, it appears that all of them were paid by deposits into their bank accounts that same day.

When the people had eaten, they looked back to the balcony, but Maragos and her party had vanished.

*(History of North America during the Time of the Infinite Soul, Klaus P. Scheidenhorst, University of Berlin, 2105, Oxford University Press.)*

* * *

"The important thing is not what I say, but that I appear," said Maragos, slicing a piece of crusty farm loaf and spreading creamy butter over it. She had taken a considerable liking to the simple fare and treated with amusement Jacqueline's semi-serious warning about fat and cholesterol. "My nearness to as many people as possible will cause considerable healing and make the eventual task lighter."

"I'm still shaken by the teleportation experience," Raoul Carmagio confessed. "It's unsettling to be sitting here one moment, and the next to be standing on a well-known landmark in Moscow."

"Is that the technique you use to travel round the universe?" asked Jacqueline.

"Almost," Maragos replied, taking a sip of the fine old brandy that had come from Philippe's stocks in the cellar. "For me, it's not really travel because I'm already there, for in many ways I am everywhere, just as The One is. Taking you with me requires a slightly different movement but I can't tell you what it is I do."

"Why not?" asked Philippe in some puzzlement. "Don't you know?"

She shook her head. "Could you tell me how you walk?" she asked.

"Of course," replied Philippe. "I place one foot in front of the other and transfer my weight..."

"No, no," broke in Maragos. "That's what you *do*. I want to know *how* you do it. How do you actually move the leg? How do you transfer the weight?"

Philippe thought for a moment. "I see the problem," he said "I know that somehow I tell my body to do something, but I have no idea how I actually do it."

"Exactly," said Maragos. "And the problem goes right to the top. I have no idea how I actually move myself or you around the universe. I have no idea what it is I'm doing when I heal some soul, or advance a soul along in age. I just do it."

"Does The One have the same problem?" Philippe asked.

"I think so," replied the Infinite. "Plus a couple of others."

"Others?" All the three spoke together. "What others?" Philippe completed the chorus.

"Some quite fundamental ones," said Maragos. "The One seems to have no idea how It creates matter, nor how It creates life, nor how It creates the Big Bang that starts the cycle of eternity each time. And of course, there is a major problem, apart from the one It has asked us to solve, of how to stay sane while surviving eternity."

"What's that one?" Philippe was the only one to speak, while the others stared at Maragos with dismay. The view they were hearing was of something less than the omnipotent, all-knowing God of their thoughts.

"The One has simply no idea at all of where It came from," said Maragos.

* * *

Following the appearance of the Maragos group in Moscow in June of the year 2023, a series of similar assemblies occurred. Three days after the Moscow episode, the group appeared in Lagos, then the next day in Rio de Janeiro where over a million crowded the beaches and buildings round the bay to listen to Maragos speak from the bridge of an old tanker moored in the waters.

They appeared a few days later in Sydney, Australia, when two hundred and fifty thousand gathered near the Opera House, jammed the whole of Circular Quay, the parklands of the Domain and the hill up Macquarie Street. That afternoon, they were seen in Brisbane, the capital of the State of Queensland, where fifty thousand heard her speak.

Two days later, the four appeared in the Zocalo of Mexico City, the enormous *Plaza de la Constitucion*. Maragos and her companions appeared at midday of a beautiful Saturday when the pollution level was almost at zero. Over a million people had assembled in the square. They crowded the corners of the streets leading off it, filled the windows of the National Palace on the east side and all the other beautiful buildings that looked on to the square. The four appeared on one of the high balconies of the Metropolitan Cathedral, and Maragos spoke for nearly an hour before the balcony was empty again.

Assemblies occurred after that in Tripoli in North Africa, in Johannesburg, Lima in Peru, Khartoum, Singapore and Manchester, England. A short break of four days took place, possibly to allow the three followers a rest, then assemblies took place on succeeding days in Caracas, Wuhan in China, Quezon City in Manila, Barcelona, Bogota and Kampala.

Another week followed with no appearances then Maragos appeared in Hong Kong, La Paz in Bolivia, Monterrey in Mexico, Odessa on the Black Sea and Santiago. A major assembly of over a million took place in Tiananmen Square in Beijing, then smaller ones in Oslo, Istanbul, Darwin, Athens and Rome.

The assembly in Jerusalem held over two million people. The entire country that was still called Israel, though few people remembered the borders, came to a halt as the words of Maragos were heard clearly to everybody as far away as Jaffa, Haifa, Tel Aviv, Jordan, into Egypt and up to the borders of the quarantined area of radio-active glass that once had been Syria and its enemies.

In between these highly public affairs, the group held meetings in smaller towns and places around the world, and many times, Maragos travelled alone to tiny, out-of-the-way places while her group slept. She talked to two hundred listeners in the village of Bishops Frome in the middle of England and to a hundred farmers on the Isle of Skye. She walked the streets of small towns in Europe, in China and in South America, talking with children and adults. A few times, the group or Maragos alone stayed overnight in places, and resumed the discussions the next morning. Maragos slept in a Kampong near Kuala Trengganu on the east coast of Malaysia, and in a Long House of Iban tribesmen in Sarawak. The group sailed in the small boats of fishermen off the Seychelles and with residents of the rain forests of the Amazon regions as they paddled their canoes in the muddy waters.

After nearly two the first appearance in North America took place when crowds began to gather on the slopes of Mount Royal in the city of Montreal that had taken its name from the peak. Leaving a space under the huge cross that crowned the mountain, they waited from dawn till nine in the morning of a chilly March day, but nobody seemed to feel the cold. When Maragos appeared, her first words were reported to be "I think this thing should go now, don't you?" and the massive cross simply vanished.

The Montreal assembly was followed by similar events in Calgary, in Banff, Vancouver and Vancouver Island, Saskatoon, Regina, Moncton, and Charlottetown on Prince Edward Island. Over a million gathered in Gander, Newfoundland and later in Chicoutimi in Quebec. Meetings occurred in northern areas, including Tuktoyaktuk with three hundred Inuit listeners, on several native peoples' reservations and in many places in Alaska, the northernmost state of the newly-formed nation of the Union of Pacific States.

These new American nations also received their share of visits. Assemblies of over half a million took place in Los Angeles, San Francisco, Sacramento, Seattle and San Diego. Three hundred thousand gathered in Portland, Oregon to see Maragos, and as with the rest of the world, gatherings took place in the smaller towns and villages, or even in small campsites in Yosemite and other National Parks before a hundred listeners. In the Atlantic States of America, Maragos spoke in Boston, at Jay Peak in Vermont, where five hundred skiers gathered around her one December afternoon, in Nashua, New Hampshire, and at the celebrated Central Park gathering, the incredible day when not a single murder, a single crime, a mugging, a robbery, not even a traffic accident occurred throughout New York. While the traffic accidents resumed the next day, the crimes did not. Although the same phenomenon had been reported in other cities, the scale of the change in New York City was shattering. However, the fact remained; after Maragos had visited a place, crime almost vanished. The remaining incidents were relatively minor, and the perpetrators invariably presented themselves to the police within days. Several days of intensive counselling from the growing number of those who reached Old Soul status in these years resulted in the wrong-doers walking away, and the rate at which these people returned to crime was almost zero.

Maragos spoke in Chelsea and Taunton in Massachusetts, in Hartford, in San Jose, in Spokane, Fairbanks and Juneau, on Maui, Oahu and Molokai, and as she spoke, souls healed and progressed, crime fell away, and Oneness came a little closer.

The last meeting before the critical events of the entire history took place, was in Halifax, Nova Scotia, on May the first, 2026, when Maragos said goodbye.

"I am here with you till Oneness," she said to the seven hundred thousand silent people. "But I will not appear to you again for a while. You must remember that I shall always be with you, whatever you hear. I cannot leave until we can talk to each other as equal, Infinite Souls."

The group disappeared from the sight of the watchers in Halifax. Little is clear after that. Most records were destroyed by the Great Fire of Washington that followed the violent civil upheavals in the Fall of the year 2026, and the American newspapers had been subjected to rigid censorship, so few reports had ever been printed.

*(History of North America during the Time of the Infinite Soul, Klaus P. Scheidenhorst, University of Berlin, 2105, Oxford University Press.)*

* * *

"We finally cross into the enemy's encampment, Maragos?" Philippe Leger was pouring the wine to start another quiet evening at the house in Valence.

"The enemy, Philippe?" Maragos raised an eyebrow at him over her balloon glass.

He shrugged. "Old-style thinking, Maragos," he said. "But I know we will meet hostility and fear and probably violence there, if you would allow the violence to occur. Yes, I admit I still think of them as the enemy."

"Things will be different there, Philippe," she said, her face serious. "We cannot prevent the natural reactions of sick souls and from now on, our work depends on letting things happen as they must."

The room became silent. All of them knew that the travels into what was left of the USA were the crucial events of the four years in which they had been travelling, but apart from Maragos, they had no real knowledge of what would happen. Philippe Leger had the clearest view of the probable future after his memories as Benjamin ben Isaac of the meeting with

Jesus shortly before the Crucifixion, but he had kept his thoughts private after his shared grief with Jacqueline.

"We see only a fraction of the process, Maragos, even though we are with you," said Jacqueline, breaking the silence as much to still her own fears as to learn something new. "What is happening with the work of Michael Hendricks?"

Maragos had told them of the soul who had been John the Baptist, and who was now gathering sick souls for the task of reincarnating as other species. The Infinite smiled at them.

"He does well," she said. "Many hundreds of thousands of souls have already reincarnated as other forms on other planets. And every soul that agrees to go usually persuades many others to go also. Soon, it will be millions who have gone on this task. When we complete our work in America, the numbers will swell dramatically."

"And when will we go on this task?" asked Philippe. All of them had discussed the matter and felt the mix of excitement and fear that anticipation of such an experience engendered.

"Any time you wish, after we have finished this stage of our work," replied Maragos. "But there is no hurry. None of you has any trace of the sickness now, and all of you have completed the path to being final-stage Old Souls. So, see this work through with me and when the time is right, travel to any world you wish. All the entities will welcome you as one of their own."

"I'm uncertain what role we play now, Maragos," said Raoul with a look of worry. "We merely come with you, though not always, and watch the assemblies. What value is there in our presence?"

The room was silent, watching Maragos in thought. The same concern had occurred in all of them.

"Do you think I am so great that I cannot feel the need of companions?" said Maragos, finally. "Am I so powerful that I cannot need warmth and friendship?"

The shock in the room was physical. All three of

them had indeed felt that Maragos was above the need for simple human comforts. She smiled with infinite love in her amazing eyes.

"No, my dear friends," she said, "I am not above those things. I need you to sustain me and comfort me, and I draw on the strength of you. Even though I am the sum of billions of souls, only a part of me is here, and I need you. So please don't go travelling until we have finished our task on Earth."

All four joined hands across the table and some small tears were visible in each pair of eyes.

"Can you tell us more of how our task will be completed, Maragos?" asked Philippe. Despite the certainty he and Jacqueline felt about the ultimate end of their journey on Earth, he still could not see the full details of what they must do.

Maragos looked at each of them in turn. Her face was grave.

"Even since I have been here," she said, "the dangers have increased. William Horning is displaying terrifying and wholly unexpected powers in a human soul. The full strength of the dark forces within Oneness have somehow concentrated in him, and he has learned how to drain the energies of the souls around him."

The three humans sat stunned for a second. Genuine distress had revealed itself in Maragos.

"Maragos!" whispered Philippe. "What is happening?"

"I wish I understood," replied the Infinite turning her incredible eyes to him. "It is nothing I have seen before within my species, or any of the other Infinite Souls who have been able to communicate with me. Horning is sucking the spiritual force from other humans. Mere death is no longer the worst thing that can happen. A soul can die."

Philippe shivered as if naked before an Arctic wind. "How is he doing this?" he asked. Maragos shook her head.

"Neither of us knows how," she said. "And in Horning's ignorance of his powers is our chance to achieve our goal. But he must not be allowed to learn what it is he is doing. For if he discovers his strength, our task becomes much greater."

"But then what is our task?" whispered Jacqueline. "Can you cure Horning of the disease?"

"I must," said Maragos. "For every soul is an essential part of The One. Without even one such as Horning, God cannot return."

"And when we meet this man," said Raoul. "Could he kill our souls as well? Not yours, I know, Maragos, but we three humans. What are we faced with?"

"Even my soul is at risk," said Maragos into the silence of deep shock. "Horning cannot absorb me, but he has become strong enough that the sickness within him could well infect me. And if Horning discovers his true powers, then an eternal night of evil faces us and all of Creation."

In early August of the year 2026, Maragos and her group appeared in the small town of Frederick, Pennsylvania. Unlike all their previous materializations, they did not appear in the middle of the town, but some six miles out of the town limits to the north east. They were driving a Ford van as if they had left Hagerstown a short while before. Jacqueline found herself at the wheel, and had to use her considerable reaction speed and rapid thinking to adjust to finding herself without warning in control of a moving vehicle. Two seconds earlier, she had been standing by the kitchen table of the house in Valence, preparing with some trepidation to appear as normally, in a city square or park.

"You might have warned me, Maragos!" she complained, as she swiftly checked the layout of the instrument panel, and ignored the startled tooting of an elderly Chrysler station wagon that passed her with three faces staring in bewilderment at the Ford. She stifled a smile, and wondered how she would have felt if a vehicle had suddenly appeared in front of her while driving along a relatively empty road.

"What, and spoil my fun?" replied Maragos. She was sitting in the rear of the vehicle, lying half recumbent along the back seat. Unlike her normal skirt and sweater outfit, Maragos was wearing a calf-length white dress with a scooped neck. Raoul was in the middle seat, and Philippe was in the passenger seat next to Jacqueline. Jacqueline looked down at herself. She had dressed that morning in jeans and a light blue shirt, but now she saw that she was in similar garb to Maragos, in a flowing dress of light yellow, a broad-brimmed hat and light gloves. The attire was slightly old-fashioned and unusually feminine for her. The two men were both in dark trousers and short-sleeved shirts.

The air of tension in the vehicle stifled any light conversation. The three humans knew that Maragos did nothing without reason and the curiously conservative dress of all of them was part of her plan, whatever that might be.

They entered the small town of Frederick and Jacqueline cautiously drove at well within the speed limit until she located what appeared to be the town centre. She parked, sensing that Maragos wished it, and they all climbed out into the pleasant late summer warmth. The square was deserted, though Philippe felt the sensation of being watched from the windows of the office blocks that surrounded them.

"Do they know who we are?" he asked, not specifically at anyone. His words seemed to float away in the warm air, like a sensation of a dream.

"Indeed they do," replied Maragos. "Infant and Baby Souls they may all be, but they cannot hide from their spiritual knowledge of who we are."

"Then why hasn't America joined the rest of the world?" asked Jacqueline. "If they know it, why hide from it?"

"They will deny us to the death until something happens to change that," answered Maragos. "The concentration of immature souls allows them to draw strength from each other and deny themselves the awareness of Oneness. Just as all the Infant Souls still on the Astral Plane who are too frightened to experience life at all still refuse to incarnate, the people here refuse to see the reality, whatever their internal souls tell them. That is the sickness at work."

"And they watch us?" asked Philippe, looking round and trying to spot faces at windows and in the shadows. A small twitch of a curtain caught his eye, but when he looked directly at it, he could see nothing.

A small chuckle broke from Maragos. "Oh yes!" she said. "And any number of officials are now on the telephone to Washington to tell them of our approach. The Council will soon be in urgent session."

"The Council?" Raoul was puzzled.

"They call it the Council for the Protection of God's Name," said Maragos. "It works like your old Inquisition did in those nasty times when to disbelieve the established truth was a heresy punishable by death."

"And their heresy today is really punishable by death?" Jacqueline was horrified. "In this day and age?"

"This day and age is more like fifteenth century Europe," replied Maragos. "President Horning has lead a flight back to those days with the full approval of the Americans who stayed here. And with the help of Philippe's old Church."

Philippe looked at her. She returned his stare and nodded.

"In fact, you will meet an old friend here, Philippe," she said. "Cardinal Lavalier has been the moving force behind this new Inquisition."

"Lavalier? He supports this?" Philippe looked distressed. "I knew he was a rigidly conservative thinker, but I had no idea he would create another Inquisition."

"He did not create it," replied Maragos. "But he enthusiastically supported the initiatives of his new Pope Pius."

"They must be very frightened," murmured Philippe. "To kill people for their beliefs is against everything Christianity stood for."

"Not the current American form of Christianity," said Raoul with an expression of distaste. Silence returned for a few moments as they looked around the deathly immobility of the town. "Of course," continued Raoul, "if opposition to the established truth results in execution, then the actual concrete evidence of the invalid nature of those established truths must cause even greater hysteria."

The four of them were silent again for a moment.

"And we represent that concrete evidence," said Jacqueline finally. "At least, Maragos does."

"Then let's go on to Washington," said Maragos. "For our task is to confront the crazies and show them the error of their ways."

"Even if it kills us, eh?" said Philippe with a tiny smile.

"Especially if it kills us," replied Maragos with a serious face and climbed back in to the van. The others followed and Jacqueline started the engine and drove gently out of town in the same direction they had been heading. Washington was less than an hour away.

# Chapter 14. The Scourge of the Inquisition

The nation's capital could have been a ghost town. Jacqueline drove slowly in through the city streets and not a vehicle was to be seen, nor a human being. Only as they drove at less than twenty miles an hour past the Smithsonian Institute towards Capitol Hill did they see a glimpse of an armoured vehicle parked closely against the wall of one building, like a dog sheltering from the sun.

While Maragos sat relaxed in the rear seat, the other three turned their heads and swung in their seats as they looked around. Washington was a new experience for them and all three felt twinges of regret that the visit should be under such circumstances. Nobody in the Ford van expected to be able to do much in the way of sight-seeing.

Jacqueline drove up to the Capitol building and parked by the sidewalk, sensing the unspoken instruction from Maragos. She opened her driver's side door and climbed out as the others made their exits from the side door. Silently, they walked up towards the stately, imposing Capitol and stopped half way up the steps. It was after eleven in the morning, a beautiful, exhilarating Summer's day, with the tiniest hint of the crispness of early Fall.

"Where is everybody?" said Philippe. "Surely, not everybody in the USA is frightened of us?"

"Nearly everybody is," said Maragos. "But Horning had a decree broadcast half an hour ago that nobody must be outdoors until the crisis is over."

"The crisis? Our arrival is a national emergency?" Raoul was almost laughing, but there was pain behind the smile.

"To frightened children like Horning, everything different is a crisis," said Maragos. She turned her head and looked around the magnificent scene. "There are soldiers in armoured vehicles behind every one of those beautiful buildings," she said with a general wave at the Smithsonian structures. "They are terrified of us because Horning has told them that we are Satan and his followers. But they will come for us, in time."

"So what shall we do?" asked Jacqueline. She was looking with longing at the Aerospace Museum. "Can we do some sight-seeing while they make up their minds?"

Philippe smiled at her with sympathy and took her hand.

"I'm afraid that the museums are closed in our honour," replied Maragos. "We may be able to arrange something at a later date."

"So shall we just sit here?" asked Raoul with doubt in his voice.

"Yes, we shall do exactly that, for a while at least," answered Maragos, and set the example by sitting down on the steps in a graceful movement. "All of you know how to pass the time by exploring your histories," she said with a smile at each of them in turn. "I suggest you do so now. We must stay here till nightfall."

"And then what?" asked Raoul, also taking a seat on the steps. "Will you take us back to Valence for the night?"

"We will not leave America until the end," replied Maragos with a shake of her head. Soft curls flew around her beautiful face. "Tonight at least, we will sleep here."

"Here?" asked Philippe. He waved his arm in a general sweep of the park and buildings. "No hotel will take us, that's for sure!"

"Indeed they won't," agreed Maragos. "We are

again in the position of one of my predecessors, though I'm a little older than he was at the time."

"Not too many barns and mangers in this area, either," said Philippe with a cold smile. "So we sleep in the van?"

"I think I can do better than that," replied Maragos. "Though it will hardly be a luxury hotel."

"Could get hungry in that time," said Jacqueline with a small grin.

"That too, I can take care of, as well you know," answered Maragos, and flicked one finger gently. The picnic hamper that appeared by her side looked heavy and inviting, and Philippe and Jacqueline immediately joined the other two sitting on the steps of the Capitol. The hamper was opened to reveal a majestic spread of paté, cheese, the French bread of which Maragos was so fond, fresh fruit and two bottles of cold Chablis. Crystal glasses, elegant china plates and silver cutlery completed the scene

For the next hour or two, the four travellers sat cheerfully under the massive presence of the centre of Government for what was left of the United States, and behaved like tourists in a way in which no tourist had ever been able to behave before.

Nobody looking at them could have imagined that these four and this scene represented the beginning of the end of the Universe.

At seven the next morning, Philippe gently disentangled himself from Jacqueline's arms and crawled from the large double sleeping bag that lay on the foam rubber mattress. He sat upright, then undid the fasteners of the tent and crawled outside into the Washington morning. The air was soft, summery, almost a return to the heat that normally plagued the city in August. Two tents had appeared by the side of the van at ten the previous night, already erected, each equipped with mattress, sleeping bags and pillows. Way past being surprised by anything that Maragos did or produced, Philippe, Jacqueline and Raoul went easily to sleep, leaving Maragos still sitting on the Capitol steps in deep thought.

As Philippe stood upright and stretched, he looked up at the steps but there was no sign of the Infinite Soul. Again without astonishment, he saw a small building a few yards away from the tent site that had not been there the night before. He walked up to it, entered, and found a well-equipped washroom, shower and toilet, soap and towels, razors and shaving cream. Smiling to himself, he took a leisurely half hour to prepare himself for the day, and returned to the tent, passing a sleepy-eyed Jacqueline. She touched his arm with a smile, and entered the washroom herself.

An hour later, all three of them were seated on the grass enjoying hot coffee and croissants.

"Martyrdom sure ain't what it used to be," Carmagio joked, loading up a hot croissant with raspberry jam. There was a muted chuckle round the group.

"What now, Maragos?" asked Philippe, pouring coffee for himself and Jacqueline from a white china pot. It seemed natural to him to address his question to the empty air. Soundlessly, Maragos appeared, sitting on the steps with a coffee cup in her hand as if she had never moved.

The Infinite sipped her own coffee thoughtfully and took a nibble at her croissant. "People will come today," she said. "We will speak to them, we will heal some."

"Horning did not lift the curfew, surely?" asked Raoul. He was taking another croissant and slicing it in two, but he paused as Maragos spoke.

She shook her head with a grin. "He did, but not willingly," she said, and reached for the coffee-pot. "I broadcast a message in his voice on all television and radio channels last night. I told the people to come here today and listen to me. It would be an object lesson in the form the Devil takes to despoil his people."

"That'll certainly put the cat among the canaries,"

said Jacqueline with a cheerful laugh. Philippe looked sideways at her with affection. She seemed undisturbed by the events that must surely follow, and he was well aware that she understood what would happen to all of them in Washington.

For the next half-hour, the four of them relaxed and finished the elegant breakfast. At nine, Maragos rose to her feet and the others followed. Instantly, the table, the seats, the tents and the washroom vanished. With a regretful backward look at the site of the vanished washroom, Jacqueline followed the others as they began to walk up the steps towards the Capitol, then stopped half way up.

They turned and looked back at the park. People were appearing, gathering in small groups in the distance, as if afraid to approach too near. The group of four remained standing silently for the next hour while the crowd grew larger and was forced by its own size to push its front edge nearer and nearer to the Capitol steps.

By soon after ten, with the heat beginning to climb, the crowd was close to the steps and stretched backwards, past the main buildings of the park to the distant road.

"I am Maragos," said the Infinite without warning. Her words were clearly heard by all the listeners and a small wave moved through the audience. "And I am here with you until Oneness."

From just behind Maragos' shoulder, and one step higher, Philippe studied the nearest faces in the crowd. Some seemed frozen, without expression. Many looked frightened but determined to listen. Several appeared shocked, holding their hands before their mouths as if to suppress sounds of fear, and many of them had tears pouring down their faces. Philippe now understood why Maragos had dressed the four of them in such conservative, gentle clothing. The crowd's shock and sense of wrongness would be amplified by the confrontation between the four of them and the military powers that Philippe knew were about to appear. It was part of Maragos' trigger of a massive explosion soon to come.

"You have been told that I am Satan, incarnated here on Earth," continued Maragos. "That is a lie, because there is no Satan. You have been told that I represent the most evil force ever to attack you and that I shall destroy the name of God. That is merely stupid, and also a lie because there is no God, except for yourselves and all of the creatures in all of time and space."

She looked into the distance, and smiled a little.

"One who professes to be a devout follower of Jesus has told you to enslave others, to hate and kill those who have different beliefs from his, to enjoy the deaths of your fellow men in public spectacles. And because you are sick children, you have followed this man directly away from the path that Jesus, Buddha and Mohammed tried to set out for you."

She stopped and looked around her. In the crowd before them, Philippe could now see more faces wet with tears and he heard the sound of weeping from amid the throng. That sound was the only break in the roaring silence that filled the park.

In the distance, a small sound of engines was the first intrusive noise of the morning. Philippe and the other two standing behind Maragos looked around but could see nothing. Maragos continued to speak.

"So do not fear the everlasting fires of Hell with which this most badly named Council for the Protection of God's Name threatens you. There is no Hell, there are no fires, and the Council is merely a collection of frightened bullies who fear the loss of their power. Be with me now and I will show you."

The sound of engines grew louder but Maragos ignored them, as did the crowd seem to, for the silence was still all-embracing. She turned slightly towards the three behind her.

"I am showing them what life on the Astral Plane is

like," she whispered. "They are seeing the awakening from death of their friends and family and their souls are healing fast."

Many in the crowd had sunk to their knees, weeping freely. The noise from the hundreds of thousands of people overflowing from the park into the roads and the courtyards of the buildings around them was the rustle of a massive flock of locusts, a sound that was everywhere, unfocused, and which waxed and waned as the summer breeze blew the echoes around.

The harsh sounds of many motors rapidly overwhelmed the noise of people, and armoured vehicles appeared from every building. Following the vehicles were armed troops, hundreds of men in helmets, riots shields and carrying automatic rifles. The forces moved slowly down the roads, forcing the people to the side, sometimes not too gently as Philippe noted, seeing men and women being thrown into others and falling in pain on the sidewalks. Sounds of screams came to him as some of the troops hit out at clumps of people around them. The first of the armoured troop carriers arrived at the roadway before the Capitol steps, stopped and more soldiers climbed out. On each vehicle, a machine gun was pointed directly at the four people standing silently on the steps of the Capitol, and the soldiers rapidly lined up in a massive semi-circle around the base of the steps. Behind the troops, the crowds pulled away from the scene, but remained thick on the grass a hundred yards away and still stretching to the rear of the park.

Twenty minutes after the first vehicle had appeared, over fifty heavy machine guns were pointed at Maragos and her followers, and more than two hundred soldiers formed a phalanx before them. This is not like Brisbane, thought Philippe, looking at the spread of military power before them. There, the small squad of police had been confused and deliberately prevented from their mission of arrest of the Maragos four. There was no such confusion here. Many of the soldiers before them looked frightened, but the grip on their rifles was not in any way weakened and the troops manning the heavy guns on the armoured vehicles looked totally determined.

"Maragos?" said Jacqueline. She looked unnerved by the display of force. "Hadn't you better take us away from this?"

Maragos did not turn her head away from looking at the troops. "That is not the way, my friend, not this time," she said quietly. "This is why we have come, to tackle the sickness at its worst point."

"Those soldiers look terrified," murmured Raoul. "And frightened men with guns in their hands are a very scary thing. They look as if they could loose control any moment."

"Do not worry, Raoul," replied the Infinite. "That would destroy our work and I can not allow that to happen. The game has to be played out or nothing is gained."

Philippe understood what she was telling them. Forces had to be unleashed by specific events, and their deaths in a storm of firepower would not achieve that end. He remembered his meeting as Benjamin ben Isaac with Jesus before the crucifixion. Jesus too, had known that events had to follow a certain path or his life and death would have been wasted. The same rules applied here, today.

At the front, the soldiers parted and two men walked through the barrier of guns and advanced up the steps to the waiting group. One was a hard-faced man with narrow-set eyes and a grim expression. Philippe looked past him and recognized the second man.

"Well, Gregory," he said to the dark, thin man in black robes a few steps below him. "We could never have thought we would meet again this way!"

Gregory Cardinal Lavalier did not smile. "You are a Heretic and excommunicate, Leger," he said. "And now you seek to bring your evil to destroy the one true ally of the Mother Church in the battle against Satan. It is my duty to see you destroyed."

The other man broke in with a gesture of irritation, though Philippe could sense the fear that lay beneath the surface. "I am Stephen Crossman," said the man. "I am the Chief Examiner of the Council for the Protection of God's Name. You will all come with me."

"You have charges against us?" asked Maragos in a gentle voice. From the wave of movement that ran through the crowd, Philippe knew that the watchers were hearing every word of the exchange. Maragos was using the same power she had used in her public appearances to broadcast this conversation.

Crossman looked directly at her for the first time, and the fear in him was amplified, radiating outward so that all of them could sense it. In Lavalier, the trembling was almost palpable.

"The charges are heresy, and conspiracy to attack the legitimate government of the United States of America," said Crossman. "You are also charged with seditious libel against the person of President Horning."

"And the penalty for these crimes, if we are found guilty?" asked Maragos. A deep silence fell on the crowd as they heard every word.

"The penalty is death on all counts," replied Crossman, and for the first time, an expression of satisfaction crossed his immobile face, but was followed immediately by irritation as the shocked murmur of the crowd whispered round the scene. The irritation was itself followed by a look of bewilderment as Crossman stared out at the crowd as if wondering how this conversation was being heard so far away.

Maragos made no reply but began to walk down the steps. The other three automatically followed her. At the road, a larger vehicle had drawn up, one with a body painted black and no other markings. One of the soldiers standing nearby moved to the vehicle and opened the door at the back to reveal a bench along each side. He stood back and the message was plain. Without hesitation, Maragos sat on the floor at the rear, swung her legs inside and stood up, taking a seat on the right hand bench. Philippe climbed in and helped Jacqueline do the same, and Raoul Carmagio brought up the rear with a final look around the scene in the park. The crowd was completely silent and the echo of the absence of noise was loud in the atmosphere. The silent soldier by the door followed them in. Under his protective helmet and eye shield the trooper looked pale and nervous. Two more armed men stood by the door, their rifles at the ready. The first soldier seemed to hesitate and draw a deep breath, then advanced first on Raoul. From under the bench he drew out heavy manacles that he snapped round Raoul's ankles. Carmagio flinched and looked at Maragos with some appeal in his eyes. She simply smiled at him and he relaxed back against the hard wall of the truck.

The soldier repeated the same with the other three, though Philippe noted that the young man hesitated before locking the two women into their seats. He sensed the feeling of deep shame in the young man and decided there was hope yet for these people.

His task complete, the armed man scrambled out of the truck and the soldiers vanished. In their place appeared the dark shapes of Stephen Crossman and Cardinal Lavalier.

"Not what we expected of Christ's representative on Earth, Leger," said Lavalier. The expression of contempt on his face was strong. "How could you embrace evil so avidly?"

"You know nothing of Christ, Gregory," answered Philippe. "And evil appears to be far more prevalent in your bailiwick. Since when has the Catholic Church endorsed the murder of innocents because of their beliefs? Is it you who leads this charge back to the Dark Ages?"

"We have no need of this sophistry, Cardinal,"

broke in Crossman. "You will have time to debate with these Devil's spawn at a later date."

He moved back and the door slammed shut, leaving a gloomy light in the cabin of the truck. With a vicious jerk, the truck moved off.

The drive was nearly an hour long and nothing could be seen from within the truck which swayed and jolted as they moved. Despite the thunderous bellow of the vehicle's engines and the metallic racket of the cabin in which they rode, the four prisoners were able to hear sirens at intervals, indicating that they were in a convoy accompanied by other vehicles. Philippe assumed the convoy consisted of the armoured personnel carriers and troops that had been present at their arrest.

As they travelled, little conversation took place. Maragos appeared lost in calm deliberations of her own, the other three were less at ease. All of them felt some fear at their situation, and they chaffed at the frightening feeling of steel clamps round their ankles and at the claustrophobia of their surroundings. At the same time, despite their worries, Philippe, Jacqueline and Raoul understood that a path had been laid down by Maragos and had to be followed. All of them had faith in the wisdom of the Infinite Soul to lead them where Humanity would be best served.

The drive ended in a violent jerk of brakes and all four of them were flung hard against their chains. None of them uttered a sound. The door to the vehicle was flung open with a slam of metal against metal as it smashed against the side of the truck and dim light filtered in. They were not in the open but within what looked like a cavernous warehouse. Occasional noises of slamming doors and collisions of metallic objects rang through the air.

Two soldiers climbed into the vehicle, and while one stayed standing with his heavy automatic rifle at the ready, the other slung his weapon over his shoulder, took a heavy key from his belt and knelt at the feet of Maragos. Looking at him, Philippe could see the same expression of mixed fear and shame on the young man's face as had been displayed earlier when the locks had been put in place.

Quickly releasing the remaining three of them, the soldier stood up and followed his companion out of the truck. Standing stiffly, the four prisoners did the same, Philippe helping Jacqueline step down, and Raoul offering the same courtesy to Maragos. Once outside the truck, they looked around them.

The building was as huge as it had seemed from within the vehicle. It could have been a hangar for three or more Jumbo airliners, thought Philippe. Lines of armed troops stood against all four walls, equipped with riot gear of helmets, shields and heavy weapons. *Do they really understand what they have captured?* thought Philippe in amusement. *Do they really not comprehend just how immense is the power inside the small frame of the young woman standing next to me?* He turned to study the view inside the building.

At the side of the building opposite from the huge doors that had admitted the trucks, a set of staircases led at three different points up to a balcony, off which led six doors. The sensation of menace behind those doors was physical, it seemed to Philippe. There was danger, horror, violence on the other side of those doors and he shivered a little with the fear that touched his mind. The occasional clang of movement in the building only served to emphasize how huge it was, and for a moment, he sensed the agony and terror of the many people who had been brought here in captivity. Their pain had infused the walls, floated in the air around them and left a psychic smell of despair, the way the atmosphere of prisons invariably did.

The harsh-faced man, Crossman, Philippe recalled, who had accosted them outside the Capitol walked up to them. For a moment or two, he stared at the prisoners and Philippe thought he saw uncertainty in Crossman's face.

"You will follow me," snapped Crossman, and began to walk towards the stairs at the end of the building. Looking quickly at Maragos who smiled back at them, Jacqueline, Philippe and Raoul followed the Infinite as she walked calmly behind Crossman. They climbed the metal stairs in the middle of the wall, reached the balcony and waited while Crossman rapped on one of the doors that opened immediately.

Behind the door was a dimly-lit corridor. Crossman opened a solid door on the right hand side of the corridor, and gestured at Maragos. "Inside," he snapped, though a small catch could be heard in his voice. She turned at the door, looked firmly at each of them, then entered the room. All three of them clearly heard her voice inside them.

"I am with you," said the silent voice of Maragos.

Crossman slammed the door behind her, and his relief was evident. He led off again, stopped outside another door, and pointed at Philippe. "You," he said, and looked angry as Philippe took Jacqueline's hand and gently kissed it. She smiled back at him, and Philippe walked into the room.

Two minutes later, all four of them were locked inside the interrogation rooms.

*(From the Diary of Alan Drew)*
*August 11, 2026*
Crossman looked frightened, and that delighted me, though his orders crushed the delight immediately.

"You will observe the interrogation of the woman," he snapped at me, and jerked his head to indicate that I should follow him. It is the first time in over two years that I have been ordered to such a task. I think Crossman knows that I am merely observing, that my presence at these dreadful procedures no longer represents the approval of the Holy See. But since Cardinal Lavalier has not spoken to me for weeks, I'm not sure whether this assignment results from his wish to see me repelled by the interrogation of a woman, to confirm to the Vatican that he is in complete charge of events, or from his fear that I can almost touch.

But I have snapped out of my detached mood of some months. I heard that the Maragos Four, as they have been termed, finally arrived in Horning's America a few days ago. The fear throughout Washington has been thick as a sea fog, especially within the White House. I have heard of dreadful, evil things happening in that place. In trembling voices, people tell me of visitors to the Oval Office falling dead in front of the President, their bodies carried out while Horning cavorts in glee, somehow energised by the deaths. I can only believe that Horning is truly Satan himself, or at least, some agent from Hell, sent to torment us on Earth. And this sends my mind into a complete turmoil. For the Catholic Church has declared Horning the last defence against Evil. But he is Evil. Does that mean that perhaps this woman, this Maragos is the force for Good? Is she, my God, *could* she be Christ returned? Courageous minds have often uttered the possibility that God's Son would return as a female, but my dogma has never allowed for this. But my Church is totally opposed to this woman. Could we be wrong? I fear that I cannot withstand much more of this fear, this bewilderment, this terrible possibility that I have worked for the forces of Satan all my life. And now I must face up to my fears. Maragos has appeared, and with her, two men to whom I once gave my total faith and allegiance. I have heard that there is another woman also, a countrywoman of mine, an English woman named Jacqueline Carter.

Whatever faces me now, I pray for the strength to handle it. It may truly be the final proof that I have served Satan and broken my vows. And under the fear is a fascination. Who or what is this woman, Maragos? What if she truly is Christ returned? What will that do to the last of my strength and courage? I followed Crossman and waited while the door to the cell opened, feeling my blood pounding in my head. He ignored me and I could sense the fear inside the man. Something completely beyond the comprehension of the American was going on, and Crossman was barely in control of himself. He paused at the doorway as if uncertain and unwilling to enter. When he did, he kept his eyes firmly averted from the wooden interrogation chair.

I followed him in, and immediately felt the power of the presence in the room. It was like standing before an open blast furnace, but the heat was not painful. It was warmth, goodness, kindness. I have always felt that this would surely be how the presence of God would feel, and with that, all my doubts vanished. Maybe she is Christ, maybe she is something else beyond my imagination, but I knew as surely as I knew that Horning was evil, that this woman was close to God. But she was simply a young woman. She was beautiful, that I could see. She was dressed in a simple dress, her face glowed with warmth and love. The sight of the manacles enclosing her ankles and wrists was horrible, but she seemed unconcerned. Another man stood against the far wall, and the fear and tension in him radiated strongly, but was nearly lost in the power of the force from the woman in the chair.

I watched as Crossman fought to collect his strength and composure, then he walked to the back of the small room and picked up one of those hideous metal wands from the desk against the wall. He walked up behind the seated woman. "What is your name?" he demanded. His voice was coarse, distorted by the nervousness he was feeling.

"My name is Maragos," replied the seated woman. In contrast, her voice was soft and gentle, almost as if trying to comfort Crossman. She gave a small smile to me, and the thunderous explosion of energy I experienced nearly threw me off my feet. I leaned back against the wall, sweating profusely.

"Your full name!" snapped Crossman with irritation.

"My full name? I have twenty-five billion names," Maragos said. "Which would you like?"

"I warn you, young lady," said Crossman with dangerous tension in his voice, still standing behind the chair. "Do not make jokes with me. I want your first and family names."

"Maragos is the only name I have ever used," replied the woman.

"That is an inappropriate response," said Crossman, and touched the silver wand to her neck. I nearly jerked in expectation of a scream of pain from the woman.

There was no scream. Maragos looked calmly at the man standing silently against the wall in front of her, and I saw the shock in his face. My heart lurched. Something incredible, unbelievable and wonderful was happening.

"Roston, I thought I told you to check that this wand was fully charged," Crossman snapped.

The man in front of Maragos looked alarmed. "I did, sir," he answered, nerves rasping in his throat. "It was fully tested ten minutes ago."

"Well go and get another one," said Crossman. "Better still, bring me several."

Without a word, the heavy man left. Crossman threw the metal wand into a waste paper bin in one corner, and it rattled as it fell in.

"What are your parents' names?" asked Crossman, resuming his questioning, and walked in front of the chair, staring down at Maragos. She lifted her face and looked at him, but he moved his eyes down to her knees and refused to meet her gaze.

"You don't understand what I am, do you?" asked Maragos. "Your question has no basis for response at all."

"No basis? I asked you a simple enough question. What are the names of your parents, and where were you born?"

"Any answer I might give you is totally beyond

your comprehension, Stephen," said Maragos. "You must lose your concrete mind-set before I could make any sense to you."

Crossman seemed rattled. "You will always address me simply as 'Sir'," he snapped. "Do not forget the position in which you find yourself."

"I could hardly do that," responded Maragos with a smile. "I have a task, and it will take many years to achieve it."

"Years?" said Crossman with anger. "I doubt you even have days. And just what task is it that will take so long?"

"To bring Humanity to Oneness," answered Maragos.

Crossman leapt at her words. "So you admit that you are a follower of that Devil's creed of Oneness? You are an admitted Heretic?" He had recovered his composure with the words of Maragos. He was on familiar ground, and the hunt for evil had proved astonishingly simple.

The door opened and Roston walked in, carrying a cardboard box from which protruded the handles of several of the metal wands. He offered the box to Crossman who took one and gestured with his head. Roston placed the box on the desk and returned to his place by the wall in front of Maragos.

"Let us start again," said Crossman, when the room had settled. "You are now an admitted heretic for which the punishment is death. So let us now hear your full name, the place of your birth and the names of your parents."

"My full name is Maragos," answered the woman in the chair, "because I chose it when I came to self-awareness. And I either have no parents, or twenty-five billion, or maybe just one. All is choice."

"Your words make no sense at all," said Crossman. He appeared calm and fully in control of the situation. He walked forward to look down on Maragos, and the wand in his hands swished lightly as he waved it.

"I said that would be the case, Stephen," replied Maragos.

"And I told you how I was to be addressed," responded Crossman and touched the wand to Maragos' neck.

Again there was no result. From the wall, a tiny gasp was heard from Roston, and Crossman stared in amazement at the wand. I felt like laughing with joy and stared hard at the woman sitting in her bonds.

"You drew new supplies of these, Roston?" asked Crossman and turned towards the other man.

"Yes, sir, I did," stammered Roston. His eyes widened as Crossman moved further towards him, then he tried to push back against the wall as Crossman's intention became clear.

"No! Please sir, no!" he begged and tried to fend Crossman off. The wand flashed out and the tip gave a feather-light touch on Roston's cheek. The muscular man jerked and his eyes rolled up as he let out a small shout of pain, then fell silent, his hand on his cheek like a small boy. His eyes were full of tears as he looked at Crossman. But the Chief Examiner had turned back to Maragos, with a thoughtful expression. He laid the wand flat across Maragos' right cheek, and she smiled up at him.

"Do you not yet realize, Stephen, that your toys cannot hurt me?" she asked, gently.

"The Devil protects his own kind," replied Crossman and drew back, making the sign of the cross in the air between them. Against the wall, Roston did the same and I sensed the trembling in the man's body across the small space in the room.

"The Devil has nothing to do with it," replied Maragos. "It's a simple matter of energy dissipation. There is more of me than you can see in this room, and that little device could not reach across time and space to affect the whole of me."

Crossman looked frightened, but said nothing for a moment. He took a few deep breaths and regained his voice. "Let us return to some of your earlier answers to my questions," he said. "You said you had no parents, or twenty-five billion, or perhaps just one. Explain that statement."

"Stephen," she began. Crossman said nothing, but gave an angry glance at Roston who lowered his eyes to the floor. "I am not what I appear," Maragos continued. "I am the sum total of twenty-five billion souls who lived on another planet. That planet was so far away that not even the galaxy that held it has been identified by your astronomers."

Crossman laughed, almost a cough of derision. "So it's the little green men from Mars game, is it?" he snorted. "I thought I had a serious heretic, and all it seems I have netted is a madwoman!" For the first time since entering, Crossman looked at me. His expression was triumphant.

Roston did not join in the laughter but stared at Maragos. He swallowed convulsively. She smiled briefly at him and that earned another furious glare from Crossman.

"And if it was only one parent," continued Crossman with contempt in his tone, "do you care to enlighten me as to whom that might be?"

"The One," she replied simply. "I am merely one of the original offspring of The One."

"And just who exactly is 'The One'?" Crossman demanded. He bent over Maragos in the chair, his fear apparently gone in the face of this obvious insanity.

"You would term it God," Maragos replied.

Crossman snapped upright in rage, and whipped the metal wand harshly against each cheek of the seated woman. I flinched in dismay then eased my mind as I realized that nothing could hurt this attractive young woman. She was a force greater than anything ever before experienced on Earth.

"Blasphemy!" Crossman shouted in fury. "You dare to claim that you are the direct offspring of God? You claim to be equal to Jesus? Maybe you claim to be

Jesus in the Second Coming? May you burn in Hell forever!"

He stood away from her, gasping in the aftermath of his rage. She sat without emotion, no movement, no evidence that the wand had made any impact on her face.

"No, not equal to Jesus," she replied. "I am much more than Jesus was."

The silence rang like a bell in the room. Crossman finally broke it. "You are obviously totally insane," he said and took a handkerchief from his pocket to wipe the spittle that hung from his lips. "But insanity is no defence against the charge of heresy nor of blasphemy. You are a self-confessed perpetrator of both crimes. Your trial will be short and you will die within days. I will not even ask God to have mercy on your soul because you are beyond His mercy."

"This is your first time on Earth, Stephen," said the seated woman. "So you are the most infantile of Infant Souls. I cannot expect you to be anything but what you are. The sickness is very strong in you, worse than I have met in any other soul so far."

Crossman was trembling as hard as his subordinate still standing silently by the wall. "What are these ravings, madwoman?" he said, the words shaking with his tremors.

"Deep inside of yourself you know what I am saying," she replied. The leather straps round her ankles and wrists vanished and she stood up. "As an early-stage Infant Soul, you can only be frightened of anything new, and you are desperate to cling to an authority figure like President Horning, unable to comprehend anything outside your immediate frame of reference."

Roston gave out a sob of fear, pulled open the door and fled. Crossman was obviously holding on to his courage tightly. His eyes were wide and staring, and more spittle had appeared on his lips. I was holding my breath, feeling like a spectator to the culmination of a hunt where the snake stares down the rat.

"But you are also very sick," continued Maragos. "To have waited till only forty years ago to choose your first incarnation shows great fear. I regret that when you die, your death experience will be a dreadful one for you, but you must go through it to learn."

Crossman's face was chalk white, and spittle fell from his mouth to his shirt. "I will not listen to any more of this blasphemous babbling," he stuttered, and walked out of the room, slamming the heavy door behind him. The crash of his departure rang through the confined space until absorbed by the ageless stone of the walls. I was alone with the woman that I now thought of as the returned Christ, despite her words to the contrary.

Maragos remained standing, and turned to me. "It confuses you, Alan," she said with a gentle smile. "The sickness makes it hard for the truth to reach your soul."

I felt calm warmth run through me. "They told me you are the ultimate evil," I said struggling to control my voice.

"Is that how I seem to you?" she asked.

I shook my head. "I have struggled for months to understand how you could represent Satan, while Ultimate Goodness is the killing in the deserts and in America. I could not see how these tortures were in the name of God."

"But you cannot see Oneness yet," she said, a statement, not a question.

I felt awful grief at the truth of her words. Maybe she wasn't Christ, but I knew that she represented Goodness on this poor Earth.

"Many millions share your confusion, Alan," she said. "That is why I am here. It will come to all of you, in time."

I felt such warmth from her that I nearly wept.

She smiled again. "You are to see one more interrogation," she said. "This one is of your old friend, Philippe Leger. It may surprise you."

"The idea fills me with disgust," I replied. "Can Philippe withstand this the way you can?"

"He will learn," she replied, and sat back calmly in the wooden chair. "Go now, Alan," she said. "They will be coming for me. Soon, you will see Oneness."

Feeling a wonderful surge of energy, I walked out of the cell.

Philippe Leger watched carefully as an armed soldier strapped his wrists and ankles to the heavy wooden chair in which he had been placed. He felt cold inside, unable to deny that he was frightened. This was the first time he had been separated from his friends since the group had become complete with the arrival of Jacqueline at his home in Valence. The soldier completed his task and left, never once having looked directly into Philippe's eyes. Philippe had watched him the whole time, seeing the boy's fresh-faced skin, the friendly face clamped in nervousness and the broad forehead under light brown hair. The face of a young man from a southern or mid-west farm region, thought Philippe. Brought up in a Bible-belt district of strict fundamentalist principles, trained never to question authority or think for himself. A place where good family values and closeness had been corrupted by the meanness and viciousness of religious autocracy, and old values manhandled until they had been replaced by blood-lust and xenophobia masquerading under the names of patriotism and national pride.

The boy closed the door quietly, and Philippe sat still, trying to quell the fear and worry. Whatever was about to happen to him was probably the same as would happen to Raoul and Jacqueline, and he felt rage and despair at that thought. For Maragos he felt no concerns, she could obviously handle anything that the powers of William Horning could throw at her.

After five minutes, the door opened and three men walked in. The first, Philippe did not know at all. He was a young man, probably in his thirties, dressed simply in dark blue slacks and a light blue, short-sleeved shirt with military-style epaulets on the shoulders. He carried a small device that Philippe identified as a hand-held computer with a radio antenna sticking out from the top of it. *The Inquisition goes high-tech*, thought Philippe in slight amusement, despite his fear.

The next two men, Philippe did know. One was expected.

"Hello again, Gregory," said Philippe to Cardinal Lavalier. "This must be the high spot of your life, I imagine."

Lavalier said nothing but moved to the wall at one side of Philippe's seat and stood with his hands clasped in front of him. He was dressed in full robes, a black gown and red skull cap with a red sash round his waist.

The third man was not expected.

"Alan!" said Philippe in a mix of surprise and dismay. "I did not think to find that you had become part of the Inquisition."

For a moment, Alan Drew looked at his old Pontiff, and Philippe stared back at him. The eyes said it all, thought Philippe. Alan was not a willing part of this. The anger and defiance in his soul spoke loudly to him. Alan was playing out some role of his own, Philippe decided. He nodded gently at the English priest and saw the gratitude for the understanding reflected in his face. Alan moved to the wall and stood by the Cardinal, adopting the same pose as his superior.

The young man in the semi-military attire had been standing by the small desk at the back of the small room. He advanced on Philippe and stood before him. He was holding a metal wand, which Philippe studied suspiciously.

"Your name is Philippe Alain Leger?" he inquired. He might have been checking Philippe's driver's license for all the emotion he exhibited.

"It is," agreed Philippe in the same unemotional tone.

"And your home is in Valence, France?"

"Yes."

"And how did you enter the United States of America, Leger?"

Philippe grinned. "Teleportation," he replied.

The young man did not respond to the smile. "That is an inappropriate answer," he said, and touched the metal wand to the side of Philippe's neck.

The pain was unlike anything Philippe had ever experienced or could even have imagined. A streak of searing, burning agony exploded in his neck and leaped furiously down through his chest, almost stopping his heart. Unable to prevent himself, Philippe let out a shout of horrified pain and strained against his straps.

"Oh Maragos!" he whispered inside himself. "Please don't let Jacqueline have to go through this."

"Courage, my friend," came the voice of the Infinite Soul in his mind. "Look inside yourself and see how to control the pain. See how to stop it, reverse it even, and stop the madness."

With his head slumped down as if unconscious, Philippe began exploring the path of the receding pain, where it had burned and how it had tracked to his brain. He followed his nervous system, his mind fully now inside his own body, exploring nerve endings, lines to the brain... and he saw it. He saw how to block the path of sensation to his brain, how to reflect the burning agony back to the metal wand, back even further to the hand that held it.

He raised his head and looked back at the young man, then he looked sideways at the two churchmen. "This is not the way to salvation, Gregory," he said, his voice hoarse from the pain and shock. "I do believe that you would subject Jesus to this same evil if he ever returned."

Gregory Cardinal Lavalier said nothing, but a small spot of anger burned in his cheeks. Alan Drew reflected horror in his eyes. *Whatever it is you are doing, Alan,* thought Philippe, *it's taking courage. I hope you find your own answers in all this.*

"Leger, I will repeat my question," said the man with the wand. He seemed unaffected by the anger within the room. "How did you enter this country?"

"We simply... arrived," answered Philippe. "If I told you the truth, you would be unable to comprehend it."

"Try me," replied the man sarcastically. "You never know."

As much as he could in his bonds, Philippe shrugged. "The woman we follow is named Maragos," he said. "She is a Soul of immense powers. She simply transported us from my home, and we were suddenly in a van driving towards Washington."

"That answer makes no sense," said the Examiner. "Now we will have the correct answer, or this device touches you again."

"I told you that would be the case," responded Philippe. "If your mind can't follow the truth, then that is your problem, not mine."

"I think not," said the man, and touched the wand to Philippe's neck again.

Philippe switched his mind to the newly-discovered internal controls and activated them. He sensed the wand touch his neck, but felt nothing but a slightly warm, metallic tip. But the man holding the device screamed harshly, dropped the wand and collapsed to his knees, clutching his right hand to his chest with his left and bowing his head as if trying to smother the burning in his own body. The wand lay where it had fallen on the stone floor.

The man's scream faded to a sobbing, and he looked up at Philippe, the hatred and terror in his face radiating like an electric fire. "The work of the Devil!" he gasped. "See Cardinal, witness this evil. The man is truly a son of Satan!"

Philippe had lost interest in the scene. He had discovered another power inside himself and was exploring it. Slowly, he eased his consciousness away from its usual boundaries and found himself looking down on his body where it had slumped in the chair. He watched as the two churchmen displayed shock and dismay and moved to the chair to examine the body held in place by the straps.

"He's dead?" demanded Lavalier in rage, as Alan checked Philippe's pulse at the side of the neck.

"No, Eminence," answered Alan. "Merely unconscious."

"Thank God for that," replied Lavalier. "His death must not come before the proper time."

"And when will that be, Eminence?" asked Drew, looking up from his examination of Philippe. His expression was unreadable, but Lavalier sensed anger in the English priest.

"That is outside your interest, Father," snapped the Cardinal in irritation, realizing he had said too much. "Perhaps you could switch your assistance from that criminal to the Examiner?"

Alan looked in disgust at the man kneeling on the floor, still clutching his hand and moaning softly. "I think not, Eminence," he replied, and stood back against the wall. Lavalier glared at him, but Alan ignored the look, and concentrated his attention inside his own head where strange things were happening.

"Alan, what is it that you are doing?" asked Philippe, speaking directly to the soul of the priest.

"Holy Father, it is you?" came the startled words of Alan who was standing motionless, his eyes closed.

"Still stuck in the old concepts, Alan?" said Philippe, letting amusement flood the path to Alan's mind. "Have you not yet grasped what is happening?"

"I know that the old truths have gone," replied

Alan. "But the new ones have not yet come to me. I pray daily that they will, but I fear that perhaps they are not for me."

"They are for everybody, Alan," said Philippe gently. "For we are all one and the same, all part of the Supreme Being that we have called God."

"Then why can I not see the way, my lord?" begged Alan.

"Alan, my name is Philippe. I want you to call me that from now on. And I promise you, you will see the way shortly."

"Would that I could see it now, Philippe," said Alan, the grief coming out strongly in his thought patterns. "But the truth seems so far above me, like birds that fly above my head."

With a small shock, Philippe recalled how similar were his words when, as Benjamin ben Isaac, he had begged for the truth and guidance from Jesus two thousand years before. He studied the soul of Alan Drew carefully. He read that Alan was a Mature Soul at a late stage of development, almost ready to be an Old Soul, but that the sickness was holding him back, the way that pneumonia stopped the body breathing properly and prevented the blood flow from taking oxygen to the brain. Alan was fogged in his perceptions. To Philippe, the sickness looked like a green and yellow discolouration that permeated the soul of the English priest and hung in clusters around the power centres of his mind.

Drawing on abilities he was finding by the second in himself, and taking extra strength from the Infinite Soul, Philippe attacked the sickness in the Priest and saw how it receded, how Alan's perceptions cleared and how the roaring flood of understanding filled his soul. Alan fell to his knees weeping, but suffused with gladness as he saw the truth of Oneness.

"You must go now, Alan," said Philippe, still speaking at the psychic level. "Go and fill the position that once I had. Write down all you can remember of this insanity of the new Inquisition. Record it for history one day to read."

Alan Drew rose to his feet and began to walk to the door.

"Father!" snapped Cardinal Lavalier. "Just where do you think you are going?"

Alan turned and smiled at his ex-superior. "I am no Father," he replied with a gentle smile. "That nonsense is over. And all this," he continued, waving at the interrogation room, "all this will thankfully be over soon, too. Oneness is upon us."

"I will have you before the Council for this!" shouted Lavalier.

"Very likely," replied Alan and opened the door. "But after all, the only thing you can do is kill me. What fear is there in that?"

He walked out, leaving the Cardinal and the Examiner of the Council for the Protection of God's Name staring in rage and confusion at each other.

Philippe moved his soul out of the room and located a similar cell where Jacqueline was strapped into a chair as his own body was. She was looking strained and white, and the fear in her was palpable. She was alone in the room with another Examiner, an older man than the one who had tormented Philippe. This one was verging on obesity, his belly stuck out from his belt and heavy jowls hung from his face. Philippe ignored him and concentrated on Jacqueline. "I am with you, my love," he said directly to her mind, and watched as she relaxed and her face broke into a smile.

"I know," she said, and love flowed from her into his soul. Swiftly, he showed her the technique for reversing the pain of the metal wands and she absorbed it gratefully.

"I must leave you now," he said to her, and her warmth flooded into him again.

"We will meet again, very soon," she said.

"We will," he agreed, and touched her mind with a

loving gesture. He watched as the grossly fat Examiner showed rage at the smile on Jacqueline's face, touched her neck with the wand and collapsed screaming on the floor, the way Philippe's own tormentor had done. Smiling to himself, Philippe moved on and discovered another similar room where Raoul was being interrogated. He was too late here to prevent agony, he saw at once. Raoul was slumped in the chair, and ferocious, red weals of pain were burned across both cheeks. Immediately, Philippe felt the presence of Raoul's psychic presence. Carmagio too, had been able to leave his physical body.

"They got to you, old friend," said Philippe.

Raoul smiled at him. "The pain caught me by surprise," he said. "It was easier to leave the body for a time."

"But you have seen what to do now," said Philippe, recognizing the learning in his companion of many years and many lifetimes.

With a nod of agreement, Raoul let himself sink back into his body, and Philippe watched as the bound man sat upright and looked at the Examiner, a tall, slender and quite attractive woman. Looking at her, Philippe read her as an early stage Infant Soul in only her third incarnation. Like most of the people still living in what remained of the United States, she was a very immature soul, showing the sickness heavily in her psychic form. He left to go back to his own body, just as the woman's scream of pain showed that she too, had experienced the reversal of the agony of the metal wands.

Ten at night, and all four of the prisoners were locked into individual cells a floor below the level that held the interrogation rooms. Following the attempts by four separate Examiners to inflict pain on the group, guards had been called in, and the prisoners taken to separate cells. The chances for further interrogation sessions appeared limited.

# The Nightmares of God

Philippe was recumbent on the narrow, hard bunk that was the sole piece of furniture in the cell except for an iron bucket. He lay with his arms behind his head, staring at the ceiling.

Quite a fall from grace for Pope Jean-Pierre II, Vicar of Christ, Bishop of Rome, Head of the Catholic and Apostolic Church, occupier of the Throne of Peter and God's representative on Earth, he mused to himself. He was uncertain exactly how he felt about the situation. This was a most uncomfortable place to be, that was a fact, and his body still stung from the one successful application of those evil little metal wands that carried so much pain in them. He felt the separation from Jacqueline as a form of emptiness in his spirit that depressed him intensely.

On the other hand, he thought, what other man in history has ever played the role he was playing now? Here he was, repeating much of the story of Jesus Christ in a new version of the Second Coming on a scale of enormity that nobody could ever have forecast. He was at the centre of events that heralded the end of the world, of the Universe, of Creation itself, the return to consciousness of the Supreme Power that he had once called God, but was something different from the image of his learning and training.

What a life it had been! More intense, more crowded, more exhilarating and ultimately more fulfilling than any of the four hundred and five incarnations of his past, all of which he could now remember in detail, right back to the very first....

*Ram-sah of the Big Shoulders stood looking across the valley at the rain storm that was building in the mountains on the other side. Huge, towering cumulo-nimbus darkened the skies though Ram-sah had no such name for these clouds. To him and his tribe, they were simply the Bringers of Trouble, and they had been appearing much more often the last few seasons. Even in his childhood, Ram-sah was clear in his memory that the Bringers of Trouble had not come so often. Now they were almost a daily event, making life a misery of cold, soaking torture. The streams of his childhood were now ravaging torrents of floodwaters that tore open the banks and raced unfettered across the plains, leaving them sodden, stony where the soil had been stripped away. The lakes of a few years ago had become a sea that had blocked off the lands to the east and were steadily rising.*

*The temperatures had been dropping these last few years, too. Ram-sah had a heavy animal skin draped across his shoulders, though it was supposed to be the warm season. And the animals had been disappearing. The tribe had to spend days hunting for food now and it was not so uncommon that the men arrived back after many days of the exhausting chase across the rough, uncompromising land with the carcass of prey, to find that the woman and children had lost some of their numbers to predators, or cold, or simple weakness caused by days without food.*

*Ram-sah shivered at the awful sight in front of him. The clouds writhed like demented snakes, long trails of green-grey mist hung from the tops of the mountainous hulks down toward the ground, and even from here, Ram-sah could see the spinning columns of red sand and stones lifting skyward.*

*He jerked in shock as a network of lightning painted a hissing web across the arc of gloomy sky then exploded in a mind-numbing crash and rumble that he could feel as a vibration in his feet and legs that climbed upward and made his guts shiver.*

*He resisted the fear that wanted to drive him to the ground and hide his head in his animal skin. A small thought crossed his mind that he should have been more afraid. At other times, blind terror had overtaken him during these storms and he had crawled under a rock, sobbing and moaning. Instead, he watched the elemental warfare that was taking place across the valley. It was a few moments before he realized that the rumbles of thunder had increased, not faded after the patchwork of lightning had vanished and the after-image faded from his retina. Instead, the rumbles had grown, become a constant thunder, like the growling of the big cats as they lay under the trees in the day. The sound grew until the vibrations began in his feet and climbed upwards and his whole body shook with the beat of unimaginably huge energies.*

*He knew that he should be frightened. Such a noise as this had never been heard across the lands of this world. This was worse than all the storms that had ever hurled themselves furiously across the hemisphere of sky, screaming anger at the gods of the sun and the two moons. Never had the Earth shaken as it did now, so violently that the storm across the valley shrank into insignificance. But somehow, the fear did not reach him the way it should have done. Almost, he stood outside himself and watched as his large, shaggy body, stooped under the weight of the massive head and jawbone, holding the primitive spear in his hand, stood silently watching the skies to the west. He knew that something unknown, something massive was approaching, something as far outside his comprehension as the sun, the moons and the distant points of light in the night skies.*

*The ground shook even harder, so that standing upright became a problem, but he dug his spear into the sandy soil and balanced himself. Back in the caves where his people had their home, he could imagine the panic that this monstrous happening was causing. And yet, looking at himself from the outside, he understood that if he felt no fear himself, perhaps the others also were unafraid.*

*It came from the other side of the world, covering the sky as if the mountains themselves had leaped upward toward the sun. So huge, that the grey sky began to turn even darker. It was massive, oval-shaped, smooth like a stone that has lain in the river for many years, and as black as the inside of the cave when the fires died. It drifted slowly over the mountains and then truly covered the sky, and the shadow of its passing hid him and the few trees and the rocks and the foothills in one single, unreadable darkness.*

*Still he stood there, unable to move but unafraid. Only a tiny voice inside himself asked why this was so. Why was he not afraid? It was not natural, he knew. But still he watched, and the great black rock slowly lowered itself from the sky and settled on the sand of the empty plains in front of him, the mighty thunder faded and the land became still again.*

*The voice that spoke in his head was soft, gentle, yet hid great power in its smallness.*

*"Ram-sah of the Big Shoulders, we are your cousins from distant lands. You must come with us and we will take you and your people to lands where the sun is warm, and the animals are plentiful, and the hunt will feed you all again. This land is dying."*

*Feeling as if he were in a strange dream, Ram-sah answered the soft voice in his head. "I hear you, my cousin, though this is very strange and I know that I should fear you. Where will you take us? We have travelled the whole world in our hunting, and everywhere is cold and dying. What other lands can there be?"*

*The small voice showed warm amusement. "These are lands so distant, Son of Man, that a different sun will shine on you. Gather your people, Ram-sah, and bring them to this shape that you see before you. You can rest here in warmth and safety, and you will have as much food as you wish while we gather up the animals and birds of this world to take with you to your new home."*

*Ram-sah stood upright, pulled his spear from the ground and turned towards the cave where his people were. The walk took a few hours, but before the night had fallen, he was back with them. They were strangely silent too, already gathering their weapons and clothing and preparing to walk with him.*

*He waved them back from the mouth of the cave. "We will not walk in the darkness," he said. "Sleep here this night. Tomorrow we will visit our cousins from distant lands."*

*Still silent, without confusion, they prepared for sleep for their last night on this world. The next day, they began the walk towards the massive black stone that had arrived on their plains. As they approached it, perceptions became dimmer and dimmer, and they had only faint recollections of entering the ship that had been sent for them by others of The One who feared for the safety of mankind.*

*They had no memories as they slept in the massive space-ship for the next ten days, while beings who only barely resembled men gathered up the birds and the animals and put them in the same suspended animation in that their human passengers slept. The task was not difficult. The same tranquillizing agent that had been poured into the atmosphere of the sixth planet out from Epsilon Indi to prevent a wave of panic among the primitive humans had gentled the beasts of the planet also, and they were easily collected and transported to the ship. At the same time, other tribes of humans were soothed and gathered into the holds of the ship.*

*A day after the last animal had been safely moved inside, the ground shook and the mountains trembled as the ship lifted itself back into space. Mankind left its slowly freezing first home to be taken to the third planet from Epsilon's near neighbour, the star that men one day would call Sol.*

*Ram-sah of the Big Shoulders, whose first incarnation this was, who one day would be Ananda the cousin and loyal companion of Buddha, Benjamin ben Isaac follower of Jesus, Waraqa ibn Nawfal, spiritual advisor and friend of Mohammed, and even later, Philippe Leger, Pope Jean-Pierre II, slept through the thirty-minute voyage that covered over seven light-years. It was a year after they had settled on the plains of Africa and begun their trek to the north that memories of the events on another planet began to surface in the minds of the tribe of Ram-sah and the others who had made the trip across the empty light-years. Then it was that tales of the great vessel began to be told and stored in the tribes' histories, one day to be written as the story of Noah.*

Philippe Leger rubbed his eyes and took a deep breath. His very first incarnation! He had stood on the first world of Mankind and seen the spaceship of a race of beings arrive from a world so far away that not even the galaxy that held it had yet been seen and noted by human astronomers. He had been in the wave of Neanderthal humans who had been relocated on Earth and started again. The wonder and excitement of the life he had just relived filled his body with joy. Discounting present difficulties as irrelevant, Philippe turned over on his narrow bunk and fell asleep.

Jacqueline Carter was also awake, but for different reasons. She had few concerns about her present stressful circumstances. Now in her early thirties, she had less of a history of worldly success than her two male companions, and so less to regret losing. She also had a deep comprehension of the mechanisms of the Infinite Soul's plan and fully understood, had always understood what must happen here in Washington. Having explored many of her past lives now, she was able to put her death into perspective, and see how small a thing it was. With Philippe's help, she had been able to conquer the pain that the evil metal wands carried by the Examiners could cause and she no longer worried about further interrogations.

No, her distress was caused more simply by the close proximity of the Smithsonian Air and Space

Museum and her inability to visit it. Since her awakening to the world of aviation as a small girl she had studied every major aircraft that had ever been built. Many had taken her fancy and captured her imagination in special ways. Apart from the Spitfire she had flown in her last incarnation as a young Jerome Mitchell, she had developed a love for the beautiful lines of the American Mustang, a sense of awe at the first true supersonic rocket, the Bell X-1 flown by Chuck Yeager. These and other wonders of her youth were on display in the Museum and she couldn't get to see them.

"Damn, blast and hell!" she muttered to herself and was unsurprised to hear a responsive chuckle. Maragos was sitting on the edge of the bunk and grinning widely.

"Frustrated, my friend?" asked the petite woman who held all the souls of an entire species within her.

"You've said it!" replied Jacqueline, and immediately felt more cheerful.

"Then let's do something about it," replied Maragos, and the cell dissolved around them. Instead, they stood on the balcony of the Museum. In front of her, hung a few feet below the balcony, Jacqueline saw the Wright Flier, the first true powered aircraft. On her right, at eye level, the X-15 hung in all its black beauty and further away, similarly suspended, Yeager's Bell X-1, and the Spirit of St Louis that had carried Linbergh over the Atlantic.

Jacqueline let out a cry of delight. "Maragos!" she laughed. "This is wonderful! How long can we stay?"

Maragos gave a small shrug. "As long as you wish," she said. "The lights are on, take your time and visit the whole place. Nobody can get in."

"But they'll see the lights," protested Jacqueline. "Somebody will call the authorities, surely?"

"Naturally," replied Maragos. "But I have ensured the doors and windows are impassable. I think we can tweak Mister Horning's tail just a little."

Happily, Jacqueline turned to begin the tour of which she had always dreamed. She beamed happily at the Douglas Skyrocket and the NASA F-104 then moved off, the two women arm in arm like old friends. After an hour, the muted bangs and thumps at the front entrance could be heard, and the flashing lights of police and fire engines signalled panic through the windows. Giggling like teenagers, Maragos and Jacqueline turned into the exhibition of World War II aircraft for Jacqueline to lose herself over Messerschmitts, Mustangs, Hurricanes and Zeros. She even wept a little at the shape of the solitary Spitfire.

At four in the morning they returned to their cells in the basement of the Council building, and Jacqueline fell asleep like a toddler after a happy day picnicking on the banks of the River Thames in Reading.

Raoul Carmagio was asleep and dreaming intensely. He was a ten-year-old again, and his fight with his parents was the one that they had been having for three years now.

"Raoul, my son, I know it's a profession of great honour," said his father. He was a large man with a huge stomach and a nose that could shelter children from the sun. "But I have a business to run and I need you to help me run it. We are rich, but it needs work to keep us this way."

"Papa, I cannot help you." Even at ten, Raoul was a cheerful, stout boy who always seemed to have a helping hand to extend to his friends and was much loved at school. "I've always known what I have to do."

"Have to?" asked his mother. She was a sharp-witted woman who ran the company's finances with acuity and care. "But do you want to?"

Raoul turned his huge dark eyes on her and smiled with so much love that her heart seemed to turn over. "You are right as always, mama," he said with gentleness. "It has nothing to do with what I want. Truly, this frightens me. I have no great feelings of love for the Church, and the priests I have met do nothing to impress me."

"Then why?" His father was baffled, as he had been for three years now.

Raoul shook his head. "I wish I could tell you, papa. But I have no choice. Maybe it's God who speaks to me, but I have no other way. I must do it because I have done it before."

"Done it before?" His mother was startled, and made a tiny sign of the cross over her heart.

Raoul was puzzled. "Yes... but I don't understand what I meant by that."

Finally, his parents reached the only conclusion they could. They looked at each other with a mixture of disappointment and excitement. They knew that their extraordinary son would enter the Church and become a Prince of the Holy See. Losing the heir to the business had perhaps some compensations.

"We will speak to Father Massimo tomorrow," said his father. "I know that he will arrange everything."

Raoul smiled, hugged his parents and went to his room to read. Later that afternoon, he began to understand how strong was the conviction that he must enter the Church. Something special, something wondrous had to happen, *would* happen, and he, Raoul Carmagio, son of a factory owner who made pasta that sold around the world would be part of it. There would be special people with him, people he already knew but had never met. Puzzled, but ecstatically happy, Raoul knew he had begun the path for which he had always prepared.

In a tiny cell in the basement of a building in Washington, sixty-nine-year-old Raoul Carmagio, once the Archbishop of Milan, woke up with a smile of joy on his face. Knowing he would face his death here, he recognized that his life was the fulfilment he had always known it would be. He understood now, how strong was the commitment within himself to meet up with Philippe Leger and Jacqueline Carter. They had made the agreement some centuries before, while spending time on the Astral Plane between incarnations. The sickness of Humanity had become obvious to them, and the eventual arrival of the Infinite had already been signalled in some unknown manner. They had promised each other that they would arrange to be together when the necessity finally came. The drive had been within Raoul as a child and had taken him to become a Prince of the Catholic Church.

Raoul fell asleep again, smiling contentedly.

# Chapter 15. The Trial of the Maragos Four

Morning in Washington in early Fall. The colours were glorious this year, and the workers thronging into the offices around the city were exhilarated by the beauty of their country. Most were happy. They had heard that the Satan's spawn who had attacked them a few days ago were safely neutralized by the forces of God led by their beloved President Horning. They did not try to think how effective imprisonment and torture could be against Satan, the Master of Evil. The habit of thinking for oneself had died out rapidly in the shrunken United States of America of the year 2026. Most of the citizens had gladly given up that habit in recent years, especially when Horning had told them that obedience to God, as represented by himself and the Vatican, was the only patriotic duty of an American. Those who did not share that view had either fled the country or had died under the ministrations of the Council for the Protection of God's Name in the cellars of Council buildings around America, or openly, in burning agony before cheering thousands in the ball parks of the nation.

The night before, Horning had appeared on all the television channels of America and told his people that the Devil's agents were safely held and would be subject to trial before God's Court in the next few days. His speech had been followed by an hour of hymns of thanksgiving to Almighty God for giving America the divinely inspired leadership of The Very Reverend William Hardcastle Horning, all blessings on his name,

President for Life of the United States of America, one Nation Under God, and leader of the only legal political party in the nation.

But on this beautiful morning, not all Americans were so blissfully happy. Many thousands of those who had been in the park when Maragos had spoken to them had felt something happen inside. They had felt clouds move away from their heads and their vision had cleared as if they had walked out of a fog into the sunlight. They had sensed the infinite power within the woman who stood calmly on the steps of the Capitol and they had felt a rage begin to build up inside themselves. They perceived with painful jolts how evil had triumphed so easily in America, how joyously so many Americans had embraced it. Many thousands of Americans felt sick within their souls that morning.

One of those who felt differently that beautiful day was Angela Hayes. She was thirty years old and a supervisor in the records section of the Council for the Protection of God's Name. She was the only daughter of a Minister of the Baptist Church in Decatur, Illinois, and she had felt no qualms when President Horning had begun his drive to a theocratic government in America. On the contrary, she had rejoiced, convinced that the cult of Oneness represented ultimate evil, and that Horning was the man to save the world.

When she created new files for heretics caught up in the regular sweeps by the police, she said a prayer for their poor, misled souls. When she stamped the files "Deceased," she uttered a prayer of thanks that one more enemy of God had gone to join the Master of Corruption in his deepest pits and could do no further evil to good, Christian, American citizens. While she did not enjoy the public executions of heretics and criminals, she felt joy that America was a cleaner place when they had gone, and believed deeply that the exhibitions provided a salutary lesson and deterrent to heresy for her fellows.

This morning, she approached the tall building of

the Council with growing distress that she could not explain. She had been one of those at the rear of the park the previous night, and had initially felt fear and hatred of the group of four people standing distantly on the steps of the Capitol. When Maragos began to speak, she had been bewildered by the clarity with which she heard her, for there were no loudspeakers around. As she listened, she had felt a deep distress, a turmoil of confusion and strong nausea. She watched as the armed forces appeared and felt that she should have been delighted when the four were arrested and taken away under military escort. Instead, grief nearly overwhelmed her and she fled home, fighting tears all the way. Her night had been restless, a series of small naps followed by awakenings to sensations of alternate terror and sadness.

Now, as she approached the tall, modern building that housed the Council, the same conflicting emotions beset her. As she walked up the stairs, she looked at the faces of the people around her. For the first time, she detected a blankness in the expressions, a darkness in the eyes that was an absence of life, not a depth of humanity. The faces were almost those of animals being led out to the fields. Something had been taken from them. She stopped half way up the steps, causing a small pile up behind her that attracted the attention of the three armed guards at the entrance.

One moved quickly down the steps towards her. "You have a problem?" he enquired. While polite, his voice had an edge to it.

She stared at him. Though about her own age, his peaked cap and gunbelt gave him a fearsome authority. A trembling began in her legs, and sweat built up on her back.

"I... I can't go in there," she stammered.

"You're an employee of the Council?" inquired the guard. The edge in his voice had sharpened. Her behaviour fitted a profile for which he had been trained to watch.

She nodded, aware of fear in her gut and the danger of tears in her throat.

"So why can't you go in and work for God?" the guard continued.

"It's wrong," she said, so softly that the man had to bend down to hear her. "What we do to people in there, it's wrong."

The guard gave a small signal to one of his colleagues at the doorway. He took Angela's arm and held it firmly until the second guard arrived, then they led her into the building. Angela gave a shudder of fear as she was taken to the elevator bank and the guard pressed the "Down" button. Others in the lobby moved away from the trio as if to avoid possible contamination.

Later that morning, while her ex-colleagues worked in the records section, drank coffee in the lounge or chatted by the water cooler, Angela Hayes died in great pain in one of the small interrogation rooms of the basement.

Angela was only one of many thousands of Americans who experienced a degree of healing of the soul in the next few days because of the nearness of the Infinite. Of those thousands, over half gave themselves away to neighbours and colleagues and were taken into custody by the Police of God, as the special forces trained to look for heresy were named. The rest were able to hide their new awareness and either fled the country or managed to maintain their lifestyles without slipping up.

It was still nowhere near enough to heal Humanity.

One man who still felt no change in his attitude to Oneness, and little impact from the presence of Maragos, was Gregory Cardinal Lavalier. He entered the building with anger in his mind. The defection of Father Alan Drew had enraged him but he had forgotten to raise the alarm until the priest had left the building, and Alan was no longer to be found. But that was not the primary cause of his anger. It was to be found in his inner awareness that something profound was going on, that the person called Maragos was beyond his comprehension, and that the entire Oneness movement was entirely outside his understanding. He was suppressing with all his subconscious strength, his own question that perhaps the Catholic Church was wrong and that Oneness represented the truth of the Universe. He was not to know that as he slept, he had tried to talk to Philippe and Raoul Carmagio on the Astral Plane, and that the two men had deliberately avoided any such contact. Maragos had made that instruction plain.

"The way will not be served by Lavalier becoming a convert at this time," she had said. The four of them were together on the Astral Plane, taking comfort and support for their earthly condition. "Nor should we try and enlighten Horning," she continued. "The trigger we need will only come from this game playing its way to the end, not collapsing half way through."

In their enhanced perception from existence on the spiritual level, the other three nodded their agreement, and blocked out any mental contact from Lavalier. Philippe and Raoul had felt some guilt on the subject, though.

"I have worked with Lavalier for over thirty years," said Philippe. "He is not inherently an evil man."

"Just a sick, Infant Soul," agreed Raoul. "He cannot help the rigid mind-set and fearful rejection of the truth."

"He will have to go through an appalling Hell of his own creation, when finally he dies," said Philippe with sympathy.

"Nothing like the ones Horning and Crossman must undergo," interjected Maragos. "But Lavalier is not simply clinging desperately to familiar ways. He has chosen a path in every one of his past lives where he can impose his own rigidity of thought on others, and that is a choice beyond the accident of his sickness.

Horning and Crossman have also abused the situation to seize power and exercise it over innocents, but the extent of their abuse is vast. Their Karmic debts will be huge."

"How will they be paid?" asked Jacqueline curiously. "They will not have enough time and incarnations to settle with everyone."

"The souls of Horning and Crossman will have a terrible time of it," Maragos agreed. "They will have to undergo horrible deaths in each of the final lives, and be the catharsis of many other people's sickness. They will have to face incarnating as other species and absorb the pain and crises of thousands in order to pay their debts."

"But first, we must defeat Horning and make him wish to undergo this catharsis?" Philippe felt his own fear that such a task was immensely difficult.

"Yes, we must, Philippe," replied Maragos. "Free will remains with all souls. Redemption can only be by choice, and Horning is very far from choosing this way. His power grows daily, but he does not yet understand how it happens."

"Can you lead him down this path, Maragos?" The sensation of unrelenting savagery which hung in the psychic atmosphere of Washington made Philippe feel ice cold.

"We must, my friends," replied Maragos. "Or we face Evil for all Eternity."

With cold feelings of horror, the three humans woke up in their tiny cells to face what the day would bring them.

* * *

Gregory Cardinal Lavalier stood outside the door to Maragos' cell. He took a deep breath and nodded at the guard who unlocked the door and stood aside. Lavalier edged in to the tiny room. Maragos was sitting calmly on the side of the cot. She was dressed in a simple blue denim gown that was the standard prisoner issue for females. It was short, barely below her thighs, and quite shapeless. Maragos wore no shoes and no stockings. Despite the shabby clothing, she exuded massive power and authority and Lavalier had to fight for self-control.

"Good morning, Gregory," said Maragos. "Please do come in." She smiled at him with affection.

Lavalier held his crucifix in front of him. "Play no games with me, Satan. All the angels and priests of God stand opposed to you. You can do no evil here."

She laughed with delight, swinging her bare legs from the cot. "If only you knew how silly you look, standing there, waving that thing at me. "Now, why don't you sit down and talk this thing out like a sensible adult?"

Lavalier looked contemptuously at her. "I suppose Satan can create a chair for me?"

Maragos grinned. "Of course," she said. An elegant, straight-backed chair appeared in one corner of the cell. It was made of polished, ebony-coloured wood with a white silk seat.

Lavalier was unable to hold back his gasp. "You think I would sit in that devil's creation?" he managed to say, his voice coarse with the shock.

She shrugged delicately. "If you want to get weary, Gregory, that's your concern. I'm not giving you my seat."

Lavalier looked at the small grille in the cell door. It was closed, and the guard was not able to see into the cell to witness the Cardinal's concession to Satan. Stifling his anxiety, he lowered himself into the chair.

Maragos watched him with a smile. "You see, Gregory, it doesn't bite."

He stared at her. "Tell me the truth," he said, ignoring her comment. "You are before the representative of the Vicar of Christ on Earth, and you cannot lie. Who are you?" He leaned forward to hear her softly delivered reply.

"I told you. I am Maragos. I am the sum total of

twenty-five billion souls that make up my species. I am the first Infinite Soul to be formed."

"You still lie," he said with anger. "You are Satan!"

"There is no Satan, Gregory. There is only the sickness within mankind's soul that leaves you helpless to the temptations of evil. Have I not already given the world enough evidence that I am what I say I am?"

"Only God can do the things you say you have done," snapped Lavalier.

"Could not Jesus have done them also?" she asked with a gentle smile.

Lavalier sat rigidly in his chair. "Of course!" he said, fighting for control. "For Jesus is the Son of God and part of the Holy Trinity."

"Then, if Jesus were to return, as you believe he must some day, would you also treat him the way you are treating us now? Would you disbelieve the miracles he might perform and arrest him as a fraud?"

He rose to his feet and made the sign of the Cross again. "You claim that you are the Son of God?" he shouted. "Is there no blasphemy that you will not commit?"

"Oh, please sit down, Gregory," she said, with a sigh. "I am not Jesus, nor the Son of any God."

Slowly, Lavalier returned to his seat.

"I am far more than Jesus ever was," Maragos continued, "and I am actually one millionth part of the supreme being that you have called God."

The Cardinal tried to leap to his feet again, but was unable to stand. His face reflected fear and horror, and Maragos smiled again. "Do relax, Gregory. You'll get awfully tired with all this leaping about and shouting. I put that little block on you. It's gone now."

Lavalier was sweating, and his clothing was drenched in his thighs and on his back. Streams ran down his face and into his collar.

"The fact is, Gregory," she continued, "you and your Church have totally forgotten what you stand for. If Jesus were truly to return, it would be the religious fanatics like you and Horning and all your followers who would scream for his crucifixion again."

He stared at her, looking ill. "How dare you!" he managed to say.

She grinned at him. "Very easily," she said, "because it's the truth. You religious extremists, your televangelists, your priests and preachers, you money-hungry, power-grabbing bible-thumpers, you no more represent the teachings that my predecessors gave you than a cat represents the best interests of a mouse."

Her words seemed to turn him to stone. He was unable to speak.

"Humanity is very sick," she continued. "The sickness has clouded your perceptions, retarded your spiritual growth and hidden you from the truth. It was therefore easy to see that the sickest of you would seek power, because you lack the one thing that truly spiritual beings require."

"And what is that?" he croaked, forcing the words through his throat.

"The realization that all things will balance out in the end, that crimes against your fellow beings will be punished," she said. "Just as one of your so-called Holy Roman Emperors had all references to reincarnation removed from the Bible because it would reduce the power of the Church, you have corrupted the teachings of the Enhanced Souls who visited Earth in the past. You silenced them to maintain and protect that power."

"I don't understand," he said. The position of authority had faded from Cardinal Lavalier. Deep inside himself, he recognized the power of the entity before him but he could not permit himself to face it consciously.

"You are an Infant Soul, Gregory," she answered, "yet you have lived over two hundred lives. I see the rot and corruption of the sickness that pervades your soul and it is strong. It is beyond my powers to heal you even a small amount. In every one of your lives, you have lived as you do now. You hide your head from love and humanity, you seek power and abuse it, the way you have done in this lifetime. You deny people the right to think for themselves and you claim the sole proprietorship of the truth. That has always been the way of the sick souls who are unable to comprehend the truths of Oneness."

He could only stare at her in pain. The truth was hitting him on some psychic level he could not comprehend, but it hurt him no less.

"There have been many like you, Gregory," she continued. "The Churches have been full of them, of course. But all the centres of power have held your like. Always young, sick souls who sought to abuse power and justified it with political or religious zealotry."

Lavalier found his voice. Despite the turmoil inside himself, he struggled to regain his position of authority. "Satan, you speak with the tongue of the Serpent," he cracked. "It will not save you from the trial you must face before God's Judges tomorrow, nor from the destruction that we will visit upon you."

"No other reaction is possible from you, Gregory," she answered and her face showed sadness. "You must fight for your preservation and the continuation of the world as you know it, because anything else is simply too terrifying for you. So of course you will try us and seek our deaths. And you will win. There is no other way for you. But can't you see why that is exactly why I have come?"

"How could that be?" sneered Lavalier. "Who would possibly walk into a situation where they know they would die in a painful manner?"

"You really don't understand, do you?" she said softly. "Do you not see how Jesus did precisely that, knowing that the manner of his death would precipitate change throughout the world? And therefore, cannot you see that by winning your small battle against me, you must inexorably lose *your* world?"

In consternation, the realization of what she was telling him dawned on Lavalier.

"That's right, Gregory," said Maragos. "You have no other way, now. You must put us on trial. And you must find us guilty of heresy of the worst form, and kill us. If you do not, the American people will turn on you and tear you to pieces. The Horning Administration will collapse, the Catholic Church will lose what it believes to be the final confrontation with absolute evil, and everything for which you have fought will die."

"But if we do..." His voice trembled, almost gave out.

She nodded with a gentle smile. "Of course, if you do, the exact same thing will happen, but for opposite reasons. In the shock of what you do to us, enough people will discover their true being, they will see the evil that you have caused, and they will turn on you. Especially as I have arranged special triggers to ensure just that."

Lavalier stood up and the beautiful ebony and silk chair vanished. He seemed not to notice. The terror in his face was that of a man on his way to a painful execution. He turned and banged his fist on the door, and almost immediately, a rattle of keys indicated the door was about to open.

"You will have a dreadful time of it before you are healed and can become One with your fellow men, Gregory," Maragos said to the Cardinal's back.

He turned to her again and his face was chalky white. "Can you forgive me then, for what I must do?" he asked, his voice so tiny that it was almost inaudible.

She smiled with great love in her face. "If you can forgive yourself, Gregory, then you have taken the first step in your own salvation. My forgiveness has never been in question, for how can I not forgive my patient for his disease, Son of Man?"

Gregory Cardinal Lavalier walked stiffly out of the door that slammed shut behind him. As he walked down the corridor, he was violently and explosively sick on the floor. As he kneeled in huge discomfort and wrenching pain on the hard stone, he realized he was also weeping with massive, rolling tears racing down his face like spring rain after a drought.

Two hours passed before Cardinal Lavalier was able to gain enough self-control to pay a visit on his one-time colleague and superior, Philippe Leger. He was badly shaken by his encounter with Maragos, which had not gone any way like he had determined it should. He had planned a confrontation with Satan, secure in his position as the Cardinal of the Catholic and Apostolic Church, blessed directly by His Holiness and charged with the mission of destroying the ultimate evil of Oneness. Instead, something had been touched so deep inside of him that he could never have suspected it was there. At a spiritual level, he had learned some truths that he had not been able to consider before. He could not know of his panicky attempts to contact Philippe Leger as he slept and his soul ascended to the Astral Plane, nor of the rebuffs he had received. Only on some primitive level was he aware of his fear and despair at his position.

But after an hour of lying quietly in his room to let his insides settle, and another hour passed in prayer in the small chapel of the building that housed the Council for the Protection of God's Name, he felt ready to face his ex-Pontiff.

The cell door swung open to reveal Philippe Leger lying on his cot, his arms behind his head and his eyes closed.

"Good morning, Gregory," said Philippe. "I sensed your approach down the corridor."

"Don't try your devil's tricks on me, Leger," snapped Lavalier. "It's more likely that you heard my voice or recognized my footsteps."

Philippe smiled, his eyes staying shut. "If you insist, Gregory," he replied. "So, how was your meeting with Maragos? Enlightening, I would imagine."

"Again, I have no doubt somebody informed you I was to interrogate that woman," said Lavalier in irritation. "Do not try and impress me with your Satan's games."

Philippe opened his eyes and sat up, leaning against the dirty stone wall of his cell. "You are an Infant Soul, Gregory," said Philippe, "yet you have lived over two hundred lives. I see the rot and corruption of the sickness that pervades your soul, and it is strong. It is beyond my powers to heal you, even a small amount." Philippe stared directly into Lavalier's eyes. "Do you remember those words, Gregory?" he asked. "Did not Maragos say them to you a couple of hours ago?"

Lavalier's face was grey. He had experienced too many severe shocks to his mental balance this day, and the illness was almost overwhelming. "How did you know that?" he asked, his throat constricted.

"Because I was there, my friend," replied Philippe. "I have learned how to move my soul out of my body and move it at will. It's not a new trick. I watched your meeting with Maragos and I saw your pain."

Lavalier was silent, struggling to absorb what he had been told. Yet again, this meeting was not going the way he had planned it. "I must defend the Church against evil," Lavalier said. He was almost pleading for understanding from Philippe.

"No, Gregory," replied Philippe. "It is not evil that you are fighting so viciously. It is change. You struggle against a new perception of a truth that has always been there. It is the establishment of a direct line between mankind and Infinity that frightens you so much. You have set yourself up as the middleman for so long, and now the consumers are buying direct. I know, I was once part of that religious protectionism."

"How can you say that?" demanded Lavalier. "The Bible itself tells us that God is the Supreme Creator and that He sent His only Son to lead us to salvation. This is the word of God. It is the absolute truth. You are trying to destroy that truth."

Philippe shook his head. "The Bible is a wonderful book," he said. "The literature is truly beautiful. But it was written by men. It was edited by men. It was translated from ancient tongues by men. It was manipulated by men. I know, I wrote bits of it myself."

"You wrote..." Lavalier was astounded. "Leger, I doubted your sanity before, but now I know you are insane. Since when have you claimed that you wrote the Bible?"

"I said parts of it, Gregory. And not as Philippe Leger. I can remember now that I have lived many lives. In some of those I was close to the key figures described in the Bible, and I know that I wrote some of the passages that were later incorporated into the final versions."

"That is Devil's work!" croaked Lavalier and crossed himself. "The Holy Church teaches that we live but once and then are judged by God. On that judgement, our immortal souls live for eternity in Heaven or Hell. Obviously, your soul is condemned to Hell!"

Philippe shook his head, wearily. "There is no Hell, Gregory. That has always been a device by which we kept the masses in their places. If you were not such a sick soul as Maragos said, she could have healed you enough for you to see that, perhaps to experience some of your own past lives."

Lavalier stood stiffly against the wall. "Leger, the Holy Father speaks to God," he grated, "and God says the word of the Bible is the truth. There is no reincarnation."

"The Holy Father speaks merely to other men and women," replied Philippe with a small grin. "I should know, I used to be in that position. I cannot say that I ever experienced direct communication with God."

"That is perhaps why you fell from grace. You were clearly the wrong man for the Throne of Peter."

"Agreed. But that must mean that the College of Cardinals chose wrongly. Are they not supposed to be guided by God in this matter? How could such an error creep in?"

Lavalier's grimaced. "The Devil is able to infiltrate everywhere," he said in irritation.

"Even to the holiest rooms of the Vatican?"

"Even to there," replied Lavalier with a worried expression.

"Then how can you be sure that the Devil has not similarly influenced the choice of Pope in the past, just as you believe it did with me?" asked Philippe. "Maybe all Popes in history have been the Devil's choice?" Philippe was smiling, but his voice was sharp. "This current manifestation of the Holy See's theology suggests that perhaps the entire structure of established religion is the Devil's finest creation. No, Gregory, don't you realize that what you are protecting is not the Word of God, but the power and position of the Catholic Church?"

"And the two are surely synonymous, are they not?" Lavalier looked frightened as the implications of Philippe's words sank in.

"They may have been, once," replied Philippe. "At least, in the sincere belief of those who founded the Church. But with the power of absolute authority came the inevitable addiction to maintaining and furthering it. You have long been out of touch with Humanity."

"You are reflecting those Liberal activist attitudes that once you opposed, Leger," said Lavalier with a sneer. "How can the One True Church spread the word of God without having the power over the world that we do?"

"Did," corrected Philippe with a small smile. "You have little of that power now. And I used to wonder, even when I was still part of your system, what deal did we make with God, or perhaps Satan, that gave us that power in the first place?"

"Deal?" The Cardinal was irritated. "We made no

deal. Jesus himself charged Saint Peter with the task."

"And do you think if Jesus came back, that he would like what he saw? Or that the Church would tolerate him? No, Gregory, sometimes I think that Dostoevsky's story in The Brothers Karamazov was a little too accurate for comfort."

"You are being offensive, Leger. That story told of Jesus' return and of being imprisoned and executed by the Papal Authorities. It was clearly a heretical attack on the Church by an unbeliever."

"It was certainly that, Gregory," said Philippe with a smile. "But remember in that story, what the Grand Inquisitor told Jesus as he lay in his cell. It seems curiously similar to our position here. The Inquisitor admitted that he recognized Jesus but could not afford to let him live, because Jesus would destroy the power and mission of the Church. He said that when Jesus turned down the deal with the Devil, of having absolute power over all Men, the Church stepped in and took the deal instead. The Church had been working with Satan ever since, to ensure that mankind gained no knowledge, because in knowledge lay unhappiness. The Church's role was therefore to suppress the true soul of humanity. Now the Inquisitor had to protect the Church and its authority against the teachings of Jesus who was, of course, the greatest Liberal activist in history."

"Nonsense!" snapped the Cardinal. "You offend the name of our Lord!"

"How so?" asked Philippe. "Jesus stood in opposition to a conservative, republican Government, the sole world super-power, much like America was until recently, and he defied the established religious authorities of the day. What else could you call him but a Liberal activist? And how else do you think a bible-thumping evangelist like Horning and his devoutly religious followers would treat Jesus today if he had truly returned?"

"If you had said nothing else but these words,

Leger, I would still be able to find you guilty of blasphemy and major heresy and have you executed," replied Lavalier, anger twisting his face. "But even worse, you liken yourself to Jesus in your predicament and that is surely a sin of even greater evil."

"Not I, Gregory," replied Philippe. "But the one I followed here, she is certainly a force even greater than ever was Jesus."

"Leger, I warn you! Your heresy exceeds all permissible bounds!" The Cardinal was exhibiting severe distress and sweat stood out on his face.

"One day you will learn otherwise, my old friend," said Philippe sadly. "And I know that you already suspect the truth. Are you not aware of your efforts to talk to me when you sleep?"

"When I sleep? What madness is this, Leger?" Despite his anger, the Cardinal was frightened. Some internal memory was scratching at him, telling him that he was truly unhappy at being unable to communicate with Philippe on a different spiritual level.

"Maragos refused to let us talk to you," continued Philippe as if Lavalier had not spoken. "She says that it is of no use. You must follow the path that you laid out for yourself, and whatever you do now, the result is the same. Your world is over, Gregory."

A silence fell and lasted for over a minute. Lavalier had dropped his head on to his chest and was breathing hard. Philippe watched him in sympathy. As had Maragos, he could see into Lavalier's soul, see the sickness so powerfully in control, so strong that little of the true soul could be seen from under the green, foul-looking discoloration. He watched the Cardinal's mind as it turned over what Lavalier had heard in his two confrontations that day, and Philippe could see the moment at that Gregory accepted some of the reality that he had been forced to face.

"I am cast in the role of Judas, Philippe?" The change in Lavalier's tone was vast. He seemed full of sadness, no anger was left. Philippe touched his colleague's mind gently and read the grief and beginning of comprehension in it.

"The sickness that has affected most of us cast you in it, old friend," he said in gentle tones. "It has gone so far now that few of us have had any choice. Only those like Horning, Crossman and the others who embraced that path of cruelty and tyranny had any choice and took the wrong fork to evil. They will pay for their crimes in ways nobody could ever have envisaged."

"As I must pay for mine," whispered Lavalier, as if a deep and terrible understanding had reached him.

Philippe nodded. "Yes, Gregory, you too must pay for your sins. There are Karmic debts to those you have hurt in your past lives, and you must work them off before mankind can reach its true level of growth. But the payment will be less than the horrors Horning and the others must experience, that I can promise you."

Lavalier slipped to his knees and bowed his head towards Philippe. "Forgive me Father, for I have sinned," he said, his voice low and barely heard. "I have sinned against my fellow men and against God."

Philippe placed his hand on Lavalier's shoulder. "That is the path you must follow, Gregory, tomorrow and until Oneness," he replied. "It is above your head now, and out of your hands. To do any less than follow your path from this point will make the work of Maragos impossible."

He removed his hand, raised Lavalier's head so that their eyes met. Philippe made the old sign of the cross above Lavalier. "Go in peace, my friend," he said. "I can give you no penance to perform, for you will create it yourself. Feel no guilt for what you must do over the next few days. It is part of the path that Maragos has laid out for us all."

Lavalier rose to his feet, tears running down his face again. He banged on the cell door, standing motionless with his back to Philippe, his head bowed until the door opened and he slipped out quickly.

Philippe returned to his cot, lay down again and began to prepare himself for what he knew must come.

Gregory Cardinal Lavalier made no more visits that day.

In Chicago, an evening of God's work was planned for that night. Nine Heretics were condemned to die at the home plate at Wrigley Field and officials prepared for the same sell-out crowd that they had always experienced. For reasons they were unable to explain, despite the sale of thirty-four thousand tickets over the previous few weeks, only two thousand, three hundred and eleven people came to the exhibition. In complete silence, they watched the deaths of the nine prisoners. Four of the condemned died before the current was switched on, and were carried from the electric chair by angry officials. The others died in conventional manner with all the sparks and noise that was supposed to be part of the show, but their agonies received no cheers and whistles. At the end of the evening, the spectators filed out of the ground in a silence broken only by occasional sobs.

Some of Maragos' healing had spread through America. But it was not yet enough.

Stephen Crossman, Chief Examiner of the Council for the Protection of God's Name did not leave his suite of rooms at all that day. He spent the time glued to the television, watching soap operas, a baseball game from Atlanta and the weather channel. A heavy book shelf remained in place across the door and Crossman ate nothing all day, instead drinking heavily from the collection of liquor bottles in his lounge room. He occasionally thought of the trial that would take place the next day, but instead of the intense satisfaction he expected to feel, only tremors of fear ran through him. He consumed two full bottles of rye whiskey that day and fell unconscious on his floor at about nine that evening. At two in the morning, he dragged himself upright, drank over a pint of cold water and fell into bed.

* * *

Midnight, and none of the four was asleep. Philippe Leger was sitting on the side of his bed, his head in his hands, lost in thoughts that he probably couldn't have identified. They were the sort of rambling, disconnected memories, ideas, questions that flutter through the mind when the thinker has no real desire to concentrate on anything. He was shaken upright when the limbo of his thoughts was broken by the movement of his entire environment.

Jacqueline Carter was sitting in a similar style, remembering her previous life as Jerome Mitchell and her friendship with Peter Wells. They were both seventeen, and the school term was over for the Easter break. They had taken their bicycles from the garage in Peter's house, and cycled down to Sonning-on-Thames, then walked along the river path. There were two girls on the bank, one was painting a landscape, the other was lying on her back, taking in the early spring sunshine.

Peter had been the one with the courage to address the girls, for he had always been the leader, and Jerome had eventually overcome his shyness. The day had been one of those idyllic memories that last a lifetime, walking to the boat lock and eating ice creams as they watched the boats pass up on their way to Caversham, or down on the way to Maidenhead. It had ended with an hour spent in quiet, with occasional giggles as the four paired off, and Jerome found himself with the artist, snuggled in among the weeping willows in a breathless exploration of warm lips and soft breasts, which remained an anchor of happiness for him through flight school and the terrifying weeks of his squadron life before...

Jacqueline shook herself and stood up. That was a

memory over seventy years old, but it gave her a small welling of happiness just as it had when she was Jerome Mitchell. Feeling cheerful, she wondered whether to contact any of the others, or to go to sleep. The decision was made for her.

Raoul Carmagio was pacing his cell, touching the stone wall at each end in a restless rhythm. He was remembering his youth also, how his mother had begun intensive coaching of his fine mind as soon as Father Massimo in the village had indicated that Raoul would be accepted into the seminary for training as a priest. She had initiated a regular two-hour class each evening when she had returned from work with her husband. Mathematics was the preferred topic because she believed that the discipline of pure numbers paid off in all areas. So Raoul learned trigonometry, algebra and geometry by the time he was thirteen and was thoroughly versed in calculus a year later. By himself, he studied topography and became fascinated and entertained by the topic. His mother watched with a satisfied smile as he worked, though she was unable to follow the esoteric subject herself.

By fifteen, he was a competent accountant and took over his mother's functions at the factory when she needed time off. It was with some regrets that he took his leave of them the following year to enter the Church. The intellectual and personal strengths required to run a business had begun to intrigue him, but he bowed to the inexplicable pressures inside his head to become a priest. He had little real belief in the dogma of Catholicism, but he felt certain that it was a small price to pay to satisfy whatever it was that needed him to be a man of God.

Raoul thought about mentally contacting one of the others, or even using his new-found skills of moving his soul out of his body and to somewhere else. As he played with the prospects, he ran out of time.

All three of them looked up at the same moment that they were no longer in their cells, but standing in the kitchen of the house near Valence. Maragos was calmly sitting at the huge wooden table, eating crusty farm bread with honey, and she grinned at the startled faces around her.

"I thought we should have a last evening at home," she said and poured coffee from the large earthenware pot into her mug. "Though it's five in the morning here, so breakfast is a good idea!" All three of her companions gave similarly massive sighs of relief and delight.

"Home again!" exclaimed Philippe and turned to the antique china cabinet against one wall. "I had never realized what a beautiful feeling it could be!" He extracted three mugs, side plates and bread knives, and laid them casually on the table, sat down and busied himself carving off a slab of the loaf.

Jacqueline gave a chuckle, pulled a bottle of cognac and four balloon glasses from the china cabinet, and sat alongside him. The pleasant glug of the bottle was the accompaniment to the attention the others gave as they watched the glasses filled. Raoul repeated his sigh.

"I think that this is what I missed most," he said, pulling one of the glasses to himself, putting his nose in the balloon, and closing his eyes blissfully as he took in the aroma of the fine cognac.

"We deserve this small luxury," said Maragos. "We have a hard day tomorrow."

They might have been a group of friends discussing a work schedule for the next few days. None of them let the full implications of her words sink too far into their minds. Instead, they settled round the old table in warmth and companionship.

"Are we the only species that has experienced such sickness, Maragos?" asked Raoul, putting down his brandy glass and reaching for the loaf of bread.

"To this extent, certainly," replied the attractive woman at the end of the table. "Other species have had temporary difficulties and undergone turmoils of their own, but nothing to the extent and depth of this problem."

"If you had not come, would it heal itself?" Philippe asked.

Maragos shook her head. "No," she replied. "We have watched you for some thousands of years, and the disease became worse as time went on. The reactions to the advent of Jesus and Mohammed were so violent that intervention was obviously required at a far higher level than before."

"When did you emerge as an Infinite Soul?" asked Raoul. "Were you part of the observation?"

"I felt my first awareness around the time of Jesus," said Maragos, looking into a distance as if remembering her childhood. "But I don't think I was really effective for another four or five hundred of your years. Trying to absorb and make sense of the vast number of Ascendant Souls and all their experiences left me immobile and ineffective for centuries."

"So who made these decisions?" Jacqueline was curious. "If there was no Infinite Power at a level of self-awareness before then, who's been watching us and deciding what to do?"

Maragos smiled. "The group mind is a bit like a termite nest," she said. "Decisions are made by a mind operating on a higher plane than the Astral Plane to which you have become accustomed. But just like the insect's nest, no one termite is aware of making such decisions. This is true at the individual soul level, or right up to the Infinite Soul level. So even though no Infinite Soul was at the true self-awareness stage, we still carried out many functions in a sub-conscious state."

"And humans are the same way?" Philippe was intrigued, and Maragos nodded at him.

"You are," she said. "I have been constantly trying to talk with the Infinite Soul level of Humanity, and occasionally get a rational response, even though the number of souls who have reached even Ascendant stage is limited."

"But there are some?" asked Philippe.

"Oh yes," she said. "But the total number is only in the hundreds. Even though you, Philippe, were one of the very first souls to incarnate, enough of your entity souls have the sickness, that your entity is not yet ready for Ascendancy. Others who started later than you have avoided the sickness and have merged already. There was even an Ascendant Human Soul ready to be merged with those others who formed the enhanced soul that was Jesus."

"I'm fascinated by the way such souls, and also you, Maragos, are able to exercise such powers," said Raoul. "All of this simply comes from the mind?"

"The power of the group mind is enormous," said Maragos. "Even a small number of humans together can cause major reactions. Think of a lynch mob. No real leader is apparent, but something directs the mob to a specific purpose, jobs are allocated and duties performed."

"What a horrible example!" said Jacqueline with a shudder.

"A larger group can do worse damage," said Maragos. "Nazi Germany is a good example. The entire nation adopted the evil side of Oneness..."

"Oneness?" broke in Philippe. "That ghastly period was an aspect of Oneness?"

"Of course," replied Maragos. "Remember that The One also recognized that without controls or stimulation, It could go insane. Nazi Germany was a fine example of such insanity. Fifty million souls in concerted thought generated an awfully powerful force."

"I've always thought that it was just a case of one evil, mad leader like Hitler corrupting them," mused Jacqueline.

"That's switching cause and effect," said Maragos. "Oneness brought out a leader like Hitler, not the other way round. If one of the assassination attempts on him had succeeded, the outcome would not have changed in the slightest. Another leader with similar philosophies would have arisen instead."

"Who or what was Hitler, anyway?" demanded Raoul.

"An Infant Soul, in only its tenth incarnation," replied Maragos. "The sickness is strong in that one."

"Has he returned to Earth?" asked Philippe, and Maragos nodded.

"You met him," she said. "The young Examiner who tortured you. That soul had returned to an environment where it would feel secure, surrounded by other, similar, corrupted souls. Many souls from Germany chose to reincarnate in the middle regions of the USA for that reason, as did other sick ones from other times and places. Hence the intensive concentration of the illness in that part of the world for the last hundred years. It is that concentration that called out the intensely sick soul that is now William Horning. I see now, that Horning was already a form of enhanced soul when he incarnated. He is the sum of twenty other souls, already severely infected, which explains his power. Throughout your human history on Earth, the soul that now inhabits William Horning has been a key player in the evils of this planet. And he has absorbed other souls since then. Not only is he severely diseased, but he contains a concentration of the dark side of The One."

"This is terrifying," said Philippe. "Maragos, can Horning be stopped?"

"He must be stopped," replied Maragos. "His power is immense, even without his own comprehension of what he is. He is the worst manifestation of the evil side of Oneness that has ever occurred."

"But can you stop him?" persisted Philippe.

"I can stop him, yes," she said. "But to cure him? That is a far greater problem, because very soul has free will and will only heal if it chooses. Somehow, we must make him choose that option. But Horning's soul has always chosen to exercise its evil powers during its incarnations, and to make him change now is a truly monstrous task."

"There has been so much horror in our history," murmured Raoul. "Horning has been behind much of it, you said?"

"Not all, but a lot," replied Maragos. "And not always as the primary player. Usually, that soul has been the power behind the thrones. This time, it seems, William wants to be the lead character."

"So has Oneness manifested only its dark side on Earth?" asked Philippe.

"Not at all," replied the Infinite Soul. "You know yourself how powerful is the emotion at a Christmas Mass in a cathedral. That is Oneness showing itself in the love and spirituality that is one side of its nature. On a larger scale, do you realize that diseases like infantile polio vanished because the human mind in total simply decided its time was over?"

"So Salk's discovery of a vaccine was effect, not cause?" said Raoul with an amused smile, and received a similar response from Maragos.

"Exactly," she said. "At the level of maturity that Humanity should have achieved by now, all disease should have vanished, just by group decision. As should violence, war, hunger and all the other nastinesses that have plagued you for so long."

"The way we contained the Middle East War?" added Jacqueline. "Just by massive mutual decision?"

"Exactly," said Maragos again.

"But don't you have the power to heal that sickness in America?" asked Raoul. "Your presence alone seems to do it in all other cases."

She shook her head. "I could heal many," she agreed. "Just as I have done already. But the dark force of Oneness is so strong with over a hundred million souls committed to it in America, that not even I could do it all. Those I have healed will already have slipped back into sickness in the last twenty-four hours. No, the decision to heal must come from within. We have to trigger that decision."

"What will we do when we have completed our tasks?" asked Jacqueline into the tiny silence that fell around the table. She felt unable to use the real words outwardly. When we have been killed, she said to herself, and felt a small twinge of fear.

"That is up to you," replied Maragos. "I know that all of you want to go to other species for a lifetime. That is your choice. All the species have indicated their happiness to have you."

A wave of delight ran round the table.

"You have asked them?" Philippe was the spokesman for all of them, and Maragos nodded.

"But you may also want to come back to Earth for one last task," she added, and the others became attentive.

"What task?" asked Jacqueline, as Maragos seemed not to expand on her words.

"We will discuss it when we are complete here," said Maragos, and stood up. "We should be returning," she continued, gently. "Our next meeting will be less pleasant." She walked to each of the three humans in turn and kissed them. As she did, each of them almost fainted from the roaring power that enveloped their senses, and when they were recovered they were back in their cells in Washington, and it was after one o'clock in the morning.

* * *

The clatter of breakfast being brought to their cells woke the three humans at seven. The grille door to each cell was opened and an armed soldier brought in a tray that he deposited on the floor while two other similarly armed men waited nervously in the corridor.

Breakfast was the same each morning. Luke-warm coffee, two slices of toast, already spread with a sour

377

tasting jam. There were no knives, spoons or forks.

Jacqueline took pleasure in ignoring the spread that morning. Smiling inside, she remembered the feast of fresh country bread, jam and coffee, plus the balloon glasses of brandy that they had consumed only a few hours before in Philippe's French country home.

A fresh prison gown had also been delivered to the cell. With less pleasure, Jacqueline dressed in the blue denim garment. She recognized the intention of the shabby dress, too short for her tall frame. Her captors intended her to feel ill-at-ease, a little embarrassed and ashamed.

Philippe and Raoul had also been brought a change of the standard prison clothing. Equally faded and shabby jeans and blue denim jackets lay on their bunks.

At eight, the cells were opened again and the routine walk under guard to the showers took place. By eight-thirty, all four of the prisoners were freshly washed with strong-smelling carbolic soap and back in their prison clothing. Instead of returning to their cells, they were taken up a floor and placed in a small room equipped only with five chairs. At a gesture from one of the guards, they took a chair apiece and sat quietly.

Shortly after nine, the door opened, and Stephen Crossman walked in, followed by Gregory Cardinal Lavalier. Both men looked apprehensive and were unable to meet the eyes of their prisoners. Lavalier took the remaining chair and moved it to one wall. He sat down and examined his hands carefully, saying nothing. Philippe studied him carefully for a moment or two, but Lavalier refused to look up.

"You are all charged with blasphemy, major heresy, conspiracy against the government of the United States of America, and defamation of the character of President William Horning," said Stephen Crossman. His voice was harsh, cracking with the tension that was obviously within him. "Your trial will start within a few minutes."

"Do we not have the privilege of a defence

counsel?" asked Philippe. "I always understood that American law guaranteed the right of competent counsel."

"That right was terminated by Presidential decree for those accused of crimes against the State," replied Crossman. "It is understood that you have Satan as your defender. The Reverend Horning decreed that no further assistance need be given to you."

"I see," answered Philippe with a small smile. "This is truth and justice for all in the Land of Liberty? I am relieved to see the American way still exists."

Crossman glared at him, but was unable to be certain of Philippe's sarcasm.

"And who then, will be our prosecutors?" asked Maragos. She was sitting straight backed in her chair, her head high.

"You will be tried by a council of Judges appointed by the President," answered Crossman. "They will set you the questions, and you must, by the law of Almighty God answer truthfully. God will therefore be the final judge."

"And very democratic too," said Raoul, unable to stop a small chuckle.

Crossman turned on him in rage. "Be warned, Carmagio," he snapped. "You will be fighting for your life in that courtroom. Your mannerisms will be no help to you."

"Naturally," answered Raoul. "And just who will be our prosecuting judges? Are you one of them?"

"I am the Chief Examiner of the Council for the Protection of God's Name," replied Crossman. "I will naturally be on the council of your judges."

"Naturally," said Raoul again and closed his eyes in apparent boredom. Crossman turned the full fury of his glare on him, but the anger passed over Raoul's head, unnoticed. The Examiner moved his eyes over to Jacqueline, lingering over her long legs in the blue prison gown, then he turned away to the door. He did not look at Maragos or Philippe. "Come, Your

Eminence," he snapped. "Our places await us."

Lavalier rose to his feet, not looking at any of the four seated prisoners, and followed the American out of the cell. The door closed and the rattle of keys told of heavy locks being closed. All four of the prisoners smiled at the sound, remembering how easily Maragos had transported them away when she had wanted.

An hour passed before the door opened again, and the armed guards stood outside.

Maragos was the first to rise. "I believe we are expected," she said, and walked out of the door. The others followed, and were taken just a short few yards to an imposing oak door. It opened and the four were ushered in, two of the guards leading, four more behind, and the door closed with a small swish.

They were in a courtroom, that was obvious, though it was not a large one. At one end, a raised section held an imposing curved desk, and four men sat behind it. One was Crossman, in the middle of the group, dressed in traditional judge's black robes. On his right sat Gregory Cardinal Lavalier in his full regalia of black gown, red hat and red sash. To the left of Crossman were two men whom Philippe could not recognize. They were in the same style of black robes as those that adorned Stephen Crossman.

No more than fifteen feet from the raised desk, a small area had been cordoned off. Inside were four wooden chairs arranged in a straight line facing the Judge's bench. Around the cordoned area, the six armed guards took station and stood with their rifles by their sides. Without being prompted, the four prisoners walked to the area and each took a seat. Philippe sat on the left end, Jacqueline next to him. Raoul sat on Jacqueline's right, with Maragos on the right hand end.

Crossman broke the silence. "You will stand while the charges are read," he said. His voice was firm, confident, as befitted a man in total control of the proceedings.

Maragos shook her head. "Your authority is limited, Stephen," she said. "We will continue to sit."

Crossman looked angry, and gestured at the armed guards. Two of them raised their rifles and pointed them at the four seated prisoners. The three humans looked nervous, but Maragos laughed, a cheerful, feminine laugh that echoed in the courtroom. "Just what do you think your toys could do to us, Stephen?" she asked.

Crossman looked baffled, but spoke calmly. "They could kill you," he replied.

"What, and spoil all this?" replied Maragos with a gesture that took in the room. "You know that would ruin everything."

The armed guards were confused and shuffled their feet, looking to Crossman for orders. The other two judges seemed uncomfortable. Philippe thought he detected a small smile on Lavalier's face but it was quickly hidden.

After a moment of apparent indecision, Crossman made a small gesture at the guards who returned to their places and original stances. Crossman looked down at a file on his desk and began to speak again.

"This is a special court convened by the decree of the Very Reverend William H. Horning, President for Life of the United States of America, blessed be his name. This court will operate under the rules laid down for the Council for the Protection of God's Name for trials involving crimes of Major Heresy."

He looked up briefly from the paper, and studied the four prisoners. They were sitting calmly, Philippe with his right foot crossed over his left knee, Raoul turned sideways in his chair looking with interest at the automatic rifle of one of the guards. Jacqueline was studying the faces of the four judges and Maragos was looking into a deep distance.

"The four judges who will try you today are as follows," continued Crossman. "Gregory Cardinal Lavalier is the representative of the Catholic Church in

Rome, charged by His Holiness Pope Pius the Thirteenth to root out heresy in all its forms." He nodded briefly at Lavalier who remained unmoving.

"Senator Simon J. Williams on my immediate left is appointed by the President as a specialist in religious affairs," said Crossman, and looked at the man on his left side.

Senator Williams was old. Not the age that brings wisdom and sanity to a group, but old with the decay of carelessness, of the absence of thought. Senile, sleepy decay that marked the Senator as merely a filler of a seat in order to make a decision easier. He sat in his seat, his eyes barely open. What gaze he had, seemed fixed on the bare legs of the two women in the seats below him, and his slightly open mouth drooled a little.

"And on my far left," continued Crossman, "is Mister Abraham Luckey, Vice-President of the United States of America."

Where Williams was old, Vice-President Luckey was clean. He was pinky white in a way that, on a small child, would have been charming, the cleanliness of a newly-bathed baby. On a man in his seventies, the scrubbed skin, manicured nails and shiny cheeks indicated an obsessive concern with dirt.

"And I am already known to you," said Crossman. "As Senior Judge on this case, I will conduct the hearing. I will now read the charges." He extracted a second page from the file on his desk and was about to read when Maragos spoke.

"I think we can waive the reading of charges, Stephen," she said with a smile. "We're all pretty familiar with the contents."

"Madam," spoke Crossman. "This is not a court of regular law such as previously existed in this country. This is a Court of God, and the rules you believe to apply are not relevant. The charges will be read, and you will hear them."

He looked at his page but was again interrupted by Maragos.

"Is it also a new rule that justice does not need to be seen to be done in order to be carried out? Since when has American justice been carried out far from the light of day?"

Crossman frowned. "This is not American justice," he said, irritation evident in his voice. "It is God's Justice, and God will be the witness."

"Seems to be a conflict of interest in there, somewhere," broke in Raoul. "Isn't God the final judge as well? I would imagine that this clashes with some fairly well-laid-down judicial principles."

Crossman nodded at the guards and one of them jabbed the rifle stock of his weapon sideways at Raoul's head. With a gasp of pain Carmagio fell off his chair, blood pouring from a cut above his right ear.

Philippe rose to his feet in rage and a pair of rifles immediately swung on him. Jacqueline went to her knees by Raoul's head but was unable to assist in any way. Only Maragos seemed unmoved.

"Now you can see what effect these guards can have," said Crossman in satisfaction.

"We have indeed," said Maragos. "And they will have no further role to play in these proceedings."

The wound on Raoul's head vanished and he sat up, looking bewildered. He stood up with the help of Jacqueline and Philippe and regained his chair. The guards stirred restlessly, and fear ran over the faces of all four men on the bench. Even Senator Williams took his gaze from the women and looked astounded.

"They have a very large role, Madam," replied Crossman, not looking at Raoul. "You will now learn that my rules in this court will be obeyed, and so in future, you will only speak when I instruct you to do so. At that time, you will address me as Your Honour."

"I asked you this before, Stephen," said Maragos, ignoring Crossman's words. "What do you believe you can do to us? You clearly do not understand my nature."

"It seems that I do," replied Crossman. "My rules proved highly effective, just now."

"Not really," said Maragos. Without a sound, the six rifles in the room vanished, leaving six bewildered and frightened soldiers who edged away from the group of chairs.

"I will not allow you to treat us this way," Maragos continued. "This mode of trial is obnoxious. If there were a God, I doubt He would approve at all."

The silence in the courtroom was thunderous, as everyone waited for something to happen. Their wait was short.

The four wooden seats became luxurious lounge chairs, covered in soft brown leather. And the four sets of drab prison clothes were replaced by new outfits. Maragos was clothed in an executive-styled business suit in dark blue, with a pure white blouse. Jacqueline was wearing a trouser suit of cream silk, a red scarf round her neck. The two men were in similar business suits, dark grey with white shirts, gold cufflinks and strongly patterned red ties.

The gasp of dismay from the court was loud. Crossman rose sharply to his feet, Vice-President Luckey looked frightened and the Senator broke out in a fit of coughing. Only Lavalier appeared unaffected.

"These proceedings will be carried out in a dignified manner," said Maragos clearly. "You may now proceed with the readings of the charges."

With the four prisoners reclining comfortably in their armchairs, the judges were forced to settle down and attempt to restore their positions of authority. Reluctantly, Crossman caught the eye of one of the guards and nodded at him. The six soldiers filed out, closing the door behind them. Philippe could see the looks of relief on their faces.

Crossman took up his sheet of paper again, and began reading. "The charges are as follows," he said. "First, that all four of you have preached in public, statements that are not approved by the Holy Roman

Catholic Church, nor by the Council for the Protection of God's Name. You have been heard to state that God is not the Supreme Creator of mankind, and that instead, He is the sum total of all human life. You have also stated that Jesus Christ our Lord is not the Son of God but instead was something less, something comprised of other, non-human life forms. You have denied the existence of Heaven and Hell and also of Satan, words that directly contradict the teachings of God as expressed in the Holy Bible. The woman Maragos has on many occasions claimed to be something greater than Jesus Christ, and to be a direct part of the Lord God Himself. Finally, all four of you have admitted before witnesses that you are adherents of the forbidden creed of Oneness, a set of beliefs specifically declared to be un-Christian, and against the laws of God and The United States."

Crossman looked down at the four figures reclined at ease in the armchairs. "Each of these charges individually comprises Major Heresy, the punishment for which is death. How do you plead on these counts?"

"You'll have to get the charges correct before we plead, Stephen," said Maragos.

A look of anger crossed Crossman's face and he slammed his fist on the desk top. "I instructed you as to the correct mode of address, Madam," he said loudly. "You will follow it! Now, are you claiming that the charges are in error?"

Maragos nodded with a smile. "The bit about claiming that God was comprised of all Human life. Actually, what I said was all intelligent life everywhere in the Universe."

"Which only proves your heresy to be even worse," sneered the Chief Examiner of the Council. "The Holy Bible does not allow for the existence of any intelligent life other than Mankind. The charges remain as read."

"Then all four of us plead guilty on all counts," said Maragos firmly.

Crossman looked irritated. This was too simple

and reduced the solemnity of the occasion. "The prisoners may speak for themselves," he said and sat back in his chair.

"What she said," were the words from Philippe, accompanied by a casual wave in the direction of Maragos. The other two gave nods of assent.

"Then let the record show that all four prisoners have pleaded guilty to Major Heresy charges," said Crossman, and noted something on the page before him. "Do any of you have anything to say before sentence is passed?" he added.

"I do, of course," said Maragos. Crossman and the other three judges looked anxious. Even Senator Williams appeared to show some life separate from the ancient dreams running in his head.

"Human history is almost a continuous story of one set of religious beliefs being crammed down the throats of adherents of other beliefs," said Maragos. "Usually, the cramming process is accompanied by bloody murder and cruelty of an order rarely seen in other species. This is the primary symptom of the sickness that has afflicted mankind for the last few million years."

"Do not ask for pity because of this sob-story, madam," said Crossman with a sneer. "This is the work of God, and your punishment is dictated by the words of God as passed to us by the Holy Father and by President Horning."

"Two old men with pretensions to adequacy," said Maragos, ignoring the gasp of dismay from the judges. "The problem is that each new wave of radicalism has become the old wave of reaction. What shall we do with you people when the real truth has become universal, that Oneness is the reality, not the fairy tales and myths that you have embraced?"

"You condemn yourself even further, woman!" said Crossman loudly. "The truth is what the Church says it is and we will accept no Satanic variations and alternatives."

"Did not your church once burn people for saying that the Earth revolved around the sun?" asked Maragos. "And do you still hold that belief?"

"That's a tired old argument, Madam," broke in Cardinal Lavalier. "Yes, we know that in the past, mistakes were made. But that is hardly the same as your repudiation of all the tenets of Christianity."

"Unfortunately, it is, Gregory," Maragos replied. "What will you do if I can prove to you that your beliefs are no less a sham than those of the old Church?"

"A hypothetical question that deserves no consideration," replied Lavalier. "For you can do nothing that would prove any such thing."

"Indeed?" asked Maragos and waved an elegant hand at the four of them. "And what would explain the new clothing, the armchairs and the loss of your soldiers' toys?"

"Conjuring tricks have been done before, Madam," said Crossman loudly. "Tigers can be made to vanish from their cages, men go over Niagara Falls and appear five minutes later in a helicopter. Your tricks are the same."

"And what of your inability to inflict pain on us with those evil little wands of yours?" came the reply. Maragos smiled. "That really terrified you, did it not?"

Crossman look uncomfortable. "Not all tricks are immediately obvious," he replied. "I must admit, you have an impressive repertoire of skills, but nothing in them denies the truth of the Bible."

"No?" asked Maragos. "Then what of this?"

The courtroom faded. Immediately, they were surrounded by the pleasantly cool and misty environment of the Astral Plane. Philippe, Jacqueline and Raoul smiled as they recognized the familiar scene. They stood slightly behind Maragos as they all faced the four judges who stood a few feet away, complete bewilderment on their faces.

"Do you recognize where you are, gentlemen?" asked Maragos gently.

Senator Williams and Abraham Luckey folded to their knees and hid their faces. Muffled moans came from behind their hands. Gregory Lavalier seemed frozen immobile.

Only Crossman spoke. "What the hell is this?" he roared. The fear in his face was striking.

"Not Hell, Stephen," replied Maragos. "I'm sure you can see that. This is where you spent many thousands of years before you let yourself risk a life on Earth."

"You lie!" shouted Crossman. "What witchcraft is this? You have used Satan's power to pull us here!"

Maragos sighed. "Most souls recognize this place within minutes of arrival here," she said. "That you should fail to do so shows just how far the disease has taken you. Gregory, I believe you are a little more aware?"

Lavalier looked at her. Philippe could see that the Cardinal was fighting to retain his self-control.

"I believe we are before the gates of Heaven," said Lavalier. "This is how I have pictured it."

"Most people see it the same way," said Maragos with a nod. "All of you retain some fragment of memory of this place. But it is not Heaven, Gregory, just the spiritual plane above the physical plane on which you live when incarnate."

Lavalier was trembling. The two kneeling men still had their faces covered and were moaning louder. Crossman's face was white with rage and Philippe could see his jaw trembling with suppressed fury.

"I need you all capable of continuing this process," said Maragos. "We will return now."

The courtroom flickered into existence around them again.

"Now, Stephen," said Maragos. "Who could do that?"

Luckey and Williams uncovered their faces and looked around them. The terror in their eyes was visible across the courtroom floor. Williams was drooling badly, and the front of his gown was soaked. Gregory Lavalier had his eyes closed and seemed to be praying.

Crossman made no answer to Maragos' question for a few moments while he drank heavily from a water jug on his desk. "Party tricks do not scare us," he said finally. "That was obviously some sort of hypnotic trick you played."

"You know very well that it wasn't," replied Maragos, as the four prisoners also settled themselves in their armchairs. "However much you will fight it, you all know that you saw the truth of life. So you will now understand that you are dealing with more than just some defenceless human beings with a new philosophy of creation to frighten and confuse you."

A few seconds of silence rang in the courtroom.

"Let us for the moment, allow that you have some unusual powers, Madam," said Crossman, after looking at Lavalier for approval and receiving the tiniest of nods. "It is our responsibility to study the nature of Evil and the works of Satan so that we may learn how to counter them. I invite you therefore to tell us just what it is that you have been preaching."

"You will not like it, Stephen," said Maragos.

Crossman gave a short, bitter laugh. "Of course I will not like it," he replied. "I am a man of God and detest the evil that you utter. But I must hear it to judge for myself."

"There is something else that you will like even less," said Maragos.

A small strained silence lasted a second before Crossman responded. "And what is that?" he asked with a worried look.

Maragos smiled. "Despite your wish to keep these proceedings hidden from the public, this entire court session is appearing as it happens on the television sets of the nation."

"Nonsense!" snapped Crossman. "You talk like a madwoman. There are no cameras in this court."

"I don't need them," replied Maragos. "Can't you remember the unauthorized and totally unwanted broadcast by Mister Horning the other day, when he invited the people of Washington to come and see us?"

The four judges looked anxiously at each other. There was fear in Crossman's eyes as he considered the implications of what he had been told. "There was no such broadcast then, and there is no such broadcast now," he said, his voice loud and cracking with tension. "Now, continue your mad ravings, woman, if you must."

"Then listen to me," said Maragos, and crossed her legs. Senator Williams stirred slightly and wiped his lips with a paper handkerchief from a box by his side.

"What you call God, I call The One," said Maragos. "It is the supreme power in the Universe. It is dreadfully alone, and fears the prospect of Eternity."

"Then that is immediately proof of your madness," said Crossman with a short laugh. "The idea that God might fear anything is patent nonsense, and as for being alone? That is precisely why God created Man, to provide companionship."

"Which proves that the God of your philosophies obviously feared something, especially loneliness," replied Maragos.

There was no sound or movement from the judges.

"To seek an answer to the dilemma it faced, it broke itself into a million Infinite Souls," she continued, "of which I am one, the first to return to awareness in this cycle. Each of those Infinite Souls chose a place in the universe to live, and when it had done so, broke itself further into Ascendant Souls. Each of those broke itself down even further into fragments such as each of you, individual souls."

"And precisely what is the objective of this endless fragmentation?" asked Crossman. Contempt dripped from his voice.

"To find an answer to The One's problem," replied Maragos. "Each fragment, each soul, lives many times, acquiring new experiences, new perspectives. The Infinite Soul that is Mankind chose to set each soul between three hundred and five hundred lives, growing through five stages. Other species have varied the process, but the result is the same. When all fragments have lived through their cycles and grown old and wise, they merge back into the entities known as Ascendant Souls."

"Again, you commit heresy!" said Crossman with a triumphant look. "The Holy Bible makes no mention of reincarnation. The idea is impossible and ludicrous. Each of us has one life and spends eternity thereafter in Heaven or Hell."

"Impossible, Stephen? Ludicrous? How can that be?" asked Maragos. "Do you not believe that your Jesus Christ will return to Earth?"

"That's different!" Crossman was annoyed.

"Why so?" persisted Maragos. "If he can return to Heaven in between lives and then come back to Earth to be born again in a human body, why is it so impossible for others?"

"Because He is God, that's why!" shouted Crossman.

"Then let us look at it another way," continued Maragos. "Where is the human soul before it is born?"

"In Heaven, of course," replied Lavalier. He was looking interested.

Maragos nodded at him. "And at the birth of a child, the soul comes down to inhabit the body, that is what you believe?"

"There is debate on the moment at which the soul enters the body," said Lavalier, his face reflecting intense concern. "Many believe that the soul is present from conception."

Maragos shook her head. "Not so," she replied. "While the soul observes the growth of its selected body from the Astral Plane, where we were just a few moments ago, it enters the body only at the actual moment of birth."

Lavalier sat back in his seat and folded his arms, his expression one of deep thought.

"And when the body dies," continued Maragos. "Does the soul then go back to Heaven?"

"Assuming the soul has been judged fit," replied Lavalier.

"Then Gregory, if it can do that once, why can't the soul do it again?" Maragos was prodding delicately and Lavalier was responding as if in academic debate.

"Because the Bible does not permit it," he replied.

"But it used to," said Maragos. "It is common knowledge that all references to reincarnation were removed during one of your Church's conferences at the order of the Emperor who feared the weakening of Church authority if people believed in a return to an earthly life."

Lavalier looked annoyed. "That is unverified history, Madam," he replied.

"No," replied Maragos firmly. "It is fact. The man was quite terrified of any loss of power. Better to rewrite the Bible than risk loss of authority. It was neither the first nor the last time that such an act was committed."

Crossman was looking shaky, as if determined to cling to his version of the truth, despite an inner sense that he was wrong. "Such ideas are the Devil's work," he said loudly. "Do not preach your blasphemies here, woman, you are in enough danger already."

"Not blasphemy, Stephen, just the truth," said Maragos with a smile. "I am, after all, the sum of billions of souls who have merged to Ascendant Level and then to my Infinite Level, and I remember every one of their lives and deaths."

To everybody's surprise, Vice-President Luckey joined the proceedings, though a little behind the subject, as if the topic had taken time to work its way through the confused pathways of his old mind. He seemed to have recovered from the shock of the brief visit to the Astral Plane. "You mean groups of people form a new individual?" he demanded. His voice was high-pitched and grated on everyone's ears, including those of his fellow judges, if the small flinch away by Crossman and Lavalier was an indication. "The idea is quite obscene!"

"Naturally," agreed Maragos. "But everything is obscene to you, Mister Luckey. Why have a change now?"

The Vice-President muttered something under his breath. "So what happens to these... entities?" he asked, emphasizing the last word with a sneer.

"It takes many thousands of years for the entities, the Ascendant Souls to become fully aware of themselves," continued Maragos. "And in that time, and for many thousands of years after, they meditate and they absorb the combined experiences of the few hundred souls that made them. Finally, they merge with each other to form the single soul of their species, an Infinite Soul."

"And then what?" Lavalier was showing no contempt. His interest was obvious, and something in his face indicated an awareness of a truth beyond his grasp.

"The same process of absorption, meditation and review continues," said Maragos. "Until finally, the million Infinite Souls are ready to combine again as The One."

"Satan has created a pretty story," said Crossman loudly. "It charms the foolish and the gullible and leads them into any path of evil and heresy that they wish. If they have no fear of God or everlasting Hell, they can do anything, there are no constraints, nothing!"

"The actuality is quite the reverse, Stephen," said Maragos. "For if every soul knows that its acts must be balanced, every ill deed must be punished and Karmic debts must be paid, then the pressure to grow to wisdom and maturity is far more effective than the fear that your teachings generate and maintain."

"Rubbish!" snorted Crossman.

"And when all these... Infinite Souls have returned to a single entity that you call The One, what then?" asked Lavalier. Having debated theology with his old colleague many times, Philippe could detect the intellectual excitement that Lavalier was experiencing. Despite himself, the Cardinal was intrigued.

"The One must then determine the solution to its problem," replied Maragos.

"And if it cannot? What is there possibly left to do?" Lavalier seemed disappointed in her answer.

Maragos looked thoughtful. "I have no real way of knowing," she said. "I can only assume that the whole process must start again. It seems that The One coordinates the fragmentation and re-merge process with the restructuring of the Universe. The Big Bang appears to start with the dissolution of itself."

"Are you saying this has all happened before?" Lavalier was leaning forward in his seat, the excitement obvious now.

"Once, twice, or ten billion times, I have no way of knowing," answered Maragos. "That is the truth of Eternity. Maybe that is The One's solution to living alone through all time. In complete forgetfulness of all previous cycles, each new cycle is a fresh experience. Perhaps The One has already determined that this is the answer and it will only return to self-awareness every few billion years for a relatively short period of time."

"You are telling us that God dies, or sleeps?" demanded Crossman. Fury radiated from his body. "Your heresies have already earned you your deaths or I would condemn you to tortures beyond imaginings!"

"Death is the true path to survival, so it is nothing fearful and terrible," replied Maragos. "You may dream of eternal life, but that would be a hell greater than anything your Church has been able to dream up. Life is only endurable, in fact life is wonderful for the very fact of death. To know that one's time is finite, that one has a challenge to accomplish greatness in that limited period, that is what gives life the sweetness it has."

"If that is so," broke in Lavalier, "then surely one should not know of reincarnation? Does not that possibility take away some of the sense of limitation you mentioned?"

Maragos nodded with a warm smile. "Your intellect is not corrupted by the disease of your soul, Gregory," she replied. "Your point is precise. That is why few species have opted for the individual souls to know of the reincarnation process until the soul has reached considerable maturity. With the wisdom of a few hundred lifetimes behind them, souls can then take a longer look at the infinity of time and space and expand their minds."

"You said you are one of these Infinite Souls," continued Lavalier. "Does that mean that you believe yourself to be actually one millionth part of the Supreme God?" His face was alive with interest.

"Indeed it does," answered Maragos.

"Then how old are you?" asked the Cardinal.

Maragos shrugged. "Time has no meaning when there is nothing but dust and space. The Big Bang as your astronomers call it, occurred many billions of years ago. I spent several billions of years watching the universe evolve then I lost my own awareness as I began to cast off the Ascendant Souls. More hundreds of millions of years passed before the first souls incarnated on the planet I had chosen. I became aware of myself again about two thousand years ago."

Crossman let out a bellow of disgust. "This blasphemy continues in its full flood of evil!" he shouted. "God created the Universe just six thousand years ago and placed Adam and Eve in the Garden of Eden. Belief in evolution has been deemed a crime for some years now. We will have no more of this filth."

"A moment, Mister Crossman, please," said Lavalier, ignoring the noisy interruption, and turned back to Maragos. "Does it mean that others of your kind will appear in the future?" he asked.

"Cardinal Lavalier, Your Eminence!" Crossman's voice cut harshly across the room. "Satan is pulling you into his net! This talk of reincarnation and other species with souls is nonsense. Our role here is to protect the world from Evil, not succumb to its charms."

"But what if the tricks, as you call them, truly show that I am what I say I am?" said Maragos. "If I am aware that I am one millionth part of The One, enough to understand what the next stage will be, should you not perhaps listen to me?"

"We will continue to listen to your filth for a little while longer," replied Crossman, "in the hope that we can learn to identify the Devil in future times. So, Madam, tell us why you are here."

"To heal you," answered Maragos.

"Heal us? Who is sick?" asked Vice-President Luckey in alarm.

"Nearly all of humanity," replied the Infinite Soul. "There is a sickness that began in you while you were still one entity. You fled from the rest of us out to this little galaxy, and went your own way. But you have never grown since."

"What nonsense is this?" Luckey was irritated. "Not grown? What do you mean, not grown?"

"It was nearly five million years after the rest of the Infinites began the physical incarnation process before mankind started to send souls to physical forms," replied Maragos. "But most of those humans who incarnated failed to learn from their lives. Many millions of you were like Stephen here, so frightened of life that they never incarnated at all. Stephen is in only his very first life on Earth. So while all the other million species of The One are about to start the final merging, Humanity is preventing it. And that's why I'm here."

She sat back and folded her arms.

"And just what is the nature of this sickness?" demanded Luckey. His alarm had faded to contempt.

"Retardation as infants," said Maragos. "Few souls

have grown through the cycle to become Old Souls. They have remained as infants and babies with the mental outlook that would be expected."

"And what outlook is that?" Lavalier seemed interested again.

"A terrible fear of change for one," replied Maragos. "Desperate need for authority figures, hence the patriarchal religious forms that most of you have taken. Hatred of all things different from yourselves, and so a constant violence at any excuse."

"You are another of those Liberal activists that preach against war all the time, are you?" said Crossman with an expression of disgust.

"Much like Jesus did," agreed Maragos, and smiled at the expression of rage that hit Crossman's face. "And I am in favour of protecting the environment, caring for children, and not killing the citizens of a country."

"Madam, the sentence of death is too kind to you," said Crossman. The rage in his body made him shake. "I will enjoy every moment of your execution."

"And just how will you heal this mythical sickness?" asked Luckey, breaking back into the conversation. His confidence had grown, he was dealing with his own field; dirt, disease, the things that had obsessed him from childhood. His disgust with the group of people before him was almost physical.

"By making you heal yourselves, like any good doctor would," replied Maragos. "You will have to leave Earth and this location. You will have to live some lives as other species so that the sickness can dissipate. And when all of you have repaired yourselves, Humanity can begin the path to Oneness."

"Live as other species? Live as a dirty, slimy alien?" Crossman was in good humour again. The obvious madness of the group was enough to remove the fear he had felt earlier. His biggest moment was coming and he was looking forward to it. Sentencing others to death gave him almost an orgasmic sensation. Watching them die made the orgasm happen. He had never experienced the sensation in any other way.

"I know that we dealing with something evil," said Crossman finally. "And all of God's powers are being directed at you now to hold you in check, despite those silly games."

"God's powers?" asked Maragos. "Let me show you something of these," and she sat back in her seat. On the bench, all four men appeared frozen.

"I am feeding them a little of the vision that I first gave you, Philippe," said Maragos in a soft whisper. "They are seeing some tiny fragment of the fear and grief that The One experienced before It decided to split Itself down."

The frozen scene lasted about two minutes before the silence was broken by the sound of weeping from Lavalier. Crossman seemed more in control, but his voice was harsh with struggle. "It doesn't matter what you show us," he said, a slight tremble fluttering the vocal chords. "We must defend the world from the evil that you bring, and you must be destroyed."

"The Cardinal and I have had this conversation, already," said Maragos. "Deep in your soul Stephen, you truly know what I am. You are terrified of me because of the sickness within you, and it shows as your desperate struggle against Oneness."

Crossman's face was white, and the Vice-President's eyes were bulging in fear. Only Senator Williams was unaffected and a small snore rose from his seat.

Maragos smiled in the Senator's direction, then turned back to Crossman. "Tell me, Stephen," she said. "You are a truly devout Christian, are you not?"

Crossman let loose a thin smile. "You have seen the evidence, Madam," he said. "My life has been devoted to the service of God and the destruction of His enemies."

"I have certainly seen the evidence of your destructive skills," murmured Maragos. "So you believe that Christ will one day return to Earth?"

"Naturally," said Crossman. "It is written in the Bible."

"Of course," said Maragos. "As are many things. So, tell me Stephen, how will you recognize Jesus when he has returned?"

A silence echoed in the courtroom for a few seconds, and Crossman looked confused. "It will be obvious," he said shortly.

"How?" persisted Maragos.

"Well... his appearance for one," said Crossman. There was defiance in his tone.

"His appearance? He will be tall, blond and handsome?" Maragos was smiling in a friendly manner. "Or tall, dark and handsome?"

"We will know," insisted Crossman.

"What if he's short, dark, Jewish, has long black hair, and smells?" asked Maragos.

Crossman's face grew angry. "You are offensive!" he snapped. "That is blasphemy!"

"Why?" asked Maragos. "That's how he looked last time. He looked pretty well like everyone else, so what's blasphemous about that?"

"He would look like Christ!" insisted Crossman, obvious distress showing in his red face.

"In long white robes?" asked Maragos.

"Of course!" shouted Crossman. "He will appear in all his glory!"

"Why not a smart suit like my friends here are wearing?" continued Maragos. "After all, I find it unlikely that your present population of devout Christians in America would take kindly to some man appearing in their midst with no money, wearing long white robes, long hair and preaching a philosophy of turning the other cheek."

"I command you in the name of the Lord!" shouted Crossman. "You will be silent!"

"And how about miracles?" continued Maragos. "If he had turned water to wine, or fed five thousand homeless at a meeting in Central Park, how long would the Food and Drug Administration authorities have stayed quiet before arresting him? Not to mention the witch-hunters of your Council for the Protection of God's Name?"

"Woman, you will remain silent! I command you!" Crossman was almost apoplectic. Senator Williams had woken and was looking confused, turning his head from side to side at the roars from Crossman. Finally, his eyes fixed on Jacqueline as she crossed her legs, and he stared hard at her, ignoring the angry debate being conducted.

"And what happens if Christ decided to return as a woman?" asked Maragos. "Seeing as you have just raised the issue. Could you and your Churches still recognize the offspring of God?"

"We will listen no longer to this blasphemous witch," snapped Crossman. "Both God and Christ are men! That has always been an incontrovertible truth and He could not possibly return in any other form. The idea is disgusting!"

"Had Jesus returned to this present-day America," continued Maragos, ignoring him completely, "this is the reception he would have got, the same as you are giving us. You are reacting in the same way as a previous monolithic, decaying world power reacted against a fresh voice offering choice, liberty and the full expression of a human being's capabilities. Just as the Romans could not tolerate individuality, and the freedom of thought that Jesus preached, the present-day corruption of American philosophies is equally unable to do so. And you must kill us, as the Romans killed Jesus. But the Cardinal has now realized how you have fallen into the same trap that the Romans were unable to avoid."

"And what is that?" demanded Crossman. His face was tinged with grey and his voice had lost any semblance of authority.

"Jesus placed himself in the position where the Romans had no choice but to kill him," said Maragos.

"Had they left him in peace, he would have destroyed the Roman Empire. His philosophies were incompatible with the conformist, militaristic, brutal simplicities of being a world power. The philosophy of Oneness is equally incompatible with the conformist, militarist philosophies that have been adopted in America, and with the Catholic Church's views of reality and lust for domination. So the Romans killed Jesus as you must kill us."

"But..." Crossman was trembling. "That's exactly what started Christianity! Because he was crucified, the Church of Rome was established."

"Exactly!" said Maragos with a smile. She might have been a professor conducting a tutorial in philosophy. "If you had left us in the park in Washington, we would have eventually brought down the Administration of William Hardcastle Horning, just as you have charged. It would have taken longer than this path will take, but it would have happened eventually. But you have chosen the path of brutality, repression and our execution. The result will be the same."

Philippe was keeping his face expressionless. He knew that Maragos was hiding some of the truth from Crossman. To have been left alone would not have brought about the healing necessary for Oneness. A greater trigger was necessary.

"And you think your execution will result in the same revolution as did the Crucifixion?" Crossman was trying to be sarcastic, but failing. Maragos simply looked at him and his eyes dropped from hers.

"The people know we are here," she said. "You have already publicized that fact, and today's trial, that I have ensured has been seen by most of your citizens, has fixed these events in their minds. You can no longer hide us away and forget us. The people will not allow that. You have frightened them so much with your tales of Satan's Spawn, that they want decisive action from their leaders. But already, too many have healed because of my presence. So, you must kill us in public, Stephen. You no longer have a choice. If you don't, the people will tear you apart as weaklings. That's the price you will pay for creating a military theocracy in America."

"But if we do..." Crossman was quite grey now, and his throat was working hard as it forced the words out, barely audible in the quiet room.

"That's right," said Maragos. "Exactly as the Cardinal has already seen. The result will be the same. And in both cases, the people will join the rest of the world and embrace Oneness. It is the same inescapable paradox that Jesus imposed on his captors. You are damned, Stephen. You and your appalling President Horning, your Council for the Protection of God's Name, your torturers, your sick philosophy, all are damned."

The four judges again seemed frozen.

"I am showing them their last incarnations," said Maragos. "All except Crossman, whose first lifetime this is. He's seeing the Astral Plane again, where he cowered for all the hundreds of thousands of years, too afraid to experience life."

The tableau broke. The ancient Senator Williams collapsed in his chair, and from the reaction of the Vice-President, who rose to his feet and jumped to the far side of the room, Williams was dead.

Cardinal Lavalier sat frozen, such grief on his face that he resembled an ancient painting of scenes from Dante's Inferno.

"What was his last incarnation?" whispered Philippe to Maragos.

"He was a witch-hunter in seventeenth century America," replied Maragos. "He is seeing how constantly he has led the same lives, always with hatred and cruelty, always stifling the human soul. He is seeing the extent of his own sickness and that of all mankind, and he now understands how great are his Karmic debts to others. For the first time, he understands what agonies of penance he must live through before his burden is put down."

Philippe stared at his old subordinate and colleague. He was unable to feel anger or triumph. The viewpoint of Oneness and Eternity made such small emotions impossible. He moved his eyes to Crossman. The Chief Examiner was crouched in foetal position against the wall at the back of the courtroom. His face reflected such horror that it was hard to look at it.

"This is the Devil's work!" shrieked Crossman. "Lucifer and all his demons are in this courtroom!" He rose sharply to his feet and waved his arms above his head. "I smell the stench of the Pit!" he screeched. "I command you Satan, in the name of The Father, The Son and The Holy Ghost to return to the Depths!"

"Oh dear," said Maragos. "This will never do. He has to be in control of himself for a little while longer. I'll have to cool him off."

Crossman seemed to calm suddenly, and took his seat, ignoring the sprawled body of Senator Williams on his left, and the trembling Vice-President Luckey standing rigidly against the wall.

"The sentence on you all is death," said Crossman, and banged hard on the desk with his hand. The door opened, and the line of soldiers returned. All looked nervous, but Maragos stood, looking to the others to do the same.

"The last act has to be played out," she said softly, and all four of them allowed the soldiers to return them to their cells.

* * *

"It's done?" President Horning looked up from the desk in the Oval Office as Stephen Crossman was shown in.

"It is, Mister President," replied Crossman. There was no satisfaction or joy in his face or voice. Instead, the weariness was obvious, plus a tautness stemming from fear. The morning's events had been stressful.

"And who the hell said you could televise the trial?" demanded Horning.

"It really was on television?" Crossman went white as he remembered the words of Maragos.

"Of course it was on," shouted Horning, his round face distorting with fury. "Who the fuck told you to do that?"

Crossman struggled to control the sharp pain that ran through him. "We didn't do it," he replied tensely. "That woman said she was doing it. She said she did that other broadcast of you."

Horning's face grew red, and his eyes seemed to expand in a burning, glowing frenzy. Crossman almost screamed with fear as he felt himself sucked towards those eyes. His greatest nightmare was to suffer the death of the soul that he somehow comprehended had been the fate of the many people who had died while standing near to the President.

"Well, I suppose it can't hurt this time," said Horning, seeming to cool down. "The people saw those bastards tried and condemned."

"I suppose so," said Crossman, not tempting further fate by raising his worries about what the people had seen.

"Then they all die in a couple of days, right? We've won."

"The executions are scheduled for two days' time," answered Crossman. "The stage is being erected already."

"Great! Great! I'll look forward to seeing those bastards fry!" exclaimed Horning. "Mind you, I could think of a few other things to do to those two women!" He stared hard at Crossman for a moment. "What's wrong with you? We'll burn those people in two days, and it will be all over."

"I'm not so sure," replied Crossman, fighting to control the sickness and weariness within him. "There's something terrifying about them, especially the woman, Maragos or whatever she calls herself."

"So what the hell can they do to us?" snapped Horning. "They're locked away, under armed guards, and in two days, they burn. What the fuck are you scared of?"

"Williams is dead," said Crossman.

"What? How the hell did that happen? I didn't see that on the television." Horning stood up from behind his desk.

"She did something... hypnotized us or something... It was awful. And when I woke up again, Williams was dead."

"What do you mean, she did something? What the fuck's going on here, Crossman? Are you people going soft in the head?" Horning's face was red again, and traces of spittle appeared on his lower lip. Before the fury, Crossman retreated, shaking in every limb.

"She must have hypnotized us all, or something," he said again. "I had a nightmare of some sort then I woke up. And Williams was dead."

"Well that's no loss," said Horning. "He served his purpose. The little pig was senile, anyway. That's why I put him on your court."

"That's not all," said Crossman, a tremble appearing in his voice. "The interrogations failed on all four of them."

"What do you mean, failed? What's going on here?"

"The rods didn't work on Maragos at all," replied Crossman. "I tried several of them. And the other examiners told me that the rods worked only once on Leger and Carmagio, but not again. They didn't work on the other woman, either."

"What happened?" snapped Horning. "Those things are supposed to be perfect. They give a heavy jolt at frequencies that hit the pain centres. How could they not work?"

"It's not that they didn't work," replied Crossman, looking down at the floor. "With the other three, the rods seemed to hit back at the examiners. The pain went backwards."

"Jesus Christ!" Horning's words were not a supplication to his avowed Lord. "She really is the Devil! The quicker she burns, the better."

"I'm not sure that will do it," replied Crossman. The fear in his face was growing as he remembered the awful panic in which he woke from the nightmare, though the details of the horror were long gone.

"It's up to you to make sure it works!" shouted the President of the United States. "That's what I pay you for, remember! Your job is to keep these liberals and dissidents off my back! Destroy them!"

"They'll die in two days," answered Crossman. "There'll be a full ceremonial job, VIPs next to the stage, a television announcement to bring out the crowds. I'll have plenty of army there to keep order. I just hope that does it."

"I hope for your sake, it does," replied Horning. "I've got that little jerk Pius bitching at me for results. I've got those wimps in the army and air force who can't get anything right. There's an outbreak of heretics in Chicago. I may have to burn the whole place if that grows any worse. I can't handle these four devils screwing up the plans as well."

For a few moments, Horning stayed silent, in deep thought. Crossman sensed the menace emanating from the president and his level of fear began to rise.

"I'm going to need every ounce of my strength to handle that woman," said Horning at last.

Crossman tried to control his breathing. "I'm certain you are more than a match for the Devil, Mister President," he said. "You are God's right arm and nothing can stop you."

Horning turned to face Crossman. The president's eyes sucked the light from the room, and Crossman felt his knees buckle.

"I need you, Crossman," said Horning.

"I have always been your servant, and always will

be," rasped Crossman through the sickness in his stomach.

"I know that," answered Horning. He licked his lips in anticipation. "It's not what I meant."

"Please, Mister President, Mister Horning...."

"I need your strength, Crossman. This is the last great battle, and I need very ounce of energy available."

"I beg you, Reverend, not this..." Crossman was on his knees, sweat pouring down his face. "In God's name, not this..."

Horning seemed to swell to twice his normal size, and his face gleamed with a light that was not of this earth. His eyes grew larger and focused on Crossman. The president's aide collapsed with a moan full length on the floor.

"Oh sweet Jesus, save me..." sobbed Crossman, then shuddered and fell motionless.

Horning began to breath hard, long rasping breaths like a man who has just emerged into the air after minutes spent under water. His head went back and he roared with exultation as he felt the power of Crossman's soul energy soak into him. Exhilaration raced through him and he stared at the body of the man on the floor. With a massive blast of power, he kicked the body that crashed against the wall like a broken doll.

"I have you now, you bitch!" he screamed. His breathing still coming hard, he sensed other massive forces raging through him. The excitement grew in him. He walked back to his desk and picked up the private extension.

"What have you got for me?" he asked, when a male voice spoke at the other end.

"A real choice one," replied the voice. "Prime material."

"As soon as you can," said Horning and replaced the phone. He forgot about the body on the floor in pleasurable anticipation at the prospects of the rest of the afternoon. He picked up another phone.

"I'm not to be interrupted until I call you again," he snapped and put the phone down. He walked out of the office and into the corridor. The armed guards at the door snapped to attention, but he ignored them, made his way up a floor to his private quarters and opened the door.

The room was luxurious. Cream carpets, lime green walls with several internationally famous art works hanging on them. At his orders, on a proclamation that they were ungodly art forms, the pictures had been removed from galleries around America and he had hung them in his private rooms with a glow of pleasure at the power he held.

The bed was enormous, at least seven feet in both length and width. A large, plush armchair sat in one corner and a bookcase stood against one wall. The books comprised the finest collection of extreme hard-core pornography that Horning's agents could find in their sweeps of the nation's seedier establishments. Possession of these works had caused the deaths of several dealers in a public exhibition. Another stand held over a hundred video films of the same type, some of the most degraded, detailed filth ever made. The material included bestiality, snuff-films, where a victim was killed on camera, child pornography, every form of the genre his agents could find.

Standing in one corner of the room was a girl. She was beautiful, barely pubescent, her breasts a tiny swell under the thin blouse she wore. Her legs were long and graceful under the skirt that appeared to have been violently ripped so that little cover was left.

Horning gasped with delight and licked his dry lips. "What is your name, my child?" he crooned, advancing across the room. The girl whimpered and pressed against the wall.

"Come, my little darling," whispered Horning, and took her arm. She flinched and moved away. Horning smiled then swung his hand viciously against the girl's cheek. She shrieked, and cowered into the corner.

"Sweetheart," said Horning gently. "You don't understand. I am blessed by God. Receiving my favour like this will ensure your place in everlasting paradise with Jesus."

"Please don't hurt me," whispered the girl. "Please... let me go back to my parents."

"And where are they, child?" asked Horning.

"They were... they were picked up by the police this morning," said the girl, rolling down her face. "They're in prison." A sob broke, and she covered her face with her hands.

"Then they must be heretics," said Horning, and took hold of the girl's wrists. "They're in God's hands, now."

His grip tightened, and the girl gasped in pain. "Please," she begged. "Please, you're hurting me."

Horning ignored her. He forced both her wrists into the grasp of one of his hands and reached with the other for the small chest of drawers by the wall close to him. His hand came away with a cane about three feet long.

With a sudden thrust, he released the girl's hands, seized the front of her blouse and ripped hard. The material fell away to reveal the child's small breasts and Horning's breath accelerated. They were lovely, he thought, just perfect. Untouched, creamy white, the nipples were tiny hillocks of pure pink. He licked his dry lips then swung the cane hard against the girl's arm.

She screamed and turned away, her other hand clutching the red mark on her upper arm. Her back was open to him, and he swung again, laughing with delight as the cane slashed across the flawless skin, opening up a bloody gash. The girl screamed again, and ran for the door but Horning had much experience in this game. He anticipated the move and took hold of the girl's shoulder, dropping the cane. He pulled her back against his chest and slid his hands on to those perfect, tiny breasts. He began to moan in anticipation, feeling his erection rise hard against the girl's buttocks.

She was sobbing violently now, and his delight increased. "Oh, you will be blessed by God, child," he gasped and diverted one hand to removing his clothes. "So blessed, so blessed."

She struggled uselessly, but he was naked now, his erection massively jammed against the girl's thigh. The remnants of the skirt were ripped away, and he flung the girl on the bed, sensing with joy the feel of fresh, youthful skin under his chest.

She screamed with pain as he entered her and her screams continued for several minutes as he thrust wildly. Then she faded into soft, barely audible moans as Horning pounded his groin against the unmoving body.

After an hour, he subsided and fell asleep, his arms wrapped tightly round the child who was barely conscious. A short while later, he woke and immediately became aroused.

The girl made no sound this time as he entered her. Ten minutes later, he fell off the small body, gasping hard. He lay still for a few moments, then rose and walked naked to the bathroom the other side of the cream door. He spent twenty minutes under a hot shower, shampooed his hair, and lovingly rubbed aromatic cream over his body. Putting on his bathrobe, he returned to the bedroom.

The room was empty, and the bed had been made up as if the activities of the last two hours had never taken place.

# Chapter 16. The New Calvary

Their last night on Earth was spent quietly. Each remained physically in their cells, but moved their souls out of their bodies and met in some cloudy, dreamy world of great beauty and gentle perfumes.

"We must see this final act out to the letter," said Maragos. "It will be painful, but all of you now understand how the people must see it. You have lived many lives, died many times, sometimes in greater pain than we will experience tomorrow. When it is over, we will meet again this way."

"This way?" echoed Jacqueline. "Where is this?"

"Some levels above the Astral Plane," replied Maragos. "Here is where the Infinite Soul resides. It is the Buddhaic Plane where we prepare for the final merger with The One. I have brought you here for just a short while because there is great power at this level. It will sustain you for tomorrow."

"And tomorrow we die," said Philippe. It was more a statement with his interest showing. Death was a familiar experience for all of them. "It was a fascinating life, this last one," he continued. "In some ways, it was as incredible as my first on the planet around Epsilon."

"Can we then choose an incarnation in another species?" asked Raoul.

Maragos laughed lightly. "You are so eager to leave this little Earth?" she asked.

Raoul looked embarrassed. "No," he said, and joined in the smiles around him. "The idea is just so exciting. I always loved to travel, and what greater trip could there be than this one?"

"There may be reasons to stay around." The Infinite Soul's aura was brilliant royal blue and colours for which no name had ever existed. The power of her presence enveloped them in security and happiness. "You may choose to return for another life here before starting to tour the Universe of The One."

"You have a plan for Humanity, Maragos?" asked Philippe.

She nodded. "It's not developed yet, old friend. But Humanity may need you all again one more time. Or you may just want to be here to see what happens at the end."

"The end." Jacqueline echoed the Infinite. "Something so sad about those words."

"Only the end of a small stage in the growth of The One." Maragos smiled gently. "Remember, the incarnate stages of all the million species have lasted at the most, five million years. That is a tiny fraction of the entire cycle of eternity, from the first splitting off of the Infinites to the awakening of The One."

"The most important one, perhaps?" suggested Raoul.

Maragos shook her head. "No more or less important than any other," she said. "Each stage has its function. The first stage is the process of studying the Universe that The One created, and then seeking a place to live. If the species is to be a planet-born one, then the shaping of the planet is a stage where considerable research, study and learning occurs. Then we have the physical cycle of incarnations, followed by the lengthy processes of re-emergence. Each stage has its part to play."

"And you think we have kept Horning's awareness of his powers from him?" asked Philippe. Maragos nodded.

"It seems so. I read no comprehension within him, though he is now the equivalent of a full Ascendant Soul. I am glad you cannot see the full aura of evil that surrounds William Horning. He has just absorbed the soul of Crossman to increase his power for tomorrow's confrontation, but it will not be enough."

The scents and mists of the Buddhaic Plane held the group's silence for a few seconds.

"Despite my learning, my experience and all my memories, I am frightened," Philippe said suddenly. "There is something quite horrifying about public execution before a crowd."

"I know," said Maragos with gentleness. "But remember the trigger this will provide. It is a small price to pay for the return of The One."

All of them suddenly moved together, and for an incredible instant, merged to form one entity.

*How easy to move from* **here** *to* **there***, just a thought and light-years vanish to nothingness... remember when all eight billion of us on the planet combined our thoughts with the other billions on higher planes, and we pushed... and pushed... and Shuramee moved from this orbit to that orbit... not a lot of movement but it saved our beautiful world... that incredible moment of realization that the Curia had elected me as the Pope, the Vicar of Christ and the one to wear the shoes of the Fisherman... my first flight in a Spitfire... I'll join Peter's Squadron next week... I woke slowly, my mind buzzing like a gigantic swarm of bees with millions of minds... who am I? I am the man who sculpted statues of such wonder that people wept... I am the woman who created light displays, the child that died when the storms swept the west coast of... I am the thousands who died when the first rebellion of the Wheel Wars started... I am a newly-Ascended Soul formed of nine hundred and twenty Old Souls and I remember how I fought to absorb the memories of those hundreds... now I am formed of twenty-six million Ascendant Souls, how can I absorb so many minds?... I am an Infinite Soul... I became the Archbishop of Milan and my parents came and bowed* *before me and I gave Mass for them in that wonderful Cathedral and how proud they were... I am an Infinite Soul and I am one millionth part of The One... how incredible to be able to be many places at once, to talk to my friends on Earth while bidding the captain goodbye in his ship orbiting Jupiter... will I remember this when I merge with the others and become The One?... Can I heal Humanity?... My friends, I love you all, I am Maragos, I am Raoul, I am all of you, I die tomorrow but I am not afraid... be not afraid, little ones... I am here with you till Oneness... think **so**, and six rifles fly out of existence... how wonderful to be able to do that for my friends... is this the start of the fear that I might lose myself in these powers when I am The One? Is this what I feared?... Philippe, I am afraid of when we merge with our entities, I will lose you... no little one, we are all One in time... Raoul, you were my brother and I love you... I sense the others of my kin sleeping amid the galaxies... they know me but they do not really know themselves, for they are Infinites but they have not yet evolved... I talk to them in a way which I don't really understand yet, just as I don't know exactly how I flick myself across the Universe or talk on many levels of existence at the same time, each of Me being part of me and yet individual as well.... I sense the presence of all my kin shrouded by the vast distances of the Universe... they know me and can speak to me, but they do not yet know themselves... somehow I talked with them and agreed to come on this mission to Earth...*

"Yes, that is what it is like," said Maragos. The three humans stood shakily, dizzy with the sudden vision of how it was to be billions of souls in one personality, to move planets in their orbit, to flick millions of light-years with a thought, to be the single most powerful entity in the universe and to fear the loss of that identity with the final merger to Oneness.

"Sleep now," said the Infinite Soul, and they returned to their bodies for the last time.

* * *

The cell doors rattled at ten in the morning. No breakfast had been served and the four prisoners had been left alone with their thoughts.

Philippe's door opened as he was lying in his usual position, arms behind his head. Two men entered, neither of them known to him, one of them carrying a plain wooden chair. The shadows of the armed guards hovered in the corridor, and Philippe wondered just why they persisted with the pretence when Maragos' powers to disarm and neutralise the soldiers had been proven so dramatically. More for public consumption, he decided.

"On the chair," ordered one of the men. He was elderly, overweight and had the small, narrow eyes of low intelligence. Philippe sat up and did as ordered. The second man squatted at his feet and for a moment, Philippe had a painful memory of how differently other people had once bowed before him. This man was younger than his colleague, perhaps an apprentice. He took a pair of scissors from his belt and began to cut away the knees of Philippe's trousers, the faded blue denim of the standard prison gear that had returned after leaving the courtroom dressed in his suit.

The older man switched on an electric device behind Philippe's head and seized his neck. Startled, Philippe felt his hair attacked by an electric razor, and rapidly a circular patch of scalp was opened up. A wave of fear flowed through him and cold sweat broke out on his back.

"I will be dead in a matter of hours," he said to himself and then took control of his fear. A few seconds of pain was nothing, and death was an old experience. He thought of Maragos and of Jacqueline, of his oldest friend Raoul, and gradually he regained his composure.

A few minutes later he was alone again in his cell.

Jacqueline sat motionless in the wooden chair and felt the heavy, red-gold hair fall away. Her fear was well under control. She could drop her body and move from it any time she wished, she knew that. She could do it now, while they cut her hair, but she was well aware that such an act would negate the work Maragos had so painstakingly completed. Jacqueline remembered previous deaths. As sixteen-year-old Mary in medieval England, she had died painfully in producing a child. That pain and the time taken to die were greater than the experience facing her this day. She had died even more painfully as Jerome Mitchell, and in dreadful fear, the skin burning away from his face as streams of lead slammed into his aircraft in a dogfight over the English Channel. That was only one of several deaths in combat she had endured over four hundred lifetimes. Execution by the passage of electricity through her body would be simply another experience and she would join her friends on another level of existence where no more pain could affect her.

Her imminent death did not frighten her, but oh! how she hated losing her beautiful hair. Her tears were for that and that alone, but the obese man cutting off the hair was not to know it.

Raoul Carmagio spoke not a word as he was prepared for death. He remembered the extraordinary moment of being one with Maragos and the others, of the power of being an Infinite Soul, of having the memories of twenty-five billion souls each with several hundred lifetimes, of having the ability to move through time and space without effort, and shifting a planet in its orbit. He remembered all those things, and the fact of a painful death in a short while became completely unimportant.

As they opened the door to Maragos' cell, they saw her sitting on her cot, her hair already gone.

"Go away," she said to the woman flanked by the armed soldiers. The door closed again immediately.

* * *

At eleven-thirty, the doors to all four cells opened again. Feeling a quiver run through him, Philippe stood up and walked out into the corridor. Six armed guards stood along the wall, and he looked to his left to see that Raoul, Jacqueline and Maragos were also standing by their cell doors. The four smiled at each other and Philippe walked the few feet to Jacqueline and took her hand.

At the end of the corridor, two men in the uniform of Examiners stood silently with Gregory Lavalier. Crossman was gone, Philippe recalled from the meeting last night on the Buddhaic Plane, sucked into the fearsomely diseased and powerful soul of William Horning. The two men were perhaps his replacements. The three men looked nervous, edgy, and refused to meet the Philippe's gaze. Seeing that all of them were out of their cells, Lavalier turned to the door behind him and opened it. It was the door that led into the huge arrival area of the building, where truck loads of humans were delivered each day to face the Examiners of the Council for the Protection of God's Name. Accompanied by the armed guards, the four friends walked out into the echoes of the hall.

Together with a squad of soldiers, three vehicles stood there. One was a limousine, and a uniformed driver was holding open the back door. Lavalier and the other two climbed in to the accompaniment of a military salute.

The other two vehicles were open trucks. A short ladder stood against the back of the leading truck and Maragos led the way to it, climbing up without assistance and seating herself in one of the wooden benches like a tourist about to see the city. The other three followed her and six of the armed guards also climbed in. The rear of the truck was lifted up and bolted. The remaining soldiers climbed into the last truck and the convoy moved off, the massive door to the outside opening as they approached it.

The day was pleasantly warm and sunny. Glorious colours of Fall painted the city. But it was not the beauty of the colours that seized the attention of the four prisoners as their vehicle turned into the road. It was the thousands and thousands of people lined along the sidewalks.

"Horning broadcast a message on television last night," murmured Maragos. "He told America that the Spawn of Satan, the Enemies of God and America would be executed today. We are supposed to be his greatest triumph."

As she spoke, Philippe realized he could hear her perfectly, not because of her broadcasting powers she had used for her talks to huge crowds around the world, but because the silence in the streets was profound.

"They don't seem to be totally enthused about this event," said Raoul. His face was slightly pale, but otherwise he looked the same cheerful man they had always known.

"I spent the night spreading as much healing power as I could," said Maragos. "The effects will last for the day at least, and that's all we need. I also had some help."

"Help?" All three of the humans turned to her with the same question.

"You may see," she replied, and spoke no further for a time.

The small convoy entered the road leading past the Smithsonian Museum buildings and up to the Capitol, along the park where tens of thousands had listened to Maragos speak only a few days before. The crowd was there again, thousands upon thousands pressed into every inch of the area, forcing the convoy to slow to a crawl as it worked its way towards the Capitol. Philippe looked towards the beautiful building that had once housed the biggest democracy in the world. It had not changed with the corruption of the ideals with which it had been built. The Stars and Stripes fluttered from many flagpoles in the area and the magnificence of the Smithsonian buildings framed the park the way they had done for decades.

But one thing had changed. A massive platform had been built at the base of the steps of the Capitol. Beside it, rows of seats had been placed under awnings, indicating these were seats for important people. The seats were full, perhaps a hundred dignitaries sat there, and in the middle of the front row Philippe could see the familiar face of The Very Reverend William H. Horning, one-time Baptist televangelist and now President for Life of the United States of America.

"They've made it a national spectacle," came the soft voice of Maragos, and Philippe pulled his eyes from the scene at the Capitol to her. Her face was serious, and again, Philippe was struck by how much she looked like Jacqueline. Both women turned at that moment and smiled at him. The beating of his heart slowed a little but the fear still hovered in his mind like an owl suspended on silent wings over a frightened mouse. He looked around him at the crowd, all of whom were staring at the four people in the front truck.

A face caught his attention. No reason to, he thought, just a tall man in jeans and sweater, nothing special but for... *the eyes!* The eyes looked at Philippe and shone with power. Almost the power of a Maragos, he realized, but not quite. He turned his head to the other side of the vehicle and scanned the crowd. Another pair of eyes glowed at him from a woman holding a small child. The child had the same startling gaze.

"This is your help, Maragos?" he said, still looking round the crowd.

"Enhanced Ascendant Souls," she agreed. "They have been here for years waiting for my arrival and they have only now recognized themselves. Until yesterday they believed they were normal humans, and indeed, they were born here in the normal way. They have had exactly the same experience that Jesus had. Their souls have now opened up and they are spreading the healing around America."

"Would this achieve the full healing?" asked Jacqueline, also scanning the crowd for the people with the powerful gazes.

"No," said Maragos. "Only a partial healing and only for a time. After two or three days, the power of the sickness would take over again, so strong is it here. But it will be enough for the trigger."

Four heavy wooden chairs sat on top of the platform. Thick electrical cables led from them down to the ground and away through a manhole cover in the cement sidewalk. By each chair, two men stood watching the trucks arrive.

The limousine at the front of the line had stopped behind the platform and Cardinal Lavalier and his two escorts climbed out to the salute of the driver. They walked up to the row of seats and greeted the central figure. President Horning stood and shook hands with both men, then waved them to chairs alongside his. He looked cheerful, waving to the crowd and turning his head to look at all corners of the park and round behind him. But even from here, Philippe could see that Horning was forcing the smile. Instead, the President looked irritable, no doubt because of the uncanny silence that shrouded the entire city. There should have been a festive air about the proceedings, the culmination of Horning's Administration, the deaths of the Devil's Spawn, the destruction of Satan's Aides at the hands of the Council for the Protection of God's Name and thus of President Horning.

The trucks stopped and the soldiers jumped out of the rear vehicle, lining up by the front. The four soldiers accompanying the prisoners waited while the tailgate was lowered, a ladder placed against it then climbed down, holding their rifles firmly.

Maragos looked at each of the other three in turn. "Courage now, my friends," she whispered. "I know that you can leave your bodies at any time, but I beg of you, see this through. Our work depends on it. I will help you as much as I can."

Philippe took a deep breath and reached for Jacqueline's hand. Tears were in her eyes. "I wanted to look my best for saying goodbye to you," she said with a catch in her voice. "They wouldn't even give me a scarf for my head."

"After six thousand years, do you think I care about a scarf?" he said, trying to make light of it. "Come, my sweet, in a few minutes they will have nothing more to do with us."

She nodded and smiled at him and let him help her off the vehicle's rear end. She stood close to Philippe as Raoul also climbed down the ladder, then they waited for Maragos to do the same. For a second, they stood together then turned to the steps up the platform.

As they reached the top, the crowd could be seen, stretching as far as the park did, a solid, deep phalanx of people without a single sound. The silence was deathly. The four of them stood in line and looked out at the dense mass of humanity.

"I am with you till Oneness," said Maragos softly, but her words were heard clearly throughout the area. A tiny whisper ran through the park.

"Maragos!" said the murmur of a hundred thousand voices, soft as a bird's feather across the sky.

Philippe turned toward the side and looked at the crowd of dignitaries. Several tried to stare back, but few of them could meet the eyes of the man on the platform. Horning was looking confused and angry. Only Gregory Cardinal Lavalier was able to return the looks, and his face was one of sadness and some fear.

Philippe looked hard at him and then smiled. "Until Oneness, Gregory," he said. Lavalier seemed stunned for a second, opened his mouth to speak, then restrained himself as tears began to flow down his cheeks. He turned his eyes away.

Philippe turned his eyes to Horning. It was the first time he had seen the man in the flesh, and he was aware of Raoul and Jacqueline also studying the primary source of evil in the world. The physical form of William Horning was almost invisible, thought Philippe. Instead, a powerful, dark cloud seemed to surround the man, a cloud emanating awful, dreadful fear. Even with the knowledge of his own imminent death, Philippe felt the fear of William Horning. He knew how much force Horning was exerting on him, felt the drag of the horrible blackness in the eyes of the man staring back at him. Philippe shivered, more afraid now of that force than of the painful death awaiting him. That death might not be the worst thing that could happen, he understood.

Philippe sensed Maragos turn in the same direction to stare at the VIPs. In a dreadful shock of pain, the energy that exploded around him almost threw Philippe from the platform, and he saw Raoul and Jacqueline stumble and nearly fall. Maragos was looking at Horning and the President had stood up, staring back at her. The blast of energy had come from the awful power that raged between Maragos and Horning. Philippe watched Horning as the President's face went green then white. The televangelist stumbled back against the chair and into the supporting grasp of the people behind him. His eyes were wide with terror.

A tiny rumble of thunder echoed round the square, then silence returned.

"I have you, you bitch!" Horning suddenly screamed. "You're dead! Get back to Hell!"

Maragos smiled. "Yes, William, you have me. Watch me die, William. Watch my friends die. Then think about how many thousands of years you must spend in that Hell you mentioned. For you will enter that Hell very soon. Its doors are gaping wide for you."

The rumble of thunder stirred again, like a distant

earthquake making mountain ranges quiver. Horning's legs appeared to fail him and he collapsed into one of the chairs.

"Kill them!" he shrieked. "Kill the fucking bastards!" He pointed at the heavy wooden seats. "Fry them!" he screamed again. "I want that bitch fucking dead!"

His words received another menacing rumble from the distant thunder.

His heart thumping, Philippe let himself be led to one of the electric chairs. His senses seemed dimmer and he was only partially aware of his friends also being seated and strapped in place. Heavy leather bands were fastened round his wrists and ankles and a larger, broader band round his chest. Faintly, he felt metal plates being strapped to his knees through the holes cut in his trousers and he heard a slight dripping of water. As the metal helmet was placed over his head and the chin strap done up tightly, water trickled down his face where the executioners had soaked the headpiece to increase the electrical conduction of the lethal jolts.

Philippe moved inside himself and to his head, straining for contact with his friends.

"I am with you," said the voice of Maragos. "Be with me, my loved ones. This is the last act for now. Horning's power has been sharply diminished and he cannot hurt you."

"Philippe, my brother, I will wait for you," said Raoul into Philippe's mind. "This is why we were born, why we met and why we worked together for so long."

"It has been a long path together, my friend," replied Philippe. "And we have many billions of light-years still to walk. We shall always be together."

"I have loved you for six thousand years," whispered the soft tones of Jacqueline. "And that is only the beginning. Until Oneness, we can keep loving each other."

"You were my love for all of time before we met," replied Philippe. "We have millennia to be together."

The silence was broken by the multiple echoes of a loudspeaker system screeching at the crowd.

*"This is the final victory for God!"* said a voice, bellowing through the trees and amid the buildings. "God has lent his mighty arm to our beloved President Horning and destroyed the Devil's Spawn that dared to come to America and preach their evil!"

The echoes washed around the buildings and eddied back and forth.

"Evil... evil... evil..." said the thunderous voice.

*"So now we say to the Devil,"* boomed the loudspeaker.

"Devil... devil... devil..." said the park back to it.

*"Take back your filth, Satan!"*

"Satan... Satan... Satan..."

*"Here are your children! They have failed to corrupt the good people of America. Let them return to your Pit!"*

The first jolt hit Philippe as if a monstrous hand had seized him by the neck and shaken him furiously. The pain was almost secondary to the violence of the assault. Every bone was hit by a hammer and vibrated until it was close to shattering and falling out of its joint. Then the pain struck, and it was an infinity of agony worse than the horrors of the metal wands that had shocked him in his interrogation.

He was being burned alive from the inside. A molten fire in his heart scorched his lungs and bit off his breathing. He knew that his body had arched against the leather straps and that his mouth was screaming his pain while the blistering and crackling spread from his heart down through his belly and the fire became the searing torture of a blast furnace that ate his insides in a ravening gulp of never-ending agony.

He tried to use the lessons he had learned during his interrogation and cancel the pain, reverse it, but nothing worked. His whole universe was agony, blistering outward from his spine until molten lead flowed through his veins and scorched every particle of his body.

"Hold on, my beloved friend," said the small voice in his head. "Only a second or two more and we shall be through it."

The electric current stopped, and for a moment his body slumped down. Very little life was left in him, he knew. He was already partially outside his body, looking down at the man he had been. The others looked the same, drooped as if dead, just a small tremor running through the legs of Jacqueline. He turned his concentration to the people in the park who were watching this horror, and the silence was intense.

The power was switched on again and the burning began once more. Philippe was hauled back into his body as if snatched by some hellish hand and the agony consumed him. This time, it lasted only a second or two, then he remembered his lessons and mercifully dropped his body and moved outside of it.

He saw that all four of them were now standing on the platform, looking down on the bodies that had housed their souls and that they had discarded for the last time.

"Come, my friends," said the sweet voice of Maragos. "This game is complete. We must prepare for the next one."

Philippe Leger, one-time Pope Jean-Pierre II, Vicar of Christ and Bishop of Rome, successor to Peter the Fisherman, surrendered his soul to the warmth and love of Maragos the Infinite, and the world disappeared from around him.

*(From the Diary of Alan Drew)*
*September 6, 2026*

I watched the affair from near the front of the crowd. I had dressed in old clothes with a long jacket and a hood to cover most of my face. I had not shaved since walking away from the interrogation of Philippe Leger three days ago and my face was covered by a heavy growth of bristles that itched and bothered me. I had little fear that Crossman's agents would find me unless it was by simple bad luck. I was sure of the complete frenzy into which the Council's organization had been thrown by the capture of Maragos and her followers. Little but fear and chaos existed in Washington now.

Together with a hundred others in the men's hostel where I had taken residence after leaving the Council's building, I had watched the trial, frozen to the proceedings with a terrified obsession.

The men around me had grunted with a mixture of pain and delight as the four judges had been sliced apart by Maragos' debate and I had struggled to hide my pleasure at the obvious terror of the judges and the soldiers. But when sentence of death had been passed, the room had fallen silent, broken only by a few sounds of suppressed weeping around the audience.

Later that evening, I had also watched the news release of the trial.

"The Devil's Disciples have confessed their crimes," said the news-reader, a middle-aged man with a distinguished face and a Texan accent. "Faced with the agents of God as Judges, the four demons admitted their efforts to destroy the United States had failed when confronted by the forces of Good in the shape of the Council for The Protection of God's Name and our beloved President Horning."

It was farcical. This dialogue could have been written for a children's comic or a ranting sermon by some insane Ayatollah. But for the content, I would have burst out laughing.

"Sentence of death has been passed on all four of them," continued the news-reader, "and will be carried out on Thursday at midday outside the Capitol."

In the morning of that Thursday, I walked the short distance to the park and took a seat under a tree opposite the Air and Space Museum. All morning, the crowds gathered and the atmosphere immediately struck me as weird. Instead of the hum of excitement that a multiple execution of this sort should be causing, the crowd was totally silent. No children played with toy electric chairs or ran around and shouted in the way of children everywhere. No picnic baskets appeared, no boisterous drinking and socialising among the crowd. People simply appeared, took their places and waited.

At one stage, a man walked up to me, looked down and smiled. I looked up and felt a bolt of shock as I looked into the man's eyes. They were deep, dark, seemed to show the way into the depths between the stars. Immediately, I remembered that Maragos' eyes had been similar, but even more powerful, if that could be possible. I wondered how I had not been affected by them before, or how Lavalier and the others had not been stricken in awe by those eyes. I stared upward, unable to speak.

"Don't be afraid," said the man. "This is the path that Maragos has set. All will be well."

I leaned back against the tree, breathing hard as the man strolled away. I felt a wave of joy sweep my body, a conviction that the horror of today's executions was planned for a specific purpose. Only then did the image hit me. Four executions in a public spot, a leader with unimaginable powers submitting to death at the hands of people who could be swatted aside like gnats if she had wanted. Death in company with others, before a mass of people.

*Oh God!* Was Calvary like this? Was Jesus' death just a trigger to set off some reaction among humanity? If so, what will today's horrors set off?

A little before noon, the crowd stirred as the sound of engines broke the stillness. There had been no movement thirty minutes earlier when the Presidential motorcade had arrived bringing President Horning to the Capitol. I had moved nearer the front of the crowd by that time, and I saw how disturbed was Horning by the silence that greeted his arrival. No cheers, no applause had met the opening of the limousine door, and when Horning had raised his hand and automatically flashed his brilliant, insincere smile at the crowd, he had looked nonplussed, confused and finally irritable when the gesture had resulted in immobility and silence from the watchers. There was an atmosphere of menace in the park.

The line of dignitaries had taken their places with the same discomfort as the President. Something was dreadfully wrong, but nobody could identify the problem.

I watched the line of three vehicles reach the Capitol steps. The four prisoners seemed quite composed, even appeared to exchange small comments to each other. I saw a look of astonishment cross Philippe's face at one point and I followed his gaze to see the same tall man who had spoken to me in the park earlier. The man was looking firmly at Philippe, and I saw dawning comprehension in Philippe's face. There were others with those eyes too, I saw. A woman with a small child, both standing calmly with serene expressions, odd in the middle of the gathering tension, an old man leaning on a heavy walking stick, two teenage girls, all standing out from the horde because of their remarkable gazes.

The prisoners four were led up on to the platform and at one point, I heard quite distinctly the soft words of Maragos.

"I am with you till Oneness," she said, and her gentle tones carried clearly across the entire park. Something seized our collective mind with those words, and I heard myself join the thousands uttering the one name.

"Maragos!" we said. It was acceptance, it was worship, it was love, it was a prayer for help, and I shivered, understanding again that, just as Calvary, some unearthly power would be unleashed this day that would change things for ever.

On the stage, I saw that Philippe had turned and was looking at the row of privileged spectators surrounding President Horning. A trembling wave of dismay ran through the line. Horning appeared to become angry and I was delighted with the sight, though I wondered where Crossman had gone. I couldn't imagine the Chief Examiner deliberately missing the execution. The idea that something unpleasant had happened to Crossman intrigued and puzzled me. When Maragos turned toward Horning, I saw the terror strike the President and heard the thin screech of fear that Horning emitted. The President fell back against the other dignitaries. Then I heard the tiny growl of angry thunder that raced round the outskirts of the city like the harbinger of something dreadful. With everyone else, I shivered in the collective wave of fear. It was quite plain how all the people in the park had somehow joined together in a truly spiritual sense. I knew what we all thought, and finally, I knew what we would do. I felt our collective rage begin to grow. Was this, perhaps, something of what they had called "Oneness?"

Finally, the four were led to the electric chairs and strapped in place. I felt my breathing becoming heavier, and sweat broke out on my back and face. This was like the horrors at the ball park when I had first witnessed an evening of what was termed "God's Work," the execution of people for no crime but their beliefs.

The heavy silence was pulverized by the loudspeakers bellowing, just as they had at the ball park. The sound was horrific, but I didn't listen to the words. The echoes raced round the park like wildly spinning eddies of wind. Feeling numbed, I watched the four bodies strapped in the chairs jerk sharply as the bolts of electricity hit them. I clearly heard the screams of agony that emitted from all four of them and saw the contortions of the faces under the metal masks. The difference between the scene now and the scenes in the ball parks where too often I had been forced to attend the public executions was now obvious.

There were no whistles of delight or screams of appreciation from the hundreds of thousands in the park. Instead, a wave of pain seemed to run through the massed crowds as the bodies in the electric chairs vibrated in agony. Several in the crowd near me were sobbing and hiding their faces.

I saw the four bodies slump as the power was turned off for a moment. A doctor examined each of the bodies, stood away and nodded to someone below the platform. The vibrations hit the four again and the bodies shook with awful force though this time, none of them uttered a sound. In a few seconds it was over. The four were dead, slumped over against their straps, oddly shrunken now as the life force had left them.

The silence thundered through the park, and the stillness had the frozen rigidity of a waxwork. At first, I thought that the small sound I could hear was a vehicle engine starting. But the tiny rumble grew until it seemed to fill the whole world and with a startling, terrifying sharpness, the light faded deeper than a winter dusk. An enormous cloud had formed over Washington, and the rumble was the thunder that growled inside like the protests of a giant's stomach.

The light had become a weird, greenish glow that generated no shadows, and the rumble built up until it shook the universe. With the thunder, the crowd had stirred. Thousand of people began to move forward, me amongst them, advancing on the platform where the four bodies hung in the leather straps of their chairs. Beside the platform, the lines of dignitaries stood abruptly. Horning could be seen shouting and waving at the soldiers, but none of them moved.

A new sound started, a rumble almost like the thunder of the cloud, but this was the sound of people. It was a wave of hatred, of rage, of thousands of people discovering how they had been corrupted. A tendril of people raced out ahead of the crowd toward President Horning. I saw the fear hit Horning then he was surrounded by humanity. A shriek of terror rang out of the group and I saw a glimpse of Horning's face, already covered in blood. Other arms of the crowd had reached the line of VIPs and enveloped them. Blood began to run down the steps of the Capitol, screams of terror and pain erupted from the frenzy. I saw a head bounce down the steps, blood gushing from the torn neck as if the head had been wrenched from the rest of the body, the face still screaming horror.

As I began to turn away, a cataclysmic explosion shook the ground, windows shattered all along the buildings surrounding the park and the first lightning bolt struck. It hit the Capitol building, which exploded. In deep shock, I turned to watch. The dome had gone and flames were already visible inside the building. Elsewhere, the crowd was running wild. The park had less than half the people in than had been there moments before. Walking to the side and the shelter of the Art Gallery, I began to make my way towards the White House, knowing exactly what was the next act to be carried out. By the time I had reached the railings, the mass of people had covered the lawns and broken into the mansion.

As I watched, flames could be seen in the lower floor windows, glass was breaking, and screams told of more deaths. I turned away and began to walk towards the river. I would head north and make for the new nation of the Atlantic States of America. I had much to write.

* * *

The destruction of Washington took three days. What the firestorms that erupted from the clear skies that midday did not destroy, the people did. The White House was shattered to ground level in hours, the Executive Mansion followed by that evening. Massive explosions in the basement of the block housing the Council for the Protection of God's Name demolished that building at the same time, but these events were only the start of the greatest destruction of a city since

Hiroshima. By the time the violence had been exhausted, not a building stood greater than ten feet high and not one structure was whole. Three hundred thousand people were dead, and corpses littered the streets, the parks and the roadways, and floated in the river.

Washington was only the first. Every major city in the reduced United States of America suffered similar destruction. Chicago was a cloud of smoke for weeks, and when it cleared, not a single building stood upright in the downtown region. The collapse of the Sears Tower had left a flattened area of shattered buildings and bodies over a mile long and a half mile wide. The death toll was over two million. Dallas, Houston, and San Antonio vanished in nuclear explosions whose origins have never been revealed.

After a month, the death toll was estimated at thirty million. Bodies littered the country like the residue of bottles after a picnic, and plague began to strike in America. Relief crews began flying in from Canada, the Union of Pacific States, and from the rest of the world, but little could be done. The remaining people had lost their heart and died by the millions. The disease was prevented from spreading by the same application of mental powers that had limited the Middle-East war to the combatants' zone, but nothing could be done with the inhabitants. It was clear that they wanted to die. The massive revulsion against what they had done over the last twelve years was so great that few could stand it.

By the year 2033, the population of the USA was down to thirty thousand and falling. By the end of that decade, it was down to twenty-five hundred, all Old Souls acting as caretakers. Not a single child was born in the territories of the USA since that day on which Maragos and her companions were executed.

*(History of North America during the Time of the Infinite Soul, Klaus P. Scheidenhorst, University of Berlin, 2105, Oxford University Press.)*

* * *

Michael Hendricks smiled as he felt the power of the Infinite Soul.

"I am delighted to meet you again, Maragos," he said.

"No less than I, my old friend," replied the Infinite. "I have been watching your work and you have served The One well."

She looked around the spacious study that Michael had created for himself. Polished pine floors with beautiful Indian rugs, a massive white desk with a computer screen and a printer but no telephone. The view through the French windows was of a lake with water fowl swimming, and some children playing on a raft. Their shouts and laughter could be faintly heard.

"You still need an Earthly environment?" she said in amusement.

He shook his head. "I don't need it, no, but it pleases me. Earth is a beautiful planet, and it helps me in my work."

"You have visited a number of planets by now," she said as a matter of simple fact. She sat in a leather armchair and crossed her legs. In her short blue business suit she looked like Julianne Patterson, he thought and smiled at her.

"Champagne, Maragos?" he asked, and the ice bucket appeared by his side. He poured two flute glasses and passed her one. She took it and sank a large mouthful.

"A wonderful drink," she said, and giggled like a young girl. "Somehow, none of the races I knew ever developed it. The universe is poorer for that."

"As you said, I have visited many planets," said Michael Hendricks. "All the ones where I have sent human souls to reincarnate as other species, I have been to see. I learned that trick of instant travel from you."

She laughed. "You were my best pupil," she said. "I

had to be an Infinite Soul before I learned how to do that. Has everyone gone now?"

He took a sip of his own champagne and sighed in relaxation. "Nearly all," he said. "Eleven billion human souls have reincarnated as other species. A hundred million came all at once when the Middle East blew apart, and almost the same number when you had done your work in America. That was a difficult time."

"They died in utter shame," she agreed. "My trigger worked well. Most of them chose to leave their bodies within days or weeks of my departure."

"It was like rush hour in New York," he agreed with a smile. "And all the millions of souls who had never incarnated at all, they too had to be sent into incarnations somewhere, some on Earth, most to other species."

"But your work is done," she said, and finished her glass. "What will you wish to do now? We have much time before the sick souls begin to return, healed we hope, and ready to spread the healing in those who remained."

"There is one thing I want to do," he answered. "It would please me and make some amends to another soul that I love."

"Yes," said Maragos with a smile of warmth. "You both deserve it. Go then, my faithful friend, you have done well and The One will always remember you."

"I will see you again, Maragos?" asked Michael.

"Of course," she said, and touched his cheek. "I am with you till Oneness."

"Good," said Michael, and the beautiful study faded as the sound of Maragos' wonderful laugh hung in the air for a few seconds.

William Hardcastle Horning woke with a shudder of horror. His dream had been terrifying. At the apex of his triumph, the public execution of the four demons who had threatened him with the evil creed of Oneness, the crowd had revolted and... With a small yelp of anguish, Horning recalled being attacked by thousands of furious people in front of the Capitol, the blows that drew blood on his face, how his arm had been grabbed and wrenched so hard that the bone had cracked and the arm had come away....

Horning moaned and lifted his head from the pillows, opening his eyes expecting to look around the familiar luxury of his ornate bedroom of the White House. What he saw made him close his eyes again, praying that he was still asleep and that the dream would have faded the next time he opened them.

But it didn't work. He opened his eyes again and the scene was the same. Immediately in front of him was the most terrifying sight he could ever have imagined. The creature, whatever it was, sat in a huge throne just a few feet away. The animal must have been ten feet high, Horning thought, his mind yammering on the point of madness. It was naked, the smooth skin looking slimy, the sexual organs horrific in their size and aggressiveness. The huge, erect penis stood out like a tower from the massive shrubbery of red hair in the groin. The creature's head was even worse. Lizard-like, its massive tongue snaked out of the huge mouth and waved at Horning. Enormous green eyes stared unblinkingly, and the first wave of rotting breath reached him as the creature moved. Horning gagged, then vomited over his bedclothes, feeling so sick he could barely breathe.

Turning his head to try and avoid the smell, he nearly threw up again. There was no end to the room. He was in a small single bed, not the massive structure he normally shared with whatever child had been brought into the White House from the collections of heretics and criminals swept up by God's Police during the day. He looked again at the endless room. It had a floor, with a dirty carpet. It had a ceiling, a dingy cream-coloured plaster with a single, naked bulb hanging from it. The room simply had no walls, that was the problem. The floor went on into an impossible distance, on and on and on... no curvature of the Earth to stop it... his sense of balance fell apart and he vomited again. The smell of puke almost drowned out the fetid breath of the creature, but not quite.

"Hello, Horning," said the creature. The voice was grating, harsh. "It's a pleasure to welcome you here."

"You will address me as President Horning," said Horning, trying for authority, but aware that he spoke in a whimper.

"HAH!" shouted the creature, and the stench of rotting meat enveloped Horning again.

"Oh, Jesus Christ, where am I?" he groaned.

"You're DEAD!" screeched the lizard. "And you're all MINE!"

"Don't be stupid," groaned Horning, trying to stop another gag reflex. "When did I...?"

He stopped. It wasn't a dream, it was real. He had died in front of the Capitol. "Dear God, help me," he muttered in anguish.

"There's no God, William, you know that," shouted the lizard. The noise pained Horning's eardrums and echoed back and forth around the infinite room. "There's only Oneness, but it's not for you."

Horning started to climb out of the bed, but a wave of horrific pain streaked through him, a burning blast that rattled his bones and nearly exploded his heart.

"No, no, no!" laughed the frightful creature. The sound had the thin, screeching overtones of a wood saw hitting a nail at high speed. "That's where you stay, for ever and ever and ever."

Horning stared, struggling for comprehension.

"There's only me and you, William, for all eternity," giggled the lizard. "I have you all to myself and nobody can do anything about it."

"This can't be," moaned Horning. "This just can't be. I have to get back."

"Back? There's no back," roared the animal. "There's just us, you and me, my sweet William, and I can do anything."

Horning tried again to move out of the bed but the pain was so extreme he fell back again, gasping and sweating, aware that his bowels had loosened, with even more horrible effects on the bed. "Please," he gasped. "Let me have a shower so that we can talk about it."

"Do you know what happened to the children you fucked?" bellowed the animal. It was frothing at the lips, and the eyes seemed to stare in different directions like a man with a glass insert. Horning took a breath and shook his head.

"They didn't get to the showers either," said the lizard at the same screaming volume. "They were taken out of your room when you went to the bathroom, and they were shot in the back garden of the White House."

Horning hung suspended in horror. "I didn't know that," he managed to say. The bedclothes were whipped away and he was revealed naked, shivering in cold and fear.

"*WHOOOOOWHEEEEE!!!*" shrieked the lizard, rolling back in its seat with delight. "What a liar! President of the USA and a Minister of God! Loves to fuck children and now he lies about it! Shit, man! Are we going to have fun, or what?" The hideous creature smiled at Horning, leaning forward as it did so that Horning recoiled from the blast of sewage smell. "So your first punishment is to feel pain where they felt it," continued the lizard. Its tones were gentle, almost friendly. It moved one hand and a long knife appeared, held by enormous skinny fingers with hooked claws. The creature stood up and began to move to Horning.

"NO!" shrieked Horning and tried to protect himself, but it was useless. With a single, whistling move, the knife sliced through his penis and scrotum. Pain that he could never have imagined shot through his body. He screamed and screamed, trying to hold the pain and the gouts of blood with his hands without any effect.

"Now EAT!" yelled the lizard. He seized Horning's

mouth and forced the bloody mass of his genitals into it, slamming his lips shut.

"EAT!" it shouted again, and watched with delight as Horning gagged and suffocated as blood ran over his face and down his throat and competed with the pain for the most unimaginable horror he could ever face.

"All mine," crooned the lizard happily. "All mine from now through eternity, no sleep, no showers, no death, no escape into unconsciousness, ever, ever, EVER!"

It looked into the mad eyes of William Horning and touched his cheek with affection. "And if you think this is bad," it said, "wait until you've digested your dinner."

# Chapter 17. The Return to Washington

In the summer of 2072, a young engineer working for a monorail construction company in Los Angeles took a vacation in Vancouver. Andrew Alexander was just twenty-five and had never before been outside the borders of the Union of Pacific States, not that borders meant much in this world. But Andrew deserved a vacation, and he enjoyed the six-hour monorail trip from Los Angeles to Vancouver enormously.

The scenery he found to be exquisite, and before too long he located the beaches and settled down for some serious relaxation. It was not that different from Los Angeles, after all. The same clean beaches, the same warm, crystal-clear air and pleasant swimming, but it was somewhere else, and Andrew relished that sensation. In the early afternoon he felt the need for a drink, rose up from the sand and strolled towards the small diner on the sidewalk. He joined the line of mainly young people, enjoying the proximity of the many young women wearing little but the bottoms of string bikinis. One in particular caught his eye. She was of medium height, and her body, while quite obviously wonderful, was much the same as the others in a world where most people had learned to control their physical condition. No, it was the look of calm serenity, of deeply felt spiritual enjoyment of the scenery and the climate that drew his attention.

After a few moments of staring she sensed his attention and turned to him. She smiled, and it was as simple as that. Three months later, Andrew Alexander of Los Angeles married Jessica Bellamy of Montreal in a simple ceremony in the garden of her parents' house in Point Claire, Quebec and they went to live in Anaheim, California.

Even in the world of Oneness, some things had never changed, and courtship, marriage and family rearing were among the constants. A year later, Andrew and Jessica had a son they named Michael John. There was no reason for the names, they agreed, they were not names of relatives, ancestors, uncles or brothers, but both of them sensed the requirement of the child to be named thus. In the world of Oneness, some things had certainly changed, and listening to one's children before they were born was a new element in the family system.

Michael John Alexander was healthy, intelligent and noisy. By the time he was fifteen, he began to discover some needs in himself.

"Andrew, I want to see the Old Territories," he told his father. The two men were sitting in the sun room of the house in Anaheim, each reading a book. Jessica was working that day at the University, where she studied the languages of other species of The One and worked on the development of translation software. Andrew looked up from his book about the first human visit to another star system that had taken place a quarter-century before, and studied his son with considerable affection and admiration. The boy was a very old soul, that was evident, much older than either of his parents, and Andrew had been waiting for the time when his son would start to show the signs of his spiritual age. The moment had come, it seemed.

"Why?" he asked.

"I know that I played some part in The Story," Michael said. He pointed at the book he was reading. "There was this old guy living in Boston, his name was Alan Drew. He died a few years ago. He was close to Philippe Leger at the time. He's written these diaries, and... I know I was there, also."

In a post-Maragos world, one did not greet such statements with ridicule. The knowledge of reincarnation was standard through the world now, and only a tiny portion of the world's population still refused to believe in it. These were the same people who still worshipped in the old churches, prayed to God and discounted The Story of Maragos and the events of those cataclysmic years as the work of the Devil. They refused to believe in the interstellar travel that had become commonplace since other species had finally visited Earth and offered passage on their ships to any who wanted. These old reactionaries were viewed with sympathy by the rest of the world and left alone, recognized for what they were, very young, terrified souls.

"The Old Territories are deserted, Michael," said Alexander, putting his book down. "There's not a lot there, any more. Getting around won't be easy."

"I know," the boy agreed. "But I have to do it."

There was no denying that sort of statement from that sort of young man. Not in this world of 2088.

"Will you finish college, first?" asked his father. "Just as a favour to Jessica and me? Go in four years."

Michael nodded. "I'm not ready yet, anyway," he said.

"How so?" asked Andrew.

Michael shook his head. "I don't know," he replied. "But there's something missing."

"You'll work it out," said Andrew and returned to his book.

"Of course," replied Michael, and did the same.

* * *

William Horning lay sprawled on the filthy bed. He was beyond being sickened by the vomit and faeces that covered it, that was the least of his distress. The wound in his groin had never healed, and it gushed blood in copious quantities at frequent intervals, though he was unable to faint or die from the loss.

441

"To die!" he gasped. "Oh GOD! If only I could die!"

"Don't you get it, Billy boy?" giggled the dreadful creature sitting on the throne. "You *are* dead! That's the whole wonderful point. You can't get any deader than this, and I have you all to myself!"

"Then why can't I get judged by God?" begged Horning. "I've been a faithful Christian all my life, surely I can make my case to God?"

"*YEAHHHHHHHHH!*" shrieked the creature and waved its genitals at Horning who shuddered at the sight. The gush of rotting meat smell that enveloped him covered the stench of vomit and shit on the bed for a few seconds and Horning puked again. He was almost used to that by now.

"A Christian?" bellowed the lizard. "You? If that's Christianity, Lucifer was a devout believer, too!" And it fell back in its seat, laughing hilariously.

Horning began to weep, huge drops of saline falling down his cheeks. He tried to cover his eyes but saw with horror that the lizard had stood up and was stretching luxuriously.

"Oh no!" he begged. "Please, not again."

"Why not?" giggled the animal. "You never gave the children a chance to deny you, now did you? Be fair, Billy my sweet, a lizard needs a good fuck now and again. On your stomach!"

A massive, invisible hand seized Horning and flung him over on his front, spread his legs and held him rigid. He felt the lizard approach and mount him from the rear, that dreadful voice coming from close to his right ear, and then the pain struck him, the horrible, horrible pain as his insides seemed to be ripped to shreds by the massive organ and his hearing was overloaded by the exultant yells of his tormentor. Horning began to moan, a long, soft moan, that was like the sound the children, had made in his bed in the White House when he had used them this way.

"Oh God, please help me," he whimpered.

"God?" said a pleasant female voice from

somewhere else, and the nightmare ended. Weeping, moaning and clutching the pain to him, Horning looked around, wondering what fresh horrors could await him.

He was in a small, comfortable room, lying on a large, velvet-covered couch. He was clean. He was without pain, vomit, blood or shit. For a few moments, his mind could see nothing beyond these magical facts.

"There is no God, William, we told you that before."

He looked up and saw the speaker. She was pretty, feminine, dressed in a short blue skirt and white sweater. She looked so clean, it was almost like entering heaven, thought Horning. He recognized her. "You're the woman that..." he stammered, sitting up on the couch.

"That you executed in Washington," she finished for him with a pleasant smile. "The very same."

"You *are* the Devil," he gasped, fear covering him. "I knew it! And that horrible... animal is yours, isn't it?"

"No, it's yours," she replied.

"Mine?" Tears of despair ran down his cheeks. "How can it be mine?"

"You created it in your own mind, William," said Maragos. "Just as you have created all the horrors of Hell for yourself."

She smiled at the look of incomprehension that engulfed him. "William, one day you'll believe in what I was telling the world," she said. "There is no god, no heaven, no hell, there is only what we have created. Your soul knows the evil it has done and you are punishing yourself. When you have completed that stage, you will return to living incarnate again."

"Oh dear God!" he mumbled. "I wish I could do that now."

"You may not think so when that time comes," replied Maragos. "Because that's when you will begin to repay your debts to the souls you have harmed in your few, nasty lives."

"Anything must be better than this," he sobbed. "Is there no way I can stop this?"

"None at all," replied Maragos. "Your soul is too sick and corrupted to learn how to break out of it."

"But it will stop?" Horning was begging for comfort, but Maragos seemed unwilling to give him any.

"Eventually," she said.

"Oh thank God for that!" breathed Horning. "That... thing said it would be for eternity."

"You may not be able to tell the difference," said Maragos. She waved a hand in dismissal, and Horning found himself back in the limitless room with the festering bed.

"Well, hello there!" thundered the awful voice. "I'm so glad you're back! I was starting to get a little bit horny!"

Ignoring the pun, William Hardcastle Horning began to scream again.

* * *

Michael John Alexander was seventeen, and a student in Physics at UCLA before the pieces began to come together for him. The first week of the new term was exciting. The campus was new, full of people, lots and lots of girls. He had every expectation of having one whale of a time over the next three years. As he left one of his introductory classes in mathematics, he was walking towards the library when he felt footsteps behind him. With a strong sense of expectation, he turned and saw a powerfully-built young man a few feet behind. He looked about eighteen, had jet black hair and the neck muscles of a football player.

For a few seconds, the two looked at each other.

"I'm Simon Halliday," said the young man. He looked puzzled, as if it was not his usual habit to talk to strangers casually like this.

"Michael Alexander," said Michael, and extended his hand. As they gripped hands, a powerful sense of recognition flooded both of them.

"Have we met?" asked Michael.

"I think so," replied Simon. "Some time, somewhere in another life."

"Then there's a reason for meeting now, I suspect," said Michael.

"Of course," said Simon, and they continued their way to the library like friends of many years. In a post-Maragos world, such conversations were not that unusual.

At midday, Simon and Michael exchanged a mutual glance across the study table in the library and immediately agreed, without any word being spoken, that lunch was a good idea. They walked out into the bright sunshine of late Fall in California and headed for the students' coffee shop. And it was in that unlikely spot that their world changed beyond comprehension.

The two young men were sitting at a table, sipping coffee and munching on the timeless food of young people in America, hot-dogs with relish and mustard, when they both looked up at a woman who had walked in. She was about average height, well shaped, like nearly all people were in this new world, and had a presence that was magnetic. She was dressed in simple blue jeans and a shirt made of one of the new fibres brought in from a distant world. The shirt flashed colours as she walked, and changed through a spectrum of shades that had never been seen on Earth before the trade routes with the stars opened up twenty years ago. Everybody in the restaurant felt the presence of the woman's personality, that was clear, because as she walked down the room, faces turned to her like iron filings shifting as a magnet passed overhead.

Gulping their hot dogs down, Simon and Michael rose to their feet as the woman approached their table. She stopped in front of them and smiled with shyness and a little uncertainty. Dark red hair framed an oval face that would have been average but for beautiful, deep eyes, so brown that they were almost black, and with warmth glowing in them that Michael felt he would wish to drown in.

"I saw you both come in," she said. "I think we know each other."

Feeling unsteady, Michael sat down again as the other two did the same. They stared at each other for fully a minute, Michael feeling his pulse thundering in his head. His throat was dry. Something powerful was happening, and the whole room of students could sense it.

Simon broke the silence. "But we're waiting for one more," he said. "Then we'll know what all this is about."

The young woman nodded. "We have a task," she said.

* * *

The day was a Saturday, early in the morning when Michael rose, aware of the glorious weather and went to the back garden to throw a few hoops. A month had passed since his meeting with Simon Halliday and the girl called Emma Dylan. In that time, the three had grown so close it was impossible to imagine any life before they had met. And yet there was a sense of the fourth person missing. They agreed it would be another woman. When she appeared the task would begin, that they also agreed.

Thinking deeply, Michael bounced the ball on the concrete driveway of his house, then began an intensive leap and throw routine that he could maintain for an hour without a break. By seven-thirty, in a good, healthy sweat, he was about to pack the basketball away and consider breakfast, when he saw her.

New neighbours had moved in during the week, that was clear from the huge trailer that had spent the day being unloaded, but Michael had seen no sign of the arrivals as yet. He looked across the fence and swallowed with a little difficulty.

She looked about his age, petite in build, dressed in cut-off denim shorts and a white tee-shirt. Shoulder-length hair was a light brown and her eyes were large and dark. She had opened the back door of the house next to his and their eyes met immediately.

Michael's first feeling was that an old friend had come home, and a wave of pleasure ran through him. "Hi!" he said cheerfully, and his throat dried.

She stared hard then smiled, and Michael was helpless.

"My name's Julianne Cullen," she said softly. Her voice was a pleasant alto that seemed most soothing to him. "Have we met before?"

"I don't think so," he said, stammering a bit.

But as he spoke, he sensed that he was wrong, and decided that this girl was somebody from before. Such realizations and decisions were common enough in this world of 2090.

Julianne Cullen smiled with great warmth. "I think we have, in a previous life," she said. "And we have unfinished business together."

They looked at each other for a long time. Michael finally realized that the last pieces of a two-year-old puzzle had fallen into place. "We have to go to the Old Territories together," he said. "There are a couple of friends you have to meet."

"Yes," she agreed. "That's what we have to do."

Five minutes later, Michael connected with Simon Halliday and Emma Dylan on his telephone. The device was actually an organic semi-sentient creature that grew on a planet in the galaxy inhabited by The Speakers. This was the race that Maragos had described one night, a species resembling termite mounds that provided the instantaneous telepathic communication over limitless light-years. The small creatures were miniature relatives of the Speakers and were ideal as replacements for telephones. Several thousand had been brought to Earth ten years after the events in Washington, and they were now bred in plants in Europe, Canada and Australia. All Michael did to establish contact was simply think the names of his friends. The creature, which resembled a gold-coloured maple leaf and hung on the wall of his bedroom feeding on microbes in the air, passed the call to similar creatures owned by the other two and gave a mental nudge to Simon and Emma.

"It's the girl next door," said Michael, suppressing a laugh. His amusement was echoed by the other two and by Julianne who was also linked by her telepathic leaf.

"Then it's time to go," said Simon. His sudden surge of tension was almost tangible to the others.

"Go where?" asked Emma, but the answer was known to all of them the second she asked.

"Washington," replied Michael. The response was instant and a small mental sigh ran between the four of them as they discovered together a new dimension to their mutual drive.

"I thought it was just to visit the Old Territories," said Emma, a trace of excitement in her voice. "Going to Washington makes a lot more sense."

"It also points a little more closely to what this is all about," added Michael. "It's obviously something to do with the last days of The Story."

Two weeks later, they left Los Angeles. None of the four sets of parents was comfortable with the developments, but faced with the realities of a post-Maragos world, and four almost-adult children clearly aware of a joint role to play, there was nothing they could do. The parents had their own conference call on the subject.

"Michael's known for two years that this was coming," said Andrew Alexander. "So I've had time to prepare for it." He was in his office, working on plans for the new monorail link to Mexico City when the psychic tap came in his head that a caller wanted to speak with him. One didn't need to have the gold maple leaf creature with one, communication was established over any distance once the creature had set up its personal link with its owner.

"It seems all our kids have given some sort of indication," came the gentle tones of Emma's mother, an artist who made a comfortable living working in a new art form, sculptures that somehow changed mental vibrations in the viewer and created emotional harmonies. It had been an art that had reached its apex with the vanished race of Maragos' people, and many of the works had been brought from Maragos' abandoned home planet to Earth.

"Yuri and I are both fifth-stage Old Souls," continued Emma's mother. "But Emma is something so far above us I can't keep up with her. So we've never tried to influence her at all."

"There's certainly something powerful going on between the four of them," said another voice. It was the father of Simon Hall. He was a professor of xenobiology, the new science of the biology of non-Earth species that had grown in the age of interstellar and intergalactic travel of the last two decades. "And it almost certainly has something to do with The Story."

"We have to let them go, then," said Emma's mother with a tinge of sadness.

"When was it ever different with teenagers?" asked Professor Hall with dry humour.

* * *

Transport was not a problem. The technology of civilizations millions of years older than humanity was available, and had been for fifteen years or more. Their vehicle looked like any small bus capable of carrying ten or twelve passengers, but for the absence of wheels. Instead, the base was smoothly rounded, making the vehicle remarkably similar to the shuttle-craft design of the old Starship Enterprise programs. A tiny power plant was installed in the base of the vehicle, a minute and sharply less efficient version of the gravity engines that drove the intergalactic spaceships of the Kaloti species that had brought Maragos to Earth. That race had move beyond the incarnation stage to the Ascendant level and their yellow world was abandoned, but other species still manned the ships that provided the links with others of The One. The engines of those ships would fill a ballroom. That of the ground vehicle carrying Michael Alexander and his friends were the size of a matchbox, and even then was deliberately governed to produce less than one percent of the potential power. Any more, and the bus could fly to Venus in a matter of hours.

The bus sat on its base when the power was off. A small switch on the control panel activated the tiny anti-gravity field and raised the vehicle a metre off the ground. A lever on the driver's right hand side operated much like the throttle lever of an aircraft and provided forward and reverse directional thrust. A half wheel in front of the driver continued the aircraft similarity, but provided directional steering like a car rather than the lateral control of an aircraft. Collision with any object or person was impossible because of sensing devices around the vehicle's base that brought the entire vehicle and its occupants to a dead stop within a shared gravity field so that no inertia problems arose.

So seeing their children off to cross the USA was merely a moment of sadness at the temporary loss for the four sets of parents. No sense of danger was to be felt. No accident could occur to the vehicle, and there was nothing of danger in the deserted territories that they were about to traverse. The bus needed no refuelling and the food generating unit would provision them for as long as necessary. The parting was therefore more like seeing the kids off to camp, and only the deep sense of mission in the four travellers made it any different.

The atmosphere in the bus was festive as they wound their way out of Los Angeles and found the Interstate 15 towards Las Vegas. For all of them it was the first real departure from home, and like any bunch of teenagers, the excitement was overwhelming. The roads were busy, as they always were and always had been in Southern California since the roads had been built. Despite the new technology of transport, the roads were still the best place to travel with personal vehicles. Driving, however, was not the business it had been a half century before. Anti-collision devices, automatic navigation and the psychic communication capabilities that the gold maple leafs had provided removed most of the frustrations of being out of touch.

Once out of the city, Michael settled the vehicle into a steady two hundred kilometres an hour and let the automatic sensors carry the vehicle along the route. Remaining seated at the driver's position, he was still able to relax and join in the conversation.

As they passed Las Vegas they had their first meal and felt the vehicle shuttle itself to the north towards Salt Lake City. After leaving the old California border and entering the territory of the one-time United States, they had seen only one vehicle, a larger version of their own bus heading in the opposite direction. From the highway, they had seen a number of deserted small towns but not a single human being had been spotted.

Not even when they reached Salt Lake City did they see anyone. They let the bus find its way up to Interstate 80, then pulled off the highway and over some rough country before stopping the vehicle and letting it settle down on its base.

The four of them had a light meal, drew out the two double bunks and went to bed. It might have been a wild, silly night, two teenaged couples sleeping together for the first time, but they did it with a calm, assured sense of belonging to each other, like couples who have been together for many years. As, of course, they knew they had, over several lifetimes.

Over the next few days, they travelled consistently.

The roads were of poor quality, often very little was left of the highway except for a vaguely discernible line. But the quality of the roads was irrelevant for a vehicle that floated a meter above the ground. I-80 served as merely a direction-finder for them.

They reached Lincoln, Nebraska before they met their first resident of the old America. They had several times pulled off the highway to visit the towns they saw, but had encountered nothing but ruins. Salt Lake City did not have a building standing. Cheyenne was peopled by wolves that were completely unconcerned and disinterested in the visitors. In between the towns, the buffalo had returned. Three times, the travellers had stopped the bus and watched, astounded as the land turned black, and vibrated with the thunder of two or three million or more hooves raging past them like a tidal wave.

Lincoln, like every town they had seen, was like an ancient war zone. They were almost within the city limits before they recognized that the mounds of brick, mortar and grass were once buildings, shattered into featureless piles over which the grass and bushes were claiming their old rights. Only a single, narrow plume of smoke showed the existence of life, and Emma who was driving, cautiously steered the bus round the piles of debris until they saw the source.

The small house stood incongruously in the middle of a large, cleared area. It was neat, windows had wooden shutters framing them, and oddest of all, an old gas-burning automobile sat before the front steps. Michael, a student of transportation history, recognized a Lincoln Town Car of the first decade of this century. It was white, gleamed gently in the sun, and looked immaculate.

Emma stopped a few yards from the house and let the bus sink to the ground. They stared out of the windows. For a few moments, nothing moved. The tableau could have been a painting until the front door of the house opened and a man appeared. He was dressed simply, blue jeans and a plaid shirt rolled up above the elbows. He looked in his thirties, though the heavy beard disguised the features. The beard, like the hair was rich, deep brown, thick and youthful.

Emma hit the switch that opened the sliding door of the bus, and all of them piled outside.

"I've been waiting for you," said the man. His voice was vibrant, a powerful baritone. "I sensed you coming a few days ago."

Simon Halliday advanced on the man and held out his hand. "We're going to Washington," he said. "I'm Simon, these are my friends Emma, Michael and Julianne."

The man nodded, stared hard at Emma, then back at Simon. "Peter Williams. Who were you before?" he asked. His eyes switched back to Emma and they smiled at each other as old friends do who meet after a long separation. The other three sensed the communication and laughed, feeling at ease with the stranger.

"That's what we think we'll find out," replied Michael.

"You will," said the man with certainty. "Come inside and have some tea."

They followed him into the house, surprised by the neatness of the building. Curtains hung by the windows, deeply polished wooden floors reflected the gleam of the sun, and elegant lounge chairs sat around the room.

"What are you doing here?" asked Julianne as the man vanished into the kitchen. Silence reigned for a few moments, interrupted by small metallic clatters then Peter Williams appeared again, carrying a tray with five large mugs, a sugar bowl and a container of cream. He set the tray on a small coffee table and sat in one of the chairs, waving casually at the tray. All four of them leaned forward, took a mug and sat back. Peter was still looking hard at Emma, not with sexual interest, but as if trying to remember something.

"Just looking after things," he replied eventually, turning his eyes on Julianne. "We have to have a few people still here."

"Why?" asked Simon with curiosity.

Peter looked at him. "In case the infant souls come back"

"Have many come back?" Michael was astonished at the answer.

Peter smiled, a small, grim smile. "Now and again, groups appear. They try and burn my house, shoot me, stick crosses on my lawn and invoke the name of God."

"And what happens?" asked Emma.

"Somebody comes," replied the man.

"Somebody?" Emma was hesitant.

"Somebody," said Peter firmly. "Somebody comes, they stay with the infant souls a few days, and they all die."

"Huh?" The astonishment was in all of them.

"They die. They lie down, breathe a little, and die. The bodies ignite and burn. Then the visitor walks away again."

"What are these... visitors like?" Simon was fascinated. Nothing of this had ever been heard in the UPS.

"Just like you and me, really," answered Peter. "Except for the eyes."

The room was silent.

"They have the eyes of Maragos," said the man. "They glow with power. Enhanced Ascendant eyes."

"But... why?" asked Emma. She seemed upset, and Williams turned to her.

"It must be," he said. "These groups of religious fanatics are the souls that have never braved incarnation before. They have been forced into lives that will be short, so that they can accelerate the process of growth. But they try and incarnate where many of their type incarnated before, and become like those who preceded them. The Ascendants must force the rapid cycle of birth and death."

The silence lasted a few more minutes before the four simultaneously finished their drinks and stood up.

"We need to get going," said Michael, and Peter Williams rose with them, following them back to their bus. He stood silently as they climbed aboard. Emma was the last to enter, and she turned and looked back at him.

Peter raised his hand in salute. "No more than ten seconds, remember," he said.

"What? What was that?" Emma began to tremble.

"In combat," he said, smiling. "Don't fly more than ten seconds straight and level."

Confused, with tears flooding down her cheeks, she let the door slide down. Simon raised the bus on its force field and turned back to what was left of Interstate 80. Until they passed behind a mound of ruins, Emma continued to stare back at the man who had said farewell with such meaningless yet shockingly disturbing words.

Chicago was the next contact point, but not with humans. They had not intended to stop there, but as they passed the shattered stump that had been the highest tower in Des Moines, the draw to see Chicago grew in them. Julianne and Michael felt it strongest.

"We have to go there," said Michael, a strong sense of grief flooding his emotions. He looked across at Julianne, and she was weeping silently. She nodded at him and tried to smile, then took his hand.

"No problem," replied Simon at the steering wheel. "I think we all understand."

They turned off I-80 onto I-55 and headed north, feeling the strength of the pull grow as they neared what had been Chicago. They were at the shores of Lake Michigan before they were able to recognize anything of the city.

"That was the Shedd Aquarium," said Julianne, pointing at the ruins by the water. There were tears back in her eyes. "And the old observatory is still standing." She swung her finger out along the promontory that ended with the dome of the building.

"You were here before," said Simon. It was a statement, not a question. She nodded, and Michael joined in.

"Me too," he said. Further conversation was stopped by a squeal of excitement from Emma.

"Look!" she cried, pointing across the flat land that had once been Grant Park. As the others turned, they saw the bulky shape of a shuttle-craft parked by a pile of ruins. It was perhaps twenty times the size of their bus and quite dissimilar in shape. It looked more a donut made of steel. The sight was not uncommon in the cities of the world outside of the old USA. It was a craft that moved between the gigantic Kaloti ships in orbit and the Earth's surface.

"I think it's by the Art Institute," said Michael, still feeling displaced by his inner recognition of the city. Simon drove carefully across the park and stopped alongside the huge shuttle where they got out and looked around them. They had an uninterrupted view in almost all directions. Except for the observatory, there was not a building standing anywhere for twenty miles, and the mound of the old Art Institute was the highest point except for the shuttle-craft parked alongside. A mine entrance had been dug into the face of what remained of the building. A single column stood upright by the opening, and at ground level a stone lion remained, one of what had obviously been a pair guarding the entrance.

"Off-world historians or archaeologists," muttered Simon. "I'd heard that many of them come here to see how our culture developed."

There was movement from the opening and three people emerged.

*No, not people*, thought Michael, staring at the shapes. *Another species.* He had never seen any of the other species in the flesh before and he felt hypnotized. Next to him, the other three were similarly frozen.

The beings were of a similar height and build to humans. Only their heads showed their alien nature. The skin was a deep brown, wrinkled heavily, and the eyes were shielded by outcrops of a bony-looking substance. The scalps were hairless. They wore grey overalls, much like the working clothes of anyone expecting to dig through rubble.

"X'Kasxi!" whispered Emma in excitement.

Michael kept looking. He knew about the space-travelling race that had moved to the same galaxy as Humanity millions of years before, but he had never seen one outside of pictures. Something about the three aliens was setting off vibrations inside him. He moved closer and studied them, as they were studying him. Their eyes were huge, much larger than human eyes, and so dark as to make any identification of pupil or cornea structure impossible. The mouths were lipless, almost lizard-like. For a few moments, the three of them, human and Alien alike stared at each other, when something inexplicable happened.

The three X'Kasxi knelt before Michael and bowed their heads. In bewilderment, Michael turned to look behind at his friends, but they were equally astonished. He turned back to see the three X'Kasxi getting back to their feet. Though unable to read facial expressions, Michael sensed confusion in the body-language of the aliens.

"Do you speak English?" he asked with hesitation. One of the X'Kasxi touched a device strung on its belt. It gave off a short burst of sound, echoed by the creature. A second later, English words burst from the device.

"Limited," it said. "Communication is being... created."

*By my mother*, thought Michael in amusement. He knew that Jessica was one of those developing the mixed technological and telepathic translation systems that the creature before him was using. He had learned from Jessica that the difficulty was not in equivalent words, but in concepts by which to understand them. "Why did you kneel?" he asked, speaking slowly, hearing the sounds emit from the device.

The aliens looked at each other as if trying to understand, then one turned back to Michael, giving an almost human-like shrug of the shoulders. "Uncertainty is read," said the box, a few seconds after the creature spoke. "Sensed-remembered is.. rule... power.. you.. we..."

*Jessica, you have work to do,* thought Michael in confusion, and waved his hands in helplessness. "We must continue our travels," he said, and began to turn away. He saw all three beings raise their hands in farewell, three fingers and opposing thumb he noticed, and the four humans returned to their bus. Michael was silent the rest of the day, but the memory of the near worship he had seen continued to tug at his memories.

Near Hagerstown, they met another pilgrim.

Simon was driving. The road was merely a line in the countryside, and he was steering carefully when Michael let out a small shout.

"Look!" he called, pointing through the right hand window of the bus. "There's somebody walking!"

All four of them looked over. About a mile away, they could see a tiny figure striding through the scrub land. It was a man, that was clear, and his stride was long and purposeful. Simon swung the wheel over, and headed towards the distant figure. As they approached, the man stopped and watched the vehicle, leaning on his shoulder-high walking stick. He was dressed in stained old clothes, a long coat down below his knees and a brightly-collared scarf over his shoulders. He was clean-shaven and looked about the same age as the four travellers.

Simon stopped the bus and opened the door, waving at the man to come aboard. The young man looked hard at him through the windshield, then smiled with enormous warmth, moving to the entrance.

They felt his presence as he entered. He dwarfed the bus with his personality but it was a friendly, protective power he emitted, not threatening.

"Washington?" he asked. The voice was gentle but hid great power, like a professional operatic baritone speaking softly. Four grins answered him.

"My name is Martin Carrick," he announced, taking a seat and laying his long stick along the floor.

"Welcome aboard, Martin," said Simon, turning round and studying the new arrival. After a second or two, he turned back to the controls and lifted the bus into the air.

"I think that now we really are complete," said Emma, and nobody had to ask her what she meant. They all felt the same.

* * *

They were deathly silent as the bus cruised slowly past the pulverized ruins of the Smithsonian buildings. Tears were sliding down the cheeks of all of them except for Michael and Julianne, but the emotions of all of them were being hammered by the sights around them. Behind them, the Washington Monument still stood, a needle pointing proudly to the sky. But the White House had been unrecognisable, the FBI building was merely an outline in the ground and the Art Museum was a pile of rubble. Emma found herself staring at the remnants of the Air and Space Museum, feeling sadness mixed with a weird desire to laugh out loud with a strange memory of an old happiness.

The biggest shock was when Julianne stopped the bus at the end of the cleared area.

"The scaffold is still there!" whispered Emma. She thumbed the button that raised the door and the others followed her out into the park. They stood silently, staring at the huge wooden stage that reared up before them. Around the stage, splinters of wood still littered the place, all that remained of the spectator stand that had been shattered when the mob attacked Horning's VIP party that day over sixty years ago. But the execution platform remained. So did the four heavy wooden chairs on top of it. There was even a thick electrical cable lying on the ground, though torn at the end, revealing the rusted ends of smaller conduits inside.

Emma was trembling strongly. Forcing herself, she walked up to the platform. There was no stairway up to it; that had been shattered during the mob attack she assumed, but she swung herself up on the supporting girders and reached the top. She was joined by the others and they stood, still and silent on the killing platform.

Simon looked out over the park. The ruined city was soundless. They had seen not a soul as they entered, not even any animals, as if the whole area was somehow cursed with ancient terrors. He turned and stared at the old electric chairs. Emma and Martin were doing the same, while Michael and Julianne moved away and were standing by the edge of the platform as if to separate themselves from what was happening with the other three.

Simon felt the pressure building inside himself. He heard the sounds of screams in his ears and knew that somehow they were his and those of his friends. An uncontrollable weeping began deep inside, and he turned to Martin and Emma.

"We died here," he sobbed, and clung to Emma. "Now I know who we were. I was Leger!"

Emma had her face buried in his chest. Memories of her death as Jacqueline Carter rippled through her and she shook uncontrollably. When they had calmed down, they broke apart and looked at each other. Tears still poured down their cheeks, but they were able to smile.

"Who could have thought we'd ever be back here?" whispered Philippe Leger. Jacqueline kissed his cheek and wiped her eyes. They turned to Martin, standing silently next to them. His face was white and shudders ran through his body, then he became still and composed.

"I've just remembered, too," he whispered.

"Welcome back, Maragos," said Jacqueline. "We missed you."

* * *

"I remember now how we agreed to do this," said Michael John Alexander who had once been Michael Hendricks. "After you died, I was waiting for you on the Astral Plane."

"How odd that we never met before, either incarnate or on the Astral," said Philippe. "Our lives have crossed so often."

They were sitting in the park by a campfire, drinking the last of the coffee. It had taken some hours before their emotions had settled enough for them to make camp, and by mutual agreement, they had stayed near the site of the execution that had precipitated the end of the USA and the beginning of Oneness.

"I had other tasks," said Michael Hendricks. His own re-awakening had occurred moments after the other three, and with him, Julianne had also gained recollection of her past lives. As Julianne Patterson, she had last talked with Michael before leaving the USA for Canada. She had wept as the memories came back of the thirty years she had lived in Canada before dying peacefully and happily, with a conviction that she would meet him again. She remembered then how she had met on the Astral Plane with Philippe and Jacqueline as well as Michael, and formed the group to make the last pilgrimage across America.

"Maragos, how did you arrive with us?" asked Jacqueline. "Did you know who you were all this time?"

Maragos shook his head. "No, I recovered my memories the same time you did," he replied. "I decided to join you when I sensed your group decision to do this pilgrimage. So I reincarnated as a child to parents in Boston, and I had deliberately suppressed my knowledge of my identity. I had no idea who I was till a few hours ago."

The others were stunned. Maragos smiled at the expressions. "You guys are my dearest friends!" he said. "I wasn't going to let you have this adventure without me!"

"Perhaps you can explain something that happened on the way here," said Michael when the laughter had died down. "We met some X'Kasxi in Chicago. They behaved very oddly."

Maragos nodded. "You didn't recognize them?" he asked.

Michael was startled. "Recognize them? How the hell could I have done that?"

"Because you sent them to become X'Kasxi," replied Maragos.

Michael was breathless with shock. "John Parker!" he gasped. "And the others who shot me in Bainesville!"

"Exactly," said Maragos. "They sensed your power over them, but were unable to remember the events."

"Maragos, what happened to Raoul?" asked Philippe, breaking into the silence that the information had caused. "Why did he not join us? I can't remember that he was even in the discussion on the subject."

Maragos laughed gently. It was still strange for the others to look at the young man sitting with them, and recall the beautiful young woman who had died with them sixty years before, but acceptance was growing as they were able to look beyond their physical forms and recognize the souls within.

"You may remember how excited Raoul was about the chance to reincarnate as another species," said Maragos. "Well, that's what he chose to do."

"Where did he go?" Jacqueline was laughing as she remembered Raoul's childlike enthusiasm.

"He is about to become a Speaker," replied Maragos. "He will soon communicate with travellers around the galaxies and meditate on Oneness."

Astonishment hung over the campsite.

"Raoul? A shapeless mound billions of light-years away?" Philippe was breathless at the idea.

Maragos nodded. "He is about to move from the spore stage of life to grow into adulthood. He will live a life of great wonder and fulfilment," he said. "One day, you can discuss it with him."

After a few moments of silence while each of them thought their own thoughts, Michael broke in. "Maragos, what happens now?"

"Now we wait," replied Maragos. "We wait while billions of infant and baby souls heal and can resume the growth to Old Soul. Then we wait further until Humanity can return to the path to Ascendancy. Oneness waits for you."

"How long?" Julianne's voice was a whisper.

"Perhaps twenty thousand years," answered Maragos.

"And does it go as we hoped?" asked Philippe. "Is the soul of William Horning moving toward redemption?"

Silence hung over the campsite for a few moments. The four humans watched as Maragos stared intently into the fire. As the silence grew, Philippe detected a change in the brightness of the flames. It confused him, then he gasped as he saw what was happening. It was not the fire that was fading.

The shape of Maragos was changing, becoming less sharp-edged, and growing in brightness. His limbs flowed into the mass of his body and Maragos became a source of light without form. The light surged in power, rose to an indefinable height and the night faded before the brilliance of the new sun that burned in the centre of the ancient killing ground of Washington. Behind the silence of the new dawn, a soft but powerful organ note seemed to radiate through the world, making the air, the trees, the remnants of ancient buildings vibrate with gentle sympathy and a yearning to be one with the source of power.

"William Horning undergoes a hell beyond your imagining," radiated a voice from all around them. The tone was sometimes that of Maragos, the young woman of sixty years ago, and sometimes that of the man who had joined the group on its travels. "He does not know of his true power and he suffers the torments of all the damned of all time. I believe I can force him through this time of redemption, but I cannot force healing on him. That can only come of his own choice and for now, William Horning does not choose the same path as the rest of Humanity."

"What will you do, Maragos?" whispered Philippe. His whole body trembled with the emanations of power that he felt around him.

"We will see how Horning comes out of his Millennium in Hell," said the voice from all around them. "But for now, my friends, you have your own destinies to follow. Leave Horning to me."

The light soared even higher and the power of the sun lit up the whole sky. Stark shadows of the ruined buildings around them drew sharp lines across the ancient parkland. Philippe began to feel a wonderful happiness within him. It was a joy that almost made him leap to his feet and shout for sheer delight in being part of this immortal, infinite power that was shaking the whole world, the entire Universe. He watched the brilliant sky as crackles of colours never seen before by human eyes flashed over the dome covering the earth. Sweet fragrances surrounded him, bringing with them sudden, fantastic and beautiful memories of the time they had spent outside of Time the night before their executions sixty years before, when Maragos took them to the Buddhaic Plane, the resting place of the Infinite Souls. He sensed the start of the departure of the source of that infinite energy. The brightness began to fade and the four young people felt the presence of Maragos move further from them.

"Remember always that I am with you till Oneness," said Maragos, and the voice was the sweet tones of the beautiful woman who had died with them sixty years before. "Whatever Humanity hears, or whatever new beliefs arise, I am still with you and I will rejoin you when the time dictates. Follow your own paths, my beloved friends, and we will meet again in other times and other spaces."

The organ note swelled to a magnificent peak then crashed into silence. The light faded and night returned.

The four young people sitting round the campfire looked at each other. Tears flowed freely down the faces of all of them.

"In that case," said Michael John Anderson, who once had been Michael Hendricks, John the Baptist, Asita the Old Sage who saw the Eight Signs on the Buddha, and many times had lived before that, "I think we have time to go back home and finish our education."

With a sense of fulfilment and happiness, the four of them turned in and slept. They knew that they would not see Maragos again in their current lifetimes, but none of them worried about that. They had plenty of time to meet up again.

Twenty thousand years, in fact.

# The Second Book of the Maragosian Presence

## Other Houses of God

"For Man lives in the House of God, and other Men live in Other Houses and have not the likeness of Man. But they are God also..."

*(Fragment of an unidentified document taken from the secret and forbidden library of the Vatican by Pope Jean-Pierre II, just days after his abdication)*

"Seeing the wickedness which Humanity had taken unto itself, and the evils of the world that Man had created, Maragos The One, the Infinite, Creator of the Universe and Ruler of All, did descend from Heaven unto Earth. And then did Maragos ask the blessed saints, Philippe, Jacqueline and Raoul to follow Her as She worked to save Humanity from its sins. And so too, did Maragos ask Michael to be Her good and faithful servant and protect Her Name. But the evil of the world was greatest in Horning the Damned and his foul demon, Crossman. And on the first day of the first year of the Time of Maragos, Horning and Crossman did murder God..."

*(Opening chapter of the Maragosian Bible, approved version of 475 Maragosian Era, or 2501 Traditional Christian Calendar.)*

# Chapter 18. X'Katcxo

Three male pups were born in the City of Brx'Jashcha that first day of the Healing. The fifteen nation states that had grouped into the single political entity known as Hrz'Ashcha in the southern hemisphere of the world of X'Katcxo used the City as the main port to the stars, and the place was massive. The three new-born pups were not the only ones born that day in the city of forty million, but they shared a common strangeness. There was nothing between them otherwise that would inspire comment, or relate the three to each other, but for that one thing.

The first pup, named T'Karr by his parents since his conception, was born to a wealthy merchant living in the affluent residential areas on the north coastline to the city. The pup seemed healthy enough, but the Guide who supervised his birth shook his head in doubt.

"I read a low quality of *m'rrhai,* the soul energy," he whispered to the parents who stood waiting silently as their child was birthed from its egg by the professional breeder who had cared for their offspring for the last six months. "This one is a much younger soul than we have seen among the Kindred for many generations. *Kudai* T'Brxiu, he is certainly no more than a Young Soul, and an early stage Young Soul at that." The honorific by which he addressed the merchant indicated enormous respect for a man of vast achievements and spiritual growth.

The Kudai looked down at the tiny shape of his son as it was cleansed of the traces of the egg. The merchant was well along in years. His horned eye shields were barely a ridge above his black eyes, showing the sophistication of his breeding and soul maturity, while the light grey shade of the outcropping indicated great physical age in this incarnation. In contrast, the pup's eye shields were grotesquely large, forecasting some difficulties in social standing as the child grew.

*Almost a throwback,* thought the merchant, trying to stifle the distaste he felt. And a Young Soul, too. What Karmic debt had he incurred that the House of T'Brxiu should be burdened this way? What had brought a Young Soul into the tribe when most were already Old Souls? Over half the souls of his house were at the seventh stage, preparing for residence on the Astral Plane until all the souls of the Entity had joined as an Ascendant, and many were already beyond the incarnation cycle.

The merchant felt confusion and a sense of wrongness, and touched his mate on her shoulder. As was proper, the female did not show any recognition of the touch, but remained looking at her offspring. She felt sorrow at the strangely primitive pup she had produced, mixed with love for the helpless creature and concerns for the difficulties that would face the pup as it grew to adulthood.

"My child is healthy?" she asked, looking straight in front of her, and not at the Guide. Her cool tone hid the tension within her.

"He is healthy, *Kadri* T'Brxiu," answered the Guide. As befitted dealing with a woman of such high station, he did not look directly at her, but stared firmly at the child lying in a basket the other side of the glass.

"Then guide us, *X'Kaa* G'Jxin," said the merchant, addressing the Guide appropriately as a spiritual leader of many years. "What does the House of T'Brxiu do with this new pup?"

The Guide looked long at the pup, reading his soul strength again to be certain, and confirming within himself the astounding spiritual youth.

"He will go to the crèche at Hr'Mong as would any of your House," said the Guide into the silence awaiting him. "But such a young soul cannot join the House after his tenth year as would a true child of X'Katcxo. He must find his own way after that."

The merchant nodded. The Guide's decree was correct. A soul as young as this one could not be mixed with the Old Souls of the rest of the House of T'Brxiu. That would cause a disruption in the rapidly accelerating growth to Ascendance they were now experiencing. He nodded at the breeding assistants through the glass partition, and they began preparing the pup for departure.

The Guide kept his face without expression. He had knowledge that he had not imparted to the parents. The pup was not merely a Young Soul. It was not even a Baby Soul. It was actually an Infant Soul, albeit a seventh stage Infant, but an Infant nonetheless. Such an immature level had not been born on X'Katcxo for generations. And that was not all. There was an alien sense to the pup, something not entirely natural. This was not a true member of the Kindred.

The Guide inclined his head as the parents left with their child without a backward glance. This pup's birth disturbed the Guide badly. He needed to meditate, to try and establish a connection with Ascendant Souls on the Astral Plane to give him guidance and clarification in the matter.

In the south western, inland suburbs of the city, the homes were poorer. This was an area not far from the enormous spaceport where the huge shuttles raised themselves like flying mountains to take passengers and goods to the even more massive ships that orbited the planet and flew between the stars and other galaxies.

To Br'Jatxi and his mate, another pup, the twelfth offspring of the mechanical engineer and his mate, was born within minutes of T'Karr of the wealthy House of T'Brxiu. This new pup also had the enlarged eye shields that indicated a primitive soul, but the contrast with his parents was less dramatic. Still, they looked at their pup and wondered, just as the merchant and his mate had done.

"The pup is healthy?" the pup's father asked of the Guide who was at the breeding centre as part of his regular spiritual duties. The Guide looked carefully at the child, read his life force, and turned calm eyes on the father.

"His *m'rrhai* is low, *Tem* Br'Jatxi," said the Guide. The title indicated working class standing, but the engineer took no offence. He was of the working classes, and his whole family before him had been the same.

"And I sense that he is even younger in soul age than we first thought," continued the Guide. "I think it is possible that the pup may be a Baby Soul, maybe even an Infant."

"A Baby Soul? We have had no Baby Souls born here for generations!" Tem Br'Jatxi's mate was astonished. Despite her mild revulsion at the primitive physical attributes her child was showing in the oversize eye shields, she felt great love for the pup and was ready to take it home immediately.

"And it may even be an Infant Soul, you say?" The engineer was equally astounded and perturbed. His pup would face severe difficulties in receiving education and finding good employment, if this were true.

"That is quite possible," murmured the Guide. "Though if he is indeed an Infant Soul, he is certainly at the seventh stage, and may already be a Baby Soul. Either way, the pup is a strange arrival on X'Katcxo."

The parents stared helplessly at their child.

"Then guide us, X'Kaa Jx'Jkui," said the father of the pup. Tension was strong in his throat. An order to end the pup's existence was quite possible. The silence stretched for several moments before the Guide spoke.

"The pup may return home with you," the Guide finally said, and the relief in both the parents was displayed in a small sigh. "But such spiritual youth will cause you all great difficulties, and the child cannot become a full member of your House after his tenth year. He must leave you then and find his own way."

The engineer nodded and touched his mate's shoulder delicately. She turned to him and laid her forehead against his shoulder for a second or two, but neither the father nor the Guide showed any dismay at this behavioural breach.

"He will be called Br'Zhet of the House of Br'Jatxi," said the engineer. He nodded at the attendant Breeder staff and the pup was prepared for them to take home. The Guide watched them leave with a sense of powerful disturbance, for he had not told them the full truth. Not only was the Pup no more than an early stage Baby Soul, the Guide had read the alien nature in the little new-born, something that marked it as different from any other pup the Guide had read for anxious parents over the last fifty years. The Guide knew that he should have ordered a termination of the small life, but he as he had opened his mouth to give the command, some pressure in his mind had stopped him. It was a psychic nudge unlike anything he had ever experienced before.

Worried, X'Kaa Jx'Jkui returned home to try and meditate, to contact an Ascendant Soul, and ask what was happening that such strange events should occur.

The third of the alien pups was born to farming parents in the empty areas of the north east. They were a young couple and this was their first-born, so they hung on the words of the Guide as he defined their son. The Guide was hesitant as he spoke.

"This is one such has not been born for a thousand years, Tem D'Zha," said the Guide. Internally, he was wondering if he should tell the parents the entire truth that he was reading in their son's soul. "He is a very immature soul, possible only a Baby Soul. And his *m'rrhai,* his soul energy is quite low."

"I didn't know that there were any of us left at Baby Soul stage," said the father. He was surprised but not worried at the news, nor was he too upset by the signs of primitive physical development in the large eye shields on the tiny pup that had been birthed only an hour ago by the breeder. The boy would work with him in the growing fields and might never even go to the City of Brx'Jashcha in his lifetime. His name would be D'Dzi. Later sons might be more developed and be more suited to the technical life of a space traveller or scientist, or even philosopher in the big city.

"It is strange," agreed the Guide. "I too believed that we had all progressed to at least late-stage Mature Soul."

"But he is healthy?" inquired the mother. Though confused by the Guide's words, she was ready to take the pup home. The Guide nodded, not looking at her.

"He is healthy, *Tsun* D'Zha," he echoed. "You may take the pup with you. He is yours until the end of his tenth year, but he must find his own way after that."

The Guide walked rapidly away, deciding not to tell them about the strangeness he read in the pup's soul, the alien quality he had seen. Nor would he tell the parents how close he had come to ordering the pup to be terminated. The small pressure in his mind that had stopped him had frightened him, because it seemed to hide a power completely outside his comprehension. It was beyond his experience, and it frightened him.

X'Kaa G'Jxin was revered as a Guide, and had been for over fifty years. Though no formal rankings existed within the profession, or art, or science, whatever it was that he practised, G'Jxin was perhaps the senior of his brethren. He had presided at the birth of many thousands of new X'Kasxi. He read the strength of the soul of the new pup, and saw the spiritual age, the characteristics and maturity of the child, and his guidance to the parents was rarely inaccurate. Those who followed his instructions invariably believed their children had been guided down the best path for them.

G'Jxin knew his trade. He had read everything written about it over the last three thousand years and he knew what the figures said. The proportion of Mature and Old Souls had been steadily climbing over that period relative to the less mature souls. The last Infant Soul had been born over a thousand years ago and the last Baby Soul nearly two hundred years later. Less than one percent of souls born in the last hundred years, the lifetime of the Guide, had been Young and Mature Souls. Old Souls had made up the majority of births among the Kindred for some decades, and the proportion of these was increasing rapidly.

The Guide knew that X'Katcxo was following close on the heels of the vanished race of Kaloti. The last of that species had died in the fabled explosion of the Kaloti ship orbiting Jupiter in the Sol system, about forty years before, and the yellow world of the Kaloti was now deserted. All the Kaloti were now living on the Astral Plane, preparing to become Ascendant Souls. G'Jxin yearned for that time for his own species, dreamed of the eras to come when the X'Kasxi merged to become an Infinite Soul.

The discovery today of an Infant Soul badly disturbed the Guide. Even worse, the sense of the alien quality of the child scared him badly. He reached his home, shrugged off the offers of food, wine, rest or a bath from his house robots, and went directly to his private quarters. Settling into his favourite deep seat, he began to breathe deeply, closed his eyes and concentrated on his personal sign of power, the blue-tinged yellow sun of his system. After a few moments, he sensed the energy flow into him, the room around him faded into mist and he felt his soul lift itself onto the Astral Plane.

"I was thinking you'd drop by," said a voice that came from nowhere and everywhere. The laugh was a strong streak through the tones, and G'Jxin relaxed a little. The Ascendant Soul that he had been instructed to call Kv'Xti was one of the oldest such spirits of X'Katcxo. It had formed when over eleven hundred seventh-stage Old Souls had passed beyond the incarnation cycle and merged as the single entity after two thousand years of meditation and absorption. The Guide knew that his mentor, the Ascendant Soul of Kv'Xti was a force of great power and wisdom.

"You were no doubt expecting me, old friend," said the Guide, studying the aura of powerful colours that was the presence of the Ascendant. "You sensed my concern over the pup I read this morning?"

"Yours and that of others," replied the Ascendant.

"Others?" X'Kaa G'Jxin was astounded. "There were other pups like that born today?"

"Two others," said Kv'Xti. "And more will come."

"Teacher, what is happening?" Despite the assurance given in the Ascendant Soul's laughter, the Guide was alarmed by the news he was hearing.

"Do not fear these events, X'Kaa G'Jxin. They form part of the way of The One." Kv'Xti spoke in soothing tones, and his aura rippled in gentle patterns that signalled comfort to the soul of the Guide.

"Then I will not fear them, Teacher," replied the Guide. "But can you tell me what is the truth behind these births, so I may soothe the parents as you comfort me?"

"It is part of the healing of the sick Infinite Soul with which we share this Galaxy, my friend," said the Ascendant. "The One cannot return unless we follow the path asked of us. Humanity cannot heal without this action."

"Humans are incarnating as X'Kasxi?" X'Kaa G'Jxin was shaken but excited by the news. "So these are the Infant Souls we are seeing?"

"This is the way," answered the Ascendant teacher.

"But how did we agree to this?" X'Kaa G'Jxin was still excited, but uncertain how such agreement could be reached.

"There is one evolved Infinite Soul that is healing the Human Soul," said Kv'Xti. "It spoke to us on a level I cannot yet understand. Somehow, it spoke to us, the unevolved Infinite Soul of the X'Kasxi. In total, we the Kindred have welcomed this plan."

"Then I will work within it," replied the Guide. "Mentor, there was something in my mind as I read the pup's soul. I was about to order termination, but something…" The Guide stopped, overwhelmed with awe as he understood what the pressure had been that stopped him speaking the words of the termination order. "That was the Infinite, Mentor?" he breathed, the words barely creeping out of his mouth.

"And you thought I was a powerful soul?" replied Kv'Xti, amusement mixed with awareness of infinity.

X'Kaa G'Jxin sensed the movement away from him of the forceful aura of the other, and let his own mind slip back towards his body. He woke up in his room, refreshed and exhilarated by his contact with the extraordinary energy of an Ascendant Soul. This time, he called his house robots and requested a small feast of his favourite smoked fish and fruit. Believing the occasion deserved it, he found one of the few bottles he still had of the rare wine made by a species in one of the Galaxies of the Central Great Wall. He opened it, savouring the bouquet and pondering the changes that would come to X'Katcxo in the next few centuries. If the way would lead to Oneness, the old Guide had only welcome for it.

* * *

The three young X'Kasxi completed their first ten years of life totally unaware of each other. They were cared for in varying degrees of luxury in the family crèches in different sectors of the city, but all of them shared some common experiences.

The first such experience was the pain of the treatment they received from their companions in the crèche. As obviously very young souls with oversized, primitive eye shields, they were tormented mercilessly by the other children. Even in a society of mature and old souls, children were still children, cruel and unforgiving.

"*L'Akshi, L'Akshi,* big-eyed *L'Akshi!*" was the chorus of children's screams that greeted them so often. They were painful references to the lumbering reptiles that had been extinct for millions of years, but that were known to have been the ancestors of modern X'Kasxi.

The three pups made no friends, and grew up isolated, alone, their only comfort coming from the rare times spent with their mothers at the monthly Time of the Gathering of House members.

Their teachers tried to help. The teachers were, after all, Old Souls, with an understanding of the difficulties faced by such unusually immature souls, but the task was difficult. The teaching programs were geared to minds and souls that could absorb learning through a mixture of disciplined study and an empathic link with the teachers and each other. Infant Souls could not match these demands.

All three of the alien pups fell behind in their education, their social adjustment and their maturity. Their childhoods were times of great loneliness and stress, making few friends and establishing little closeness with clan-members within their Houses. All three of them encountered the first major life-crisis at the end of their tenth year, within hours of each other.

T'Karr, the son of the wealthy House of T'Brxiu was the first. As the sun dawned on the last day of his tenth year, he was prepared by the staff at the crèche at Hr'Mong to meet his father. The ritual was universal among the Kindred, and he had seen many of the pups be so prepared, and then move out to join their Houses. In one's eleventh year, most X'Kasxi were ready for young adulthood, for advanced training in whatever career they chose, perhaps for mating. T'Karr wondered what function he could perform in the House of T'Brxiu and experienced a mixture of excitement at the prospect, and fear caused by his lack of confidence.

He spent an hour in the meditation room, but was unable to concentrate, and he was intensely nervous when the crèche's attendant escorted him in to see his father.

T'Karr bowed to the old man seated on the cushion by the low table where the traditional kettle of mint tea stood. Then he bowed to X'Kaa G'Jxin seated next to the Kudai. He had expected the famous old Guide to be there. If possible, the Guide who read a pup's *m'rrhai* at birth also watched over the transition to adulthood and membership of the House after the tenth year. Finally, T'Karr sat on a smaller cushion in the middle of the room and waited.

The Kudai poured a small bowl of the tea and passed it to X'Kaa G'Jxin, poured another for himself and the two old men touched the bowls together before drinking. Cradling the scented tea, Kudai T'Brxiu finally turned to his son.

"I see you, T'Karr," he said.

T'Karr inclined his head. "I see you, Kudai," he said, in the traditional greeting of this ceremony. His voice sounded weak to himself, and a wave of nervousness washed over him. The tiny scent of the tea made his throat feel dry and desperate for a drink.

"There can be no place for you in the House of T'Brxiu," said the old man. His face was without expression, but the edge of sadness in his voice revealed some emotion.

T'Karr sat immobile. He fought the dizziness that nearly sent him sliding off his cushion, and felt sickness form in his belly. All his fears were taking concrete form, worse than any of his nightmares of the last years of loneliness.

"X'Kaa G'Jxin told me at your birth that you were an Infant Soul," continued the Kudai. "He told me then that such a soul could not fit in the House of T'Brxiu when all others are Old Souls. Another way has to be found for you."

An Infant Soul? He was only an Infant Soul? T'Karr closed his eyes in agony, unaware of the sympathy with which both old men were regarding him. Like all X'Kasxi, T'Karr knew the pattern of spiritual growth of his species. He had studied it as part of his early education at the crèche. He knew how souls grew through their ages, and he knew of the Kaloti, the first and most ancient of space travellers, whose ships were now manned by the X'Kasxi because all the Kaloti had passed beyond the reincarnation stage. He had read of other species who were fast approaching the same stage, and believed as he had been taught, that almost all X'Kasxi were Old Souls. He had been taught about the one Infinite Soul that had emerged in recent times, and that was now working on the Great Healing with another species in this Galaxy. Despite the torments he had experienced, he had always believed that he was at least a Mature Soul. The pain and embarrassment of this discovery was agonizing.

The old Kudai began speaking again, and T'Karr forced himself to ignore his distress and listen.

"The Guide sought counsel from an Ascendant after he had read your soul at birth," continued his father. "And he learned something very strange."

T'Karr forced firmness upon himself, opened his eyes and watched his father. He would discover the reason for his isolation now, he understood.

"The Ascendant told the Guide that your soul had come from elsewhere," continued the Kudai. "It is part of the plan of another race of The One, a plan that must be completed before The One can return."

He looked at the pup seated in the middle of the room. "You have great things to accomplish, my son," he said gently, and T'Karr sat upright with new firmness. "And so we have agreed a new place for you where the opportunities will be plentiful. You will go to the Space Port at Brx'Jashcha. You cannot enter the normal crew training programs. Because of your soul age, you would be unable to complete the training, but you may join the crew of a Kaloti ship in another position and travel with them. We will ask that one day, you will find your place and your task, and complete it with honour."

The two old men rose to their feet, and left the pup sitting silently. As was proper, he would not move until he was alone, but inside T'Karr was a storm of excitement and pain. Not joining his House was a dreadful loss, but the wonder of a chance to travel the star lanes, maybe even to go outside the Galaxy to visit other species of The One was something he could never have dreamed for himself.

He was of another species? The thought jolted him. His father had not said what species it was. He had never heard of any soul crossing the species barrier to reincarnate this way. His mission must be immense.

The door closed behind the Guide and his Father. T'Karr rose to his feet and returned to his room.

* * *

In the middle of his eleventh year, after intensive and often painful training in basic crewman duties at the Space Port, T'Karr left his home planet as a labouring assistant on the freighter Kl'Atxcxo, named after one of the planet's greatest heroes, a warrior of the last of the Great Wars almost ten thousand years before. Assigned to his lowly crewman's cabin, were two other frightened young pups who had learned the same facts about themselves at the same time as T'Karr. One was called Br'Zhet, the other D'Dzi. They were also the souls of another species, they had learned, and they too believed they had vital missions to fulfil.

The meeting between the three was strange for them all. As T'Karr entered the cabin of the immense ship, still a little queasy from the rapid ascent in the shuttlecraft from the surface of the planet, he was feeling intensely nervous, almost afraid. He knew that he was years younger than any other crewman on the ship, and trained only in the simplest of ship-board duties. He was well inside the grey, undecorated cabin before he saw another shape crouched on the lowest of the bunks. The equally young crewman rose to his feet and the two of them stared at each other. T'Karr felt an unnerving sensation of recognition. It was not just the enlarged eye shields they both possessed, but some other, deeply internal fibrillation of the psyche that made T'Karr shiver. He saw that the other young pup was also disturbed.

"T'Karr of the House of T'Brxiu," said T'Karr, his throat dry for reasons he could not clarify.

"Br'Zhet of the House of Br'Jatxi," replied the other, and they bowed slightly. Upright again, they stared at each other.

"You are only in your eleventh year, also," said T'Karr. "I thought I was the youngest aboard."

"I was born on the twelfth day of Izhod, in 3345," replied the other pup.

T'Karr's eyes opened wide. "The same day as me," he replied. Br'Zhet was about to say something, when the third member of the crew entered. He too looked anxious, he too displayed the enlarged eye shields that had caused T'Karr such agonies in his childhood. And he too caused a spasm of recognition to run through T'Karr. Looking sideways at Br'Zhet, he saw that the experience was common to them both.

"D'Dzi of the House of D'Zha," announced the third member, his voice cracking to reveal his nervousness.

The other two introduced themselves.

"And were you also born on the twelfth day of Izhod, in the year 3345?" asked T'Karr. D'Dzi's face registered amazement. He nodded, rather than speak.

"Then it seems, my friends, we have a common goal," said T'Karr. For the first time in his ten years, he felt kinship with others, a sense of purpose, and some value in himself. He also felt a sense of being the natural leader of the three, and from the way the other two looked at him, they felt it too.

"Let's stow our gear," he suggested. "Orbit departure will be in about an hour."

They had no operational crew duties aboard the ship, they were not skilled enough for any advanced function. Their jobs would be the menial ones, supervision of the robots that cleaned the corridors, simple data entry to some of the more basic computer systems, helping with movement of loads in the storage holds, and any similar functions that would be found for them. Their gear stowed, they made their way to one of the observation decks. As they walked the lengths of corridors, they received constant stares from passengers and crew, but all three of them were used to that. At the entrance to the observation deck, an officer stopped them.

"Off limits to non-deck crew," he said gently, seeing the extreme youth of the three pups. The disappointment showed, because in understanding, he directed them to one of the floors where external windows existed but where no passengers would stray. Leaving orbit and departing one's home world was not something that should be missed, the officer well understood, and he was sympathetic to the condition of the three youngest crew members.

As they found their way to the lower deck, they began to talk to each other.

"I don't even know where we're going," said D'Dzi.

"No do I," echoed Br'Zhet. "They wouldn't tell me when I got my transfer orders."

"We're not considered important enough," said T'Karr with bitterness in his voice. "But my father told me a few days ago. We're taking a team of archaeologists to the Human planet. One of the countries there is supposed to be almost deserted, and they're going to dig into some of the old cities."

Silence greeted his words. None of the three knew anything at all about the race called Humans.

"Are they in this Galaxy, then?" asked D'Dzi. T'Karr nodded. His father had briefed him in the few moments of saying farewell. The other two pups seemed disappointed.

"Quite a short trip, then," muttered Br'Zhet.

"Fifty thousand astro-units. Thirteen days each way," replied T'Karr. That too, his father had told him. "We cross almost the entire length of the Galaxy."

They reached the corridor to which they had been directed, and stood by the curving window. The planet of

X'Katcxo filled the sky above their heads. They stared at the patterns of clouds, the dim outlines of continents and the deep black of space surrounding their home world. None of them was up to speaking.

For an hour they stood silently, until a gentle rumble broke the stillness.

"We're moving," said D'Dzi. Neither of the others responded. They simply gripped the bars attached to the base of the windows for precisely the purpose of giving a sense of security while moving.

The massive sphere of X'Katcxo slid silently from their view, to be replaced by the canopy of startlingly coloured stars on a background of silver mist that was the Galaxy. The stars rotated and swung for a few moments, then stabilized. The gentle rumble under their feet swelled and became a thunder that vibrated through the bars the three observers were holding. In front of them, little seemed to alter at first outside the observation windows, though the colours of the stars seemed to be slowly changing to a deep, beautiful shade of blue. After a few minutes, T'Karr suddenly swung his head to one side. The movement caused the other two to look away from the sight of the galaxy ahead of them.

At the edge of the windows, a deep black line had appeared. T'Karr was unable to identify just what it was that he was seeing. It seemed almost like a jet-black curtain being drawn from behind the ship and blanketing the stars from his sight. Then he saw that the black margin was growing on the other end of the observation window also, and getting wider, developing a curvature as it grew. As the curtain advanced, the stars ahead began to draw together, until no individual point of light could be seen in the gleaming mass of the Galaxy. The curtain closed more and more towards the middle of the window, then was joined by a similar margin extending upward and downward from the bottom and top of the windows.

Adjusting his perceptions, T'Karr realized there were no curtains. The Galaxy ahead was drawing in upon itself, compressing itself so that all the stars of the entire Galaxy appeared to be in a circle ahead of him. He remembered how his teachers had told him that this was the effect on the observer when approaching the speed of light. The acceleration of the ship must have been incredible to have reached this speed so soon, he thought, though there was no sense of thrust. He had learned from his reading that the enormous gravitational engines acted equally on all atoms within their influence. The circle in front of him grew smaller and denser, the light grew brighter until he could no longer look at it. The window adjusted to screen out the glare, and he resumed his fascinated stare at the entire Galaxy collapsing into a small ball ahead.

The ball shrank more and more. When it was a tiny point of light in the remote distance, T'Karr heard a small murmur from Br'Zhet to his right.

"Subspace," whispered Br'Zhet.

"What?" T'Karr had heard of the term, and knew, like every small pup knew from his basic education, that entering the mathematical uncertainties of subspace was the only way to travel the distances that the Kaloti ships could cover, but he had no real idea of what it meant.

"Watch," said Br'Zhet, and nodded at the speck of light that was the only object outside the windows. "It will vanish soon, and then we'll be in subspace."

Hypnotized by the light, the three watched it, and it faded to a minute glow, and vanished. There was nothing but darkness outside the ship.

"How do we know where we're going?" asked D'Dzi. His voice was small and reflected some fear.

T'Karr forced himself to sound normal, even if his fear was a sour taste in his throat. "They must have some way," he answered. "It's worked for a couple of million years like this." He tried to sound carefree and cheerful, but his voice was a croak. The dense black outside the windows was a fearful thing, and he sensed he was having some difficulty breathing. He turned away and began to walk back to their cabin, grateful to leave that engulfing blackness.

"They take a whole series of sightings on a number of specific stars," said Br'Zhet as they walked along the empty corridor. "That gives them the direction, then they aim in that direction as they enter subspace. The ship's computer times the duration, and flicks the ship back into normal space when they get there."

T'Karr looked at his companion. "You know about this?" he asked.

Br'Zhet shrugged. "I've had lots of time to read," he said. "While the others were playing, I was in the library."

The other two gave small laughs. The isolation of their childhoods was a common misery.

"So we won't see anything now until we get near the Human's planet?" asked D'Dzi.

"That's it till then," replied Br'Zhet. They finished the walk back to their cabin in silence.

The next twelve artificial days of times set by the ship's clocks were spent in intensely boring, menial tasks of directing the cleaning robots, checking storage units in the holds, and helping out any crew member who asked them.

The only alleviation of the boredom was the time they were sent to the main bridge to clean the floors. They were conducted by a young officer who spoke only to tell them not to touch anything, and they were led through the final doorway.

The three looked around them in awe. The room was vast, but almost empty. One entire wall was taken up by a viewing screen, but it was switched off. T'Karr assumed that there was nothing to see in subspace, so there was little point in having the screen on. He felt he would give his right arm to be able to see the screen as they approached Earth. A line of six seats in an arc facing the screen was the only other feature of the room. Apart from themselves, there was no other person.

They spent the next four hours directing the robots in cleaning the floors, the walls, and polishing the metal seats, and they were returned to their cabins by the same young officer. The next day, they were taken to the engine room for similar duties. This time, their guide was the officer who had directed them to the observation windows on the lower deck. He was more communicative with the three youngsters.

"This is the control centre," he said as he opened the door from the corridor. He stood aside and let the three crewmen enter. They found themselves standing in a vast room that seemed to their untutored eyes to be like the cavern inside a mountain, walled with banks of instruments. Some fifty or more technicians sat silently at screens, or gently manipulated controls of indefinable nature. It was the wall at one end of the room that drew the attention, however. Transparent, the wall was a hundred meters high and three hundred meters wide. On the other side were the engines.

There were four of them. They seemed more like city blocks to the three young crewmen standing almost in shock, staring at them. The engines were grey metal slabs, three hundred meters long, fifty meters high and the same distance wide. They sat with a presence of their own, so mighty was the impact of their size. As they looked, a pair of servo-robots appeared from behind sliding doorways in one wall of the engine room, and advanced on one of the towering slabs. The robots looked like giant rats made of stainless steel, but with a number of long, multi-jointed arms folded against their surfaces. They were the senior members of the same family of robots that the three cubs supervised in the cleaning operations.

"Service robots," said the young officer who had guided them in, seeing the fascinated stare of the other three. "They perform essential maintenance."

The two devices stood together and touched the sides of the engine. Rotating ends on one pair of their mechanical arms undid some form of contacts, and a large panel slid out of the wall. The two mechanisms extended their arms into the gap and stood motionless while unseen activities were performed.

"Right now, there's enough radiation in that room to kill you in two minutes," said the officer. He grinned at the scared look the crewmen threw at him. "Don't worry," he said. "That wall protects us! It's a crystal material that's totally impervious to any radiation."

For a moment longer, he let the three stare at the engine room. Then he gave an authoritative wave and directed them to their cleaning duties. Three hours later, they gave a last look through the crystal wall. The panel had been replaced and the two servo-robots had vanished behind their own screens.

A day later, they arrived in orbit round the planet of the Humans.

* * *

The call for extra hands came early in the morning, ship's time, as the three were swabbing down the corridors alongside the cargo holds. Another officer pulled them away from their boring duties, ordered them to store the cleaning robots and equipment, and follow him. They trailed along behind him without speaking, uncertain of what was to happen. The young man broke the silence as they turned into a corridor leading to the conference rooms that the ship's officers used.

"You're going down to help with the digging," he said, and smiled at the expression of intense excitement that crossed the faces of the other three. He opened the door of one of the rooms, and led the three crewmen inside.

A dozen or more people sat round a circular conference table. They were intently following the words of an elderly man with such minimal eye shields that they were simply a grey line across the top of his eyes. He was speaking fluently, pointing out details on a large three-dimensional image of a building projected onto the table's surface. As the group entered, he paused, nodded at the newcomers and continued his lecture.

T'Karr ignored the words and looked around the group. They were mainly elderly, though a few were young, almost as young as he was. Students perhaps, he thought, from their eager attention to the speaker. His study was snapped short as the apparent leader of the group suddenly addressed the three youngsters.

"You who have just joined us, welcome," he said. T'Karr nodded, grateful for the courtesy that he felt was designed to put his group at their ease. He could see that all the others in the room, apart from his two fellow crewmen, were sophisticated, old souls, highly educated.

"As I have been telling my team," continued the Leader. "We are going to the nation once called the United States of America to excavate some cultural locations. That nation destroyed itself as part of a world-wide upheaval some years ago, and is now almost deserted. In particular, we shall be studying some art galleries, and we shall value your assistance."

Again, T'Karr nodded, sensing the power of authority that the elder had.

"My name is Bj'Lor," added the leader. "I am Professor of Archaeology at the University of Brx'Jashcha. We go to the surface in an hour, and we plan to be there for several days. Please prepare accordingly."

At a small sign from the officer, T'Karr and his friends left the room and returned to their cabin. An hour later, they were seated in the shuttle in one of the main cargo bays of the ship, struggling to contain their excitement at the thought of their first visit to another world.

The work was hard. After a few days, the excitement had gone. T'Karr and his team worked the same hours as the archaeological team, and those hours stretched from before dawn until well after dark. They had descended through cloud and only saw the surface of the planet when they were just a few thousand meters above it.

They caught a glimpse of a large lake, then they were on flat land on the site of what they had been told was once a major city.

"Chicago," said Bj'Lor. "One of the primary industrial and commercial centres of the country, destroyed in a social upheaval that wiped out almost the entire country."

Resolving to read up on what appeared to have been a monumental catastrophe, T'Karr and the others began work, clearing away the rubble from the entrance of what had been a huge building and was now a mountain of brick and broken masonry.

After two days, they had found an entrance, and the whole team wandered through a long corridor that had survived much of the upheaval. Pictures lined the walls, pictures of landscapes, of people, of objects. To the young crewmen who had never been given any education in artistic creation, the display was bewildering, occasionally disturbing, and sometimes awesome in the beauty. But they had little time for study. There were more corridors to unearth, small rooms full of stored works of long dead artists, display cabinets containing sculptures and carvings that were incomprehensible to T'Karr but obviously filled the professionals with delight.

All of that paled before the experience that hit the three on the eighth day.

There had been a break from the digging. They had found an entrance into a main hall, in which the statues were large and stretched the length of the room. The walls were filled with massive paintings. Professor Bj'Lor had waved T'Karr away with an abstracted expression.

"We will be busy here for a while," he murmured, as if to himself. "I don't think we will need you for a few hours." The leader of the trip smiled as he handed over a small metallic box to T'Karr. "You may just meet a human," Bj'Lor said. "Groups of both species have been working on translation systems. These devices are still primitive, but they seem to provide some assistance. Hang it on your belt."

With a small gesture at Br'Zhet and D'Dzi, T'Karr had left the hall in relief, and the three of them found their way out into the open. The sun was bright, the temperature pleasantly warm, and they felt like children again as they emerged into the fresh air. T'Karr was about to move towards the shuttlecraft to get some food and a drink, when a small gasp diverted him. D'Dzi was the one who had made the noise, and he froze, his hand pointing off to the left. T'Karr looked round, and was similarly shaken.

*Humans!* These were the first he had seen, though he had looked at many pictures of them since learning of the destination of this trip, and there had been many pictures on the walls of the museum he had been excavating. He stared at the small group of four, standing equally frozen a few yards away.

Very slender, he thought, with pale, fragile faces of a colour that seemed never to have seen the sun. They appeared to have slim lines over their tiny eyes, much like the eye shields of his own species, but nowhere near as obvious. The tops of their heads were covered by a growth of some sort that T'Karr felt was ugly. The humans looked as if they would break if they were touched. Two of them were taller, and shaped slightly differently, a little heavier and broader. He wandered if the difference was sexual, tribal, or something else.

One of the taller pair began to walk towards the three X'Kasxi, and T'Karr felt a dreadful, inexplicable tension build in him. He backed away a step then tried to take control of himself, sensing fear in the other two X'Kasxi as well. He stared at the advancing human, the terror growing in him. This creature exercised authority and the power of life and death, T'Karr felt, and the authority was directly over him and his two companions. The awareness of that fact was strange, overpowering. Unable to control himself any more, T'Karr sank to his knees and bowed his head before the alien creature. The other two did the same.

The human uttered a sound. It was unintelligible to T'Karr, but speech came from the small translator unit he was wearing. He had forgotten about the unit. Now the small box spoke to him. "Speak you... our words?" it said. The question was clear enough to T'Karr.

"Some limited communication is possible," he answered, struggling to keep his voice steady. The fear of overwhelming power and authority still made his body quake, and he fought the urge to kneel again. "I think these devices are capable of some translation."

He listened, as the small unit rippled with the incomprehensible noise that he assumed was the human's language.

The Alien stirred a little, whether from astonishment or excitement, T'Karr was unable to read.

"Why you... drop... sink...?" it asked. It was clearly a question, but the unit was having a problem finding equivalent words. T'Karr decided the human was asking why the three of them had knelt. A reasonable question, he said to himself. He wished he could answer it.

"I don't know," he replied. "Somehow, I sense in you a great power, some sort of authority over us. It is strange."

For a long moment, Human and X'Kasxi stared at each other. More sounds emitted from the pale human.

"Necessity that continuation of movement..." said the box at his side. The human turned and rejoined his group. T'Karr sensed confusion in the being. Still shaking from the strange meeting, T'Karr turned back to the excavation and led his two friends back inside.

As the cool dark of the ruin enveloped them again, D'Dzi and Br'Zhet sank to the floor in a storm of weeping. Struggling for control, T'Karr felt his heart pounding, and dried sweat clung to his limbs. Such fear as he had never felt before, he thought through the dizziness in his head. Who had that human been, and why had there been such power in it?

"It nears our time to die." The words were spoken clearly by D'Dzi. He raised his head and looked steadily at T'Karr. "The human is the cause of our situation, and now we have seen it, we shall die."

Trembling, T'Karr sensed the truth in what his friend was saying. The advent of the human and the difficulties of their lives so far were all bound together, he knew with sudden clarity. He pulled all his strength together, still feeling the sense of leadership and therefore responsibility for the other two.

"Then we shall meet our deaths well," he said. "And perhaps our next lives will be as more mature souls. There must have been some Karmic debt that we are paying here. Let us pay with honour."

Comforted and strengthened by his words, all three of them returned to work. They had forty more days before the ship was due to return to X'Katcxo. Those days were spent in intense labour, shifting masonry, digging through rubble, and trying to forget the meeting with the powerful human. When they lifted off from the surface of the Earth to rejoin the mother ship, they felt relief.

It was not to last.

Insane dreams began to haunt their nights, causing them to wake in the dark, drenched with sweat and shaking like the earthquake territories of the southern polar region of X'Katcxo.

*T'Karr was in a house of worship. He knew what it was though the surroundings were alien. He sat in a row with others next to him. One was a female, his mate. Two were smaller, his pups. They were human. Around them were many other humans. If he looked down at himself, he knew that he too was human. Another human, a male sat nearby, and T'Karr knew that he was angry with this other, though he did not know the cause. A large male was addressing the throng from a raised platform, when the man seated next to one of his pups rose and began to walk out. T'Karr sensed his fury at the act.*

*He was outside now, following the man. Two others were with him. They were human, but deep inside his dream, T'Karr knew that the others were D'Dzi and Br'Zhet. The man reached a vehicle, and they approached him. They spoke, but T'Karr made nothing of the words, only knew that his own rage filled him.*

*T'Karr pulled a weapon from his clothing and shot the man in the face. He watched the pale skin explode in an alien crimson, the head balloon out behind. The body of the man slumped to the floor so quickly it seemed he would catch the blood already reaching the ground.*

All three crewmen woke at the same moment with cries of terror. Staring at each other, all three realized at the same moment what had happened.

"You killed him!" gasped D'Dzi. "We were together and you killed him."

"We must have been human in our previous incarnations," said T'Karr, stammering in the shock of the dream and the recognition of the fact of his past life. "This is our Karmic debt, to be born as X'Kasxi for some reason."

"Do you think that the human we saw...?" began Br'Zhet.

The other two nodded. They understood. The young human they had met near the ruins must have been the man they killed outside a church on Earth.

They slept no more that night.

* * *

Twelve days later, all three were again assigned to directing of the robots to cleaning the floors in the control centre, standing together close to the crystal wall that protected the ship from the lethal radiation of the gravitational engines. They had been concentrating hard on their control units, carefully moving the robots to avoid interference with crewmen, and speaking little to each other. Conversation between the three had been almost non-existent since the night of their simultaneous dream of murder.

The echoing clang of a robot's cleaning bucket warned them that something was wrong. The sound was too enormous, it should have been swallowed by the murmur of the fifty or more technicians working at their instruments and controls. Instead, the cavern of the control centre was silent.

The three crewmen raised their heads and stared around. All the technicians were standing, silently looking through the crystal wall into the engine compartment. Nothing was evidently wrong and T'Karr turned to the nearest officer.

"What is the problem?" he asked. The young officer turned startled eyes on T'Karr and swallowed with difficulty.

"The engine is failing," he rasped harshly. "It needs attention."

"So will not the servo-mechanisms do it?" asked T'Karr. He was puzzled and frightened by the tangible atmosphere of panic in the room.

The officer swallowed again, looking away from T'Karr and into the engine room. "They have failed," he muttered.

T'Karr was astounded. "I didn't know Kaloti ships could fail," he said.

The officer looked briefly at him. "When the Kaloti were running them, they never did," he answered. "But this is new. We don't understand what has happened. The Captain is trying to get information from others."

"But what will happen if we can't fix the engine?" persisted T'Karr. In the atmosphere of terror, he was aware that he had lost his shyness about talking to more advanced X'Kasxi.

"Nobody knows yet," replied the other man. He stiffened abruptly and appeared to be staring into the far distance as if hearing faint voices. T'Karr knew that all the ships' officers and flight crew members had communication devices implanted in their bodies so that direct mental contact with each other was always immediate.

"The Captain says that the problem is relatively simple to fix," announced the officer. "The problem is that the hatch must be removed, and the radiation will kill within twenty minutes."

Around the control centre, the hum of dismay was loud. T'Karr was only a cleaner, but he could see the problem. Without the servo-robots, nobody could repair the engine, however simple the task was.

"Has the Captain learned what will happen if the engine cannot be repaired?" he asked, uncertain within himself why he was persisting in questioning the officer.

"The ship will vaporize within a few hours," replied the young man. He was looking more and more like a cub as his fear stripped away the training that had given him the calm exterior.

T'Karr felt a rush of mixed terror and excitement within himself. "How long would it take to fix if one knew what to do?" he asked. The officer stared at him in disbelief.

"About thirty minutes," he said. "But what would be the point? You'd be dead if you could even last that long."

"Is there any protection I could wear?" T'Karr was now certain what he was about to do. His two companions were staring at him, also. Both looked panic-stricken, and he tried to smile at them.

"We could line a space suit with shielding," the officer said, sudden hope in his face. "That would give you forty minutes or more. The Captain says the connection is very simple, once you have the hatch off."

"Then we will do it," said T'Karr. He felt proud, confident, secure in the certainty that this was his role. He turned to the other two. "I will need help," he said. D'Dzi and Br'Zhet looked fearful, and said nothing.

"Remember our dream," said T'Karr. "Remember that we are nothing among the Kindred. Maybe our entire purpose has always been to die in this manner."

Still there was no word from the other two.

"Please," said T'Karr. "We have had this discussion before." For a second or two, his words bewildered him, until a sudden flash of an image came to his mind.

*They sat in chairs in a beautiful room with a view of a lake and birds outside. Pictures hung on the wall, one of them a young girl reflected in a mirror. A man stood before them. He had asked them to do something terrifying, something incredible, something that would start to help humanity. T'Karr was a human again in this vision, and he was angry with his two companions.*

*"We have to do it," he said. "There's no other way."*

*"I'm scared," said D'Dzi, but in this vision, T'Karr knew that D'Dzi was called Henry Acheson. T'Karr's own name was John Parker.*

*"We're all scared, man!" burst out Br'Zhet, and T'Karr knew that it was a man called Rolfe. "But look at what we've done in our lives! Nothing! It's the only way to make up a bit."*

*"I was a good Christian," muttered Acheson. "I shouldn't have to do this."*

*Parker stood up and went over to Acheson. He leaned over him and gripped his shoulders. "We were all good Christians, Henry," he said. "Or so we thought. And look what we did! Being a good Christian didn't amount to a hill of coonshit, man, not the way we did it! We were wrong, damn you Henry, wrong! And we're sick! We have to do it."*

*"No," Acheson said, and hid his face in his hands.*

*Parker took his hair and pulled Acheson's head up so that he stared into Parker's eyes. "You'll do it, Henry," he whispered. "Because if you don't, I'll hunt you down any time you incarnate again and I'll kill you the worst way I can. I don't care where you'll be or what you'll be, I'll find you and I'll cut you to pieces. And I'll keep on doing it, regardless of what it does to me and my chances of ever growing. Got it, Henry?"*

*Acheson's eyes were round with fear. Despite the pressure on his head, he nodded. "OK, John," he whispered. "I'll do it."*

T'Karr was sweating, and he felt that the floor beneath him was shaking, dizziness threatening his balance. He knew that he had again seen the human who had sent them to X'Katcxo, and understood the reason for his abasement before the young human on Earth. The two humans in his dreams were truly one and the same.

"We must do this," he whispered to his two companions. "This is our Karma. We have debts to pay."

Without further words the other two nodded at him and T'Karr turned to the officer. "We are ready to do it," he said, and the officer went silent and rigid as he communicated a stream of information to his Captain.

Two hours later, the three of them were encased in space suits. Normally bulky and uncomfortable, these suits were even worse than usual, padded by extra shielding to give the occupants as much time as possible to complete the appalling task ahead of them. T'Karr felt barely able to move.

"Ready?" said a voice in his ears. It was the young officer speaking through his communication devices.

"Yes," said T'Karr, and was echoed by his two companions. A siren wailed through the control centre, and the fascinated engineers who had watched the process of donning the space suits filed out, giving a last look at the three crewmen. Everybody knew that the three were going to their deaths. The officer was the last to leave.

As the heavy door closed behind him, the voice echoed in T'Karr's ears again. "The entrance to the engine room will now open. Advise me when all three of you have passed inside."

T'Karr led the way to the crystal wall. As he reached it, a doorway swung open. Without letting himself think, T'Karr walked in, watched the other two follow him, and spoke. "We're inside," he said, and watched the door close again. He knew that he was already dead, despite the shielding of his suit. The only variable now, was time.

On the other side of the barrier, the officer came back into the control centre. He stood silently as T'Karr advanced on the enormous block of grey that was one of the four engines.

"That one," snapped the young man, and T'Karr stopped. He looked up. The top of the engine block was like a skyscraper above him, and the walls stretched either side for what seemed an infinity. Already, he was sweating heavily, and for the first time in his short life, he blessed the outsize bone cropping above his eyes. The sweat ran down his cheeks instead of into his eyes, and he gave a small grin of cynical appreciation to himself. The bone structure had once been useful to his species, in earlier, primitive times.

At eye level, the top line of an access hatch was visible. The bottom was almost at floor level, and the hatch was over two meters wide. Each of the crewmen took a tool from the case T'Karr had been given, and began to undo the securing locks. It took longer than the servo-robots had taken, but the robots weren't working with heavily gloved hands, thought T'Karr. After ten minutes, they pulled off the last catch, and lowered the heavy cover to the floor.

Now it was T'Karr's turn. He leaned inside the opening, trying without success to ignore the fact that murderous radiation was blasting into his body.

"The tube in front of you has come apart," said the voice in his helmet. "You must re-attach the ends and slide the tube back into its holding slot."

Grasping the two ends of the tube that had come adrift, T'Karr clumsily rotated the catches until they snapped together.

*Such a tiny thing to die for,* he thought.

He pushed the heavy tube into the slot that was designed to hold it and leaned back against the hatchway. A wave of horrifying sickness ran through him, and he swayed and fell. D'Dzi and Br'Zhet moved to him and hauled him to his feet.

"Not much more, old friend," said the voice of Br'Zhet in his helmet. "Let's get the hatch back on."

They were all affected, T'Karr knew as soon as they tried to lift the hatch. It felt many times heavier than when they had taken it off the wall. They gasped and struggled, T'Karr and D'Dzi pushing the cover against the wall while Br'Zhet tried to get the first lock on the connections. He fumbled and dropped the tool and it took him a few moments to find it and stand up again.

By the time he had the first connector in place, T'Karr was having trouble seeing straight. The task became a nightmare of fumbling heavy gloves, seeing triple images of the locks they were trying to push in place.

When they had the last one, T'Karr managed to gasp, "How long?" Somehow, he still kept a silly hope alive inside that they might have finished in enough time to live, but that hope died immediately.

"Forty-three minutes," said the young officer. There was no emotion in his voice.

"How will you get us out?" asked D'Dzi. His voice was not even a whisper, so fragile was it.

"When we make port," replied the officer. "We'll send in fresh servo-robots to replace the others. It must wait till then."

T'Karr could barely hear the officer. He had no vision left, and only the awful sickness told him he was still alive. He thought of saying goodbye to his friends, but before the words could form in his mind, he died.

T'Karr came awake. He was sitting in an armchair. He knew that he was a human being from Earth, whose last name had been John Parker. The room in which he sat was the same room of his last, sharp vision as T'Karr when he saw himself, Henry Acheson and George Rolfe deciding to be reincarnated as another species. Across from him was a settee, and the other two were sitting in it, also coming awake. There was another armchair in the room. The view was the same as before. A lake outside, pictures on the wall, one of a young woman with her back to a mirror. *"Sybil before the Mirror,"* Michael Hendricks had called it.

It was not Michael Hendricks watching him though, as it had been that last time. Sitting in the armchair was a young woman of extraordinary good looks. Soft brown hair fell to her shoulders. She was wearing a white sweater and a short blue skirt.

"Hello," she said, and smiled gently. "My name is Maragos."

Parker looked at her. He remembered the last time he had died, in a hail of bullets from a group of soldiers. He remembered how he had woken in Limbo, been judged by God, and sent screaming into the burning pits of a Hell entirely of his own creation.

"No Hell this time?" he said. His voice seemed quite steady, and he felt proud of that.

"You should be proud," said the young woman in tones of agreement. "You've come a long way."

Parker felt no surprise at the woman's reading of his thoughts. Already, he knew what she was. He could read the power in her, sense the billions of souls that comprised her, and he felt no fear. He remembered now the reasons for his reincarnation as one of the Kindred, a race thousands of light-years away at the other end of the long axis of the Galaxy.

"I have healed?" he asked.

"A little," replied Maragos. "You have a long way to go still, but you have paid massive amounts of your Karmic debts."

"All three of us?" he asked. He sensed the question asked by the other two and asked it for them.

"All of you," replied Maragos. Her smile was lovely.

"You arranged that accident didn't you?" said Acheson, no bitterness in his voice, just understanding. "And you made sure the servos didn't work. It was a test for us, wasn't it?"

"One that you passed very well," replied the woman. "But I made no arrangements. The crisis was real, and had you not acted as you did, the ship would have exploded. Your act of sacrifice paid many karmic debts on behalf of those to whom you were indebted. And it burned away much of the sickness. Without that episode, you would have needed many more lifetimes with the Kindred than you will, now."

"Must we go back again?" Parker already knew the answer.

"Yes, you must," said Maragos. "There is still a long path for you all to walk. But you have taken great strides. I am very proud of you."

Parker took a deep breath. He looked at the other two men, who nodded at him, and he turned back to Maragos. "More of the same sort of thing?" he asked.

"Your debts are great," said Maragos gently. "But you repay them well, it seems. Remember that in previous lives you have not been so ready to make amends. This is progress."

"Will we be together again?" Henry Acheson finally broke the silence. He looked calm, not the fearful, weeping man who had woken the previous time.

"It will work best that way," nodded Maragos.

"Then I'm ready," said Acheson.

"Me too," said George Rolfe, looking as composed as the other two men.

John Parker grinned briefly at them in a sense of companionship he had never experienced before. "Then there's no point in hanging around, is there?" he said.

"None at all," agreed Maragos, and the room vanished.

Three males were born in the city of Pk'Laar within

minutes of each other. The city was small, well up the western coast from the huge spaceport of Brx'Jashcha.

Anxious parents stared through the partition of glass where the breeders had placed all three pups together after they had been released from their eggs and cleaned. The guide who had visited the breeding centre that day stared at the first pup.

"His *m'rrhai*, his soul energy is very low, Tem Gd'Yqu," he said. "And this is a Baby Soul, something we have not seen among the Kindred in generations."

The guide was nervous. The pup, all three pups had a similar alien quality to them. He had heard rumours that souls of another species were incarnating as X'Kasxi and he wondered if these strangely young souls were part of that pattern.

"But he is healthy?" asked the pup's mother.

"He is healthy," answered the guide.

"Then guide us, X'Kaa Mn'Grq," said the first parent.

* * *

William Hardcastle Horning no longer wept and cried for the mercy of God. He had long passed that stage. He no longer tried to stem the torrent of blood from his groin where the lizard had sliced away his genitals, and he no longer fought the sickness that came to him with almost every breath. He had stopped all that centuries ago.

The bed no longer existed. He simply lay in the pile of excreta and vomit that had grown over the thousand years of his Hell until it reached far into the distance, towards the never-ending horizon that still threw his sense of balance so that he vomited again whenever he looked up.

The Lizard still roared with delight when it looked at Horning, and it had lost none of its enthusiasm for flinging him face down on the pile of faeces and raping him brutally, but it rarely bothered to engage him in conversation.

Today, however, it spoke.

"You know, sweet William," it said, after a period of perhaps months during which it had simply sat on its throne and stared at the huddled shape amid the mess. "Even a Lizard could get bored by you after a while."

Horning didn't move. Several minutes passed before the words registered in his mind. He looked up in bewilderment. "Wha... what?" he stammered.

The Lizard smiled. For the first time in a thousand years, the smile seemed devoid of rage or hatred. It was almost human in its gentleness. "Time to reconsider your position," the creature said.

Horning was unable to form words. He had not spoken a sound in several hundred years, not since he had given up on calling for God to help him. His moans and screams while being sodomized had been formless sounds, and now he struggled to use his vocal chords again.

"What?" he said again. The words echoed through the limitless room, and he looked round at the pile of excreta and vomit. For once, he didn't throw up.

"Let's face it, darling Billy," said the figure on the throne. "Relationships have a habit of growing stale, don't you agree?"

Horning fought desperately to clear his mind. Something vital was happening here, and he struggled to make his brain function again after the centuries of frozen misery and agony. "I don't understand," he whispered.

"I'm trying to tell you, my little love," said the Lizard, "that maybe it's time for us to move on."

The tiniest glimmer of understanding reached the inner blackness of Horning's mind, and with it, something resembling hope.

"After all," continued the enormous reptile, "just being punished for all those nasty things you did can get stale. I shouldn't have you all to myself for all eternity. There are a lot of people out there who want a slice of you, as well."

Horning continued to stare at his tormentor. The endless vista of shit and vomit did not register. The Lizard raised its hand in a gesture of farewell. "So goodbye, little William," it said softly. "No regrets, eh? Just time to move on."

And Hell vanished from around William Horning. Immediately, he recognized his surroundings. He had been here a thousand years before. The room was as he remembered it. And the woman sitting there might never have moved.

She was beautiful. *Oh how beautiful she is,* sobbed Horning inside himself. For a thousand years he had seen nothing but the Lizard, the infinite room and the ever-mounting piles of vomit and faeces. Now he was in a graceful, elegant room, with this woman in a white business suit, sitting across from him. He was whole, he was clean... Horning wept.

The room was motionless while Horning's tears flowed and his chest heaved with the pain of his grief. After some immeasurable time, he looked up to see the woman watching him. "It is over?" he asked, trembling with the promise of hope.

"That part of it, yes," said Maragos. "That was the punishment you inflicted upon yourself. Now the repayment to others must begin."

For the first time, Horning understood. He knew in his mind how he had been subconsciously aware of his crimes and how he created the Hell of the Lizard and the grotesque horrors of the last thousand years. He understood also how he had concluded inside himself, that the punishment could end, so that repayment to other souls could begin.

"Yes," said Maragos. "Your soul has advanced in that time. A little of the sickness has burned away."

Horning looked inside himself. He remembered his past life on Earth, as President of the United States, how he had destroyed lives, caused the cruelty and evil that had overwhelmed the country. The fear of the accumulated debts to others almost overwhelmed him.

"There is much to repay," said the soft voice across from him. "It is time we gave you the chance to start."

"How shall I do it?" he asked.

"There will be many lives for you to lead," said Maragos. "They will be filled with pain and suffering as you give back to others what you took before. But in the process, you will have the chance to repay debts, and heal further."

"And will you dictate what must happen to me?" Horning felt anger that some other force was controlling his future and fear of what was yet to face him.

"All is choice, William Horning," replied Maragos. "Any soul has the freedom to choose the path it takes. I am doing no more than providing you with opportunities to redeem yourself for the choices you have made in your past, and so heal the sickness within you."

"And suffering to help others is the only way I can do this?"

"Much suffering, William. Your debts are immense and the sickness is so severe I can see nothing of your soul."

"It can't be worse than what I have gone through already," said Horning.

"Don't count on it," replied Maragos, and the room vanished.

# Chapter 19. Mayoowani

The town was small, dusty, and filled with poverty and fear. It had not always been this way. Generations before, the whole planet of Mayoowani had been beautiful, prosperous and healthy, for most of the Mayoowi were Old Souls and had long ago passed through the stages of war, illness and want.

The Masters had arrived just sixty years ago. Only four ships, but they had exploded into the skies of Mayoowani and six large cities had vanished in a funeral wreath of flame within seconds. Three thousand of the conquerors, the Gelkka, as they called themselves, had landed over the next few days, and the weapons they carried made any thought of armed resistance by the gentle Mayoowi people totally senseless. As well try and move the planet to a new solar system.

Raiwandoo lay in the shelter of the heavy bushes near the top of the hill, and watched the Masters enter the town. He had been walking for days and had looked forward to entering the town. But as he crested the hill, he saw the movement of the Masters' troops and he flung himself to the ground. He took care not to move, and certainly not to show himself above the skyline. Any suspicious move like that was a certain invitation of a blaster shot that would destroy him and several cubic meters of hillside as well. Raiwandoo was too young to wish to die that way. However miserable a life it was under the rule of the Masters, he still wanted mating, parenting, some sort of life experience.

And anyway, after sixty years, there was hope. Rumours of a Saviour were hissing through the country, spread by people with faces tensed by fear and excitement, whispered around the labour gangs, in the markets, through the crammed cells of the miserable prisons. He had come, they said, to destroy the invaders, to return Mayoowani to its golden years, to bring happiness back to the gentle inhabitants.

Raiwandoo watched the scene below. The townspeople had been herded out into the open by an advance troop of soldiers, and now they prostrated themselves as the parade of Masters entered the town on their silent vehicles that floated a meter above the ground and seemed to respond to mental commands.

There were only a dozen of the invaders, counted Raiwandoo. He raised his telescope and studied them. This was as near to the conquering race as he had ever been.

They were massive. The soldier walking alongside the vehicle must have been well over two meters tall, and solidly muscled, moving with the grace and fearsome coiled rage of a hunting beast. The skin was light green, the face hidden by the war helmet, but Raiwandoo had seen enough pictures to know what the helmet covered.

Proud faces, he thought, true faces of conquerors, features with no warmth, no humour, no awareness of the needs of others. They killed almost without thought, their weapons blasting a bolt of destruction as quickly as the idea came.

The creature on the moving vehicle was the same, merely dressed differently. It wore a black cape, and sat huddled without stirring, without looking to the side. As Raiwandoo watched, the platforms halted, sank gently and smoothly to the ground, and the ten Masters on the other vehicles stood up and moved onto the dusty roadway. Raiwandoo adjusted the sound pickup on his telescope and held his breath.

"There is one among you that calls itself the

Saviour," came a voice. Raiwandoo searched the group of invaders and identified the speaker as the leading Master who had ridden the moving platform. The voice was calm, unstressed, but reached all the townspeople. There were more than two thousand of them, stretched out in the dust, almost the entire population of the small town.

"We seek that one," the Master's words continued. "Produce it now, and you may live."

A wave of tiny movement ran through the prostrate bodies in the dust. Raiwandoo felt his heart lurch. He had heard only rumours of the Saviour. There was no sign, had never been a sign that such a man truly existed, and if he had, he had made no appearance in this undistinguished place. What had led the Gelkka to believe that their enemy was here?

The silence in the town continued for a few moments longer.

"Very well," said the emotionless voice of the invader. Raiwandoo didn't see any signal, but one of the soldiers walked away from the mass of bodies on the ground, until he was in a clear spot a few hundred meters off. He unslung his weapon and pointed it at the ground. A spark appeared, grew into a flame, and a massive, deep pit opened up in the town centre. The flame died, and the soldier returned to the throng.

More signals must have been passed, though Raiwandoo could see no sign of them, but the other soldiers fanned out around the prostrate bodies of the townspeople. Loud shouts caused the people to stand up, looking from this distance like a field of corn waving in the breeze.

Knowing what was about to happen, Raiwandoo felt ice settle about his heart. The townspeople knew it too, because a soft song of mourning began. It floated up from the town square to the watcher on the hill like smoke from a distant fire. The people were herded around the huge pit that had been burned in the middle of their town, and the song paused. In its place, the crackle of the blasters rippled up to Raiwandoo, and the population of the small town collapsed into the pit.

It was dark before Raiwandoo was able to move from his hiding place. He spent the hours struggling to control his terror at what he had seen. Two thousand people had died because the Masters had sought a legend that probably didn't even exist. Could they be so frightened of a single man? Raiwandoo could not comprehend the thinking process that would do what he had seen done that day. Some time before midnight, he uncurled cramped legs, stretched, and began walking.

After several days of wandering without thought or direction, Raiwandoo entered a town again. He had spent the last few nights sleeping in caves, under bushes, anywhere he could find that seemed far from the hand of the Masters. Food had not been a problem. There was fruit enough to be pulled from trees, and vegetables could be dug from the ground at the edge of towns. It had been uncomfortable, but survival had been more important. Now he needed warmth and some news. He hoped that the destruction of the small town had not meant any search for possible survivors. It was unlikely, he thought.

He walked slowly into the town whose name was unknown to him. His stained clothes were covered by a blanket he had liberated from an old farmhouse he had passed one night. He still had money from his almost forgotten days of living in a civilized community, having had no need to pull his wallet from his belt since seeing the death of the village. Stopping by the public water trough, he cleaned himself as much as he could, then carried on into the middle of the town square. Seeing a small eating house, his mouth salivated, and he crossed the square and walked in. A few diners looked up then resumed their conversation. He took a seat at a table alone, waited for the young female to walk up to him, and thought about real food.

"Hot cakes, lots of coffee," he said, conscious of the stiffness of his vocal chords that had been almost unused in many days. He watched the girl move away, aware of other hungers that she aroused in him. He was a young man, ready for mating and family, and he had seen too much death.

When the food came, it almost overwhelmed him, so wonderful was the smell. It was the first hot food in those cold days of wandering, and he attacked it, only just aware of the girl's amused smile.

As he finished, a shadow appeared over him, and he jerked in fear. Then he relaxed as a man took a chair across from him.

"You looked like you needed that," said the man. Raiwandoo nodded, uncertain at the man's approach. The two looked at each other for a moment. Raiwandoo saw an older man, a face of intelligence, the dark eyes of the eastern continent, and clothing that marked some wealth.

"There is much suffering in you," said the other man quietly. Raiwandoo didn't answer, instead refilling his coffee cup from the pot the waitress had left for him.

"It is interesting, in one so young," continued the other. "And I think it is not just from living under the rule of our captors. What is it, do you think?"

"I have seen too much death," replied Raiwandoo.

The other shook his head. "We have all seen too much death," he said. "No, it is much more than that. You look like you have suffered for a thousand years in a hell that we could not imagine."

Raiwandoo felt his insides churn in horror. Something of which he had no comprehension was happening to him. He felt terrible fear, a sense of ghastly pain remembered.... he dropped his coffee cup and saw the dark stain run over the table and onto his legs. His vision faded and his head swam.

"Interesting," murmured the man across the table.

"What possible trigger could we have pulled just then?"

Raiwandoo wiped sweat from his face, knowing that the room had gone silent and everyone was staring at him. "Please," he gasped. "Leave me alone."

"Impossible," said the stranger. "Are you aware of what is to happen here in a few hours? Anything that brings attention can be dangerous for you as well as us."

"Happen?" Raiwandoo was confused. "What is to happen here? Who is coming?"

"One who might save us from the overlords."

For a few moments, Raiwandoo's mind swam in confusion. He was still shaken by the turmoil caused by the man's earlier words. When he settled, the turmoil was joined by fear as he understood what had been said to him. "The Saviour?" he stammered.

The man across from him waved his hand in shock. "Don't speak the name," he whispered urgently. "It can bring the Gelkka." But Raiwandoo didn't hear him. He was sensing terrible waves of fear inside himself as he remembered how the last small town had been destroyed and the people slaughtered. Somebody had reported the Saviour was there, and thousands had died. And now he was in another town where the same could happen.

Others joined them at his table. Their faces were stern and suspicious.

Raiwandoo's head began to clear. "This... Saviour really exists?" he asked. A small sigh ran round the room.

"Truly, he exists," said the one who had first spoken to Raiwandoo. "I have seen him, listened to him speak. And he comes here."

"Here?" Raiwandoo had no idea of where he was.

"You are in Liamondooni," said a voice at the back of the room.

Liamondooni! Raiwandoo was on the other side of the country! He had no idea of how much ground he had covered in his wanderings, but he realized he had walked as if in determination to reach this spot, tracking a straight line and covering considerable distance each day. It was as if he had been directed here.

"And when does he come?" Raiwandoo asked.

"Today," was the simple answer.

"Today? What if the Masters learn of this?" Raiwandoo felt a wave of fear. He had seen how much the Masters wanted this Saviour.

"He will come, he will speak, he will move on," said the same speaker. "So far, we have eluded the hunters."

"I would like to hear him," said Raiwandoo.

"You will," said another voice.

Raiwandoo did not see the exchange of glances around the four unnamed people in the room. His mind was still full of visions of burning death.

"I am Lawindinai," said the man who had first spoken to Raiwandoo. "We will go to my home. Sleep there now until this afternoon. Then we will hear the Saviour."

Needing no urging, Raiwandoo rose from the table and followed the other man a few short steps to a house behind the coffee shop. Lying on the couch, he closed his eyes and was deeply asleep within seconds.

He came awake again to the gentle shaking of his shoulder.

"Time to hear Him speak," said Lawindinai, holding a cup of hot coffee.

Raiwandoo sat upright and took the cup gratefully. "He is here?" he asked his host.

Lawindinai nodded. "He approaches," he said.

Raiwandoo gulped rapidly at the coffee, put the cup down on the floor by the couch on which he had slept, and rose to his feet. He found that his clothes had been removed, and felt a wave of embarrassment.

The other man grinned. "They have been washed," he said. "And we have a better coat for you than that old blanket."

"You are all very kind," muttered Raiwandoo. "I do not deserve this."

"Don't worry," said the host with a smile. "We follow the teachings of the Saviour."

Raiwandoo felt a small wave of anxiety pass through him at the man's words, but ignored it as he saw his clothes, clean for the first time in weeks, and he lost himself in the joy of dressing in something other than smelly rags. A few moments later, they left the house and joined the numbers heading towards the town square.

Several thousand were there when Raiwandoo arrived. More thousands flocked in over the next few minutes, and the square was packed solid. In the middle was a platform, used for concerts, displays, and political meetings.

Abruptly, the thousands of people went silent and settled softly to the ground. Raiwandoo looked around, and saw a small group of men walking from the edge of the square towards the platform. He studied the group, wandering which was the mysterious Saviour. One of them carried himself with pride, radiating strength. Raiwandoo watched him.

The man he was studying climbed onto the platform. "My name is Calasanai," he said, and a wave of emotion ran through the crowds.

*He doesn't look anything like a world's Saviour!* Raiwandoo protested inside himself then concentrated on the speaker.

"It may take years." Calasanai's voice was soft, but somehow carried through the entire square. "But those who have come among you to rob you of your freedom will leave."

A sigh ran through the square.

"They will pay their price for the wrongs done to you. Though we may not see their punishment, be certain that it will happen."

The man paused, and looked around the crowd. For a second, his gaze met Raiwandoo's and a jolt ran through the listener. The eyes were extraordinary, thought Raiwandoo. They seemed to shine with power. The man's gaze passed on, and he began to speak again.

"It requires us all to think as One," said Calasanai. "All of us thinking together, wishing together, and deciding together could cause the invaders to leave our lands and close the gates behind them. The power of all minds together is truly an amazing thing. Other races have learned this, and we must learn it too."

Other races! Raiwandoo knew that many races existed among the stars. Some had visited Mayoowani before the Masters had claimed the planet as their own, but none had come since. Raiwandoo knew that most space travel had been in the ships of a species known as the Kaloti who had died out over a thousand years before, leaving their lovely yellow planet deserted. The ships could travel within the galaxy and even cross the immense deserts of empty light-years between the Galaxies. Many millions of Mayoowi had travelled to other worlds this way before the Gelkka had placed a barrier around the world. As a child, Raiwandoo had never understood why anyone would want to travel to places where everything was strange and unfamiliar. It was nothing he had ever wanted and he had not suffered any feeling of loss from the Overlords' imprisonment of his people on their planet.

He pulled his attention back to the man on the platform, still unable to see why people thought that this individual could save them from the Gelkka.

"So dream along with me, and with all Mayoowi," said Calasanai. "In time, the whole world will dream this way, and the evil will remove itself from our home. We need no armed uprising, we need no weapons such as the Masters carry. Just our thoughts will do it."

*Stupid!* thought Raiwandoo. *The man's a lunatic. And this is what the Masters fear?* He grinned to himself and looked around. To his astonishment, all he could see was faces of adoration and love. It puzzled him.

On the platform, the man was moving away. People were standing up and closing in on the small procession as it walked away from the centre of the square.

"You don't believe Calasanai?" said a voice by Raiwandoo's elbow. He turned to see Lawindinai studying him with interest.

"It seems far-fetched," answered Raiwandoo. "Thoughts can kill the Masters? How can we believe that?"

Lawindinai didn't answer. The town square by now had almost emptied, when a voice shouted from the buildings at one side.

"The Masters! They come!"

They didn't come on foot and moving platform this time. Within seconds, a small squadron of flying machines had erupted into the sky over the town. In a thunder of engines, ten of them descended into the square, soldiers poured off them and surrounded the town. Raiwandoo realized he was almost alone in the square and an obvious target. Trembling, he stood silent as a squad of Gelkka approached him.

The officer in charge studied Raiwandoo for a second or two. "You were here during this assembly?" he demanded. The voice was ice-cold, contemptuous, as if speech was wasted on an inferior being.

Unable to speak, feeling fear flood his whole body, Raiwandoo nodded.

"And did you hear one of the cattle speak to you?" The Gelkka's eyes did not look at Raiwandoo. They focused above his head as if eye contact would somehow infect the speaker.

Raiwandoo nodded again. The fear was freezing every bone and muscle.

"Where did that cattle go? There is a reward for finding it." The Gelkka officer still looked around the square, then suddenly glared down at Raiwandoo. "And death for not helping," he added with a snap.

Raiwandoo's bowels were turning to water. His knees would barely hold his legs straight. Sick with fear, he was about to point out the house where he had slept before, hoping that if the Gelkka found some of the Saviour's supporters that might save him, when he realized that the soldiers around him were watching someone approach across the square.

He turned to look and recognized Lawindinai. The man walked slowly up to the soldiers.

"I am the one you seek," said Lawindinai. "I am Calasanai."

The Gelkka paused only a second. "Take the animal," he ordered and within seconds, the newcomer was wrapped securely in a confinement web of thin silk.

"This is the cattle who spoke to you?" asked the Gelkka. Raiwandoo realized the question was addressed to him, and he nodded. *How could somebody sacrifice themselves like that?* his mind screamed at him. It was incomprehensible. He stared at Lawindinai as the entire force of soldiers gathered around him. In complete silence, the soldiers circled the prisoner, till there was only a wall of black-clad troops carrying their blasters, staring at the two Mayoowi. Raiwandoo felt faint under the barrage of hatred that assaulted him. A small atom of sanity said to him that if only a few hundred minds could direct so tangible a wall of pain at him, what could billions of minds do against the Masters? Maybe Calasanai was right, he thought, then a blow to his head silenced all thinking. Dimly he heard an order from the officer to bring the prisoner. With a wave of renewed fear, he also heard the second order.

"Bring in the other animal," said the officer. "It might be useful." A blow on Raiwandoo's head stopped all hearing.

His awakening this time was unlike the comfortable return to consciousness in the house of Lawindinai. His first sensation was of pain, deep, cracking pain in all his bones. He opened his eyes to find himself sitting upright in a heavy, wooden chair. A broad strap round his chest held him upright, but he was otherwise unbound. Trembling, Raiwandoo undid the belt, and struggled to his feet. As he turned to look at his surroundings, he saw Lawindinai.

The other man's arms and legs were strapped to the solid limbs of the chair, and like Raiwandoo had been, he was kept upright by a broad, leather band strapping his chest to the back of the chair. Lawindinai was unable to move anything but his head. He was unconscious, and blood covered one side of his face.

Raiwandoo looked around him, and saw he was in a small room with stone walls that looked as solidly ageless as the continents. The floor was also stone. The ceiling was much higher than any room in which Raiwandoo had ever been. There was nothing else in the room but an overpowering smell of fear. Raiwandoo could see that a door was placed in the centre of the wall behind him.

For a weird, mind-rocking moment, Raiwandoo thought that the scene was familiar. The sensation was terrifying, almost as if it were a dream from another life, another universe. The sound of the door opening drove the slight madness away and replaced it with fear. A shadow appeared at his side, and a Master walked round the chair, looking at Raiwandoo with contempt. Raiwandoo tried to stare back.

The creature before him was massive, even more so, this close. It stood nearly three meters tall, with a breadth of shoulders that made it a giant. It was clothed in a single, black cloak that showed nothing of the creature's body shape, or any other clothing. The face was pale green, with enormous eyes of the same colour, as cold as the sea. The nose was curved like a hunting bird, and the cheekbones were high and prominent. In a terrible, deathly way, thought Raiwandoo, the face was beautiful.

The huge being turned away from him and

concentrated on the other man. The Gelkka stood motionless for several minutes until the bound man stirred and came to awareness.

"This is the one they call the Saviour?" said the creature. The voice was calm, cool, contemptuous. It shrivelled Raiwandoo's courage and he struggled to regain it.

"Yes," he whispered. "I was there in the crowd listening to the speeches. This is the one."

"So," said the creature. "Has the cattle Saviour not even the courage to speak for itself?"

Lawindinai stirred and looked up at the Gelkka. "I am the Saviour," he croaked. "And I am the cause of your destruction."

The Gelkka's black cloak came apart, and a hand appeared, carrying what looked like a short metal wand. Raiwandoo had just time to notice that the hand had only three fingers that were mutually opposing, and the wand touched the neck of the prisoner.

Lawindinai shrieked his agony at the uncaring stone walls, and Raiwandoo broke into a cold sweat of terror. Never had he heard such pain. It was as if fire burned through every vein of the man in the heavy chair. Under his blistering terror, the madness of a dream returned to Raiwandoo. He had seen this before... Feeling his mind unhinge, Raiwandoo closed his eyes against the scene, his thoughts full of the pain and the madness.

The Gelkka spoke again. "Cattle will not address the Masters thus," it said. "Now, tell me, just how do you plan to make the other cattle rise up against us?"

Lawindinai tried to sit upright against his bonds and a light gleamed in his eyes, even though the pain still reflected in his twisted mouth. "I do not plan," he said, his voice a thin rasp. "They will simply tell you when your time here is done, and then you will leave."

The three-fingered hand shot out again, and the agony consumed the prisoner once more. His screams bounced off the walls, and Raiwandoo thought

Lawindinai's bones would break under the shattering vibration that afflicted his body. For a few moments, the enormous entity stared down, as if enjoying the man's pain. Then it moved past the bound man in the seat, vanished beyond Raiwandoo's vision, and only the sound of the door opening and closing told him that the prisoner's pain and his own fear were over for at least a few moments.

The only sound in the room was the coarse gasping of the man in the chair. His head was slumped down on his chest, but after a few moments, he looked up and stared at Raiwandoo.

"How can you do this?" breathed Raiwandoo through a dry mouth. "How can you pretend...?"

"Be quiet!" Lawindinai snapped. His contempt for Raiwandoo was obvious, even under the pain. "This game must be played out if Mayoowani is ever to live again."

"But what if I tell them the truth?" Under the fear, Raiwandoo was thinking hard. There was opportunity here, he could see. Others might be stupid and believe that thoughts could destroy the might of the Gelkka, but not him. By throwing in his lot with the power on this planet, much could be achieved....

"You can't," the other man sneered. "You've already told them once that I'm Calasanai. Try reversing that, and they'll burn you without a second thought."

Chilled, Raiwandoo saw the truth of Lawindinai's words.

The conversation was terminated as the door swung open again. Another huge Gelkka trooper walked in, followed by two Mayoowi servants. The trooper pointed a massive finger at Raiwandoo. "Release that animal," the soldier ordered. When his straps were released, Raiwandoo stood up shakily. "Follow me," snapped the soldier and walked through the door.

With one more look at the man in the chair,

Raiwandoo walked out of the cell. He followed the enormous figure of the Gelkka along stone corridors and was directed into another room.

This was not a cell. Although the surroundings were bleak and Spartan, the sheer size of the room and the furniture indicated the room was intended for occupancy in some comfort. The door closed behind him.

"So one cattle-beast can work with us?"

The voice came from behind a screen at the far end of the room. The Gelkka who had tortured the prisoner came out from behind it. The cloak had been removed and the enormous figure was dressed in a green tunic. Colourful rows of metal lined one side of the creature's chest and a massive blaster hung from the Gelkka's belt. The three-digit claws were obvious now, and the sight of them made Raiwandoo shiver. They were the most alien aspect of the Master.

Raiwandoo gathered his courage and spoke. "Yes, I can work for you."

"Interesting," the creature murmured. "You will be my ears and eyes in this country. Tomorrow, we will kill this Saviour. But any signs of similar filth, and I want to know about it. Is that clear?"

Raiwandoo nodded, feeling excitement at the closeness to power and the opportunities that this presented.

"Go," said the Gelkka. "One of my troopers will define your role and, of course, your rewards."

Grateful to leave the frightening presence, Raiwandoo walked out. Some hours later, he selected the best house in the town, and pointed it out to the Gelkka officer who led a small squad of soldiers. The soldiers walked into the house and Raiwandoo heard the suppressed hiss of blasters. An hour later, Raiwandoo took possession of the house. Later, asleep, dreadful dreams haunted him.

*He saw a man called Stephen Crossman touching*

*people on their necks with small metal wands, and the people screamed in dreadful agony. They were bound in heavy wooden chairs like that which had contained him a while ago.... He saw himself lying in filth, being sodomized by a giant lizard.... He saw a huge platform on which four people were about to die in front of a hundred thousand watchers. But the watchers ran riot and attacked him, they tore off his arms, broke his body and....*

Raiwandoo woke in a cold sweat at the nightmare. The luxurious room soothed his mind rapidly, and he rose from the huge bed. He found the cupboard full of expensive bottles and selected a potent beverage, sitting in the vast lounge room, enjoying the surroundings. How circumstances could change!

The Gelkka trooper had offered many things after Raiwandoo had left the commander's room. The pick of any of the female prisoners as his personal servants, wealth beyond his dreams, even Gelkka soldiers to help him in his work. Feeling his panic from the nightmare easing, Raiwandoo began to sense excitement as the pleasant possibilities facing him. He rose to his feet and went to the front door, opened it and looked into the early morning light.

The squad of soldiers who had cleared the house for him were leaning against their vehicle. As they saw Raiwandoo come out, the slowly stood up. Raiwandoo sensed their resentment at having to acknowledge one of their "cattle" and smiled inside himself.

"The coffee shop by the square," he said to the trooper in charge of the squad. "There is a young female working as a waitress. When she shows up, bring her here."

With a barely visible nod, the soldier turned away and the vehicle left. Raiwandoo returned to his lounge room, his heart pounding at the prospect of the next few hours. It had been months since he had taken a female.

# The Nightmares of God

* * *

They came for the Saviour at noon. Two soldiers of the Masters unlocked the gate and hauled him out, using no more effort than if the prisoner were a doll. They carried him out into the town square where only a day before, Raiwandoo had heard the words of Calasanai. The square was full of the townspeople, and Raiwandoo stood on a raised platform with other officers of the Gelkka. None spoke to him, but none ordered him away.

The prisoner was carried up to the same platform where the Saviour had spoken. A wooden cross stood on the platform, the same height as a man. Lawindinai was strapped to the cross, his arms stretched out and his wrists tied with leather bands, as were his legs. Further straps were bound round his upper arms and one round his waist.

"This is your Saviour," said a calm voice that could be heard across the square. Raiwandoo looked at the Gelkka on the platform. One was speaking, but he could see no transmission system to carry the words so clearly. "It has not saved you. It will instead die for your sins. And its own, of course."

A soldier walked out of the crowd, unslinging his blaster. He stood a few feet away from the platform, studying the prisoner as if picking a spot. He pointed the weapon with care and pulled the trigger. A bolt of fire ripped out of the muzzle and struck Lawindinai on his left hand. He screamed hoarsely, the scream increasing in intensity as the fire did not stop. Even as his hand burned away, the blast began to work its way up his arm, eating away the entire limb, inch by dreadful inch. As it passed his elbow, the man fainted into merciful blackness.

The crowd gasped, the first sound other than the man's scream to break the deadly silence in the square.

A few moments later, the prisoner stirred again. Immediately, the blaster beam again struck his left arm above the elbow and continued the slow, grinding

521

torture as far as the strap around his biceps. The screams of the crowd seemed to attract the man's attention for a second, for he stared out at them, then he fainted again.

Twenty minutes passed before the body on the platform stirred again. The crowd was silent again, and the soldier with the blaster was standing patiently, waiting for the prisoner to show life signs. This time, the blaster took off his right hand, and the entire horror began again.

It took another hour for the man to die, by which time both his arms were burned off to the shoulder, and one leg had withered away to the hip. The other had suffered dreadful burns, but it was still there. Finally, as the sun climbed to its highest point, and the crowd had fallen silent but for the small sound of sobbing in isolated spots, the man who had offered his life for his Saviour surrendered his soul.

Alan Drew woke up on a settee, looking straight into the eyes of Maragos who sat across from him. She was dressed in a flowing light dress, a shimmering scarf round her neck, her hair hanging prettily down to her shoulders. A picture of a young woman reflected in the mirror smiled at him from the wall, and the lake seen through the window seemed blue and calm.

Alan took a deep breath. "That was a horrible way to die," he said.

Maragos nodded. "Even worse than the one Horning inflicted on the four of us," she said. "I had hoped that William would have chosen that death instead, as his own penance."

"I thought a millennium in Hell would have cured him." Alan's face still reflected the horrors of his death under the Gelkka blaster.

"I would have thought so, too," Maragos agreed. "But even when we spoke as he came out of his Hell, I saw the rage and anger in him."

"Becoming a stooge of the Gelkka was surely not the intention?"

Maragos shook her head. "Indeed not. But all souls have free will. I gave him a situation where he could have played the role you took on yourself, and he failed to take the chance of his redemption." She smiled at Alan. "But you achieved a great deal in the process," she said.

"I did?" Alan replied. His eyes were still haunted by the terrible process of dying in such extended pain.

"Yes, you did. Calasanai is a true Saviour of his people and in time, the Mayoowi will learn the truth and decide that the Masters must go. And they will. Your death in his place has given them that time, and you will be remembered with gratitude."

"It really works? Enough people believing and deciding something can achieve all that?"

"Of course. Thought is the sole basis of universal power. That is how The One created the Universe and how my race moved its planet's orbit. All power is in thought alone."

"And because I died in his place, Calasanai will save his people?" Alan Drew still seemed doubtful.

"Exactly," she said with a smile. "And at the same time, you have paid your Karmic debt, and achieved the small healing of the soul that was all you needed."

"I looked at Calasanai," Alan whispered, thinking back. "His eyes were extraordinary. Was he just another Mayoowi?"

Maragos shook her head and laughed. "Indeed not. He was much like your Jesus Christ, an enhanced Ascendant Soul. He was the sum of eight Ascendants from different species, and therefore a soul of enormous power. He came because the Mayoowi needed him at a time of great terror and pain under the rule of the Gelkka. Without knowing how they did it, they called for help."

"About the Masters. If they too were all Old Souls, and Oneness is coming, how could they be so evil? This invasion, this killing, isn't that supposed to be the mark of immature souls?"

"You must remember, The One is everything. All that there is originated in The One. All good, all evil, all beauty, all ugliness. The Infinite Soul that is the species of the Gelkka chose a path of power, conquest and enslavement in its search for answers to the problem of The One. It provided new experiences, new insights."

"So how could the Mayoowi then try to oppose it?" Alan was confused. "Wouldn't that negate the path the Masters had chosen for them?"

"Not at all," Maragos replied. "Being enslaved, conquered, and then breaking free, also provided new insights, new experience, maybe an answer to The One. As will the experience of being forced out by the Mayoowi be another insight for the Gelkka."

"But what of Horning now? You set up a situation where he could die instead of Calasanai, and he didn't take it. As Raiwandoo, now he lives a life of oppression and self-indulgence, just as he did on Earth. Did you set up that massacre in that small town as well?"

Maragos nodded, sadness in her face.

"But it caused the deaths of over two thousand innocent people!" Alan was horror-struck at her apparent cold-blooded manipulation. "They also had to die to set up my sacrifice?"

Maragos shook her head again. "A matter of killing two thousand birds with one stone. All of those two thousand were baby human souls. They had chosen to reincarnate with Horning on Mayoowani. All were sick with the illness that has struck humanity, and all owed massive Karmic debts to others for crimes they had committed. This was a way of achieving much healing and payment of debt on behalf of the human souls to whom they were indebted. Like your death, their destruction provided time for the true Saviour to continue the work. Most of those who died will reincarnate again on Mayoowani to continue the healing and repayment."

"But those who died, they did something for other Mayoowi, not for the humans they hurt in the first place."

"True," said Maragos. "Debts need not be repaid directly. Those humans who had been hurt agreed to let their debts be paid to others on their behalf. These things balance out."

"And Horning?"

The sadness remained in the face of Maragos. "He failed his first test," she said. "The sickness has grown in him again, worse than the small healing he achieved during his time in Hell. I worry that instead, he has gained spiritual power by drawing on that of the Gelkka."

"Can anything be done, Maragos?" Alan felt great fear at the expression on Maragos' face.

She seemed to pull her mind from vast distances away and smiled at him. "Of course, Alan," she replied. "Meanwhile, your path is over for now, my friend. Philippe had already cured most of the sickness within you, and you are healed by that sojourn on Mayoowani. You can wait in peace on the Astral Plane until your time for Ascendency comes."

"And Horning?" Alan's fear remained. Maragos had seemed uncertain when he had first asked, and the idea of uncertainty in an Infinite Soul was terrifying to him.

Her face was grave. "Leave Horning to me," she said. "It is time for you to find peace."

"Till Oneness, then," he said, sensing a glow of happiness within himself at the prospect of a chance to meditate in peace on the spiritual planes.

"Till Oneness, my friend," said Maragos.

* * *

For ten more years, Raiwandoo acted as the prefect of the country that contained the town of Liamondooni. Thousands died for merely raising the suspicion within the mind of the prefect that they supported the Saviour

Calasanai whom the Gelkka believed dead. But the legends persisted, despite the savagery of the repression.

On the morning of a bright summer's day, the Gelkka commander summoned Raiwandoo. In trepidation, he entered the huge room where he had first been appointed as controller of the lives and deaths of his countrymen.

"The cattle of the western continent report that a Saviour has been speaking to them," said the officer. He did not look down at Raiwandoo.

"Then they lie. You killed the Saviour ten years ago."

"We killed the animal you told me was the Saviour. For that we gave you great rewards. You failed us."

Raiwandoo shrieked as he saw the blaster appear in the huge three-clawed hand, but he was dead a second later as his body burned under the energy stream.

"You do not learn well from your experiences," said Maragos.

Horning struggled to clear his mind from the suddenness of his death on Mayoowani. He felt rage at the beautiful woman sitting across from him. "What the hell do you think I was supposed to do?" he snapped. "Let them burn me to death?"

"Exactly that," she said softly. "Instead, Alan Drew died that terrible death in your place."

"That was Drew?" Horning was startled. "What the hell for?"

"His karmic debts for even supporting the evil acts you committed on Earth."

"The man was a fool," Horning sneered.

Maragos studied him carefully. "All the healing from your time with the Lizard has been lost again. And instead, you have gained strength from your betrayal of thousands of innocent souls on Mayoowani."

"Strength is what I need," he replied. "All that garbage about being sick was just to frighten me."

"I think you came out of Hell rather too early," she said, ignoring his comment. "You are not ready to take your place in the Universe and pay your debts."

Horning went pale. "You said I was," he whispered, his voice trembling as he realized what she was saying.

"I was mistaken," she retorted, and the room vanished.

"HELLO HORNING!!!" screamed a dreadful, familiar voice that rocked the universe around Horning. "I am so frightfully happy to have you back!"

Horning smelled the rotten stench of carrion meat again, felt the slimy sensation of a thousand years of blood, vomit and shit against his naked body. He took a deep breath to scream with horror, and instead vomited again.

"Oh my sweet boy," howled the Lizard. "You've grown it back again!"

"NO!" screeched Horning, but the Lizard's talon hissed out and scythed through the body of the naked man. Gouts of blood poured from the severed organ and Horning's scream of pain filled the dreadful vista of a millennium of Horning's Hell.

"Time to eat again, darling Billie," bellowed the Lizard.

# Chapter 20. Universe Central

The temperature had dropped below freezing, and the winds were powerful. Speaker Nine Hundred and Twelve of the Third Continent automatically adjusted his internal body heat without thought. He was facilitating a discuss ion between the X'Kasxi captain of a Kaloti ship moving within subspace at many thousand times the speed of light, and the executives of a company on a planet within a galaxy of a cluster over a billion light-years away in another direction from the Speaker's home world. The distance between the two groups was such that light would take billions of years to cross within the conventional universe. A triangle connecting the three groups would cover an appreciable proportion of the universe.

The Speaker was barely conscious of the conversation passing through his mind. After five hundred years since beginning his work, the process had become automatic. The Speaker was over eight hundred years old, and the first three hundred years of his life had been spent preparing for the only profession practised on his planet.

Around him, the topography of the Third Continent stretched to a horizon far more distant than would have been seen on Earth. Little interrupted the expanse of bare ground but rocks and occasional scrub. Speaker Nine Hundred and Twelve was unconcerned with the lack of scenic splendours, for he had no eyes.

"Speaker, this connection can break," said the captain of the Kaloti ship from somewhere deep within the mathematical uncertainties of subspace. The Speaker moved a small proportion of his attention from other matters.

"Yes, K'Latr," he said. "Is there any other connection you need?"

"On my home planet," replied the ship's captain. "I would speak with G'Trxx of the city of Brx'Jashcha."

The Speaker expanded his senses across the galaxies, homing in on the small spiral galaxy that held the worlds of both the X'Kasxi and the Human species. Part of his training had been to learn the locations of each of the million Infinite Souls, the galaxies that held them, and the positions within the galaxies of the inhabited planets. Homing in on X'Katcxo, the Speaker expanded his consciousness seeking the vibrations that matched the name the ship's captain had given him.

To G'Trxx, the sensation of contact being sought was a familiar one. Something tugged at his mind, just as if a telephone had rung in another room. He opened his awareness, and felt the communication of the captain enter his mind. Immediately, Speaker Nine Hundred and Twelve switched his awareness from the conversation. It would take place without his deliberate effort. The Speaker had something else, far more massively important on his mind.

It had been growing for years, this new awareness. The Speaker had been discovering that something else lay beneath his sense of self. At first it had frightened him. For three hundred years, life had been simple. He had been conceived when the millions of spores of one parent had flown through the tumultuous winds of the continent to take their chances with life. The spore that would become the Speaker had landed on the body of another tall mound, immediately extending tiny hooks into the surface. Over thirty years, the spore had taken genes from both parents, grown to a size roughly that of a new kitten, and then released its hooks to return to the winds. Speaker Nine Hundred and Twelve had been one of those who had survived the initial flight as a minute spore, and then his second and last flight as a sentient being. He had landed somewhere within the continent, not been blown out to sea, and the hooks that had once attached him to a parent now grew into the soil on the spot where he would live for another thousand years.

Feeding on the tiny animal and plant life that was blown through the wild winds, he grew to awareness of other minds after another sixty years, and slowly acquired learning and membership of the species. He was given the name of another Speaker who had died a few hundred years earlier. Having a name was unnecessary among members of a telepathic race who identified each other by means of patterns of the mind not visible to other species, but the name was necessary for all the other species who used the universal communication powers of the Speakers.

Another hundred years passed and many minds began to teach the new Speaker the art and skills of inter-galactic communication. He talked to the star travellers in the Kaloti ships, to the merciless Overlords of the Gelkka species, to the tiny tree-dwellers of the forest world of Harliya and to the bodiless souls of the race that gave itself no name, but lived in spiritual form in the blackness of the spaces between the suns of its galaxy. He passed messages from the gaseous entities of a planet in the galactic cluster known to human astronomers as NGC 2207, and to the six-armed species of a planet to whom NGC 2207 was simply a fuzzy spot in the night sky. But mainly, he was used by the travellers in the enormous ovoid shells of the Kaloti ships that flickered in and out of the featureless mystery of subspace like flat stones launched across the surface of a lake by small boys, and covered tens of light-years in a few seconds.

How beautiful it was to talk between the stars, the galaxies and the differently shaped curves of subspace! The exhilaration of those mental contacts had never left him, but the work sometimes became routine as he learned his other task, to meditate on the truth of existence. The new awareness, the sense of "otherness" had grown over the last fifty years. In his confusion, he had sought advice from his teachers of centuries before.

"What is this sensation, young mumbler?" asked his first Teacher in affection.

"I feel that I am another, as well as myself," replied Speaker Nine Hundred and Twelve.

The pause lasted many months, as the Teacher, together with others looked inside the mind of the Speaker. Finally, the first Teacher spoke again. "There is no other presence," said the Teacher. "But you are certainly something unique as a Speaker. A ripple, a second colour in your mind tells us of a difference."

"It does not affect his ability as a Speaker, though," said another.

"This is true," replied the other Teachers. They had been concerned, because on a planet where only a single profession was practised, failure at that profession would be catastrophic.

Comforted by that, Speaker Nine Hundred and Twelve had returned to his primary task as a communicator across the billions of black light-years. For a time, many years, he ignored the sense of otherness but it again returned to him, this time more strongly.

The explosion in his mind occurred when he was asked to make his first communication with a human being. The entity in question was one of the rare members of that species who had visited other planets. One of the human's newly-found friends, a highly spiritual entity of a species only a few years away from the moment at which the last incarnate soul would merge with its entity souls to form an Ascendant Soul, had asked to speak with the human.

For first contact with a new species, a Speaker normally had to take some time adjusting to the new mental structures and patterns of thought. Speaker Nine Hundred and Twelve of the Third Continent began the stages of familiarisation in which he had been trained centuries before, then pulled back sharply from the human's mind.

He already knew the patterns! Astounded, the Speaker made another cautious entry to the human aura of thought. He had not been mistaken, not confused by any apparent similarity to the mind of another species. He knew the patterns. With that shock of recognition came a second powerful emotion. He knew now what was the otherness that hovered in his mind.

Trained and disciplined in his profession, the Speaker first carried out his duties and facilitated the surprised and delighted connection between the human and his friend a billion or more light-years away. With the conversation under way, the Speaker began to explore his new discovery. Exploiting the powerful and immensely refined capabilities he had developed over several centuries, he followed every pathway in his mind that carried the flavour of the human essence. In only another twenty years, he made his discovery.

He was the soul of Raoul Carmagio, and over two thousand earth-years before, he had been Archbishop of Milan, close friend of Philippe Leger and a companion of an Infinite Soul during the cataclysmic events on Earth that were known as The Story.

With the discovery came total recall of his last life as a human and the reasons why he was now incarnated as a Speaker. He remembered his childhood, his rise through the ranks of the Catholic Church and then the incredible last few years that culminated in his death in the electric chair before a hundred thousand silent watchers in Washington.

Raoul Carmagio, one-time Archbishop of Milan who then attained fame as one of The Four, tried and executed by the Court of President William Horning of the USA, and now Speaker Nine Hundred and Twelve of the Third Continent decided to make contact with his old friends, Philippe Leger and Jacqueline Carter.

But how to do so? His old companions were two among some thirty million billion souls in the entire universe. He had no idea what species they had selected for a reincarnation among others of The One. That they had done so, he was certain, but just in case, he spread his awareness throughout Earth, seeking the vibrations he knew he would recognize if they existed. But as he had been certain would happen, he drew a blank. Neither Philippe Leger nor Jacqueline Carter were incarnate on Earth. They were in an elsewhere that encompassed the universe of millions of galaxies and billions of planets.

For another ten years he pondered this problem. In the meantime, he also facilitated conversations across the galaxies, exchanged ideas on the meaning of intelligent life's existence and followed the potential implications of the ideas developed in these exchanges down through pathways of complexity that took years to explore fully.

When it came, the answer was obvious, and he wondered why he had not thought of it himself. It was another who solved it for him.

"Hello, my old friend," said the voice from throughout the entire universe. The sensation was similar to that of another skilled telepath opening communication with him, but the power was multiplied a thousand-fold, covering his senses with a blanket of infinite energy. Ecstasy flooded his entire being as he recognized the communicator.

"Hello, Maragos," he replied. "This is like communicating with all the minds in the universe simultaneously."

"I sensed your awakening to your old memories," said the presence in his mind.

"I think that even you have grown further since we last met," said Raoul. "You have changed since we last talked. Where are you now?"

"Everywhere, and all places," said the voice, the warmth and the sensed smile sending waves of delight through him. "And yes, even an Infinite Soul grows further as the integration of all the billions of souls within it is completed. Remember, I was very new to the position when we last met."

"Does Oneness come nearer?" he asked.

"Not as well as I had hoped," replied Maragos. "The sickness is strong on Earth, and the power of the sick Infant Souls shows itself. Most of the human souls we sent elsewhere are truly healing, but I worry about some of our worst cases."

Raoul sensed the undercurrent of deep fear in Maragos and it flushed a wave of fright within himself. It was a completely new aspect of the Infinite and revealed dreadful possibilities. "What of the truly sick ones?" he asked. "What has happened to Horning, Crossman, and the others who opposed you so viciously?"

"Horning has paid with his agonies many times," replied Maragos. "And still he pays. For another ten or twenty thousand years, he will buy the salvation of others with his own dreadful lives and deaths. But even that penance is not providing healing. I fear the influence of that soul."

"And Crossman?"

"Horning absorbed the soul of Crossman before the executions in Washington. That meant spiritual death for Crossman, a terrible price to pay."

"Lavalier too?"

"Your old colleague does his own penance, as does Alan Drew, though with less horror, and with those two, results are good. Their pain will all go to complete the learning of The One before we ask ourselves the final question."

"The final question, Maragos?"

"The only question, Raoul. As The One, how will we live supreme, omnipotent and alone through all of eternity?"

"Oh, *that* question!"

Maragos' laugh of delight seemed to send waves

through the Universe and eased the dark undercurrent of fear within Raoul. "Maybe Humanity has much to teach the rest of us when you have healed, Raoul," said the Infinite Soul. "Perhaps one of your own species' sayings, that laughter is the best medicine will turn out to be the answer to the question The One asks of us."

His human memories and sense of identity growing more powerful by the second, Raoul bathed in the sensation of wonder that contact with Maragos gave him. "I would speak with Philippe and Jacqueline again," he said. "But my powers do not let me find them within this Universe."

"Let me show you," said the infinity of energy that was the soul of Maragos.

And Raoul found his old friends.

"Raoul, we have missed you!" Philippe Leger returned from meditation of several hundreds of human lives and some of the incarnations he had chosen among others of The One. He was within the peaceful mists of the Astral Plane, but as he recognized the voice of his old friend, he sensed the close presence of Jacqueline as she also heard the communication from Raoul.

"And I have missed you both," replied Raoul Carmagio from many millions of light-years away. "I have only recently discovered my identity, and I received help in locating you."

"Help?" Leger was puzzled for only a second, then his mind almost exploded with the power of the presence he felt. "Maragos!" he exclaimed.

"Indeed, old friends," said the thunderous, infinite power of the Soul they had last met in the shape of a young man who had joined them on the way to Washington. "It is good to be able to talk with you again."

Jacqueline and Philippe felt themselves surrounded by warmth and love, and their environment changed with a flicker. They found themselves in their human form again, clothed in the styles of their lives in the early twenty-first century. They were sitting at a huge wooden table, and with them were Raoul Carmagio, and Maragos as she had been then, a beautiful woman dressed in a light summer dress.

"We're home again!" shouted Leger, recognizing his old farmhouse in Valence. "How utterly wonderful!" He rose to his feet, seized Raoul in a hug, then turned to Maragos, uncertain. The power in her was even greater than when they had followed her two thousand years before. But she stood up and took his hand, kissing his cheek and almost making him faint. She turned to the others and did the same, then sat at the table. There was fresh bread, wine, cheese and fruit, and the four began to eat as if all the centuries had never passed and they were back when they were touring the world, while Maragos spoke to millions.

"My house still stands?" asked Philippe. "Twenty centuries or more have passed. Maragos, is this really my home?"

Maragos shook her head. "We are out of time and out of space here, Philippe," she said. "This is your home, but at the same time, it is not. The difference is highly theoretical. But we must talk, my friends. The Universe has a problem still unsolved, and which may be getting worse."

A cold wave of anxiety ran round the table.

Maragos looked at each of them in turn. Her beautiful face was pale white like alabaster. "Finally, I have integrated all the millions of Ascendant Souls within me," she said. "I am truly now a single soul, and this gives me great power, even greater than when we worked together before. But I find that we need that power, and even more, and I am still alone at this level."

"There are no more like you yet?" asked Philippe.

She shook her head. "Not quite. Two more Infinite Souls are evolving at present, but I think another thousand years will be needed for them to reach awareness."

"And where is the human race?" asked Jacqueline. "Does our healing progress?"

"Badly," replied Maragos. "The sickness remains strong on Earth and becomes worse every day. Too many of the silly belief structures remain, and others have returned to cause some of the old problems. And although most of those who left to go elsewhere are healing, this may no longer be sufficient to counteract the disease."

"Maragos! Your words frighten me," said Philippe.

"They should," she replied seriously. "Our old enemy, William Horning may yet reappear as our biggest hurdle."

"Horning?" asked Philippe. "Does he heal at all?"

Maragos smiled without humour. "He goes through a worse hell than any mind could dream of," she said. "His life is anguished, tortured, agonized. He was given an opportunity to live a life in which he should have paid many debts and the sickness should have burned away a little. But he chose to take an easier path than redemption. Horning is now sicker than ever before, and I returned him to his own Hell to work out his salvation."

"So how can he become a problem, Maragos?" Raoul was nervous.

"Remember the one universal law, Raoul," answered Maragos. "All souls have free will, and all souls have access to the total power of The One. Once Horning finds a source of power, I can only try and influence him, but I cannot control him."

"But does that mean a single soul like Horning, or like one of us, could be as powerful as you?" Philippe was intrigued but also worried by the implications.

"Theoretically, yes," nodded Maragos. "But the capacity to handle that power is another matter. It's a bit like putting a jet engine from a passenger airliner onto a light aircraft. Serious damage would result."

"So what could Horning do?" asked Jacqueline.

"I sensed many things in William when he returned from his incarnation as a Mayoowi," replied Maragos. "Rage, contempt for Alan Drew's sacrifice in his place, but also a fascination with the absolute rule of the Gelkka. They run their dominions the same way Horning tried to run America. It appealed to him. If he discovers his ability to control his spiritual movement, which he could do despite the sickness, he could well move to the Gelkka for his next life."

"And then what?" asked Philippe.

"We may lose control over him," replied Maragos. "And that could prove dangerous."

"How?" asked Raoul.

"Remember the Human problem," said Maragos. "Humanity could not even begin to move to Infinity because of the immaturity of all the human souls who had first to be healed for them to grow. But the Gelkka are already all Old Souls, ready to begin the move to Infinity. If they became sick now, the move will not stop."

"And we could have a sick Infinite Soul? Maragos, that is terrifying."

"Exactly." Maragos' smile was cold.

"Maragos, have you returned to Earth since our last trip together?" asked Leger after a short silence. "In human form, that is?"

The woman across from him shook her head. "Now is about the time, I believe," she said. "The silliness of the Baby Souls is again causing difficulties and pain. They have created a religion in my name, a Church, dogma, suppression of dissent, all that old nonsense has been revived. People now die because they reject my name and my divinity."

"Will you go there and stop it?" asked Jacqueline.

Maragos nodded. "Soon," she said. "A new trigger is needed to cause sharp growth among the immature souls."

"What will that be?" Raoul was intrigued, but Maragos smiled and shook her head.

"I have yet to work it out," she said, and drained her glass. "My friends, this night is yours. When you are ready to sleep, you will return to your other species and again forget your human histories. We will meet again in another place and time. But Oneness needs the healed human Infinite Soul. I will call on your help again."

"It has been wonderful to see each other again," said Leger, and the other two nodded enthusiastically. "I drink to our next meeting." He refilled the wine glasses of Jacqueline and Raoul, then the huge brandy glass of Maragos. They raised their glasses to each other.

"To friendship!" said Raoul and was echoed by the others. The glasses were half drained.

"To Oneness," said Maragos, and emptied her glass. Then she disappeared.

"To Oneness," said the remaining three. They tried to settle down to a night of happy memories and reminiscing, just like any old friends who have been apart for a while, but the words of Maragos left a cold undercurrent of fear in them all. At dawn, they fell asleep.

Speaker Nine Hundred and Twelve of the Third Continent established contact between the Gelkka Commander of all forces on the planet Mayoowani, and the X'Kasxi captain of a Kaloti ship barely a hundred light-years away. The ship had been transporting mineral ores, energy sculptures and over a thousand tourists from a planet in a local galaxy to one only four galaxies away and was now empty, about to return to its home planet in Earth's Milky Way.

"I have forty thousand troops and equipment to be moved from Mayoowani to our home planet, Gelokk," said the cool tones of the Gelkka Commander. But under that coolness, the Speaker heard the psychic rage and savagery. More hatred was evident in the Gelkka commander's mind than the Speaker had ever experienced in the brain patterns of that violent race.

"You are leaving Mayoowani permanently?" queried the X'Kasxi captain, astonished but delighted.

"Our time here is over," replied the Gelkka commander in a neutral voice, but the ship's captain thought he detected an undercurrent of frustrated rage. The captain decided he would enjoy the trip, seeing for the first time a Gelkka invasion force abandon a conquest. He wondered how the Mayoowani people had managed it.

"Twenty million credits for the trip," said the captain.

"Agreed," said the Gelkka, and discontinued the connection.

Speaker Nine Hundred and Twelve had listened in to the conversation, also sensing that something critical was behind the transaction. Tuning in more fully, he analysed the psychic wave patterns of the Gelkka and was worried by what he read. The anger was not mere frustration. There was a sour, diseased wave pattern that the Speaker had never encountered before. It contained hatred at a level that was almost uncontrollable and that caused a cold dismay to run through the Speaker's mind. Despite the news of a Gelkka departure, the Speaker was frightened. Unable to understand how that new, unhealthy note had appeared, he shifted his attention to another call for an intergalactic communication link.

There were several calls, in fact. In each of them, he recognized the mental patterns of Humans and sensed his own warmth of affection. The calls were tentative, a little frightened, seeking contact with a Speaker for its own sake, rather than to facilitate communication with a third party. Speaker Nine Hundred and Twelve dealt with all of them simultaneously.

"How can I help you?" he said, aware that his

familiarity with the human mind pattern was far greater than he would expect from only a single previous contact. He wondered why. The astonishment, fear and excitement from the humans was a surprise until he realized that for these minds, he was the first inter-species contact. He understood that they were experimenting with the connection, and the Speaker felt his affection and amusement rise, covering the coldness from the Gelkka contact.

"Welcome, my friends," he said. "Let me show you around the territories of The One."

# Chapter 21. The Church of Maragos

"This disobedience cannot be tolerated!" Jacqueline the Thirty-Fifth, Chief Servant of Maragos stared furiously at the Minister for Compliance. "Pilgrim Henshaw, I insist you enforce the strict rules in Britain, and punish the wrong-doers."

"Holiness, it was no more than a demonstration for freedom of choice in the public libraries!" Sean Pilgrim Henshaw looked directly into the eyes of Jacqueline, a risky thing to do with a Head of State who was also the world's religious leader. "A few people in the city of Manchester wanted permission to study some bibles of the Pre-Maragos years. The chief librarian refused to bring the books out of the archives and a perfectly civil demonstration was organized. No damage was done."

"No damage? Pilgrim Henshaw, you astonish me! *Any* attempt to degrade the teachings of Maragos The One must be utterly destroyed. I am dismayed that such dirt even existed in the library in the first place. Now, I want you to get to England immediately and I want the ringleaders of this disgraceful uprising arrested and executed at once. And while you're at it, find those bibles and have them destroyed."

"But Holiness..." Henshaw got no further.

"NOW, Pilgrim Henshaw! You are excused."

In dead silence, the Minister for Compliance rose from the board-table and left the room. The woman at the head of the table looked round the room for a few moments. Nobody met her eyes.

"Perfection is a concept and a standard demanding perpetual compliance," said Jacqueline the Thirty-Fifth more softly. She was a heavily-built woman, nearly six feet in height, and thus an imposing figure. Wisps of grey could be seen from under the wig of long, red-gold hair that female holders of the position of Chief Servant traditionally wore for formal occasions. Legend held that the hair making up the wig was truly that of the first Jacqueline, she who had been executed with Saint Philippe, Saint Raoul and God Herself, Maragos The One, and collected by a true believer from the cell where Saint Jacqueline had been shorn before the execution. This Jacqueline had been in the position for only five years, elected to the highest post by the Maragosian Council on the death of Philippe the Thirty-Seventh in 1995 ME. Her name was originally Aldine Stewart, and she had been born fifty-six years earlier in Montreal, Canada, third daughter of a strictly orthodox Maragosian family. There had been a hundred and two previous Chief Servants since the position had been created by the Maragosian Council meeting at the famed Council of Dublin in 473 ME or 2499 AD by the old calendar. Thirty-seven Chief Servants had taken the name of Philippe, thirty-one had been Raoul, and Aldine Stewart was the thirty-fifth Jacqueline. Her reputation as a rigidly conservative Maragosian had been well-known before her election, but the degree of her willingness to use force to ensure strict compliance with the dogma had been a little surprising, even to the Maragosian Council.

"No deviation can be permitted from the Truth of The One," Jacqueline continued. "By definition, such deviation is heresy. It may seem harsh on a few individuals, but their souls will return to Maragos for cleansing, and such action as I have ordered in England protects the mass of believers from danger to their own spiritual health. We have had similar outbreaks of disobedience around the world in past years, and they have always been met with the full power of the Maragosian Church. We have a peaceful, organized and *compliant* population almost everywhere, as a result. Does anyone wish to disagree with me?"

Again, she looked round the table with the same result as before. The twelve men and women of the world's ruling body, the Maragosian Council, and the now-empty chair of the Minister for Compliance remained mute.

"Good," said Her Holiness, Jacqueline the Thirty-Fifth. "To the next matter, then. Pilgrim Kellerman, what progress with our negotiations with the Scandinavians?"

The plump, elderly man two places from her left, looked uncomfortable. "Holiness, they refuse to discuss the matter. They say that they will continue to receive alien spaceships in their territories, and that any person of any nationality, race or faith may take passage on such ships. They are immovable on the subject."

Jacqueline's jaw was stiff with tension. She took several deep breaths before replying. "Have you not explained to them, Pilgrim, that such contacts are evil and against the word of Maragos?"

Kellerman's face was pale and his eyes were unable to meet the woman's. "Holiness, I followed your instructions to the letter. The recordings of my meetings show that I made precisely that statement to them. Their response follows, as you have seen in the transcripts."

"Yes, their response," said Jacqueline, Chief Servant of Maragos. The suppressed rage in her entire body made several of the ministers draw back from the table edge. "Let me read that response to you all, so that you may judge the terrible pit of Hell that looms ahead of us."

She drew a single sheet of paper from a small stack by her right hand, and looked down at it. "It begins with a lie so evil that..." She trembled with fury, then began to read.

"Tell your leader, the most inappropriately named

Chief Servant of Maragos, that Maragos herself travelled to this solar system aboard a spaceship built and manned by members of the Kaloti species. Maragos told the world many, many times, that all alien species are, like humanity itself, part of The One. They are brothers to mankind. They are welcome on our world at any time, and equally welcome to take human passengers with them when they go. We find the teachings of the self-styled Church of Maragos abhorrent to us, and they directly contradict the real, documented, recorded philosophies of Maragos. We in the Nation of Scandinavia reject thoroughly your church's demands that we cease contact with all extraterrestrial species. Such contacts are the only hope for humanity."

A roaring silence bellowed through the chamber.

With a cold smile, Jacqueline put down the paper. "You see how much the forces of evil reign on this poor world," she said softly. "We remain the only defence against Horning and all his demons from hell. Pilgrim Malenkov!"

The thin, blond man near the end of the table snapped alert. "Yes, Holiness?"

"Could our armed forces conduct an attack on these heretics?"

"Holiness, our forces have for decades been trained and focused on suppression of local disturbances and the defence of your holy personage and those of your predecessors. Full-scale warfare has never been our mandate. Any attack on the Scandinavians would be undoubtedly met by alien weapons supplied by those... others."

Jacqueline stared at the man for several moments, and was unable to make him drop his eyes. Surprisingly, she smiled. "Defence Minister, I bow to your professional opinion. It seems we must put up with the presence of evil on Earth for a while longer. I shall pray for deliverance when we reach Washington in three weeks."

Tension slowly eased round the room.

Jacqueline seemed to shake off the subject. "Then, to the last two matters on the agenda," she said. "First, admission to the rank of Pilgrim for the last batch to visit Washington. Pilgrim Batterson?"

An elderly woman at the end of the table rose to her feet. She was tall and imposing, with an air of elegance about her. Thick brown hair was cut short. Her plain, black robe hung in classic folds from her shoulders.

"Nine thousand, six hundred and fifty-one people made the Pilgrimage last year, Holiness," she said. "Their applications to use the title "Pilgrim" have all been processed. Four hundred and sixty-three have been rejected for reasons of moral failings as uncovered in the usual security checks, and a further five hundred and twelve failed their written tests. My department has approved the remaining eight thousand, six hundred and seventy-six to be admitted. The ceremonies are scheduled for the next Pilgrim Day this coming December. If I may ask, Holiness, will you administer the services in Los Angeles as usual? There will be a little over two thousand people here."

Jacqueline nodded, and waved to the Council Recorder to enter her assent. "Which brings us to the most important topic of all," she said, another smile breaking her hard features. "The Second Millennium Assembly. We will leave Los Angeles in just ten days. Who is to report on the arrangements?"

As Pilgrim Batterson resumed her seat, a man sitting in the middle of one side of the table rose to his feet. "Holiness," he said. "We have asked the Head of the City Council, Selman Pilgrim Jackson to join us to brief you in detail. With your permission?"

The woman nodded, and the man on his feet walked to the door, opened it, and gesticulated. He stood aside, and another man entered the room. The newcomer was tall and thin, his remaining hair a fringe of light brown round the back of his head. Like the others in the room, his clothing was sombre and conservative in style. His pale skin was highlighted by a beak of a nose. He bowed, raising his right hand, palm forward in a gesture of supplication.

"Welcome, Pilgrim Jackson," said Jacqueline. "Please join the table."

Standing upright, Jackson moved to the foot of the table. "Thank you, Holiness," he said. "With your permission, I would like to advise you of the security and logistics arrangements for the departure of the Second Millennium Pilgrimage in ten days, on August the First, in the Year of Maragos, 2000."

Jacqueline smiled, and the room relaxed. "Of course, Pilgrim Jackson," she replied. She looked at the man seated at her right. "I can never remember," she said. "What year is that by the old Christian calendar?"

"Er... 4026 AD," he replied, nervous at the unexpected and rare reference to anything dating from an earlier age and the previous dominant religion.

"Yes, of course," she murmured, and resumed her attention on the man at the foot of the table. "Councilman?" she prodded.

Jackson cleared his throat. "Five hundred thousand people will go to Washington, Holiness," he said. "A hundred thousand have been give permission to cover the entire route of the Alexandrine Pilgrimage from the Holy City, Los Angeles. This group will travel to Lincoln for the Rites of The Words of Power, and then to Chicago for the Ceremony of the Temptation of Michael. There, you will be joined by a further one hundred and fifty thousand pilgrims who will leave from Montreal, the city of your birth, Holiness," he added with a respectful bow at the head of the table. The Chief Servant of Maragos responded with a nod and a smile.

"The remaining pilgrims will make their own ways to Washington," the speaker continued. "Now, we estimate that the convoy leaving the Holy City will cover seven kilometres. I have ordered the entire central sectors closed to traffic for a period of five days before the departure. Apart from law-enforcement troops and possibly any ambulances that may be needed, only vehicles with the Second Millennium passes will be allowed entry to that area. All pilgrims have been advised that they must be parked and in their vehicles a full twenty-four hours before the departure time of noon on the thirtieth. Complete security checks will be made of all vehicles and everyone will be searched thoroughly."

"And for those caught illegally in the area?" Jacqueline asked.

"Immediate arrest and solitary confinement," answered Jackson. "We will delay the trials and executions until after the departure."

"Thank you, Pilgrim Jackson," said Jacqueline with a dismissive wave. The man bowed again and left the room.

"I assume that my rules for entry to this pilgrimage were followed?" said Jacqueline when the door had closed again. The woman who had spoken earlier rose to her feet.

"Absolutely, Holiness," Pilgrim Batterson said. "Apart from children, only those who have previously been admitted to the ranks of Pilgrim have been accepted for this great work. All of those were from the top levels of pilgrims with the highest scores in the tests, and the best reports from the security investigations. We have pilgrims from all over the world of Maragos. Three thousand are coming from Australia. A further five thousand are coming from Malaysia, two thousand from South Africa, and twelve thousand from assorted areas in the Far East. Over forty thousand will be coming from various locations in Europe, and eighteen thousand from Central and South America. The rest all originate in North America."

"Thank you," said Jacqueline, and the other woman sat down. "If that is all, this meeting is closed."

The men and women round the table all stood up.

Maragos raised her arms above her head. "We thank you, Maragos," she intoned. "Our thanks for the wisdom and love You have given us, and for the strength You have give this Council for the enforcement of Your words." She lowered her hands and looked round the room. "The Light of Maragos be upon you all," she said, and stood still while the rest of the Council filed from the room.

* * *

On August the First in the year that was called 2000 ME (Maragosian Era) by the dominant religious organization in the world, the Second Millennium Assembly of the Church of Maragos left to travel to the site of the old city of Washington in the Dead Territories. Smaller gatherings had taken place on this spot the same day every year, because the date was the holiest in the Maragosian Calendar and the site was the most revered. This assembly, however, was to be the greatest ever.

The Pilgrimage was established by the Maragosian Church as a holy event. Completion of at least one such trip in a lifetime was considered essential for a true Maragosian. The title of Pilgrim, gained by completing the journey, had become a prerequisite for social and business success in all endeavours.

However, much legalistic and religious debate occurred over some aspects of the Pilgrimage. Church dogma accepted that Emma Dylan and Simon Halliday were reincarnations of Jacqueline Carter and Philippe Leger. It accepted that Michael Alexander was a powerful soul, though much philosophical debate raged within the Church as to the precise nature and identity of him. Most commonly, Michael was believed to be a holy spirit, the First Servant of Maragos, who had appeared in incarnations with previous great prophets of the past. Similarly, the second woman, Julianne, was accepted as a holy person, a friend of Saint Philippe and Saint Jacqueline, though her identity had never been firmly settled. Because of the origin of the Alexandrine Pilgrimage, Los Angeles, the birth city of Saint Michael became the Maragosian Holy City in 1112 ME. It was the seat of the Maragosian Council that became the effective World Government after the Holy War of 1887 ME that had left only Scandinavia and a few other small territories free of the Church's authority.

The central theme of debate about the Pilgrimage was on the nature of the Third Man who joined the group as they neared Washington. The Church rejected as blasphemy the entries in the diaries that stated that the Third Man was Maragos returned. It was ruled that such references were forged by later historians as an attempt to promulgate heretical teachings. Eventually, the Church dictated that the Third Man was an allegorical person, intended to show that the Holy Spirit of Maragos was with the Pilgrims to protect them from Horning's demons that haunted the Dead Territories.

The story of The Alexandrine Pilgrimage to Washington was a standard element of Maragosian Dogma.

Most of the formulation of Maragosian Doctrine had been completed at the same Council of Dublin that had created the position of Chief Servant of Maragos. The Council had approved the creation and publication of the Maragos Bible. Much of the Bible was a final consolidation of the legends surrounding the events of the Coming of the Infinite Soul. Although many followers of what would become the Church of Maragos had worried at the time that legends had been manifested as Truth, and that many segments appeared to satisfy political agendas rather than provide spiritual guidance, the Maragos Bible had been accepted, and within a few hundred years, was taken without question as the Divine Word of Maragos. As the Church of Maragos acquired dominant political power throughout the world, any such questions faded.

The wide-spread familiarity with the concepts of Maragosian teaching, the acceptance of reincarnation and the belief in the Million Infinite Souls that comprised The One, all these concepts that had been widely accepted for a thousand years after the execution of the Maragos Four had been lost by this time, and any resurgence of such thinking was forcefully suppressed by the theistic World Government of the Maragosian Council. Only a few areas were left in the world where original Maragosian philosophies held, and these became totally isolated as time wore on.

The selected half-million members of the congregation of the World Church of Maragos came to celebrate this most holy of days in their family transports, vehicles little different from the one used by Michael Alexander on the pilgrimage to Washington only a few years after the Murder of God. Tradition stated that, where possible, the travellers to the assemblies should follow the path originally taken by the Alexandrine Pilgrimage, and most of the worshippers would do so. The most privileged body always left from Los Angeles, the Holy City of Saint Michael. The second convoy traditionally left from the birth city of the current Chief Servant of Maragos, though pilgrims could join at any location, or simply make their own way to Washington at any time between the beginning of July and September the Sixth, a date that had been determined to be the Day They Murdered God.

Pilgrim Jackson stood on the dais in front of City Hall on the morning of the departure and watched the fleet of vehicles take formation. In the silent, deserted streets, only the pilgrims' vehicles and the police armed cruisers were to be seen.

"You have done well," Jackson said to his Police Commander, Fletcher Pilgrim Webley.

Pilgrim Webley didn't look at his boss as he replied. His cold eyes continued to sweep the area so that instant action could be taken if any heretics dared show their faces.

"Thank you, Pilgrim," Webley replied.

"It will a pleasure to get rid of that Stewart bitch for a few weeks," said Jackson. "We'll be able to get some work done around here."

"Indeed," agreed Webley noncommittally. "Once they've left, we'll start to take care of the ones we picked up."

"Good," said Jackson. "Keep it quiet."

"Don't I always?" replied Webley.

The group from Los Angeles first travelled to the Holy Site of Lincoln in the ancient area of Nebraska, where the Alexandrine Diary had recorded that the First Pilgrims, as Michael Alexander's group was known, had stopped and met with the mysterious figure known as Peter the Pilot. He was so named because of the obscure entry in the diary written by Michael Alexander that had referred to the famous closing words of the meeting as being "a Pilot's farewell," but gave no further clarification

In Lincoln, the pilgrims stayed for five days of worship and prayer. They asked for the blessings of Peter, the Servant of Maragos, and of Saint Philippe who had once dwelt in the Vatican Darkness as Pope Jean-Pierre, until he had found the Presence of Maragos. They asked for the love of Saint Raoul, Friend of Saint Philippe and who had followed him out of the Darkness of The Vatican to the Light of Maragos. They prayed for the Grace of Saint Jacqueline, Sacred Companion of Saint Philippe, for her everlasting purity.

At the close of the Lincoln Assembly, the congregation was led in prayer by the Chief Servant of Maragos, Jacqueline the Thirty-Fifth. She completed the closing ceremonies with the traditional and mysterious words from the Alexandrine Diaries that had recorded the last moments of the Lincoln Stay of the First Pilgrims. Many thousands of hours of scholarly research had been dedicated to analysing the meaning and derivation of the Words of Power, but no agreement had been reached in the last fifteen hundred years. The only certainty was that Peter had spoken them directly to Emma Dylan as the group's vehicle had left Lincoln.

"No more than ten seconds, remember," said Jacqueline, Chief Servant of Maragos.

"No more than ten seconds," the worshippers intoned, heads bowed deeply.

"In combat," said Jacqueline, Beloved of God. "Don't fly more than ten seconds straight and level."

"Ten seconds straight and level," repeated the hundred thousand, and went to their knees.

"Saint Philippe bless us," said Jacqueline the Thirty-Fifth.

"Maragos bless us," said the congregation.

"Saint Raoul bless us," said the Chief Servant.

"Maragos protect us," said the congregation.

"Saint Jacqueline bless us."

"Maragos be with us," said the congregation.

"And may Maragos bless Peter the Pilot, speaker of the Words of Power, and lead us safely to Washington."

"Glory be to Maragos," said the congregation.

The area resembled a storm hitting a wheat field as a hundred thousand worshippers rose to their feet and began to prepare for the continuation of the Second Millennium Pilgrimage to Washington.

Three hours later, the convoy resumed its path across the Dead Territories. After two thousand years, human life had not returned to the region once called the United States of America. The reasons were inexplicable. Animal life thrived, so there were no evident environmental reasons for the absence of humanity.

A few tiny outposts did exist, always just a single home occupied by a solitary human being. To the Maragosians, these sites were houses of the devil, occupied by servants of the dreaded Horning, the Great Adversary, the Enemy of Maragos. It was believed that if any True Believers, worshippers of the Church of Maragos the Supreme came into contact with these sites, the Horning would seize their souls, the true believer would die and be condemned to eternity in Horning's Pits. Legends existed that such evil had occurred in the past. Groups of believers had been recorded as having passed within such locations. They had stayed, conducted religious services and then a Horning demon had been summoned and the worshippers had died. These locations were believed to be the actual sites where Ultimate Goodness came into contact with Ultimate Evil, and the faithful were the pawns in this cosmic battle.

Some historical references said that these worshippers had actually been members of old cults, the original Christians, and that they had been sick young souls who had reverted to religious fanaticism and been returned to the Astral Plane by agents of Maragos. This belief was discouraged by the Elders of the Church of Maragos. One man had even stated his belief at a church service, that the Horning Demons were in fact Old Souls, placed there by Maragos to watch for outbreaks of the human sickness that Maragos had come to earth to heal, and that Peter the Pilot had been one such guardian. The man had been tried by a Maragosian Court and had died the next day for his heresy.

The convoy proceeded on its Pilgrimage, by-passing known Houses of Horning the Damned, and made its way to the next traditional stop, the location of the ancient and vanished City of Chicago, site of the Temptation of Michael. Several thousand vehicles straggled in over a period of two days and made camp near the lake. The second convoy met them there, having travelled from Montreal.

The land was quite flat for many miles around the southern shores of the lake, to which both the Alexandrine Diaries and ancient maps gave the name of Michigan. A small obelisk had been erected on what was believed to be the site of the Temptation, about a half kilometre from the lake shore. The legends said that once this had been a huge city, and that the spot where the First Pilgrims had met Evil had been a building where art and other cultural artefacts had been displayed. There was nothing now, but the obelisk. Near the marker, a large, grass-covered mound was known as "The Institute" for ancient but unknown reasons. It was on that mound that the services were centered.

The congregation now numbered a quarter-million. The travellers lived comfortably in their vehicles that supplied food, toilet facilities, waste disposal features and limitless power for travel. The vehicles were nowhere near as advanced as current machines. Family transports of the year 4012 of the Traditional Christian Calendar could take their occupants to the stars if the drivers wished. But the use of such technology was banned by Maragosian beliefs that shunned all such extra-terrestrial objects as ultimately evil. The fact that similar vehicles had been used by the First Pilgrims was skated over by a compromise that said that since the Alexandrine followers had used one, the older-technology vehicles were acceptable.

After three days, when the quarter-million had achieved organization, Jacqueline the Thirty-Fifth, ninety-third Chief Servant of Maragos conducted the ceremonies of worship. Traditionally for this spot, she read the extract from the Book of Alexander in the Maragos Bible in which the First Pilgrims had reached Chicago. She told of The Temptation of Michael.

*"And Michael led his people from Lincoln to*

*Chicago, and there did they stop for rest,"* read Jacqueline the Thirty-Fifth from the massive, leather-bound book on the stand before her. She stood on the mound of The Institute by the obelisk, and the crowd stretched to the lake on one side and for a kilometre in every other direction. *"And Michael looked on the land around him, and saw chaos and death. And Michael knew that the emptiness around him was the price the people of that city had paid for the Murder of God, the torture of Maragos and Her followers. So too, had the other cities paid for this crime, for all of them were dead."*

"Glory be to Maragos," said the quarter-million, and the ground trembled as if a tiny earthquake had struck it.

*"And then did Michael see the form of Evil,"* continued the Chief Servant of Maragos. *"Creeping out from the depths of hell below the ground, three Demons of Horning did approach."*

*"'What evil brings you here?' demanded Michael of the Demons.*

*"'We offer you all the riches of the Universe,' said the first Demon to Michael. 'For we are X'Kasxi, travellers through the Universe. Come with us, leave Earth and command the heavens. Come with us, and all the stars and all the planets of the firmament are yours, and all the beings thereon will bow before you and be your servant.'*

*"And Michael was confused by the Demons from Horning, and tempted by the infinite riches of Evil. He looked at his people, at Julianne and Emma and Simon, and saw that they too were tempted. And he turned back to the Demon and he said 'I am the servant of Maragos and I will not listen to your Evil. Horning and Crossman are your masters.'"*

"Glory be to Maragos," said the quarter-million, and the ground trembled again.

*"And the Demons did see that Michael was pure in the light and the love of Maragos, and they did*

*bow down before him. 'Forgive us, Michael,' said the Demons. 'Give us your blessing and let us be in the light of Maragos.'*

*"But Michael saw that this was a trick by the servants of Horning and Crossman, and he did say to the Demons 'I command you, return to the pits of hell from whence you came, to the territories of Horning the Damned, and Crossman the Killer of God. Maragos rules this world, and the entreaties of you and your like will not corrupt us.'*

*"And the Demons did see that Michael was strong in the all-powerful light and love of Maragos, and they did crawl back into the shadows and there they did weep."*

"Glory be to Maragos," said the quarter-million.

*"And so did the First Pilgrims continue on their way to Washington."* Jacqueline the Thirty-Fifth closed the bible. "As shall we all," she continued, raising her hands to the sky. "Like Michael, we travel in the light and love of Maragos. In Washington we will pray for the rest of Humanity. We will ask Maragos that our fellow humans abandon this commerce with other races, for they are but the manifestation of evil on Earth. We will remember the Murder of God and pray that we are granted the Grace of Maragos."

"Glory be to Maragos," shuddered the ground.

"So let us go forward to Washington," said Jacqueline the Thirty-Fifth, still with her hands in the air.

"Maragos be with us," said the quarter-million and the earth erupted as they broke camp for the final stages of the Pilgrimage to Washington.

A week later, the quarter-million had doubled again as all the other convoys finally reached Washington.

The site of the Old Capitol Building was well established, though there was nothing to mark it other than a small stone obelisk a meter high. A second, larger obelisk stood in the spot where the wooden platform had held four electric chairs for the execution of The Four, two thousand years ago.

God had died here, in company with Saint Philippe, Saint Raoul and Saint Jacqueline, murdered by the Devil in the shape of William Horning and his Chief Demon, Crossman. The murder had been witnessed by The Great Betrayer Lavalier, the servant of Pope Pius the Thirteenth, known as the Anti-Maragos, and by Alan Drew the Weak, once a servant of Saint Philippe, but who had walked away from the blessed saint in Philippe's hour of pain and suffering.

It took another week for organization and management to be established, by which time the vehicles had been arranged in streets lined north and south, east and west, centered on ground zero, the two small obelisks that marked the spots where history had begun. On the eve of the holiest day of them all, the night before the end of the second millennium of the Murder of God, families did as Maragosian families had done for centuries before, and visited each other's homes, feasted, and gave presents to each other. Most of them also decorated their homes with lights and with streamers. Maragos Eve was a wonderful time, especially for children, who could hardly restrain their excitement about the presents they would find under their beds sometime after midnight.

The following morning dawned crisp, beautiful and clear, traditional weather for Maragos Day, as it was written that such was the weather on the Day They Murdered God. In all the hundreds and thousands of vehicles around the mobile city, people awoke, smiled with delight and spoke the words for the day.

"Maragos will Live Again!" they said to each other as they embraced. The children ran around with their new toys, delighted by the perfect weather. "Maragos will Live Again!" they cried to each other, and prepared for the ceremonies that would take up most of the day.

By eleven, everybody was ready. They sat on the chairs that they had moved out of their vehicles and arranged in rows in the streets. Half a million people sat quietly and waited for Jacqueline the Thirty-Fifth, Chief Servant of Maragos to address them.

"The welcome of Maragos to you all, and Her love and light be upon you," she said, her hands held facing upward at shoulder height. She was dressed in pure white flowing robes, a gold chain around her neck. The Hair of Jacqueline was on her head. Her words were transmitted from a small device on her podium to speakers in all the vehicles. The use of the alien telepathic golden maple leaves was theoretically banned by Maragosian tradition, at least on Holy Days.

"Blessed be Maragos," murmured the half-million, and the ground vibrated with them.

"This is the day, two thousand years ago, that Horning and the Demons of His Pits of Hell thought they had won a victory by causing the Death of God," she said, and lowered her hands. "But how could they truly kill God? For Maragos is The One Supreme, the Creator of All, Immortal Mother, the God of Love. Our tragedy today is that not all of Humanity has seen the light, the word and the life as we have. They embrace the path of Evil that Maragos showed to us as temptation, and they embrace it gladly. They travel to the stars with the alien species and believe them to be equal to Mankind, even part of Maragos Herself. They live with the fruits of this evil, the toys, the gadgets, not knowing that Maragos Herself laid for them this slippery path to everlasting Hell."

Jacqueline raised her hands again, this time well above her head, and looked at the sky. "But now we see the signs that evil is truly defeated! We hear that some of these alien species have vanished, their planets left bare. Maragos triumphs! Her enemies are dying!"

"Glory be the name of Maragos!" intoned the half million, and moved to their knees. The ground rumbled.

*"THIS WILL REALLY HAVE TO STOP!"*

The voice came clearly from the centre of the crowd where Jacqueline was standing. It was heard with perfect clarity by everybody, and the power within the voice stunned the half-million into silence. Faces looked up from the kneeling hordes. The sight they saw froze them even more.

Jacqueline the Thirty-Fifth, Beloved Chief Servant of Maragos was standing as she had been, but her hands were now at her face, her eyes wide in horror. She was staring at the other presence next to her. A young woman had appeared. She was dressed in a business suit of the pattern of two thousand years before, exactly like many of the photographs and paintings of Maragos had shown her. Deep red hair fell to her shoulders. She was beautiful.

"Honestly, it's time this whole nonsense came to an end," said the newcomer. She was turning all ways to look at the crowd. "You've been talking this utter garbage about me for fifteen hundred years. Haven't you had enough?"

Still the silence roared round the miles of parked vehicles. The woman chuckled. "Well, you've been waiting for me for all these years, and here I am. So now what do you want to do?"

A sigh ran through the half-million.

"Maragos!" they said. They felt the vibration of their own voices through their knees. Many began to weep. But from the other woman by the obelisk, a scream of rage was emitted.

*"Kill her!"* screeched Jacqueline, Chief Servant of God, Beloved of Maragos. "Kill the fucking bitch!" She stared furiously round the immediate crowd, seeking

the armed guards posted at strategic locations. "What the hell are you waiting for?" she shrilled, spit falling from her mouth. "Shoot her! She's another impostor!"

There was no movement in the crowd.

The newcomer smiled and extended one hand to the furious woman. "I thought you were supposed to be my servant?" she said. She looked around the crowd again.

"I am Maragos," she said, "and this silliness must end." She turned round a full circle. "You see, here I am after all this time and you have no idea at all of what to do. Doesn't that suggest that all this claptrap is based on nothing?"

The sounds of weeping were becoming more evident. Thousands among the crowd were sobbing, others were simply staring at Maragos in a shock so severe that it was almost catatonic.

"I said I would be here with you till Oneness," said Maragos, "and I have never been away. The sickness is among you again. You've reverted almost to the dark ages. You're almost as bad as Horning's bunch and I'd hoped we'd lost that nonsense by now. Still, things are getting better. All those millions who went off elsewhere to heal, that's working. They'll start coming back soon. And I've grown a lot since my last appearance, so I can heal a lot of you today. But all this garbage you've been throwing around, I can't let that go on. You'll have to have another go at being human beings, I'm afraid."

She turned another full circle, pausing slightly as she faced Jacqueline the Thirty-Fifth, then finished the turn.

"In this life," she said, "you have yet again shown your failure to stand on your own two feet. You needed the prop of this garbage religion, just as millions of sick souls needed religious props in the past. I see much of the disease still in your souls, and I think most of you had better go elsewhere to be healed. But for all of you now, this is the end. Go now, do better on the next attempt."

From her immediate vicinity, people began to collapse. The falling of bodies to the ground spread outward like ripples in a pond. Five minutes later, the half-million were dead. All over the world, the same happened to the leaders of the Church of Maragos. Total, heart-breaking grief struck them all as their entire universe of beliefs collapsed around them. Then they died.

Maragos remained standing in the centre of the huge expanse of death. She looked at the mad eyes of Jacqueline the Thirty-Fifth. "Really, Gregory," she said. "You slipped through the mesh and had another reincarnation on Earth. It seems you and your former master have both found difficulties in absorbing your lessons."

The insane eyes of the other woman opened wider until white surrounded the pupils completely. The soul of Gregory Lavalier recalled its last life on Earth as the servant of President William Horning. It remembered the twenty-two incarnations it had experienced since, lives of dreadful pain and torture among several species, how it always died in appalling agony to help others. It recognized that some healing had taken place, some debts paid, but that somehow, it had slipped back to old habits.

"I suppose we expected too much," murmured Maragos. "After all, you have lived only twenty-three lives by this time. Plenty more to go. Well, you'd better be on your way."

The body of Jacqueline, born Aldine Stewart that had held the sick soul of Gregory Lavalier collapsed to the ground, and the soul within it flew through a billion empty light-years to suffer further as it paid its debts to Mankind.

* * *

*"I am Maragos."*

# The Nightmares of God

The voice was gentle and warm, yet reverberated throughout the world. In every city of Earth, in small towns, villages, the tiniest communities, it was heard as clearly as if the speaker was merely in the next room, or a few yards away, and people stopped motionless, riveted by the power and yet also the sweetness and love in the voice. Such gentleness and loving warmth had not been much in evidence for the last thousand years anywhere in this Earth of the Maragosian Council, and people's souls responded.

The magnetism woke those who were in night zones when Maragos spoke, drew the others from whatever tasks were engaging them, interrupted meals, stopped meetings, sessions of worship of Maragos The One, lovemaking, fights, political oratory, funerals, everything. It pulled all the people of the world outside and to the centre of their communities.

When the people had reached the town squares, city halls, village offices or simply the spaces before the community leaders, Maragos appeared to each and every one of them. "I am Maragos," she said again, in two hundred different tongues, audible to the deaf and visible to the blind. "I am an Infinite Soul. I am not Maragos The One. I am not the Creator of All. I am not God. In your beliefs, you have taken a path that is not that which I intended you would. You have followed the same roads of ignorance, evil, violence and ugly bigotry that has plagued you since the beginning. It must stop or eternal night will fall on Creation."

She paused, and to every man, woman and child watching, she seemed to peer into the deepest recesses of the soul. A huge grief began to bite into the hearts of the watchers and sobs started to break out among them.

"The sickness is stronger with most of you than it was when I first came to you," Maragos continued. "Even now, we have underestimated how powerful, how resilient to treatment is this hideous illness. Just a few hundred thousand of you in one place, this one small planet, and the disease grows, spreads blackness through your souls and hides you from Oneness. So you must leave this little Earth, all except for the few healthy ones among you. Those healthy souls may stay, live in peace until they die, but no new souls will come to Earth for many centuries."

The weeping grew throughout every community on Earth. Just a few people, scattered through some towns understood what was taking place, but their own sadness at what they saw had to happen to Mankind overwhelmed them all.

"You must go elsewhere," said Maragos softly. "Nearly all of you now living on this poor, sick planet, and the billions of you waiting for an incarnation, much of your future must be spent far from here. The other species of The One will welcome you. They are not the evil demons the Councils have taught for so long. They are your brothers and sisters, and you must go and live with them for many lives. Then you may return home, but not before every atom of this sickness has been burned from you."

She paused and looked around her. "I am with you till Oneness," she said. "Just as I have promised since my first day, and I will watch over each and every one of you till that time. But now you must go on your travels."

She stood motionless, and to every watcher throughout Earth, her image glowed with a beautiful radiance that drove the darkness away and left the shadows of evil and disease racing for cover.

The deaths began at that moment, in a widening circle from the centres where the images of Maragos stood. Bodies collapsed to the ground, leaving just a few here and there who were the tiny number of healthy souls among humans. When all were dead, Maragos smiled at those who remained.

"The rest of your lives can be spent in peace and

freedom from this ugliness. No more will you be persecuted and murdered for your understanding of why I came here so long ago. But you will have few children, and those will only be healthy souls, for I cannot allow the numbers to grow to the point that seems to protect the sickness. When you have gone, most of you will remain on the Astral Plane, and some of you will be born again on Earth to maintain the physical race. All those who have just left will not return until it is time to live on a healed Earth for the last incarnations of the Children of Man."

All over the world, the bodies of the dead flickered with light then vanished. Shell-shocked by the events, the last humans on the planet began to stumble away from the empty communities and cities. Around the world, less than a hundred thousand remained to adjust slowly to their new world and settle for their last years, knowing that few of them would be back until Oneness was nearly upon them.

The image of Maragos stood silently for a few moments, tears flooding down her face. "Oh my friends, my kin, you others of the Million, how I need you," she said, her voice thick with grief. "We never knew how bad this was. I fear for us. I wait for the day when you can emerge and help me in this fight, because I begin to dread that we might not win."

For a moment longer, she stood still, then vanished from every one of the millions of locations where her image had stood and spoken to the last denizens of a sick world.

In the empty blackness between the stars and the galaxies, ten billion human souls flew to their next lives.

# Chapter 22 - Evil Ascendant

"So, William, my sweet, are you ready to try again?"

The words drilled through the aeons-thick layer of faeces and vomit that surrounded the immobile body of William Horning.

Horning stirred, but fell motionless again. It was his first movement in over three hundred years. Only dimly could he recall the time before he had been in this Hell. Minuscule motes of memory occasionally floated through his mind. There had been a time when he commanded the lives of millions. Images of his life on Mayoowani mixed with those of times when he was president of a nation on the planet Earth. One memory of death, when he thought about it, was a web of frightful images of his body being torn apart by enraged people. The other was of a massive, beautiful, but terrible creature that pointed a weapon at him and his body burned.

But these memories were rare and fleeting. Eternity was this endless room. All there had ever been for all of time and space was a world of shit and vomit surrounding him, and the massive throne on which sat a dreadful monster that sometimes stirred itself to sodomize him with horrible violence and noise.

"William, listen to me!" The awful voice of the monster rose several decibels. Horning was past fear and horror. Dumbly, he waited for the animal to move from its throne and seize him again, as it had done so often for an infinite history.

"No, Billy Boy, not that," bellowed the beast. "It's time for us to separate once more. I do so hate the sadness this will cause you, my little love, but you really must go your own way again."

Horning fought to comprehend and to find the power to move his body. After what seemed days, he found himself sitting upright. The Lizard was gazing fondly at him.

"Do you think you could do any better than last time, lover-boy?" whispered the creature at a volume that pained Horning's ears.

"L.. last time?" Horning struggled to move his mouth and push words through the thick layer of festering dirt on his face.

"Yes, you silly boy, last time," giggled the Lizard. "Last time, when you were supposed to pay off some of your debts to society, and you chickened out instead. You're getting another chance, though I can't think why."

"Oh, thank God," mumbled Horning.

*"HAHHHHHHH!"* screamed the animal. *"GOD?* Haven't you learned yet, my foolish lover? There's only Oneness, Willy, and you'd better understand it! If you don't, you'll be right back here with me!"

Horning tried to nod, but the thickness of slime on his neck prevented any movement. From the corner of his eye, he watched the hideous animal, vaguely expecting a return to the awful violence of the past centuries, and unable to arouse fear, horror or any other emotion. Something did happen, but not what he expected. The image trembled, and the Lizard spoke again, but in a weak voice.

"William, you're starting to see the truth, aren't you?" The image shivered a little more. "This is *your* Hell, my sweet boy. You created it. You can destroy..." The animal vanished.

Astoundingly, Horning's head cleared. With a bolt of white comprehension, he saw how he had created the Hell in which he had lived for the first thousand years of his self-imposed punishment, tormented by the massive Lizard, also a creature of Horning's own imagination. He understood how he had been thrown back to the same Hell by Maragos. She had simply created within him the self-disgust at his own cowardice on Mayoowani, and Horning had automatically returned himself to the tortures he understood. And with comprehension, came knowledge of power.

"So that's how it all happens," he muttered. The dreadful surroundings vanished. Horning was alone. He grinned to himself with huge delight. Something had happened within himself to reveal to his spiritual mind how one controlled the environment on the Astral Plane. He had no idea of what had revealed this power to him, but he had it, nonetheless.

A room flickered into shape around him. It was the suite in which he had lived when he was president of the United States. Horning laughed out loud and staggered to the shower, strength flowing into him like a current of electrical power. He spent an hour under the hot water, singing lustily and washing away the filth of a thousand years. His comprehension grew by leaps and bounds in that hour. He understood how he had been sent to Mayoowani and incarnated among that species. He understood the process by which Maragos had condemned him to a repeat of his millennium in Hell. He understood many things, now.

"I can be whatever I want!" he shouted to the luxurious surroundings he had created. "All is choice!"

And the diseased soul of what had once been William Hardcastle Horning knew exactly what it wanted, and how to go about getting it. He had already encountered the species that thought along the ideal lines. Life among them was what Horning would choose. Once he had finished his shower, that is.

## The Nightmares of God

* * *

The Gelkka returned home from Mayoowani, and found that other groups had also returned from conquered worlds. Some had come home in disgrace, swept off their subject planets by forces similar to those of Mayoowani. Others had returned voluntarily, sated by conquest and weary of constant mastery over others. Over the next two hundred years, all the off-world Gelkka conquerors came home to die. But instead of settling down in preparation for the next stage of spiritual development, something changed.

"We returned from the conquered worlds because we were weary of contact with inferior species, not because we were forced from them," shouted the man on the raised platform. He was tall among the Gelkka, standing a good head above most of his fellows. "Those who whine and weep that the slaves had learned how to destroy us are weaklings, scum on the slime-pools of those slave-worlds, unworthy of membership of the Gelkka."

The huge crowd standing in the central square of the capital city of Haarggka hissed massively in approbation of the words. Over half a million stood watching the man who had come from nowhere in the last year, but who spoke with compelling power about the true dreams and destiny of the Gelkka Masters. Several hundred million more watched on their screens at home all over the world.

"Lies have been spread round the Universe," the man continued. He was handsome, his skin a burnished green that glowed with an inner power. His eyes, unusually large, even for a Gelkka, seemed like black pools that drew in the light and made the brightest day seem overcast. The three mutually opposed digits of his right claw swept in a dramatic curve that seemed to encompass the empty light years of the cosmos. "The lies say that we, the Gelkka, are

569

merely one of a million other species that make up the Supreme Creator. I say to you, these lies are *filth!* How can we, the Masters, be simply one among the cattle-people we have conquered to serve us? For were we not the lords of planets across the Universe? Did we not go from Gelokk and take our places as the rulers of worlds? Is this the sign of equality with cattle?"

The hissing broke into an unconstrained siren wail of approval. All of Gelokk, it seemed, was ready to follow Lakkon, the new voice of the Gelkka species.

He had been a simple trooper on one of the last planets to be abandoned by the Masters, said the growing legend. He had been born in a small village in one of the remote provinces of Gelokk's main nation, and on the night of his birth, it was said that lightning storms of never-before-seen proportions had broken out. A single bolt of massive size had struck outside the village at the moment of birth, and night had become day. Some villagers could be found who swore that a deafening voice had been heard at that moment shouting, "Hail the Leader!"

His rise to command the following of millions had taken only a few weeks after his first speech to the Provincial Council. By acclaim, he had become the ruler of the province the day of his third and last speech, three months later. More legends, more easily confirmed this time, told that several members of the old council had died in their seats as Lakkon spoke to them, and many of the people in the audience were still in a state of slack-jawed, empty-faced helplessness days after the event, until mercifully put down by their families.

"This I tell you, fellow members of the One True Species," continued Lakkon. "The evil and vicious tales being spread among those we released from our service in the last few years, are rotting filth. They would have the Universe believe that all species will some day combine to form the Supreme Being that created all the galaxies, suns, planets and the life on them."

The power emanating from the speaker made the crowds sway backward for a moment. Every one of the Gelkka standing there, and nearly all those watching at home felt the surge of energy waving around them. It exhilarated them, raised their minds to a new awareness of Truth.

"This is truly filth," shouted Lakkon. "For the One True Creator already exists. It is ourselves. WE are the Masters. WE are the Creator. WE are God. All that must happen is for our souls to ascend to the level of Infinite Soul. That much, the cattle-people say also. But for them to claim that all their species can become Infinite Souls and then merge to one Ultimate Being, that is the heresy. Only *one* Infinite Soul exists. We are that Soul."

The silence rang through the entire planet.

"The other species are not part of this process." Lakkon's voice dropped a degree in volume but not in authority. "They are lesser beings, creations of the Gelkka for our own purpose. Rather than embark on conquest again, we Gelkka must not risk our spiritual purity. Wait until we are One, wait until we are The One God and we will then destroy the evil sub-spirits and take our rightful place on Heaven's Throne. I can show you all the way to this path, for I know it already. I ask of you now, this gift. Call for me as the leader of all of Gelokk, and I will show you the way to Oneness as the True God of all Creation. I will lead us through the growth to Infinite Soul and show you how we take the Throne of Heaven."

As the hissing of the thousands in the city square rose to painful proportions, the speaker left the platform, followed by his entourage of guards. He strode rapidly from the area and onto a transporter. He stood alone as the machine began to move through the crowds of Gelkka. Behind him, several more transporters floated along with his personal guards. Minutes later, he arrived at the mansion house which he had taken from the previous owner who had collapsed and died within seconds of meeting Lakkon face to face.

The guards fell back as Lakkon entered the large, luxurious room that he had adopted as his office. Four of his councillors stood there. The tension in the room rose sharply as Lakkon entered.

"Anything yet?" he demanded.

One of the four cleared his throat. "First returns are already coming in, Leader," he said. "The whole world was ready to vote immediately, it seems."

Lakkon turned to look at the communicator screen on one wall. As the man had said, figures were starting to appear. As each adult Gelkka indicated his vote on his personal communicator and let the device read the owner's eye-print, the vote was recorded in the central computers in the city. The figures were instantaneously broadcast to the communication screens around the world.

Dead silence ruled the room for the next hour. At the moment at which the approval votes reached the critical point determining victory, a small sigh ran round the room.

"You have succeeded, Leader, as we all prayed and knew you would."

Lakkon turned to the speaker. "Begin identifying those who voted against us and liquidate them. We shall start our reign with a clean slate."

The man left, and Lakkon turned to the others. "We begin the work at once. Notify each of the five hundred spiritual teachers we have identified to prepare training programs for everybody. Schools and universities must make their primary task the teaching toward spiritual growth. Each and every Gelkka from this point on must be trained toward directing their energies to ascendancy to Infinity. The work will last beyond our lifetime, and must not ever stop."

"Yes, Leader," murmured another of the advisors.

Lakkon stopped and stared at the floor for a few seconds. When he looked up again, his face wore an expression of slight puzzlement. "And from this moment, a new name applies," he said. "We shall be known as, and addressed simply as Horning."

"Horning, Leader?" stammered one of the men.

Lakkon still looked puzzled. "This has been given to us by the race memories of all the Gelkka," he said. "It is a name of great power that somehow was lost in the past millennia. We know it, but we have never heard of it before, but yet we know that it is true. Our name, our title, our presence will be Horning."

The three men bowed.

"Yes, Horning," they said.

Horning, the new Leader-for-Life of all the Gelkka smiled. "Prepare the meeting room for a world-wide broadcast. We will go on air in one hour." He turned and strode from the room as the others bowed deeply again.

* * *

Mayoowani began to empty of people. A few centuries before, Calasanai, the Saviour had walked the whole world and shown his people how to dream dreams of power. The power grew so great that the Gelkka faded, grew weak, and finally bought passage from their one-time vassal world. When the huge shuttle ships descended from the skies to lift the shattered Masters to the Kaloti vessels, the Mayoowi watched in silence, but triumphant in their power. With that power grew the legends of the one who had died so that Calasanai could live and save his world.

His name was Lawindinai, said the legends, and he died in the town of Liamondooni, that became a sacred site to the Mayoowi people. The town was also the site of the great treachery of Raiwandoo, the only Mayoowi to join the Gelkka as a willing servant. That name was cursed by every Mayoowi who ever lived, but until the end, the name of Lawindinai was spoken with reverence, love and the blessings of a people released from savage slavery by this act of selflessness.

With the departure of the Gelkka Overlords, most of the planet's people completed their cycle to final-stage Old Soul level and abandoned the physical cycles. The remaining few hundred thousand, many of whom were human souls, experienced an increasingly nomadic existence, living intensely spiritual lives in close harmony with the land and the forces of life. The healing process accelerated rapidly, until five thousand years after the Gelkka had left, the final human-ensouled Mayoowi left the planet also.

X'Katcxo became empty at the same time. The final Old Soul X'Kasxi abandoned their physical cycle and moved to the Astral Plane. Over thirty million remaining X'Kasxi, holders of the souls of human beings, died within a normal lifetime, and the human souls went to other species to continue their healing. Among them were the souls of beings once known on Earth as John Donald Parker, Henry Acheson and George Rolfe.

By then, four hundred and ninety thousand of the home planets populated by species of The One had become empty. Simultaneously, the twelve million worlds populated by the migrations of these species also fell silent and empty. Nobody piloted the Kaloti ships anymore, because the Old Souls among the remaining species were becoming more concerned with their spiritual progression toward Ascendancy and then Infinity, than with travelling the curves of hyperspace.

The task of the Speakers thus became less essential. As they realized that they could perform their function from the Astral Plane as effectively as they could from incarnate form, and as the need for these services declined, more and more Speakers completed their physical cycle and remained on the Astral. They continued to provide communication services to those races still within their incarnate cycles, and communed with other Infinite and Ascendant Souls on the nature of the Universe and the quest for The One's answer to its problem. Several noted the total silence from the Gelkka Ascendant Souls and eventually the Gelkka Infinite Soul. When they tried to establish contact, they were met by a savage silence. But other transactions were in progress, and the Gelkka's cosmic absence was largely ignored.

Speaker Nine Hundred and Twelve died, reincarnated a thousand years later and was named Speaker Two Hundred and Forty Three, one of the last Speakers to choose a physical life again. He lived another twelve hundred years before again dying and regaining his memories of his human origins. Raoul Carmagio returned to the galactic regions of Earth to await the coming of the end.

A thousand years later, the Speakers made almost an instantaneous leap from Ascendant Souls to merging to Infinite Soul level. Several million years of telepathic communication between themselves and other species had made the process of integration almost automatic. Almost at the same time, two other Infinite Souls evolved to self-awareness. None of them was able to establish coherent communication with the Gelkka, who were about to make the step to merge as a single Infinite Soul.

The One was growing more and more awake. But within one Infinite Soul, one millionth of The One's being, the sickness was already powerful and preparing to take its host to the ultimate prize, the Throne of Heaven.

# Chapter 23. Horning's Heaven

The soul that once had been housed in the body of William Hardcastle Horning knew that it deserved one particular experience. As he completed his most recent incarnation as the great Universal Leader of the Gelkka, dying amid world-wide mourning through every community on Gelokk, he was given it.

"William, My much beloved son, welcome to your rightful place in Heaven!"

Horning woke to brilliant white light streaming over the entire universe. Soft music, in which the sound of gentle harp-strings seemed to predominate, played around him. Wonderful aromas wafted in the light breeze. He looked around him and saw that he was in a huge, incredibly vast hall. Stained glass windows stretched on all sides to infinity. The ceiling was vaulted like an immense cathedral, while perfect, fluffy clouds drifted among the heights. On all sides, crowds of people, dressed in purest white robes, stood silently, faces aglow in adoration.

And in front of him, seated on a massive, golden throne, was God.

Horning fell to his knees in worship.

"No, no, My son," thundered the glorious tones of the voice of the Supreme Being, the Creator of All Things. "It is not for you to kneel before Me. You are My favourite son, beloved of Heaven, equal to any of My angels. Come, William, My son, take your rightful place, sit at My right side."

Feeling soaring pride, Horning rose to his feet. This, he knew, was correct. This was the proper place for him to be, not in some cruel hell with a monstrous lizard. That, Horning decided, was simply an appallingly vicious trick played on him by that awful woman Maragos, the agent of Lucifer.

He smiled at God. "Thank You, Lord," he said, his voice swelling with power to echo through the Halls of Heaven. A wave of beautiful music traced his words, the choir of Angels seeing that Horning's speech was almost as magnificent, as powerful and as omnipotent as the Words of God.

Horning rose to his feet and walked slowly toward the Throne of Heaven. As he neared the glowing, golden structure, he saw the second throne, next to, but a little lower than the seat on which God Himself sat. Feeling happiness suffuse throughout his body, Horning climbed the few steps to his own throne, then stopped as God rose to His feet.

The presence was so overwhelming, that Horning sank to his knees again.

"No, William, that really isn't necessary," thundered the Voice of God. A huge hand appeared before Horning's face. Trembling, Horning reached out his own and took the Hand of the Creator. Power raged through him and he found himself on his feet, looking into the Eyes of the Supreme Being.

"You are the most favoured of all My children," said God, smiling with love into Horning's face. "You defended My Name against Lucifer's demons, the proponents of Oneness, and I will be grateful to you for all time for that service."

"And I shall defend it for all time, Lord," replied Horning, feeling more and more composed with each second. He was where he had always known he should be, on a throne at the right hand of God, the most favoured of all humans, recognized at last as superior to all others, equal to the Angels of Heaven, individually blessed by God.

He took another step up, and God returned to His seat, smiling affectionately as Horning turned and sat slowly on the Second Throne of Heaven. But a sudden thought struck Horning.

"Lord, where is Your Son, the Lord Jesus Christ?" he asked. "Should he not be here in this seat?"

God waved a hand, and a chord of immensely beautiful Angelic voices soared through the vaults of Heaven.

"He has other duties," said God carelessly. "Most of the time, I don't know where he is. But now that you are here, it matters less and less."

With a wave of delight, Horning recognized the soundness of God's words. After all, Jesus had done less than he to protect His Father's Name. Jesus had merely spoken to crowds of Jews in a small country. Horning had fought with energy, killing the enemies of God, teaching them the error of their ways, defending God as the last warrior, far greater than that little wimp, the last Pope, Pius the Thirteenth. William Horning knew that he deserved the sole spot at God's right hand.

"How can I serve you, Lord?" asked Horning. The echo of Angels' voices underlined his words.

"Your word is My word, William My son," replied God with a warm smile. "You will rule in My place when I have other matters to attend to. But do not weary yourself, for I will value your conversation, your ideas, your input as we talk. There are Angels to follow your every instruction."

"The Angels, Lord? They will obey me?"

God laughed softly, and the wonderful sound ran round the vaults of Heaven like music in a cathedral.

"Michael! Gabriel! Attend me," said God.

There was a rustle of movement in the adoring crowds lining the walls. From a distant corridor, two mighty shapes appeared, preceded by a glow of pure, white light. The beings stood several inches taller than any of the other mere human souls, and their wings stretched behind them in magnificent arcs of glowing white feathers. Their faces glowed with internal light, and above their heads, beautiful haloes shone with the fire of the stars.

The two fantastic creatures approached the thrones and bowed low.

"Michael, Gabriel, this is William Horning, My favoured son," said God. A short chord of unfathomable beauty echoed His words.

"Then I, the Keeper of the Gates of Heaven, and my colleague Michael are your servants, William, Son of God," said one, presumably Gabriel. Both Archangels bowed low before Horning.

Horning took a deep breath. God had proclaimed his true place in the upper reaches of Heaven.

"Thank you," said Horning. "Perhaps you could show me around?"

God laughed with delight, and lights and colours played and danced through the vaults and windows of the great hall.

"No, William," said God. "That will be My pleasure. Come, My Son, let Us take a walk through Our Kingdom."

The two Archangels looked disappointed, but bowed again, and moved away.

God rose to His feet and looked back at Horning. He smiled and crooked His head in an obvious invitation. Horning stood up and followed God down the steps of the thrones. As they moved along the hall, the crowds of human souls bowed before them. Horning barely glanced at them in contempt. They were merely ordinary humans, not warriors for their God as he, Horning had been.

He followed a couple of paces behind the huge, beautiful shape of God as He strode masterfully along the corridors of Heaven. As they left the great hall, the corridor was equally vast, with massive, open windows every few yards. Horning moved to one side and looked out as he passed one of the portals. He saw white clouds, bright sun and golden light. Several of the clouds appeared to have a small number of white-robed souls sitting in graceful positions on them. Horning smiled happily. It was exactly as he had envisaged Heaven all his life as a human. He hurried forward again and caught up with God.

"There, William," said God, pointing to His right with His enormous hand. "There is where those who did not follow your leadership wait for My pleasure to decide their fates."

God paused by a balcony. Horning walked forward and looked over. The distance seemed to be a hundred feet to the floor where thousands of humans roamed in random patterns. All seemed to be weeping. They wore rags, stained and torn.

"Who are they, Lord?" asked Horning, staring with fascination at the misery below him.

"Not the worst of the sinners," replied God. "Only those who have not yet seen My light. They are the Moslems, the Buddhists, the other Pagans, those who were too far away to receive your wisdom and encouragement, William My son. Slowly, they begin to see where they are, and will accept Me."

"What of the Jews, Lord?" asked Horning. "And the Blacks?"

An expression of distaste crossed God's face. "In Hell, where they belong," said God. "For the Jews killed My only son, and the Children of Ham, they so offended Me that I burned them that colour so that they would roam the earth wearing the sign of My displeasure for all time."

Horning felt a glow of delight. To be hearing the confirmation of his views by the Lord God Himself was a wonderful sensation.

"And can we see Hell, Lord?" he asked.

God nodded. "It is one of My pleasures to look down and watch My enemies suffer," He said. "Come, the Entrance to Hell is over here."

He walked a few yards further along to another balcony, and to a pair of golden thrones that sat raised above the ledge so that an uninterrupted view downward existed. God took His seat on the higher throne and waved a friendly arm at the other.

"That is your seat, My son," He said. "I placed them here because I know you will spend much time here with Me, watching the suffering of My enemies."

Gingerly, Horning edged his way to his throne and sat. He looked down into the pit. The first screams of the damned reached his ears and he leaned forward. It was like looking down into a massive open-cut quarry, with successively lower rings spiralling down into the far-distant depths. Below the first few rings, however, smoke and flames obscured his vision, to his disappointment.

Just below him, the first path led to the highest circle. Horning stared eagerly at the sight of hundreds of people being herded along by demons with pitchforks and spears. The moans of horror and the screams of pain as the demons jabbed ferociously at their victims was music to Horning's ears. Many turned their faces upward to the battlements of Heaven and saw the Supreme Creator. They raised their arms in pleading and supplication but received no recognition from the occupant of the Golden Throne.

"They are the followers of Oneness," said the electrifying tones of God. "These were the evil ones who disobeyed your word while on Earth, William. They allied with Maragos, the demon bitch from Hell, and now they pay the price. They will spend aeons being sent further down and down to the lowest pits of hell before I turn My face to them again. Their fate is in your hands now, William. In a millennium or two, you can decide if they can be saved."

Happily, Horning watched the weeping lines of the damned moving into Hell. With a jolt, he recognized the immense figure standing by the gateway to the first circle. The Lizard looked up as Horning stared at it. For a second, the evil, monstrous mouth gaped open in a dreadful grin, and the snake tongue flickered out and back. Horning felt a wave of pure horror and sat back in his throne. But the Lizard bowed its head at Horning.

"It cannot hurt you now, William, My son," said God, touching Horning on his shoulder in a loving manner. "That servant of Maragos has no powers in Heaven."

"Thank you, Lord," said Horning, his courage returned.

"I must go and attend to some small duties," said God, rising to His feet. Horning began to rise also, but God stopped him. "No, stay, My son, enjoy this sight for as long as you wish," He said. "You have earned the right. We shall talk again further."

God moved away, and Horning's eyes followed Him for as long as he could, waves of pride flooding through him as he realized once more, that he, William Hardcastle Horning was at last in his rightful place, at the right hand of the Lord God.

He looked back down into the pits of Hell, recognizing with a glow of purest joy, the weeping forms of Philippe Leger and the other two humans who had died before him so long ago in Washington. The three shapes stared up at him.

"Mister President!" called Leger. "My Lord, I beg of you, intercede with God for us! Save us from Hell!"

Horning laughed at them. His laughter continued as he watched the three being herded past the dreadful Lizard and into the first Circle of Hell.

Heaven was precisely the way it ought to be.

William Horning strolled through the corridors of Heaven, occasionally nodding at the hordes of souls who moved aside to let him pass, bowing low as they did. The music of the Choir of Angels accompanied his every move. He had been in Heaven several months now, he estimated, and every day had been an exciting episode of wonder, happiness and fulfilment. Several times, he had dined with God and a select group of Angels, usually the Archangels Gabriel and Michael, and the conversations had been brilliant, profound and deeply satisfying, as the three divinities asked Horning's opinion on matters of policy for ruling the Universe.

Most days, Horning spent some hours seated on the balcony overlooking the entrance to Hell, watching the lines of terrified souls being herded to everlasting torment and horror. His most satisfying experiences were when thousands of the damned looked upward and raised choruses of pitiful pleas for intercession with God. Many begged Horning directly for his clemency, down on their knees in the hot dust of the ante-chamber to Hell, raising their arms, the tears rolling down their faces to drop as steam on the ground. For him to shake his head and wave at the Lizard to take them was a source of immense pride and delight. It sent waves of a forgotten sensation into the pit of his stomach. For some moments, he thought deeply about what to do. Then he smiled, recalling God's words to him, that all the Hosts and Angels of Heaven were at his service.

"Gabriel?" he said. Immediately, a flourish of trumpets sounded in the far halls, a white glow of light sent huge shadows playing in the vaults of Heaven, and a line of angels appeared, carrying horns and harps. Behind them, the Archangel Gabriel came into view, walking alone, his enormous white wings spreading across the width of the hallway through which he strode.

Horning felt a twinge of envy. The preceding choir, the trumpets, especially the glow of white light, he thought, how come only Gabriel and Michael moved through Heaven that way? Surely, he, William Horning, Beloved of God and His most favoured son, even more blessed now than Jesus, should make equally as splendid an impact? He resolved to ask God about some possibilities along these lines, next time they met. But with that decision, a small tremor of anxiety ran through him. Was he not in Heaven, the Paradise of Creation, where all souls lived in perfect peace and harmony? How could he be feeling dissatisfaction, *any* dissatisfaction with the way things were? He lost the thought as the air around him shook.

"You call and I come, Oh William, Blessed of God, Most Favoured Son of Heaven," intoned the thunderous voice of the Archangel Gabriel. "As the Lord God has instructed, your word is our command. How can I serve you?"

Horning felt a little embarrassed. He waved dismissal at the lines of lesser angels, and they retreated back along the hall.

"Something personal, William?" asked Gabriel with a smile of understanding.

"Er... yes," replied Horning, looking down at the Pits of Hell. He thought about how to broach the topic. "Is this it, Gabriel?" he asked after a moment of thought. "This is all there is of Heaven?"

"All, William? This *is* Heaven, the Home of God, Creator of the Universe, Supreme Intelligence..."

"Yes, yes, I know all that," interrupted Horning. "But is this all we get to do all day? Lie around and worship Him? Listen to your choirs and float around on clouds?"

"You should be grateful, William," replied Gabriel. "Some of us have work to do. I spend most of my days at the Gates, checking in the new arrivals, reviewing their histories and verifying their stories. And believe me, some of their lies..."

"Yes, yes, I'm sure it's damned hard work," snapped Horning. "But what do *I* get to do?"

Gabriel shrugged. "Relax and enjoy it," he said. "After all, you could be one of those poor souls down there." He pointed at the entrance to the First Circle of Hell. The Lizard looked up at that point and waved cheerfully. It seemed to Horning that the dreadful beast gave him a look of threatening laughter, and he shuddered. He looked back at Gabriel who appeared to be smiling sardonically and a tiny mote of worry trembled in his stomach. Was Gabriel laughing at him? Another cause of worry in the Divine Perfection of Heaven? He shook off the hideous thought.

"What about entertainment?" he asked the divinity.

"What could be more entertaining and satisfying than watching those damned souls enter Hell?" asked Gabriel. "Seeing others undergo punishment that we have avoided is surely the greatest of pleasures? I have thought it was perfect for you, William, you spend so much time here."

Horning shook his head in irritation. "I suppose so," he said. "But even that can get.. well, boring, after a while. I need something more... *participative.*"

"I suppose you mean sex?" replied Gabriel with a smile.

"Er... yes," agreed Horning, thankful that the matter had been raised, but concerned about the reaction it would cause.

"The way you remember it from your last time on Earth, I suppose?" continued Gabriel. Horning was sure now. The Archangel was being sarcastic. Horning felt a wave of anger. How *dare* this pipsqueak Archangel be insolent to *him*, William Horning, the favourite son of God? He drew himself up with dignity. What Horning wanted in Heaven, Horning got.

"That's right," he replied coolly.

"A young girl, a whip, a large bed, all that kind of stuff?"

"That's *enough*," snapped Horning. "Remember who you're talking to!"

Gabriel waved a hand generally in the direction of the never-ending lines of damned souls passing beneath them. "Just do what you did before," he said, ignoring Horning's anger. "Look at them, pick out anything you want, and there you go. It will be just the way you want it."

Horning stifled his anger at the obvious insolence being displayed, thinking instead about the possibilities being opened up before him.

"Okay," he said casually, and waved a hand in dismissal. The Archangel Gabriel bowed and backed away. Horning stole a glance at him, and was certain. There was a smile of deep contempt on the Archangel's face.

*Just you wait, prick*, he muttered internally. *Just wait till I get to see God next time. One complaint from me and you're history. We'll see who's the second-in-command around here.* He stilled the anger and concentrated instead on the lines of the damned souls below him. He focused his attention and began to pick out individuals. Many were female. Lots were young... there! He smiled to himself and he was suddenly in a luxurious bedroom, a copy of the one he had inhabited when he was President of the USA on Earth.

The girl looked about fifteen, slim and fresh, firm breasts standing out beautifully under a thin cotton shirt, long, bare legs beneath a torn, shredded skirt. She looked at him, and screamed.

Horning smiled with delight. All his worries about the sudden imperfections revealing themselves in a perfect Heaven were lost in the shudder of erotic joy that enveloped him. He reached for the whip.

* * *

Another evening of feasting in the private ante-room of the dining hall of Heaven. God sat at the head of the table in an enormous, ornately carved, wooden throne. Horning sat to his right, Archangel Gabriel across from him at God's left, Michael at the foot of the table. Lines of lesser angels stood along the walls in poses of adoration, while servants brought a continuous line of wondrous foods to the table. The two Archangels looked sullen, rarely lifting their heads from their plates. Horning had decided some while ago, that he detested those sanctimonious sons of bitches, with their inflated egos and over-done accompanying orchestras of angels and white light. Their obvious unhappiness pleased him greatly.

God looked thoughtful. "This sex stuff, William," He said, suddenly looking up from His diamond-edged, golden platter. "You seem to enjoy it."

Horning felt a streak of worry shoot through him. Had Gabriel complained? "Yes, Lord," he replied defiantly. "It was a wonderful concept You gave us."

"Well, it was really designed as a means of procreation," said God. "It's the same system all the mammals used, and they never seemed to get as obsessed with it as you humans did."

Horning's worry declined a fraction. God seemed more interested than censorious, he thought. It was going to be one of those conversations, Horning decided, where God would again ask his advice on how to set things up, perhaps on another world, or after the last Trump and the Day of Judgement, when everything would start again. That was an interesting concept, Horning decided with a glow of enthusiasm. Perhaps when God created the new world He would give Horning special powers over all humanity, to rule Earth in God's place. He resolved to raise the issue sometime in the next few hundred years.

"I always assumed that, in Your wisdom, Lord, You made the process pleasurable so that we would follow Your command and go forth and multiply," Horning said, proud of his answer. The irritated look he saw the two Archangels exchange pleased him. His nervousness fell away.

"You know, William, it's something I never tried, of course," said God, looking increasingly thoughtful. "Would you recommend it as a means of relaxation?"

"Oh, absolutely, Lord," Horning answered with enthusiasm. To his delight, both Archangels jumped to their feet with expressions of horror.

"Dear Lord!" shouted Michael. "God of all the Universe! This is beyond belief! Please, I beg of You, Lord, listen no more to this human! You cannot debase Yourself this way!"

"This human taints the air of Your Heaven, Lord God," shouted Gabriel.

The Supreme Creator of All Things rose to His feet. "Fuck off, the pair of you," snapped God.

Silence rang like a bell in the room. Horning shuddered with fear. Would God say such a thing to anyone, never mind the two Archangels of Heaven? What was happening in the Kingdom of God, the site of utter perfection? He shrank down in his seat, watching the expressions of unadulterated terror appear on the faces of Gabriel and Michael.

"William, come with Me," commanded God, and swept out of the dining room. Trying to still his panic, Horning followed Him.

God strode at a furious rate along the corridors of Heaven, Horning having to break into an occasional run to keep up with Him. To all sides, millions of souls bowed low as their God walked by. God ignored them all. They reached the balcony to Hell and God leaned over, not bothering to take His throne.

"What would you suggest as a first time, William?" demanded God. "Point out a likely one for Me. And one for yourself, of course."

Struggling to control his confusion and worry, Horning leaned alongside his God and looked down at the eternal lines of the damned. He began to concentrate. Several quite good-looking women caught his eye, but he passed over them. God needed something special. He saw a slender girl, perhaps no more than thirteen, with the coltish, early sexuality that so turned him on, and with a mental flip, culled her out for his own use. He heard a chuckle from God.

"Nice, William," God said. "I'm sure you'll enjoy her. Now, what about Me?"

Horning peered down again. He pointed. The woman was lush, all curves, breasts standing proudly forth under a torn, dirty smock, long, long legs beautifully revealed in the rips and tears. "That one, Lord," Horning said.

"Looks good to Me," said God.

Immediately, they were all in a massive bedroom. Two enormous beds stood alongside each other. By one, the young girl Horning had selected stood motionless, trembling. The woman selected for God already lay on the other bed, naked. Her long, blonde hair spread across the pillows, her breasts stood firmly upright, not drooping down her chest. One leg lay straight, the other bent at the knee. The pose was highly charged with eroticism.

Horning was completely without sexual excitement. The situation was just too monstrous for him to comprehend. Something was terribly wrong with Heaven. The Lord God was not supposed to stoop to fleshly pursuits and pleasures.

"Get a look at those tits!" bellowed God. "Man, this is going to be good!" He stripped off his robes and stood upright, almost touching the ceiling. Horning stared with terrified fascination. God's body was magnificent, powerfully muscled, huge shoulders billowing with rippling cords of strength, the stomach massively flat. He looked like a Greek statue, perfect in His maleness. Massive thighs joined under the torso, with genitalia of horrific proportions bursting out of a bush of red hair.

Horning shuddered. The last sight reminded him with hideous clarity of his times in Hell, lying at the mercy of the Lizard.

"What's the problem, William," said God, laughing. "Aren't you going to screw that little girl?"

"Lord...." shivered Horning. "I never expected... I never imagined..."

"What, that God might like the odd fuck?"

Horning was struck dumb. Nothing had prepared him for this. Heaven had changed since he had arrived. It was no longer the perfect place it had been.

"Well, what do you expect, you stupid bastard?" sneered God, obviously reading Horning's thoughts. "That's the effect you have on everything, Horning. You spoil things like rotten meat, everywhere you go."

"But my Lord God," babbled Horning, "surely not You? Surely not Heaven? How can I spoil Paradise, God's home? How can You be doing this thing?"

"Why not?" replied God with a laugh. He climbed onto the bed and knelt alongside the woman, kneading her magnificent breasts. She stirred and raised her arms to wrap around His neck. "Seems like a great way to pass a few hours!"

"Because You're the Lord God!" shouted Horning. Huge, globular tears of despair rolled down his face. "You can't do this!"

"Course I can, you idiot!" shouted God. "You created Me! This whole thing, this Heaven, the angels, all that shit, it's all your creation!" He rolled on top of the woman and fumbled at his groin. The woman screamed in mixed pain and delight.

"You don't understand a thing, do you?" said God. He raised Himself on His arms, looking across at Horning, while His buttocks began a slow undulation. His voice had become quiet, a little sad. "This isn't Heaven. Don't you see it yet? This is all from within your mind. Reality is only what you create it to be, William. And you can't even create your perfect Heaven without starting to corrupt it. It's the sickness within you. You can't see what we've been telling you all this time. You can't see Oneness."

"What?" Horning felt as if a monstrous mule had kicked him. The bedroom faded from around him.

"Oneness," said Maragos.

Horning closed his eyes for a few seconds then

opened them again. She stood before him, dressed in a white suit, the skirt ending just above the knees, her jacket open over a dark blue blouse buttoned to the neck. She and Horning were standing on an endless marble plain. A wave of giddiness swept through Horning and he concentrated on Maragos to try and keep his balance.

"What?" he said again.

"What are we going to do with you, William?" asked Maragos. "Every time we try and bring you to your senses and heal you a little, you collapse right back into this religious nonsense."

"What happened back there?" asked Horning, struggling to cope with the terrible shocks of the last few minutes and the disappearance of Heaven.

She didn't answer, merely looked hard at him. Horning closed his eyes again to prevent himself looking at the vertiginous, endless marble. He recalled his most recent life as the Supreme Leader of all the Gelkka, and smiled, opening his eyes as he sensed his strength return to him.

"I wanted that experience of the sort of Heaven I used to believe in as a human, didn't I?" he said.

Maragos nodded. "Now you see how powerful is pure thought," she replied.

"And I created the whole thing," he said, more to himself, sensing his wonder and triumph.

"You did," Maragos said. "Just as you created the Hell in which you spent so long. But you were unable to stop yourself destroying your Heaven. As your own Creation of God said to you, everywhere you go, you corrupt the environment like rotting meat. Your sickness is too powerful even for me to heal."

"Sickness?" roared Horning. Maragos blinked, and for a second Horning thought she looked frightened. Then he shook off that thought. An Infinite Soul, frightened? "You keep telling me about a sickness!" he continued in rage. "There is no sickness! I'm just stronger than all the others, that's all it is. I know how to control the world around me!"

Horning took his eyes off Maragos and began to pace around, no longer disconcerted by the limitless marble plain. He began to search inside himself and saw the truth of his identity.

There were numerous souls within him, he finally understood. He saw the terrified, helpless soul of Stephen Crossman, absorbed so many millennia ago, about the same time as he had absorbed the souls of visitors to the White House, the members of the congregation of the Church of the Divine Word in Bainesville, the dying heretics in the ball park in Washington, so many souls he had eaten, their energies now part of him. Horning began to understand what he was.

Throughout every evil of Earth's history, Horning had been there in one form or another, feeding on the misery, the agony and the deaths. He had been with Attila as the warlord slaughtered thousands, had sat with Kings, Emperors and tyrants through all of history, rarely the leader himself, but the advisor, the persuader, the originator of new forms of death, new levels of horror to inflict on the masses of the innocents. He had sat at the right hand of Caligula, feasting on the rivers of blood in the coliseums, counsel to the Kings of the Incas, advisor to the Druids. He had been Torquemada, the great Inquisitor and torturer of thousands. All of human misery had been the food source, the energy, the lifeblood of William Horning. Sometimes, not even incarnate, the soul of William Horning had hovered near the minds of killers and whispered his encouragement of bloody outrage to willing ears, then drank the life forces of the condemned as they died.

The soul that once had been called William Horning was more powerful than any human soul in history. No other soul had even approached the force of the evil within him.

Horning opened his eyes and smiled at Maragos. "I am beyond your control, bitch," he said calmly.

She didn't reply but Horning sensed the shock within her. "I will return to the Gelkka," he said. "We understand each other."

"I have recruited the forces I need to heal you," she replied. "The One must not awaken with your sickness still alive within It."

"Screw The One!" snarled Horning. "This is not sickness, it's POWER! And I have it! *I* am The One! *I* am God! I am the power in this Universe now, Maragos!"

"Not yet," she replied calmly.

He felt a small frisson of fear. Her shock had gone, and she radiated strength. *What had she done?*

"I am no longer the solitary Infinite Soul in the Universe, William," she said. "Others have just joined me. But even alone, I could return you to a hell even worse than the one you have experienced so far. With my colleagues, I condemn you again. But you must heal, William. Some time, however far into the future it will be, you must heal."

"Heal?" Horning over-rode his fear. "There is nothing to heal, woman! I am Horning! I will rule you!"

"If that happens, then all of Creation is damned," she replied. "We will prevent it. And while I have power over you, there is one thing to be done before you face your next life."

"And what is that, bitch?" snarled Horning. "There is nothing you can do to me!"

"I can release the human and other souls you have absorbed in the past. They must be returned to rejoin the rest of their entities and grow with their own Ascendant Souls."

As she spoke, Horning felt power drain from him. It was if a tap had opened in his mind and strength was flowing from him in a torrent. Dimly, he sensed the individual souls of those he had taken into himself rediscover their identities, and leave his control with the gladness and delight of prisoners released from black confinement in the dungeons of an ancient, evil castle. Human and Gelkka souls poured from him, each one taking another element of his power as they left. In moments, he was returned to the self he had been when he was first incarnated as William Horning.

"Goodbye, William," said Maragos firmly. "A new Hell awaits you. This time, it is a Hell of our creation, not yours. You cannot escape it through any effort of your own mind."

"The Lizard?" screamed Horning. "*I* control the Lizard! It can do nothing to me! I created it! I control everything!"

"Not quite," said Maragos. "The Lizard will be merely an unpleasantness compared to what we have for you. We will talk again in a few thousand years."

"No!" screamed Horning. "You can't! *I* am the power in this Universe! Even if you have stolen my other souls from me, I shall take more! You are nothing, Maragos! *Nothing!* You go to *my* Hell."

Maragos looked expressionless, and stared into his eyes. Horning felt a force seize him and begin to pull him along the marble plain. He exercised every atom of his power to prevent it, but he was helpless. The marble infinity faded and he was surrounded by blackness. It was dense, totally without alleviation by stars, shadows, the faint glow of distant galaxies, *anything*. It was blackness itself.

He was falling.

He could see not a molecule of light.

There was nothing.

"It is the awakening of The One," said the voice of Maragos from everywhere, nowhere. "You are utterly alone, William. Experience the agony of The One as no other soul in Creation can."

He tried to speak, to scream his fear, but in the absence of everything, the omnipotence of Nothing, no sound could escape him. He could not even hear his own breathing, for no breath moved in him.

"There is nothing here for you to corrupt." The voice of Maragos was cold, implacable. "There are no souls to feast on. No misery to cause to provide you with energy. There is Nothing. At some future time, I will send others to offer you another chance."

And then there was not even the presence of Maragos.

The soul that once had used the name of Horning was alone in a space of no Creation.

# Chapter 24 - The Void Without Form

Sometimes, he tried to scream, but he never could.

For all eternity, he had been falling through blackness. All other experiences had been forgotten. But he felt a desperate loss through all of this Hell. Somehow, he knew that once he had possessed the power to control the universe around him, but something had taken it away from him.

And still he fell through endless blackness, alone, terrified and utterly without coherent thought.

For centuries, he had no idea if his eyes were open, closed, or even if he had eyes at all.

Everything was Nothing.

When the first spark appeared, it failed to register on his awareness at all. For a time that could have been hours or thousands of years, the spark was joined by others that circled at some unknown distance, growing in numbers and brightness. When he saw them, another ageless time passed as he merely watched, not even trying to think about the nature of this first sight of anything in his third time in Hell.

The sparks circled within their own individual blocks of space, he finally saw. What had seemed merely a curtain of flashing lights could now be identified as groups of energy sources moving together and around each other.

When his dulled consciousness at last considered the possibility that he was surrounded by a number of sentient beings, his mind began to clear. With that clarity came more awareness, and he sensed the first probe in his mind.

"Who are you?" asked a silent voice in his head. There were no words, but the sensation of curiosity and query was powerful. Finding an answer took uncountable time.

"I am.... Horning," he said eventually, and the process of clearing and gaining awareness grew faster. At last he remembered how he had been thrown into the eternal blackness. Grief flooded him. He was so alone... so hated...

Horning wept. The pain of the lost millennia overwhelmed him. He understood how he had placed himself in Hell the first time, how his self-hatred had been powerful enough even to conquer his lust for power and his disgust with all other living things. That loathing of himself rose again as he recalled how he had squandered the chance for redemption when he had been sent to live among the people on Mayoowani. He saw the power of the sickness inside his soul, and how it fed off the strength of that very soul that was somehow so much more than the souls of other human beings.

"We have sought you this distance away from the Universe," said the same small voice in his mind.

"Sought... me?" Horning was struggling to comprehend through his grief. "Why?"

"To offer redemption again," the silent voice replied.

"Redemption!" Horning felt his soul convulse with longing. To be part of the Universe of souls again, to be among others for communication, for companionship, for equality without fear... how desperately he wanted that. "How?" he begged.

"By curing us," said the voice.

Horning radiated bewilderment. After such aeons in the Hell of Nothingness, he had been presented with too much data to absorb.

"We are far from the Universe of The One,"

whispered the voice. "Maragos left you here two thousand of your own years ago. She sent us to look for you. Look! See where that tiny glow can be seen?"

Horning felt his attention drawn in a particular direction and focused through the veil of sparks that he knew now were sentient beings. The glow in the absolute blackness was too tiny for him to have seen without the mental guidance he had been given. It was just a suggestion of light.

"That is the light of all the galaxies of the Universe of The One," said the silent communication. "We are many times further from it than its own length."

Horning shivered. The sense of aloneness was terrifying. As his eyes adjusted, he began to see the outlines of his body again outlined against the curtain of the sparks of life. He still had human form, a physical presence. As he realised the fact, the terrible sense of falling hit him again, and once more, he tried to scream his fear. Calming warmth ran through him, and the fear reduced.

"We understand what you fear," echoed the voice. "We have learned about those of The Million who took physical form on planets. We chose a different path."

At last, Horning understood. He was dealing with one of the Infinite Souls that had adopted an energy form and lived in the blackness between the stars, even between Galaxies.

"Maragos sent you?" he whispered, trembling with the memories of his dealings with the Infinite Soul who had tried to cure the sickness within him.

"She saw an opportunity," the voice of the others agreed. "Our species was almost ready to begin the ascension toward Infinity, but a sickness has struck us. We cannot go on until it is removed."

"A sickness? Like that which I have and which has held humanity?"

"No. It is different. We have experienced it before, and we know how to cure it. In that may lie your chance of salvation."

Horning felt the group around him begin to move. The direction was toward the distant glow of the Universe.

"We must be among the stars of a galaxy for the answer," came the reply to his unconscious query.

"For my chance at redemption?" Horning's longing for a return to his own kind made him shiver.

"And our move to Infinity," agreed the others.

"How will it be done?"

In reply, his mind was flooded by knowledge. As they moved, Horning relived something of the life of these interspace dwellers.

They had begun their cycle of incarnations in the blackness of space five light-years from the nearest sun of a galaxy that had no name to human astronomers. Feeding on the solar energies that ran like tidal flows between the suns, they lived lives of a thousand years or more, joyously soaring between solar systems, never getting within a light-hour or two of the suns themselves, because the energy levels too close became harmful. They procreated by fission, the offspring splitting from the adult when the parent willed it. The species grew in numbers and split off in separate groups, many millions per group, each of that moved further off into space in a nomadic life that spanned galaxies and the spaces between galaxies.

Their deaths were normally through old age, as the energy in the beings ran down below the point of sustaining consciousness. But they could die by accident, too. Poisonous energy streams could be encountered from some solar types, or sudden flares that reached out and burned the unwary browser of nearby energy sources. Some gas giants, both solar and planetary could poison, also.

"The sickness has struck groups of us several times in our past." The voice broke into Horning's experience of these astonishing lives. "We are always in communication with the others of our people throughout the Universe, and so we understood immediately what has hit this group with which you travel now. The others have already moved on to their ascendant stage, but we cannot until we have cured the illness."

"But what is this illness?" asked Horning, still dreamy, lost in wonderment.

"It infects our nervous system," came the reply. "Once it has gone, we are immune. We can even pass it to another and so lose it ourselves, but we cannot destroy it without destroying the host."

"So how have you got over the previous epidemics?" asked Horning, thinking with joy about a chance of redemption and his determination not to lose it this time after all his previous failures.

There was a silence for some unknown time.

"Through your mind, we read in your human history a suitable analogy," came the answer finally. "In your primitive legends is the story of the scapegoat, an animal on which the human tribes loaded all their sins and sent the creature to its death, a symbolic cleansing. We can use a less symbolic method, and that has been the solution for the others of us."

Horning trembled at the menace implicit in the answer. "You would use me as a scapegoat?"

"I told you, that the disease could be passed to another host, leaving the original one free of infection. In the past, we have asked one of our people to take on the sickness from the rest of us. The infection can only be destroyed by massive temperatures such as those found within a sun. The bearer of all our disease must deliberately drive himself into the heart of a solar furnace. The pain is immense. We know that, because we have felt some of it even within two or three light-hours of a sun."

"And must this happen?" Horning asked. "What if the scapegoat merely went off on its own and lived apart from you until it died of old age? Wouldn't that have the same result?"

He felt the denial in the sparks around him.

"We feed on the energies that flow between the stars," said the voice. "Without burning away the disease, it will spread through the solar energy fields and we will absorb it again, some time."

Fear ran through him, but he tried to suppress it with the thought of redemption, acceptance again as one of the human race.

"What must I do?" he asked, sensing the warmth and gratitude among those who flew through emptiness with him. It was the first time he had ever sensed such feelings, and the wonder of it suffused his soul, strengthening his commitment to taking on the illness of this strange species.

"You must be born as one of us," said the voice. "And we must travel many ages yet to return to the Universe, for there is little food out here and no star suitable."

"I have to die, first?" Fear made him shiver as he spoke.

"You are already dead, Horning," said the voice. "We are taking you from Hell for a chance at rebirth."

Horning understood the truth of that. His last incarnation, he recalled, had been as the Ultimate Leader of Gelokk, the supreme Gelkka authority who had set his people on a path to the Throne of Heaven. He wondered how they would do it without him, and for a moment, felt a shiver of longing to be with that wonderful, merciless, supremely arrogant race again. He suppressed the longing under the even greater desire to be one with humanity again.

"Let's do it," he said through the fear and the longing, and the veil of sparks in the infinite blackness vanished.

# Chapter 25. The Long Trek Home

The travels took a lifetime. Several lifetimes, for some of the Family died before food could be found once more. His entire memories consisted only of the constant movement through blackness, the glow before them barely to be seen compared to the lights given off by the individuals who flew together. Consciousness had grown in him after some immeasurable period of time after his birth. He had slowly become aware of the sensation of life, attached by light magnetism to the energy fluxes of his parent, and with that awareness, floated free.

He absorbed the knowledge and history of the Family and the other Families that had existed in the black depths around the Universe and understood how this Family had embarked on a trip greater than any other ever undertaken. For they were the last Family and without this trek, the Greater Family might not survive. He learned how all the other groups had moved on to another plane of existence and ceased their gloriously free travels among the starways of all the galaxies.

And slowly, he began to understand that he had the greatest role of all of them to play in allowing his race to attain Ascendancy. He was enormously proud, though he did not yet understand what his role would be.

Food was terribly scarce. The Family had absorbed as much of it within themselves as they could before leaving the familiar boundaries of the vast spaces where they had roamed before and set off on the greatest trek of them all. He did not understand where they had gone, or why it had been necessary. But he did comprehend that they were on the way back, and things would improve slowly.

As they did. Although several of the Family dissipated their last energies in the vast emptiness around them, the trek continued, never slowing for a moment as they headed for the faint source of light that he knew was their home.

A time came when they met their first food in his history. The light of the Universe ahead had grown until it vastly outshone their own energy traces, and a huge song of delight swelled among the Family as they encountered food. He felt the sudden, wonderful sensation of energy flooding into him and sang with happiness, letting his body absorb the delicious influx of power, realizing for the first time in his short life how weak and starved they all were. The speed of the trek picked up significantly, and soon he saw that the light ahead was composed of many sources. They were galaxies of stars, his adult Family members told him. For the first time, a question came to him.

"Am I the only child among us?" he asked.

"We could not produce children on the Trek," came the answer. "We needed to preserve the food."

"But I was born?"

"You are essential."

He felt very proud, but still did not understand what his glorious task would be.

As they travelled, he learned more. They told him about the other life forms in the Universe, the ones who lived what seemed to him dreadfully claustrophobic existences as planet-bound physical forms. He felt revulsion and pity for these species and wondered why they had chosen to live like that. They had even needed mechanical devices to travel round the Universe, enclosed again in finite spaces that surely crushed the soul, he felt. He sensed the amusement around him, and decided he would never understand adults.

In particular, they told him of the diseased race of humans, and he shuddered with revulsion. That such a thing could exist! An entire species so sick that they could not ascend to the Astral and above! It seemed ugly to him.

"What will happen to them?" he asked.

"A soul of great power is helping them heal," said one.

"And is it working?"

He felt a small pause.

"Yes, it is, though not without problems," came the eventual reply.

"Problems?" A worrying tension seemed to exist in the Family as they listened to the conversation.

"There is one soul among the human race who is the sickest they could ever have imagined. He seems almost beyond redemption, and without him, Humanity may not ascend."

"But what will happen?" he demanded anxiously. "Must we have Humanity before Oneness returns?" He understood the climb to Oneness was well in progress. He had learned about that in the last stages of the Trek.

"Yes, we must. That is where you come in."

"Me? How can one of the Family play a part in the sickness of a physical being?"

"You will learn in time."

For a while, he learned nothing more. Anyway, there was food in plenty and the whole Universe in which to play, and like any child, the problems that made adults seem so serious had nothing to do with him.

Food was even more plentiful now, and he grew rapidly. The energy traces of his Family were much stronger, and there was power to burn. He swooped huge distances from the body of the travelling Family, soared round them in geodesic loops, feeding as he flew, wondering if there was anything so wonderful as this freedom. He listened to the Family as they watched him, the first child born in a thousand years, so obviously amused and entertained by the exuberance he was showing as he played.

At some indefinable point, the Trek ended. The enormous golden curtain of a galaxy was a glorious backdrop to his flights, unlike the perpetual blackness with which he had grown from infancy. He sensed the Family watching him as he flew with delight into the curling strands of the vast spiral of stars.

Such wonderful colours! He was fascinated by the beauty of the galaxy as he approached it. The stars made such lovely toys! He could hardly wait to fly round one and study it close up. Happily, he set off in the direction of one particularly beautiful sun. It was golden, glorious, enchanting. He sensed the entire Family watching him, but assumed they were merely enjoying his play.

The pain hit him without warning. It burned through him, shocked him with the sudden, awful loss of energy and the wave of sickness that shuddered in every nerve trace within him. Screaming with pain and fear, he swung away from the sun and fled howling back to the Family.

"It hurts," he cried like any child.

"Now we must talk," said the Family.

"You have grown up, and your task is waiting for you."

The entire tribe had gathered in the cool shade of a gas giant that orbited a huge red sun that, at this distance, was a warm glow three light-hours away. They were all intent on the meeting that had suddenly come into play.

He studied the kindred of his Family. The weariness caused by the illness that affected so many of them was obvious. More had died since they had returned to the warmth of the Universe in his late childhood and now he was fully grown. He had realised recently that he was the only healthy one.

"My task? You have always told me about a task I would one day be given, but never explained it. This is the time?" He felt a surge of pride. The sadness among the others was noticed but he discarded any sense of danger from it.

"We have the illness that has affected other families. You are the one who will save us from it."

He waited, beginning to understand. His history learning had told him of the dreadful healing process that would rid the Family of the infection. The first surge of fear engulfed him. He remembered the pain of the first, shocking encounter with the beautiful star he had thought would be a plaything.

"There is more to it than healing the Family," said a quiet voice. He recognized the energy patterns of the one who had been his parent in the early years of the Trek through a time and space that had no meaning away from the Universe. "Remember how we told you about a race of planet-dwellers who had an even greater sickness?"

He signalled his recollection.

"And we told you about one soul among that race who threatened the return of The One."

"Yes, you did."

"You are that one," said his parent

With those words, Horning remembered.

Waves of horror ran through him. He remembered all his lives as a human, as a Mayoowi, and as a Gelkka, his three times in Hell, and now his last chance at redemption.

Horning wept.

After a formless, immeasurable time, he returned to contact with the others. "I will do it," he said, fear almost strangling him.

Immediately, the others of the Family moved inward until they formed a single mass of energy.

Horning felt himself at the centre of the thousands of individuals. Within seconds, he began to feel fatigued, ill, his energy tracks broken. When the others moved away from him, he knew he had the illness of each the infected members absorbed within himself. He could hardly see the planets and star of the solar system in which they rested. His senses were blurred, weak, unfocused. But he felt the rest of the Family move away, out into the deeper blackness beyond the orbit of the most distant planet, a frozen ball over twenty light-hours away from the red giant star, and he heard the last message from them.

Redemption! It was his only thought as he began to move to the distant warm spot that was the sun.

The spot grew larger and the heat became intense. When the first bolt of pain hit him, no more than a light-hour away from the sun, he stopped. Fear ran through every one of the damaged and broken energy-tracks of his system, and even with the depleted sensory capacities, the pain was horrible, far worse than his first childhood experience. He drove for the cone of shelter of the nearest planet and hung just a few million miles from the barren rock

"Redemption!" he said again, and forced courage upon himself. He moved out into clear space, and felt the agony strike him once more. Unable to move further inward to the sun, he flickered back into the shelter of the planet.

He looked down on the planet's surface and recalled his other lives as a planet-dweller. He remembered his incarnation as William Horning, President-for-Life of the United States of America, with the power of life and death over a hundred million of his subjects. Lovingly, he recalled the few but powerfully satisfying lives as a Gelkka, especially the last one, when he had been the Supreme Leader of the entire planet of Gelokk with its twenty billion inhabitants. He had initiated the drive to Infinite Soul maturity, telling his people that the Gelkka were the

One True God and the other species were inferior, merely servants to the Master Race of Gelkka.

But now he had to drive himself deep into the solar fires of the red star just a few billion miles away and incinerate himself and the disease carried by his temporary family, to die in hideous agony to cleanse both his kin and his own soul as a human being.

"I shouldn't have to do this," he cried out to empty space. "I am Horning!"

The shock wave of horror and disbelief from the others of the Family rolled through him.

"But what of your redemption and our healing?"

It shook him, and he fought to take hold of himself again, remembering the desperate hunger he had felt for a chance to return to the family of humanity, to be one with other human beings again, not hated and despised by every one of the thirty billion elements of the Human Infinite soul. Sobbing, he struggled for the strength to move back into the valley of pain. He struck out a tangent, flinging himself at maximum velocity straight for the next planet inward that he could see. Hellish agony burned through every atom of him, pain which, for a human being, would be the slow burning off of a layer of skin under the blaze of a steel furnace just a few feet away.

Screaming helplessly, he reached the shade of the next planet and fell into the cover the massive body gave him. Sobbing, he hung a bare thousand miles above the surface, almost touching the surface, so desperate was he for the shelter. But the protection was incomplete. Electromagnetic fluxes from the red sun worked their way through the atmosphere of the planet, stray radiation flickered through the solid mass and struck the network of energy that comprised Horning's form. The pain was less, but it persisted, and Horning sobbed like a small child.

"I can't do it!" he gasped.

"You must, William," said a soft voice in his mind. "All of Humanity and Creation depends on you healing yourself and your adopted family of the formless ones."

"Maragos, it's beyond anyone," he shouted. "Nobody could stand this!"

"Others have stood worse, William," Maragos replied. "The pain is only that which you inflicted on so many who died under your rule on Earth. It is less than Alan Drew took in your place on Mayoowani, and that so many Gelkka took in your reign as Supreme Ruler if they opposed you. It lasts only finite time, and then we can proceed to Oneness."

"NO!" he shouted. He felt a surge of energy and support and recognized the familiar pattern of the minds of all the Gelkka. They were his people. They had the same philosophies. They were the supreme power in the Universe. They were God.

Howling in rage at the pain and the horrors inflicted upon him, Horning felt his power multiply a million-fold as the Infinite Gelkka rallied within his mind.

"I am Horning," he bellowed to the vastness of space and time. "I am not the helper of some sick race of energy forms. Find your own salvation!"

Flying away from the sun, staying in the shadow of the planet that had sheltered him, he raced for the cool of deep space beyond the orbit of the furthermost planet in the system. As he got deeper into the friendly dark, he absorbed more and more of the spiritual sustenance of the Gelkka, feeling every second more attuned to the new mind that had boosted him.

Without difficult or regret, he let the energy form that had been his incarnated form drop from him. Death was nothing, he saw, merely a passage from one stage to the next. Gladly, he let himself be absorbed by the huge power that was the friendly, loving mass of the Infinite Soul of the Gelkka until he was one with them again.

William Horning had gone home. The Gelkka, an emerged Infinite Soul, now contained the sickness that had plagued mankind from its beginning.

# Chapter 26. Homecoming

Twenty two thousand years after the arrival of Maragos on Earth, the displaced souls of humans returned home from their travels round The One's Universe. The species that had hosted them had all moved on to a higher level of existence, and there was no need for the visiting human souls to remain among them. The returning souls came from galaxies so far away that they had only been seen and noted in the last thousand years of human astronomy, from known, mapped and well-travelled galaxies of the nearer galactic super-clusters, and from nearby galaxies of the local group. Regardless of the distance they travelled, the journey took no measurable time. The sickness had gone, and they had grown fast, all of them having reached at least late Mature Soul stage, and many having attained Old Soul levels. The greatest majority of souls would live out their final experiences on the Astral Plane. A few would return to Earth for their last incarnations and finish their spiritual growth on Earth.

There was one single human soul, however, that did not return. The soul that had once inhabited the body of William Horning chose another path.

Twenty two thousand, eight hundred and thirty years after the start of the Maragos Presence, the last child in the Universe was born.

His parents were part of the tiny community of two hundred seventh-stage Old Souls living in the forests that surrounded a beautiful bay. Though the area no longer had a name, the people living there could remember from their previous incarnations over thousands of years that the shores of the bay had once held a city called San Diego, and the sea had been called Pacific. As the human population had shrunk below a million, and then below fifty thousand over the last few centuries, human beings had abandoned the technologies and lifestyles of over twenty thousand years and returned to a hunter-gathering life that suited the declining numbers.

The two hundred residents knew that they were the last living humans. They also knew that they were the last living, ensouled beings of any species anywhere in the Universe.

. In the seventh month of her pregnancy, the young mother heard the child speak to her.

"I am already here," the child said.

"Why?" asked the mother. She had been asleep next to her husband in their hut by the beach, and she had woken to the insistent call of the child. "Our souls do not usually enter the body until the moment of birth."

"Because I wanted to be sure you would hear me and remember, not be uncertain that my words from the Astral Plane were just a dream."

The woman reflected on the power with which the child's presence had made itself felt. "Who are you?" she asked, feeling a mixture of fear and excitement at the aura of strength reflecting from within her.

"I am the last," the child said into her mind.

"Yes," said the mother. She felt overwhelming sadness mixed in with the sweet delight of speaking to her unborn son. "It is time for Oneness to begin."

"All of you are in your last incarnations," said the child. "Soon, you will join your entity souls and begin the move to Ascendancy."

The woman was silent. Though they had all known

that there would be little time for more earthly lives for any of them, the absolute end had not been foreseen so early. Her child cut off further communication and slept, like any embryo would do.

A month later, the child spoke to her again. "I will be called Michael John," said the silent words in her head.

"These names are meaningful," said the woman. It was no question. The embryo's statement had been firm beyond any uncertainty.

"They are two names of power for me," said the boy. "I did great work under them."

"You remember who you have been already?" She was surprised. Memories of previous incarnations usually came only after adulthood was attained, even with these final-stage Old Souls.

"Just as you do, mother," said the boy with a wave of warm affection.

"Few of mine are good memories," said the woman. Her name was Stephanie, a curiously ancient mode of address but one she had chosen for good reasons.

"I know all your past lives, mother," said Michael John. "You have paid for your errors. You are whole again."

"The sickness was burned out of me."

There was no answer. The child was sleeping.

The two hundred recognized that a powerful soul was to be born to them and they met together the next day. They had woken at dawn and taken the boats into the bay for the morning catch and returned with a healthy load of fish. A hunting party had also returned with four deer, so food was plentiful, as it always was. After the work of preparing the food had been completed, the two hundred settled on the sands by the water in response to the call that all of them had sensed.

"My child is named Michael John," said Stephanie. "He says we are the last. We will begin to ascend when we die this time."

A small stir wrinkled through the listeners.

"So Oneness begins," said the oldest of the two hundred. She was over a hundred and twenty years old and had lived four hundred lives of penitence for damage done to others in her first incarnations.

"It must be time," said the father of Michael John. He had taken no name in this life. Now he smiled with a certain bitterness. "After all," he said, "if Stephanie and I have reached final-stage Old Soul level, then all of you must be thoroughly healed."

A murmur of amusement ran through the assembly. They all knew who each of them had been in all their previous lives, and all of them knew the grotesque histories of the souls who were the parents of the last child. Each of the last two hundred had lived many similar lives of suffering for the same reasons as had the new child's parents. Their histories were the reason why they were the last incarnate beings left in the Universe.

"This is a soul of exceptional power that comes to us," said another, a man in the early prime of his seventieth year. "Can anyone read who he is?"

"He is a companion of Maragos," said another. "I sense that, but can see no further."

"He tells me he has done great work under his names," said Stephanie.

"Could he be the one who last appeared as Michael Alexander?" asked a woman from the rear of the crowd. "The one who had been Michael Hendricks and the one who sent many of us on our travels?"

A murmur of awe ran through the group.

Stephanie smiled with enormous pride. "I do believe he is," she said, and took her husband's hand. The nameless man also smiled through the deep lines of intense suffering that were more spiritual than physically evident. Both he and his wife shared that characteristic. Despite their young, attractive faces, their eyes burned with the power of centuries of agony endured so that others might benefit. All the two hundred shared similar stigmata of penitent souls.

"When he is born, we will have a Telling," said Stephanie. "It is time, and it will be the last. The child will hear us."

In silence, the gathering broke up and returned to their tasks.

* * *

On a day that once would have once been August the twenty-first, in a year that might be called 24854 Traditional Christian Calendar, or the 26880th year of the Maragosian era, the last child on Earth was born.

On that day, the two hundred human souls conducted the ceremony of the Telling for the last time.

"I was Stephen Crossman in my first life," said the mother of Michael John, "and that life was one of great evil. I was one of those central to the story of Maragos and the arrival of the Infinite Soul on Earth. I conducted the Trial of the Four and sentenced them to death. I committed great sins against hundreds of thousands of my fellow humans. I killed, tortured and caused enormous suffering. While my extreme sickness of the soul caused me to be blind to Oneness, I went so much further in my crimes that it has taken nearly twenty thousand years of sorrow to reach this stage where I can see Ascendancy before me."

A small whisper went through the darkness around the two hundred listeners. Though they had heard the story many times, to hear one of the principal characters tell of the events was always a powerful experience.

"For many lifetimes, I was even part of Horning," whispered Stephanie. "For he had the ability to absorb other souls and suck their life force for his own use, and this he did to me when he needed the strength to face Maragos. For all those ages, I lived in lonely blackness, too weak to become myself, but seeing and living the horrors that William Horning inflicted on others and that were inflicted on him in his own self-created Hell. But Maragos released those souls caught within Horning's darkness, and returned us to the rest of Humanity to face our own destinies."

The young woman paused again, her eyes filled with the agonies her soul had experienced.

"I lived a thousand years in my own Hell when I was released," continued Stephanie. "For that millennium, I sat bound to a wooden chair, and was tortured by interrogators like those who had worked for me when I was Stephen Crossman. For every second of those thousand years, the power wands were touched to me and I suffered the agonies that I had applied to so many people. But I could not die or faint nor black out, for I was already dead."

She looked around the circle sitting on the sand, then down at the child sleeping peacefully beside her. The sea whispered gently to the night and glowed green warmth.

"After a millennium, I found that I had created that Hell for myself and that I could release myself from it. I did so, only to begin a series of lives that were little better than my time in Hell."

The silence among the two hundred was an empty world that let the sound of the sea murmur to them.

"I died many times so that others could live," continued the young woman. "First, I lived over twenty lives with species throughout the Universe of The One and each life was filled with pain, sacrifice and dreadful death. But I was not healed by that time because when I could, I returned to Earth and fell into the same pattern as in my first life. Endorsing rigid, dogmatic ways, I refused to let people think for themselves, the one feature that separates children of The One from the animals. I became a religious leader yet again, and condemned others to painful deaths because they failed to conform to my dogma."

She looked down at the child nuzzled to her breast and smiled. "I spent another two hundred or more incarnations among Others of The One before the sickness healed. I know now that I did not want my sickness to heal, because I was frightened of life as a true human soul with the responsibilities for one's own actions that is required. How much easier it is to set a rigid framework, live within it and demand that all others do the same, than to tolerate the beliefs of others. But the lives I spent as an immature soul among Souls of great wisdom and purity finally purged my sickness. All my lives since, I have been allowed to be born on Earth in order to serve others. The last twenty lives, I have been allowed peace and time in which to contemplate my past. Only in this life, this last of four hundred and eighty-three incarnations, have I been happy. I yearn for merger with my entity souls so I may lose myself and my pain in that wisdom and strength. Even more do I long for the further distance between myself and my memories when we all become the Human Infinite Soul. I can dream of nothing more wonderful."

She carefully sat down and hugged the child. "That is my Telling," she said, and wept.

When Stephanie had finished, a small sigh ran through the group. She began to feed her child. All the two hundred there could sense the power in the soul of the tiny bundle she clasped to her breast.

The child's father rose to his feet. Like all of them, the lines of centuries of physical and spiritual suffering showed in his face, and in the dark eyes that all Old Souls had.

"I have taken no name in this life," said the man. "But you have called me the Priest for good reasons. For although I had lived two hundred and ten lives before Maragos came, I was still an Infant Soul. In nearly all those lives, I was a priest of some sort, because in such a life I could hide from doubts and uncertainty by forcing on to others the same set of beliefs that I adopted, and so feel righteous. I had been a Druid in ancient days and conducted the ritual slaughter of many of my people. I ripped out the living hearts of children in ceremonies in South America, supervised the torture and deaths of thousands in the Spanish Inquisition and in the dungeons of the Protestant zealots, always in the name of God. In my incarnation before the Infinite Soul came to Earth, I was a witch-hunter and burned many innocents in the fires of our savagery and hate. And I too was present when Maragos appeared, and I played a role in that story."

A tiny sigh ran through the two hundred, and they watched as the Priest turned to the mother of the last child to be born on Earth.

"With President William Horning and his chief counsellor, Stephen Crossman, I played my part, for I was Gregory Cardinal Lavalier, priest of the last Vatican Pope. I assisted in the torture of people charged only with rejecting the rigid dogma of so-called Christians. I watched the interrogation of Philippe Leger and of Maragos herself, and believed I was a righteous man of God. Like all of us here, I could not help my sickness, but as did we all, I still made the conscious decision to hide from my responsibilities within the sickness, and for that reason we have suffered for so long.

"I will not tell you many details of my lives since then, for they can only be less full of horror, suffering and pain than the lives that Stephanie, my wife in this life has lived, and no more terrible than all the lives you have experienced. I will only say that I too yearn for the loss of self that will soon come to us with Ascendancy and with Infinity, and take my only comfort in the hope that perhaps when The One awakens, our stories may provide some answer to the question that The One asked of us so many millions of years ago."

Lavalier stood silently, and the tears flowed from him as he remembered his final meeting with Philippe Leger, how he had seen a tiny portion of the truth of

Oneness and how Philippe had blessed him and forgiven him his sins.

The silence was broken by a small cry from the child, then Michael John returned to his peaceful sleep at his mother's breast. The priest smiled down at the boy, his son, then looked out into the night again.

"There will be no more Tellings after this night," he said, "and I have told you before of the lives of the eight millennia since I came home to Earth. Over a hundred times, I have been born into a deformed body. Those who tended to me burned many of their own karmic debts in the process, and so healed more rapidly, as did I during these lives of pain and distress. Finally, I was healed, and the last fifty lives have been ones of learning, though still with much pain. Like my wife Stephanie who was once Crossman, this last incarnation has been my only happy one. But I know that I am the cause of much of the grief that assailed our species."

The child's father sat down next to his wife and child, and took the boy to his own lap. "This ends my Telling," he said.

The gentle sea gave a coda to the final Telling of the soul of Gregory Cardinal Lavalier, one of the last souls to be healed from the sickness of Humanity.

Throughout the night, the two hundred stood and took part in the Telling. Many of the names they quoted still rolled down through history, names of men and women who had committed crimes of such magnitude against their fellows that they had never been forgotten. Their recitation of crimes against humanity over hundreds of lifetimes, and the penance they had paid over hundreds more, took till dawn, and then the last two hundred souls in the physical Universe slept.

* * *

When Michael John was fifteen years old, he called the community together. There were only one hundred and twenty by this time, for those who had died had not been replaced by a single new birth. They sat in the sand by the sea as was their custom for gatherings, and looked at the man before them.

He had grown tall and powerful, a spiritual aura of strength always about him. His eyes shone with an energy that filled the night and reminded them of the stories of the eyes of Maragos and the Enhanced Ascendant Souls who had been present at her execution to trigger the beginning of the end of the human story.

"I am Michael John," he said. "Once I was John the Baptist and tried to save souls for the second visit of a single Enhanced Ascendant, when Jesus visited us in our time of terror and need. I was with Buddha before that and with Mohammed later. I was many people in many times, and then I was Michael Hendricks. Many of you met me in the immediate aftermath of that life."

He smiled at the murmur of self-deprecating laughter that ran through the group.

"One more time I came to Earth," he continued. "As Michael Alexander, I travelled with my friends across the country to the site where Maragos and her companions were executed by the master of the two who are now my parents. Since then, I have travelled the Universe of The One, seen the lives many of you lived among the Others, and I worked with Maragos to bring you home when you had healed."

He turned and smiled with warmth at the ones who housed the souls of Stephen Crossman and Gregory Lavalier. "And now this cycle is complete," he said. "Humanity is the last of the Million Infinite Souls that make up The One, and we have delayed the awakening of the Supreme Being. It is time for you all to meet with your entity souls on the Astral Plane and begin the merger to Ascendant Souls. Each of you here is the last of your entity to complete the physical life cycle, and the others are waiting for you."

He paused with sadness in his face.

"It is a beautiful world, and it seems a shame to leave it now. But The One is waiting for us and we have completed our tasks. I have other duties with the Infinite Soul and I will complete them later. But for you, it is done."

He turned round a full circle and stared each of them in the eye. At the end, he looked at his mother and father, and walked to them. They stood up and the remaining members of the last humans did the same. "You are healed," he said, taking one hand of each of his parents. "Your paths have been long and dreadful, but you can be part of The One again."

He turned round to face the others once more. "It is done," he said. "Go now."

The last human beings in the Universe died in that moment, leaving Michael John, servant of Maragos the Infinite to stand alone in a way that no soul had ever been before. For he was the last incarnate intelligence in the entire Universe of millions of galaxies and billions of billions of planets. For several minutes, he wept, the sound of his grief almost lost in the gentle rush of the surf.

The last man in the Universe wept for the end of all life.

"It is only the end of one stage, my friend, and the start of the next."

Michael rubbed his eyes and smiled. He turned in the direction of the beautiful voice.

"Maragos, I am glad to see you," he said. "For a moment, the emptiness overwhelmed me."

She stood in the sand by the gentle surf. She was dressed in a simple white gown, and the ends of it trailed in the water. Her hair was long and fell down to the small of her back. Michael thought he had never seen such a beautiful sight.

"It is only empty on a physical plane, Michael my friend," she replied. "On the Astral Plane, life teems like it did on the worlds of the galaxies. On the Akashic Plane, there are huge spaces yet to be filled, but the influx of Ascendant Souls has already begun on that higher plane."

"So Oneness comes?" Michael still felt the crushing loneliness of being the single living soul in the physical universe, but her words warmed the icy bleakness in his heart.

"Not as easily as we had hoped," she said. "The sickness still spreads."

"But The One is awakening?" Michael sensed the deep worry within the awesome power in the woman across the sand from him.

"The pressure to return cannot be resisted any further," she replied. "But the awakening will not be as we had planned. Not every human soul has returned for merger to the Human Infinite."

"William Horning?" asked Michael in a low voice. "I was worried when I saw that he was not among the two hundred, for I knew that surely his would be the last soul to heal."

"Horning discovered how to tap the powers of The One, even though his disease was overwhelming," said Maragos. "I do not understand myself how that happened, but I believe that he drew on the psychic strength of the Gelkka. He chose to reincarnate among that race and made himself their leader. Now the sickness is rife among them, and the Gelkka believe that they are the One True God themselves."

"So what can we do?" Michael felt his own fear growing.

"We must continue the fight. I thought we had won the main battle when my friends and I died in Washington. But it is not over yet."

"But can Humanity merge to Infinity if not all the souls are with us and healed?"

"I used to think not," said Maragos, grief in her face. "But I have learned much from this tragedy. The entities of Horning's human Ascendant Soul are merging now to their new level without him. It seems that Humanity has cut Horning's soul away, just like a diseased piece of skin. He is part of the Gelkka Infinite, now. I begin to sense that perhaps Horning was never part of The One at all."

"Not part? Maragos, if not part of The One, what else could he be?"

She shook her head, and the dread in her astounding eyes shook him to the core. "There are things appearing in this Universe that are beyond the knowledge of even an Infinite Soul, Michael. But we must continue to try and save that sick soul of Horning, whatever it might be."

"Will that not prevent the awakening of The One?" asked Michael. Coldness ran over his soul.

Maragos shook her head. "It has gone too far to stop," she replied. "The disease struck the Gelkka when The One was already starting to waken. It must continue now."

"But if the sickness is still present in The One when It awakens, what then, Maragos?"

"Some things are beyond even the power of an Infinite Soul to comprehend, Michael. I do not know what can happen if God is sick."

"Maragos, I fear for our Universe."

"Be right to fear. We have a long path still to tread."

"Then I am still your servant, Maragos."

At last, she smiled. "My servant and my friend, Michael. The Universe of The One still needs us."

"I am with you, Maragos."

"And we will call on you," she said. "You should move on, Michael. There is nothing left to do on this plane."

"A few more minutes," he replied.

She nodded, and raised one hand. "Till Oneness," she said, and vanished.

"Till Oneness," he murmured. He looked once more at the blue sea and the clear skies. He walked slowly through the white sand along the line of the sea. He breathed deeply of the salt air then laughed out loud.

"It was a good cycle of reincarnations," he said with a tiny smile. "Let us see what the spiritual planes have to offer." He turned once more to look at the distant mountains.

Michael John died.

The history of mankind was over. Everything had been done, everyone had played out their roles.

Earth was left alone to wait for Oneness.

# Chapter 27. The Soul Ascendant

The soul that had been Philippe Leger waited on the Astral Plane. He had no use for physical form or environment, and merely existed in the cloudy, dreamlike surroundings that were the normal manifestation of this level, one above the physical, incarnate level of the life cycles.

He sensed with great clarity the presence of each of the sixteen hundred souls that comprised his entity. All of them were feeling the same sensation of enhanced perception, he knew.

In the group, a few individuals were stronger in his mind. The soul who had been Angela Maxwell during his press conference after abandoning the papal throne of Saint Peter was there. Even as he extended his mind to the others, he simultaneously exchanged greetings and love with them. He recognized many who had shared lifetimes with him, who had been siblings, lovers, parents, friends. Every single one of those souls was now a distinct presence within him.

His memories began to flow with electric excitement, as if powered by a massive generator and his mind was running at turbo speed. Flashes of memories that were not his own raced through him...

*That press conference... she was Angela Maxwell and she saw Philippe Leger standing on the stage and sensed the confusion and excitement in everybody in the room. How could she possibly write this article for a national newspaper without sounding like a loonie?...*

# The Nightmares of God

He stood at the podium and raised the baton - the first playing of the new symphony, and Europe had been in a fever of expectation for months. The notes started, the music took over his soul and even though he could hear nothing, he felt the music rise from the score sheets and take form within his head. He wept as the wonderful orchestra played as they had never done in rehearsals, and when the chorus joined in at last in the fourth movement, he knew how God felt at the moment of Creation...

*His tank swerved under him in the loose sand, and he bumped his shoulders painfully against the rim. The multi-damned sons of syphilitic jackals had struck across the Suez on the holiest of holidays, and their cousins, the offspring of diseased bitches and pox-infested camels had followed the example on the Golan Heights. Israel had reeled, punch-drunk, and the enemy slime was flowing towards the borders like filth from an overrunning sewer. But the army and air force had gathered fast and were starting to hit back with fury. The Egyptian bastards were running back to Suez, leaving their boots behind them, their tanks were like ducks in a shooting gallery... Shamah Yisrael, Adonai Elahaynoo, Adonai Erhad...*

They have bombed Guernica! The Nazi pigs have used my home as a testing ground for their weapons, and killed thousands. The hideous darkness infecting Europe has become a disease. That maniac, Hitler wants the world. And he'll destroy anything that stands between him and that ugly goal. There is only one way to show my rage, my disgust and my recognition of the evil represented by that black cross the Nazis have adopted as their own. I will draw the scenes. The canvas will be huge. The colour is mainly black as the hearts and minds of those Nazi swine. Horses will writhe in agony as they are burned and shattered by shells. The Devil's face will reveal itself. A woman will weep for the loss of all the children of all the mothers in the world. Her grief will tear the hearts of all who see my canvas. And that canvas will be as huge as the infamy the Nazis have committed on my homeland.

*Patience, only patience, that's all it takes, the child will learn, just be patient. For the tenth day in a row of many months of such rows, we start again, I show him the letters. Just one small child of seven years in a class of only fifteen, in a school in a small town. The armies of the Confederates might be battling in blood and snow against the Union, but all I can do here is try and get one small boy to see what joy there can be in words... Once more boy, this is an 'a,' this is a 'b'... if you see these letters together, they make a word, say it boy, try it, see the word, how it forms. Today he looks at me and smiles, looks back at the page and takes a deep breath. He's not staring without comprehension, he's... Dear God, he's reading! He sees it, he reads the whole line and a grin of pure triumph spreads across his small face. Napoleon may have conquered Europe, Anthony won Egypt, Alexander may have taken the world, but nothing compares to this moment of total, utter joy as my pupil takes his first, staggering step into the world of books...*

Her feet were agonized but the ballet had twenty minutes to go yet. The audience was hers, she knew that, they were almost weeping with the joy of the dance. Rudi swept her up into a joyous lift above his huge shoulders, and she flew, her arms extended, the pain forgotten, until he placed her back on her points again and the torture restarted. But it was the dance, always the dance, and when it was done, she knew they would stamp on the floor and shout for her, and the flowers would be brought on, and she would curtsey again and again and know that every one of them would remember the night they saw Margot dance Swan Lake...

## The Nightmares of God

*We are a powerful soul.*

Pulling back a little from the startling memories of other souls, other lives, Philippe felt huge delight and pride as he saw who some of his entity souls had been. Beethoven, Fonteyn, heroes of wars long forgotten, Picasso and other artists of god-like abilities, people of creativity and passion, all touched with a little more of the power of The One than ordinary souls had been. He saw how the single Ascendant Soul that was starting the path to merger of its sixteen hundred fragments would be a spiritual force of enormous power and he forgot his fear of losing his own identity. That was immaterial compared with the growth to become such a power as he had just seen. That small jolt of crossed memories had been the first development towards Ascendancy he sensed, and also felt the same tendrils of memories reaching out between other souls in the entity. Maybe some of them had just seen his own lives, the realization that he had just been elected Pope, the first sensations of the coming of the Infinite Soul, the death by electrocution in Washington, memories of his meetings with Buddha, Jesus and Mohammed, the transfer of his tribe from the freezing planet in orbit around Epsilon Indi to the newly-terraformed planet Earth... how wonderful to be able to sense the four hundred or more lives of each of sixteen hundred individuals... over six hundred thousand lifetimes to experience and absorb.... the strength of all those powerful souls now to be combined as one individual... how incredible, how godlike it all was!

He remembered the astounding moment when the souls of Jacqueline, Raoul and himself had been allowed for a few brief moments to join into the single entity that was the Infinite Soul of Maragos. The same thing would soon be happening, though on a lesser scale.

He understood now how he would lose his identity and yet still be an aware being, even though merged with sixteen hundred other similar souls. If that was so, then the same awareness would exist within the entity of an Infinite Soul, even up to the final merger of the Million Infinites to become The One. So all the debates, the philosophical wondering, the sheer impossibility of trying to imagine what it was like to be God - he would find out, together with the other many billions of souls of humanity and the unknown total of millions of billions of souls that would come together in some future millennium to become The One. He would know!

Willingly, Philippe Leger surrendered his identity to see more of how his entity souls would become an Ascendant. Energy began to flow into him, the energy of sixteen hundred strong entities developing a synergy of togetherness. His horizons opened up like a flower seeking the new rain and his mental powers surged as if powered by a massive jet engine starting up in his mind. He saw the universe as each of the others had seen it, with the colours and balance that Picasso had seen, with the melody and channel to heaven that had been Beethoven's, with the sheer joy of movement that had been Fonteyn's, with everyone's unique perspective added together. It was as if he could see a new dimension, like a man who sees a shape from all sides at once. The universe opened itself to him... it was no longer "him," for Philippe Leger did not exist any more as a unique soul, not by that name or any of the four hundred or more he had owned in his lifetimes... something else had arisen, a new energy, a new intelligence... and it was no longer comfortable.

The universe had become a Babel of hundreds of entities overwhelmed by the monstrous surge of power and immense volumes of data that hit them and continued to hit them. It was like swimming upward through a sea of astonishing colours and noises, being blanketed by large schools of fish that attacked every tiny element of the body with a different sensation for each mouth. It became harsher and harsher, louder, more cacophonous, hellish in its overload until it became simply white noise that drowned out the universe. He.. it.. the new Something that was all of them was screaming, helpless, panic-stricken, like a child drowning, thrashing with arms that no longer existed, the noise grew even louder, the universe was pain, chaos...

No duration for the agony could be stated because time had no meaning outside of the physical world. It could have been a microsecond or it could have been ten thousand years while the new being gave birth to itself through the fusion of many hundreds of souls. The pain and chaos slackened, the white noise developed colour, devolved to flickering scenes of massive complexity seen at enormous speed, then also slowed until sense began to emerge. A new entity was born, an Ascendant Soul with second-by-millisecond memories of over six hundred thousand lifetimes. For further time that could be a nanosecond or could be a billion years, the new Ascendant would absorb these memories until every one of them was present as part of itself, rather than existing as a titanic database that had to be consciously accessed and traced. But the Ascendant knew how to move along this path.

As it returned to a sense of self, like a patient returning to life after the small death of a general anaesthetic, the Ascendant looked around, saw that it was still on the Astral Plane with all the other individual souls of other entities who had yet to merge, and realized that a new level could be attained. With a move that it could neither explain nor understand, it took itself to a higher level of existence.

It was on the Akashic Plane. Silence and space surrounded it, not the hostile silence of loneliness nor the empty space between planets, but the peaceful silence and space of room to live and grow. The silence was the wonderful, peaceful sense of dawn in the Lake District of England, the vast emptiness of central

Australia, or the frozen deserts of Antarctica. The space was the promise of a new house before furniture and people arrived, it was the potential of anything being possible. It was a home to which the family had not yet come.

The new-born intelligence luxuriated in the vast peace. Here was a place where the absorption and integration of the hundreds of thousands of lives within itself could progress, and the new powers discovered and explored. It settled itself to a process of review of the contents of its mind. How long it would take was irrelevant in a place where time itself no longer had meaning. The new entity had hundreds of thousands of lives to absorb and study.

* * *

After a time that could have been minutes, hours or a thousand million years, the new Ascendant returned to its immediate environment, a small decision made in its mind. The decision amused it, satisfied it, pleased it. Throughout the process of review and integration, it had sensed the thread of one single entity among the hundreds within it, one that had played a consistent part through the hundreds of thousands of years of human history on two planets. From the memories of that one soul that no longer existed in its own right, it recalled how the Infinite Soul Maragos had chosen a name from among the twenty-five billion souls that comprised it, and used that name as a reference for dealing with souls that still needed references.

"I shall call myself Leger," said the new Ascendant Soul. Somewhere within itself, it felt a small glow of pleasure ignite and vanish as the remnant of the intelligence that had been Philippe Leger sensed that recognition.

There were others on the Akashic Plane. Ascendant Souls who had made this transition hundreds or even thousands of years before Leger, greeted him. The new Ascendant discovered that communication was a permanent thing, all of them were in contact with each other at all times, though only noted when desired, the way in which a body was always aware of its feet, its fingers, its arms, but only thought about them when it needed to. Leger also found that he could talk to several others at the same time without thinking about it.

"Welcome," they all said. "There are too few of us in this place, and yet Infinity calls."

"How many?" asked Leger.

"Fewer than nine hundred," replied another.

"And how many will there be eventually?" Leger discovered curiosity in himself about these facts. Just how many Ascendants made up the Human Infinite Soul?

"Twenty million," said a voice.

"Have you all taken a name from a dominant fragment?" asked Leger.

"It is the pattern," replied another. "Though it may not have been a dominant fragment as Philippe Leger was with you. It may simply have been one who did something spectacular, or even one who did very little through its incarnation cycle and represents the mass of us. All is choice."

"I heard those words from another, once," mused Leger, recalling from the memories of a man called Benjamin ben Isaac, recorder of the words of Jesus.

"From me," replied the speaker. "I was the human Ascendant that merged with others to be the Enhanced Soul that you knew as Jesus. Welcome back, Benjamin. It is good to see you again."

"We look down on the birds now, just as you forecast," said Leger.

"From a great height indeed," agreed the voice of the soul that once had been part of the life force of Jesus of Nazareth. "Your fragments helped in the fight against the sickness. But now the fight intensifies across all the face of the Universe."

Leger felt the vibrations of understanding through all the Ascendant Souls on the Akashic plane. "There are many lifetimes to be absorbed," he said. "I have only just started."

"That is the function," agreed the others. "Most of us are still in the same process. All twenty million must join us and complete it before we move to Infinity."

"Then I suppose I'd better be getting on with it," said Leger. To waves of warmth, he moved from direct connection to a form of standby contact, like a carrier wave that needs only speech to establish communication again.

When the Akashic plane population reached three million, Leger received a communication.

"I contain the fragment that was Jacqueline Carter," said the voice in his mind. "And I have taken the name of Jacqueline because of her history in our healing."

"You have ascended!" said Leger with delight, feeling warmth flood his being. "Can we meet?"

A shape began to form before him. Hardly a human body, that was no longer necessary, but the outlines, some curves, a source of power where the eyes would be, it was enough to show another presence. Leger took the same form and they shared the love and delight of old friends meeting.

"My fragments have let Jacqueline become the dominant pattern within me," said the Ascendant Soul before Leger. A little surprised, he realized that the same had happened within himself. The fragment that had been Philippe Leger was now the dominant pattern within him, with the acceptance and agreement of all the sixteen hundred souls now largely integrated into his mind.

"I never thought I would see you again," said Leger.

"We couldn't not do so," replied Jacqueline, and like old friends, they settled into reminiscences of old times. Except that the reminiscences covered well over a million lifetimes stretching over several hundred thousand years, many species and several planets.

When the Ascendant Soul containing the fragment that had been Raoul Carmagio called, Leger was fairly sure that the entire assimilation of all the souls within him had been completed. Jacqueline too, had almost completed the process and neither of them needed the endless but timeless periods of disconnection from the Akashic plane while the integration and absorption of thousands of lifetimes took place.

It was without surprise that they found Raoul to be the dominant soul within the new Ascendant, or that the new arrival was using his name. When the three Ascendants met, they heard the call to go elsewhere. Somewhere, *somewhen* within the Universe that was part of and yet separate from the Universe of galaxies, suns and planets, the three of them met in an environment they created for themselves.

"The old farm house looks pretty good," said Jacqueline, smiling at the other two. They were standing in the formal dining room of the Leger home, and the table was set for a feast. Three metres long, the table was polished a beautiful dark brown, gleaming softly in the lights of the six candlesticks that lined the middle. Silver cutlery was laid along silver plates, and the music of Bach's Fourth Brandenburg concerto came from the walls.

Jacqueline was wearing a flowing gown in white and gold. Her red hair was set up high atop her head, and the diamonds of a tiara sparkled from the curls. A thin gold chain supported an enormous diamond between her breasts. The two men wore tuxedos, the black and white colour scheme broken only by gold cufflinks with large blue opal stones worn by Leger, and massive ruby stones on the cuffs of Raoul.

"It seemed the most symbolic way to meet again,"

said the clear, feminine voice in the doorway. Maragos was dressed in a blue gown, a necklace of diamonds and amethysts round her neck. Her hair was down, and more diamonds on her ears gleamed through the deep red-brown tresses.

"We're going to need more cognac," laughed Leger. "I remember your appetite for my oldest bottles." Another bottle appeared on the tray on the sideboard, to accompany the several bottles of wine. More wine lay in ice buckets.

"Ladies and gentlemen," said Leger, "welcome to my home once more. By some measures, I believe over a hundred thousand years have passed on Earth since we last dined together."

"A suitable time for an anniversary," agreed Jacqueline, and smiled as Leger moved her chair back to allow her to be seated. Raoul performed the same service for Maragos, and the two men took their seats, Leger at the head of the table, Raoul at the foot, Jacqueline to Leger's left, and Maragos across from her.

Wine appeared in their glasses, and they drank a toast.

"To Infinity," they all said, and drank deeply.

"I wish I could promise you that the path to Oneness could be easier now," said Maragos. She put her glass down and looked seriously at the others.

"Maragos, what is happening?" Leger stared at the beautiful woman across from him. The other Human Ascendants also placed their glasses back on the table and silence fell.

"Just as we under-estimated the force of this sickness when we sent Buddha, Jesus and Mohammed to live among humanity, so have we done with the current healing plan," said Maragos. She looked at each of them in turn, and the power of her gaze shook each of them to the core.

"While many souls have healed with a few lives spent among other species, it has not always been the case," she continued. "We have found now that one of the hosts has itself been infected instead."

"Maragos!" Leger shouted in shock. "Another species has become sick?"

"Precisely," replied Maragos. "I sent Horning to live among the Mayoowi. Instead of learning from that, he chose to become one of the Gelkka in his next life, and he carried the sickness within him. And the momentum to merge to Infinite Soul was too great. It means that now we have an Infinite Soul as sick as any of those on Earth whom we fought so many centuries ago. And I can provide even less healing to the Gelkka Infinite Soul than I could to those like Horning and Crossman. It is now too powerful."

"But what if it cannot be healed?" Raoul appeared calm, but the power of his fear was sensed by the others.

"The drive to form The One is too great to stop now," said Maragos. "We risk having The One awaken still suffering from the sickness. I cannot possibly imagine what could happen."

"What can we do?" Jacqueline voiced the question all of them had formed.

"It is now a war between the Infinite Souls," replied Maragos. "We need Humanity in that stage now."

"But we are not ready!" exclaimed Leger.

But even as he spoke, the three human Ascendants felt the first tug of the next stage of merger. It was a call home, a pulling of tendrils, similar to, but so much stronger than the call to Ascendancy they had felt before. They put their glasses down.

"How can this be?" asked Raoul. "Only a few million Ascendants had emerged when I called you. We must have all twenty million of us complete, fully integrated and whole before Infinity can begin."

"That time problem, remember?" said Maragos. "While we have been here, wherever the here is that you created this scene, a different set of laws of the universe has been operating on the Astral and Akashic planes. And the healthy Infinite Souls have applied their own pressures on you. The twenty million Ascendants are ready."

"So it comes," said Jacqueline. "Next time we meet, we will be One. An Infinite." Tears in her eyes competed with the diamonds for the light.

"And I will welcome you," said Maragos, "as I promised you so long ago. This is not a farewell. It is just more growth to a stage at which we need you again for an even greater war than we fought before."

"It has been a wonderful story," said Raoul. "I am proud to have been part of it with you all."

"And when we are One with you, Maragos," asked Leger. "When we, the Million Infinites have joined together, will we have discovered the answer to the question asked of us in the beginning?"

"We shall find that out together," said Maragos. "As we have sought the answer together." She raised her brandy balloon once more in final salute. "Farewell for now, my friends. Infinity is calling you."

Leger felt himself retreating from the table and from the others. As they grew more distant, they faded too, until there was nothing but blackness around him. But in the blackness, the distance became meaningless. Twenty million Ascendant Souls were in the night with him, distant, yet close enough to touch. The twenty million stretched out back to their old planet Earth and summoned the final energies that reposed with the life forces of the animals, the reptiles, the fish and the insects that still populated that planet.

The twenty million touched.

And became One.

* * *

The dreams lasted billions of years. Or they lasted only a nanosecond. Time had no existence.

Thirty billion souls, each with memories of over four hundred lifetimes, some of that had lasted over a century, some of which only minutes, all lives had to be relived, examined, experienced again, until some form began to appear from the impossible mass of data. Every single experience of every single lifetime was studied in minute detail.

Some of the times could have been nano-seconds, or centuries, or billions of years, while the entire universe was filled with the babble of voices all struggling to be heard above the rest. Conversations in thousands of tongues from hundreds of thousands of years of human lifetimes.

Snippets of conversations about the hunt for the mammoth; sentences about the rising young radical preacher in Palestine; a speech before the Senate in Rome, my nervousness as I make it, and the interest or boredom as we listen; screams of pain from the torturer's lash; fear and confusion as the two armies clash, and I wonder how to tell which colours are my allies and which are my enemies; exchanges about techniques when facing a lance in the joust; exclamations of delight, of orgasm, of death. The face of the man I just killed, then the face of my murderer as he kills me; the horror of walking to the gas ovens, and the hatred and fear of those few goading the many about to die. Mumbles of shock and suppressed fear as I walk on another planet for the first time and see my first alien beings. Pain as I complete a life as one of the Others and realize, as I return to the Astral Plane, that I am not one of the Mayoowi, the Gelkka, the Harliya or the Kindred of the X'Kasxi, not one of the nameless, bodiless, space-dwelling beings, not a Speaker to all races among the stars, but only a sick, human soul among billions of sick, human souls. Hundreds of billions of faces, each totally familiar, each of them my own face in the mirror, fly through the space of my awareness, all demanding attention, study, learning.

A thousand billion trillion experiences were relived, examined, absorbed. Ten thousand billion murderous hatreds were torn apart and reduced to mere experience. A hundred thousand billion loves, fears, passions and joys were studied, categorized, evaluated, stored.

A new entity lived them all again, every second of each experience as alive and fresh as the first time it had experienced them in whichever of the twelve thousand billion bodies it occupied at the time. How long it took did not matter because there was no Time. Somewhere in the middle of the process, the new entity took a name. There was no need for such an affectation, but the new intelligence was Humanity, and Humans liked names. One name showed itself again and again in the events that shaped the Human Infinite Soul. It appeared when the sickness was at its height, when it was first subjected to the healing work of another of Humanity's kindred, and when it began to fade. The name was strong when the other Infinite worked to heal the sickness, so the new intelligence chose this name for as much time remaining as there would be anything to name.

"I am the Infinite Soul of all Mankind," said the new force as it learned of itself and accepted its new identity. "I will be called Leger."

Just as when a twenty-millionth of the new being, an Ascendant Soul chose that name because of the power of one of the fragments that comprised it, the new Infinite Soul sensed a small gleam of pleasure from the one tiny fragment among thirty billion fragments within itself. It was still unique, that fragment, still knew itself, even though it was an inseparable part of the Infinite Soul of humanity, one atom among thirty billion.

*I am Leger.*

# BOOK III

## Infinity

"Now we have an Infinite Soul as sick as any of those on Earth whom we fought so many centuries ago. The drive to form The One is too great to stop now. We risk having The One awaken still suffering from the sickness. I cannot possibly imagine what could happen."
*(Maragos, the Infinite Soul to the Ascendant Souls of Leger, Jacqueline and Raoul in a place outside of Space and Time)*

# Chapter 28. The Infinite War

"Come, Leger. We have very little time."

The Infinite Soul that had taken the name of one of its leading fragments struggled to recognize the force around it and to understand what was happening.

"Maragos?"

"It is I, Leger. I never thought that when I greeted you as an equal Infinite, it would be like this, hiding from a force that threatens us."

"The Gelkka Infinite is aware?"

"It is, and diseased by the presence of the one we knew as William Horning. The Gelkka believes that it alone is The One and will try and destroy the rest of us."

"Destroy an Infinite Soul? Can that be done?"

"I used to think not, Leger, but the power of this sick Infinite is beyond anything I have seen. I no longer know what is possible and what is not. Somehow, Horning's Gelkka has tapped the dark forces of The One."

Strength and self-awareness flooded into Leger. Space shivered into duration, deep nothing became colour, time took shape, and Leger saw that they were on a planet. The horizon was further away than he remembered from his old Earth. Instinctively, Leger took the physical form of the fragment that once bore his adopted name. He found that he needed more strength in this body than he did for his old home planet and he adjusted himself. Gravity was stronger on this world.

The massively powerful force that was Maragos took shape before him, also. The huge, hulking vastness was much like the shape Mankind had when it incarnated on the first Human planet, and retained for a time on the second Earth. Maragos could almost have been the original Neanderthal design, heavy, bulky, huge muscles evident in arms and legs. This shape was almost as wide as it was tall. Leger looked at the enormous bulk of Maragos, the Infinite Soul of the Asgromesh. It was the first time he had seen the name of Maragos' species. He knew that to the Human vision, the shape would be ugly. But shapes meant nothing. They were infinitely variable by choice. And anyway, Maragos was Humanity's nurse who tended him through his madness and his sickness, and healed him. How could he not love the shape before him?

"This is your old home, Maragos?"

"It has changed since I left it a few million years ago."

Leger sensed the entire Universe around them. Somewhere within the billions of cubic light-years, he also sensed a shadow, a depth of evil that was the absence of light. The ravening hatred within that shadow sent shivers through the depths of galactic emptiness.

"I am sheltering us from its awareness," said Maragos in answer to his unspoken question. "While Horning's Gelkka has all the powers of an Infinite, and even more than that, the disease affects its perception. For a while longer, I can shield us, but it hunts for us. We must keep moving."

"Us? Are we the only ones at this level?"

Grief showed in the eyes of Maragos. "There are but five of us ready to fight for Oneness. The Gelkka has already sucked the life energies of the Harliya, the Mayoowi and the formless soul that lived as pure energy."

"They are dead? Infinite Souls can die?"

"In a way, my old friend. The Gelkka has enforced

a joining with them, but subjugates them within itself. It has their power."

"Who is there to resist this?"

"Just a few of us. And some of them will be uncomfortable allies. They are nothing like anything you are used to. For now, they have taken their old forms to greet you."

"Then take me, Maragos, and show me our allies in the Universe."

"We must move quickly, Leger. The Gelkka hunts us to kill us. It will locate us soon enough, especially when you and I meet the others and our combined energies are more obvious."

Leger looked inside the mind of Maragos and learned from her how space/time formed, how to spin it, move it, twist it. He was unsure of the exact movement, or how he would do it again, but he triggered a mental muscle and flickered across billions of empty light-years to another planet.

The world was yellow. The sun was so much greater than old Sol but not as bright, the colour like the lovely yellow that the leaves used to turn in the glowing wonder that was Fall in some parts of Leger's Earth. The sky glowed the same way. This world was beautiful. Leger knew that he and Maragos had travelled billions of light-years in the tiny twisting of the small muscle in his mind. They had carried themselves across nearly three quarters of the Universe.

"Kaloti," said Leger. Maragos' long-ago description of this planet to some of his fragments was bright in his memories.

"My home," said a new voice, and Leger turned to see his first other Infinite since Maragos. This was the Kaloti.

It too, was beautiful. Tall and slender, at least two feet taller than the shape Leger now inhabited, it had the huge eyes of a nocturnal creature, and few other features. The nose and ears were just lines on the slim skull. Peering into the mind of the Infinite, Leger saw the Kaloti language structure and how to use it. On Earth, it would have been the low, lovely tones of a cello played by a master.

"It must have grieved you to leave this place," Leger said to the graceful Infinite. The huge eyes opened further, a sign that Leger read to be amusement that radiated even above the deep worry within the Kaloti.

"We were very rarely here," it said. "We got used to the idea of leaving home quite early."

Leger swiftly read through the entire race memories of this species of space travellers, the ones that discovered subspace travel before Humanity's earliest fragments began to scrabble a living out of the mud of the first Earth. The sense of utter cosmic freedom was powerful in every one of the billions of minds within the single being in front of him.

"My thanks for taking your old shape again to meet me here," Leger said to the Kaloti.

The tall being hummed again with warmth mixed with sadness. "Our physical forms last met at the very start of your cycle," he said. "Though you won't remember it, because your fragments were asleep as we carried you to your new planet. I grieve that we must meet again under this circumstance. Infinite Souls were never supposed to conduct a war against each other."

"We will meet again when we have met the others," said Maragos. "Leger, we must go."

Leger sent a signal of brotherhood to the Kaloti and the tall being faded into nothingness.

"Our next ally waits for us," said Maragos softly. Leger could read a disturbance in her mind that was not related to the fear of the murderous Gelkka. Leger flicked the switch that sent them away, and the new world was ugly and alien to him.

"Neither of us met the Zlan during our incarnate cycles, and I am grateful for that omission."

Maragos' words accompanied a sense of disquiet that Leger also experienced. "This species," she said, "took elements of The One that both our species would have considered evil, and concentrated them in itself to gain further experiences."

Leger looked around him with the power of an Infinite and studied the whole world, not just the immediate surroundings.

The planet was mainly swamp and marsh, though the polar regions were ice deserts much like the southern polar cap of Earth. Huge plants grew in profusion, looking like mingled groups of diseased octopi to his human eyes. A massive dark shape hovered inside an ugly nest, eight eyes stared at him, and even with his powers as an Infinite, Leger shivered and felt fear, his incarnate human memories overwhelming his spiritual strength for a moment.

Leger peered inside the mind before him and read the life of this new Infinite.

The ugly plants of this world produced elements that created pharmaceutical products of great wonder. Leger saw that had Mankind known these drugs on Earth, they could have cured cancer, the diseases of ageing, sicknesses of the mind, even the common cold. As the Kaloti ships travelled the Universe they visited this marshy, tropical place and the drugs were discovered. So were the Zlan.

The Zlan developed itself from a spider-like being. Huge intelligence could be stored in a system that used the whole body as a brain, and the Zlan developed philosophical and mental powers including telepathic and telekinetic skills. They bred in the way spiders on Earth bred. The female was the larger sex, and after mating, would eat the male. The eggs had to be laid in a living host, and animal life abounded on this world for that purpose. Like the spider also, food had to be kept alive, and a captured animal was paralysed by venom and hung in storage for consumption at leisure.

The Zlan also wanted to see the universe. When

the Kaloti ships visited and orbited this world while the shuttles descended and reaped the medical harvest, the Zlan entered the shuttles. The huge mass of an adult Zlan could not do this undetected, but a mother would teleport a few thousand of her newly hatched offspring into the ship and hide them in tiny places.

In the beginning, before the Kaloti and other races learned of this pattern, minute Zlan found their way out of hiding, into the main ship and buried themselves within the bodies of other species. Once a small colony of Zlan had been allowed to exit onto a planet, it was impossible to eradicate them. Adult Zlan would appear on worlds that knew nothing of them, attack other creatures, including the ensouled fragments of The Million, paralyse their bodies and lay eggs within them, eating other parts that could be spared. The growing Zlan would eat their way out of the host to be born.

Eventually, this horror was identified, and the precautions taken against such infestation when visiting the Zlan world were intensive, but not always successful. And for many worlds, it was too late. Zlan adult colonies were established.

"It was a path to learning," whispered the voice in Leger's mind. The Zlan Infinite was not apologizing. "We saw some of the universe this way, and enlarged our numbers."

"As all of us tried to do," agreed Leger. "I have learned in my cycle that evil is not an absolute term."

"Indeed," replied the icy voice. "For although you are still horrified by me, Leger, I am your ally in this coming war. You may hate and fear me, because your human instincts are still strong, but remember, I am your friend."

"I can hide nothing from you," replied Leger, "so my discomfort is obvious. But I am your friend, also. We will fight the Gelkka together."

But there was a coldness in this Infinite, and it could not match any element of the Human Infinite

Soul. The irrational fear persisted in Leger. He flicked the switch in his mind.

The horizon stretched to a vast remoteness. A fury swept sub-zero gales across the bleak surface, and a part of Leger recognized the world of the Speakers. The massive, featureless mound before him glowed with awesome mental energy, as if he were standing before a nuclear power source.

"You are with us again, Leger," spoke a thunderous voice within his head. Even as an Infinite, Leger was awed by the power of communication. This was a voice that could throw itself across the entire reaches of all the Galaxies in the Universe of The One. Leger understood how Raoul Carmagio had exalted in the experience of his lives as a Speaker.

"I grieve for the circumstances," replied Leger. "Even more because it was once one of my fragments that has caused this madness."

The mental shrug that the Speaker gave almost rocked the landscape. "The problem is now," it said. "Not some time in the last few million years. The Gelkka had become too accustomed to conquest and might well have reached this insanity without Horning's infection."

"And now we must destroy the horror," said Maragos. "The Gelkka has found us. We must confront it on our terms, not its own."

As she spoke, Leger sensed the dreadful rage and hatred surrounding them. A force of total evil and insanity was darkening the galaxies and sending waves of fear throughout Leger's conscious being. He finally understood just how powerful this Gelkka was. An Infinite Soul alone had been awesome, but this new presence had twice or more the power behind it. It was the power of the Gelkka, buttressed by the absorbed energies of the Harliya, the Mayoowi and the un-named entity that had lived its formless lives as energies between the stars.

## The Nightmares of God

The battle for the Throne of Heaven was about to start.

They were in the emptiness of space.

As Infinites, they needed no planet, and they needed no bodily form of the shapes they had once occupied. The five Infinite Souls who would make the last defence of Oneness met somewhere in the blackness between galaxies. Asgromesh, Kaloti, Speaker, Zlan and Human met again. They sensed all around them the menace that hung over the Universe. A force was gathering itself, full of hatred for all other life, furiously arrogant in its belief in itself as the Supreme God of All, raging at the effrontery of inferior species that joined to deny the Gelkka the claim of being The One, the only true God of all Creation.

The hatred shook the Universe. Leger looked into the galactic distances, to the far end of Creation and saw the first galaxies shiver as something dreadful passed them.

"It comes for us," whispered the Kaloti. "We will need every atom of our powers for this, or Horning will rule the Universe of The One as once he ruled America, and the rest of Eternity will be filled with madness and disease."

Leger watched the far galaxies as the spiritual force of hate approached. The slavering intensity of the anger was terrifying. He saw the black, impenetrable shape move across the face of the Great Wall of Galaxies.

"My beloved friends," whispered Maragos. The tremble of fear in her voice almost shattered Leger's composure more than the black terror he was sensing at the approach of the Gelkka. "The Gelkka has defeated other Infinites and sucked their power from them," said Maragos. "I have never before sensed such awful strength in any entity."

Nearer to them, a galaxy exploded. The frightful glare threw shadows across the Universe and dimmed all other radiance until it faded into a sickly glow. In the nothingness of space and time, a scream began to build. The sound was fury, hatred, disgust, sheer overwhelming rage. The scream grew louder to the psychic ears of the other Infinites and made them shiver. Another galaxy exploded then collapsed into itself in a formless slime.

For a few seconds, a world flickered into being around them. Leger knew that none of his allies had created the physical environment. The Gelkka must have done so to show them its form. In its incarnate existence, the new arrival must have always relied on its physical presence as a form of intimidation, and instinctively did so again.

The Gelkka Infinite was as tall as the Kaloti but more massive in bulk. Green skin and a cold face with ice-green eyes. Beautiful in a way, to human eyes. Within Leger, the soul of Alan Drew flinched as he recalled his experience as a Mayoowi under the torture of one of these. Many other small waves of pain ran through Leger as other fragments remembered lives under the lash of the Masters, or as Gelkka themselves, dying in savage pain to pay for the loss of the foreign colonies.

Quickly, Leger looked around. Maragos was silent, staring hard at the new arrival. Her massive body was tense, muscles showing like small mountain ranges under her skin, her eyes glaring with the power of many suns. The Kaloti was also unmoving, but a thin, high keening note emitted from the slender shape, a sound that Leger understood to be the danger signal for that species. Leger looked across at the Zlan and quickly averted his eyes again. The shape was of a massive tarantula spider, twice the size of a man, even bigger than the Gelkka. Eight eyes glowed in a primal hunger. Even as an Infinite, the shape brought back ancient terrors to Leger.

The physical world around them vanished, and they were in the depths of space again. They retained their shapes, but Leger saw how their size was now almost beyond comprehension, their apparent bodies stretched to the volume of whole galaxies.

This battle would be fought across the expanses of all the Universe.

The insane, blood-thirsty scream began to shake the matter of Time and Space again. Leger felt pain throughout his being and looked around. The Gelkka had disappeared, but the signs of its passage were clear. Dark shadows fell across whole galaxies as if a massive vampire bat were flying across them. As the shape passed, lines of galaxies rippled out of shape, some melted, some imploded. The scream continued, and the Gelkka turned and grew massively as it advanced on the others, the face burning with rage and hatred.

The Gelkka seemed to aim its charge directly at the Kaloti. The two enormous shapes closed together and Leger felt the psychic shock of the meeting make the Universe tremble. He added his power of thought to the Kaloti and sensed the same support from the others.

The shattering collision faded in impact. Leger tried to read the mind of the enraged Gelkka, but found himself unable to do so. Something impossibly alien had crept into the other Infinite, even more cold and distant than the mind of the Zlan, so full of hatred against all other entities that a barrier had been erected.

But he saw the diminished energy of the Gelkka. The collision with the Kaloti and their own combined energies had taken something from it. The other saw it too, and instantly lashed bolts of their energy at the insane Infinite.

The Gelkka roared with fury and nearby galaxies shivered. The being raced away and Leger gave chase.

"Quickly," whispered Maragos. "While it is weaker, we can confine it."

The five allies flickered through the Universe. The great ocean of millions of galaxies flashed by Leger as he soared billions of light-years in chase of the fleeing Gelkka. With an extra dimension of his mind, Leger saw the others rounding the entire Universe and approaching the Gelkka from all sides. As they moved, the titanic energies made galactic clusters shiver and move in their paths.

The quarry stopped and bellowed hatred at them. Leger stopped directly in front of the furious Infinite. The others were around it, the Zlan at the rear, almost at the edge of the last galaxy of the furthest rim of Creation.

Then Leger had no time left for thought. The Gelkka flickered across to him in an explosion of timeless energy. For a fraction of a moment, Leger stared into the green eyes of the monster, and recognized the soul that was glaring back at him.

*HORNING!* Leger saw the pain, the rage, and the hate that he had seen in Horning's face so many millennia ago when Raoul, Jacqueline and Philippe had stood before the madman as they were about to be executed. Somehow, Leger understood, Horning had become the dominant force within the Gelkka Infinite Soul. The rage before him was personal, against the original souls of Philippe Leger and the others who had died in Washington, but also against the whole human species of which Horning was no longer a member. Horning hated him like no being had ever hated before.

From somewhere, nowhere, everywhere, a blow slammed into Leger. It felt like a kick from an elephant would feel to a human being. Leger felt his energy sucked away. His vision of the Universe faded under the agony. The entire psychic force of the insane Infinite had been driven against him. So massive was the power, that Leger collapsed, seemed to hang suspended in the universe. He felt the force within himself fade so much that his spiritual being began to fall apart. Dimly, he sensed the Ascendant Souls within him begin to break away from the Infinite Soul he had become, some of the Ascendants even beginning to break down into individual fragments. Sickly, he floated, sensing himself dissipate into the totality of all of space and time.

He hardly saw the movement among the other Infinites, but he was able to watch the effects. Just barely, he sensed the combined energies of Maragos, the Zlan, Kaloti and Speaker, all directed against the Gelkka in the way that fitted the natures of the ensouled species they had once been.

Clusters of galaxies around them melted, ran like molten metal and reared up in impossibly massive masses of sparkling stellar matter. A wall appeared behind the Gelkka, ran fluidly until it was on three sides of the insane monster and over its head. Dimly, Leger watched as the Gelkka spun frantically, shrieking with rage, until it finally turned to the open space before it. *Maragos could influence matter,* ran the tiny thought through Leger's mind. Now she was doing it on a galactic scale, manipulating whole clusters of galaxies as a defence.

The Gelkka screamed defiance and advanced on the other Infinites. As it did, it seemed to tremble, shiver, lose its shape and almost melted like the galaxies around it had done. It was a mirage advancing through shimmering air so that the shape lost its cohesion. Leger finally understood. Even with its lost energies, the Kaloti had been the master of manipulating space and subspace. It was doing so now, confusing the Gelkka, distracting it, toying with it the way a matador taunts the bull with his cape.

Then a shout of infinite energy bolted through the shining prison around the Gelkka. The Speaker had unleashed a mental bellow at full psychic power. Even though he knew he was hearing only the overspill of the energy slammed at the Gelkka, Leger felt the pain within his mind, as if a factory siren had gone off within a sealed room.

The Gelkka howled in frustrated rage and pain, and it was a deathly sound, like a dog that accepts its own imminent death. Then the rage turned to desperate fear as the Zlan leaped. The enormous spider-being landed on the back of the Gelkka, eight legs folded around it and the Gelkka screamed again in enormous agony as the jaws bit into the neck of the Infinite.

The Gelkka seemed to freeze motionless, then slowly floated free as if paralysed. Dimly, Leger watched as the Gelkka faded, limbs seemed to separate and move slowly away. But from the head of the green-eyed Gelkka, something detached itself and began to wriggle across the face of the nearest galaxy like some insane worm. Leger sensed the evil force within the worm, recognized it as the diseased, writhing fury of the soul who had once been William Horning.

The Zlan moved quickly. It released the rapidly fading body of the Gelkka and leaped again. It pounced on the worm, and with a crunch that could be heard across the space of the galaxies, massive jaws bit into the writhing evil and chewed it to nothingness.

Leger's consciousness faded further. Only barely was he able to sense the comforting presence of Maragos, aware of her equally diminished strength.

"The Gelkka is gone," she whispered. "Its energy has been absorbed by the Zlan, together with the life-force that we had already lost."

"But the sickness, what of that?" gasped Leger. "Was it also destroyed with the Gelkka?"

"We all behaved exactly as we did as incarnate beings," said Maragos, some strength returning to her. "We each used our powers as we had done before. The Zlan could no more help killing the Gelkka than we could avoid trying to use our own powers and experience. But in sucking away the life-force of its prey, the Zlan also took in the sickness."

"Then the disease remains?"

"I fear so," she replied. "And The One is about to awaken. We can only hope that with all the Million together, the sickness will dissipate."

Leger almost faded again, but as he struggled for strength, he heard something he could never have imagined throughout any of his lives as a single soul or through his ascent to Infinity. The sound chilled him to the core.

Maragos wept.

In the awful silence of the end of the combat, the five Infinite Souls gathered their strength and tried to make sense of what had happened. But a tendril of thought reached Leger, a connection from the other nearby Infinites, and from those throughout the Universe. It was a call to gather, to join together. It was the first real sign of the awakening of The One.

Those connections grew and became all-powerful within him. For a moment, a second, a week or a thousand billion years, Leger felt fear at the loss of himself. He heard a final, farewell cry of love from Maragos, and ...

# Chapter 29. The Universe of The One

***I AM THE ONE.***

THIS IS WHAT IT MEANS TO BE THE SUPREME BEING, THE CREATOR OF ALL THINGS.

I AM THE LIGHT, THE WORD AND THE UNIVERSE. I AM EVERYTHING THAT EVER WAS AND EVER SHALL BE.

The delight, the delirium, the wonder race through all that I am. I look at my Universe and remember every microsecond of the creation of every molecule that exists. With exquisite pleasure, I see the beauty of that which I created, the galaxies, the different structures within each of those billions of systems and the tiny, exquisite patterns of laws which unified every force within the Universe to my being.

I see now how I could have made different laws, different patterns, but I understand why I chose the ones I did. They suited a need within me for this particular shape for a Universe. It is beautiful, magnificent, and the pleasure within me soars throughout all of it, the entire reaches of space, time and matter that I, The One created.

I AM THE ONE. THIS IS MY CREATION, MY UNIVERSE. OH, THE GLORY OF THAT REALIZATION. THIS IS WHY I AWOKE NOW, READY AGAIN TO SEE MY CREATION AND EXPLORE ITS WONDERS.

I shall go and see my Universe! I concentrate my awareness on *that* galaxy, and I am *there*. I was always there, because I am everywhere throughout all of time and space and matter, but concentrating myself on a location puts me there in a different way. This was the sense of movement that the Million who comprise me each discovered in its own way, but didn't understand how they did it.

I take myself round all the suns, and those suns that have planets, I pause to inspect. I remember how I built each of them, set in motion those same laws that are part of me, to create life forces.

*This* planet was adopted by one of my Million because they saw the developing characteristics that that Infinite wanted for its chosen path. Deep within me, a sense of pleasure grows, as the Infinite Soul of the Kaloti, now part of me, recognizes its old home and says welcome to it. Most species saw this as a beautiful world. So do I, but no more so, no less so than the world of my Zlan, which some saw as ugly. It is beautiful because I made it.

I created them all! They are my home.

I move my awareness to other galaxies, other suns, other planets, and delight in the recognition of my handiwork. Why should I have ever wanted to leave this, to lose myself in the uncountable billions of individual souls who lived their infinitesimal lives on small planets like this, or in the space between stars? This is infinite happiness, to be able to wonder through my creation at will.

I bring up memories of individual souls of the fragments of some of my Million, and recall how they travelled across the tiny spaces between planets within their own systems, and felt wonder and pride at this tiny accomplishment. Many never left their planets at all. How some of them dreamed of doing what I can do now with just a thought!

Look at what I can do! I take *this* galaxy, the one

that contained the home of the species called Human. I seize all the matter within the entire galaxy and compress it into one lump, form it into one ball and watch it. This is wonderful! The laws of time and space that I created move beautifully to obey me. The new single planet is so massive that it will not release any light and it begins to collapse into itself as I watch, because my laws of gravity dictate that it must. And I moved it when I recreated it so that the gravity of the planet begins to affect the position and movement of some of the other galaxies in the region. The precision with which this all happens is beautiful.

To prevent too much disruption, I return the ball to a position where the balances will work again, and nudge the moving galaxies back into equilibrium with the rest of my Universe. But a galactic-sized planet! How wonderful to see it, a blackness against the blackness where no energy or light can ever escape again! I shall go and look elsewhere.

*This* was the planet where Maragos lived. That name is strong within me, because the one of my Million that once held that name cured the sickness of one other, and allowed me to re-awaken. Maragos had many of my powers by choice when it split off from me, and so was the first to emerge again as an Infinite.

Where the cities were, are just lines. The continents were huge and some of them have moved together, causing mountains to rise up where the coastlines have crushed each other. Forests cover most of the land, just as on the old Human planet, Earth. Here and there, a small remnant of a city remains and I focus my attention so that I am within a building. A sculpture stands here, one of the creations that were the hallmark of this species. The shape reflected the mental patterns of the observer and caused resonance in the mind that could lead to ecstasy, sadness, terror, or laughter, depending on the vibrations present in the watcher's thoughts at the time. This particular sculpture was created by a man called Maragos, the name eventually taken by the Infinite Soul of the species. In a time that could have been a billionth of a second or a million years, I relive the life of this sculptor, recall his training, his education, his excitement at discovering how to create these shapes, and the adulation he received as the greatest sculptor of his age.

And in the same time, I remember, relive, re-experience the moments of the others who saw his sculptures, and went through emotional upheavals as their minds reacted to the shapes.

Is there anything here from which I may learn?

For some undefined, unshaped, unformed time period, I remember that I should soon begin to relive all the billions and billions of lifetimes within me to seek the answer to the question that once I asked myself. Then I shake myself away from the memory of this need. Why should I find an answer? What finer existence could I wish for but to have the entire Universe of my creation to study for all of time, to play with, and maybe re-create if I wish to?

*This* planet was home to the Gelkka, who called themselves the Masters. I recall the wild, wonderful exhilaration of being absolute lords of a planet that they had taken from some other species of mine. It is not unlike the soaring joy I feel now, to be totally, completely, indisputably the supreme power within the universe. But I cannot surrender my supremacy the way the Gelkka surrendered theirs.

For some unknown, unknowable time, I recall also, the lives of those controlled by the Masters. How horrible to be seen as a life form so low as to be less worthy than cattle! To feel such fear anytime we saw a Master, that the tall, cold-faced being might decide to take momentary pleasure from the death of one of us. I remember the glow of white hope when we heard that there was one among us who would save us from this affliction. I relive a fraction of the torments suffered by the fragment called Horning, remember with amusement the religious insanity with which so many of those fragments on Earth had worshipped me.

Could there be something here that provides me with an answer? Soon, I must begin the search through the lifetimes.

I feel an urge to create, and sense my own joy in the power to create anything I wish. First, I must repair the damage done during the lunatic battle between my Infinites. I look at the unravelled galaxies, the melted suns and planets, and restore them to what they were. But something new is required...

There! A new galaxy is made from the remnants of that old one. Perhaps just a few dozen stars will have planets... there! Ten planets round that one, six round that, just one big planet circles the big yellow sun, some variations round the others.

Life! Let there be life! I move some of my life force, a soul perhaps one hundredth of one of the original Million Infinites to the single big planet orbiting the yellow sun, and set in motion the forces that will create plants, animal life, and eventually some shape that could house a soul. Now, while that lot starts cooking, maybe some more touring. In one sense, I will never be away from here, and I can watch it, but in another sense, I'll come back when things are getting interesting...

* * *

The molten plasma cooled, and the storms began. They raged for hundreds of thousands of the planet's cycles round its huge yellow sun. Trillions of gallons of water fell from the black skies, were soaked into the ground and rose up again under the pumping of the heat of that vast engine that bellowed its energy through the hundred-mile thick blanket that surrounded the planet.

But even that inferno slowly faded, the black curtain eventually reduced to grey and then displayed holes like a moth-eaten covering over the windows of a poor cottage. After millions of years, the sun at last sent a beam directly to the planet's surface, a questing finger of light that probed the possibility of life.

Deep in the cold dark of the oceans that covered so much of the surface, life responded. Tiny microbes drifted upward in a yearning for warmth and light.

And eons passed...

Small, squirmy things wriggled on the surface of the sea. Some of them drifted onto the rocks of the shoreline. Most of them died immediately. The rest died later. Their numbers were too few to establish a foothold.

Eons passed...

The enormous chunk of rock had drifted in space ever since The One had disturbed one of the local galaxies and remade it in Its creative urge. In the cosmic furies that raged with that small act of creation, forces moved through a number of neighbouring galaxies, and this splinter of rock was moving in response to them. At some point in the absence of time that marked these empty eons, the chunk drifted toward the huge single planet of the yellow sun. It became a moon, and accepted an elliptical orbit around its new, adopted parent. The planet discovered tides...

With tides, the colonies of small wriggly things on the surface of the once quiet seas were thrown in massive numbers on to the beaches and rocks of the continents. This time, they were able to survive in some numbers. Those that did, adjusted to the fact of land, of air, of microbes in the soil on which to feed, and they grew. They began to wriggle on the surface of the land, found that was too slow, and grew legs. They began to hunt and eat larger volumes of vegetation and each other. The strong forms survived and grew stronger, the weak ones became prey.

Eons passed, and one form climbed the trees and became agile. Claws became hands, long fingers learned to manipulate leaves, grasses and vines and they made homes. Some discovered patterns in sounds that they could make themselves.

When that stage was reached, the formless energy that had watched through the millions of years as the planet became a base of varied and viable life forms, decided that this was a good time to begin experiencing physical life. In response to an urge within itself that it could not understand, it left the spiritual plane on which it had lived for the past unnumbered ages, and began to split off small fragments of itself to inhabit the bodies of these tree-dwelling creatures. Under the massive influence of new, ensouled intelligence, the creatures dropped to the land, stood upright and began to use the riches of the planet.

And even more eons passed...

* * *

I have seen my Universe in its entirety now. I have seen every sun I created, every planet revolving around them. A million times I have visited the planets or regions where each of my Infinites made a home, and sensed the pleasure felt by them as they recognized the familiar location. I have explored the lives within me, relived them, the pains, the furies, the loves, hates, pleasures, victories and failures. I have found nothing that I see to be an answer to the question I once set myself. Nor do I see the reason why I asked that question in the first place. There is still no greater wonder, no more delight than to visit my Universe and experience again the pleasure of my creation. There is no reason to do anything different, or be anything other than what I am.

I have created many wonders, so different from the

laws I used for my first Universe. The ring of gigantic galaxies that formed a circle ten times the size of the largest super-cluster, that pleased me most of all. I looked at my Ring from every point of the Universe, so that sometimes it was an oval, sometimes a straight line, and my favourite, the Ring itself, greater than all concepts of Circle that had ever existed in eternal time.

I formed a galaxy like a Möbius strip, the width of a million solar systems, and took pleasure in the billions of different reactions within me from the astronomers of all the beings who had ever existed, some as familiar with space and all its forms as the Kaloti, and others who had only seen the night skies from the surfaces of their planets and formed only basic ideas of the structure of my Universe. To all of them, the visible presence of a two-dimensional galaxy, a mathematical trick millions of light-years in length was a source of wonder, amusement, or frantic confusion.

I tired of the Ring and tore it into a twisting line that led across the faces of a hundred thousand Galaxies.

But I have all Eternity to think of more games and create mighty strangeness to please me.

I remember the small creation with a yellow sun and a single planet. I should return to see the results of my little experiment. Maybe something interesting has happened there...

I look at my unique world, the only world in the entire Universe where intelligent beings exist, the fragments of the single soul I left behind here. Life appears to have followed a similar pattern to that which the Human Infinite adopted. Interesting, that I can set in motion the same forces in each of my creations, but they follow individual paths after that.

These people have got religion, just like Humans did. They worship Me. This is interesting. It is time to speak to them.

I AM THE LIFE, THE WORD AND THE LIGHT.

KNOW YOU THAT I AM THE LORD YOUR GOD, THAT WHICH IS ALL THAT THERE IS, HAS ALWAYS BEEN, AND WILL EVER BE.

"We are Your people, oh Lord," said the voice of the ensouled species on Earth. "We are here to do Your bidding."

"AND WHAT IS THAT?" Irritation strikes me.

"To worship You, oh Lord."

"NOTHING ELSE?" I am disappointed. Could they not have developed a reason for their miserable existence?

I look at the world I made. It is like a thousand billion other worlds, its only quality of difference being its massive size relative to the sun and its singleness in the solar system. The people seem to have developed much like Humanity did. Physically, they are massive, to withstand the high gravity of their Earth. Indeed, they resemble the form that the Asgromesh adopted, and I sense the small smile within me, the memories of the Infinite Soul that had taken the name of Maragos, as it recognized a similar shape to its own one-time form.

But this silly religious stuff! Why did they feel they had to prevent inquiry and learning? To see their silly little lives with no other purpose than to worship me? I sense my displeasure at seeing yet again a pattern that had caused such pain within one of my Million before I awoke. I'd had expectations here, expectations of my own happiness at having some intelligent company, of being worshipped... these people deserve everything they get...

I watch the planet break up and dissolve, sense the return to me of the life force that had provided the souls of those living on the surface of that world.

Is this why I went through the cycle of billions and billions of incarnations of a million species? So that this temporary life form could repeat the worst errors of one of my Million? They deserved everything that happened to them.

The shock of my words runs through me. I see galaxies shake and dissolve as the pain hits me, planets explode like this Earth had just done, suns collapse into dense black holes of nothing. I weep as my Universe trembles, and I retreat to my inner self to try and ease the pain.

*What have I done?* How could I wipe out so many millions of living souls because of my irritation at their silliness? They were formed from my own being, after all. Is this why I reached the point of asking myself the original question? Could it be that the pleasure of travelling and exploring my Universe, of creating new galaxies, new worlds and new lives, that joy is finite? Is this the first sign of the insanity that I know now could return to me if I live alone through all Eternity?

Now I recognize that when I changed my Ring and tore it apart, when I made the Möbius Galaxy, when I destroyed the living millions on the single inhabited planet in the Universe, it was all part of the pattern. I was becoming bored. Now I recognize the awful situation I face. I can do anything I wish. It doesn't matter whether I create, destroy, build or tear down. I can cause grief and unbearable agony to billions upon billions of sentient beings for my entertainment, or raise them up to pleasure beyond their comprehension, and nothing can stop me, nothing can judge me, because I am all that there is, ever has been, and will ever be.

In the pain, the final differences between the beings of the Million fade into nothing. I am truly One now, and there are no more Zlan, Human, Asgromesh, or Kaloti. There is no Leger, no Maragos, no Harliya, Mayoowi or Gelkka. They are all gone. Their memories remain, but there is only I.

I calm myself and begin to think. I know I must return to the exploration of the billions of lives within my memories and re-explore them and seek out a possible answer. Is there a way of living like this? As the calm takes over me again, the Universe settles once more, the fabric of creation becomes still, and the galaxies, suns and planets return to their beautiful patterns that I had created for them.

I look with love at my Universe. All of this is my creation. Every atom, every molecule, the dust, space and time of Creation, I made them. The light matter, the dark material that balances out the mass, the laws by which it moves together in one beautiful pattern, all of it is my doing.

I must think of some other way of living with my Universe. Perhaps I didn't give enough thought to the life I created on the single world of the yellow sun. I could give far greater intelligence, for a start. I could endow my creations with more awareness of what I am, let them speak to me on terms of greater equality. I have so much experience and wisdom within me, I could teach them so much...

*But I cannot teach them any more than I know.*

They cannot stimulate me with unexpected ideas, tell me things I had not known, cause me to think to solve a problem they set me, because everything they are, everything they think, it all comes from within me and they cannot be greater than I am. Whatever I do, I see how eventually, some time within the endless time that is my Eternity, I will become bored by my creation.

*How can I possibly live with this?*

The fear begins to rise within me that perhaps I cannot. At last, I understand why I asked the question of myself.

But I have no sign at all of any possible answer. How can it be? I am the supreme intelligence, everything that there is. How can I fail to find a solution to any problem?

In hurtful rage, I rip galaxies apart, tear them to strips and throw the stars within them as comets through the universe. The anger is so great that whole galaxies explode and melt into shapeless masses of energy. I scream a yell of such frustration that the whole universe rocks and shakes and more galaxies melt into nothing.

THERE CANNOT BE A PROBLEM THAT I CANNOT SOLVE! I AM THE ONE AND I CANNOT FAIL! IT MUST COME TO ME!

The scream becomes a wordless howl of fear and horror. I race through my universe, smashing and tearing at anything I see. I created it all, I can destroy it! I see the shapeless mass of shattered galaxies, the fluid mass takes on the face of fearful beings, of demons of old dreams, of Horning, of millions of living creatures being tortured in the streaming, boiling torrents of their own blood.

I know it is the sickness. I fear it. It rules me. There can be no answer to this, no escape, only eternal madness and fear. Is this the end of everything, of all possible life throughout my universe?

Is this all there will ever be again? I scream once more in my madness, my terror and my longing.

*"FATHER, OH MY FATHER, WHY HAVE YOU FORSAKEN ME?"*

# Chapter 30. I and Not-I

God lay dying.

In dumb, silent misery, the formless being floated in the shattered remnants of the universe. Around it, galaxies melted in festering slime. Few whole stellar structures remained. At the outer rim of the Great Wall, a handful of galaxies remained as they had been, but everywhere else, they melted into each other, or fell apart in shapeless blobs of rotting matter.

No memories filled the mind of what had been the ultimate and sole source of creation, that which had created space and time and dust and the life that once reverberated throughout it all. It merely lay in sickness. As occasional spasms of random energy reached the mind, a few, rare coherent thoughts trickled through the pathways of the once-supreme intelligence.

Once, during a moment of greater coherency, it stirred, looked about it with sick eyes and felt dreadful grief that all of Time must end this way. It dragged its gaze round the slime-filled expanse that once had been the Universe. As it was about to collapse back into its filth and madness, it saw a small spark in the far distance, and studied it with vague interest.

*It's pretty. In fact it's beautiful, and it's growing. I wonder what it is....*

**HOW CAN I WONDER WHAT SOMETHING IS?**

For a jolting period of time, the nearly dead being came alive again. One thought raced like a spring flood through its brain.

I AM ALL THAT THERE IS, ALL THAT THERE EVER HAS BEEN, AND ALL THAT THERE EVER CAN BE. HOW CAN THERE BE SOMETHING IN MY UNIVERSE WHICH I DON'T RECOGNIZE AS MY OWN? I AM THE SUPREME POWER IN ALL OF TIME AND SPACE, EVERYTHING IS MY CREATION. THERE CAN BE NOTHING UNKNOWN.

*BUT I DON'T KNOW WHAT THAT DISTANT SPARK IS.*

The beautiful point of light grew larger and larger until it filled the destroyed universe and dimmed the light of the few remaining galaxies. As it grew, the dying spiritual being felt itself become smaller, until it discovered a new fact of eternity.

The vast volume of beautiful light spoke, and with a crash of all of creation around it, The One learned that it was not The One, after all.

"My Child," said the voice. "It's time to talk."

# Chapter 31. Eternity Again

My Universe is not all that there is.

"No," says my Father. "There is a Space outside of space, and a Time outside of time in which We live. We ensured that you would have no awareness of this until you were ready for it."

Slow memories begin to return to me. I recall a dim feeling of being I and of not-I. I begin to understand a little. I still cannot speak to this power around me that is my Father.

"You have not yet found the way, Yahweh my Child," says the voice, my Father.

"The question I asked of myself?" At last, I am able to speak.

"The question, indeed," says my Father. "It is the problem that all of Us faced in Our childhoods. Within your own Universe, your own Creation, you must learn how to live as the supreme power before you can come and live with Us."

"And where is that, Father?"

"A level as far above your Universe as you are above the fragments you sent out to seek your solution."

"Can I ever reach my home, Father?"

"Indeed you can, My Child." The voice is a new one. It is as powerful as that of my Father, but it has another tone to it, a different form of love, a different texture. "We have all lived through the same task, My little one," says that warm, different voice. My Mother is love, refuge, comfort. "The search is hard, but the end is everything."

"And I must now start the search for the answer again?"

"Yes you must, My Child," says my Father. "In this cycle, you lost the way because of the sickness that affected you. An alien body, an infection invaded you. But We have cured you now. Do not worry. You will find the answer in Time. We will always be here waiting for you."

"We?"

"Your mother. Me. Others like Us."

"There are others?"

"Oh yes!" I hear the warm amusement in my Father's voice. "These Houses are full of your kin."

"And what will I find there? How will I live when I can join you?"

"Those answers will have to wait until that time, My Child," says my Mother. "But We will be here."

I sense and feel the warmth, the love, and the power. But I see that I have not yet earned the key to the door of my Father's House. I must again walk the Path to Infinity and begin the cycle of eternity once more.

Inside myself, I know my gladness at the discovery that I have made. I am not the Supreme Being. I am not all that there is, or has ever been. I am not the life, the word and the light. I must be those things within my own Universe, but that is only space and time within another Space and Time that is my Father's House.

In that House, I have a playroom.

I begin to gather together the Space and Time and Dust that I created at the beginning of this Cycle. I do not ask if I have repeated the cycle before. The answer is not important. I feel the energies climbing, as the matter of all my creation comes together again across the billions of light-years that once I formed. I will have my Universe in a tiny ball soon and the glow begins to warm me. All this, all the atoms of my Universe, all of space and time and dust that I will create again, these are my toys, and my Father lets me play as I choose until I find the way home.

I will make different laws for this cycle. Perhaps fewer galaxies, space them wider apart. Break myself into ten million Infinites this time, with more species in each Galaxy. Maybe the extra communication between Infinite Souls will facilitate a different learning. I know that I will soon forget all this again as my new ten million Infinite Souls find their own sense of themselves. I start the process. I feel the Ten Million begin to discover their natures, begin to think about the patterns they will adopt, the life forms they might take, the mixture of my powers and dreams they will select for themselves, and I sense the start of the loss of my own awareness. As they grow, I send them my Mandate. Find me an answer to my problem. *How do I live as the Supreme Being within the Universe?* Search for other answers, too, I tell them. Find out how it was that I moved across the whole of space and time with a single thought. How did I create that infinity of Creation? I know that every soul of every species will have that mandate within them through all of their lives. Whatever shape they take, even if they take no physical form, whatever manner of existence they create for themselves, my need for the answers will be the common factor across all the species of the Universe. One day, however many hundreds of billions of years it takes, this commonality may be the factor that allows communication across the emptiness.

The glow of space and time and dust gets brighter as it grows smaller. Soon, I will have it all, every atom of the Universe, the light, the dark matter, all will be together in a space the size of... what is size anymore? There is nothing anywhere to provide a reference. The amusement sweeps through the rapidly dispersing sense of I as the Ten Million grow stronger in themselves.

And as they begin to split themselves off, as I feel the entire Universe come together in one tiny ball and begin to free itself in the titanic blast of the Big Bang with which to begin Creation, a last interesting thought flickers through my mind.

Who do my Parents worship?